ORCHID BAY

ORCHID BAY

Patricia Shaw

HEADLINE

First published in 1999
by HEADLINE BOOK PUBLISHING

10 9 8 7 6 5 4 3 2 1

British Library Cataloguing in Publication Data

Shaw, Patricia, 1928–
Orchid Bay
I.Title
823[F]

ISBN 0 7472 2247 9 (hbk)
ISBN 0 7472 7413 4 (sbk)

Typeset by
Letterpart Limited, Reigate, Surrey

Printed and bound in Great Britain by
Mackays of Chatham PLC, Chatham, Kent

HEADLINE BOOK PUBLISHING
A division of Hodder Headline PLC
338 Euston Road
London NW1 3BH

For Evangeline and Benjamin Shaw.
With love.

The Times, London, 4 October 1867

The Patrons and Members of the Female Middle Class Emigration Society have this week farewelled six more governesses who have gone forth to the Colonies to take up employment in their chosen vocations.

Four of these gentlewomen embarked in the Pacific Star *and two others sailed from our shores in* City of Liverpool.

Members of the Female Middle Class Emigration Society are to be commended for their dedication to the well-being of their less fortunate sisters, for it is a sad fact that there is little employment in this country for educated ladies who have fallen on hard times.

We are advised that the last time the Society advertised for governesses to go abroad an astonishing three hundred and six applications were received, many of these females forced to admit they were reduced to penury.

Much as the Society would wish to assist all of the applicants, budgetary considerations keep the number of those who are successful at a relatively low level.

Because of this, however, females who have received approval can lay claim to expertise in English Studies, Latin, French or German, Music, Painting, and Elocution.

It should be said that our loss is the Colonials' gain, for what family would not consider themselves truly blessed to be able to welcome such paragons into their homes? We wish the emigrants Bon Voyage and every success in the Antipodes.

Chapter One

The dazzling white lighthouse at Cape Moreton blazed a warm welcome to the weary passengers and crew of the *City of Liverpool* as she sailed sturdily into the bay on this glorious sunny morning, and they were pathetically grateful for its reassuring presence. The dangers of the great oceans were behind them. The voyage of fifteen weeks to the day was almost over.

They had been warned that this wide bay could be rough, but today it was kind as the ship left the shelter of Stradbroke Island and headed for the mainland, rocked by a gentle swell. High above, pelicans drifted in the depths of a flawless blue sky, and sleek dolphins flashed through the clear waters as if challenging the vessel to race them to the mouth of the Brisbane River.

Two young ladies in dark bonnets and capes stood at the crowded rail of the small section of deck allotted to second-class passengers, eagerly viewing their progress.

'Shan't be long now,' Emilie said to her sister, excitement in her voice.

'Thank God for that. I can't wait to get off this dreadful ship.'

They passed several islands and Emilie consulted her notebook.

'It says here that one of those islands is called St Helena and it is also a prison. How extraordinary. And the other one is a leprosarium. What a horrible place that must be, Ruth.'

'Terrifying. But I suppose the poor things could be in worse places. The islands themselves appear pleasant.'

Other passengers began moving about, bringing cabin luggage up to the decks, gathering family and friends together to engage in lengthy farewell conversations and comparisons of further travel plans. But the Tissington sisters remained aloof. They were on their way to find employment as governesses in Brisbane or the vicinity, and in deference to their calling, they deemed it important to learn as much as possible about this new land. They had both kept journals of the voyage, and read everything they could find about Australia, but now they could physically expand their knowledge by not wasting a minute as they travelled down the river, taking note of its course and the unusual flora that bordered its muddy shores.

It must be said, too, that though they gave the impression of sophistication, neither of them was above a childish searching of those same shores for a glimpse of the famous kangaroos or koalas, but unfortunately not one marsupial as much as showed a nose from the greenery. Birds, however, were not in short supply. On past the coastal mangroves Ruth recognised stately eucalypts towering over bushland lit by clumps of startling red flowers, obviously a source of nectar for the thousands of brightly coloured birds that screeched and chattered along the banks.

Emilie was charmed. 'Will you look at those parrots! Aren't they just gorgeous?'

'Lorikeets, I believe. It's wonderful to be able to see them in the wild. Excellent subjects for your watercolours.'

They returned to their own thoughts, gazing at the unfamiliar country-side, Ruth's mind drifting unwillingly to the unhappy chain of events that had forced them to go abroad in search of a decent living. She shuddered. Had they not gained the support of the Female Middle Class Emigration Society they would by now have reached the end of their tether in London, living in hideous poverty, unemployed and desperate. She mourned their dear mother. Alice Tissington would have turned in her grave had she known the misery her two daughters had endured since her death. She had been an educated woman, her father a philosopher and mathematician, and she had seen to it that Ruth and Emilie received comprehensive tutelage in the arts in addition to the knowledge they acquired at the Brackham village school.

Three years ago . . . a lifetime ago, Ruth mused . . . their widowed father had remarried. The shy girls made their stepmother welcome, only to find that this woman begrudged their presence in the small household, and they were soon to hear in the village that she was given to gossiping about them, claiming that they were lazy and indolent, a couple of budding old maids who were a burden on their dear father. The twenty-three-year-old Ruth was shocked and embarrassed. In her quiet way she reminded the new Mrs Tissington that her earnings as a music teacher contributed to the housekeeping and that Emilie, only nineteen, was already taking private pupils in French and art appreciation.

'That's another thing,' the woman had retorted. 'I won't have my home turned into a schoolroom with all sorts marching in and out. Take your lessons elsewhere.'

Ruth appealed to William Tissington, who pointed out that his wife was within her rights. 'How can she entertain in her own drawing room if you've got juveniles plonking away on the piano in there? Besides, the poor woman is suffering headaches from the constant jangling.'

Confrontations between the women became more frequent. Emilie objected fiercely to their stepmother's constant carping, while Ruth endeavoured to solve the problems as a gentlewoman should, but to no avail. Naively, the sisters did not understand that a wife could undermine them, chipping away at their security until their base became very fragile.

When Emilie announced that she had invited friends to another of their musical evenings, Mrs Tissington flatly refused permission.

'I am informing you as a courtesy,' Emilie flared. 'Our musical evenings are highly regarded in the village, they always have been. Ruth

4

and I are entitled to a social life. We don't need your permission to have a few friends over; this is our home too, you know.'

'We'll see about that. I shall speak to Mr Tissington.'

'By all means!'

Their father's decision still rankled.

'I cannot put up with this constant bickering. This lady is my wife. She shouldn't have to put up with it either. She has done her best with you girls, but apparently you do not reciprocate her attempts at goodwill. It will be better if you find other accommodation.'

After the initial shock had subsided, the two young women agreed that a move wasn't such a bad idea after all. It would be pleasant to have their own home, to be independent, and wonderfully free of that dreadful person. However, they decided against renting accommodation in the village because it would soon be common knowledge that they had, in effect, been evicted from their own home. Neither of them was willing to suffer that humiliation. Better to go straight to London, where they knew a few people and where there would be a much wider scope of opportunities for them to seek engagements as tutors or day governesses.

Tissington gave Ruth twenty pounds to begin with, and a promise of further financial assistance, which never eventuated. He also arranged for a carrier to take their trunks and furniture to London. Furniture, his wife was quick to point out, that she was sparing them from her home, out of the goodness of her heart.

Thinking back now, Ruth realised how foolish she'd been to expect to arrive in London and find suitable employment with only personal references. As they were told time and again, by prospective employers and agents, they lacked experience.

She choked back a sob. But what else could they have done? Abandoned by their father, funds dwindling, they managed to earn a few shillings here and there, working at stop-gap jobs, assisting in libraries, letter-copying in offices, minding children in the absence of their nannies, and other insignificant posts, but desperation had set in. They sold their books and as much of their furniture as they could spare, moved to a bleak basement room, and sat in the dark at night, half starved, afraid even to waste a candle, and all the while their pleas to their father for help were ignored.

It was Emilie who heard about the Female Middle Class Emigration Society, Emilie who contacted them and stumbled on the first glimmer of good fortune the girls had encountered for such a long time. One of the members, checking their applications, had known their late mother. She was distressed to find that her friend's daughters had fallen on hard times, and immediately recommended that they be accepted into the emigration programme. They were soon deemed to be ideal to take up positions as governesses in Queensland, travelling under the auspices of the Society, and were offered a loan of two hundred pounds to cover their passage and expenses. The two girls were overjoyed. Not only had they narrowly escaped penury, but now they heard that they could expect to earn at least one hundred pounds a year as governesses in the Colony. They discovered, however, that there was one last hurdle to overcome. They had to produce a guarantor for the loan, in case they found themselves unable to refund the money within the specified three years. The guarantor would then become liable.

'What can we do?' Emilie had wailed. 'Who would guarantee us such a large amount?'

'Father.'

'Who? Definitely not! I wouldn't ask him if my life depended on it.'

'We have to try,' Ruth said gloomily. 'Our lives *could* depend on it.'

'He won't answer.'

'He just might. Don't you see? If he knows we're leaving the country, and that the Society has assured us of positions in the Colony, he'll be rid of us. No more begging letters. We will be able to repay the loan ourselves, with three years in which to do so. He's got nothing to lose. I believe he will write a guarantee for us. It's the least he can do now.'

Emilie finally agreed that they should ask him, but she had another plan in mind as a fallback position. 'Very well, write to him, Ruth. But if he refuses, I'll write the guarantee myself, and forge his signature.'

'Oh my Lord! You wouldn't!'

'I certainly would. By the time he found out, we'd have left the country.'

As it turned out, William Tissington did guarantee them, causing his daughters to despise him for that as well.

Now Emilie nudged her sister. 'Penny for your thoughts.'

Dismissing the past, Ruth smiled wanly. 'I do hope that when we take up our engagements we shan't be too far apart. They say that distance is a hard master out here, and travel is expensive.'

'Cheer up. We might even be employed by neighbours. I think we are coming to the outskirts of the town now, judging by those farmhouses.'

No matter how she tried, Ruth couldn't match Emilie's enthusiasm for this venture. She had only gone along with it because they had no choice. As the ship berthed at the Brisbane wharves, however, she felt a rush of relief. The town seemed pleasant, if countrified, with low white buildings surrounded by a backdrop of distant hills.

Some of the expenses incurred on boarding the *City of Liverpool* had been cabin fittings. They had managed a half-cabin to themselves, separated from two rowdy women by a canvas curtain, and had purchased mattresses for the bare bunks, as well as life preservers, lanterns, a toilet pail and various other shipboard necessities. However, they had saved money by bringing their own linen and crockery, lamps and candles. None of these items would be any use to them ashore, since they'd be taking up live-in positions, so Emilie was engaged in arranging their sale to the second mate, who would resell them to outgoing passengers, at a profit, no doubt.

Ruth waited for her sister in the cabin, to make sure that none of their belongings left the ship in the hands of the other women, who were great borrowers and poor returners. She took this opportunity to complete the letter she had written to Jane Lewin, director of the Society, thanking her for their kindness, promising to repay the loan as soon as possible, and describing the voyage as absolute misery from beginning to end. She made it very clear that ladies should not be sent out second class.

The company they'd been forced to endure for months had been inappropriate and intolerable. She described them as vulgarians of the lowest order, and their attitude to the only two *ladies* in their midst as disgraceful. She had no qualms about sending this information, as Miss Lewin had specifically mentioned that reports from their governesses would be appreciated.

When Emilie came down, grumbling that she'd only managed to prise two pounds out of the second mate, Ruth blushed.

'Oh well, that will have to do. You can hardly haggle.'

'I did haggle. He only wanted to give me one. We can go now, the steward will bring up our trunks. We're here, Ruth, do you realise that? We've arrived on the other side of the world. Isn't it amazing? I can't wait to explore.'

'I can't wait for the taste of fresh food again,' her sister said drily.

Contrary to expectations, there was no one to meet them. They stood forlornly on the wharf in the staggering heat, waiting for the agent, or at least an associate of the Society, to come for them, but no one appeared, nor had anyone enquired after them on board. As the afternoon shadows grew long, they had no recourse but to seek advice from the ship's captain, who recommended them to a boarding house in Adelaide Street.

'Best you retire for the evening, ladies, so that I know where you are when your tardy friends come a-searching. Then in the morning the sun will shine again and all will be well.'

He arranged for them to travel to the oddly named Belleview Boarding House in a horse cab, and they enjoyed the short journey until they discovered it had cost them three shillings plus seven pence for their trunks.

'We should have walked,' Ruth whispered.

'We couldn't, we might never have seen our trunks again.'

They were met by their landlady, a Mrs Medlow, who informed them that her tariff was four shillings and sixpence each overnight, or one guinea each at the weekly rate, full board. They took the overnight rate, explaining that they were unsure of their plans, and were shown to a large room on the ground floor.

The room, with its inviting single beds and immaculate appointments, was a godsend for the Tissingtons, but they simply accepted quietly, rather than give any indication that they'd recently emerged from second class.

'Dinner's at six. The bell will go any minute,' Mrs Medlow told them before departing.

'Oh, heavens!' Emilie cried. 'Real beds! Privacy. Cleanliness is next to godliness indeed. No more stinks and smells.' She pulled back the white counterpane on one bed. 'Do feel the sheets, Ruth. They're soft and sweet-smelling, not stiff from the salt wash. I may never leave here.'

Ruth laughed. 'I can smell the cooking. We must change quickly before I faint from hunger.'

Properly attired in dark taffeta dresses, tiny toques set primly on upswept hair, the Misses Tissington were ushered to their corner table in the dining room, under the curious gaze of other diners. An elderly gentleman sitting alone at a nearby table greeted them.

'Evening, ladies. Just off the boat, eh?'

Unaccustomed to being addressed so boldly by a complete stranger, Emilie could only manage a curt nod, while Ruth fumbled for her napkin, not a little shocked by his temerity. Dinner was a set menu, but the fare was excellent – rich broth, roast lamb with a tureen of fresh vegetables, and lemon pudding – and the girls ate as delicately as they could, reluctantly leaving a small portion of each dish in deference to propriety.

The waitress informed them that coffee would be served in the parlour, but they declined politely. Suddenly they were both very tired, the strain of the long, exhausting voyage taking its toll.

'I'm glad now that we weren't met,' Emilie sighed as she closed the bedroom door behind her. 'It is so much better for us to have this time to ourselves to recuperate.'

Before they retired, they kneeled to pray, giving thanks to the Lord for delivering them safely to shore, but the rest of their prayers were lost to weariness. In a matter of minutes they were both asleep, luxuriating in the peace and comfort of the unassuming boarding house room.

Julius Penn, Employment Agent, beamed at the long queue of females lined up outside his Ann Street office, greeting several of the regulars by name.

'You back again, Dulcie?' he said to a blonde woman as he unlocked the door. 'What went wrong this time?'

'They never paid me, that's what's wrong. I been cooking for them for a fortnight and all they can do is cry poormouth, tell me I have to wait for me money. How am I expected to pay me rent, I ask you?'

'Very well, very well, I'll cross them off the books. We'll find something else.'

'Seems to me half the bosses you got on your books oughta be crossed off,' she snapped, but he merely looked at the wall clock in his office and closed the door behind him, leaving her outside to compare complaints with the other hopefuls. Ten minutes to go before opening time.

He hung his hat and cane on a wooden peg, then removed his jacket and hooked it on another peg before taking his place at his desk in his shirtsleeves. As he lit a cheroot, he surveyed the rows of empty seats in front of him and shook his head. Dulcie was right: half the employers on his books would pull any trick to avoid paying servants. On the other hand, half of the females he sent out wouldn't know how to do a decent day's work, so it was tit for tat. He just moved them all about, collecting a shilling for each appointment from both employee and employer. Amazing how they added up, all those little shillings. Julius, now in his fiftieth year, wondered why he hadn't thought of this lark years ago. He'd had a hard life, he was wont to bewail, nothing had ever seemed to go right for him, though he'd had any number of jobs, from clerking to roaming the outback as a travelling salesman. Many a grand plan he'd had too, guaranteed to make his fortune in double-quick time, but they always fell flat. Take his invention of alcohol-free ale. He still couldn't figure out where his formula had gone wrong. The Temperance Society had run him out of Parramatta when several of their ladies had got roaring drunk.

He sighed, and sucked on his cheroot. Finding this business was sheer accident. He'd come to Brisbane to escape the burden of pressing debts in Sydney Town, and had gone in search of an employment agent only to discover that no such person existed. Within days Julius had set up this office, with his desk in the centre, facing his rows of applicants, and behind him a battered Chinese screen providing privacy for hopeful employers, who were afforded better seating on a couple of dingy sofas. After that, it was only a matter of ins and outs, he explained to the publican next door, who got the pick of the staff in return for the occasional free brandy. Julius ran a couple of advertisements in the *Brisbane Courier*, but there was no need to continue. Word of mouth did the rest. Everyone complained about his fees, but as he pointed out, in his best bank manager voice, they were inevitable. Whatever that meant.

The clock struck eight and that damn Dulcie was banging on the door, so he shouted at her to enter, sitting back with his thumbs in his braces as an avalanche of females burst into his office, jostling for positions.

'I'm first,' Dulcie yelled, plonking herself in the lone interview chair in front of his desk, while the others squawked and settled as if it were dusk in a chookhouse.

'Let me see.' He turned the pages in his neat employers' register. 'You could go to the Ship Inn. They want a cook.'

'I'm not goin' there. That bastard would bash you soon as look at you.'

'There's not much else for a cook at the minute. Unless you're prepared to go out to the bush.'

'The hell I will. Most of them out there got two heads.'

'Country towns aren't so bad. I get plenty of letters from people in country towns, they're desperate for ser . . . staff.' Julius had to watch what he was saying. Talking to employers, he always referred to 'servants', but after ten months in this business, he knew better than to use the word in front of these women. Cooks were cooks and maids were maids, or even domestics, but they balked at being labelled servants. Too close to the word 'servile' for these beauties. Red rag to a bull, in fact.

'What country towns?'

'Toowoomba, Maryborough.'

'Nah. I'll stick in town awhile.'

9

'I could place you as a housemaid. The Victoria Hotel.'

'I'm not a bloody housemaid, I'm a cook. How often do I have to tell you that, Julius?'

'All right. But there's nothing doing at the minute. Hang on to the job you've got.'

'With no pay and her entertaining all the toffs with lobsters and oysters and champagne like she's a Russian empress?'

Julius understood. Mrs Walter Bateman, wife of Chief Inspector Bateman of Customs, was an ambitious woman, famous for her parties but also well known to staff and tradesmen as a skinflint.

'Tell her you'll put the bailiffs on to her,' he murmured.

Dulcie stared. 'Jesus. That's ripe. I'd be out the door with a boot in me bum.'

'What have you got to lose?' he grinned, stroking his clipped grey moustache. 'She's good at sacking people when their pay is due. She'd be hard pressed to find anyone else. You could warn her.'

'I'd like to see her face if I try that one on her.'

'Up to you.'

Dulcie pulled a pink crocheted shawl over her shoulders and stood up. 'Doesn't say I'm gonna stay there, mind you. Pay or not.'

He nodded. 'We'll see. Who's next?'

Before Dulcie had even vacated the chair, a thin girl confronted him. 'You've got to help me, mister, I'm bleedin' desperate . . .'

The governesses peered in the agent's shopfront window, disbelieving.

'This can't be the place.' Ruth backed away.

'Yes it is. This is the address Miss Lewin gave us, and there's the name.'

'I am not going in there. It is obviously an establishment for servants. We can't be seen in that company.'

'Oh well, stay here! Perhaps there's another office. I'll enquire.'

Julius was interviewing a plump woman who required a position as a children's nurse. He was nodding cheerfully as he leafed through her references. He'd have no trouble placing this one.

When the door opened, he didn't bother to look up, but a stir in the room took his attention. A young woman with an air of authority approached his desk; a very pretty young woman, shapely too, in a neat-fitting navy-blue dress, brightened by a ribboned hat atop thick dark hair.

Taking her for a prospective employer, Julius was out of his seat in a second to escort her to his inner sanctum.

'Are you Mr Penn?'

The voice was cultured, as sweet as the owner.

'At your service, dear lady. Do be seated. It's very warm today. May I offer you a glass of water?'

'No thank you, Mr Penn. I fear I must be in the wrong place, but perhaps you can redirect me. I am Miss Tissington; my sister and I were referred to you by the Female Middle Class Emigration Society. We are the governesses you required, but we appear to have intruded upon the wrong section of your agency.'

'Gawd!' Julius said under his breath. He remembered that Society now. They had written to him months ago – it must be six months ago – asking if he could place highly recommended governesses in suitable positions, and he'd replied in the affirmative, flattered that his fame had spread to London. He guessed someone had sent them his advertisement. Having heard nothing more, he had forgotten all about them.

'Dear lady, you are not in the wrong place, and I must apologise for these premises. We are only in a small way here. My head office is in Sydney.'

From women travelling interstate he'd heard that there were separate employment agencies for a better class of female, but he couldn't afford to rent two premises. The few well-educated women who came his way seeking engagements did not warrant such extravagance, even though it would add to his prestige.

'I see.' Unimpressed, she handed him a neatly bound file. 'Here is my letter of introduction from the Society, and the originals of my references. You *were* expecting us? Miss Lewin did write to you?'

'Well, she may have done, Miss Tissington, but I have not heard from the Society in quite some time. It is possible that advice of your imminent arrival is still on the high seas. Or it may have accompanied you on your ship. When did you arrive?'

'Yesterday. We were distressed that we were not met. We were given to understand that we would be met and taken immediately to our places of employment.' Her confidence was ebbing. 'Is no one expecting us?'

'Not right now, but of course that's temporary. I just need a little time to look into this, you understand.'

'My sister is outside. Shall I ask her to come in? Or are you too busy? There are so many people waiting.'

Julius was anxious to please, and he felt sorry for her, but the people waiting meant shillings if he could separate the wheat from the chaff. 'Tell you what, why don't you take a stroll for a while, familiarise yourself with the town? I'm sure you'll find Brisbane most interesting. Then I'll meet you at twelve noon at the little café down the street, where we can talk. In quieter surroundings.' His waiting clients were becoming restive.

'We do not have positions to go to?' Ruth was horrified. 'Are you sure?'

'No, I'm not sure. He confused me. He wasn't expecting us.'

'Even so, he does have positions available? He assured the Society of that. You should have insisted on knowing what they were so that we could discuss them.'

'Why didn't you go in yourself, if you're so smart? At least I made contact with the agency.'

11

'Such as it is,' Ruth sniffed. 'I'll have something to say to Miss Lewin about this state of affairs, too. And how dare he expect us to cool our heels until midday in this heat.'

'I doubt our heels will cool,' said Emilie with a wry smile.

'Don't pun.'

'It wasn't a pun. We could go in search of the post office, that will fill in time.'

The morning was hot and humid. As they walked up the main street, Ruth regretted the addition of a short cape to her day dress, but she could hardly remove it and carry it through the town. Surreptitiously she dabbed with a gloved hand at beads of perspiration under her eyes, while observing the contents of shop windows. They were all well stocked with quality goods, surprising for an outpost like this, but prices were high.

'Have you noticed that ladies here are wearing much larger hats?' Emilie asked her. 'Do you think we are out of fashion?'

'No. I believe it's more to do with the sunlight. We'd be better advised to do likewise in the future or risk sunburn.'

They found the post office, sent Ruth's letter on its way and explored the neat grid of streets that composed the business centre, but a few blocks away from the river took them into high residential terraces, so they turned back. Taking another route downhill, they were buoyed to discover a town hall and a cathedral, and they agreed that the town held promise. They found evidence of culture: a museum, a playhouse, even an advertisement for the Brisbane Philharmonic Society. Unaccustomed to the heat, they were both tiring when they arrived at the impressive Parliament House, which was surrounded by huge trees on the banks of the river, but they still had more than an hour to fill.

'We should go back to the boarding house and inform Mrs Medlow that we'll probably have to stay another night,' Ruth said.

'Not yet. Wait until we hear something definite from that wretched Mr Penn. We might be better to take the weekly rate after all.'

'Weekly? Surely not.'

'We just don't know. And the overnight rate is expensive.'

'Not as expensive as paying for accommodation we may not need.'

In the end they proceeded to nearby public gardens, where they seated themselves disconsolately on a shaded park bench.

Penn was waiting for them when they arrived at the café, and he waved a letter as he placed them at a corner table.

'What did I say, ladies? Here's the advice from Miss Lewin. You might as well have delivered it yourselves. I believe I am meeting the other Miss Tissington now. A pleasure. Not often I make the acquaintance of two such charming ladies in the one day.'

Ruth was cool. Sitting stiffly in her chair, she acknowledged his greeting with a curt nod. Her references were in her handbag, rolled up and tied with cord, but she had no intention of producing them in public.

'Now,' he said, 'will you have tea? Yes, tea and savoury scones, I think.

Excellent here.' He waved to the waitress and gave the order, then turned to Emilie.

'I must say, Miss Emilie – may I call you Miss Emilie? To differentiate, you understand – your references are excellent. Quite remarkable, in fact. I see that, besides the three Rs, you teach music, piano I hope. Not a decent household in this neck of the woods lacks a piano.'

Emilie ducked her head at him to interrupt the flow. 'Piano. Yes, we both teach piano, and singing.'

'Quite so. And French, elocution, dancing and drawing.'

'No, painting. My sister teaches drawing.'

'Indeed, yes, of course. Very talented ladies.'

'Thank you, Mr Penn,' Ruth said. 'But I was wondering, do you have any news for us?'

'Not as yet, I've been exceeding busy this morning.' He rambled on as the waitress served them, describing the delights of Brisbane and the families they were likely to encounter, in town or in the country, until Ruth again intervened.

'But you have nothing definite?'

'Oh, early days yet.'

Over tea, he asked a lot of questions. How many children could they cope with? What ages? Did they prefer city or country? What remunerations did they require? Emilie responded until she began to realise that he was only stalling for time.

'Surely you would have received this information from the Society, Mr Penn?'

'Yes, but it's just as well to hear it from the horse's mouth, so to speak. I want you to be happy, Miss Tissington.'

Wearily Ruth watched as he took the last scone. 'We were hoping you might be able to arrange some interviews for us this afternoon, but am I right in assuming that you do not have any vacancies for governesses on your books?'

'Temporarily, Miss Tissington. But that is not to say I won't have them. Now that you have arrived on our shores, word will go out. I will see to it. Right away, in fact. Now, where are you staying?'

They gave him the address, and he nodded sagely. 'An excellent address. Mrs Medlow is well regarded. Now, I have to leave you, ladies. Duty calls. But I'll be in touch. You make the best of a little holiday before your duties commence.'

They watched him stop by the counter to pay, collect a battered top hat and hurry out.

'The man's a blowhard,' Ruth said, exasperated, but then she saw that Emilie was upset. Obviously she had come to the same conclusion. 'I daresay he'll make an effort now, though.'

'What if we can't find work here, Ruth? Is it happening to us all over again?'

'Certainly not. You saw his reaction to your references. I don't think there are too many ladies here who are as well qualified as we are. Oh dear, I must give him my references, but tomorrow will do.'

As they left the café, which was now crowded, a little bell over the door tinkled, and the waitress came running.

'Ladies. You forgot to pay.'

Ruth bridled. 'We did not. The gentleman paid.'

'Mr Penn? No, he paid for himself. He didn't want you to have to pay for him. You owe four shillings.'

Embarrassed, they scrambled for the coins and made a hasty exit.

That afternoon, when he had closed his office, Penn did make an effort. The Tissington girls were high-class clients, and he was certain he could place them, and charge a little more. He went first to the gentlemen's bar in the Victoria Hotel to begin his enquiries and spread the word about the newcomers, and while he did raise interest in the ladies themselves, he found nothing in the way of possible employment. But as he had warned them, these were early days. He also visited the bushmen's bar in the Royal Hotel, since that was the meeting place for wealthy graziers, but the result was the same. Undeterred, he planned to further his enquiries at the Turf Club on the morrow, it being Saturday, certain he'd have more luck there with the well-to-do society types who turned out in force for the races. They'd pass the word along.

Emilie bought a paper on the way back to the Belleview, delighted to be able to catch up on world news again, but as she folded it, she noted the day.

'Oh my goodness. It's Friday! Unless he can place us tomorrow, we'll have to wait until Monday to see people. I think we'd better ask for the weekly rate after all.'

Their landlady did allow them the weekly rate, until next Friday, she emphasised.

'No, that will be Thursday,' Emilie said firmly. 'Since we came in yesterday. Here is the balance for the week, in advance.' She was canny enough to know, from their London difficulties, that 'cash up' was always a telling point with landladies, and Mrs Medlow was no different.

'This is highly irregular,' she grumbled, 'but I suppose it will have to do. You can have the same room.'

'Thank you.'

'Do you expect to be staying on after that?'

'No.'

'You have friends here in Brisbane, Miss Tissington?'

'Of course,' Emilie lied, and Ruth, standing back, was shocked.

'What did you say that for? Mr Penn knows her. He could tell her the truth.'

Emilie shrugged. 'Who cares? She shouldn't be so inquisitive.'

For her part, Mrs Medlow watched them disappear down the passage to their room and muttered, 'Hoity-toity pair!'

She looked at their neat signatures in her lodgers' book. The taller one with the dark hair was Emilie, and the elder of the two, fairer and more on the chubby side, was Ruth. Had she to make a choice, she preferred Ruth, but they were both too high-and-mighty for her liking. Nevertheless, she was immensely curious about them. Their clothes were good quality, full skirts only lightly hooped in the new fashion, but they wore no jewellery of any sort, not even rings or earrings. Some of her boarders thought they might be missionaries, but Mr Kemp had laughed at that.

'Not them. They're too poised. Schoolteachers, I reckon.'

'You're wrong about that,' said his wife. From her recollections, schoolteachers were old, ugly and dowdy, not genteel like these girls. She was already aware that her large flounced crinolines would have to be modified eventually. 'I think they're society ladies just waiting for transport to one of those big sheep stations out west, where all the nobs live. We must get to know them.'

Mrs Kemp was delighted to hear that the newcomers were staying on. Her husband had been transferred to Brisbane only recently, and had taken up his new appointment as Superintendent of Police as a favour to his cousin, Charles Lilley, the Queensland Attorney-General. At this late stage in his career, Jasper Kemp would have preferred to remain in his beloved Sydney, a city remarkable for its beauty and contrariness, but his wife suffered from severe arthritis, and the doctors had advised that a move to a warmer clime would be beneficial. As well, Lilley had offered him an excellent salary, and a new house, which was already under construction in Fortitude Valley, not too far from the town centre. The Attorney-General had good reason to import an experienced New South Wales police officer, because, as they all well knew, bad lads from that state were crossing the border in search of easier pickings in Queensland, where the distances between towns, and goldfields, made communication more difficult. And where they stood less chance of being recognised.

Kemp knew he had a tough job ahead of him, enforcing law and order in a state that wasn't even fully explored, with poorly trained men and a slack administration, especially since British troops were being withdrawn. Ever since the first colony was settled, troopers had been the mainstay of law enforcement throughout the country, but it was time now for the colonies to take charge.

The Attorney-General had approved the intake of more police, but on another matter he and Kemp were already at odds. Legislation known as the Felons Apprehension Act was already in force in New South Wales, and Lilley was determined to introduce the same law in Queensland despite Jasper Kemp's opposition. This Act stated that bushrangers could be declared outlaws and shot on sight. Kemp was appalled. He argued long and hard that it would give any trigger-happy policeman, or civilian, for that matter, licence to take the law into his own hands. But the Superintendent could make no more impact on the decision here than he could as a lowly chief inspector in the south.

On the Saturday morning he was standing on the veranda of the boarding house, taking the air and mulling over this very problem prior to setting off for a meeting with local inspectors, when the English ladies

15

emerged, making straight for the garden gate, to turn right, heading into town. Despite their sedate appearance, he could see by their faces that they were troubled about something, and wondered what it could be. His wife followed them out of the front door, bristling like a testy bantam hen.

'Those girls!' she said to him. 'They're so rude. I only asked them if they were off out for a walk, and they ignored me. Walked on past as if I didn't exist. What have I done that they should be so rude to me?'

'Nothing, love. Seems to me they've got a lot on their minds. Worry makes people standoffish, you know.'

'First I heard of it.'

'Well, now you know. I'll be back for lunch, then do you feel like coming with me to see how the house is progressing?'

'Oh, yes. Mrs Medlow wants to come too. She's very interested.'

I'll bet she is, he thought. Boarding house life didn't appeal to him, too many hangers-on, and Medlow was one who'd stick like glue.

Ruth and Emilie did not realise they had serious adjustments to make. They were unaware of the propensity for colonials to address strangers at will, and the necessity to respond politely. They did not appreciate that woman's inquisitive approach, asking what they were about, and their own rules of propriety required that they simply proceed. By the time they were out of the gate they had forgotten her.

'Did you bring your references?' Emilie asked Ruth.

'Yes. I have them. And this time we will sit down in his office and discuss the matter properly. He did advise Miss Lewin that positions were available.'

'But that was months ago.'

'Nevertheless, some of those posts could still be vacant. They mightn't have found suitable governesses. We must pin that fellow down.'

There were to be no discussions this day, though. Penn's office was firmly closed and the blinds drawn.

'It's Saturday.' Emilie wilted. 'Obviously he doesn't open on weekends at all.'

'He could have told us! It just goes to show what a lackadaisical wretch he is. Well, we shall be here first thing Monday morning.'

A low cover of cloud hid the sun but gave no respite from the heat. Instead it blanketed the town, steaming it to the point of perpetual damp. Ruth could feel a trickle of perspiration between her breasts, and it annoyed her that Emilie could manage to look so cool. The younger girl didn't perspire to this extent, yet another one of the advantages she had over her sister, trivial though it may be.

She sighed. 'We might as well go back to the room.'

'No.' Emilie was definite about that. It was Ruth's answer to every setback, in London and on the ship, and Emilie had had enough of hiding behind closed doors, cringing from the world.

'What else can we do?'

16

'We could go for a walk.'

'In this heat? The humidity is suffocating.'

'I know, but we'll just have to get used to it. It isn't going away. This is their summer, after all.'

'So it might be, but we don't have to be foolish about it. Anyway, we took the measure of the town yesterday.'

'If you don't want to walk, then you go back. I've plenty of time. I'd like to go a little further and see what the suburbs have to offer.'

'You can't go wandering about on your own.'

'Oh, for heaven's sake. Sooner or later we'll be working in places on our own. A walk won't do any harm, and at least I'll know a bit more about the town.'

Huffily, Ruth turned away. 'If that's how you feel, go ahead, but be careful and don't get lost.'

As they parted, Emilie was delighted. She and Ruth got along very well, their fondness for each other matured by shared adversity, but in truth, Emilie had long been tiring of their forced closeness. They had their occasional spats, but that wasn't the problem; she felt that her sister was becoming more and more withdrawn, and she was dragging Emilie back with her, suffocating her. Emilie likened their relationship to this suffocating heat, which she felt just as much as Ruth, but one had to break free, overcome it. Move on. She would be glad when they were both placed so that they could get on with their lives separately, not tied together, too dependent on each other. She walked up to the main street, which she now knew to be Queen Street, determined to follow it to the end and beyond. It was just so good to be alone, and free to go wherever she wished without an argument.

Charles Lilley might be the Attorney-General but he was also representative in Parliament for the good people of Fortitude Valley, a riverside electorate a stone's throw from the more dependable Brisbane constituency. When he'd first been elected to the State Legislative Assembly, he'd been proud of the Valley voters for their confidence in him, but ever since then it had been an uphill fight to maintain his hold on the shifting sands of public opinion. He groaned as he wrestled to fit a gold stud into a heavily starched collar that was already softening in a sweaty hollow created by his beard. Fortitude Valley had begun life as an almost palatial residential suburb, but its main street had been invaded by shopkeepers unable to get a foothold in the Brisbane commercial centre. Stables, saddlers and small factories had also taken advantage of this handy suburb, and workmen's cottages crowded in behind them, taking over the gentle open fields. Riverside residents hung on, jealous of their fine views, cooling breezes and magnificent Moreton Bay fig trees, steadfastly turning their backs on the broil of humanity building up in the Valley commercial centre. Hotels and gaming houses abounded; mysterious Chinamen brought their wealth from the goldfields, but made no show of it, preferring obscurity in laundries and dingy shops. Houses of ill repute blatantly muscled their way into the forefront, beside drapers and tailors, while their ladies hung boisterously over high balconies, calling to the worldly sailormen from merchant ships who cocked a sly eye at them.

And over this predatory and opinionated mob reigned Charles Lilley, Esquire. He wished to hell he'd taken up a constituency on the other side of Brisbane, where new suburbs like Paddington and Toowong and Yeronga were remaining staid and decidedly decent, but there it was. He had won Fortitude Valley, and he was stuck with it. Stuck with shouting workers who'd rather have a fight than feed. Stuck with genteel residents who wanted no part of his battles with socialist elements that harangued him at every turn. Fortunately, though, women, renters and the young spoilers didn't get votes, although one would think they did judging by their mass turnouts at public meetings demanding all sorts of justice, which could be translated as money. Charles was always astonished to see women out there, joining with their menfolk, shouting him down as if they were enacting some replay of the French revolution.

'Dreadful people!' he sniffed at the mirror as the stud fell into place at last.

His stalwart riverside residents were with him, as, oddly, were the Chinese. Charles had been horrified to find so many of them moving into his electorate, God only knew how many, but strange elderly gentlemen with long pigtails and bowing minions had called at his home by appointment, and in their heavy-lidded way had set him straight on a few things.

They did not want trouble.

They were, despite wild rumours to the contrary, law-abiding citizens.

They had bought their unassuming homes and businesses and wanted no further advancement. Most of their money, he learned, went back to support relatives in China.

They would be honoured, great sir, to pay their dues to him as gentlemen and representatives of honourable families.

'And by God,' he said to the mirror as he straightened his frock coat and adjusted the folds of his black tie, 'they are right. How many Chinks in jail? None. Seems they attend to their own villains.' Charles shuddered. He preferred not to know too much about their methods. On the face of it, they were model citizens, contributing to his election funds and minding their own business. They wouldn't be among the rowdies guaranteed to turn up at this morning's public meeting.

His secretary, Daniel Bowles, met him at the gate.

'What are you doing here? I thought I asked you to go straight to the park . . .'

'I did, sir. The dais is set up. It's quite firm . . .'

'I hope it's in the shade.'

'Yes. And I hung the flag on the tree behind where you stand. But Mr Lilley, the Mayor has decided not to speak.'

'What? He was supposed to introduce me. Typical of that fool to renege on a commitment. Only yesterday he promised he would be there.'

18

Daniel shook his head. 'He was there earlier. There's a big crowd gathering, Mr Lilley, and the mood is not good. The Mayor asked me to tell you he thought it would be wise to call the meeting off.'

'Call it off? After an advertisement in the local paper specifically stated I would be speaking at ten a.m. this morning? I can't do that. It's unheard of.'

He set his black top hat firmly on his head and began striding up the street.

Daniel hurried to keep up with his boss. 'Mr Lilley, having seen that mob, I'm inclined to agree with the Mayor. As he says, discretion is the better part of valour.'

'Discretion, poppycock! The man's a shirker. I am aware that people have good reason to be alarmed, that's why it is necessary for me to speak. I have to explain that though unemployment is rife at present, these things do right themselves.'

Angrily he plunged round a corner. 'It's not our fault that blasted bank collapsed, taking the government credit with it. We simply couldn't pay our workers. But we are re-establishing credit and all will be well now.' He looked at the gold watch that was strung across his waistcoat on a gold chain. 'It's ten to ten. Come on, Daniel, get a move on. You will have to introduce me.'

'Me? I'm not a public speaker, sir.'

'You are now.'

The crowd was ominously quiet as Lilley strode into the park with his secretary, lifting his hat in cheerful greeting to sullen faces as they parted to make way for him, but at this point Daniel was more concerned with his new role than with the hostility that confronted them.

As he stepped up on to the platform, he looked back to see Lilley in earnest conversation with Joe Fogarty, a waterside worker and a rabble-rouser of the first order. Apparently it wasn't going too well, because Fogarty was shouting and waving his arms at Mr Lilley, who finally shrugged and marched up to join his secretary.

'Go ahead.' He nudged Daniel. 'Deep breath. Loud voice.'

'What will I say?'

Nervously, Daniel stepped forward. He raised his arms as he had seen politicians do. Quickly he looked out over the crowd, realising in fright that there were so many they spilled out into a nearby street. They were a drab lot, poor-looking, in shabby clothes, but not all workmen: there were clerks among them, and teachers, some of whom he recognised, and even a few women. That set the tone for him.

'Ladies and gentlemen,' he cried in a voice that sounded too high-pitched, 'thank you for coming along today. This is an important meeting, as no doubt you all know, and I . . .'

'Who are you?' a voice shouted, and roars of laughter drowned Daniel's attempt to introduce himself, which he had thought necessary.

A woman shrieked at him, 'Go home to your mother!'

Red-faced, clutching his straw boater, Daniel plunged on, though he could hardly hear his own voice over the bellows of derision. 'It is my pleasure to introduce to you Mr Charles Lilley, Member of the Legislative Assembly for the State of Queensland, and . . .' But Mr Lilley came forward at last to rescue him.

There was a sudden silence as Lilley stood tall, nodding his thanks to Daniel, who drew back swiftly.

'Ladies and gentlemen, your government is well aware of the problems you are facing . . .'

'Since when?' a raucous voice shouted, and others picked up the call, but Lilley waited until the noise died down.

'I am here to listen to what you have to say and to seek out solutions with you, but we can't do that if agitators among you are determined to drown out reason.'

'Then give us your reasoning,' Fogarty yelled. 'The banks are operating again. Why is it taking so long to reinstate workers who were put off?' He acknowledged a cheer from the crowd with a wave of his cap.

'It's not that simple. We will be starting public works shortly: new roads, a new General Post Office to be built in Queen Street . . .'

'When?'

A hard-faced group of men had moved to the front of the crowd. Daniel didn't like the look of them and he wondered if Mr Lilley had noticed them.

'They're in the planning stages now.'

'In the meantime people starve while you go to the races,' one of these men shouted, deliberately misunderstanding as Lilley shook his head to point out that he was here now.

'Don't lie! You're off to the races today. You've got a horse running, Lilley.' The stranger climbed on to the dais to grab the limelight, annoying Fogarty, who was rousing the crowd for his own purposes, rounding on Lilley as a charlatan, a bigmouth, a rich fool who didn't care a whit about the workers.

Lilley called down to Fogarty, 'Who's this fellow?'

But Fogarty shrugged, frustrated by the knowledge that the meeting was almost out of hand, with men jostling in the forefront and placard wavers pushing at the rear.

Daniel noticed that a horseman had reined his mount in at the entrance to the park, and now another joined him, both watching curiously but taking no part in the action. Fogarty was still down there, quiet but scowling, and Daniel realised that the waterside worker must have had a plan of his own to grab an opportunity to address the crowd, because he was known to have political ambitions. Obviously in all this confusion he'd given up, and Daniel wished Lilley would too, but his boss was still speaking, shouting now, as angry as his audience.

Suddenly the crowd erupted, surging forward with shouts of 'Grab the bastard!'

'We ought to hang him!'

They were yelling, 'Lynch him!' and swarming up on to the dais.

Daniel jumped clear to land among the mob surrounding the platform, but nobody cared about him. Fogarty was shouting too, but he was trying to stop this onslaught, grabbing at men mounting the steps, pulling them back, while Lilley was getting the worst of it, caught in the fiercely jostling mob.

Then one of the horsemen plunged forward with reckless disregard for people scattering to safety, heading for the dais. After a couple of minutes' delay, the second horseman must have decided to assist as well. He was only a young fellow, big, fair-haired, riding into the mob cracking a stockwhip, and Daniel noticed, as he ran backwards from the mêlée, that he was laughing. Thoroughly enjoying himself.

'It's no laughing matter,' Daniel muttered, worried about Lilley, feeling guilty that he'd run away, but what could he have done against that mob?

The Parliamentary representative was furious to be manhandled by these thugs, and he gave as good as he got, punching wildly, hearing his coat rip as he wrenched hands from him, kicking vulnerable ankles with his hard leather boots, swearing and shouting at his attackers to desist. He heard the yells of fools threatening to lynch him, but was more concerned with remaining upright for fear he could get trampled underfoot. He was saved from being dragged from the platform by the sweating sway of the mob, coming at him from different directions.

He glimpsed a red-bearded horseman looming up almost level with the affray and took him to be another thug, part of the crowd menacing him from below. But the fellow leaned forward just as Lilley realised that the crush had him dangerously close to the edge of the dais. He felt the man grab his arm in an iron grip.

'Climb aboard, mate!' he shouted, indicating the horse's rump.

The intervention caused a slight lull of surprise, giving Lilley enough time to assess the situation.

'Certainly not!' he shouted. He had no intention of being rescued like some silly maiden.

Instead he jumped down to the safe space provided between the horse and the platform, and grabbed for the stirrups to steady himself.

Already the horse was moving forward, sheltering him, but the mob would not give him up so easily. Clods of dirt were hurled at them and men began lurching against him.

Then he heard the crack of a stockwhip, and another horseman reared up beside him, ignoring the screams of pain as the vicious whip connected at will. The second rider jumped down, handed Lilley the reins to his horse and dived away into the crowd before anyone had a chance to grasp what had happened. This time Lilley consented. He flung himself into the saddle and the two plunging horses soon parted the crowd and galloped away to the exit from the park, leaving the mob to sort itself out.

Once free, they rode into a quiet street where Lilley reined in his mount and turned to the other rider.

'I have to thank you, sir. Those thugs might have done me a real damage.'

'Why?' the man asked him.

'Political unrest. What they call bread-and-butter riots.'

'I get you. I thought you must be some sort of politician.'

'I am Charles Lilley. I am the Member for this electorate. I was trying to explain to those fools . . .'

'Better you do it with an armed guard next time. Never met a politician before. Pleased to meet you.' He reached over to shake hands with Lilley. 'Do you live around here? I'd better get you home. Reckon you'll startle the ladies walking the streets like that.'

Only then did Lilley remember to take stock of his dishevelled appearance. He had lost his hat, and his clothes were grubby and torn.

'Oh God! I've lost my watch.'

'Worth a bit, was it?'

'Worth a lot. Watch and chain were gold. But I prized it because it belonged to my late father.'

'No point in going back to look for it,' the stranger said ruefully. 'Someone will have snapped it up by this. It'd buy a lot of bread and butter.'

'Damn shame. Oh well, best we move along. Who was your friend? I'd like to thank him too.'

'Never seen him before in my life. Only a kid. Smart, though. Smart enough to get himself out of there fast too. He was bloody free with that stockwhip.'

'Serves them right,' Lilley grumbled. 'But what about his horse? What should I do with it?'

'Don't worry. You can ride it home and I'll take it back. I'll find him.' He glanced at the chestnut horse with a white flash on its face. 'He's only a youngster, and as cheeky as his master. Didn't flinch at that mob at all. My old nag, she's been a stock horse; two-legged animals don't bother her.'

When they reached Lilley's gate, Daniel came running from the other direction.

Lilley had regained his composure. He dismounted and clapped his secretary on the shoulder. 'At least you got out of it unscathed. Have you got any money on you?'

'I've only got about ten shillings.'

'That will have to do. Give it to this gentleman here. Small tribute for his troubles.'

Daniel hoped the fellow would be a gentleman and refuse. It was difficult to obtain reimbursement of these borrowings from the great man, who usually forgot all about them. But this was no gentleman. He accepted the ten shillings as his right, took the other horse, bade them good day and rode away.

James McPherson considered it was a good day's work. He'd earned ten shillings and a new horse.

Emilie made sure that she would not get lost by keeping the river to her

22

right, if only managing to glimpse it through uncleared blocks, because there did not appear to be riverside walks. Once she left the town centre, there were no footpaths, so she kept to the side of the sandy roads for shade and safety. The few riders and vehicles she saw tore past at a pace that seemed odd, considering the somnolence of the day. But then, Emilie decided, maybe she had not quite adjusted to traffic after months on the ship. And, after those months of inaction, it was truly wonderful to be able to step out so freely; the exercise was doing her good already. The heat didn't seem so bad now either, since her face was protected by a silk-lined straw bonnet and there was a slight breeze to accompany her.

The contrast in flora was quite amazing. The blocks of land that had not yet met the axe were overgrown with matted bushes, tangled grass and tall, skinny trees, eucalypts, which looked as if they had just escaped for air, with thick green vines hanging relentlessly from their sides like malevolent bonds. Had she not known better, Emilie would have referred to this almost impregnable bushland as jungle. The fact that there were no palm trees or other such tropical plants was, however, a surprise to her. Thinking back now, she'd expected this town to be awash with waving palms but there were few to be seen except when planted in private gardens. She peered, interested, into those gardens, noting that apart from the occasional palms she might as well be back in England, since the residents preferred roses, lavender, hydrangea and their fellows to native plants. Emilie thought that was rather a pity, and quite unadventurous, because she'd already noticed some superbly perfumed native plants growing in wild profusion by the wayside.

Drawn in by the heavenly fragrance, Emilie couldn't resist the temptation to pick a few delicate white frangipani flowers to take back to the room, but as she stepped towards the huge bush through a fringe of dried grass, she gave an almighty shriek. She was shocked at herself! Never in all her life had she screamed as loudly and as vulgarly as that, but she was confronted by the head of a huge snake, mouth hanging open, cold eyes staring. It didn't move. Neither did Emilie. She couldn't, she did not dare, the snake had her transfixed. Emilie had seen snakes before, but never one with a head that size. The skin looked as grey and tough as chain mail, and those eyes still stared balefully at her.

A woman came running. 'What's wrong?'

'Snake,' Emilie whispered, hardly breathing.

'Are you bit?'

'No.'

'Are you standing on it?'

'No.'

'I can't see a decent stick anywhere,' the woman muttered, as if to herself. 'You'll have to jump away from it. They're more scared of you than you are of them.'

Emilie didn't believe that for one minute, nor could she move.

The woman behind her waited, but when it became evident that neither the snake nor the girl was giving way, she said, 'Oh well . . .'

In a second it was over. The woman had grabbed Emilie and flung her away. The pair almost toppled over in the scramble, but when they found their feet the woman stunned Emilie by turning back: 'To get a look at the rascal.'

Then she laughed. 'Come see, girl. That's no snake. He's a big old goanna, like as not the one that robs my chicken coop.'

Snake or not, Emilie had no intention of going near the monster. She shook her head and stayed back.

'Be off with you then!' The woman waved her arms and stamped her feet, and the goanna disappeared, rustling into the grass only to emerge speeding up a nearby tree.

'There he goes.' Her rescuer was excited. 'See! He's a big fellow. You never seen one before?'

'No.'

'Then remember, lizards have legs, snakes don't. And lizards won't hurt you.'

In her defence, Emilie wanted to point out that she hadn't been able to see the goanna's legs in the undergrowth, but that seemed rather petty, so instead she thanked the woman for her kindness, and there they stood, watching, interested, as the goanna clung to the tree, its head moving slowly from side to side as if to detect further assaults on its dignity.

Each to her own, they parted with smiles, and Emilie set off again, heading away from the river, pleased to have a tale to tell Ruth on her return. She had only walked a few more blocks when she saw a young man racing down the street towards her. He gave the impression that someone might be chasing him, but there was no one in sight. As he reached her, though, he looked back and slowed, puffing, almost out of breath, then stopped to speak to her.

'I wouldn't go that way, miss. There's a mob in the park and they'll be likely to spill out into the streets.'

'I beg your pardon!'

He grinned. 'Only a suggestion, miss. A detour might be in order.'

Emilie stared, half believing him, but detour? Where? She was confused.

'Come on, I'll walk you back to the corner.'

He was about her own age, tall, with longish fair hair under a wide hat, and, she had to admit, the sunniest smile she'd ever seen on a man. His face was tanned and he had twinkling blue eyes. But he was no gentleman: his clothes were rough and he had an ugly leather whip coiled over his shoulder.

Taking his advice, Emilie had no wish to proceed, nor did she want to be seen walking with him, but he gave her no choice. With a light touch he turned her about, fortunately not taking her arm after that or she'd have had to shake him off, and then, as casually as you like, strolled along beside her.

'Just taking the air, miss?'

'Yes.'

24

'Nice day for a walk.'

Emilie refused to engage in conversation with this upstart, but it didn't seem to bother him; he simply walked along beside her. There were only about twelve houses between where he'd forced his company on her and the next street, but they seemed like forty to Emilie, who was in an agony of embarrassment.

At the corner, though, he stopped again. 'Where are you headed?'

Emilie had had quite enough of him. 'Back to the town centre,' she snapped.

'That's good. You'll not be inconvenienced. Just go up this way and turn left.' He laughed. 'You were going in the wrong direction anyway.'

Her temper spilled over at that. 'I was not! I was going where I chose.'

His face fell as if she'd hurt his feelings. Emilie was exasperated. What about her feelings? Being accosted by a stranger in a quiet street, with some tale about a mob.

'I'll leave you to it then,' he said sheepishly, tipped his hat to her and strode away.

As she resumed her walk, taking the direction he had indicated, she couldn't resist a glance back at him, and then she blushed. He'd caught her! She could see his amusement as he waved to her. So much for his hurt feelings! To shut him out, Emilie held her bonnet fiercely with one gloved hand and stamped away, head in the air.

'Now there goes one pretty lady,' the young man said to himself. Still thinking of the English girl, he gave an appreciative wink to an old biddy hobbling down to her gate,

'Ah, get out with ye!' she responded with a toothy grin.

He wished he could have stayed with the girl. He'd have walked her all the way into town if she'd asked him; if she hadn't been so high and haughty. He'd even have told her his name, his real name, Mallachi Willoughby, and that was a rare thing, he pondered. An event, you could say.

As he strode along, being in no hurry now, he even considered dodging up another street and coming upon her again, as if by accident, but he knew better than to push his luck. She was a real lady, no doubt about that, and no doubt either that she wanted no truck with the likes of him. He supposed he couldn't blame her. After all, he was only a drifter. These last five years since his pa had died in an alcoholic stupor, way back at Gurundi Station, he'd been on the road.

Once, the Willoughby family had lived on a small farm two days' ride out of Sydney. Right from the start his sister had called him Sonny, and the name had stuck. That had been a good time, he recalled.

He'd loved the small timber farmhouse with its warm kitchen, its cramped bedroom where Ma and Pa slept and its sleepout that housed the two children. The farm was dry and dusty in the summer, cold and soggy in the winter, but he'd never noticed; he was always busy, finding things to amuse himself in the barns or the cowsheds, or wandering the fields far and beyond the creek.

'A happy child,' they all said, and recalling, Sonny nodded. It was true enough even now. He couldn't see the point in being miserable. He'd been the odd one out at the single-roomed schoolhouse only a mile from the farm, attended by eleven kids of various ages. They'd hated school with a vengeance, plotting interminably about getting their own back on their teacher, Mr Patterson, whose main teaching aid was his strap. Not that they'd ever succeeded. Sonny was the only one who liked school; he didn't even mind old Patterson, who reciprocated by seeing that he always won a prize at the end of the year and informing his proud parents that he'd go far. Sonny never forgot that. He was quite convinced he *would* go far. It was just taking time.

They'd been poor, dirt poor it was said, but that had no impact on the boy. So was everyone else of his acquaintance. Then, when he was ten, his mother took sick. She was a-bed a long time with her sickness, growing paler and thinner every day until she gathered him to her and told him she would be going to heaven soon. That was a shock, a bad shock, for he couldn't imagine life without his sweet mother, and Sonny was scared for the first time in his life. But she talked to him, calming him, telling him that when she went to heaven she would be free of the pain that she couldn't shake off, pain that had her moaning and sobbing through the long nights, so he mustn't be upset. Pa would look after him and his sister, and she would be up there in heaven, safe and comfortable at last, looking down on them with a smile on her face and angels for company, as well as her own ma and pa, who had gone on ahead of her. So he must be a good boy, and not cry when she was gone.

Sonny had felt privileged that she'd talked to him, because she'd obviously forgotten to tell the others all that. They wept and wept, and Pa had a good excuse to get sorrowful drunk again.

Not long after that his sister, Maggie, got married and left, and Pa sold the farm. That had been on the cards, because he'd never liked farmwork, especially a dairy farm that wasn't worth the hours, as he always said.

He took to the road with Sonny in tow as his best mate, a decision that infuriated Maggie, who wrote angry letters demanding that the boy be sent to live with her, but Pa ignored them, and Sonny didn't mind. He was excited by Pa's boast that they were as free as the breeze. In the season, Pa worked as a shearer, moving from station to station, with the ten-year-old son Sonny in charge of their two horses and their swags. The rest of the year they travelled about, finding odd jobs in town and country. Soon the lad was beginning to pull his weight too, working as a dumpster in the shearing sheds and then as a labourer, because he was growing big and strong.

Sonny was Pa's mate all right. His best friend and backstop, who soon became more of a keeper because Pa kept falling back into the drink. He stole Pa's money when he was drunk and hid it in a slit in his saddle to keep them fed. On the weeks when there was no work, or the old man was too wheezy to leave camp, he went off on forays, always managing

26

to come back with food of some sort, filched from farms or from under the noses of shopkeepers. Pa never enquired where the eggs or the meat or any of the provisions came from, and Sonny never volunteered the information in case he got a belting. As he grew older, Sonny was offered permanent jobs but he always had the same answer.

'What about my pa?'

It seemed no one had a place for Joe Willoughby, and few had a good word for him, so his son could hardly desert him. Drifting became their way of life. And not a bad life at that. They had their ups and downs, he and Pa, but as Pa used to say: 'There's always someone worse off.' With that, Sonny had to agree. He'd seen some real unfortunates in his day.

They buried Pa in the Gurundi Station cemetery up by the big old pepper tree and stuck a wooden cross over the spot. One of the shearers carved the name on it with the letters RIP, which he told Sonny meant 'rest in peace', and Sonny thought that a good thing to say.

At the end of the week, when he lined up for his pay, the squatter glared at him.

'What pay? Your old man owed me more than ten quid, not to mention the bill for grog and tobacco he ran up with my storekeeper. You owe me, son, but you can stay on and work it off. Meantime, I'll impound your horses for security.'

Sonny was furious with his pa. It was this booking things up and the borrowings that had kept them broke. Hadn't he promised on their ma's blessed head never to be at it again? And that was only last month, for the umpteenth time. Nevertheless, he put it to the squatter that a man wasn't responsible for another man's debts, even if it was his pa.

That brought a laugh from the squatter. 'The bills are in the name of Willoughby, and that's your name, son. You have to learn to live up to your responsibilities. And anyway, you got the funeral for free, so don't come whingeing to me.'

A lesson well learned that was, the older and wiser Mal – short for Mallachi – Willoughby mused. He had a string of names at his command now; they rolled off his tongue like he was born to them, so that he could move on without having to look over his shoulder.

But he fixed the squatter. Mal Willoughby couldn't be made to work for nothing. He'd gone to the storeroom and booked up a bottle of whisky and two bottles of rum.

The storeman had frowned. 'Here now, lad, I thought you was a teetotaller. I don't want to be the cause of sending you down the road to ruin like your dad.'

'Ah, no. I wouldn't do that, Charlie. Didn't I see enough of it? But it's said out there among the shearers that my dad shouldn't go off lonely like that. They're planning a wake for him.' He smiled sadly. 'I've got responsibilities now. On behalf of the family, I have to make a contribution. The grog's for the men.'

And so it was. Mal sold it to eager shearers at half the going price, pocketing the cash. Then, when the wake was well under way, and the singing a discordant lament, he collected his swag and rig, even the other saddle and bridle that had belonged to his father, and slid out into the darkness. He took the chain off the gate and whistled up the horses, laughing to himself. By the time they woke up in the morning he'd have put too many miles between himself and the hard-hearted squatter for anyone to care.

Mal Willoughby had only been in Brisbane a few days this time, just looking about. He was a countryman, no fan of big towns like this, but he had enough cash to rest up awhile before heading out again.

He had seen the mob in the park, but whatever they were doing didn't interest him. He'd heard there was a buck-jumping contest being held that day on the other side of town, and he was riding out to take a look. Not that he had any intention of entering and collecting broken bones for his troubles.

'Bums for brains,' Pa had always said about those blokes.

No. Those sorts of gatherings were always a good place to find out where he could make a quid. Unofficial horse races, foot races, fairs, and even better pickings out on the roads. Mal didn't work for anyone any more. He worked for himself. A dedicated loner, with a face that was his fortune, a face of such sweet innocence that women took him under their wings and tough men were fooled into thinking he was an easy mark. An amateur. Which he was not, in his chosen fields. He could run like the wind. He always had good horses, but when he entered a race on makeshift courses he would turn up with a poor-looking nag and make the switch later. Or he'd grease up his horse's mane and tail to make it appear unkempt, adding neat touches of grey, even a well-trained limp. Mal knew so many tricks, especially with cards, the only entertainment he and his pa had had on lonely nights, that challenges were more fun to him even than the payoff.

Oh, no. He wasn't interested in the crowded park; he'd almost passed on by when he spotted the bloke sitting astride his horse, watching proceedings. And he recognised him.

Jesus wept! It was McPherson. In the flesh.

Mal didn't know McPherson personally, but he knew of him, and he'd come close enough to him at times to be tipped off as to his identity. Now here he was, large as life, red hair and bushy beard still intact, calmly surveying some sort of half-baked riot.

James McPherson was a bushranger, wanted in the southern states for all sorts of crimes, from horse-stealing and robbery under arms, to shooting a man at the Houghton River. Whether all the tales Mal had heard about McPherson were true, he could not be sure, but he'd heard enough to know that this bloke was a true, dyed-in-the-wool outlaw. And he was still free.

'Come at anything,' they said of him. 'Steer clear, mate.'

Next thing, there was McPherson playing the gallant. Plunging into the mob on his horse to rescue that fool spruiker in his fancy clothes, so Mal decided to join the fun! Laughing, he wheeled his horse and sent it racing across the park, straight at the mob, his stockwhip cracking.

Mal forgot about the English lady. He had to go in search of his horse. He wasn't worried about it; he'd find it. Either the spruiker, some politician, had his mount, in which case that bloke wouldn't be hard to find and he'd take his horse back with grateful thanks and a tip; or McPherson did. His bet was on the latter. He broke into a run, now that he had his breath back.

He knew it wouldn't be wise to charge into a pub asking if anyone had seen a bloke answering to McPherson's description, in case he ran into any of the bushranger's mates, who might think him to be an informer, and Mal would never do that, not being in love with the law himself. Instead, he scoured the area from pub to pub, checking hitching rails front and rear. It was at the back of the Royal Mail Hotel that he spotted his horse. Now he could have taken his mount and gone on his way, but that wouldn't have been much fun, and what if someone reported it stolen? Besides, he dearly wanted to meet his hero. That would be a tale to tell your grandkids: 'I knew the wild Scotsman himself . . .'

He rewound the long whip into a neat coil and looped it back on his shoulder, the plaited leather handle to the front, a weapon in an emergency. Not that he foresaw any trouble here, but you just never knew. Taking off his hat, he combed his hair back with his hand and headed for the back door of the pub.

No one took any notice of the country lad who strolled casually through the Saturday crowd of drinkers in the bar, squinting at the sudden switch from glare to gloom. Not even McPherson, who was standing with a mate in a far corner, and who glanced at Mal and turned away without so much as a blink of recognition. He pressed through to the counter and bought himself a lemonade then he turned, looked directly at McPherson and strolled down. 'How're you going?'

The Scot glared at him through heavy-lidded eyes. 'Who are you?'

Mal grinned. Good, he thought. That's good. Pretend you don't know me. But it won't work.

'The name's Ned Turner. And I've come to thank you for taking care of my horse.'

'What horse?' McPherson growled.

'The chestnut outside, with my rig on him.'

'That one?' The Scot turned to his mate. 'When a man deserts his mount in a public place, you'd think he didn't want it any more, wouldn't you?'

'You would,' his bald companion replied. 'Like he's givin' it away to the first comer.'

'That's what I'd say too. Finders keepers.'

Mal laughed as if he thought the two older men were just teasing him. 'Fair enough any other time, but not when it's my horse. Who was the spruiker?'

29

McPherson was slightly taken aback by the lad's amiable attitude.

'Some bloody politician,' he allowed.

'You saved his life. I hope he did the right thing.'

'Since when do those bastards do the right thing?'

Mal gaped in wide-eyed innocence. 'You don't say! You shoulda dumped him back there, sir. Can I buy you a drink? Least I can do.'

The Scot winked at his mate. He looked at their beer glasses, almost drained. 'Yeah. We'll have whisky. Doubles.'

'Right you are.' Obediently Mal made for the counter and returned with the drinks as ordered, and by the time he got back, McPherson had had a change of heart.

'Tell you what, Ned. If you're in need of a mount, you can have mine.'

'That's good of you, sir, and I'm sure it's a fine animal, but me and my horse, we're sort of used to one another. You know how it is. I'm right fond of Pally.' The worst name Mal could think of for his horse, Striker, rolled off his tongue, and McPherson roared with laughter.

'God Almighty! What sort of a name is that for a horse? He's a thoroughbred. Ain't you got no respect for the animal. Pally! I never heard the like.'

'We've always been pals, you see. He's inclined to go lame, got a weakness there, but I look out for him.'

The Scot turned back to his drink to give this some thought. He hadn't necessarily swallowed the lame bit, Mal guessed, but then again, how could he be sure?

Eventually he lit his pipe, sucked heavily on it and gazed at Mal.

'Do you know what I think? I think you're a bloody shyster with them baby-blue eyes of your'n. You don't fool me for a minute. Do you know who I am?'

'No, sir, I don't.'

'Creepin' Jesus. Will you listen to it?' He mimicked Mal's voice: 'No, sir, I don't! Just as well you don't. Now let's get down to business. You can have your horse. But I'll have the watch.'

'What watch?'

'The one you lifted from Lilley. Mr Lilley to you. Along with his gold chain that belonged to his dear departed dad.'

'I don't know anything about a watch. I only went in there to give a hand.'

'Like hell. You saw the glint of that watch from the sidelines same as I did. Now hand it over or you lose the horse.'

'The horse is mine.'

McPherson sighed. 'We could turn you up and shake it out of you right here . . .'

Reluctantly, Mal slid the watch over to him, and the Scot pocketed it swiftly. 'There's the lad. No hard feelings. You want a drink?'

'No thanks.'

'Hey! What happened to the sir?' McPherson grinned. 'Where do you live, Ned?'

'Here in Brisbane.'

'You got a job?'

'I work mainly on stations when there's work.' More lies. 'I'm thinking of going north.'

'So are we, as a matter of fact.' McPherson looked to his mate for approval, and the bald man nodded. 'You could ride along with us if you like.'

Mal swelled with pride. To be accepted by the famous – infamous – James McPherson, that was really something. To ride out in this company would be a real feather in his cap. And madness. Mal knew that outlaws could be shot on sight, even if he wasn't sure that this law had been extended to Queensland. It was his understanding that laws were laws wherever you went, and he had a lot of respect for his own hide. He had no plans to get shot in the crossfire.

He shook his head. 'Can't. I've got a girl here. I'm hoping she'll come with me.' He had a vision of the English girl, and grinned. 'She's hell bent on putting me on the straight and narrow.'

They laughed. Conspirators now.

'That'll take some effort,' McPherson remarked, and dismissed Mal. 'We'll see you around, son.'

'I hope so.' Mal smiled. Hoping he didn't. Enough was enough. He was sorry about the watch, but there were other watches, and who else could say they not only knew the wild Scotsman, but he was a friend? He'd actually made a friend of the bugger. And he had his horse back. Fair trade.

Thanks to their bitter experiences in London, the Tissington sisters were aware of other avenues that might lead to employment if, or maybe when, Mr Penn failed them. While Emilie was out walking, Ruth scoured newspaper advertisements for suitable positions, but employers seeking females required only domestic or factory workers. She did, however, find that a governess with excellent references sought employment with a family, live in. Remuneration by agreement.

Ruth nodded. She could improve on that. If they were forced to invest in an advertisement, she would state that they were English governesses. Not that they would advertise in the plural. It was better not to confuse people by allowing that there were two ladies interested in such engagements. But surely, to emphasise that a governess was English would appeal to a better class of employer, and possibly wealthier.

Then there were church people. They might assist. It was through the minister at the Anglican church in the Edgware Road that they'd found some employment to sustain them in London, and they should do better here. At least they had the necessary excellent references from the Society this time.

Unfortunately, the fine cathedral they'd passed previously turned out to be Roman Catholic, so on the Sunday morning the two girls attended the Anglican service at St John's Church. They never liked to miss Sunday services, but on this occasion they didn't consider it unworthy of them to make sure they were seated in a pew close to the pulpit, where they would be noticed as newcomers. Only a small and possibly helpful ploy. They took communion trying to keep their minds on prayer, rather than the all-important necessity of earning a living.

After the service they lingered in the church, leaving only with the last of the worshippers, pleased to see the minister already there, chatting to members of his congregation. He was a sprightly fellow, with wispy white hair and a cheery disposition.

When they emerged into the sunlight, he was there to greet them.

'Ah, ladies, you're new, I see. Welcome to St John's.'

They learned that he was the Rev. Forrester, and much interested in his new parishioners.

When they'd covered the introductory conversations about who they were and where they'd come from, and the discussion on their long voyage, which they were at pains to say was extremely pleasant, Ruth managed to tell him that they were governesses.

'Both of you. Governesses! Well, I declare. I'm sure you ladies will make a remarkable contribution to the education of our youngsters. We're very fortunate to have you choose Brisbane.'

Suddenly Ruth was tongue-tied. It didn't seem right to be burdening him with their troubles outside the church, with other people still waiting to talk to him, but Emilie felt they couldn't afford to waste time.

'I hope so, Reverend. I hope we are able to make a contribution to this community. However, we have been let down. We were given to believe that we had definite engagements here, but on arrival we found that this is not so.'

'But then I suppose it is early days yet.' Ruth found herself echoing Mr Penn, while Emilie frowned at her.

'Yes, of course,' he said. 'I am sure you ladies will have no trouble finding suitable employment.'

'Yes.' Ruth nodded politely.

'But if you hear of anything suitable,' Emilie said, 'we are staying at Belleview Boarding House for the time being.'

'Excellent. By all means,' he said vaguely, anxious now to move on to another group. 'Now you must excuse me, ladies.'

'Not much luck there,' Emilie grumbled as they walked down deserted Ann Street.

'You never know.'

'Who were they?' Mrs Walter Bateman asked the Reverend, who, having done his duty, now wished to continue discussions with her husband about the building fund.

'English ladies. They only arrived on Thursday. Came in on the *City of Liverpool*. The Misses Tissington.'

'Really? I had several friends disembark from that ship. I gave them a splendid welcome-home party on Saturday night. They brought along several other passengers as well, but I never heard that name mentioned. What are their connections?'

'They're governesses, and charming ladies they are too.'

Annie Bateman was intrigued. 'Goodness me, they look too upper class to be servants.'

Her husband sighed. 'Governesses are hardly servants, dear. Not that sort especially. They educate in the grand style.'

'Well I never. And I suppose they'd be well paid too. Who are they working for, Reverend?'

'I don't believe they have accepted a post yet. They'd be rather particular, I'm sure. Now, Mr Bateman, we really ought to have a committee meeting as soon as possible . . .'

'Indeed we should, Reverend, but building a cathedral is an immense task, in more ways than one. I've been delaying because we need the Governor and the Premier of the state as patrons. Once we get them signed on the dotted line we'll have lawyers register the fund, and make our committee an official body. Just one committee; there are too many willing hands at present forming their own little fund-raising circles. They have to be better organised.'

'You can be the chairman of that committee, Walter,' his wife proposed.

He grunted. 'That remains to be seen.'

'I can see our great project is already in good hands,' the Reverend said, delighted.

While the two men talked about architects and the necessity for a worldwide search, Annie was more interested in the governesses. She wondered who could afford such brilliance in their households, and imagined what a social coup it would be to have an English governess on the staff. There were schools in the town, so she supposed the ladies would go to wealthy country folk. But who?

A week later, thanks to Mr Penn's efforts, Annie Bateman's gossip and the Reverend's gentle enquiries, the English governesses were the talk of the town. But they had no idea. With their funds dwindling, they informed Mr Penn that they'd go out to the country. Anywhere.

He was surprised. 'That's why my enquiries are taking so long. It takes time to get the word out there and receive responses, ladies. There are no jobs for governesses in town. I thought you knew that.'

Ruth had no choice, when she booked in for a second week, but to ask the landlady if it would be permissible to use this address in the advertisement they intended to place in the *Courier* newspaper.

Mrs Medlow was impressed. 'They might be uppity and real cold fish,' she told Mrs Kemp, 'but by God they got manners. No one else would bother to even tell me about an advertisement, let alone ask my permission to mention Belleview.'

'What do they want in the paper?'

'Jobs. You coulda knocked me down with a feather. They want jobs as

33

governesses, and here I was thinking they were ladies of leisure. I can't wait to see the advertisement.'

By Friday morning almost everyone in the boarding house had read the advertisement and there was a guilty fluster when the ladies came down to breakfast, quietly composed, as usual. Although Mrs Medlow had a *Courier* at the ready, they did not enquire if there was a newspaper in the house.

'Cool customers, that pair,' she said, disappointed.

But she began watching the mail, with the other boarders and Cook looking over her shoulder.

Annie Bateman saw the advertisement too. She didn't have any children, but she'd written to her sister out at Lindsay Downs, via Nanango, giving her all the town gossip, including the news that two high-class governesses were in town. She'd made some enquiries, just out of curiosity, and discovered that English governesses taught the normal lessons, but on top of that were good at music, languages, elocution and all sorts of social graces. This she passed on to her sister Leonie, who had two daughters, and added the catch: English governesses had to be paid at least a hundred pounds a year, plus bed and board. Which unfortunately Leonie couldn't afford.

More than a hundred miles away, Leonie Stanfield read the letter and smiled sadly. Her daughters, aged twelve and ten, did have a governess, who was already under notice. She was her husband's cousin and not worth half of the fifty pounds a year they were paying her. As a teacher, she was useless. It hadn't taken Leonie long to see she might as well give the lessons herself. She agreed with Annie. It would be wonderful to have a real governess for the girls. Not as a social coup, though; Leonie totally rejected that foolish attitude.

Lindsay Downs was an established cattle station, not the biggest in the district but considerable, extending over twenty square miles. The homestead was comfortable, more of an overgrown cottage with shingle roof and, as Leonie knew, nothing special, but she didn't mind that. She was content: they were a close, happy family, and despite a long drought and the slump in beef prices, Jack Stanfield was managing to keep going. He was an incorrigible optimist, taking these setbacks in his stride, taking for granted the cycles of nature.

'What goes round comes round,' he liked to say with his patient smile. 'We can ride out the poor years by squirrelling away enough nuts in time of plenty.'

He was a good manager and a good man, and Leonie loved him dearly. She knew that a hundred pounds for a governess was an extravagance that Jack could not countenance. No one on the station, not even the overseer, earned that much. But in her heart she lamented. A yearning came over her at quiet times, a vague yearning that she'd like to know more about things . . . She wished she was more – even the word caused her to cringe for fear of derision – cultured. There, that was it. She'd decided on the word one soft night between dusk and sunset when the skies were flooded with red and gold, with such beauty that she wished she had a painting of the scene, to keep forever.

There were a few books in the house, only the Lord knew where they came from: poetry by Wordsworth, her favourite, Bibles, the lives of great generals, a history of England, a Shakespeare anthology, Jack's books on farming and animal husbandry and a few romantic novels, the latter contributed by the present governess as light reading for the girls.

Leonie would have liked more books. Good novels. Books on art and beautiful things. But she didn't know what to order, nor could anyone of her acquaintance enlighten her, even if she did ask. But it wasn't just books; there were those things, indefinable for a countrywoman educated in the bare essentials in a small bush school. Things she wished she knew about, that she wanted her girls to be aware of, that an English governess would have at her fingertips. Culture. She wouldn't dare mention the word to Jack, for he'd laugh at her, thinking she was going the same way as Annie, whose affectations amused and sometimes irritated him.

She replied to Annie's letter, remembering to remark that her governess was leaving. She refrained from writing that they'd sacked the girl, because she didn't wish to give her a bad name in Brisbane. Annie talked too much. And she did mention that an English governess would be ideal for Jane and Jessie, but who could afford one? Not the Stanfields.

Nevertheless, in her daydreams, Leonie had a beautiful picture of her daughters in white muslin out under the wisteria with their elegant governess instructing them in art. Paints, brushes and easels completed the languid scene. At other times she could see them at the piano, playing beautifully for guests, with the governess standing by, beaming on her pupils. At present, the only one who could play their piano was Jack, and he played by ear. She sighed. How wonderful it would be for her daughters to grow up elegant, cultured ladies, with full lives, no longer restricted to station talk of the weather, cattle and kids.

Then Annie wrote again, full of excitement, homing in on only one subject.

> Listen to me Leonie . . . The Misses Tissingtons I wrote you about. The governesses. They haven't got jobs yet at all. They are advertising for jobs. That says they haven't got any offers yet. I'll watch and if they advertise again, then you could be in luck. I mean, you might be able to get one of them cheaper. I know you were paying the cousin fifty pounds. What if you could get one of these English ones for fifty pounds? Which I reckon is fair enough anyway. Send me a telegram if you want me to enquire . . .

Leonie was delighted. Jack wouldn't balk at fifty again. She sent the telegram but was not hopeful. Since the ladies had advertised, they'd probably be swamped with offers. She told Jack what Annie was up to this time.

'Annie and you,' he corrected. 'But if she can talk one of them into coming out here, at our set wage, then it's all right by me. What do the girls think?'

'I haven't told them yet. I don't want them to be disappointed.'

Responses to the advertisement were delivered personally to their door by the landlady, who kept asking them if they were having any luck. Ruth, embarrassed, had a set reply.

'We haven't decided yet, Mrs Medlow, thank you.'

Every day they received at least three or four letters, which were opened with eager anticipation only to disappoint. The girls thought they'd made their requirements quite clear, but these writers didn't seem to understand. They were offered positions as nursemaids, even as cooks. One woman said she was a widow, she had a very nice house, and would appreciate a companion in her home, but she couldn't afford to pay anything. They received two marriage proposals from strange men which sent them off into fits of laughter, despite the seriousness of the situation. Someone wanted news of his sister who had gone to London, hoping the English governess could oblige, and two female teachers wrote asking if they could assist them in finding employment. Those requests were depressing.

The second advertisement that they placed, at the end of the week, told the tale, and Mrs Medlow was quick to comment:

'Still no luck?'

Ruth admitted then that they hadn't yet been able to find suitable engagements. She wondered if perhaps Mrs Medlow had a cheaper room?

'A cheaper room? I don't know about that. All our rooms are the same price, except for a back room off the kitchen. It's got two single beds but not much else. I usually only let it to commercial travellers. You know what they're like. Don't see much of the bed anyways. But your trunks wouldn't never fit in it.'

'Oh.' Ruth was inclined to take the room, but she knew Emilie would never agree. 'Oh well, never mind. We'll stay where we are.'

'I'm sorry,' Mrs Medlow said, genuinely concerned for her, and Ruth was touched. By the time she closed the bedroom door behind her, she was in tears.

They still haunted Penn's office, more from habit and something to do than hope, but this morning he was waiting for them with good news.

'Didn't I tell you I'd find you an engagement?' he crowed, using the word he'd gleaned from their vocabulary. 'And not just one. Two. In the same town. Go on through, ladies.'

They sat on the lumpy sofas in his anteroom, staring at one another, barely able to speak in their apprehension, listening to his swift and impersonal dealings with wretched females who, depending on their situations, laughed, wept or shouted at him.

36

Emilie raised her eyebrows and whispered sarcastically, 'All in a day's work.'

He came back with a shabby ledger. 'Now, let me see. Maryborough, that's the town. North of Brisbane, only a couple of hundred miles. It's a wool port. Very important it is too, some say a bigger port than Brisbane. See, you shouldn't have wasted your money on those advertisements. I saw them. No offence taken, ladies. But I placed my own in the *Maryborough Post*. Have to charge you for that. Three shillings. All right?'

They nodded.

'Cheaper than the *Courier* anyway. Now there are two positions, as I said. And they're both plums. The first is with Mrs Manningtree. She's got three kids, seven, eight and ten, the eldest a boy. Lives right in town. A tasteful house, you'll be pleased to know. So she says anyway. No proper schools up there, so she's desperate for a governess.'

'That's wonderful,' Ruth breathed.

'Good. Now I put the wage you want in the paper . . .'

'You didn't!' Ruth was appalled.

'No use wasting time. Your time or hers. Better to lay it on the line. Anyways, she won't come at a hundred pounds but she will pay eighty. Is that all right?'

'Yes. Emilie will take that position.'

'No. You take it, Ruth.'

'Definitely not. I promised myself that you'd take the first, no matter what eventuates.'

'Good,' Penn said. 'That's Miss Emilie settled. Now the other position is with Mrs Mooney. Live in too. She'll pay seventy pounds. No more. But she's only got one kid. A thirteen-year-old daughter. Says she doesn't have time to keep an eye on the girl herself . . .'

'Did you say Mooney?' Ruth asked. 'Is that an Irish name?'

'Yes. Peculiar there's only one kid, but I suppose there'd be a reason . . .'

'Mr Penn,' Emilie intervened, 'Ruth is trying to tell you we didn't envisage working for Papists.'

He blinked. 'Why not? Can't see they'd be trying to convert you.' He didn't wait for a response. 'Now this Mrs Mooney has the Prince of Wales Hotel. I've heard about it. One of the best in town, they say, guest rooms, dining room, the lot.'

'And where do they live?' Ruth asked.

'In the hotel, of course. You'd have your own room there. You'd live well.'

Ruth shook her head. 'I'm afraid not. I wouldn't consider living in an hotel. Or with those people. You'll have to find something else.'

Penn was annoyed. He leaned forward. 'It seems to me, ladies, that beggars can't be choosers. I've found two jobs for you, as I said I would do. You either take them or you're on your own.'

'Can we have a day to think about it, Mr Penn?' Emilie asked.

'Tomorrow. Yes, tomorrow. Or I'll be advertising Mrs Mooney's job myself. That's my business, you understand. I can't let situations go to waste.'

The Tissingtons were not abstainers. Wine was served on occasions at table, and William enjoyed his after-dinner ritual of pipe and port. On the ship, the girls had their own ritual of a glass of wine a day, one of their few pleasures. The wine was passable good, they found, and the price in their range very low, bought from the first mate free of excise duty. They were heartened, too, when he provided them with an excuse to imbibe, informing them that doctors recommended wine for medicinal purposes on long sea journeys to counteract the lack of fresh vegetables.

'Many doctors own wineries in the colonies these days and are doing very well,' he told them. 'But in the first place they only began their winemaking to provide ships with wine on the return journey.'

However, while they approved of alcohol in its place, neither of the girls could contemplate actually living in a hotel. Apart from their personal abhorrence of such an idea, they feared for their reputations. By the time they reached the boarding house they were still wrestling with this dilemma. Emilie was placed, she would go to Maryborough, but what about Ruth? Would she have to remain behind and take her chances on finding another position, or accept this dreadful offer as a last resort?

Emilie went through to collect their washing from the line, and Ruth was making for their room when she was waylaid by Mrs Medlow.

'Miss Tissington, I've been watching out for you. There's a lady to see you. She's in the parlour. Come along and I'll introduce you. She's got a job for you.'

Ruth winced. She wished the woman would not refer to *jobs*, as if they were labourers or the like.

As soon as she was introduced to Mrs Bateman, she recognised her as a woman she'd seen outside St John's Church the day they'd met the Reverend. How could she forget? she mused. The woman was wearing the same garish hat overloaded with striped ribbons.

'I'm so pleased to meet you,' Mrs Bateman gushed. 'And to find you're still available, as a governess I mean. Mrs Medlow was telling me . . .'

Irritated at the cheek of the landlady, who was still standing there as if she intended to take part in the interview, Ruth looked at her sternly.

'Thank you, Mrs Medlow. That will be all.'

Dismissed and displeased, the landlady flounced away, and Mrs Bateman raised her eyebrows, obviously impressed by the governess's authoritative tone.

'I have to tell you, Mrs Bateman,' Ruth began, 'that my sister and I had two excellent positions offered to us this very morning.'

'Oh no. Don't tell me I'm too late.'

'Not necessarily. We have until tomorrow morning to make our decisions. Perhaps you might care to tell me what you have in mind. This chair by the window is very comfortable; do be seated.'

'Thank you, Miss Tissington.'

While Mrs Bateman settled herself and her voluminous skirts, Ruth sat primly across from her in a straight-backed chair, allowing the prospective employer to speak first.

'My sister, Mrs Stanfield, needs a governess. She lives on a cattle station out west. Not that far, mind you. Only about a hundred miles or so. North-west really. She has a very nice home and two lovely young daughters. She has a piano too, and would like the girls to learn music as well. Do you teach music, Miss Tissington?'

Ruth nodded.

'I knew you would do, of course. They live near the town of Nanango. Only a little town really. More of a settlement. But very pleasant. And it's drier out there. Not as humid as Brisbane. We're in a valley here, you see, that's why we don't get much of a breeze on hot days. My own home here is very spacious and cool, I must say, but you can't really expect that standard in the country. Well, not in the average household, so to speak. My dear husband is the Inspector of Customs in Brisbane. He has his offices in the Customs House, a fine building, you may have noticed . . .'

Ruth let her rattle on, deeming it impolite to interrupt this person, under the circumstances. She didn't like Mrs Bateman, finding her rather common, but then she was not the employer. The position sounded ideal, and perhaps the sister would be an improvement.

'Is there anything else I can tell you?' Mrs Bateman asked her eventually.

'I was wondering. Is Nanango anywhere near Maryborough?'

'Maryborough? Well, that's a port. Nanango is inland. No, there's a fair distance between them. I suppose as the crow flies you'd find Maryborough is as far north again. So to speak.'

'Oh. My sister is considering taking up a post in Maryborough, but I'm not sure that I wish to accept the other post available in the same town. I must say, Mrs Stanfield's position is much more in my line.'

Mrs Bateman was thrilled. 'Then you'll take it?'

'There are other things to be considered. What salary is Mrs Stanfield prepared to offer if she decides I may be suitable? I have excellent references, Mrs Bateman. You may view them if you wish.'

'No, no, no, that won't be necessary. I am an excellent judge of character, if I say so myself. And I am sure that as an educated lady, you would be very competent. And let me tell you, you wouldn't regret accepting this post. Mr Stanfield is a charming man, the girls are well behaved, you'd have your own room, and my sister would be delighted to have you join them out there. One big happy family, so to speak.'

'And the salary?'

'She's offering fifty pounds a year. Quite a sum, wouldn't you agree?'

'Oh. That's very much under the going rate.'

'But you'd only have two pupils, and you'd be your own boss. And you do get bed and board free.'

'That's taken as a matter of course.'

'I'm sure you'd enjoy the life out there. If it was me, I'd much prefer Nanango to Maryborough.'

'Really? Why?'

'Well, Maryborough is a port after all. A river port. Rather rough, not the same sort of people you find in decent country towns.'

That settled the hotel offer for Ruth. Obviously it was out of the question. Emilie's employers, though, sounded reasonable, since they had a big house. There had to be some decent people there. She worried about accepting a figure as low as fifty pounds, keeping in mind that the debt to the Society had to be repaid. It wouldn't leave much to live on, even with free board. There were always other expenses, like clothes and so on. Emilie would advise against accepting such a low wage.

She looked to Mrs Bateman. 'Would Mrs Stanfield consider seventy pounds?'

'Oh, she couldn't. They're a good family, but not wealthy. Comfortable, you could say, and that's all. They've had bad seasons, drought, hit their finances hard. Fifty pounds it would have to be.'

Mrs Bateman's sharp eyes were set in a take-it-or-leave-it expression, and Ruth made a decision. She would tell Emilie that the Stanfield offer was seventy pounds, to stop her worrying, and she'd just have to scrimp as much as possible to try to put money aside for the Society.

'Your description of the position and the family makes it very hard for me to refuse,' she told Mrs Bateman. 'I should be honoured to accept the position.'

'At fifty pounds?'

Ruth nodded. 'When would I be required to commence?'

'Right away, Miss Tissington! I can't tell you how happy I am for you.' Suddenly Mrs Bateman was on her feet, as if afraid the governess would change her mind. 'I will advise my sister and find out about coach transport for you. You won't be sorry, I assure you, and Mrs Stanfield will be looking forward to meeting you.'

'Just a moment, Mrs Bateman. Could you tell me how my sister can get to Maryborough. We didn't think to ask. Would she take a coach also?'

'She could, but it would be a long journey with coach changes. She'd be better off to go by ship. Much more comfortable.'

When the woman had left, Ruth went down to tell Emilie that, at last, they were both placed, but she couldn't find it in her heart to be pleased. They would be parted now, each one to fend for herself among strangers in strange environments. She prayed to the Lord to watch over her young sister and keep her in good health and happiness.

Chapter Two

The sweltering weather inevitably brought misty rain, which soon deepened into a heavy fall, and by the time Mal arrived at the makeshift fairgrounds, tents were coming down and patrons were trudging away. But nothing could dampen his spirits on this Saturday afternoon. It had been an interesting day. He turned his horse about and allowed it to amble back up the road, ignoring the rain, for there was no malice in it, no chill to torment the bones, not like the bleak rains down south.

At a street corner he saw a very strange contraption of a vehicle and once again marvelled at the peculiar things a man could come across in big towns, where everyone was trying to outdo everyone else. It appeared to be a large lorry drawn by four horses, but the tray was enclosed by a high canvas canopy, something in the style of a covered wagon. Ever curious, and with nothing better to do, Mal dismounted, tied the horse to a hitching rail and strolled up under the awnings to investigate.

A large sign resting against one of the wheels read: ALL ABOARD FOR GYMPIE, GOLD TOWN EXTRAORDINAIRE.

'What's this?' he asked a man in a white coat who was collecting fares from a couple of customers, while a small crowd gathered to watch proceedings, or maybe just to shelter from the rain.

'Gold!' the man said. 'And you look a likely lad. You've got the muscle for it, but have you got two quid?'

'Better still, I've got a horse, mister. But where's Gympie?'

'Up north, mate. Not too far for a man with a horse, but too far for foot-slogging diggers, unless they want to wear themselves out before they get to the diggings.'

'And you're taking them up like on a bus?'

'Like an express bus. Cheapest way to get there. Coach is the only other way, and that's too dear for the working man.'

'Well, I'll be blowed. And there is gold in this gold town extraordinaire?'

'Richest find yet, they say. My customers'll come back millionaires. You want to ride along with us?'

'I might.' Mal wouldn't commit himself. This bloke was too much of a fairground spruiker to be trusted, but it mightn't be a bad idea to take a look at the goldfields. He stood back, noting the pinched eagerness of men counting out the two pounds in coin, some even passing the hat round to raise enough for the fare, with plaints of poverty and starving

41

families. They reminded him of mad punters at the races.

When a proffered hat reached him, Mal dug out five shillings.

'Do you reckon it's a good bet, mate?' he asked.

'Too right! A man'd be crazy not to go. Never get a chance like this again.' He saw the shillings drop into the hat and looked up at Mal gratefully. 'You're a gentleman, lad. Barney Magee won't forget you when he's made his pile.'

Mal grinned. A born cynic, he noticed Magee hadn't bothered to take his name so that the donor wouldn't be forgotten when he made his pile at Gympie, gold town extraordinaire.

As Magee was clambering aboard, the lorry owner was still spruiking for passengers: 'Roll up! Roll up! Only a few seats left! Don't get left behind. What about you, mister?'

A skinny bloke with a gaunt, sad face asked if he could pay the fare at the other end, but he was ignored. Mal strolled back to his horse. He didn't have the gold fever, as it was known, nor was he ever likely to, but the interest remained. He might as well take a look.

The trek north was more of an obstacle race, Mal soon found, beginning with the route itself, which was only clear to men who knew the area. Rough dray tracks veered off in all directions, many coming to a dead end faced with primeval bush that hid marauding Aborigines. Stock routes, leading only to outback sheep stations, created more confusion and ill temper. Rivers swollen by the onset of the wet season, a phenomenon new to despairing southerners, barred the way, and sodden camps lined the shores as travellers bargained with ferrymen for the cost of crossing. Harassed by the incessant rain and mud, footsloggers and vehicles alike straggled on, beset with fear.

Mal realised that fear was worse than fever. Fear that the gold would run out before they got there. Fear of a sudden raid by Aborigines on lonely campers, which caused them to try to band together for protection. But the banding together only caused more hardship. Too many woke in the morning, after wild and horrific dreams of murder and mayhem, to find they'd been robbed of their desperately needed food and equipment, and, even worse, of their guns. On country roads, where it was usual to pass the time of day with strangers, meanness and suspicion rode the route. Everyone knew that bushrangers wouldn't bother with these miserable wayfarers when real pickings were there for the taking between the goldfields and the port of Maryborough, so they looked cautiously into the faces of so-called friends. They shunned the Germans and Swedes on the road, and most of all they turned their frustrations on enigmatic Chinamen padding by as if oblivious of the hazards. Fights broke out in camps and wayside shanties, but the Chinamen, determined to press on, would not get involved. They flitted away in the darkness and disappeared, amid fears of their knives so sharp they'd slit a man's throat.

Mal rode on, taking his time. If the gold was gone, it was gone, He picked up a few quid as a ferryhand for a week, and got himself and his horse across for free. He wandered on to a stock route, finding himself confronted by the biggest sheep drive he'd ever come across. Amazed, he talked to the boss, who told him he was taking twelve thousand sheep, thereabouts, to open up a station in the far west of the state, and that he could do with another drover . . .

'Since some of my bastards have shot through to Nashville.'

'Where's Nashville?' Mal asked.

'About sixty miles upriver from Maryborough, where Nash found the gold. They call it Gympie now. An Aborigine word for "stinging tree". Is that where you're going with the rest of them mongrels?'

'Might as well.'

'Listen, son. Give me a week. I'll make it worth your while. This is a big mob and the coastal terrain is hell. Once we get over them hills we'll be into more open country. You can turn back then.'

As he expected after they'd struggled over the hills, Mal was asked to stay on, but he didn't fancy months droving over barely explored country, so he took his pay and headed back. Once on the Gympie route again, he took up with a couple of diggers, riding with them to pick up on the latest news, pleased to hear the gold strikes were continuing. He'd been comfortable with the sheepmen. Spoke their language and enjoyed their cameraderie, so back in this country his guard was down. Also, on the return ride across trackless country, he'd encountered two groups of tribal blacks. They were fierce-looking blokes, carrying spears and waddies. He'd guessed – hoped – they were hunting parties, and had greeted them with a smile and a wave. They hadn't bothered him, but in case they decided the lone rider was fair game, he hadn't slept for two nights, only resting, one eye open and a rifle at the ready, beside his horse. He was tired. Stupid, he told himself later.

The drover's cook had given him some salted mutton and a few tins of food to see him on his way, and this Mal shared with his new mates, before unrolling his swag and drifting into blessed, relaxed sleep by the embers of their campfire.

In the morning, the diggers had gone. So had his money, his food supply, his rifle and ammunition. Amateurs, they'd left him his horse.

It occurred to Mal that these blokes might have been plain old robbers, not real diggers, preying on other prospectors as they wended their way north, so, on the off chance, he backtracked. When he came across a troop of Chinamen, he gave them their description, and sure enough his former friends had ridden south. Unlike so many of his colleagues on the road, Mal had no problem with Chinamen. Many of the stations had Chinese cooks, who had always been kind to the kid travelling about with his old man, with the result that Mal probably knew more about them than his father did.

Mal found the elder of the Chinese party and engaged in formal conversation with him, mentioning the sad fact of the robbery and asking if he might be permitted a small favour. After giving the matter some thought, Mr Xiu spoke rapidly to a coolie, who returned with a small

43

bottle of pills. He then put a few of the pills in a fold of rice paper and, at a nod from his master, handed them over to Mal.

The weather had cleared and the sun baked the muddy tracks into uneven furrows, hard on the swagmen but making life much easier for riders. Mal was able to travel fast now, in his search for the robbers, but he'd covered more than twenty miles before he caught sight of them, leaving a wayside shanty with a sugar bag full of supplies.

'Probably bought with my money,' he muttered, watching them from the cover of the bush.

They made camp about a mile down the road, so Mal detoured into the bush, where he left his horse, and slid quietly through the undergrowth to watch. When they finally had a billy boiling over the fire and a pan of meat sputtering beneath it, he made his move. First the horses.

He undid their halters, slapped the animals on their rumps and withdrew to watch the fun. The two men heard the disturbance and were on their feet in seconds, racing to catch their mounts, which were zigzagging, bewildered, out on to the road. They soon caught the horses but were away from the fire long enough to provide Mal with the time he needed. He dropped the opium pills into the tea and disappeared, hoping they'd work. It would have been futile trying to take on two armed men with his only weapons, a pocket knife and his stockwhip.

But it seemed Mr Xiu knew his business. Before long the pair were stretched out by the smouldering fire, snoring away in beatific slumber.

The thieves were robbed of their money, the best of their supplies, and their horses. Mal rode through the night, all the way back to the last ferry. When the ferrymen turned out from their huts to begin work, he sold both of the horses to the boss for ten pounds each, five below the going rate, no questions asked.

After that, for safety, Mal kept to stock routes, further inland than the dray tracks but, as he figured, much more peaceable.

He rode through the Gympie hills, eyes wide with wonder, looking down at bustling tent villages and gaping slopes shorn of trees. He followed a track through two rows of tents and mounds of rubble where workers, like ants, crowded by the river with large sieves, and others laboured with picks and shovels as if their lives depended on it. Right from the beginning, the country boy hated the place. It was worse than the slums of a real town. It stank like a sewer. Raw meat hung outside makeshift butcher's shops, dogs and goats dragged at refuse between the tents, aggravated by crows, drunks reeled about sly grog tents and slovenly women hung on their arms, for what they might yet have to spend.

But he was here, he decided, and he might as well see what he could do.

While the whole area gave the impression of chaos, Mal soon found that regulations did exist and good-natured diggers were free with advice. He bought a miner's ticket from the registrar's office, a square shack built of shingles, and no sooner was he out the door when he was approached by a young Englishman.

'On your own, sir?'

'I could be. Who wants to know?'

'Clive Hillier. At your service.'

'For what?'

'As a partner. You'll do no good here without a partner.'

'And you're nominating yourself?'

'Exactly.'

'Why?'

'Because I have a claim and I need someone to work it with me. Perhaps we could have a drink at that grog shop and discuss our business?'

Mal laughed. He wasn't about to fall for that one. A freeloader, after a free drink. 'Sorry, I don't drink.'

'Better still,' the Englishman said in his toffy way of talking, 'if you'd rather, we could go up to my tent and have a cup of tea.'

He wasn't a bad-looking chap, dark hair, clean-shaven, slim build, and he wore his moleskin trousers tucked into knee boots that must have cost a pretty penny before they hit this territory. He reminded Mal of the English chaps who came out to the sheep stations from the Old Country, friends of the squatters, new chums, anxious to learn how to make their fortunes.

Mal decided he had nothing to lose and a cup of tea would go down well.

What he learned over the cup of tea in the neat tent was that Hillier was broke. The lease on his claim had run out and he couldn't afford to renew it. In fact, he couldn't afford to stay and he couldn't afford to leave.

'Maryborough's sixty miles downriver,' he said. 'As a last resort, and with more luck than I've seen to date, I might be able to cadge transport . . .'

'Haven't you got a horse?'

'Sold it, old chap. Hard to leave here when daily, right next door to you, some damn fellow goes shouting mad that he's struck colour. Gets to you, believe me.'

'Not me it won't. What do you want me to do? Bankroll you?'

'I would say invest, if you have any money.'

Mal had more than forty pounds in his money belt by this, but if the Englishman had designs on it, he was out of luck again.

'A couple of quid,' he allowed.

'Then why not renew the lease in both our names? In return, you can share this tent. And we'll go halves in whatever the mine returns. I'd appreciate it, to be truthful, if you could stake us for some grub. My larder is bare, or I'd have offered you lunch.'

Mal blinked. This fellow, who, he guessed, was about twenty-five, was not only broke but apparently out of food, and yet he was quite cheerful about it. Not the usual tale of woe, by any means.

45

'What's the point of renewing your claim if it's no good?' he asked. 'You've just said you haven't found a speck of gold. Why don't you forget about it? I'm not buying into a dead hole.'

'Will you join me then?' Hillier asked, relieved.

'Not there. Can't we find a better spot?'

'No. I'm right down by the river. Gold keeps popping up either side of me. I just haven't found the reef yet. Please stay with me on this, if only for a few weeks. Once I quit that mine, someone else will move in and I'll kill myself if they make a strike.'

Mal lit a smoke, checked the tent. It was still in good nick, no telltale leak signs, and big enough for two men. Hillier must have started off well, because he even had a table and two chairs, and a couple of decent lanterns. And another bunk.

'What happened to your partner, then?'

Hillier shrugged. 'Oh yes. My partner. She left.'

'She?' Mal's eyebrows shot up.

'Yes. I was very attached to Fleur. A sturdy lass. Met her in Brisbane. We came up here together, by ship. Very romantic. Women can be useful here if they have the stamina for it, and Fleur was never short of stamina. Lovely girl, believe me. But unfortunately one of my neighbours struck it rich and waved goodbye to the diggings. Sad to relate, Fleur went with him. Silly girl.'

'She doesn't sound too silly to me.'

'I suppose that's true. But I really did care for her. What did you say your name was?'

'I didn't. Mal Willoughby.' He'd had to register with his correct name.

'Then you will partner me in the claim?'

'Might as well.'

Hillier burst out laughing. 'My luck's changed at last. Did you see the other men waiting outside the claims office?'

'Yes. I saw some blokes hanging about. What of it?'

'They're on the breadline too. That's where you watch for new partners not already spoken for. You didn't appeal to the hard men of the fields. They thought you were too young, too soft. I hope you're not.'

'I'd have to be an improvement on a woman.' Mal shrugged, wondering what sort of a fool he was to be getting entangled with this loser. But Hillier had the makings of good company, so a few weeks on the diggings wouldn't do any harm.

Mal wasn't averse to hard work, he just didn't like prolonged doses of it. Swinging the pick and shovelling loads of rubble into heavy buckets was testing on the muscles for a start, but he soon found his rhythm, and went at the job cheerfully, watching for the famed glint of gold in their rocky lair. He also saw where a woman could be useful, pouring rubble down the chute for crushing, endlessly washing and sluicing for alluvial gold and generally helping out on lighter duties, noting without comment that Hillier seemed to have assigned himself that role.

46

With time for his mind to roam, Mal wondered about this girl called Fleur. Aside from the prostitutes, the other women on the goldfield were wives, hard, worn women, desperately struggling beside their men for that pot of gold, but Hillier kept insisting that Fleur had been different.

'A great beauty,' he'd claim sorrowfully. 'Marvellous coppery hair, lovely face and figure, and full of life.'

An adventuress, more like it, Mal thought, with enough good looks to addle Hillier's brain. Because the Englishman was of gentry stock, that was obvious, so it was a wonder that he'd taken up with a woman of that type in the first place. Mal often thought about his English lady, the one he'd met the day of the riot in Fortitude Valley. Hillier would have liked her. She was young and beautiful, and a lady. She wouldn't dream of setting foot in a place like this, let alone stoop to labouring. One night, when Clive was boring him with his daydreams about striking it rich and finding Fleur again, Mal told him about *his* friend.

'She's English. Very pretty and dainty. With the nicest voice. And dresses very fashionable. Smart as paint.'

'Really. She sounds charming. What's her name?'

'None of your business,' Mal growled, rather than admit he had no idea.

Her secret admirer would have been broken-hearted could he have seen his English lady now. He probably would have downed pick and shovel and immediately gone to her aid.

Emilie was at the docks, fighting back tears as she farewelled her sister, no longer so eager to be on her own.

'I'm so sorry it has come to this,' Ruth groaned.

'Don't be. We knew this was a big country and that it would be difficult for us to find positions close to each other. I'll keep an eye out for a place for you where I'm going, in Maryborough, and you can do the same for me in your country town.'

'But you're so young.'

'I'm twenty now.'

'Yes, at an age when you should be enjoying a decent social life, not dragging about in the wilds.'

'Please, Ruth. Don't go on so. You'll make yourself ill. Brisbane Town is hardly the wilds, and they say Maryborough is busier still. You're the one going out into the wilds.'

'Don't forget, if you're unhappy, you leave, Emilie. You come right back here to Mrs Medlow and I'll send you some money. She's agreed to put you up.'

'You've told me that before. Now I must go, Ruth . . . they're boarding.'

Emilie had to admit to a small sense of relief when she boarded the crowded schooner *Miriam*, because their funds had been dwindling again. They'd had to buy lighter clothes to cope with the heat, almost complete wardrobes, adding to the expense of rent, but that worry was behind them now. Salaries at last.

★ ★ ★

47

Since the voyage would only take a few days, Emilie had paid the cheapest fare possible, nineteen shillings, and had steeled herself for horrible accommodation, but even so she wasn't prepared for the chaos aboard this ship. Apart from a few families, the passengers were mostly men, who were lounging about the deck among mounds of luggage as if prepared to spend the whole voyage up top.

She found a steward, who directed her down a narrow gangway to what she expected to be a cabin, only to find it was kind of a dormitory for females. And it was already crowded with women who had hurried to claim the best positions. They all looked very poor, but not troublesome.

An Irishwoman beckoned her to a spare bunk.

'Grab this while you can, love. There's not much room in the men's quarter, it's my guess they'll be pullin' spare bunks out of here for the lads pretty soon. Then where will you put yer head?'

Emilie sat down with a bump on the hard ticking. 'There is no linen. I was told it would be provided.'

'Tell you anything, they would. Don't worry about it. Just pray we get there safe.'

'But my trunk. It's not here. Where will I find it?'

'It'll find you.'

Sure enough, the trunk was brought down with other luggage and stored in a heap by the bulkhead. There was no privacy at all; whenever Emilie wanted anything from the trunk, she had to shift other women's belongings to unearth it.

The Irishwoman, Mrs Delaney, made the journey bearable for Emilie, though. She explained that most of the passengers were immigrants, invited to Maryborough by the town council, which was desperate for workers at the port and the inland farms and stations. She was going to join her husband, who had already found a good job as a timbergetter, and she was so happy, she wouldn't allow anything to bother her.

On this short voyage, which would have horrified her sister, Emilie slept in her petticoats on a bare mattress, she washed in buckets of sea water behind a long curtain strung up by resourceful women, and she queued for food with them in the galley. In all, she had to admit, these plain women were kinder and more generous than the posturing second-class passengers she'd encountered on the previous voyage. When they did mingle with the men, to take the air, Mrs Delaney was at her side, a self-appointed chaperone, casting indignant glances at the men who eyed up her pretty young charge.

'They're not for you, Miss Tissington,' she warned. 'You keep your sights high.'

The port was quite a picture the day they arrived, with several great sailing ships swinging at anchor, long bullock trains hauling huge loads of wool along the wharves, lorries carting stacks of timber and, among the crowds on shore, a general air of bustle. It did seem a much busier port than Brisbane.

Mrs Delaney saw to it that Emilie's trunk was put ashore before she left with her husband, who'd been waiting anxiously for her, and Emilie found herself, once again, standing hopefully on a strange wharf. Only then did she look about her, to take in this new community, and the realisation that there were hundreds of black men on the wharf was a shock. She and Ruth – trying not to stare – had seen quite a few Aborigines in Brisbane, poor, ill-kempt people but obviously harmless. These fellows, though, were lighter-skinned, and bolder, peering at her with wide grins as they milled about. She would have moved away but she couldn't leave her trunk, so she called to a crewman from the ships.

'I'm waiting for a Mr Manningtree. Do you know him?'

'Can't say I do, miss.'

'Should I move from here?'

He saw her look nervously at the natives surrounding her. 'Don't worry about them kanakas. They won't hurt you. Their bosses will round them up soon. They've been brought in from the islands to work on the sugar plantations.'

No sooner had he spoken than a burly man with a red face came towards them, pushing the natives aside as if they were inanimate.

'Would you be Miss Tissington?' he asked.

'Yes. Mr Manningtree, is it?'

'In the flesh,' he said, looking her up and down in a manner that Emilie certainly didn't appreciate. 'Well now. I didn't expect a filly like you. But welcome to Maryborough. Is this your trunk?'

Emilie nodded unhappily. She didn't like this man: he was rough and uncouth, in a collarless shirt, no jacket and gaudy braces on show. He wasn't even wearing socks, just a pair of raffia sandals. She looked about her, desperately hoping to see someone she knew, wishing Mrs Delaney would find some reason to come back, wishing she could rush back aboard the *Miriam*, but that was not to be.

Mr Manningtree hauled in two of the kanakas to carry her trunk to a waiting buggy, and flicked them a coin for their trouble, laughing as they both dived for it, then he calmly climbed aboard to take up the reins, calling to Emilie to hop in.

As they drove away, her new employer lectured her. 'I own the sawmill here, doing well it is, and a few other businesses. And I'm on the town council, be Mayor one of these days, but I don't put on no airs. Do you get me?'

She nodded. That was obvious.

'And I don't want my missus puttin' on no airs either, so don't be puttin' notions in her head. It was her idea to get a teacher for the kids, there being no schools here worth their keep, and I'll go along with that. I never had no education, neither did she, but you have to look ahead in this world. Get in early like I did with my businesses. See what's needed. My kids will grow up moneyed, second-generation cash, so it won't do for them to grow up ignorant, if you get what I mean. It's all right for me, I'm doin' better than most here, but the town's growin' up too. In a few years this'll be a real city, you mark

49

my words, and I don't want my kids to be left at the post.'

While he was talking, Emilie was peering at the town from behind the rim of her bonnet. It was an awful place. Not at all like Brisbane. They seemed to be travelling up the main street, a wide, ugly thoroughfare bordered by odd buildings ranging from shacks to two-storeyed edifices in need of paint, and in between there were vacant weed-ridden blocks, like gaps in teeth. It was very hot, even worse than Brisbane, but not a tree in sight, just this miserable, dingy street, no smart shops and a populace that looked as dreary and unprepossessing as this member of the town council.

'She says you teach manners too,' he was saying. 'That's fair enough, won't hurt them to learn some manners, but you can learn them to speak proper. That's important. I taught meself to read and write, and add up, and I'm good at adding up.' He laughed. 'You can bet your britches on that. I don't need to speak proper – I'm my own boss, you see – but I don't want my kids making fools of themselves. You got that?'

'Yes, Mr Manningtree.'

'That agent fella, he wrote to the missus all fired up that you teach French too. Is that right?'

'Yes, Mr Manningtree.'

'Well, I won't have that. Waste of time. What he didn't say, and what I want to know . . . can you play the piano?'

'Yes, Mr Manningtree.'

'You can? By God. Now we're on to something.' He pulled the horses abruptly to a halt, threw her the reins and jumped down.

'Wait here.'

He disappeared into a general store, leaving Emilie clutching the leather straps, hoping the horse wouldn't decide to bolt. She saw all sorts of weird people wandering by: women in flat, serviceable skirts with no hint of hoops, floppy hats; rough men, some even wearing jingling spurs; groups of Aborigines and, worse, Chinese; some of those kanakas were idling on a street corner; and on top of all that, horsemen cantered down the main street as if they were out on country roads, unsettling her horse, causing it to whinny impatiently.

But then he was back, pleased with himself. 'I just bought a piano,' he exulted.

Emilie had to ask. 'Do they sell pianos in there, Mr Manningtree?'

'No, girl. I ordered one. The best he can buy. He'll ship it up to me. Always wanted a piano. So did the missus, but I said it was a waste of money with no one to play it.' He wiped the perspiration from his moustache and rubbed it on his shirt.

'Hot out here, we'd better get going.'

They drove in through an open gateway and along a muddy drive that tunnelled through a steaming forest of limp greenery which Emilie found unpleasant. A confusion of ferns and larger plants with wide leaves crowded patches of mushy lawn, under a canopy of misty trees. There was an eeriness about this garden, as if ghosts of another time still lingered in the half-light. She thought this might be the outskirts of an estate, but suddenly there was a clearing and the house loomed into view. A large timber house, and, like other buildings she'd seen in the town, unpainted, giving it a grey, listless appearance. She wondered if perhaps paint was not procurable in these parts.

It was a single-storeyed house, quite big, with a wide covered veranda across the front, but they did not enter from that direction. Mr Manningtree swung the buggy around to the rear of the house and into a large unfenced yard bordered by sheds and, further back, rows of unkempt banana trees.

Mrs Manningtree was standing by the kitchen door with three children gathered about her when the buggy pulled up, and as Emilie turned her gaze towards them with a smile, she saw the flash of a frown on the woman's face, and instinctively knew it for what it was. The lady of the house, pretty in a fussy sort of way, did not approve of a young, good-looking governess.

Emilie retained her smile as she was introduced by the husband, but she already knew she would have to watch her step with this one. Keep her head down. Mrs Manningtree was about thirty years old, at least twenty years younger than her spouse. She was wearing a busy pink floral dress, tightly boned to show off an ample bosom and small waist, and a rope of pearls which Emilie found odd for this time of day. Her own travelling outfit of dark navy with a white blouse looked dowdy beside this apparition, and Emilie was grateful that she had, eventually, succumbed to Ruth's insistence that governesses should never stand out. Her best dresses, relics of the good old days back home, were tissued in the depths of her trunk.

The children, all in clean smocks, but barefoot, grinned at her enthusiastically as their mother identified them.

'This is Jimmy, and Alice and little Rosie. Say hello to Miss Tissington.'

Their chorus of 'hello' was cheerful and friendly, and Emilie responded that she was pleased to meet them, but was cut short by Mrs Manningtree, who sent the children off to play.

In contrast to the decrepit garden, the house was neat and clean, and the timber floors shone and gave off the reassuring smell of beeswax. They'd entered through a well-scrubbed kitchen, and as her employer showed her through the house, Emilie wondered if that meant she was to use the tradesmen's entrance, or whether she'd been delivered that way for convenience.

As they toured, they peered into well-furnished rooms, parlour, dining room, sitting room and so on. Emilie fought off an overwhelming tiredness to listen dutifully to her employer.

'I entertain quite a lot, Miss Tissington. We have a social position to uphold. Coming from England, you may think that we're in the back-blocks here, but do not be deceived. I maintain a certain standard and expect my staff to do the same.'

'Of course.' Emilie nodded, then added diplomatically, 'Your home is very gracious, Mrs Manningtree. After the rigours of shipboard life, I count myself fortunate to be invited to join your family, and promise I shall do my very best for the children.'

The woman was mollified by this speech. 'You do? Oh, well, good. But you have to be firm with them, and I want a report every week. They did attend a small private school here, but the damned woman ran off with some low fellow and left us high and dry.'

She looked at Emilie suspiciously. 'I hope you're not here on a husband hunt.'

Taken aback, Emilie stared. 'No, madam.'

Mrs Manningtree seemed unduly pleased by her response. 'I don't suppose you are, you don't look the type to be chasing after the men in this town. But you beware, decent women are in short supply, so they'll be sniffing about after you. Just make it plain to them that under no circumstances can you entertain gentlemen in or around my home and they'll get the point. Now I'll show you your room.'

Back down a passage, Emilie found her room was adjacent to the kitchen, but it was like the rest of the house, neat as a pin. Her bed, with its white counterpane, was swathed in a generous mosquito net, a washstand sat under an open window, and a matching wardrobe and dressing table stood sturdily side by side on the far wall.

'It's very nice,' she said as Mr Manningtree lumbered in with her trunk.

'You got your bearings?' he asked, setting it in place, but before Emilie could respond, his wife dismissed him.

'You promised to fix the roof in the laundry, Bert, so get on with it. Next rain it'll be flooded again and my linen ruined.'

By the way she spoke to him, Emilie guessed that there was more than an age difference between this pair, but she found herself on the woman's side. Mrs Manningtree might be overbearing, but she had attained a household with a decent standard, which could not be easy in a dreadful outpost like this, and she at least tried to make herself presentable, if lacking in taste. Her husband, on the other hand, was uncouth. A ruffian. An arranged marriage, perhaps.

In a fit of relief at finding a friend Emilie took off her gloves and extended her hand to Mrs Manningtree.

'I can't tell you how pleased I am to meet you. And how happy I am to be here.'

The woman blinked, but took her hand in a firm shake. 'I'm not accustomed to shaking hands with women. But is that etiquette?'

Not really, Emilie thought. It was spontaneous, in lieu of an urge to hug someone. To care. To have someone care.

'Yes,' she lied, embarrassed.

'That's nice to know. I hope you'll be happy here, Miss Tissington. And another thing. You called me madam. I appreciate that. I hope you will continue to do so. Give an example to my cook and maid. They're dailies and very hard to train. Being locals, you see. Do you have a watch?'

'No,' Emilie admitted, remembering how she and Ruth had pawned their watches and what little jewellery they'd owned in London. 'I lost it on the ship.'

'Probably stolen. You have to learn to beware of low people. But never mind. I'll have the maid call you for dinner at six, and I'll put a clock in the classroom – that's over the back, where you won't be interrupted.'

Emilie, poised at her door, thought the woman would never leave, having launched into the subject of the classroom and its new, expensive fittings, with blackboards and slates and desks and maps of the world . . .

An hour later, she lay on her bed, intrigued by the misty veil of the mosquito net, and wondered about Mrs Manningtree's reference to husband hunting.

Was she after a husband? This was a matter that she and Ruth had never discussed, because their reduced circumstances had placed them beyond any care other than survival. Than being thrown into the streets. But before their father had remarried, the girls did have a normal social life and, if not exactly gentlemen friends, friends who were gentlemen. Friends they'd known all their lives. And, in the usual eventuality, gentlemen who would have proposed marriage. Ruth had been quite enamoured of shy John Perigree, son of Dr Perigree, and he of her, if the truth were told, but John was following in his father's footsteps, studying medicine in Birmingham, and his visits to their village had become less frequent. They had corresponded, but it had ended when Ruth advised John that she and Emilie were leaving for London.

Often Emilie had wondered if Ruth had told him why they had to leave, but Ruth would not discuss him. She was so stiff-necked about things like that. John, a student, had little money, not enough to take on a wife, and Ruth had lost her home, and her inheritance. It was a hopeless situation all round. Maybe that was why Ruth would not talk about him. Too sad. Too private.

For her part, in those carefree days, Emilie had wasted precious time, she now knew, playing the giddy lady with beaux aplenty. Dances, parties, picnics . . . Emilie Tissington was never short of attentive young gentlemen, of friends, friends who fell by the wayside when the new era of the stepmother took control, curtailing the pleasantries of the hospitable Tissington household, and making it common knowledge in the village that the daughters, however socially acceptable, would carry little in the way of dowries.

'What friends?' she asked herself dismally. 'Male or female, they all proved fairweather.'

When they'd written to friends from London, with overly cheerful accounts of life in the metropolis, they'd received no response, except from dear Biddy Halligan, a neighbour, who was saddened to hear from their stepmother, Mrs Tissington, that they could not find employment. That had hurt them atrociously. Biddy was a nice girl but famously tactless. To have her feel sorry for them was too much. Their letters home ceased.

But husband hunting? Maybe eventually, Emilie thought. Had they been able to travel first class, they might have had a chance to meet eligible gentlemen, the type that would not dream of travelling second class. All of a sudden it occurred to Emilie that the Society may have had its reasons, not necessarily economic, for sending its educated middle-class women that way. So that they would not come in contact with eligible men. So that they would land in the colony uninvolved, eager to conform to the rules of the Society, as single women.

Although she was weary, although the bed was comfortable and it was mid-afternoon on a very hot day, Emilie could not sleep.

Without Ruth's restraining influence, she saw herself as being caught up in a cruel conspiracy, sent off in the prime of her life to a life of service, bowing to the will of a strange woman and her ruffian husband. There were no tears. Just anger, as Emilie allowed herself to indulge in a rare bout of self-pity.

Husband hunting? Emilie asked herself again. Maybe I am. But Mrs Manningtree is right. Not in this apology for a town. Not in this rough place, where they don't even paint their houses.

Unwittingly, Mrs Manningtree had prodded her into rising above the flat feeling of doomed servitude Emilie had experienced since their devastating expulsion from home. That frown she had encountered from her employer on first sighting had been the only encouraging sign Emilie had seen for such a long time. It had been jealousy. Plain as that.

Emilie stood before the mirror and loosened the plaits wound into a neat circlet to her crown, allowing her hair to fall in dark, shimmering waves. The voyages had been good for her. No pimples remained; her skin was fresh, unblemished, even a little tanned. Shiny and healthy-looking. Emilie knew she had something in her favour now. She had blossomed into a rather nice-looking girl. Woman.

Miss Ruth Tissington was surprised at the warmth of her welcome in Nanango after a fascinating coach journey inland that had taken two and a half days. All four of the Stanfield family, and their two excited dogs, were at the depot to meet her, rushing at her as if she were some long-lost friend. Mrs Stanfield actually hugged her.

'I'm so thrilled you're here, Miss Tissington. Did you have a good trip? I hope you didn't find the travel too difficult. Did they look after you?'

'Indeed, yes, very kind . . .'

They were turning her arrival into quite a circus, making such a fuss that people were staring, hardly giving her a chance to farewell her kind fellow passengers. Discovering that she was new to the country, the two couples travelling with her had gone out of their way to assist her at the various coach stops, as well as pointing out landmarks and delightful fauna. Ruth was happy to have seen, at last, mobs of kangaroos and emus racing across the countryside, quite a few sleepy koalas and more livestock than she'd ever come across in her life. The journey had been a real adventure, which she must write up in detail in her journal when she found time.

Mrs Stanfield had introduced her husband, Jack, and the two young girls, Jane and Jessie, adding:

'And you must call me Leonie.'

Ruth was startled. 'Thank you, but I should prefer not. It would be a bad example for the girls.' She doubted that Mrs Stanfield had taken note of that directive, and though a small matter, it bothered Ruth. She was determined to prove her excellence as a governess and she couldn't begin by bowing to brash colonial ways if she was to be any use to these girls at all. Already, she'd noticed that Jane and Jessie, aged nine and eleven, were sorely in need of training, interrupting their parents and romping about the depot as if they were in a playground.

Finally she was borne over to a wagon, where Mr Stanfield managed to find room for her trunk among boxes and bags of supplies, and then took her by the arm.

'You sit up front, Ruth,' he said, obviously having gleaned her Christian name from his sister-in-law.

This wasn't the time to tell him she could not approve of her Christian name being used either, so she sighed and allowed him to assist her up, only to hear an argument break out.

'No, Dad. We want Ruth to sit with us,' Jessie cried. 'She's our teacher.'

Their mother shushed them. 'Be quiet and sit still.'

'No, you change places with her.'

'It's too late. Shut up.'

Their father ignored them and the wagon rolled out of the depot, turning right on to a long country road.

'That's the town down there,' he told Ruth, pointing back with his whip. 'We'll bring you in another time to have a look around. There's a storm coming there, from the east, and I want to beat it home.'

Jane began to wail. 'Aren't we going into town? I wanted to see Elsie. You promised we could go into town.'

Her sister joined in, crying that it wasn't fair, while their mother argued with them, instead of, as Ruth thought primly, putting a stop to this behaviour. Stanfield drove steadily on, taking no notice at all.

Then Jessie used the age-old child's plea. 'We have to go into town. I want to pee.'

'No you don't. You went at the depot,' said her mother.

'I do so. If you don't take me I'll wet my pants.'

Mrs Stanfield sighed. 'Pull up, Jack. I'll take her behind those bushes.'

She hustled the child down, and while they waited in the wagon, Jane giggled. 'I bet she doesn't go. I bet she doesn't.' When they returned, she nudged her sister. 'You didn't go, did you?'

'I can't go behind bushes, that's all.'

'Don't tell lies. You can so.'

Ruth listened in horror to these exchanges, sitting straight-backed on the seat, gloved hand holding the rail, watching the horses pound down the road.

55

This part of the journey took two hours, and Mr Stanfield was right: they were no sooner inside the house – very similar to large farmhouses back home, Ruth was pleased to find – when the storm broke. The skies darkened, ear-splitting cracks of thunder followed shafts of lightning, and the rain began to fall, deepening into torrents. She sheltered in the small bedroom allotted her, completely unnerved, not only by the terrifying storm but by these atrocious children.

One of the gentlemen on the coach, eager to provide the young Englishwoman with as much information as possible, had purchased an up-to-date map of Queensland for Ruth, and now she took it out from her overnight bag to study her exact position in relation to Emilie's destination. Maryborough was much further north, even further than she'd imagined. Only now was she beginning to understand the size of this country, where her three days' travel had only covered a minute area of this state.

She hoped that Emilie had managed the sea journey without her support, and that her pupils would be less of a challenge than the Stanfield pair.

Just as well, she thought, that it was I who took this position. Emilie mightn't have been able to control these girls. They need a firm hand, and I'll see to that. I don't want to let Mr and Mrs Stanfield down. Despite their overly effusive attitude, they were quite nice people. The pay was not what she'd hoped to receive, but Ruth resolved not to allow that to matter; she was a responsible person and would give of her best.

She finished her unpacking and steeled herself to go out to the family, dressed now in her uniform of white blouse with a navy bow at the high neck, and navy skirt, her hair parted in the middle and wound into two neat plaits over her ears. Miss Tissington, the English governess, had arrived.

Chapter Three

The liveliness and sheer energy of the goldfields kept Mal there longer than he had intended, happy enough to keep working with Hillier, but once he became aware of the undercurrents of violence, he decided it was time to get out.

'This place is getting too big, too crowded,' he warned Clive. 'We ought to move on. We've not doing any good anyway.'

But Hillier wouldn't hear of it. 'You've got an investment here, Mal. You can't walk away now. What difference does it make if more diggers come here?'

All the difference in the world, Mal knew, as he watched fights break out, claims jumped and everyday brawls deteriorate into gunfights. The Chinese camps were attacked by gangs of angry miners with no logical reason other than that the Chinese had no place in the white world, and robberies were daily events, not only on the fields but out on the roads. Bushrangers menaced the stagecoaches carrying gold consignments to Maryborough, and the police were kept busy searching the hills for their hideouts in vain attempts to recover stolen gold, with the result that the fist and the gun were at once law and disorder on the fields. Colt revolvers became currency in themselves, and Mal was angry one afternoon to come back to the tent to find Hillier proudly displaying one.

'What the hell are you doing with that?'

'You know what's happening round here, old chap. We have to protect our claim.'

'Are you mad? We've got nothing to protect. And what did you pay for it?'

'I said you'd give the fellow ten pounds. Cheap at half the price. And I'll have you know, I'm quite a good shot. He threw in the ammunition.'

The fellow who came with two mates to collect his money was in no mood to take the gun back, but Mal managed to break the price down to a more realistic four pounds by grumbling that the Gold Commissioner was threatening to send out deputies on the search for stolen guns, which was not true but rattled the sellers enough to allow the price to slide, on condition that Mal kept his mouth shut.

'I paid for it, it's mine,' he told Hillier. 'And I'll sell it first chance I get. But as of today, I'm giving you a fortnight, then I'm on my way. You can come with me or stay, please yourself.'

Late that night, he and Hillier were resting in their tent with the flaps down for some protection from insects when they heard shrieks and shouts: another fight.

Suddenly a Chinese coolie staggered into their tent, bleeding profusely from several wounds.

Clive leapt up, shouting at the coolie to get out, but Mal cut him short. 'Leave him be!'

They heard men running, shouting, searching, and Mal quickly pushed the coolie aside and strode out. 'What's going on?'

'You seen a bloody Chink anywhere?'

'No. Why?'

But they rushed on, about ten of them, wielding heavy sticks and ropes.

'Now you've torn it,' Clive complained. 'What if they come back? They'll beat us up too.'

Mal ignored him, lifting the young coolie up on to his bunk. 'God Almighty, he's taken a hiding! Reckon his head's broke, and an arm. You mop up the blood and I'll get help.'

'What help? No one will help a Chink.'

Mal slid the gun out from under his bunk, loaded it and handed it to Clive.

'Now you're going to need this.'

'What for?'

'To protect yourself. If they come back. But if you chuck him out, you'll need more than that to protect yourself from me. Now make yourself useful. Look after him.'

He slipped away into the darkness, heading for the Chinese camps, but as he neared their tents he knew they'd be alert. A white man might not even get a chance to explain. On the outskirts, he whistled a few times to gain attention, but it came faster than he'd expected. A Chinaman loomed up beside him in a crouching fighting stance, so Mal shouted the only name he knew.

'Mr Xiu! Mr Xiu!'

The sentry seemed uncertain, but he did not attack.

'Bossman!' Mal insisted. 'Mr Xiu. Me, friend. You take, pretty bloody quick.'

There was a swish in the undergrowth and two other men materialised, keeping Mal at bay while they discussed this situation in their own language.

'You speak English?' he asked, and realised that with coolies, even that was a waste of time. Had they asked him in their language if he spoke Chinese, he'd have looked equally mystified.

He stood tall then, and with an imperious gesture indicated he wished to see Mr Xiu.

They made him wait outside Mr Xiu's tent until the gentleman was ready to receive him, and when at last he was permitted to enter, he understood why. The highborn Chinese was fully dressed in ornamental robes, giving no indication that he might have been sleeping, and seated on a beautifully carved chair in the most luxurious tent that Mal had ever seen. Golden filigree lanterns revealed a carpeted retreat lined with red and gold silk drapes. From the exterior, standing under guard by the tent flap, Mal hadn't noticed how large this tent was, nor how ornate, because the outer drab canvas had seemed to fit in with the general dark and crowded surrounds.

Smelling incense from candles lit in the far corner, he gazed astonished at the formal black furniture, low tables, carved chairs and a long, low daybed upholstered in red satin. His curious stares were interrupted by Mr Xiu.

'We meet again, Mr Willoughby.'

'Yes, sir. I didn't know where else to go. One of your diggers has been hurt. They beat him up. He needs help bad.'

Xiu seemed unimpressed, so Mal continued. 'Well, I don't know if he's actually one of your men, but . . .'

'Where is he?'

'In my tent.'

'And where is that?'

'Down by the river. What they call Elbow Bend.'

Until then Mal hadn't realised that several black-garbed Chinamen had entered the tent behind him; they all moved so silently.

Mr Xiu spoke to them and then turned slowly back to Mal.

'You will show them?'

'Yes. He needs a doctor.'

Mr Xiu nodded. 'You have repaid the debt.'

'I would have done it anyway.'

'Yes, Mr Willoughby, I think so. Now if you would be so kind, my men are ready.'

The audience over, Mal turned on his heel to leave, but it wasn't in his nature to allow himself to be dismissed like that.

'Good to see you again,' he said to Mr Xiu with a grin, and was rewarded with what could have been interpreted as a smile from the elderly, thin-lipped Chinaman.

He was hardly aware of the silent men who loped along behind him as he dodged through the rutted streets and mullock heaps to Elbow Bend and on to his tent.

Clive stood back, amazed, as four Chinamen in their sleek, pyjama-like suits slid into the tent behind Mal, picked up their fallen comrade and disappeared into the night without a word.

'Where the hell did they come from?'

'Friends.' Mal shrugged. 'They'll take care of him. I'm tired. Let's get some sleep.'

It irked Mal, it really annoyed him that it had to be Hillier who'd stumbled on the gold, and not the man who'd bankrolled the enterprise and had been doing most of the work. A matter of principle, you could say. He'd been chipping away in the mine, forming an ever-widening arc,

59

while his partner was supposed to be removing mullock with a borrowed wheelbarrow but had instead been pottering about in the cool shallows at the river's edge. And stumbled was the right word. The banks had been subjected to so much traffic and shallow digging that a section had collapsed under Hillier's weight, causing him to slide into a muddy hole. And there it was, glinting like stars against the dark earth . . . specks of gold as fine as dust, merry grains of gold masquerading as sand, heavy golden pebbles rolling about untarnished by the mire.

Hillier was given to crying wolf, as well as shouting for help when confronted by real wolves in the shape of sleek water snakes and the families of vicious rats that infested the diggings, so when Mal heard the shouting he took his time, ambling down to see what the fuss was about. But Hillier was ecstatic, yelling his head off, all words unintelligible except the one that brought other men running as well.

'Gold!'

Mal dropped to his knees, staring, disbelieving, as his partner ran his hands through the treasure trove of mud.

'By all that's holy! It is gold!'

'Of course it is, I told you there was gold here!' Hillier shouted gleefully. 'Get the sluice, quick. Borrow another one. Make a sluicegate there to stop any of this ore running out. Get a shovel. Build a levee. Move, Mal, move!'

Clive became the boss and Mal his willing labourer. They forgot the dry hole and, working carefully behind the high levee the cautious Mal had constructed, began, inch by inch, to extract the gold, their gold, a long, slow process but wildly rewarding.

The next morning, bright and early, Mal delivered their first gold to the shanty bank: fine alluvial gold in matchboxes, and the rest in the bottom of a scoured and dried jam tin. He watched suspiciously as it was being weighed, to make certain specks didn't drift off on to sticky fingers, and breathed a sigh of wonder when he was handed ninety pounds.

But the bank teller wasn't impressed. 'Don't go yet, mister. I have to take your particulars and enter them in the register.'

While he waited for the relevant book to be unearthed, a tall, grey-haired man entered the bank from the rear door, and with a genial nod to Mal went over to talk to the teller. After a few minutes, the teller found him a file and the older man left.

Mal was surprised to see that this bloke was somehow connected with the bank, because he knew him to be a rather heavy gambler. To ease the boredom of stagnant tent life, Mal had often played cards in a nearby saloon, small games with a few trusted players, where he could do little damage and keep clear of trouble, and he'd seen the older man there. Playing at the back table, though, with the big guns. Sometimes Mal had even gone up to watch as cash and pouches of gold piled up on the green baize cloth, a luxury afforded those gentlemen.

'Who's he?' Mal asked the teller.

'Gold Commissioner Carnegie,' he replied, opening his register. 'Now,

I want your licence number, claim number, owner's name or names, signature, or thumbprint if you can't write.'

Mal provided the information and signed the book, mildly surprised that such an important gent should be mixing with the common mob, but then, he supposed, big boss or not, he probably wouldn't have much to do of a night either in a dump like this.

There wasn't much left of Clive's half-share of the ninety pounds by the time Mal had extracted his expenses, but he didn't care; tomorrow was another day.

By the end of the week, Mal had sewn an extra pocket into his money belt to carry more than four hundred pounds, all bounty from the strike, but by then the gold was becoming harder to find. Daily their take dwindled, until after a few blank days Mal was only able to hand the teller less than an ounce of gold.

Commissioner Carnegie was in the bank again, and he looked at Mal with interest.

'Running out, is it?'

'Yes, sir. Looks like it. But no complaints. We've done all right.'

'Good attitude, son. The smart ones take their luck and go while they can.'

Mal pushed his hat back on his head and grinned. It always amused him when men talked to him as if he was just out of knee pants. 'I reckon I might just do that,' he said, to impress the big boss.

'Let me know if you decide to leave. I might have a job for you.'

Mal nodded, obliging as always, but the last thing he needed was a job. It was too soon to give up on the claim, but if it stopped producing, he was off. They said Maryborough was a good town; he would take a look and then go on out to the sea coast. His card-playing mates had told him that that coast was the prettiest place a man ever did see.

'Not much in the way of company, though,' they warned him. 'Barely a white man in sight, save a few squatters that have swiped all the land.'

That didn't bother Mal. One of his pleasures was to seek out scenic spots in his travels, to see these talked-about places for himself. His favourite was the Blue Mountains outside Sydney, with their truly magnificent views, but being a countryman, he had an abiding interest in the sea, a curiosity about what it would be like to live by the seashore, even for a little while . . .

Clive was shocked 'You can't go! We'll renew the lease and dig deeper. We have to keep going.'

'We didn't hit a reef, mate, we struck a patch, that's all. We've been searching around for weeks now, and not a glimmer. The claim looks as if a mad ploughman's been at work. We couldn't even sell it.'

'Then we'll stake another claim, further downriver.'

'They're not finding gold so far out, and you know it.'

'Somewhere else then. These goldfields aren't finished, Mal. Look about you. More diggers are turning up every day.'

Mal shrugged. 'I can't argue with you on that, but I don't want to stay. It's no life, living on this antbed. We've made a pile. Time to go.'

'But we can make so much more. What's a few hundred pounds when a good strike sets a man up for life? They're still finding real nuggets here, Mal . . . big ones . . . we could be rich. Don't you understand? We can afford to stay on now.'

Mal shook his head. He'd almost become accustomed to the stink of the place, but he yearned for clean air, for solitude, for fresh food, for his life back. Clive could stay, but he was leaving.

That night, rather than endure more of Clive's arguments, Mal wandered up to the saloon for a game of cards.

Carnegie came striding along, and was just about to enter the saloon when he noticed Mal, who was standing outside, waiting for the call to take a turn at the table.

'You still here, Mr Willoughby?'

Mal blinked. 'How do you know my name?'

'It's my business to know names. I thought you'd be well gone by this.'

'Tomorrow.'

'Ah. That's interesting. Would you care to take a stroll with me?'

'A stroll? Why?'

Carnegie frowned. 'Because there are big ears all about. We can go this way.'

They walked to the end of the dingy lane and stood under the awning of a deserted butcher's stall. Though the wooden benches were now empty, the smell of raw meat lingered, and flies buzzed in droves. Revolted, Mal suggested they move on.

'Just bear a minute,' Carnegie said. 'Since you're leaving, the job's still open.'

'With all respect, Mr Carnegie, I don't need no job.'

The Commissioner brushed flies away from his face. 'Are you going south, or on to Maryborough?'

'Going on.'

'Well then, all I ask is that you make yourself useful *en route*, and you'll be paid.'

'How?'

'As you know, it is my duty to take the gold consignments into Maryborough under escort. I'll be leaving with another consignment shortly and I need a deputy. You look an honest chap, so the job's yours if you're willing.'

'Why me? You must have your own deputies.'

Carnegie shook his head. 'They come and go. The gold escort only leaves every three or four weeks, so it's just casual work for most of them, except for Mr Taylor. He works in my office full time, and is very reliable, but it is our policy to choose different men each time. Men who are not known to each other, so there's no fear of collusion.'

'You mean there's a chance they might gang up on you?'

'It has been known to happen. Not to me, of course, but Mr Taylor and

I take precautions, and we're always well armed.'

'Why don't you use police?'

'When they're available we do, but that's rare.' He swatted at flies again. 'This place is quite dreadful. We'll have to go.'

Before they reached the saloon, Carnegie turned to Mal.

'What do you say then? Will you take the job?'

'You want me to be an outrider for the gold? Just like that?'

'Not quite. Are you interested?'

Mal stopped to give this some thought, digging a thumb in his belt and leaning on one hip. If he travelled under escort he'd have protection for his own considerable funds. Come to think of it, he was a walking bank himself. He couldn't cart all this money about indefinitely, and not being one to squander it in pubs like the mad miners round here, sooner or later he'd have to think what to do with it. Maybe put it in a bank. That was a novel thought.

'Well?' Carnegie asked.

'Why not? When do we go?'

'I decide that. But first I want you to report to Mr Taylor. He'll need to know a bit more about you. I'm just making a suggestion at this point. If he approves, you've got the job. But I don't want you discussing this with anyone. If I get wind that you've talked, you're out.'

Taylor was a lantern-jawed man in his forties, a fearful-looking gent with dark hair, a dark moustache and cold grey eyes that seemed to look right through the young man as he tramped across bare boards to the deputy's desk. Mal thought he looked more like a policeman than a public servant and was instantly uneasy.

'What do you want?'

'Mr Carnegie told me to come and see you. For the job, riding escort. The gold . . .'

'He did, did he?' Taylor glared, and Mal had the impression that Carnegie wasn't popular with his offsider.

'Who are you?'

'Mal Willoughby, sir.'

His polite tone did serve to soften that glare but not the snapped interrogation that followed. Where had Mal come from? His family? What work did he do? Had he ever been in trouble with the police? Did he drink? Gamble? Any success on the goldfields? His partner's name? Background? And so on.

Amused, Mal spun a fine tale about a family hotel in Ipswich, his life as a shearer on big stations and his home base with his Uncle Silver down south in Chinchilla. That would be news to Silver.

Taylor bit his lip, sizing him up. 'Where did you meet the Commissioner?'

'He saw me in the bank. Then I suppose he saw me a few times in the saloon, at the tables.'

'I thought you said you didn't gamble?'

'Me? No, sir. I only play a small game, a friendly game there

63

sometimes, with a few mates. To pass the time, so to speak. I couldn't sit in on the big games like Mr Carnegie.'

That hit home. Taylor scowled and slammed down his pen. He pushed aside the notebook that now contained details of this applicant.

'The job's dangerous,' he grated. 'You're not so wet behind the ears you don't know that. Why would you want to take it on?'

Mal grinned. 'If you look at your notes, and at the bank register, you'll see I'm carrying more cash than I ever earned in my life. I want to get out of here while the going's good. My partner, he's staying. I can't think of a better way for a cashed-up lone man to travel than with a gold escort. Can you?'

Taylor nodded. 'You'll need your wits about you. But you seem alert, not like half the drunken clowns around here. Can you handle a rifle?'

'My word.'

'All right. I'll be in touch.'

'When do we go?'

'When I say so. I know where to find you. Settle up with your partner and keep your mouth shut.'

Commissioner Carnegie quit the poker table early, blaming the heat, which was terrible, still in the nineties, though the sun had set hours ago, with not a breath of wind for relief. He mopped his sweating face with a large handkerchief and called for a brandy to ease his thumping headache.

'Getting old,' he said. 'I haven't got the stamina of you lads any more. I swear this heat is crushing my head.'

The headache was true enough, but it was also being fed by a succession of losing hands, and he dared not borrow any more from the saloon keeper. Until Taylor had descended on him, a couple of months ago, Carnegie had kept the books himself, neat accounts that allowed him to pocket cash and to collect bribes, which he referred to as stipends, from miners who needed favours. The additional income had proved helpful because Carnegie needed every penny to make this job work for him; letters from his creditors in Brisbane were pressing. Gambling debts were, of course, a gentleman's privilege, and it would be a while before any of them took real action, because Allyn Carnegie had a good name and powerful friends.

That damned Taylor, hovering over the journals and registers like a hawk, would have noticed if a halfpenny went askance, or if claim jumpers suddenly came into legal possession of mines, so that source had dried up.

He sighed. Thanks to Taylor, he had been forced to turn to Chinese moneymen for loans to keep himself afloat, and now he was in so deep only a miracle could save him from ruin.

Since miracles were hard to come by, the Commissioner was preparing to stage his own, a daring plan, so simple it couldn't go wrong. All he needed was the courage, no, the guts, to carry it out. To make the decision.

Carnegie was sweating so much he was already shedding his jacket and tie as he stepped into the two-roomed timber shack known as the Commissioner's residence. He threw them on to a chair and was fumbling for matches to light a lamp when he heard movement in his bedroom.

'Who's there?' he called. 'Come out and show yourself.'

A burly, bald-headed man loomed up in the doorway. 'Ease up, it's only me.'

'Dammit, Perry! What are you doing here? I told you never to come here.' Relieved, though, Carnegie lit the lamp, closed the door and dropped the canvas blind over the small window.

'No one saw me. I want to know if you're gonna move on this or not. I can't hang about forever.'

'There are things to consider . . .'

'You've been saying that for weeks now. You get your considerin' done and stop wasting my time. When's the next shipment going out?'

'When I say so,' Carnegie retorted, but he was suddenly nervous. He reached into a box and took a cigar, his hands trembling as he lit it.

Perry took a cigar as well. 'Don't mind if I do,' he grinned. 'Are you gettin' cold feet, Commissioner? It weren't my idea, it was yours, remember? And I don't recall you picked me for my good looks. You wanted a good backup, and you've got it. I'm your man. Now what's the problem?'

Carnegie sucked hard on the cigar. Perry *was* the man to help him; he was a hard-faced brute, a criminal type no less, but exactly the sort he needed. And if he didn't go with Perry, having discussed the plan with him, he'd never get another chance. He would never be able to attempt such a coup with anyone else because Perry would hear of it, and would be able to point the finger right at Commissioner Carnegie from a position of innocence. Uninvolved, and therefore dangerous.

He had chosen Perry with care, just as he'd chosen the yokel Willoughby as a foil. The kid was as dumb as they came.

'I'm getting there,' he said slowly. The next shipment of gold to leave the diggings would be in excess of eight thousand pounds. He'd have to give half to Perry as promised, because the papers would release the amount stolen, but four thousands pounds would solve all his problems.

'I have to trust you,' he said. 'I have to let you take the gold. How do I know you won't take off with it? All of it.'

Perry lolled back against the wall. 'Never fear. You'll have your half. You can trust me on that. And do you know why? Because this is the smartest deal I've ever come across. I have to hand it to you, Commissioner, it's a beauty. How much do you reckon I'll get?'

'About four thousand,' Carnegie said dully.

'Jesus! Four thousand! I'd have come in for half that. Jesus! We pull this off and you'll never see me again. I'll be going home to Tasmania and you'll be a hero, while the police are chasing through the hills looking for some big bad outlaws.' He laughed. 'Crafty it is. Real crafty. Then I suppose a man doesn't get big jobs like yours unless he's smart.'

Carnegie needed that flattery, and he was relieved that Perry under-stood the logic of not trying the double-cross. That was crucial. He would claim they'd been attacked by bushrangers but never give Perry's descrip-tion. By the time police got wind of the holdup, Perry would be in Maryborough, not racing for the cover of the hills.

There would also be a consignment of cash from the small goldfield bank, sent to town at the same time – a bonus. It would be Perry's job to take the gold, and the cash, hide it in a site they had previously chosen and then resume his job in Maryborough.

In four weeks, exactly twenty-eight days after the fuss had died down, he was to retrieve the bags of gold and cash and bring them to the Commissioner's bungalow in Maryborough. They both knew it was important that there was never any connection between the two men, so the delivery had to be made in the dead of night. All Perry had to do was simply hide the haul under the back steps of the bungalow and slip away. They had to trust each other; the stakes were too high for mistakes, and neither man could take the risk of double-crossing his partner.

In the privacy of the bungalow, Carnegie would divide the takings as best he could, given his experience with gold, and repack Baldy Perry's share. This would be replaced under the steps and Perry could collect it the following night and be on his way. No contact between them ever established. It would work. The plan was foolproof.

Carnegie was glad now that he had bought that bungalow, as a respite from the miserable conditions on the goldfields. It was proving to be very useful. Though by no means up to the standard of his spacious house in Brisbane, it was a little home away from home.

He smiled. And very convenient it was.

As he mulled over his plan, his only real worry was Perry. Trusting Perry.

But who else? Either Perry or another of his ilk.

He stubbed the cigar. 'Saturday. We go Saturday.'

Perry was straddling a chair. He knocked it over in his excitement. 'You mean it? It's on?' He was on his feet. 'I tell you, Mr Carnegie, you won't regret this. We'll pull it off and we'll be free and clear. Not a soul in the whole damn world will be able to point a finger at either of us. By God, we'll be rich.'

Four thousand pounds wasn't rich to Carnegie, but it was a fine start. 'Let's go over it again. You will be waiting for us at Blackwater Creek. On Sunday night. With the rowboat.'

'Yeah, I've got it. I'll have it there. How many men will you be travelling with?'

'Taylor and three deputies. Two I've used before and one new fellow.'

'Who's he?'

'A kid called Willoughby.'

'What about Taylor?'

'He goes by the book.' Carnegie smirked. 'And so will I. We wait for police reinforcements at Blackwater Creek.'

★ ★ ★

The coach, with its extra-strong straps to cope with the rough track, had no passengers this trip. It was loaded with steel trunks and ready to leave before dawn on the Saturday morning. Taylor himself took the reins, and the other riders, led by the Commissioner, took up escort beside it. There were no farewells. They simply turned on to a back road out of the diggings and were on their way.

Mal was excited. This was something different, riding shotgun, as it were, along with a gold consignment, although he and the other deputies were only armed with rifles.

There had been no notice to speak of. One of those deputies, who hadn't even given his name, had barged into the tent while it was still dark.

'Willoughby?'

'That's me.' Mal had been groggy but awake enough.

'Commissioner wants you. Get movin'.'

This was it! He'd only had time to pack his swag and wake Clive to tell him he was off. Of course, he'd already told Clive he'd taken a job as a guard to get him to Maryborough. Clive was disappointed but Mal's mind was made up. They shook hands and parted friends.

Then he was outside the Commissioner's residence, trying to keep his horse still as the coach came out from cover, and the other horsemen, who were not introduced, jigged about, their horses also smelling action. Mr Taylor was driving the coach, but the Commissioner, on a sturdy grey, was the leader. He spurred his horse, and they all shot down the road before there was even a stir in the camps.

The ladies of the Female Middle Class Emigration Society had not only provided their governesses with references; they had also impressed upon them the necessity to retain a certain standard, so that all of their employers, and future employers, would understand and accept a governess's correct status in a household.

Emilie had read and digested the list of rules without concern, because she found them quite sensible and normal, exactly as one would expect in the pattern of life for a governess. Very soon, though, she discovered that Mrs Manningtree was not aware of these rules, and Emilie was too intimidated by the woman to attempt to right matters on her first day.

At five that afternoon, the maid came for her.

'I'm Nellie. Mrs Manningtree said to take you through to the kids. They've had their baths, miss, so you'll only have to do their hair and bring them down to dinner.'

Emilie clocked up the first error. Governesses were not nursemaids, they were teachers. But she followed obediently to the bedroom, where she was ambushed by her three charges, all talking at once. They rained questions on her, obviously fascinated that she had come such a long way on a big ship.

She held up her hands for quiet. 'I can't answer everything at once,' she

67

smiled. 'Tomorrow I'll tell you all about the ship and the long, long voyage. It will make a good geography lesson for you. But now you must get dressed.'

The room with its three beds in a row looked like a small, untidy dormitory, with clothes and towels strewn about. She began picking them up. 'What do you wear to dinner?'

'What we've got on,' Alice told her, 'but Rosie's got hers on back to front.'

Emilie gasped. 'But they're your nightgowns.'

'Yes, because we've had our baths. We waited for you but Nellie said you were having a sleep.'

'Do you always go to dinner in your night attire?'

They nodded, and Emilie shrugged. 'Very well. You'll all need to brush your hair first. Can you find me a brush, Alice, and I'll do Rosie's.'

She took the youngest child aside, rearranged her nightgown and waited until Alice found a soiled brush and a broken comb by scrambling through dresser drawers, then attended to Rosie's tangled curls as gently as she could.

Rosie was pleased. 'You do my hair real good. Nellie hurts, she pulls at the knots.'

Emilie wondered then if the maid was pushing one of her chores on to the governess. Something that would have to be sorted out.

It was quicker to take on the hair-brushing of all three than to wait for Jimmy and Alice's vague efforts to produce a result. That done, Emilie lined the children up.

'Good. Now where are your slippers?'

They stared. 'We don't got no slippers,' Jimmy said.

'We do not have . . .' she corrected.

'That's right,' they echoed.

She soon discovered that shoes were only for Sunday school, that they were hot, uncomfortable and caused big blisters that had to be pierced with a needle to let the water out, then they hurt more. Emilie could relate to blisters – she'd had a few herself in her day – but barefoot children in a classroom? That did not sound right.

Instead of leading Miss Tissington to the dining room, the children escorted her through the kitchen, where she met Kate, the cook, a capable-looking woman with fair hair in a tight bun, and a thin smile. Hardly stopping, the trio marched on past a pantry, to an inner window-less room, where four places were set on a bare table.

As the children took their seats, Nellie came in.

'You sit here, miss,' she said kindly. 'Me and Cook, we eat later. Do you want soup?'

Taken aback, Emilie nodded, but still stood uncertainly by the table. Governesses take their meals with the family, she recalled, not in the nursery with the children.

But this was worse. This was evidently the servants' dining room. Didn't Mrs Manningtree understand that she was neither a nurse nor a servant? Emilie felt she should tell the cook there had been a mistake, but she knew better than to offend household staff. She would have to take this up with her employer in the morning. In the meantime, she was hungry.

The classroom, in a shed with an iron roof, was a furnace, but the children didn't seem to notice. Their parents had at least made an effort to furnish the room, with one long table for the pupils and a neat table up front facing them for the teacher. On a ledge under the window were notebooks, a box of pencils, slates and slate pencils, and a jumble of school books. Beside them was a large new blackboard on an easel with a box of coloured chalks.

Alice, who seemed to be the leader, brought chairs from the back and placed them at the table, and another one for 'miss', who thanked her as she placed her own collection of readers and textbooks on view. Books that she and Ruth had purchased in London before they left, hoping they would be suitable.

The new teacher called the children to attention, asked if they had a favourite morning prayer, and since it didn't seem they did, had them recite The Lord's Prayer with her. Then she began the day with a short talk to introduce herself, pleased that her pupils were very attentive. So far, anyway.

Her plan was to give each one a little writing test to see where to begin with them, but before she could do so, Mrs Manningtree appeared in the open doorway.

'Good morning, Miss Tissington. I'm glad to see you're under way. No use wasting time. Are they behaving?'

'Oh yes indeed, Mrs Manningtree. They're very good children.' She saw them glow at the praise, but their mother didn't appear to notice.

'Have you got everything you need?'

'I think so. Yes.'

'If you want anything else, tell Kate. She'll see to it.'

'Thank you.' Emilie took a deep breath. She had to speak up, she had to. It was now or never.

'Mrs Manningtree, I was wondering. About dining arrangements. Do you wish me to join you and Mr Manningtree at meals?'

'What? Good Lord, no. The kids eat in the servery. I thought you knew that.'

'Oh yes, I understand that. But where do you wish me to take my meals?'

The woman bristled. 'Are you saying that you want to eat in the dining room? Is that what you're saying?'

'Well . . . it's usual,' Emilie stammered.

'Not in my house it's not. We often have guests to meals. Business people. Important people. They would regard your presence as an intrusion. I don't know where you got that idea from. An idea well above your station, believe me. I hope you don't have any more such notions . . .'

Emilie was stunned by the tirade. 'I just thought . . .'

'You'll find your meals are just as good in the servery as at my table, if that's what's bothering you.'

'Oh no . . .'

'Then we'll hear no more of it.' She turned on her heel with a flourish and strode up the path to the house.

Tears brimming at the injustice of such insults, Emilie kept her head down as she went back to her table, but the children had been listening.

'*We* like having you with us, miss,' Alice said, in an attempt to cheer her up.

Emilie gulped, composing herself. 'That's very kind of you, Alice, I like being with you too. Perhaps you and Jimmy could start with some writing while I see what Rosie can do.'

The children became Emilie's friends. They were all very forthright, but not bold, and they were earnest in their endeavours as long as she didn't allow them to become bored. Often Emilie broke the routine by telling them stories, taking them for nature walks through the huge garden, which she soon realised was partly cleared rainforest, and introducing them to physical jerks, which they thought was fun, although she allowed they were a healthy crew, hardly in need of more exercise since they ran wild about the place after school.

After hours, though, Emilie's time dragged. She went for walks, taking the children with her, as a break from her dreary room, since she seemed to be denied entry to the front of the house. By this, she had only a few shillings left and was afraid to ask when her pay would be forthcoming, for fear of annoying her ill-tempered employer. Soon she discovered that Mrs Manningtree was even nastier to the maid and the cook, who disliked her intensely, but Emilie was careful not to become involved in their complaints about the mistress. She also realised that being relegated to the staff quarters could be a blessing in disguise.

Her employers certainly entertained. Lunches with raucous women went on all afternoon, but the nights were worse, with drunken shouting and roistering echoing throughout the house. Kate and Nellie remained in the kitchen until all hours, but then they could escape, go to their own homes, leaving Emilie wishing she had a lock on her door when she could hear men stumbling about the passages and muttering in the yard outside her window.

Sometimes Rosie, frightened by all the racket, would sneak down to Emilie's room and climb into bed with her. Emilie never had the heart to turn her away.

One morning, after a particularly rowdy party, Nellie made an observation to Kate while Emilie was in the kitchen.

'It's a wonder she doesn't invite miss to her parties. There are always more men than ladies in there. You'd think she'd want to even it up a bit, and miss is as nice as any of them.'

The cook raised a caustic eyebrow. 'That's why. She wouldn't want no competition. Not with our miss as pretty as any of them.'

'Goodness me,' Emilie exclaimed. 'I shouldn't think so.'

'It's true. You mark my words. You got more class than the lot of them put together, and that woman knows it. Nellie hears her in there boasting about her governess, but no one gets to meet you. No bloody fear.'

'It's just her way,' Emilie protested.

'I'll say it is. But you watch out for the boss, missy. I seen the way he looks at you. Taken to calling into the classroom, hasn't he?'

'Yes, but just to see how the children are coming along.'

'Tell that to the birds,' Kate laughed. 'Just keep the hatpin handy.'

Even Emilie had to laugh at that, and Cook nodded approval. 'Good to see you laugh. You're too serious, miss. You ought to get out more. A young girl like you. Not right that you be sitting in that room every night.'

Emilie couldn't agree more, but there was nowhere to go. And she wouldn't dare venture alone into the dark streets at night. Worse still, stuck in her room, she had nothing to do. She had no money to buy books or even embroidery. Hoping to do some painting, she put in a request, through Kate, for paints and brushes and sheets for water colours, claiming it would be in Alice's interest to learn the rudiments, but that request was ignored.

Then, after weeks, there was much excitement in the house. The piano had arrived! Emilie had forgotten all about it, but there was Mr Manningtree fussing and jumping about as two men carried it into the house, warning them not to mark it or he'd have their hides, arguing with his wife about where to place it in the parlour, and when it was finally planted, ripping off the protective tar paper to display his pride and joy, a shiny black upright decorated with brass candleholders.

Mrs Manningtree stood back, Nellie and Kate gazed in awe, and the children dashed around it, demanding to have a go, but their father waved them away.

'No. We've got a real piano player here. Miss Tissington! Step forward, young lady, and let's hear how it sounds.'

Emilie was only too pleased. To her the piano was like an old friend entering the house. She opened the lid, took Nellie's duster and wiped the keyboard carefully before running her hands over the notes.

'Oh, it has a lovely tone,' she said.

She began with a Chopin étude, then switched to some melodious Lizst, and everyone was thrilled, except Mrs Manningtree.

'Can't you play something we know?'

'I think so.' Emilie played some Irish ballads she'd heard people singing on the ship, surprised to hear Mr Manningtree burst into song in a passable tenor voice.

'Sing up, you lot,' he called, and before long everyone was ranged about the piano singing heartily. Everyone except Mrs Manningtree, who stood by the door with a face like thunder.

'What time should we expect lunch today?' she asked acidly.

Kate took the hint and, nudging Nellie, edged out, but the boss had his new toy and he wouldn't allow Emilie to leave until they'd happily exhausted every song he knew.

'By Jove,' he said. 'This is a great day. Nothin' like having a piano in the house. Do you reckon you could teach the kids, Miss Tissington?'

'Yes, of course. We can start lessons whenever you like. Although Rosie might be a bit young yet.'

'No I'm not!' she said stoutly.

'You can start lessons when I say so,' Mrs Manningtree announced. 'And that means when the parlour is free. And not during school hours. You may go now, Miss Tissington, and take the children with you. They've missed half of their morning's lessons.'

Emilie was still entranced by the appearance of the piano. Off her guard. 'Oh, I'm sure we'll make up the time,' she smiled.

'You certainly will. There's a pile of ironing in the laundry. Nellie hasn't got time for it. You can do the ironing after lessons today.'

In his gauche way, Mr Manningtree didn't notice anything amiss. He thanked Emilie for 'christening' the piano and made her promise she'd play for them again.

'I should be delighted,' she said calmly, refusing to allow his wife to see that she was furious at this latest instruction. 'Now, if you'll excuse me . . .'

It was the piano that brought about the changes in Emilie's life, but not changes for the better.

Late on the following Saturday night, when she had just finished a letter to Ruth extolling the virtues of this job, mostly fibs, Mr Manningtree hammered on her door.

'Are you in there, miss? It's Bert here. We want you to come up and play for us.'

She hugged her dressing gown about her and opened the door a few inches. 'Mr Manningtree, I really can't. I'm not dressed.'

'Never mind. We'll wait.'

'Perhaps another time.' She could smell the alcohol on him.

'No time like the present. Come on now. Don't be shy . . .'

'I really can't . . .'

'Yes you can.' His voice was firmer. 'Be a sport. No getting out of it. I'll give you five minutes.'

Madam's dinner guests had left the dining room in disarray and were assembled in the parlour when Emilie appeared in the doorway. The women were all dressed in their finery, loud taffetas being the mode, she noted crossly, while the men were in their shirtsleeves. She waited, deliberately, not saying a word until someone noticed her and she was rushed across the room and plonked at the piano amid cheers.

Obligingly, she played requests, suffering the press of bodies around her as the boss led community singing, time and again refusing the glasses of wine offered to her, and fending off the advances of a bleary-eyed young man with slicked-back hair and a thin moustache.

The other male guests were greybeards, city fathers, she guessed, content to enjoy the singalong, but the young man, whose name, she learned, was Curtis, was a nuisance, whispering inanities in her ear and putting his arm about her shoulders.

'I'd prefer it if you didn't do that,' she said, stopping to remove his arm for the third time, but her action only caused laughter.

'Watch out, Miss Tissington,' a greybeard warned her with a smile. 'The Captain is a great one with the ladies.'

Unabashed, Curtis turned to his hostess. 'How can I not be when we have a lovely English rose in our midst? You've been keeping her from us, Violet. And such a talented lady . . .'

Mrs Manningtree shrugged. 'I think we've had enough music for one night. Thank you, Miss Tissington, we did enjoy your little performance.'

Emilie was glad to escape, regardless of the offensive dismissal and slammed her door hard when she got back to her room, furious that she'd been forced to endure such a thoroughly unpleasant evening.

In the morning, still angry, and needing to talk to someone, she told Cook about the experience, but the response was depressing.

'Well, I'd say the die is cast now, miss. You'll be dragged up whenever it suits 'em. Nothing you can do about it, same as me and Nell. Whenever she has a dinner or a supper party we have to stay on till late. No extra pay and never a word of thanks. Nothing much you can do about it.'

She was right. At least once a week, sometimes more, Emilie was called upon to play, without warning. She got to the stage that when she heard the revels at the front of the house, she remained dressed, waiting wearily for the inevitable knock. But through these appearances, and watching proceedings, she did get to know her employers better. Mr Manningtree, despite his rough ways, was really quite kind. He was proud of her, and in sober moments did manage genuine thanks. He even brought a box of chocolates down to the schoolroom.

'You're a good girl,' he said. 'These are for you. Our mayor thinks you're a topnotch musician, so that's a pat on the back for you, isn't it? Anything I can do for you?'

Emilie blushed. 'There is, sir, if you wouldn't mind. Could you tell me when I can expect some salary? I've been here six weeks now . . .'

'Eh? Short of cash, are you? Why didn't you say so? The wife looks after the household bills.' He dug in a pocket and counted out five shillings. 'Will this do to go on with?'

'Yes, thank you. But I was wondering at what intervals I should expect to be paid?'

'I'll ask the wife. Leave it to me. How are the kids getting on?'

'Very well, sir, they're a pleasure to teach. Perhaps I could arrange for you to hear their reading and arithmetic . . .'

'Yeah. One of these days. Very good. Very good.'

Apparently, their education was her department, not his, so Emilie didn't press the point.

On the other hand, Emilie found the mistress, in a social setting, very interesting. While endeavouring to play the great lady, she drank a lot and flirted surreptitiously with Curtis, also known as Captain Morrow, who was an army officer and a regular at these functions. She was also very critical of her husband, ordering him about as if he were the butler, but he didn't seem to mind. It was obvious that he was very fond of his wife, and that she could do no wrong in his eyes.

That evening, when Emilie was having dinner with the children as usual, Mrs Manningtree barged in, eyes blazing.

'How dare you complain to my husband about not being paid, you little upstart!'

Emilie stood up quietly. 'I did not complain, madam. I enquired as to when I could expect to be paid some part of my salary.'

'I'll tell you when you'll be paid. Every quarter. Every three months, you will receive one quarter of the arranged salary. Is that clear?'

'Yes, madam. Had you explained that to me, I wouldn't have had to ask.'

'Are you correcting me?'

'Certainly not.'

'I hope you're not, because you're only on probation. Three months' probation, so don't go putting on airs. My husband gave you five shillings; that will be deducted from your first pay, and I don't want you begging from him again.'

'Begging? I did not beg, Mrs Manningtree, and I resent such a remark. Now if you're quite finished, the children are ready for their dessert.'

The woman stood, affronted, for a few seconds, then slammed through to the kitchen to berate the cook about a pie she'd served for lunch. Taking it out on Kate, thought Emilie, but she was quaking, worrying that she had gone too far. Worrying that by the end of three months there was every chance that this harridan would terminate her employment. And then what?

Emilie wished there was some way she could beat her to it. While she was very fond of the children, this was no life, living in a back room, in fear of being dismissed. She soon came to realise that the more Mr Manningtree sang her praises, the more his wife found fault with her. She insisted on weekly reports of the children's schoolwork, and took to testing them herself. Tests that were too hard, causing Alice to weep and Jimmy to cringe. Emilie felt so sorry for them, knowing that this cold woman was using them as a weapon against her. She tried to console them, without criticising their mother, who never bothered with them at any other time, and they rarely saw their father. But then, she soon came to realise, children forget easily, and not knowing any better, they were content under the care of Cook, Nellie and Miss.

Finally Emilie wrote a long, miserable letter to Ruth, wailing about this terrible job, the loneliness and, worse, that she only had eight shillings to last her for the next six weeks, when she hoped to receive twenty pounds, less five shillings. But what if she was dismissed? Would she be within her rights to ask for the nineteen pounds, fifteen shillings? Or did dismissal at the conclusion of probation mean she would not be entitled to pay? She poured her heart out to Ruth, who was happily settled with an ideal family, though the children were very spoiled and inattentive.

How fortunate she is, Emilie sighed, rereading the letter. Then she tore it up. What was the point in burdening Ruth? What could she do?

One Sunday the young governess took a quiet walk through the town of Maryborough, standing to stare up at the imposing Prince of Wales Hotel, a two-storeyed building with verandas across the front. Remembering that Ruth had been offered a position there, Emilie wondered if working in a hotel *and* for Papists could be any worse than her present situation. She almost went in to enquire if the situation was still available, but decided against it, for any number of reasons. What if Mrs Manningtree found out? And besides, the children would be hurt if she deserted them. But she might be forced to leave them anyway. Would she dare go in there, just to ask? No, better not.

As she walked on, she heard a voice calling her.

'Miss! Miss! Hang on a minute!'

From across the street, she saw a young man leap down from his horse, leaving the bridle dangling as he raced towards her.

Emilie looked about, expecting to find that he was addressing someone else, but there were only a couple of churchgoers walking serenely in the other direction.

He hurtled over to her and came to a stop, wrenching his hat from his head. 'Miss! Don't you remember me? I'm Mallachi Willoughby. I met you in Brisbane. In the Valley! In the street. You were going the wrong way. Remember?'

Emilie shook her head, trying to step around him, but he persisted.

'I'm sorry. You don't remember me. But I remember you.' He was breathless, excited to see her, as if she were a long-lost relative.

'Would you excuse me, please? You must be mistaken.' She was about to brush past him when the Brisbane incident came back to her, and she was so surprised, she did stop.

'There you are!' he cried gleefully. 'You do know me.'

'I don't know you at all, and please don't tell me I'm walking in the wrong direction again.'

'Never! I'm just pleased to see you. I'm a stranger in this town. What are you doing here?'

It was difficult to remain cross with him, since the proprieties didn't seem to mean a thing to him, and he obviously meant well.

'I'm employed here,' she allowed.

'You are! What luck. What do you do?'

Emilie sighed. She remembered the face only too well now – incredibly handsome in a guileless way, with those trusting blue eyes – but that gave her no excuse to stand about the street talking to him in this common manner.

'I'm a governess, and I was just on my way home.'

75

'A governess, isn't that nice? I'll walk you home then.' He looked about the empty street and joked, 'I wouldn't want you to get run down by the crowds.'

He whistled to the horse and it ambled over. 'This is Striker,' he told Emilie. 'Striker, say hello to Miss . . .'

Mr Willoughby was not to be shaken off, and anyway, Emilie thought, making excuses for herself, why shouldn't I have a young man walk me back? Even if he was a stockman; the town was full of them. The children had taught her the word, explaining why horsemen like this carried whips and ropes on their saddles.

'Tissington,' she said.

'That won't do for a horse. Too hard. What can he call you?'

She smiled. 'Emilie.'

'Emilie,' he told the horse. 'Now isn't that a beautiful name? Just like its owner.'

He took the reins and led the horse as they walked up the street, turning into the road that led to the Manningtree house, and all the while Mr Willoughby chatted happily, not even noticing, or maybe not caring, that Emilie was too reserved to ask even the most trivial question about her companion. He had too many questions of his own. But she was surprised that she felt so comfortable with him; he made her feel very much at ease.

'So this is where you live?' he said, peering down the drive. 'Looks very grand.'

Emilie shrugged, dreading having to return to her lonely room.

'Not for me,' she suddenly blurted out. 'My room's out the back by the kitchen. I only work there.'

He frowned. 'It's a good job though. I've met governesses on the stations out west. They seem to like the life.'

Emilie was suddenly interested. 'You have? Where?'

'Lots of places.'

'And you know these people?'

'Sure I do.' Mr Willoughby looked at her, troubled. 'You don't like this job?'

She shook her head, his kindness triggering an emotional surge of self-pity. 'I have to go in.'

'No, wait a minute. We should talk about this. If you don't like the job, why don't you leave?'

'I can't.'

'No such thing as can't. Listen, I have to go too. But I'll be back in town tonight. Might be late, though. What about tomorrow night? Can I call on you? I don't mean to be disrespectful, nothing like that.'

Emilie could just imagine Mrs Manningtree's reaction if he came to the door asking for her. Bad news. Very bad news. But Mr Willoughby knew about those stations where governesses could find good jobs. He might be able to help her.

'Do you know a place called Nanango?' she asked him.

'Yes. Not a bad little spot. Squatter country. Why?'

76

'Oh. No reason, really. My sister works there.'

'Don't you want me to call on you?'

'I'm sorry. It wouldn't be a good idea. They wouldn't like it.'

'Could you meet me then? Here at the gate? What time do you knock off?'

'I couldn't get out before seven. I have to put the children to bed.'

'All right. I'll meet you here at eight.'

Now Emilie was worried. It would be dark by eight. She didn't approve of girls sneaking out at night. It was so common. And to meet a strange man. She could be taking her life in her hands.

'What would we do?' she asked as some sort of precaution.

He laughed. 'You'll be safe with me, Emilie. We could walk down to the waterfront and look at the ships, or we could go anywhere you like.'

'I wouldn't know where to go,' she said. 'I don't know anything about this town.'

'Neither do I. Let's just have a look around and a bit of a talk, eh? Is that all right with you?'

'Yes. And Mr Willoughby . . .'

'Call me Mal.'

'Mal. Thank you.'

He watched her step sedately up the drive – a pretty, petite figure in her neat skirt and crisp white blouse, straw hat atop her glossy hair – until she disappeared from sight, and then he reeled about in excited abandon. If only Hillier could have seen him today with his lady. If only he could have seen them, walking along like the ideal couple. Mal wished he'd had the courage to take her arm, believing that was the right thing to do with ladies, but Emilie made him nervous, she was so beautiful. He worried that he'd talked too much.

Needing to know more about her, and this place that had her so unhappy, he led his horse off the road and hitched it to a tree before setting out on a reconnaissance of the unfenced property, slipping quietly through the grounds. Here, Mal saw the beauty of the area that had so unnerved Emilie, at first glance, with its gloomy appearance. Choking undergrowth had been cleared, giving way to coarse lawn, in spots where light could filter through, but the grand old trees, dripping in creepers and Spanish moss, had been allowed to remain. He recognised huge native figs and red gums, bloated bottle trees and sheoaks, and squelched through mulch under a wide flame tree with its carpet of rusting red blooms. He was in time to see Emilie detour round the house, past a straggling hedge of banksias, making for the back door, and that irritated him.

What sort of people would make a fine young lady use the back entrance like a maid? And what did she mean when she said she couldn't leave? What sort of a hold did they have on her? Whoever these people were, her employers, Mal was sure Emilie was too good for them.

Then he remembered that he had to be back at the Maryborough police station within the hour, and raced back to do his duty.

At Lindsay Downs, via Nanango, the atmosphere of the household had undergone considerable change since the advent of the governess, and Leonie was worried. It was unlike Jack to complain – he was always so easy-going – but after dinner last night, he'd put his foot down.

'I want you to speak to Miss Tissington. I can't sit through meals listening to her carping any longer. Tell her she has to stop criticising the kids. It's worse than being stuck in a schoolroom.'

'Oh, Jack. Don't be so hard on her. She means well. She's only trying to do the best for the girls. Improve their manners.'

'I don't care what she's trying to do. I'm sick of her nagging.' He mimicked Ruth's voice: 'Elbows off the table. Hold your knife correctly. The soup plate is tilted away from you. Do not speak with your mouth full. Manners if you please!'

'Perhaps if you spoke to the girls and told them to obey her, they'd be trained more quickly and she wouldn't have to be nagging them.'

'Ha!' he said. 'So you do admit she nags.'

'Only because she feels she has to. She's very particular about her job, trying very hard to do the right thing by us.'

'Then tell her to stop doing the right thing. She's got me jumping too. I put an elbow on the table myself and I feel she's got her beady eyes on me as well. All she's doing is making us cranky. Jane and Jessie deliberately play up on her. When you speak to them, they whine and pout, the woman never lets up, and I have to listen to all this. It's damned unpleasant, Leonie. No fun any more. If I can't enjoy relaxing meals at my own table, I'll eat with the men.'

Leonie sighed. She wasn't looking forward to having to confront Miss Tissington, who flatly refused to have anyone, family or staff, address her by her Christian name. The woman intimidated her. Woman? She mused. Miss Tissington was only about twenty-four, but she was so rigid and humourless, so convinced that her English ways were superior to those of colonials, that she was old before her time. Typical, already, of the stereotyped old schoolmarm.

She was doing well in the classroom, though. Under her rule the schoolwork of both girls had improved tremendously. They hated her, but she made them work, and the proof was in the neat books, and the weekly tests in a number of subjects. She combined botany classes with sketching, and they were all surprised, and pleased, to find that Jane excelled at drawing.

'Oh dear,' Leonie worried as she made her way through the house. She was pleased that Jack was out of the house during the disastrous piano lessons that took place each week. Noisy hours of banging scales and the governess's angry complaints that neither girl had done her practice. Which was true. Once freed from the classroom, they'd run for the stables, saddle up their horses and disappear, well out of the teacher's reach. They'd learned not to stay about the house or she'd collar them.

Nervously, Mrs Stanfield waited until the girls emerged for lunch, then went over to the classroom to do the deed.

After indulging in small talk, in which she told Miss Tissington how very nice she looked today, that the country air must be agreeing with her, and how interesting the classroom looked with pictures and sketches and weather calendars on the walls, Leonie finally broached the subject.

'Miss Tissington, I wanted to talk to you about mealtimes.'

'Yes, by all means,' the governess smiled. 'Are there to be changes in the times?'

'No. It was something else. I wonder, would you mind not correcting the girls at the table?'

'Not correcting them? I don't know what you mean.'

'I mean I'd prefer that you didn't give them orders at the table . . . I mean, about their manners.'

Miss Tissington digested this, then said, 'They need to be taught, Mrs Stanfield. How else are young ladies to learn?'

'Perhaps you could instruct them in here.'

'I do that. Endlessly. But I'm afraid they forget, so I have to remind them. If we persevere you'll find it becomes second nature.'

'I realise that, but I find the constant corrections disruptive.' She hadn't meant to say that, to say 'constant', it did sound too severe, but she'd been so busy making sure she didn't blame her husband for the complaint, and create embarrassment, that it had slipped out.

'My corrections are disruptive?' Miss Tissington's voice was icy. 'I rather thought Jane and Jessie's constant sniping at each other, and their tendency to interrupt and even answer back their parents, far more disruptive. I am very careful not to comment on that side of things, because that is up to you . . .'

'Of course. I understand that, but still . . . I just wish, I mean, it would be better for all concerned if you didn't make such a fuss about their table manners.' She tried to smile. 'They do get quite wearying.'

Leonie had meant to ease the situation, to blame the girls for being so wearying, but it hadn't come out that way, and now Miss Tissington was offended.

'Am I to understand I am not to correct them at all? That *I* am being disruptive?'

'Not exactly,' Leonie quavered.

'I can see no other interpretation. You specifically told me when I first arrived that you wanted the girls to behave in a more ladylike manner. I consider table manners absolutely basic for any young lady.'

'Of course. You are right. But it's not working, really it isn't. For the sake of peace during meals, I have to ask you not to correct them. Please.'

Miss Tissington nodded coldly. 'Very well, if that's what you wish, I shall refrain. Let us just hope they can learn from good example.'

'Thank you. It's only a small matter, so don't be worrying about it.'

To Ruth, this was far from a small matter. She was hideously embarrassed that she should be corrected because of the ill-mannered daughters, whose table manners were still atrocious. She found Mrs Stanfield's complaint, for complaint it certainly was, unfair and hurtful, when she had been trying to do her very best for the girls. And she was not unaware, by Mrs Stanfield's approach, that this criticism was not sudden, that her employers must have been disapproving of her for some time. That made her cringe, because she'd thought she had their full approval.

In her own way, Ruth really was enjoying living at Lindsay Downs. The girls were a trial, a challenge, but she was managing, and after lessons, in her own time, she found life on a cattle station extremely interesting. No one bothered her as she walked about, observing all the activities that took place in the management of thousands of cattle and, from her calculations, hundreds of horses, as well as a small dairy herd with the duties that they entailed. It was a man's world out there, brawny and dusty and rough, and though Ruth was too shy to get too close, she was fascinated to see so many riders forever on the go, and all those lowing cattle constantly being herded through the maze of high-railed pens, for whatever reason. Not a talkative person, Ruth never needed company as she strolled through the orchard and down to the stream that ran through the property, enjoying what she liked to call her nature walks.

Of an evening, she was free to join the family in the parlour, but they never stayed long after dinner, because Mr Stanfield rose at dawn, so they all retired early. Then Ruth had the parlour to herself, to do some sewing or read one of the books that Mrs Stanfield had kindly ordered at her request. She had even been invited to join the Stanfields when they visited friends in the tiny town of Nanango, and Ruth had found those people to be very kind, although of course she had little in common with them.

Now Mrs Stanfield had upset her. Ruth was not equipped to deal with censure. Convinced that she had been playing her part in an exemplary manner, she was so shocked at the rebuke that she could not face the family just yet. She hurried over to the kitchen to inform the cook that she wasn't hungry, she wouldn't be in for lunch, and fled back to the schoolroom.

That night, the governess did not correct the girls, but the atmosphere at dinner was even worse. She sat through the meal in stony silence, except when Leonie directed the odd question at her to try to break the ice. Even then she only replied in monosyllables, her face grim.

'She's hurt, that's all,' Leonie explained to her husband later. 'She thought she was doing the right thing with the girls. But she'll get over it.'

'I hope she does. Tell her it's a bad example to sulk in front of her pupils.'

'She's not sulking.'

'Looks like it to me.'

After a while, though, Miss Tissington's reticence became more of an irritation. Denied the right to correct her charges, she seemed to have little else to contribute, never volunteering conversation and sitting rigid and upright in her place beside Jane, as if aloof from the proceedings.

Leonie didn't know what to make of her. Was she shy? Or maybe punishing them, as Jack had said, calling her Miss Gloom. Whatever the explanation, Leonie had to agree with him that it couldn't go on. The girls had noticed how quiet Miss Tissington had become, and began to needle her with flippant questions, finally causing their father to explode in her defence.

'That will do!' he roared at Jane. 'If you and your sister can't behave, leave the table.'

Miss Tissington didn't bat an eye; she continued to eat her meal with delicate precision.

'Find her a boyfriend,' Jack said to his wife. 'Someone to put a spark of life into her. She's in the running to be a typical old maid, and yet she's not bad-looking, if she'd only relax.'

Ruth knew she was making a bad impression on Mr Stanfield these days – she'd seen him glance sharply at her many a time – but she didn't know how to retrieve the situation, and she wasn't sure that she wanted to. It was easier to sit at table and say nothing than to think of some foolish remark to contribute to their conversations, which were mainly to do with country affairs. Also, to her horror and acute embarrassment, once she'd stopped correcting the girls, Ruth had realised what a bore she must have been to parents and daughters alike, since she now could find no substitute for her alert attention to the girls.

She was depressed, very depressed, and although she didn't realise it, was becoming withdrawn. She was now in receipt of about four pounds a month, and she worried about her obligation to repay the loan to the Society while coping with necessary personal expenses; there always seemed to be something, especially in the replacement of clothes to keep up appearances. Her goal of earning a nest egg, and the fare back to England, seemed far beyond her reach.

Mrs Stanfield had instigated another quiet chat. She had taken Ruth aside and suggested that since they regarded her as one of the family, she could be less formal.

'In what way, Mrs Stanfield?'

'Christian names really are acceptable here. Except for my daughters, of course. It will be nicer for us to call you Ruth. That goes for you as well, I'm Leonie, and my husband is Jack.'

'I thought we'd already discussed this.'

'Yes, but you'll find it more comfortable, you'll see.'

'I'll try.' Ruth still disapproved, but if they insisted . . .

'And there's another matter. If you require a cup of tea or coffee at any time, you're welcome to get it yourself from the kitchen. There's no need to call the maid.'

'They've been complaining, have they?'

Leonie gulped. The two maids had indeed both complained that they were not 'her ladyship's' servants, ready at her beck and call. The house staff disliked the governess and her superior ways.

'Not at all,' she said. 'I just want you to feel more comfortable.'

'I have been going out of my way not to intrude on the cook's domain.

Where I come from, it is best to ask a servant.'

Leonie shook her head, defeated. 'You are not where you came from, Ruth. Things are different here. We live very informally. Don't take this to heart . . . There's no need to be so serious about everything. A smile here and there will do wonders. Now, we're going into town tomorrow, and staying over for a dance in the hall. Would you like to come? I'll arrange your accommodation.'

'I don't dance,' Ruth lied. Still smarting from the lecture she'd just received, she fancied herself a wallflower at such a function among strangers, and couldn't abide such exposure.

'But I'm sure you'd enjoy yourself.'

'I'd rather not, thank you, Mrs Stanfield.'

They left for Nanango on a dry, windy morning after Mr Stanfield had made a last-minute plea for Ruth to join them, which she steadfastly declined. He was very nice about it, though, smiling at her.

'Next time then, Ruth. I won't take no for an answer.'

She was disappointed in Mrs Stanfield, not only for the unfair criticisms but for failing in her own duty. Since the governess was not permitted to teach those lumps of girls how to behave at the table, their mother should. But she did not. She had allowed them to fall back to their old slovenly ways without a word of admonishment. Watching them in silent disapproval and counting their digressions had become an obsession with Ruth, so she had taken to listing them and placing the ever-growing list on the classroom wall. The girls ignored them, and Mrs Stanfield appeared not to notice, but Ruth felt she had made her point.

It seemed to Ruth, eventually, that all the females in the house were against her, but she was comforted by the fact that Mr Stanfield, the boss, as he was referred to by the staff, was on her side. He was always kind. In fact, he was so sweetly genuine in his insistence that she accompany them to the next dance that Ruth was allowing the possibility that perhaps next time she just might accept. She could wear the blue silk with its fringed cape, which hadn't seen the light of day since the ship. It was rather fetching, and would be entirely suitable for a country dance.

The wind was stronger as the morning progressed, so Ruth took refuge in the parlour until just before lunch, when the maid stuck her head through the door.

'Cook says to save me setting up in the dining room, you can have your meals in the kitchen while they're away,' she said brightly.

Ruth bristled. It was not her place to take meals in the kitchen. 'The dining room, please.'

'What?'

'I shall take my lunch in the dining room, *if* you please.'

The girl shrugged and marched away, but then Ruth had second thoughts. Mrs Stanfield had said she should be less formal. Maybe this was a concession she could make, in their absence. After all, it was a large kitchen, and a staff table was neatly placed in a far corner under a window. She could eat quickly and remove herself without fuss.

Having made the decision, Ruth went down the passage to the kitchen, just in time to hear them laughing at her.

'Her ladyship won't budge,' the maid was saying. 'I can't go back and insist. She'll sit up there on her own with a face like a sour lemon.'

'Oh well, leave her be,' said the cook. 'Any wonder the boss calls her Miss Gloom.'

Ruth was shocked. The derision of the servants didn't bother her, but surely Mr Stanfield wouldn't say that about her? Surely not! She couldn't turn back, she was halfway through the door as they were speaking, and she caught their guilty looks.

She spoke quietly, forcing herself to face them with dignity. 'I have changed my mind. I don't feel like lunch today, thank you, I had quite a large breakfast. I think I'll go for a walk.'

In an effort to retrieve the situation, the cook tried to be helpful.

'Oh, Miss. I wouldn't go out there today. That wind is building already into a dust storm. They roll in here pretty fast, them storms . . .'

Ruth turned abruptly and made for her room. She was so upset, she had to get out of the house. Wind would be welcome now to take her mind off the hurts these people kept inflicting on her. Solace, in fact.

She put on a jacket, tied a scarf under her chin and set off through a side door, along a path that led down towards the barns. The wind was very strong, and there was grit in the air, but it wasn't too bad. The sky had taken on an orange glow – unusual she noted, determined to distract herself – deepening towards a reddish brown at the horizon. Quite beautiful really, a painter would glory in it. Though the wind whipped about her, Ruth pressed on, realising that she was headed for the areas where the men worked, but since there was no one about, she could use this opportunity to take a new direction.

'Something different,' she said to herself with a sob. 'How dare they make fun of me!'

She charged past the shelter of the barns, on past the deserted cattle pens and out across wide pastures that had seemed smooth from a distance but were bumpy and uneven, causing her to stumble a little. She wouldn't allow such minor difficulties to stop her, though. This was exhilarating. She was out in the wide-open country now, leaning into the wind, putting that house and those ungrateful people behind her, at least for a while.

Treetops swished overhead as she left the cleared land, admitting that it was a little easier to proceed through the sparse bush, guessing that she would emerge at the creek that seemed to twist and turn through the property. She decided that when she came to the creek she would rest awhile, and then turn back. Reluctantly.

It seemed to be getting darker by the minute, and dust was infiltrating the bush, creating an orange mist. Ruth was beginning to think maybe she ought to turn back when suddenly, through the gloom, she was confronted by a huge beast with massive horns, its eyes red and threatening.

83

She screamed and ran, tripping over a fallen branch, picking herself up, too terrified to look back and see if the bullock was lumbering after her, hearing only the roar of the wind, which now threatened to smash down the trees that surrounded her. She ran wildly until she was out of breath, then collapsed, cowering behind a stark white tree trunk. Panting, she peered back, but there was no sign of the animal. How many more of these huge cattle would be roaming through here? she worried, castigating herself for being so stupid as to march blindly into their territory. Only areas around the homestead were fenced. She had been lucky not to run into a mob of them.

While the dust storm raged, Ruth pulled the scarf over her face and remained crouched by the tree. With no prior knowledge of this phenomenon, she had no idea how long she'd have to endure the torture of dust-laden air and the miserable itch of fine brown dust seeping into her clothing, but she determined that no matter how long it took, she would stay exactly where she was. Nothing would entice her to take the chance of running slap bang into a ferocious bull again; she would have to wait until she could at least see where she was going.

More than an hour later, the dust clouds passed over, the wind dropped and the sun came out again as if nothing had happened. Wearily, Ruth disentangled herself, shook the dust from her hair and clothes and stepped out, only to give a shriek of pain as she clung to the tree for support. Her ankle was swollen, sprained, probably from when she'd tripped and fallen over the branch.

'Blast!' she said, grimacing with the pain as she limped away. Every step was agony, but she couldn't stay in the bush forever; she had to get back.

Struggling along with the aid of a stick, Ruth realised she was taking far too long to reach the open pastures, and Stanfield tales of people being lost in the bush began filtering back, frightening her.

'It's what they call the sameness,' Mr Stanfield had explained to her. 'Hundreds and hundreds of look-alike trees can confuse anyone if they don't know the area, especially on foot.'

'Well, it's not going to confuse me,' Ruth said now, glaring at her bleak surrounds. She hung her scarf on a tree.

'Now, I'll walk in one direction for a while, and if I'm not clear of the bush, I'll come back to this point and start again in another direction.'

When she was forced to retrace her steps, Ruth was shattered to admit that she couldn't find the tree flagged with her scarf. Somehow she must have missed it.

Ruth Tissington would not cry. Shadows were deepening, birds were fluttering in to roost with noisy chatter, the afternoon was deserting her. She was lost, but she refused to cry.

'You got yourself into this mess,' she said, 'so get yourself out of it.'

Exhausted, she tested a fallen log, and finding it firm, sat down to rest. Her ankle throbbed and her head ached; she felt dizzy from the anxiety of this interminable search. The dust hadn't helped. Ruth had never been so thirsty in all of her life. If only she could have found the creek, she lamented, as she sat, desperately staring about her for some clue that might provide deliverance. A small movement startled her, but it was only a little kangaroo, or maybe a wallaby, she didn't know. It looked at her with soft, dewy eyes, as if commiserating, and then it hopped gently away. Ruth wished it had stayed. Later she saw two of those bullocks shouldering through the scrub, and thought she should follow them, that they might lead her out of this maze, but she was afraid they would turn on her. Cattle here were like huge wild animals, a breed far removed from the meek cows that trundled over the fields at home. She remembered a stocky bull that had frightened them as children, a miniature compared to these hulking brutes. Better to let them go their own way. As soon as she felt better, Ruth decided, she would start the same process again, this time building a heap of brush as a starting point, and she would be more careful.

When Miss Tissington was found to be missing at six o'clock, the cook raised the alarm. Being Saturday, quite a few of the men had been given a half-day off, to ride into Nanango and attend the popular annual Cattleman's Dance at the Freemasons' Hall, but several of the older stockmen were on hand. They'd entertained themselves during the dust storm with round-robin card games, and were just sitting down to dinner in the cookhouse when she clanged the alarm bell.

Someone went to investigate, and on hearing that the governess had apparently wandered off during the storm, and with the boss away, it was unanimously agreed that they might as well have a meal first. This looked like being a long night.

And it was. Five horsemen carrying lanterns, led by old Thommo, a veteran station hand with some experience as a tracker, gleaned from the Aborigines who had previously inhabited the area, fanned out over the immediate area surrounding the homestead. Since neither the cook nor the two maids could give him any clue as to which direction the girlie could have taken, Thommo could only go about the search in the accepted manner. Slowly and methodically. They probed sections with the bush call of 'coo-ee, coo-ee', gradually widening the arc across the pastures into bushland rarely entered by these men until mustering time came around. Then it was hell-for-leather riding when a man proved his worth by flushing out belligerent cattle and their bellowing calves that had mistakenly believed they were safe from the general muster by sheltering in the scrub.

Tired and angry, by no means impressed by this duty, they searched for hours, until one of the men spotted the scarf. Then at least they could concentrate the search in that area.

They found her asleep in the scrub, and Thommo was called, because they had trouble waking her.

'She's got a fever,' he announced. 'Bung her up in front of me and I'll take her in.'

85

★ ★ ★

Ruth had no recollection of being rescued from the bush. She was very hot, pleading for water. She could not control the shivering; it was so cold, the nights were so cold in the bush, freezing, and they wrapped her in blankets, but then she was too hot, throwing them off, begging to be left alone because her head ached, and her bones, not her bones, that ankle, that's what it was. She perspired horribly, as if she'd wet the bed, and she was so humiliated she kept asking Mrs Stanfield to forgive her, to please forgive her, but then they'd go away and the nightmares would begin again. Dreadful nightmares. She called out for her mother, for Emilie, but they turned their backs on her, ashamed that she should be making such a fuss in front of strangers. Appalled by the sight of her, the vomit, the stink.

'It's the yellow fever all right,' the doctor told Leonie.

'Jaundice?'

'No, not jaundice, I'll bet on that, but a yellow fever. Some say it's brought on by mosquito bites, and there's plenty of them to bear that out round here.'

'But she's yellowed like jaundice . . .'

'So she is, Leonie, but the yellow fever can do the same thing. I saw it in Java, where there are more mosquitoes than air.'

'What can we do?'

'Keep her warm. Keep her cool.'

'You won't go? You won't leave her with this sickness. I wouldn't know what to do.'

'No, I won't leave her. Or you. We can only sit by and wait. She's young and strong. I reckon she'll ride out the fever in a day or so.'

Chapter Four

'Where the hell have you been?' Sergeant Pollock shouted at Mal. 'I told you to give me a half-hour, not a bloody half-day.'

'Had to see to my horse.' He looked over at the other two mounted police waiting with the Sergeant. 'Anyway, there's three of you blokes; you don't need me any more.'

'You'll finish your job!' Pollock spurred his horse and the four horsemen galloped down the street, turning swiftly on to the road to Blackwater Creek, the road that led to the goldfields.

Mal didn't really mind; it was just worth a try. He was safe in town now, and had hoped to be spared doubling back to meet the Commissioner and his entourage. For that matter, today he didn't mind a thing. It was the happiest day of his life. And to think he'd bucked when Carnegie had instructed him to ride on ahead early this morning.

'What for?' he'd asked groggily, when Taylor had shoved a boot at him, telling him to get up. It wasn't even dawn, only the barest glimmer of colour in the eastern sky.

They'd come through from the goldfields without any problems. Despite the rough road and the inevitable obstructions of dry gullies and rocky streams, the coach with its precious load had held up well, and there'd been no sign of bushrangers, for which Mal had been grateful. Then they'd camped overnight by the creek. More of a little river, he'd thought, because it was flowing well down there, almost hidden by lush rainforest. The other two offsiders had been assigned as guards through the night while the bosses slept in their tent, and Mal was allowed to stretch out under the cart. He was pleased about that too.

Then he found out why.

'You're to go on ahead,' Taylor told him.

Mal shivered in the pre-dawn breeze and drank from a pitcher of water as Carnegie came out of the tent to give him his instructions.

'You mount up, Willoughby, and get going. Follow this road direct to Maryborough, ride fast and don't stop anywhere. When you get to town, go straight to the police station, find Sergeant Pollock and report to him.'

'Why? What's wrong?' One of the guards grinned at him as he strolled over to the ashes of last night's campfire and prepared to relight it. For breakfast, Mal thought angrily. He was hungry.

'Nothing's wrong. And it's going to stay that way,' Carnegie said. 'The next leg of this journey could spell trouble. It's the last chance for bushrangers, and even some town ruffians have been known to try their luck between here and Maryborough. A gold shipment was robbed on this stretch some months back and any number of miners have been held up, so we don't attempt it any more without full police protection. So don't waste time. Sergeant Pollock and his men will patrol the road and bring us in.'

Mal wasn't worried about their gold; he was more concerned about his own stash. A money belt fat with cash.

'Why can't one of those blokes go?' he asked Taylor. 'They know the road better than me. I've never even ridden it before.'

Taylor shrugged. 'The Commissioner's orders. A precaution. Always a last-minute decision. Now go. The sooner you get back, the sooner we can move on.' He looked about him. 'I'm not keen on this latest plan. I'd far rather keep moving.'

As he rode out, Mal saw Taylor and Carnegie loading their guns to back up the tired guards. He was armed with a rifle himself, but he didn't figure on using it. He rode fast but carefully. He was well aware of road tricks to trip a horse or slow up vehicles like a coach carrying gold consignments, so this was no time to be admiring the scenery. As he covered mile after mile and the sun edged up into the sky, he began to feel better. Then, when he noticed isolated farmhouses here and there, he knew the worst was over; he was nearing civilisation. No bushrangers, no ambushes, the coach could have been brought on after all.

Then again, he mused, most of the time that damn track was like a hollow through heavy scrub; anyone could have been lurking there. Someone, or two, not interested in a lone horseman.

The road improved, flattened by farm wagons, and flourishing market gardens tended by Chinks in their coolie hats appeared by the wayside. He passed a bullock train, twelve lumbering animals hauling a high load of wool bales, and flicked a salute to the driver. Rounding a bend, he came upon a huge sawmill. He wondered why it was so quiet, then realised it was Sunday. So it was. Not a bad day to bring in a load of gold. Most of the bad lads would still be drunk from the night before, unless they were the dedicated bushranger type. Like McPherson. There'd been plenty of talk of him on the goldfields. He'd robbed the Maryborough Mail only two miles out of town, not once but twice. That remembrance caused Mal to sit up and start paying attention again. Only two miles out of town! God Almighty! No wonder Carnegie had the jitters.

The river led him to the wharves, and a gasp of surprise to see so many ships at anchor, but he couldn't delay. A fisherman directed him to the police station, which was closed, being Sunday, but Mal found the residence next door, and knocked.

A Paddy-looking bloke with ginger hair poked his head out of the window. 'What do you want?'

'You Mr Pollock?'

'Sergeant Pollock.'

'Yeah, well, Mr Carnegie sent me.'

'Where is he this time?'

'Blackwater Creek.'

'Everything in order?'

'Yes. He's waiting for you.'

'Righto. Give me a half-hour, I'll round up the lads.'

And that half-hour gave Mal the gift of a lifetime. He'd only been walking the horse through the town, looking for somewhere to grab a feed, when he'd seen her. The English lady.

Emilie Tissington. He knew her name now and, joy of joys, would be seeing her again tomorrow night. Nothing in the world would stop him from meeting her at her gate tomorrow night. He bet she was ten on Clive's girl.

Mal angered the Sergeant even more by stopping at a trough to allow his horse to drink.

'I thought you'd seen to that!'

Mal shrugged. 'He's a thirsty beast.'

Right up to the last minute, Baldy Perry had expected the plan to fizzle out. For the Commissioner to lose his nerve. He'd been waiting all night with the dinghy hidden at the Blackwater Creek bank, under an overhang of foliage, and hadn't been able to sleep a wink. At times he thought he ought to give it a go himself if Carnegie changed his mind, but he knew that was only idle imagining. Perry was a follower, a foot soldier, and he accepted his limitations. He wasn't resourceful, but he did as he was told, and if plans went awry, as they often did, it wasn't his fault.

When at last he heard voices, he stole up through the scrub, barefoot and rifle in hand, to watch and wait. That was all he could do; the gold was there in the coach, but he wasn't brave enough, or foolhardy enough, to attempt to ambush four armed men on his own, so it was up to Carnegie to make the first move. He shinned up a tree and steadied himself into position as Carnegie had instructed. He'd claimed that the guards might get a chance to return fire, but in their panic they'd be firing into the scrub, not at the sniper above it, and Perry supposed he'd be right. He didn't panic, nor would he. This was just a job. Shoot a couple of blokes. Get the gold, and get out of there.

The first shot almost jolted Baldy off his perch.

As he settled quietly in the early dawn, he heard a rider leave the camp and began his watch. He saw Taylor come out of his tent, and the two guards relaxing their vigil as they lit the campfire for breakfast. He checked his rifle again and waited.

The bacon smelled good. Then came the shot! Carnegie shot Taylor in the back, and he fell by the coach. The guards swung about, confused, reaching for their guns. In a second, Baldy had gunned down the first one, and as the other man tried to run for cover, Baldy picked him off too. Wary now, he took in the scene, but Carnegie was frantically waving him down.

It was all over. As simple as that. Perry nodded in appreciation as he lumbered out of the bush. A smart man, Carnegie. As neat a job as he'd ever seen.

Perry hardly had time to glance at the bodies sprawled about the clearing, because Carnegie was in such a panic, all jittery, his voice barely a whisper. Baldy Perry grinned. You'd think them dead 'uns could hear.

'Quick, pull out all the trunks, get them out, quickly!' Carnegie snapped, but Baldy ignored him and went over to make sure the men really were dead. Taylor was finished, he noted, and so were the guards. The first shot through the head, and his second shot had got the other dead in the chest. Damn good shooting, he mused, I always was a marksman, if I say so meself.

'Get over here!' Carnegie was almost screaming, dragging at a steel trunk himself. 'We have to get them all out.'

'Have they all got gold in them?' Baldy worried. That'd be too much for him to carry.

'No, you bloody fool. The gold's in this one. There's a consignment of cash being transferred from the bank in this second one. The others are full of registers and reports from the bank and the Mines Department.'

Baldy soon had the two interesting trunks out of the coach, and the Commissioner was fumbling to unlock them.

'Get the rest,' he hissed.

'We don't need them.'

'Get them out. We're not supposed to know what they contain. Get the damn things and tip them out, as if we're searching.'

Books, papers and thick ledgers were soon strewn about in untidy heaps by the upturned trunks, but Baldy had his eyes greedily on the leather bags of gold that Carnegie was dumping frantically on the ground beside the lighter bank bags containing a bonus of good old cash. What a haul! What a bloody haul!

Carnegie flung down the keys of the trunks and turned to him. 'Now, you know what to do,' he was saying as he pulled a hessian bag from a seat in the coach, one of the bags used to protect the upholstery. 'Grab all those bags and stuff them in this one.'

Dutifully Baldy grabbed the first bags, surprised that they were half empty. 'Is this all the gold?'

'It's plenty, more than a thousand ounces. The others are sovereigns and banknotes. Now don't forget. When you get across the river, bury the lot under the big fig tree I showed you. Sink the boat and get out of there. Go back to work tomorrow as if nothing has happened.' He was panting as if he'd run a mile. 'Wait twenty-eight days, exactly twenty-eight days, then go back and dig up the bag . . . Your horse is still over there, isn't it?'

'Of course it is.' For Baldy, this was the easiest part. And it had been easy to bring the dinghy up river from Maryborough and hide it in readiness on the other side of the river, but he'd really earned his share in the long tramp back to town from there. No horse that time, only a trek that had taken him a full day, and half the night, to reach the ferry.

90

As Carnegie went over the instructions, Baldy knew he was stalling, dreading what was to come. Scared.

'Pay attention,' the Commissioner snapped. 'Bring this bag to my cottage in Maryborough, hide it under the back steps during the night. You mustn't be seen anywhere near me. I'll divide it all, equally, as best I can, given the gold weights, and put your share back there.'

'It better be,' Baldy growled.

'It will be. We have no further contact from this minute. You do not know me, whatever happens.'

'All right, all right, let's get on with it.'

'Very well. But first I'm going to lie down and you're to throw Taylor's body on top of me.'

'Jesus! Why?'

'Cover for me. It will look as if he fell on me. Blood, too.' He shuddered. 'And while I'm thinking about it, here's my rifle. Take it with you and dump it in the river. Afterwards . . .'

Carnegie lay flat, shivering, as Taylor's body was dumped on him, then, white-faced, he pushed his deputy's body aside and stood. 'God, I feel sick.'

'It was your idea.' Baldy shrugged. He picked up Carnegie's rifle, loaded it and stood waiting. 'You ready?'

'Yes. Get back a bit more.' Carnegie steeled himself. 'Go ahead.' He closed his eyes as Baldy, grinning, raised the rifle. He considered killing Carnegie right there and then, but the plan was too good to muck up. Carnegie had to be found alive, to give a description of the outlaws and to point the finger at the young bloke he'd hired as a guard, blaming him for tipping them off. They'd be looking for outlaws, not just one bloke, and Carnegie would be able to send the police off the wrong way. He couldn't have them thinking in the direction of the river. Besides, as Baldy knew, things worked out better for him if he did as he was told. The plan was smart.

Carnegie was holding out his arm, his face creased, ready for the pain.

Perry fired and put a bullet through Carnegie's upper arm, a bit lower than instructed, but what was the difference?

'Oh Jesus! Oh Christ!' Carnegie had collapsed and was weeping and moaning as Perry grabbed the hessian bag containing their treasure and ran through the bush towards the creek, well away from the clearing and down the banks to his dinghy. He dumped the bag aboard and then, breaking a large leafy bough from a tree, hurried back to brush away his tracks in the mud. As soon as he was in the dinghy, he hurled the branch far into the creek.

Pulling strongly on the oars, Baldy was soon on his way to the mouth of the creek, grinning at the cleverness of all this. His old mate McPherson was in for a shock. Baldy had contributed to Carnegie's tale with a description of the Scot as one of the outlaws who had attacked the party. What with McPherson to chase, and that bloke Willoughby accused by Carnegie, the police would be hot to trot as soon as they discovered the raid, with two candidates for the rope in their sights. And he, Baldy Perry, had had nothing to do with it. No reason for them ever to come after him.

The Commissioner was stumbling about the bloody scene almost delirious when Pollock rode in with his men. They were all stunned, leaping down from their horses to check to see if anyone else was alive, sickened by the flies and the smell.

Pollock gave orders for the dead to be lifted into the coach and covered while he saw to the Commissioner's wound, shaking his head at Carnegie's pathetic attempts at a tourniquet and bandage, not upsetting the poor bloke any further by telling him that a tourniquet on the wrong side of the wound wasn't much help. But then poor Carnegie was a city bloke, and in a lot of pain. The bullet had gone right through his left arm, shattering the bone. Pollock reckoned angrily that the bastards had made a right mess of it – it wouldn't be much good after this – but he made appropriate clucking noises as he cleaned the wound, dousing it with salt and bandaging some whittled sticks into place as a sort of splint to keep the arm firm until they got the poor bloke to a doctor.

While he worked, Carnegie, not a good patient, screamed and yelled, near to fainting, so Pollock called to Willoughby to search the tent for some grog to ease the pain.

Willoughby, shocked and eager to help, found a bottle of scotch whisky and ran over with it. They poured some of it down Carnegie's throat and he swallowed it greedily, then suddenly started shouting again, pointing at Willoughby.

'He's one of them. What are you doing back here, you bastard? He was with them! He brought them back! Arrest him!'

Carnegie fell back, almost frothing at the mouth in rage, while Mal stood staring at him.

'You got it wrong, Mr Carnegie. I wasn't here. You sent me to town, remember?'

But Carnegie wouldn't let up. 'It was him, I tell you! Don't be trying to make out I don't remember. I remember every second of that vicious attack.' He began to weep. 'You thought I was dead, didn't you? Shot like the rest.' He clutched at Pollock. 'He'd only been gone a half-hour at the most, Willoughby! Him! When the shooting started. Taylor was on guard. They got him in the back after they shot me. He fell on top of me . . .'

Pollock helped Carnegie to take another swig of whisky. 'They thought I was dead. Down there, under poor Taylor. I thought I'd be sick, he was bleeding on me, but I stayed still, playing dead. They didn't care, they didn't even check.'

'Willoughby couldn't have been with them,' Pollock said. 'You sent him to town.'

'Like hell he wasn't. Of course he left. Then he brought them back. After the shooting, I saw him. We were set up like dummies in a shooting gallery. We didn't have a chance. They were laughing, the bastards. Then he left . . . Oh, God. Taylor's dead, isn't he? And the lads? I think they're dead too. Will you make sure, Sergeant? I tried . . .'

'Just take it easy, Mr Carnegie, just you take it easy. We'll look into this. Mike . . .' He called to one of the constables. 'You get Mr Carnegie up front in the coach. And you, Gus, place Willoughby under arrest until we sort this out.'

As the constable drew his revolver and grasped his arm, Mal stepped back, outraged.

'He's mad! I never had nothing to do with this. I never killed anyone in my life. I wouldn't do this!'

Carnegie was being assisted to the coach. He turned back angrily. 'You were the Judas! They must have been out on the road ready to ambush us, but you warned them we were back here, waiting for the police escort. So you brought them back while there was still time.' He leaned heavily on the constable before being lifted up beside the driver's seat of the coach. 'I saw you with your mate. A big red-bearded fellow with a Scottish accent.'

Pollock was all ears. 'You can describe the bushrangers?'

'My bloody oath I can. There was him, and the Scot, I saw them. There could have been more. I didn't dare lift my head. After the shooting it was so quiet it was shocking. I could hear them dragging out the trunks. I was feeling faint, then I heard them ride off . . .'

'And one of them was our mate McPherson. Who else?'

'But not me!' Mal shouted. 'Carnegie's imagining things.'

The Commissioner lurched against the coach. 'To my dying day I'll never be able to forget this nightmare. Joseph Taylor was my best friend . . .'

Mal turned squarely to face Carnegie. 'Since when?' he sneered. 'Taylor hated you.'

'You shut your mouth,' Pollock said angrily. 'Rope him and put him on his horse, Gus. And Mike, you finish up here. Shove all those papers and books back into the trunks, and shift them into the scrub for the time being. No one will be interested in them. We'll send someone out later for them. We have to get Mr Carnegie back to town. And the other poor fellows.' He shook his head as if he could hardly believe this calamity, and walked wearily about the camp, noticing that the men had been in the act of preparing breakfast. A billy of water had boiled dry over the now cold embers, and a pan resting below contained bacon burned almost to ash. Unused pannikins and mugs lay near to where the bodies of the guards had fallen.

'Who was on guard?' he asked Carnegie abruptly.

'Taylor was. Or he should have been. The guards had been up all night. They were tired.'

'Who shot you?'

'How would I know, Sergeant?' Carnegie cried plaintively. 'The shot came out of the blue. I didn't know what happened, I was swung about by the force of it and fell, and almost simultaneously there were more shots and Taylor fell on me. The weight landing on me was so sudden I thought it was a tree falling, and you can imagine my horror . . .'

Pollock was locked into his own thoughts. 'If the shots came so fast, there had to be more than one shooter. They came from different angles, two at least, maybe three.'

'I only saw two . . . I played dead, too terrified to lift my head, as I told you. Lying flat on my face.' He began to weep. 'I'm sorry, Sergeant, I'm making a perfect fool of myself.'

'No. It's all right. It's the shock.'

'We ought to hang you here and now,' Mike snarled as he looped narrow strips of hide round Mal's wrists and bound his hands together in front of him, pulling the cord tight with a vicious tug. 'Three good men dead and you breeze into town thinking you've got away with it, you bastard.'

He jammed his rifle butt into Mal's back, sending him sprawling in the dust.

'That's enough,' Pollock shouted. 'I don't want any rough stuff. Get him up, Gus.'

Dragged to his feet, Mal called back to Pollock: 'Carnegie's either off his head or he's dead blast lying. I never saw any bushrangers.'

'Tell that to the hangman,' Gus muttered, shoving Mal towards his horse.

As soon as Mal was mounted, Gus tied a rope round his left ankle, took the rope under the horse's belly and secured it to his other ankle, making sure he was bound tightly to the animal.

'Just in case you think you can jump and run for it, you bloody murderer. I never seen nothing like this in me life.'

Mal ignored him. He was trying to think. Why was Carnegie blaming him? He wasn't all that bad hurt that he could make a mistake like this. The party had camped in this siding, off the main road, for cover and security, the guards had told him. It was a natural clearing, used by bullockies with their teams, as a camp site, to avoid jamming up the narrow road. Even Pollock hadn't known exactly where they were. But someone had known. Someone had been tipped off. And how? Mal supposed that would have been easy enough, back at Gympie. Maybe one of the guards had talked before they left, and they'd been followed. And a wrong word in the wrong ear had cost the poor bugger his life. But that didn't explain why Carnegie was so adamant that Mal had been the Judas.

The men were clearing up the camp and Pollock was still peering about.

'They would have headed for the hills, one or more of them,' he said to Gus. 'No point in going the other way, into town. And they've got a helluva start.'

He came over to Mal. 'How many were there?'

'I don't know. I wasn't here. Carnegie told me to go and get you, and that I did. I never doubled back.'

'So the bushrangers just happened to turn up, did they? Waiting here for weeks on the off chance that a gold consignment would come along.'

'Give me a go! I had nothing to do with it. Someone was tipped off back in Gympie, I reckon.'

'Amazing. So all you had to do was ride out and alert your mates. I never said anything about doubling back. Neither did Carnegie. He just said you came back. Is that where they were? Out on the road on the Maryborough side? Did you warn them you were being sent for reinforcements?'

'No. Carnegie's got it all wrong. He must have seen someone who looked like me.'

'Oh, sure. Lots of blokes look like you. Especially bushrangers. But I'll get the truth out of you, you bastard. I'm arresting you, Willoughby, for murder and robbery under arms. You thought they were all dead, didn't you?'

'No!' Mal tried to free himself from the ropes but they only cut deeper. For the first time he began to realise that he was in trouble, terrible trouble, and all because of that idiot Carnegie mixing him up with someone else. Someone who was now well away from here, with McPherson.

No matter how he argued and pleaded, none of them believed him. He was their Johnny-on-the-spot, and they had a witness, and their certainty of his guilt was set in stone. They tethered his horse to the rear of the coach and the party set off on their dismal journey to Maryborough, travelling slowly, almost at a funereal pace in deference to the slain men occupying the coach. Mal was mortified at being stuck bolt upright in his saddle, tied to his horse. Knowing all eyes would be on him as soon as they met people on the road, he began to feel like a circus clown, a distraction for the police. There would be a huge outcry over a crime of this magnitude, but at least they could produce one of the outlaws. They had a prisoner to show off. At the goldfields, he'd read that miners and townspeople had been complaining about lack of police protection from bushrangers, and Mal felt he was being used to shield them from the force of public opinion.

Wildly, he worried that the police themselves might be mixed up in this. What hope would he have then?

Riders stopped. He saw them talking to Pollock. Saw their shocked stares at the coach. Saw their hatred as they looked back at him. One man rode round the coach and spat at Mal, spat at him fair in the face, and Mal, with his hands tied, could do nothing but allow the phlegm to slide down his cheek. And fear began to seep in. On this road they would meet more and more travellers, who would have the same reaction, or even worse. For the first time in his life he was really scared. Towns meant crowds, and in this situation, ugly crowds. Trussed up like this, he'd be at their mercy. He wondered if Pollock and his two constables would be prepared to defend him if push came to shove. Why should they?

He had thought of insisting that Pollock check his gun, which they'd grabbed earlier. They could see it hadn't been fired. But then they'd say

95

he'd had time to clean it, or he'd used another gun.

He thought of Carnegie, sitting up front beside Gus, who was driving, his horse trotting obediently beside Striker, also tethered to the coach. The Commissioner was a gambler. Everyone knew that, at the goldfields anyway. And a loser. How deep did his gambling debts go? Nothing new about gamblers turning to crime. But the Gold Commissioner? Hardly likely. And anyway, a partnership between bushrangers and the Gold Commissioner would be dicey. They'd have made sure he was bumped off.

But why hadn't they checked? Pollock had been careful, immediately, to make certain that those three men were dead, even though it seemed obvious. How come the outlaws hadn't done the same? Too much of a hurry, Mal guessed. He remembered his pa saying that most outlaws got caught, sooner or later, because they were just plain stupid. So he hoped they'd catch McPherson quickly. Apart from Carnegie, he was the only one who could clear him.

'Oh, Jesus!' he muttered, hanging on to the saddle awkwardly. What if they dragged him through the town with everyone watching? What if Miss Emilie saw him? Mal was devastated.

By dusk they were on the outskirts of the town, meeting up with riders, wagoners, miners, all sorts of people who, on hearing the awful news, joined the party, travelling with them, hurling abuse at Mal, until Pollock sent Mike back to ride alongside the prisoner, his horse acting as a buffer, keeping the anger at bay, warning off riders who came too close, holding his rifle under his arm, his hand near the trigger.

There was one small ray of hope for Mal when he heard a stranger's remark: 'He don't look much like a bushranger to me.'

That brought shouts of derision, but Mal thought he recognised the voice. He looked about but saw only angry bearded faces, and turned back to stare fixedly at the back of the coach.

At the big sawmill, Pollock suddenly called to Mike to pull in, and the coach rattled into the yard, coming to rest between stacks of timber.

'What's up?' Mike asked him.

'We can't take the bodies into town like this. It's not right. Their families are going to feel bad enough without having to see them just lying in the coach. Besides, we'd be looking for trouble. Bringing Willoughby in with the murdered men would cause a full-scale riot. Wait a minute.'

He turned to the crowd of hangers-on milling about them, and delegated a man to ride into town to fetch the mortician.

'Tell him to get out here quick and take care of the bodies.'

He then ordered two men to remain at the sawmill, which was now closed down, and stand vigil over the bodies until the mortician arrived.

While this was going on, the bystanders had, temporarily, lost interest in the prisoner, except for one man, who brushed past Mal and punched him in the thigh. He seemed about to add abuse to the blow, but what he actually said was:

'Barney Magee never forgets a favour.'

Mal glanced down and recognised the little bloke who'd passed round the hat hoping to earn the bus fare to the goldfields. Mal had given him some money, he couldn't recall how much.

'Some favour,' he retorted, but the prospector had already disappeared into the crowd. As he rubbed his thigh, awkwardly forced to use both hands, he felt an extra weight in his jacket pocket, and outlined it with his fingers.

Jesus! A knife. It must have been Magee who'd said he didn't look like a bushranger. He had a friend after all. The knife mightn't help, but he could try. He manoeuvred it into his sleeve, while appearing to concentrate on Pollock, since all heads were turned that way.

The Sergeant was dispersing the mob, ordering them to be about their business, determined not to allow them to interfere. Reluctantly, they backed off, but Mal noticed that they all turned towards town, their previous destinations forgotten, so that they could witness the prisoner being brought in.

Along with a million others, Mal thought miserably. But the knife was sharp; small, slight, but very sharp, like the one his pa had used for whittling, and it slit the cords about his wrists so fast, he had to grab for them to make them appear to be still in place. His rifle had been taken from its pouch by the saddle but this stockwhip still hung lazily from the peg. Mal looked at it, wondering what to do next.

'Are you up to riding?' Pollock asked Carnegie.

'No, Sergeant, I feel too faint.'

'Righto. You stay here by the coach. Mike will drive you in when the mortician gets here with the hearse.'

'That will be a relief. It's been unbearable to have to travel with these poor men. I'm grateful to you, Sergeant. It's much more appropriate to bring the dead in with some dignity.'

Pollock nodded and jerked his head at Gus. 'We'll take Willoughby in ourselves. We don't need a lynch mob as an escort. And when we get closer, we'll detour round the back roads to get this bastard into the lockup before they wake up we're in town. Let's go.'

Mal didn't feel like waiting for the back roads.

They were riding three abreast most of the time, a policeman either side of him while Mal forced himself to make a decision. He'd have to try to get out of this. Once in jail, no one would listen to him; he could swing. But if he tried to escape now, they'd shoot him.

Not a lot of choice, he decided. And time was short. There was still enough bush on the far side of the road to cover him if he made it that far, but soon they'd be coming to open fields, only a few miles ahead.

He waited until the three horses were spread out enough to enable him to use the whip.

Both of his captors were taken by surprise. The whip suddenly whirled and snapped across Gus's back with such ferocity that he screamed, crashing from his horse while Mal's arm went round to lash the rump of

Pollock's horse. It bolted, streaking down the road with Pollock fighting to regain control and the riderless horse bolting with it. But Mal was gone. He didn't dare look back as he sent his horse for the bush, galloping wildly for freedom. For his life.

Compared to the endless scape of virgin forests surrounding it, Maryborough was just a speck clinging to the river bank, so Mal knew that if he kept plunging on they'd have little hope of catching him. He thanked God for the dense sub-tropical vegetation as his horse dodged and fenced through the trees without losing pace, like the skilled stock horse he'd been before he became Mal's friend and companion.

At first the shouts of his pursuers had seemed dangerously close, then they'd faded, but Mal knew they wouldn't give up yet. There were still wisps of golden light trailing through the trees, tantalising him as he prayed for the sun to get on with its setting, to shut the forest down into darkness. He clung low to the horse's neck, urging it to keep going, like a jockey heading for the winning post, and then suddenly, there it was. No twilight to speak of in the north; the light faded before his eyes, causing him to blink, adjusting to the gloom. The horse slowed as if it knew the race was over, and so it was, Mal thought. For now. There'd be posses out for him tomorrow. Big posses, armed, with the right to shoot on sight.

This was the worst trouble he'd been in in his whole life, and there seemed no way out of it. Escaping had probably branded him guilty as sin, but what was the alternative? Maybe Pollock could have prevented a lynching by irate citizens, but courts of law might approve. Mal had no inkling of how they operated, but he didn't want to wait about to find out.

He came across a creek glistening in the moonlight, drank heavily to allay his hunger, since he'd been deprived of food for a whole day, and stood studying the position of the moon as the horse took its fill of the fresh water.

A bushman, Mal didn't need a compass, but he did need a plan. Eventually, he'd have to find McPherson, if he could stay at liberty long enough, because they were bound to put a price on his head, but for now: a decision. They'd expect him to head inland, to make for the distant hills that could shelter a man for years, so it would make sense to double back. That was what he told himself anyway. Risky but good sense, if he moved only at night, because the posses would be searching this country to try to head him off before he made it to those hills.

And then there was Miss Emilie. Ashamed of his present status, he had taken to thinking of her, with more respect, as Miss Emilie, because she was rarely out of his thoughts. If he doubled back, he could still meet her. Keep his promise. Beg her to trust him. Pray she hadn't heard about his difficulties.

God, he was hungry; his belly felt as if his throat was cut. That was one of Pa's favourite sayings. They'd often gone hungry for days on end in lean times.

Lean times? Mal patted his money belt and laughed.

'Jesus! I must be the richest starving fool this side of the equator.'

Then he thought of the Chinks. The market gardeners. They never gave a tinker's kiss for what went on in the white man's world. He could slide into one of their huts for a few minutes. They'd sell him some tucker as long as he didn't hang about and involve them. And after that he could survive on bush tucker, given a chance to fossick about in daylight.

He picked up the bridle and fondled the horse's ears.

'Come on, mate, I'll lead for a while. Let's give the bastards a run for their money.'

That night at dinner, Mr and Mrs Manningtree had the most ferocious row. The children had gone to bed, and Emilie, having given up all pretence of being above the domestic staff in her need for company, had sneaked into the kitchen to find out what was going on.

The cook grinned when she walked in. 'Wake you, did they?'

'No. I wasn't asleep. I thought you would have gone home by this.'

'Ah, no. I have to stay until I serve the pudden, but she hasn't given the nod yet. With a bit of luck they'll kill each other.'

Emilie distinctly heard the crash of breaking china and fled to the other side of the kitchen as Nellie came through the door carrying a tray of glasses and plates.

'Who's in there?' she asked.

Nellie grimaced angrily. 'The Captain came for dinner. By the sound of things the boss insulted him, so he took off, and they've been having this barney ever since. She reckons he was rude to their guest and he's been shouting that she's having it off with the Captain. Which she is.'

'What?' Emilie was amazed.

Nellie shrugged. 'That's been going on for a good while. And he's not the first. Takes time for the boss to wake up, that's all. Then he gets boozed and starts smashing things. He busted up a chair and the mirror over the mantelpiece, then he turned on the dessert dishes. I'd forget the pudding, Cook. They're past it.'

Nellie took off her apron and Cook followed suit, but the shouts and bellows from the dining room continued. Emily was frightened.

'You're not going to leave me? I don't want to be alone in the house with them.'

'You'll be all right,' Cook said. 'Lock your door.'

'It doesn't have a lock.'

'Then put a chair up against it. But they won't bother you. They're always fighting.'

'I haven't heard them before.'

Nellie packed the dirty dishes on a bench. 'They can stay there until tomorrow. I don't care what she says.' She ran a comb through her wispy hair and turned back to Emilie. 'Come to think of it, neither you have. They've been on their best behaviour since you got here. But I knew it wouldn't last.'

'Go to bed and forget about it, Emilie,' Cook said. 'It's nothing to do with us, or you.'

'Ah, but it is,' said Nellie, and the other two turned to stare at her.

'What do you mean?' the cook demanded.

'Well, I got a real earful, waiting outside the door to go in and get the dishes from the main course. He was shouting about her being a whore and she says: "What about you? I know you're on with that prissy Miss Tissington. You're always carrying on about her, how pretty she is and so clever . . ." '

The cook gaped. 'She never?'

Emilie gaped too. 'That's dreadful. How could she say such a thing?'

But Nellie wasn't concerned. 'You know how it is. Tit for tat. He starts on her. She starts on him. Who cares? I'm going home.'

'I care,' Emilie snapped. 'It's not true.'

'Nothing much you can do without dobbing Nellie in,' the cook advised. 'Take no notice, Emilie. You'll hear worse than that if you hang about here long enough. Last time he caught her out, Christmas it was . . .'

'No, New Year,' Nellie corrected.

'Yes, they went to some New Year party and when they got home he gave her such a hiding, she was in bed for a week.'

'Oh, dear God!'

Emilie did put a chair up against her doorknob when she ran to hide in her room. Apparently the violence had subsided, but angry arguments still continued spasmodically, through the night. She jumped in fright when she heard a timid knock on her door, but it was only Rosie.

'Will you let me in, miss? I've had a bad dream. I'm frightened.'

Emilie took the child into her bed to comfort her, and in the doing, slept more soundly herself.

The next day Mrs Manningtree was in a vile mood, finding fault with everyone, especially the children, invading their lunchtime, screaming at them to eat their meals and complaining that Alice hadn't done her chores, which included collecting the eggs from the chook pen. When Alice whimpered that she couldn't find any eggs today, her mother slapped her face.

Emilie had had enough. 'Don't hit the child, please. It's not her fault that there were no eggs.'

'Really! Then how did Nellie happen to find more than a dozen a few minutes ago?' She rounded on Alice. 'You didn't go at all, did you?'

'I forgot, Mum,' the child wept.

'There, you see, Miss Tissington. She's a liar. So don't you go telling me not to chastise my children. You mind your own business or your days here are numbered. Numbered, do you hear me?'

'Yes, madam.' Emilie felt stifled. The bare little room seemed to close in on her. She wanted to push the woman out of the doorway and rush outside, to run and run until she could breathe again, but that she could not do. Angry with herself for being so weak, for putting up with this common woman, she stood stolidly by the table, eyes downcast, studying her shoes.

'And we won't be needing you at the piano any more,' her employer sniffed, adjusting a comb in her puffed-up hair. 'One becomes rather bored with it after a while.'

After she left, the cook brought in some hot buttered toast. She winked at Emilie.

'No more piano? Oh well, every cloud has a silver lining.'

Emilie managed to raise a small smile. 'I suppose so.'

All day she fought off a determination to march into the house and give notice. Surely they would have to pay her something. If not, she could write to Ruth for enough money to return to Brisbane to find another job. Any job. She no longer thought in terms of situations or places of employment. She had learned from Nellie and Kate that no one differentiated out here, not in this backwater anyway. One either had a job or one did not.

And then there was Mr Willoughby to worry about. Could she really go to the gate to meet him?

Her anger provided the answer. No matter who came to visit her, even Ruth, for that matter, they would have to come to the back door of this household, not the front door, so she might as well go to the gate. And why not? She wouldn't be doing anything wrong. But a strange man?

Crossly she shrugged off the arguments that had been pestering her since Sunday. Besides, he might not even turn up. She decided she would go to the gate at exactly eight o'clock, but she certainly would not wait around. If he was not there, she would come straight back in. It was too silly to think that a stockman could help her find another situation . . . job.

So why was she bothering about him at all?

'Because I can do what I like in my own time,' she answered herself, defiantly, rather than admit she was desperate for a friend, someone beyond this prison of a household who would talk to her, who liked her. Even Mr Willoughby.

He was there an hour early, keeping well back in the shadows, waiting for her. He saw two people go out in a fancy gig, obviously Miss Emilie's boss and the missus, both lit up like Christmas trees, heading, he supposed, for some town beano. That gave him heart. She seemed scared of them. Now that they were out of the way, the coast was clear.

Mal wasn't nervous about being in the town. This was the last place they'd be looking for him. And after he left here, he'd head for the coast. That was risky too, he could be trapped in that direction, but posses were set in their ways. It was a pretty safe bet they'd be belting through the inland scrub having the time of their lives chasing a so-called murderer.

He wished he hadn't thought of that.

And now there was no time to do any more thinking at all, because she was coming up the drive and he wasn't ready. How could he explain this awful turn of events to her? And would she listen? Were it not for the fact that he would never let her down, he would have retreated into the night, because his self-confidence was ebbing away, deserting him when he was most in need of it.

Mal felt weak at the knees as he walked out to greet her. It wasn't only the meeting with Miss Emilie, though. The full force of the gravity of his situation had suddenly struck him again, like a physical blow, and he could only nod when she addressed him.

'Good evening, Mr Willoughby.'

He was encouraged when she added: 'It's a very nice evening, isn't it?' to cover the silence, and he had to make an effort. He looked about him. A squat stone fence, more ornamental than useful, jutted out for a few yards either side of the gateway, and he decided that would do. He couldn't walk her into town on this night.

'I have to talk to you,' he said with a rush. 'Can we sit here?'

'If you wish.' She sounded very shy.

He saw that she was comfortably seated on the flat stone and almost collapsed beside her, keeping a space between them in case she thought he was being too forward.

Emilie was surprised by the change in him. Nothing brash about Mr Willoughby this time; he seemed worried.

'Is there anything wrong?' she asked.

He nodded. 'Yes and no. I'm sorry, I don't have much time after all, but I wanted to ask how you're getting on. With your job, I mean.'

'Oh, I'm coping.'

'Doesn't sound like it to me. What's wrong?'

Emilie hesitated. Then she decided she might as well tell him. Tell someone. And with him it wouldn't go any further. He didn't know these people.

'The job itself is fine. I enjoy teaching the children, they're all rather sweet. But it's difficult living here. My employer, Mrs Manningtree, is an unpleasant woman, not just to me, but to the domestic staff as well.' Emilie sighed. 'It's just her way, I suppose.'

'And what about the husband? Does he bother you?'

'No. Not really. I don't see much of him.'

'What about your family? What do they have to say about this?'

He was so interested in her, intrigued really, that Emilie found herself answering all of his questions candidly, as freely as she would have spoken back home, before she'd become intimidated by poverty. She recalled that she used to be a forthright young woman, never afraid to speak her mind, as her stepmother had discovered, and it was refreshing to be able to breathe like this again, to talk about these things, if only to Mr Willoughby. She even told him about the Society, about being assisted to emigrate with her sister and their shock at finding they were not expected and the promised good jobs did not exist.

'We were rather naive,' she said ruefully.

'No. They let you down. I think you were very brave, coming all this way. That's a big step. How's your sister getting on? Does she like her job?'

'Yes. She's very happy.'

'And she can't find anything out her way for you?'

'She would have told me if there was an opening. But really, I'm talking too much. What about you? Did you say there was something wrong?'

He took a deep breath and shifted uncomfortably, stretching his long legs out in front of him. 'There surely is. And I guess you'll hear about it before long, but Miss Emilie . . .' he turned to her, 'whatever you hear about me, don't believe it. I'm in trouble, really bad trouble.'

'What sort of trouble?'

'There was a holdup, a gold shipment was taken, some men were killed. I'm being blamed but I had nothing to do with it.'

'When did this happen?'

'The very morning I saw you in town. I was only a guard. Only because I was on my way into Maryborough anyway. I should never have taken the job. They set me up.'

'Who did?'

'I'm not sure yet, but I'll find out. They arrested me . . .'

'Oh my Lord!'

'But I got away from them. I just wanted you to know that I had nothing to do with it, I swear I didn't . . .'

'Are they looking for you now? The police?'

Mal stood up and took her hand, assisting her to her feet. 'Yes. That's why I couldn't take you into town. I'm sorry, very sorry. I'm going away now and it would be best if you never tell anyone you know me. Not that you'd want to,' he added lamely.

Emilie was bewildered, wondering if any of this was true. She didn't know what to say.

'I hope you'll believe me,' he was saying. 'I wouldn't lie to you. It's bad luck, the lot of it. I've been out on the goldfields and I did all right. My partner was an Englishman, Clive Hillier. You might meet him one day. If you do, I know he'll speak for me.'

'Where will you go?' she asked, resisting the urge to glance about, for fear police might be watching them even now.

'I'm not sure.' He thrust a small package into her hands. 'I want you to have this. I came by it honest. Clive could tell you that.'

Emilie stared at the package tightly wrapped in newspaper and secured with string. 'What is it?'

'It's yours. If they catch me, I'll never see it again, someone will pocket it. So you might as well have it. I'm sorry, I have to go now.'

She was still holding the package as he clasped both of her hands in his.

'Don't forget me. I'll figure a way out of this. And I was thinking about you. You ought to get lodgings in town, then you can keep your job and you won't have to live in her house.'

Then he was gone, and Emilie was left standing, dazed, in the gateway, surrounded by tall trees that shivered in the moonlight.

103

Beyond checking occasionally to see if a governess was required anywhere in the district, Emilie had paid scant attention to the local
newspaper, but now, with news of the ambush and murders blazoned
across the front pages, she was suddenly interested.

At first she could only listen intently as Kate read out the tale of horror,
until she could get her hands on a copy and read it for herself, furtively
studying every word. She grew pale when she read that the outlaw, Mal
Willoughby, was still at large, as was his partner in crime, James
McPherson, another outlaw with a price on his head.

'They say he's vicious,' Kate said as she sliced expertly at a side of
lamb. 'A real killer.'

'Who?' Emilie asked, quaking.

'That Willoughby fellow. A friend of mine saw him out at the sawmill,
at Mr Manningtree's sawmill. He said he's got the face of a fiend, ugly as
sin with yellow eyes.'

Emilie stared at the cook but dared not remark.

For days she followed the story, reading much the same thing over and
over again about the stolen gold, the bravery of a Mr Carnegie, the Gold
Commissioner, who had been wounded in the attack, and the continuing
search for the two outlaws. There were sad stories of the bereaved
families and a report of the funerals, attended by all Maryborough's
leading citizens, including the Manningtrees, who were delighted to have
been mentioned. By the end of the week, though, another tragedy of far
greater import stole the limelight. A steamer from Sydney, the *Java
Queen*, with forty-two souls on board, was well overdue and feared lost.

One of the passengers was Captain Curtis Morrow, and as the days
dragged, and other vessels searched the coast without success, it became
clear that there were no survivors.

Distraught, Mrs Manningtree wore black and seemed inconsolable,
although her cynical cook regarded the mourning as an act.

'Anything for a bit of attention,' Kate said.

All this time, ten days to be exact, since Emilie's friend had bade her
farewell, she had not been able to bring herself to open that parcel. She'd
kept it hidden in the bottom of her trunk, hoping he'd come back for it,
and yet hoping he'd keep away, for his own safety, because there was a
poster outside the police station offering a reward of fifty pounds for the
apprehension of the outlaw Mal Willoughby. Emilie had only seen it
once, but it had given her such a jolt, she'd walked on the other side of the
street ever since.

It was probably stupid of her, she worried, and naive, but she believed
Mr Willoughby. She was certain that he couldn't have been part of that
ambush, that he couldn't have killed anyone. She'd spoken to him only
hours after the ambush was said to have taken place, and no one could act
that well. Surely there would have been some darkness evident, some
strain of guilt following such a dreadful deed. He couldn't be that
cold-hearted, that brutal.

Weary of the worry and the constant misgivings, Emilie finally took out the parcel. It was late, the house was quiet and her door was firmly closed. Guiltily she unwrapped it. Embarrassed, because he'd given her the impression it contained money under the wads of newspaper, and she didn't want his money. What on earth had she said that Sunday morning to have him believe she needed money from him?

The notes fell out on the bed. A jumble of notes. Not just a few pounds, a lot of money. Frantically Emilie searched through the wrappings for a note, for a letter of some sort that might give her directions on what to do with it. Did he want it banked? Or placed somewhere that he'd have access to? But there was nothing, only these large, familiar Bank of England notes, crisp and new, amounting to four hundred pounds.

Emilie took fright, thinking they might be ill-gotten gains, proceeds of that robbery, because she recalled the robbers had stolen gold and currency. She leapt up and closed her window, shutting herself in with this secret.

'It's yours,' he'd said. 'If they catch me, I'll never see it again.'

Panicking, she rolled it up in her underwear, deposited it deep in her trunk again and closed the lid with a bang.

Was he quite mad? Or very clever? No wonder he'd said not to mention that she knew him. Not that she would, with this infamy running riot. But now, by giving her this money, he had involved her in his wretched life. What on earth was she supposed to do with it? Imagine if she told Cook that she had a fortune in her room, courtesy of the fiendish outlaw?

Emilie didn't sleep a wink that night.

At Lindsay Downs, the governess was recovering slowly from the fever, but she was weak, and only able to take light foods, since her stomach seemed to revolt at anything substantial.

The doctor didn't feel there was much more he could do.

'She seems to be suffering from melancholy,' he told Mrs Stanfield. 'Not unusual in these cases. Protracted weakness in people is apt to lead to such a state, for they wish themselves to be healthy, and when they are not, they become impatient and that causes misery, which is in itself melancholy, if you get what I mean.'

Leonie did not. She thought his explanation was a lot of rigmarole but was too polite to say so. To her mind, Miss Tissington was simply feeling sorry for herself. She needed to get out of her sick room, to allow them to place her on a chair on the veranda where she could get the air, and start building herself up again. It had been weeks since she'd been lost in the bush and gone down with that fever, not an uncommon ailment. But no, she simply lay there, determined to remain the invalid. For how long?

A few days ago, the governess had managed to write a letter to the sister in Maryborough, and her employer, having promised to post it for her, had sneakily steamed it open. Leonie had never intruded on anyone's privacy like this before, but she was desperate to find out what Miss Tissington had to say. Since she was still too weak to emerge from her room, maybe she would give some explanation to her sister.

The letter was a disappointment and rather sad. It only told Miss Emilie Tissington that her sister was very happy but had been too busy lately to do justice to their correspondence, so a more interesting epistle would be shortly on the horizon. Obviously she had not told her sister that she'd been ill, and Leonie supposed that was understandable. But what to do with her now?

The doctor was half right. Ruth was melancholic, but not quite as ill as she might seem. She was simply so mortified by all that had happened, she didn't have the will to face anyone. She still saw herself as being superior to these people, these colonials, better educated, better informed in all manner of things, an English gentlewoman, and she could not bend. She did not know how. She kept promising herself that she would get up shortly, any day now, and when that happened, she would call the Stanfields to account.

She would not brook any further criticism from them. She would require an apology from Mr Stanfield for referring to her as Miss Gloom, thereby undermining her authority not only with the children, but with the domestics. She was horribly disappointed in Mr Stanfield and she would say so. She would also point out that far from relaxing her discipline, the daughters needed more. A great deal more. And she would see to it. She had been engaged to turn them into ladies and she was quite capable of doing so, if the parents desisted from interfering.

This was the plan that Ruth mulled over all the time she remained in her room, but to actually go out and confront them required a strength she didn't feel she had just now, because she was not well. But she would soon. It was just a matter of time. And a cycle that she was unwittingly forcing on herself. A treadmill. Something akin to the doctor's diagnosis.

But the household had lost interest in Miss Tissington. A spring clean was under way as they prepared for an important visitor. Jack's mother was home from her travels and on her way to Lindsay Downs, and as Leonie knew only too well, Lavinia Stanfield was very particular.

This station, one of many owned by the Stanfield clan, was Lavinia's favourite because it had been her first home after she'd married Lindsay Stanfield, and the first of a chain of cattle stations the couple had acquired over the years, as their wealth increased.

Like everyone else, Leonie looked forward to seeing the visitor again, and hearing all about her travels. Mrs Stanfield, now a widow, had set sail for London with a niece as companion, to call on various relatives who were very highly placed in society, and had received a warm welcome. From there the travellers had toured the Continent before spending a month staying with friends in their beautiful villa in Florence. Leonie had seen sketches of the villa, and she envied her mother-in-law; she would adore to visit Florence.

'One day,' Jack had said, 'when the girls are older, we'll all go.'

Leonie did like her mother-in-law, but Lavinia made her nervous. She was a formidable woman, imperious and never backward in lording it

106

over her family with advice, opinions and instructions. At first Leonie had thought her arrogant, but Lavinia did have a sense of humour, which took the edge off her high-handed attitude, so that was some consolation. But right now she had to have the house shining to avoid fingertip inspections and sniffs of disapproval.

Jack wasn't immune either, she smiled, even though he professed not to be concerned. The gardens and grounds had been weeded and tidied, fences mended, and sheds painted. Lindsay Downs would pass muster this time.

When the great day arrived, they were pleased to see that Lavinia looked remarkably well, and was in excellent spirits. She greatly enjoyed the special luncheon Leonie had arranged for her, set splendidly on the cool veranda with a view out over the valley. There was only one glitch, when Jane and Jessie, not interested in their grandmother's recounting of the fascinating cities she'd visited, interrupted with their questions.

'Where are our presents, Grandma?'

'What did you bring us?'

Her withering stare was lost on the girls, who continued to badger their grandmother until Leonie had to order them to be quiet. As a result, they had to wait for days until they saw any of the gifts Lavinia had brought home for them, until all the other presents had been distributed. Not even the family retainers had been forgotten. The overseer received a pewter beer mug from London, and the cook and the maid were each presented with Swiss music boxes. Eventually, though, tailored riding habits were taken out of their tissues for Jane and Jessie, and Leonie was delighted, but her daughters were unimpressed, even though they fitted them perfectly. They were happier with the boxes of trinkets Lavinia had collected for them.

During this time, of course, Lavinia heard all about the governess, and one day she visited the sick room without warning.

Ruth was nonplussed when the woman she'd already heard so much about suddenly appeared by her bed. Mrs Stanfield senior was a tall, dignified woman with softly coiffured grey hair and steely blue eyes. She was dressed as if for town, in an expensive black dress with a finely pleated bodice lit by a double row of pearls and pearl earrings, and she wore a huge diamond ring beside her wedding ring.

The governess had been dozing, and her hair was loose, placing her at a disadvantage, she felt. She resented this woman's intrusion.

'Good morning, my dear. You are Miss Tissington, I believe. I'm Mrs Stanfield. They tell me you haven't been well.'

Ruth struggled up, dragging at a pillow for support. 'Yes, but I'm improving now, Mrs Stanfield.'

'That's good. These fevers can be very nasty. But tell me now. Do you still feel bilious? Do you still get temperatures? Chills?'

The questioning, like a medical examination, went on and on. Mrs Stanfield felt Ruth's forehead, her throat, her pulse, and eventually stood back.

'These days people have no idea how to cope with sickness, or the aftermath of sickness. They can't lift a finger without calling for doctors. In my day there weren't any doctors within a hundred miles. One simply had to learn what was best. I must apologise for my son and his wife, leaving you here to waste away.'

'Oh, no,' Ruth cried. 'They've been very good. Very kind.'

'Not kind enough. I'll have you well in no time. Now you get yourself up and I'll have the maid run a bath for you. Then you can have a cup of tea and perhaps an egg and lettuce sandwich, out on the back porch. It's shady there at this time of day, and very pleasant. You need to get the air, my girl.'

'I don't really feel . . .' Ruth began, but Mrs Stanfield overrode her objections.

'Yes you will. You must be up and doing. Sickness must be fought, Miss Tissington. Not endured.'

Protests were useless. Ruth had no choice but to bathe, dress and make her way out to the veranda, where she found that a bulky armchair had been transported there from the sitting room for her comfort. A small table was set with an immaculate cloth and a china tea service, and there was even a tiny vase with a bouquet of sweet peas, but Ruth was in no mood to appreciate such niceties; she felt very shaky and put upon.

She did manage the tea, though, and the sandwiches, thin and crustless, were quite delicious, only four, cut in corners. She really hated leaving one, but dignity prevailed.

For a while she was left in quiet contemplation until she was joined by Mrs Stanfield senior, a cruel imposition because she didn't feel up to making conversation.

'How do you feel now, Miss Tissington?'

'Rather shaky, I'm afraid.'

'I'm not surprised. Your poor legs must be weak from inaction. But they'll soon pick up. I recommend a short walk this afternoon. Only once round the garden, rather bracing, this country air, but not what you're accustomed to, I imagine.'

To Ruth's horror, Mrs Stanfield settled into a nearby chair. 'I mean, you must miss the cooler weather.'

Ruth was forced to respond. 'I do rather, but one acclimatises.'

'I'm sure you do. What part of England do you come from?'

For the next half-hour Mrs Stanfield engaged her in conversation based mainly on Ruth herself, since the woman was genuinely interested in her background, but it was conducted in such an amiable, genteel manner that Ruth could not take offence. In fact, it became obvious to her that Mrs Stanfield liked her, and was impressed by her qualifications, and that made her feel better. Much better. This woman understood her. She had recently returned from England and she would be very much aware of the cultural differences that Ruth was confronting. She promised she would take that walk to please Mrs Stanfield.

★ ★ ★

108

Lavinia was indeed very much aware of the cultural differences when she went to find her daughter-in-law.

'We have to sort out the situation with Miss Tissington. She can't be allowed to loll about feeling sorry for herself forever. I'll get her up within days. She's not that sick, only crushed.'

'Why? I've done everything I can to make her happy, Lavinia, but she's very difficult. She takes umbrage at the slightest thing.'

'That's understandable. She's young. She has led a sheltered life and is very much steeped in protocol. She had no idea how to unbend to what she would consider our lax ways, and I'm afraid with someone as rigid as your Miss Tissington, the transition will be difficult. She has a great sense of herself.'

Leonie shrugged. 'Jack agrees. He says she's too full of herself.'

'Then he's wrong,' Lavinia snapped. 'Miss Tissington is a very nice young woman. A gem, in fact. Well read. She even speaks French fluently. What couldn't I have done with her on my travels on the Continent instead of silly Monica, who kept getting herself into fixes. Miss Tissington is not full of herself; she has a standard to maintain, and that type of woman will do just that, if it kills her. She doesn't know any other way. She even worries about her young sister, who is also a governess and apt to be flighty.'

'She told you all this?' Leonie was astonished. 'I can never get much out of her, she's like a clam about her personal life.'

'Because she has been too busy trying to please you.'

'Oh dear. Has she complained about us? Or the girls?'

'Of course she hasn't. You still don't understand, Leonie. She's very aware of her responsibilities. It would not occur to her to criticise any of you. But this isn't solving the problem. I don't know why you brought a person like her out here in the first place. You should have gone to town and interviewed her yourself, instead of taking the word of your sister.'

'I was just trying to do the best for the girls,' Leonie said miserably.

'Ha, yes! The girls. I take it they don't like her, and Jack disliked her attempts to teach them table manners. He told me that himself. Well, that's just too bad, isn't it? What do you propose to do about it?'

Leonie sat back and sighed. 'I really don't know. She's got everyone on edge. She doesn't even get on with the maid and the cook.'

'Why should she? In her world they don't exist. But you listen to me, my girl. Miss Tissington is right. I've been here long enough to see that Jane and Jessie have disgraceful table manners. It has been all I could do not to bring a ruler to the table. If ever two girls needed a Miss Tissington, they do. Even to just listen to her. She has the most beautiful speaking voice, and they talk like a couple of navvies. I intend to tell Jack myself that I consider Jane and Jessie ill-mannered wretches.'

Leonie bristled. 'You're being unfair, Lavinia. They're just tomboys. They'll grow out of it.'

'They won't, Leonie. They need to be taught how to behave, since you and Jack aren't up to it.'

'You want us to keep Miss Tissington on?'

'No, I don't. She's a square peg in a round hole here. And she's wasted on that pair, because their parents won't back her up.'

'We try,' Leonie said defensively, 'but she's so strict, and she takes offence if I make the slightest suggestion. We'll have to let her go and find someone else.'

'No you won't. Jane and Jessie belong in boarding school, and the sooner the better. I will speak to Jack about it myself.'

Chapter Five

Clive Hillier didn't believe a word of it. Mal was no murderer. Nor was he an outlaw given to robbing gold shipments.

'Why would he?' Clive argued with other miners. 'He left here with plenty of cash on him. He took the job because it was safer to travel to Maryborough in company. For God's sake, you blokes know Mal. This is all wrong.'

'Then why did he bolt?' he was asked.

'Wouldn't you? With all the cards stacked against you? They were all so riled up about the murders, they could have lynched him. Wouldn't you bolt given half a chance? He's innocent, I tell you. He's just a patsy. The police had to produce someone to prove that they can protect travellers on these roads, because they've failed miserably up until now. Outlaws are having a field day up here; they come and go as they like, robbing where they please, and they're never caught. McPherson is a prime example.'

Some men listened. Some even agreed. But they all had their own problems, and anyway, what could they do about it? Willoughby was on the wanted list, with a price on his head.

When he heard that Sergeant Pollock was on the goldfields, Clive sought him out, insisting he be heard, and Pollock, liking the cut of the Englishman, agreed to listen.

From this man, Pollock managed to glean some background on the elusive Willoughby, who had disappeared without a trace. He argued that just because Hillier saw the outlaw as a 'good fellow', it didn't make him innocent. The backblocks of the Australian countryside were already infested with bushrangers, beloved of the populace, heroes in fact, who were out-and-out criminals. They raided authority – banks, mail coaches, gold or cash shipments – never the small man, and for that they were cheered by the battlers. They obtained succour from isolated farmhouses by paying their way and by treating the womenfolk with respect, even with such courtesy that women were known to swoon over them. On the other hand, police or troopers trailing them, met a wall of obstinate silence or, worse, outright dislike. They were not welcome, they were not fed, they were informed by suspicious homesteaders that they could water their horses and move out. A thankless job.

Pollock understood this. His grandfather had been a convict, transported for the theft of clothing from a rich landowner, separating him

111

from the family he'd tried to support. This turned Jonah Pollock from a quiet farmhand into a hard-timer who fought his jailers at every turn. He'd ended up on the notorious Norfolk Island, known for its vicious treatment of convicts, where he'd fathered a son by a female prisoner before he was flogged for insubordination and died. The son, Joseph Pollock, had ended up in Sydney Town, where he made his own way as a blacksmith. He was not a bitter man. Far from it.

'Whatever happened happened,' he used to tell his own son, young Joe. 'I could have gone the same way as my old dad. Cursed the bastards till the day I died. But it wasn't in me, see. It all worked out all right. I got my own blacksmith's shop. Your ma, she's a good woman, came out free she did. We could have been worse off back there. Nothing wrong with Sydney Town.'

And so it seemed, until the day young Joe Pollock told his father he was joining the newly formed police force.

Then Joe saw the real side of the family story. His father shouted and raved, threatened to belt him, called him a tout and a traitor for going over, while his mother wept, trying to keep the peace. Joe understood then that his father had accepted the circumstances of his birth, but could never forgive the authority that had so penalised and eventually killed his father. It was called the law, or authority, or whatever name you cared to put to it, but high on the list were judges and policemen . . . Joe senior hated them.

It was still the best chance available, though, and Joe Pollock took it, moving eventually with his wife and children to Queensland. His mother kept in touch, but his father never forgave him. Oh yes, Sergeant Pollock understood this antipathy towards authority, he knew whence it came, but he had no time for it. Transportation of convicts from the British Isles had ceased, it was all over. Generations now had to get on with their lives, and that included folk who sheltered outlaws in a misplaced sense of payback against authority. Most of them had never even met a transported convict; they just paid their dues to folklore, to an inbred opposition to authority. And Sergeant Pollock wasn't about to put up with it. He encouraged his superiors to bring in harsh punishments against anyone, man or woman, who aided and abetted outlaws, and he stood by those extreme measures.

Now he had to listen to this Englishman singing the praises of another outlaw who had seemed a very nice fellow.

'Aren't they all?' he asked Hillier.

'I wouldn't know about that. I'm just telling you that Mal Willoughby isn't your man.'

Hillier insisted on going over every detail of the ambush and the killings, again and again, searching for some clue that might assist in proving his friend's innocence, and while Pollock listened patiently, the conversation was going nowhere. Willoughby was up to his neck in it, and Carnegie was still alive to prove it. Fortunately.

'How do I know you're not still his partner, Hillier?' the Sergeant barked, fed up with the arguments.

112

'Because I haven't left the goldfields and I can prove it.'

'So you say, but I'm wondering if you're holding out on me. You were his partner here, but you can't tell me anything about him. I'm getting less from you than from poor Taylor's notes about him, and I'm finding a lot of that was hogwash. Why would he lie to Taylor?'

'Because he didn't take anything seriously. That's typical of Mal. He was a very private person.'

Irritated, Pollock turned on Clive. 'And what does that mean in plain English?'

'He minded his own business.'

'Or he had plenty to hide. He's only a young bloke; where's his family? He must have family somewhere.'

'I don't know. He never mentioned them.'

'Or you're not telling. You would do well to remember, mister, that the law comes down hard on anyone aiding and abetting outlaws. You're not in the clear by any means. You still working a claim here?'

'Yes.'

'Doing any good?'

'That's my business.'

'It's my business if you leave here. I'll want to know when, and where you're going. Got me?'

'Of course.' Clive was furious. 'I'm sure you'll carry out the usual police investigations, harassing the easiest targets and making a big noise chasing an innocent man. Looks good in the papers, though, doesn't it?'

He marched away, leaving Pollock standing, not caring that he had antagonised the man in charge of the investigations. Why couldn't the thick-headed Sergeant get out there and find the real outlaws. They certainly wouldn't be hanging about the goldfields.

But Pollock didn't mind the Englishman's reaction. It was mild compared to the usual sneers his enquiries engendered round here. Few were co-operative at the best of times. Hillier was important, though. Hillier was his only link with Willoughby. Taylor's notes of his interview with the fellow had been brought to Maryborough, and Pollock had studied them carefully. Then he'd telegraphed the information to the new Superintendent of Police, Mr Jasper Kemp, pleased that they had a good lead on the escapee, but the response had stunned him.

No one knew a shearer called Willoughby. Some of the stations he'd mentioned ran cattle. Not sheep. His father did not have a hotel in Ipswich, nor was his family known in that town. Kemp seemed to think that Willoughby could be an assumed name, and Pollock was inclined to agree. It seemed rather highbrow for this lying lout. And it all pointed to a man carefully blotting out his real identity for criminal purposes. He began to think that this raid might have been in the planning stages for quite some time. But Willoughby, or whoever he was, didn't fit the profile of the brains behind the outfit.

Pollock strode back to the Commissioner's offices and slumped into a

113

chair in Carnegie's room. The new Gold Commissioner would be arriving any day.

He had to admit that had he been Taylor, he'd have approved the baby-faced Willoughby as an outrider. A last-minute casual employee, unknown to the other guards, for safety's sake. If not a shearer, he was definitely a bushie, cool and calm, not likely to panic if there was trouble. Pollock had the advantage; he knew Willoughby, he'd ridden out there with him, and he knew that the big lout was not the boss. But who was?

McPherson. James McPherson. That could be . . . and who else? And what was the connection between McPherson and Willoughby? If he could pin that down, he'd have them both. He had a small problem with this scenario, though . . .

McPherson wasn't a planner either. The Scot's escapades had placed him in New South Wales, as far south as Cowra, and in Queensland west to Roma and in the far north at Mackay, even Bowen, hundreds of miles north of Maryborough. Then he'd turned up here and robbed the mail coach two nights in a row.

Pollock studied a map on the wall. A map of Queensland. It was obvious that after every robbery, or maybe two, McPherson took off. He didn't just head for the hills; there was always a gap of hundreds of miles before he surfaced again. So why would he be hanging about this district for weeks, waiting for a gold consignment?

He shook his head. The description sounded like McPherson, but the robbery didn't.

Something else about that raid bothered him, something he'd missed and he knew he'd missed, but he'd think it through. Given time. Only Pollock's wife agreed with him that he was good at his job; he was seen by others as a plodder, very methodical, someone who didn't go in for the big show, the limelight. That was why he was now being criticised, very severely, for dismissing the men accompanying him with the prisoner, Willoughby. Had he allowed the crowd to stay, Willoughby would never have escaped.

Pollock had good reason to be very angry with Mal Willoughby.

Yes, Allyn Carnegie was satisfied with Perry when his present sufferings allowed him to think of anything other than the condition of his arm. The local doctor had treated the wound and reset the arm to the best of his abilities, causing the patient considerable pain and anguish. Having no confidence in this doctor, whom he referred to as a butcher, Carnegie complained bitterly that the fellow was making it worse. So much so that the doctor offered to send to Brisbane for a bone specialist.

'Do you think I'm made of money?' Carnegie shouted. 'The cost would be exorbitant.'

'You could go down and see a specialist,' the doctor retorted. 'I have no objection.'

'I could not. I am not well enough to travel.' Apart from which, Carnegie had no intention of leaving Maryborough. Not without the gold.

Willoughby's escape had been fortuitous. That, and the funerals, had directed public attention away from the actual raid, and sent Pollock off on the chase. The Sergeant's questioning had been interminable, too much for a sick man to have to endure. As well as the injured arm, Carnegie was suffering from severe dysentery, and he blamed that on the disgusting potions prescribed for him by this doctor.

Feeling very sorry for himself, Carnegie remained in his Maryborough house, being cared for by a daily, worrying about the gold, worrying about Perry. Though they had agreed that Perry should not have any contact with him, Carnegie could not be absolutely sure that the rogue had not absconded with the proceeds of the robbery, the only soft spot in his plan. Therein lay the difficulty. One could hardly engage an honest man for this duty, hence Perry and the necessity to take a chance on him. The absolute necessity. But then, as a gambling man, Carnegie knew the odds were in his favour. Perry was a foot soldier, a bonehead; he'd obey. Half of a haul this size, without fear of ever being accused of involvement in the crime, was his ultimate reward. The brilliance of the plan had produced a rare smile of appreciation from the brute.

All this worry gave Carnegie a constant headache, and as he sat gloomily at his window watching the activity in the busy street, he began to hate this town.

In an official letter to the Minister of Mines, he resigned his commission, quoting serious injury and nervous exhaustion, and removed his effects from the Maryborough office.

It was accepted with commiserations and grateful thanks, as well as assurance that his salary would be paid for the full year instead of the nine months that he had actually served.

Carnegie thought the payment just. But the suggestion of seeing a specialist had given rise to another possibility. When he had his hands on the gold he could use his injury as an excuse to rush to Brisbane, but instead of remaining in that town, where creditors lay in wait, he could take ship to other lands. China maybe, there were plenty of ships travelling to and from China, and thence to America. It would be much easier to dispose of the gold in China. Before he'd embarked on this plan, Carnegie had made sure there were shady dealers in Brisbane who would buy gold, no questions asked, but this was a much better idea.

To his horror, he received a letter from his wife, shocked to hear of the ambush and of his injuries, which were greatly overstated in the newspapers, and offering to come up and care for him. Carnegie had answered that quickly. He did not need her, and a rough town like this was no place for his wife. She should stay in Brisbane and he would be home as soon as his health permitted.

He sighed. The woman was a constant irritation.

And where was Perry?

No one working on the wharves with Baldy Perry had any idea that he was a rich man now, an important man, and though he had the sense to

115

keep quiet about it, he developed a swagger that did little to endear him to his workmates. At his best, Perry was an aggressive man, relying on his bulk to see him through, and he was never fond of hard work, but for the present he had no choice. He'd only taken the job to avoid suspicion; it gave him a reason to be hanging about Maryborough. He kept telling himself that it was only a matter of time before he marched away from this backbreaking slog, sorted the share out with Carnegie and headed for a life of luxury. But the waiting was a strain.

He kept thinking about the gold, deposited under a tree by the river, but he didn't want to think about it . . . the way you thought about a woman when there was none to be had, sweating and prickling, nights of torment . . . and he'd wake feeling like death warmed up. That didn't help his disposition.

Mahoney, the gang boss, had been on Perry's tail for three weeks now. He would have sacked him if he hadn't been so short-handed. It was hard to keep men working here, within striking distance of the goldfields. Perry was trouble, a bully; he caused fights and menaced other workers, and seemed to think he could pick and choose which ship he worked on.

Finally the boss was fed up. 'If you don't want the bloody job, Perry, say so and get the hell out of here!'

Surprisingly the bruiser backed down, muttering something about wanting to keep his job, words that almost amounted to an apology, and Mahoney stared, shaking his head, as Perry slouched away.

But the backdown couldn't last. For Perry, the humiliation in front of all the other men, who *had* to work, was hard to bear. All day it irked him, like worms writhing in his big belly, worms that he tried to ignore because he had to stick to the plan. He cast his mind back to the elation he'd felt when he'd buried the treasure under the tree. Not exactly the same tree that Carnegie had chosen, but it would do as a marker. He remembered Carnegie's spot with a shudder. He'd never moved so fast in all his life. Just as he was about to burrow a hole among the roots, he'd spotted crocodile tracks in the mud, leading up from the river. Big, deep tracks! He was out of there in a second, not even bothering to look about for the monster.

Knowing crocodiles could move at a terrifying speed, Baldy burst up the bank, high up, ploughing through the thick scrub until he was out of danger.

'Jesus!' he gasped. 'I ain't going back there.'

When he'd recovered from the fright, he searched about for another hiding place, deciding on an ancient Moreton Bay fig tree with roots knotted and splayed for yards around it. Ideal.

The booty was soon buried in the deep hollows; no need to disturb the dirt or even a leaf. He patted the gnarled trunk.

'There's a good old fella. You mind this stuff for me.'

Baldy had shuddered as he looked back at the river. He'd dumped Carnegie's rifle in the water, but when he'd rowed ashore, he'd unpacked the dinghy, bashed a hole in it and sunk it, without giving a thought to the bloody crocs!

116

'A man can be lucky,' he muttered as he found his horse and released the hobbles.

It was an unusually cheerful Baldy Perry who mounted his horse and headed back along the river track towards the ferry and the safe haven of Maryborough.

He was still thinking of that good old tree when the whistle blew for knock-off time. Perry dug his grappling hook into his belt and headed for a pub, not the Port Office Hotel, where all the dockers drank, but up the road to the Criterion, to dodge the gibes and sly taunts of his cronies, who had heard the exchange with Mahoney.

He drank three pints in quick succession as he stood in the far corner of the bar, a lone, brooding drinker, thinking of Mahoney and what he'd do to the Irish bastard one of these days. Thinking of Carnegie, who was the cause of his shame, keeping him roped and tied with what he could and could not do. He, Perry, who'd pulled off a robbery that had outdone McPherson's exploits.

Perry switched to rum. Overproof rum. Maryborough's best. He figured he ought to go see Carnegie. It had been three weeks now, and the robbery was all but forgotten, what with the sinking of the *Java Queen* and the opening of the Town Hall. Willoughby barely got a mention any more. The dummy had scampered for the hills, and if he knew what was good for him, he'd stay there, Perry chortled. That was a good move, implicating a dumb kid like him. Carnegie had said the police would fall for it, and they sure had, heading off on a wild-goose chase. Geese looking for a goose. He called for another rum. It was real firewater, this local rum, but by now Baldy had swallowed so many it was tasting like nectar.

A crowd of men stumbled into the bar and Baldy scowled. He knew some of them, and resented them invading what he now regarded as his space. Obviously they'd been drinking somewhere else and decided to repair to the Criterion, but it was only a small bar and already they were crowding to the counter, shouting for service. Deliberately Baldy stood firm, widening his elbows to reserve plenty of room for himself, and inevitably someone pushed in beside him.

'Who do you think you're shoving?' he growled.

'No one, mate. Just move up a bit.'

Yet another man pushed in, ignoring Baldy's elbows, so he used a hefty shoulder to bump back, sending the intruder staggering.

'Watch it, you bloody idiot,' the stranger shouted, but Baldy rounded on him, grabbing him by the shirt.

'Who are you calling a bloody idiot?'

He was only a small man, but feisty. Angrily, he broke free.

'Keep your fat hands off me, mate.'

Baldy reacted by punching him in the stomach, causing him to crash into other drinkers. Immediately the barman was shouting at them. 'No fighting in here! You, Perry, get out. Go home to your mother.'

Perry was highly insulted. He'd been here first, minding his own

117

business, then this mob had come along, most of them already boozed, and he was being told to get out. Well, he wasn't putting up with humiliation twice in the one day.

'Who's gonna make me?' he growled.

A ginger-headed bloke pushed through the crowd. Mahoney! The Irish bastard! 'I will. We don't need any trouble here, Perry. You've had your fill. Now go on home, man.'

In a second Baldy had his grappling hook out, holding it in front of him like a claw. 'Let's see you try! You're not the boss now.'

Exasperated, Mahoney turned towards the barman. 'Give him a drink for the road . . .'

But Baldy didn't wait to hear what Mahoney had to say. He struck out at him, trying to catch him off guard, but the feisty stranger was fast. He sprang forward to push Mahoney out of the way, but in doing so took the full force of the hook across his neck and back, blood spurting everywhere.

Infuriated, the mob closed in on Baldy, punching and kicking him into his corner.

Next morning Baldy woke up in jail, battered, with several ribs broken, hungover, sick and hungry, charged with assault and battery. His victim was in hospital with serious injuries.

'How long do I have to stay here?' he groaned.

'What's it to you?' Constable Gus Frew shrugged. 'You're only on loan to us until the magistrate arrives, then you'll be doing a stretch down south.'

'When does the magistrate get here?'

'All in good time. You made a right mess of Jackie Flynn. He was getting married on Saturday. That's off now. You wrecked a good party, mate, there's no one will have a kind word for you, so start getting used to the bread and water.'

Several days later, Baldy tried to appeal to Frew. 'You gotta listen to me. I can't stay in jail. I got things to do.'

Frew laughed. 'Sure you do. The ships can't sail without your help. You're an important man, Baldy. But didn't you hear? They say Jacky's so bad hurt he'll never be able to turn his head again.'

'No, listen. I can pay. If someone can get me out of here I'll make it worth their while, if you get my meaning.'

The constable ignored him. Hearing the exchange, Baldy's fellow prisoners tried to borrow money from him. The magistrate took his time coming to Maryborough, but the hearing lasted only a few minutes. Baldy was sentenced to six months at St Helena Island prison, located at the mouth of the Brisbane River.

Angus Perry was illiterate. He'd grown up on a wretched farm south of Sydney, where book learning and boots were not considered necessary by his struggling parents. They saw merit, though, in their only son's development from a flabby toddler into a tall and muscular youth who soon outgrew his father. Their lad was strong, an ideal farm labourer, and they put him to work at an early age. Or rather, they tried to. Angus was lazy and defiant, and it was only constant use of the whip that could get him through his chores. Complaints began to come in from neighbouring farmers who were no better off than the Perrys, all battling a devastating drought, that Angus was a thief, that every time he called on them something would go missing . . . a bridle, a leg of ham, a chicken, fencing wire . . . the list seemed to be endless. At first his parents protested Angus's innocence – the boy was only going on fourteen – but when his father found a stray saddle in the barn, he went after his son with the whip, determined to teach him a lesson he wouldn't forget in a hurry, before sending him off to return the saddle to its owner.

But it didn't work out that way. Angus wrenched the whip from his father, hurled it away and battered him with an axe handle. It was only Mrs Perry's screaming intervention that saved her husband from more serious injuries. The battle was over, though. Angus walked off the farm, never to return.

He joined gangs of brutish youths who hung about the Sydney docks and eventually made his way north, a shady character, mixing with his peers, criminals and other lowlife.

Like so many of his ilk, Baldy graduated to the goldfields, where he hoped to make a quick fortune, one way or another. He and a mate tried prospecting, and to their delight they did find a few ounces of alluvial gold. But it was there that he met Mr Carnegie, an important man, who took an interest in him when he applied for another lease.

Baldy was impressed that Carnegie, a genial sort of bloke, had taken a liking to him, had even filled the forms in for him. He often gave Baldy the time of day when he walked about inspecting the fields, so much so that Baldy began to be suspicious of the great man, wondering if he was snooping. Perry the prospector was still Perry the thief, and empty tents were fair game.

It was after the fight with his partner, who had since taken flight, that Carnegie found Baldy sitting disconsolately by his dilapidated tent.

'How's the prospecting going, Mr Perry?'

'Ah, it's no good. A waste of time. I think I'll give it away.'

'Yes, it's all luck, I think. Some have the luck, some don't.'

Baldy shrugged. He was in no mood for niceties with this snoop.

'I might have a job for you,' Carnegie said.

Unimpressed, Baldy scowled. 'Look elsewhere.'

'Only a one-off job. Plenty of cash in it.'

'You don't say.' Baldy was even less impressed.

'Very well. If you change your mind, come to my rooms after ten tonight. But don't let anyone see you.'

Baldy rolled a cigarette, not even bothering to look up as the dapper Commissioner strolled away. He wondered if this bloke was a pervert, and grinned. Perverts were money. You could bash them senseless and

119

they'd never give you up. Especially this sort. He decided he might just turn up later, sneaking around to the Commissioner's rooms. Could be worth his time.

That was how it started. Carnegie wasn't a pervert. He had a bottle of whisky and he talked a fair bit, but he didn't make any pervert moves. He did talk about this job, though, in a roundabout sort of way, until Baldy started to get the gist of it, and he slowly came to thinking that this bloke was a crook. That had him grinning, eager to find out more, and so it went on . . .

All the time he was in Maryborough lockup, Baldy had hoped that Carnegie would rescue him. Pay off some of the bigwigs and get him out, but there was no sign of his partner. He couldn't trust anyone to write a letter for him; what could a letter say? It would be dangerous for him to draw attention to the acquaintance between them. Then again, it would be equally dangerous for Carnegie to speak up for him, when the crux of the whole plan was no obvious contact between the pair.

Just the same, he worried angrily, Carnegie could do something behind the scenes, surely? He was an important man.

When he was taken from Maryborough and chained in the hold of the ship, Baldy was grateful to that lurking crocodile. Had it not been for the beast, he would have left the gold exactly where Carnegie expected it to be. Where Carnegie could have grabbed the lot for himself, in the absence of his partner. Now it could stay there until he was free.

It was a sour, bullish Perry who was shoved, with the other prisoners, into the longboat at the Brisbane Quay to be carried downriver to the dreaded penal island of St Helena, from where the only escape was a swim through shark-infested waters. Even as he stepped ashore, his belligerent attitude earned him the first of many floggings by his warders, who warned him they were in no hurry to have him leave.

'We know your type,' they said. 'Bully boys learn to jump to attention here, or they do their time and some.'

As the time approached, Allyn Carnegie became so impatient he took to sitting on his back porch of an evening, watching for the late caller, watching for Perry to slip into his yard, even though they were not to meet. Perry had agreed to rely on the practised eye of the former Commissioner to divide the spoils evenly. As evenly as one could, Carnegie mused, given that the bags contained weight-measured pouches of alluvial gold as well as graded nuggets, coins and banknotes. This was his right as boss of the enterprise, and Perry had no complaints; he was so overawed at the prospect of a foolproof robbery, he would have agreed to anything.

When he eventually took to his bed, wearied by the vigil and the constant ache of his limp and misshapen arm, which was taking a very long time to heal, Carnegie slept fitfully. He kept listening for Perry, dragging up at every sound, every living thing conspiring to disturb his sleep. Small animals fossicked in the bushes, birds screeched at some unexplained disturbance, dogs barked, cats yowled, and Carnegie's pillow became wet with sweat, for night brought its demons. Cruel dreams assailed him in short, stark dramas, always incomplete yet terrifying in their intensity, until he came to dread sleep, but he kept telling himself it was only nerves. When Perry came, it would all be over.

So he waited and he waited. Days dragged and the nights were only endured with the company of the whisky bottle. He discouraged visitors and anyway, his fame as a victim had diminished, so few bothered to call any more. The goldfields at Gympie were still producing, but the excitement of the rush was over, as all eyes turned to a new place called Charters Towers, where it was claimed there were massive deposits of gold, eclipsing other fields.

Pollock called again, an unofficial visit, he said, to check on the patient, but he was insidious, that man, and Allyn was wary of him. He delivered mild questions with an equanimity that might have put a lesser man off his guard, but Carnegie was not to be fooled. He could play the game too, welcoming the Sergeant with pitiful gratitude, for few cared about him any more, not even the witless doctor. And he talked about the raid and poor dead Taylor and the other two men, to the point of being repetitive and very very boring, as if he would never recover from such an outrage.

The Sergeant sat on the porch with him, drinking his good whisky, seeming to be in no hurry to leave.

'A shame they were so quick to appoint a new Gold Commissioner,' he noted.

'Not at all. I resigned. I'm no hero. They can have that job.'

'I realise that, sir, but it was well paid. Unfortunate to have to relinquish a salary like that.'

'Not for me. I do have means, you know.'

'That's good. I was under the impression that you have a few debts out there at the fields. Gambling debts.'

Carnegie laughed. 'All gentlemen seem to have gambling debts. I had a bad run with those wily fellows. I have been too ill to think about them of late, as you can imagine, but only today I was arranging to make payment, since obviously I am not able to return. I never welsh on gambling debts, I consider the practice abhorrent.'

'Of course. But would I be correct in mentioning that you are already overdrawn at our local bank?'

Carnegie was furious that this upstart should be investigating his finances, but he laughed it off.

'What's happening? Is that wretch at the bank becoming peeved that I might up and die on him? I have just received a substantial cheque from the Mines Department, plus a bonus, so there isn't even any need for me to contact my Brisbane bank to forward funds. By the way, do you have any shares in the Ballarat gold mines?'

'No.'

121

'Then take my tip. Invest. After the riots there by the miners, investors lost confidence. My wife wanted me to sell but I would not; now my shares are worth a packet, and still climbing. I have it on good authority that Ballarat is still knee-deep in gold. Not like the Gympie shallows. By the way, Sergeant, you travel about a bit. I should appreciate your thoughts on this Charters Towers strike. Is it as big as they say?'

'I don't know.'

Carnegie could see that talk of shares had little meaning for a poorly paid policeman with a family, so he persisted.

'I wonder if you'd be good enough to let me know if you hear anything. A few thousand shares in a solid mine out there wouldn't go astray . . .'

Pollock finished his drink. 'If you'll excuse me, sir, I have to go. The magistrate is in town and we have to prepare for court tomorrow, but thank you for the drinks. I hope you'll be feeling better soon.'

He stood, picked up his hat and strode across the porch.

'Just one more thing . . . the keys to those bank trunks, the ones that contained the gold and the bank papers. Where were they? The locks weren't smashed.'

'I had them.' Carnegie looked at him, unconcerned. 'They were in the pocket of my jacket.'

As he said that, Carnegie's stomach lurched and he felt the bile rising. But he fought it down, not even permitting himself an obvious swallow, feeling his throat restricting as if he were being strangled. The keys. The damn keys.

'But if they'd taken them from you as you lay wounded, they'd have seen you weren't dead . . .'

Carnegie saw himself lying there in the dust. Had he been wearing his jacket? No! He wouldn't have wanted a bullet hole in his good serge jacket, where he kept his keys, attached by a chain to a buttonhole in case they fell out of the pocket. He shaded his eyes as he sucked on a cigar, hating this prig, hating his audacity, and shaking his head in kindly admonishment. 'You're quite right, Sergeant. I do believe those keys saved my life. It was a very hot morning; my jacket was hanging by the driver's seat of the coach. A quick search by those bastards would have unearthed them. God help me if they hadn't found them,' he ruminated. 'But then they had Willoughby to point them in the right direction. Haven't you caught that bastard yet?'

'No. But we'll get him.'

'I hope so. I really appreciate how much you have done for me, Sergeant Pollock. If you ever do decide to invest in those very worthwhile gold shares, keep me in mind, I shall be only too pleased to show you how to go about it. But I mustn't keep you, you've been too kind . . .'

The four weeks had come and gone. Interminable hours stretched into days and fear had Carnegie resting during the day and keeping vigil at night. Fear kept him checking and rechecking; he couldn't allow himself

122

to consider that Perry had double-crossed him, the man couldn't be that stupid. He extended his searches to the surrounds of the house, beating about the bushes with an obsession born of panic, but there was no sign of any of the gold. He kept telling himself that it was possible that Perry had misjudged the time, miscounted the days, he *was* that stupid. He was. But even so . . .

In this frontier town, drunken fights and brawls were commonplace, and unless guns were used to settle arguments, such incidents were not reported in the local newspaper, so Carnegie, who read the paper inch by inch to fill in time, had no way of knowing that his partner had already been scooped up by the law and whisked out of town. No way at all of knowing.

When despair began to overtake the former Commissioner, he paced the house restlessly, chewing his fingernails, knowing that he would have to ride out of town to that spot by the river to check for himself. To see if the gold was still there. But he procrastinated, wailing inside. What if someone saw him? Guilt had him in a vice, unable to separate a casual ride into the countryside from a very suspicious assignation with a tree. He was well enough to ride, that wasn't a problem, but dare he go? Still he waited, praying plaintively for Perry to do his part, threatening to give the man a good telling-off when he did see him. He even considered, during those long, mad hours, punishing the man by docking his pay, his share of the gold.

He worried about mistakes. He'd told Perry to weight the leather bags and dump them in the river, and hide the gold in the hessian bag in his swag. No one took any notice of the pathetic bundles carried by tramps and bushmen, even by prospectors these days. What if Perry had kept the bank bags and been investigated? No, that couldn't have happened. That would be headline news. Headlines.

All of this thinking and worrying and figuring and rehashing occupied his waking hours and demonised his sleep until it was fined down to the one common denominator. Perry was now two weeks overdue. Allyn would have to go out to that tree himself. But what if the police had already found the gold and were lying in wait by the river to trap the robbers, the murderers?

While he was thinking of the many reasons not to go, and trying to gather his courage to make the effort, another visitor came to his door. A decidedly unwelcome visitor.

Chapter Six

Mr Xiu was highborn. He travelled in style as befitting his rank. At any given time he had with him at least forty coolies, several stewards to attend to his meals and his living quarters, two bodyguards and his major domo, Chung Lee. Early to these fields, Mr Xiu had done well. He considered this exercise a good proving ground for his men, but was now preparing to move on. His astrologers and geologists in Shanghai had advised him that this state of Queensland would produce untold wealth in gold, and he had no reason to doubt them.

Chung Lee had studied his maps and recommended a route they could take to this far-off place called Charters Towers if his master, in his wisdom, decided to go north. Mr Xiu nodded; he had a good feeling about that place. It would be suitable.

An educated man, Mr Xiu was literate in English, as was, to a lesser extent, Chung Lee, who also performed secretarial duties for his master. Official forms and registrations that required attention in this country held no fears for Chung Lee; in fact he thought they were rather slack compared to the bureaucratic mazes at work in his own country, and he was able to provide smooth passage for Mr Xiu and his entourage. He found the countryside not unlike areas of China, but was astonished that it was so sparsely populated. Even with both the black men and the white men, there seemed to be hardly enough residents to stock a village in China. He and Mr Xiu often discussed this matter with interest, remarking of course on the lack of reliable water supplies, which could become a problem for future generations as the population expanded.

Every evening Chung Lee read newspapers to Mr Xiu, whatever newspapers he could find. Sometimes they were only a day or so old, but others he'd managed to scrounge from miners came not from Maryborough but from the big cities, and were weeks out of date. There were days, though, when he was not able to find a newspaper for his master, so with apologies, he reread items that had been of especial interest to Mr Xiu, and that was acceptable. Of course Mr Xiu was capable of reading them himself, Chung Lee knew that, but a gentleman of Mr Xiu's noble family could hardly be expected to dirty his hands with them, and being only a servant he regarded this nightly duty as an honour.

Mr Xiu was greatly interested in the matter of the attack by bandits on the gold shipment and the killing of the guards, though Chung Lee didn't regard the incident as of any great moment. China's bandits were far more plentiful and decidedly more bloodthirsty; it was almost a way of life to have them attack caravans of varying value. However, he read and reread the accounts dutifully, and was even asked to give his opinion of the episode, which he did by repeating comments he'd read and then, on the insistence of his master, offering a personal comment.

'A difficult situation to understand, sire. Why would the bandits leave one man alive, I might ask, when they take no pride in the ambush? When they have a desire to remain anonymous and not boast of their success in their own haunts. A few sword thrusts in all victims would have ensured secrecy.'

It was not for Chung Lee to ask if his master agreed, but his subsequent silence did leave the subject open for discussion.

'I have my own thoughts on the matter,' Mr Xiu said eventually. 'You may withdraw now. I have much to consider.'

Everyone was packing up, and to Clive it was almost a relief. He knew he could never have torn himself away from the prospect of gold without the finality of official opinion. As far as the experts could make out, Gympie had given up most of her treasure and prospectors must look elsewhere. The winners had taken their spoils and headed home, all flags flying. Other winners had returned to the fray, having roistered their new-found wealth on the finest wines money could bring to Maryborough, and high-priced women who introduced their gentlemen to the bordellos and the town jewellers.

Not that the miners complained. They'd blown the lot in Maryborough but they'd had the time of their lives doing so. No regrets. They simply joined the ranks of prospectors faced with a real endurance test, the trek to Charters Towers. Only about five hundred miles north as the crow flies. Some took ship from the port of Maryborough on to Townsville and trekked inland from there, but whichever route was chosen, the rush was on and Clive wondered if he should follow.

After Mal had left, he'd kept going alone, and had picked up a few more ounces here and there, enough to keep him in food without touching his nest egg, earned in Mal's days. In the days when Mal, his lucky mate, had been around.

But Mal wasn't so lucky these days. Where the hell was he? Clive worried about him.

He knew he ought to take his nest egg of more than four hundred pounds and go home, but where was home? London? Where his own family had fallen on hard times after his father, the Colonel, had died. He planned to send his mother half of his earnings as soon as he reached civilisation, but how far would he go in London with the rest? Clive, the eldest son, had resolutely refused to join the Guards.

'I've nothing against the military,' he told his mother with a grin, 'except for the discipline, the poor pay and the life-threatening hazards.'

As he recalled, he had also mentioned the food, but he doubted that army victuals could be any worse than the wretched fare he was forced to consume in this place. The thought of similar conditions on the Charters Towers goldfields, which were even further from civilisation, helped him make the decision to take a break in Maryborough before heading north.

Unwilling to rush off before his lease ran out, since it was bought and paid for, Clive was still picking away at the gloomy walls of his mine when a Chinaman arrived bearing a message from a Mr Xiu, who would like Mr Hillier to call on him.

'Who's he?' Clive asked.

'Our gentleman, sir. He wishes a conversation with you.'

'What about?'

'You will come?'

'Now?'

'I will guide you.'

Clive was intrigued. 'Very well. Just give me a minute to wash up and we'll see what this is about.'

Mr Xiu was obviously the boss of the Chinese outfit. Clive thought he was an evil-looking fellow, with a gaunt face and a thin black moustache that drooped like fine cords down the sides of his mouth. His dark eyes were hooded, expressionless, even when the visitor was invited to join him for tea in the shade of a canvas canopy.

The host wore a heavy skirt and a padded silk jacket, topped off by a round embroidered cap which allowed his pigtail to fall down his back. Clive thought it seemed a thicker edition of the moustache and wondered idly if they were supposed to match.

Clive didn't go much on Chinese, he thought they were a weird lot, but this was the first time he'd met one socially. He took his place in a smooth, polished chair opposite Mr Xiu, and they drank remarkably good tea, poured by a servant, but apart from the introductions, little was said.

Refusing to be impressed by this little show, Clive came to the point. 'What can I do for you, Mr Xiu?'

The Chinaman turned his gaze on him for several minutes, as if he was sizing up his visitor, before replying.

'You were the partner of Mr Willoughby?'

'Yes.'

'Are you still his partner?'

'You mean in the outlaw business?' Clive snapped. 'No, I am not. And if you are interested in the reward, look elsewhere.'

'You regard Mr Willoughby as an outlaw?'

'I do not. Others do.'

Mr Xiu nodded slowly. 'If not an outlaw, then just a criminal, perhaps?'

Clive replaced the delicate china cup. 'Listen, Mr Xiu, I don't know what you're getting at, but believe this. Mal Willoughby is no criminal. He is neither a robber nor a murderer. I don't believe he had any part in that raid.'

126

'You have proof of this?'

'Only my word. I know him, he'd never kill anyone, let alone get involved in a holdup.'

'Then it is all unfortunate. Where do you go from here, Mr Hillier?'

'Charters Towers, perhaps. I believe that field could be worthwhile.'

'Indeed, so it is said. A difficult journey ahead. I shall travel inland. You will take ship?'

'Yes. There must be a port up there somewhere.'

In deep, sonorous tones, like a clergyman from the pulpit, Mr Xiu proceeded to explain the route, and Clive was surprised by his knowledge. He heard that he should take ship to the port of Townsville, which would place him approximately four hundred miles north of the Tropic of Capricorn, that the goldfields were then about sixty miles to the southwest. He was advised to beware of the wet season on the coast and the dry season inland, of one big river that could bar his progress when the monsoonal rains brought floodwaters south. He was also advised about the climate, the terrain, until his head spun, and all the time the servant kept pouring tea into those tiny handleless cups.

Eventually Mr Xiu stood, his hands in his sleeves, the audience over.

'You will sail from Maryborough, Mr Hillier. Perhaps you will take a few days' rest and respite there after these hardships.'

'I am looking forward to that.'

'And perhaps you will find time to call on Mr Carnegie.'

'Why would I do that?'

'Why would you not? You are a gentleman, it would not be impertinent for a gentleman of his same class to make a visit. Mr Carnegie is the man who was there. He alone knows what happened on that Sunday.'

'You mean I could persuade him that he made a mistake about Mal?'

'Sometimes mistakes are not what they seem.'

Clive was astonished. 'You don't believe Carnegie? The Commissioner?'

'My humble opinions are of little note. You should draw your own. Do you wish an escort back to your tent?'

'No, thank you. No . . .' Clive had taken the hint and was on his feet too, still not sure what to make of this lordly Oriental who seemed totally out of place in this bush setting.

Mr Xiu reached down and rang a small brass bell. The sound was more that of a tiny gong, sweet and melodious, and it brought the first Chinaman from a nearby tent. He bowed to his master and, at a nod of approval, handed a sealed roll of parchment to Clive.

'What's this?' Clive asked. He was suddenly nervous, as if he'd been handed an order by a bailiff.

'It is yours, Mr Hillier,' the Chinaman said, not seeming to notice that his master was padding quietly away. 'Mr Xiu had a request to pass it to you, sir, but he is a wise and cautious lord. He thought it best to look into your heart before complying.' He bowed. 'You will excuse me.'

He too slipped away before Clive had the opportunity to ask the obvious. Their attendant was now whisking the tea things on to a black

127

lacquered tray, but Clive guessed it was no use asking him. He had the feeling that their mysterious world was now closed to him, and he was already trespassing, so he slipped the light parchment into his pocket and walked across the clearing to the track, sure that he was being watched and not prepared to give anyone the satisfaction of seeing him rip into the parchment like an eager child. Though he was just that. He was bursting to know what it contained. A gift of some sort, maybe. Or a map of that little-known northern area round Townsville, since the Chink had been so knowledgeable. He trudged down the track, past deserted campsites now being prospected by noisy crows, past the turnoff to what was jokingly known as the town centre, where officialdom and the grog shops, saloons, stores and brothels bunched together. No doubt he'd see all the same faces up there in Charters Towers.

The sunset was short and spectacular. Streaks of gold and pink lit ribbons of cloud in the western skies, in stark contrast to the ugly, ravaged countryside, littered with the greying debris of occupation by men who had come through like a plague of locusts.

It was more than a mile back to his tent. Clive lit the lamp and poured himself a couple of fingers of questionable gin before fishing out the parchment, crushing it a little to discover that the gift, whatever it was, had no substance. He grinned. Probably a collection of Chinese words of wisdom for his edification. He would have preferred a pound of that delicious tea.

Then he remembered that Mr Xiu had been requested to pass it on to him.

'What in the world?' he asked as he stared at the parchment. It was not addressed to him, in Chinese or English. There was no writing on the outside at all.

He slit the seal, staring at the parchment as another page fell out. That was empty too. It was just a blank page. Irritated, he picked up the inner page, which was much flimsier paper, and gazed at the writing in an unknown hand.

Dear Clive,
    I hope you are well and doing well. I'm real sorry about what happened. True I am. I didnt want you to think bad of me. It might be hard for you to swallow after what the papers say but I never had nothing to do with that business. Not the killings and not the robbery. I was just the bunny. Me, I should of knowed better. Real fool I am, I dont know who done it, but theres a man I have to find. He might help but its not a good bet.
    I am hoping you will do me a favour. Call on my friend Miss Emily Tisinton who lives at Lennox Road Maryborough. A governess. I told you some bit about her. She is English too but pretty miserable, dont know nobody and lonely. You see me, not much of a friend now for anyone. Bad luck eh. Hope you find Fleur again.
    Mal

128

Clive read and reread the letter, wondering how Mr Xiu had come by it, remembering that Mal had seemed to be accepted in that closed-shop community for some reason. He understood now why Xiu had been cautious. Had he found Mal's former partner no longer a friend, who could have passed this letter on to the authorities, it would never have reached him. It might even have led to harassment of the English girl by the police as a contact. From Mal's own words and the oblique remarks of the Chinaman, it became obvious to Clive that Mal really had been set up. By whom?

Xiu had suggested he visit Carnegie. The wily Chinaman had seemed to point the finger at the Commissioner. But that was stretching a long bow. The man had been wounded in the affray. And Mal hadn't mentioned Carnegie.

So where was he? Still hiding in the bush somewhere out here? Mal had never talked about himself; as Clive had told Pollock, he never said much about anything, and the only thing Clive really did know about him, he hadn't told the Sergeant.

Willoughby was a superb bushman. From the day he'd agreed to be his partner, Clive's living conditions had improved out of sight. He smiled, remembering. Mal had swept the tent and surrounds, dug a proper latrine, insisting it had to be shut down in so many days – which Clive had already forgotten – the length of the life of the fly. He could cook bread of flour and water in the coals of the campfire, a bread he called damper. Quite delicious when served with a treacle called Golden Syrup, which Clive had never heard of until then. He'd taken days off to find bush food when he could no longer stomach the turned meat on sale at the butcher's shop, and come home with fish, kangaroo meat and an astonishing collection of edible plants unknown to the average digger, even wild honey. That was something he did talk about. At length. He was amused that so many diggers regarded the bush as a desert, a place that could not provide sustainable food, relying on high-priced and almost inedible fare to be brought to the fields.

'How do you think the Abos live?' he'd asked Clive. 'They got no shops.'

Left to his own resources, after Mal left, his partner had fallen back to his old ways, eating rancid meat when he couldn't find better, stale bread covered in the now famous Golden Syrup. He'd lost weight again, and now he began worrying about his survival in those northern goldfields, north of the Tropic of Capricorn. That meant heat, much worse than this place. If only he could persuade Mal to come with him. If only Mal wasn't a wanted outlaw with a price on his head.

Suddenly a thought struck him. The man Mal had to find! Surely it wasn't Carnegie? Fear gripped him.

'Oh, Jesus, no!' Surely Mal wouldn't be crazy enough to confront Carnegie? Who was still in Maryborough, last heard. He would be mown down on the street. And Carnegie would have the right to shoot him on sight. Would he do that? Clive shuddered. If Mal stuck to the endless, isolated bush, he could survive, albeit with no future at all. Or would he take a chance and go and see the Commissioner?

Clive then realised that he really didn't know Mal Willoughby. As a friend even, he could not guess what Mal would do. For that matter, he had no idea where the lad was now. He could be anywhere in this vast country.

The next morning Clive packed up, for real this time. He rolled his few belongings into the ubiquitous swag, strapped it to his saddle, mounted his horse and set off on the road to Maryborough. He too had a man to see. And a young lady, by request.

The young lady in question was convinced she was a magnet for confusion. She saw herself as a calm being, one who preferred an ordered existence. But how was that possible when people kept disrupting her life? Things were bad enough with the difficulties of her position and the worry about Mr Willoughby and his money. Now there was another aggravation to contend with.

Mrs Manningtree had made a great show of her mourning for the late Captain Morrow, sighing and sobbing and clinging to the black garb, but suddenly she seemed more cheerful . . .

'All of a twitter,' Cook said. 'What's she up to this time?'

They were soon to find out. Apparently Captain Morrow's grieving mother was coming to Maryborough to visit his memorial site in the local cemetery. At Mrs Manningtree's instigation, his friends had contributed to a marble gravestone in the Captain's honour, and erected it in a prominent position by the gate. Out of curiosity, Emilie had gone with Nellie to view this wonder that their mistress kept talking about, and they were saddened to read the melancholy words: *Lost at Sea.*

Nellie, being a sentimental girl, even shed a few tears.

However, while she remained faithful to mourning black, Mrs Manningtree's tears vanished. She could hardly contain her excitement. She sped to the kitchen to break the latest news to her cook.

'Not only is the poor dear Captain's mother coming to town, she has accepted my invitation to stay here with us. She is a countess, you know, an aristocrat. She could hardly stay anywhere else in this town. But I must do all I can to make the poor dear as comfortable as possible.'

Listening to this, Nellie was concerned. 'What room are you going to put her in, madam? You've turned the second bedroom into your dressing room, and the kids have the other one.'

'I have it all worked out. The children's room is the most suitable; it's big and airy, and the Countess will be comfortable there. We'll take out two of the beds to give her more room. Great ladies like the Countess travel with a lot of luggage. I want that room scoured from top to toe. It'll need new curtains and a better dressing table. I saw a beautiful Indian rug at the store which will go nicely in there. And new lamps . . .'

'Excuse me, madam, where will we put the kids?'

'They can go in Miss Tissington's room.'

'It'll be a crush. It might take two more beds, but not three.'

'That's all right. Rosie can bunk in with Alice.'

'What will Miss Tissington say about this?'

'Miss Tissington is an employee. She will do as she's told. It's only a temporary arrangement.'

The children were thrilled at the prospect of being 'all in together' with their governess, finding fun in the arrangement, but Emilie was not. Apart from the inconvenience of having three beds jammed together in her room, she objected to the invasion of her privacy. Then there was Mr Willoughby's money. What if the children started fossicking about the room in her absence? What if they found it? Emilie knew there was nothing wrong with owning money, but this cash had an aura of guilt about it. She had hidden it so often in various niches of the room that days went by when she was upset that she couldn't locate it. Couldn't remember where she'd hidden it. Finding it again always brought immense relief, so it went back, for a while, in its more obvious hiding place. The trunk.

She knew it would be no use arguing with Mrs Manningtree, but she did feel she should speak up, have her say, at least. Why couldn't the woman vacate that dressing room instead? Nellie said it was only laden with clothes and boxes of junk. Apparently Mrs M. was one of those people who never threw anything out.

When the new rug arrived, ready to take the floor when the children's room was cleared out, Emilie went in search of Mrs Manningtree.

'I was wondering if there isn't any other room in which the children could sleep, madam? As their governess, I have to point out that sharing my room with the children is very inconvenient for me.'

'Pity about you, miss. A little inconvenience won't hurt you. As I told Nellie, it's only temporary.'

'How long is temporary, madam?'

'How do I know? And I certainly wouldn't dream of asking the Countess how long she is staying. She is coming all the way from Melbourne, she may stay as long as she likes. Probably a month or so. After she settles down, we have plans to introduce her to local identities and show her about the countryside. We have quite beautiful scenery here . . .'

Emilie was appalled. She had thought in terms of a couple of days. But weeks? She couldn't allow Mrs Manningtree to impose on her that long. It was ridiculous. She found herself saying something that Mr Willoughby had suggested to her. It just came out as if he was nudging her to make a stand.

'In that case, madam, I think I ought to take lodgings in the town. Let the children have my room. It's not big enough for all of us.'

Mrs Manningtree was startled. She frowned, but then it gave way to a caustic smile. 'Very well. That might be a solution.' She warmed to it. 'In fact, it's an excellent idea. I could do with a spare room again. Yes, you find lodgings and we'll work out your hours here.'

We didn't work them out, Emilie mused now. The mistress did, and very quickly. That afternoon, in fact.

Emilie's hours were weekdays eight to seven, and Saturday mornings. Since her salary had included bed and board, she would be permitted to take her meals with the children. There was to be no compensation for accommodation not required. And the arrangement would not be temporary, as Emilie had expected it to be, but permanent. She had no choice now but to find those lodgings.

Kate and Nellie were upset. 'She's throwing you out?'

'No. It was my idea.'

'But where will you go?' Kate said. 'There are no decent lodging houses in this town; they're only for miners and all sorts of fly-by-nights.'

'I'll find something,' Emilie said gamely. 'Don't worry about me. I'm perfectly capable of looking after myself.'

But was she? She was afraid now that she'd made a dreadful mistake. She couldn't blame Mr Willoughby for putting the idea into her head. He was a man, he wouldn't think of the hazards for ladies in these lodgings, if they were as bad as Kate painted them. On the Friday night, she sat nervously in her bedroom wondering what she'd let herself in for.

Paying weekly rent would be almost beyond her means if she was not careful. But then there was the money. His money. Or her money? Would he mind if she used a little of it? Emilie was sure he would not mind at all. In fact, he'd probably be pleased. But still she was uneasy. Too late to back out now, though; decisions had to be made, and right away.

She always found this town intimidating. As if she was just a small creature, like an ant, trudging its streets. Insignificant. It bore no resemblance to country towns of Emilie's acquaintance, where the pace was slow and people went about their business in mannerly fashion. Riders ambled and vehicles were careful not to cause any aggravations; unwritten rules of public behaviour were stringently observed. But here! There were no rules. Nor was there even a footpath; one took one's life in one's hands venturing into the main street, where horsemen went by at the gallop, wagons piled ridiculously high with bales of wool swayed and blundered *en route* to the wharves, and the drivers of gigs and buggies seemed to think a wide street was an invitation to speed.

There were far more men than women in the town, men who crowded outside pubs or loitered in groups, intent on their own affairs, but it didn't seem to bother the women, who strode out gaily, unconcerned, even calling to friends in loud greetings, which shocked Emilie. She had, by this, become accustomed to walking head down, gloved hands clutched together, like a nun, to avoid any untoward attention.

And that was another thing, she wrote to Ruth. No one wore gloves here, no one at all, and she wondered if she should discard hers. She was even able to tell Ruth that she had seen women riding with groups of men, riding astride their horses, wearing men's trousers and men's hats. Truly a sight to see. The children had identified them simply as 'bushies',

132

as though the practice was normal. Such a bad example.

Ruth had been horrified. Apparently her little town of Nanango was much more civilised. She advised Emilie to keep wearing her gloves and not, under any circumstances, to lower her standards, even though she had found herself in the sort of frontier wilderness that one had only ascribed to America. She begged Emilie to be very, very careful in her associations, adding that even though her employers were common, she should be thankful that she was safe in their household. Ruth had heard of governesses on outback sheep stations who'd been subjected to unmentionable advances by male family members, causing them to flee and thereby face serious financial difficulties.

As Emilie tripped quietly along the street, dodging wares stacked untidily outside shops like dusty jumble sales, she trembled at the thought of Ruth discovering who she did know, and was quite acquainted with: a real outlaw. Then, when she walked into the Bank of New South Wales, she had to dismiss Ruth from her thoughts altogether. Ruth would never understand this situation. She'd be shocked. Appalled. Furious.

Nervously Emilie approached the counter, nodding politely at the cheery teller, a bewhiskered gentleman with very red lips, and handed over the money. *His* money. Whether she was in lodgings or sharing with the children, this money had to be made safe. She glanced about her as he started counting, expecting to be arrested on the spot, but he glanced at her kindly as he flicked the notes.

'Four hundred pounds, Miss . . .'

'Tissington,' she said quickly. She couldn't bank the money in his name. The name of a wanted man. 'Emilie Tissington.'

There were no questions. No curious blink as to why a young lady should be in possession of such a large amount of money, just a reassuring nod. The bank, only a shopfront really, was hot, her face was red, burning, and her teeth chattered as she signed a form. He disappeared for a few minutes, a smelly man behind her sneezed and wheezed, the big clock on the wall took an age to move a hand, then he was back, still smiling, handing her a bankbook, looking over her head at the next customer, inviting her to move on.

There was a seat by the door, a polished seat like a church pew, and Emilie managed to get to it before her legs gave out. She balanced her serviceable black handbag on her knee, slipped the bankbook into it and took out a handkerchief to gain time. She had done it. The money was banked.

Only then did she understand what he'd said to her. That if they caught him, he'd never see that money again. The startling conversation she'd had with Mr Willoughby was only coming back to her in bits and pieces. Now she felt immeasurably sad. She realised he'd been trying to tell her that when, or if, he was captured he could expect brutal treatment and, in their turn, the captors would rob the 'robber' of anything valuable.

Emilie looked down at the shiny leather bag. Ruth had bought two at a market just before they sailed. She couldn't resist them; they were so cheap, but they looked expensive, in keeping with their new roles as elegant governesses. She thought of Mr Willoughby and his sweet, open face, without a trace of the cruelty he was being accused of. She saw his eyes again, big, blue, innocent eyes, and felt he was there with her, agreeing with her, pleased that she was being sensible. Emilie hoped she wasn't imagining this, and promised that if he ever needed the money, she would return it to him. But for now, it was she who needed it.

As she walked out of the bank into the glare of the day, Emilie had her benefactor in her heart. She knew he was fond of her, that was obvious, but now she was afflicted with a yearning to see him again, and it had nothing to do with the money. Long starved of love, Emilie yearned to take that sweet young man in her arms and comfort him, care for him. What were her troubles compared to his? Mr Willoughby was in danger of his life and she was whining about her wretched problems. It was time she stopped feeling sorry for herself.

Maybe Mr Willoughby had infected her with his good humour, with his incredible self-assurance, Emilie couldn't be certain, but now she stepped out with new resolve, no longer keeping her eyes on the sandy ground. She was no shy girl any more, but a woman, and out there was a man who loved her.

Emilie blushed at the thought. It was true. Fond was a silly word, an old-fashioned euphemism for what she'd seen in his eyes and was too shy to interpret. Emilie had found romance at last, not the heart-fluttering, bosom-clutching romance of her dreams, but a bittersweet love for a man so handsome, she'd been dreaming about him for weeks. She allowed herself to think of his Christian name, which she had been avoiding in the name of protocol. He was Mal. Her friend.

'The money in the bank is ours, not mine,' she whispered to herself as she stopped at the steps of a lodging house. 'I have to do the best I can with it. But one thing I promise you, I won't leave this town until I hear from you. It's our only point of contact. God bless and preserve you, Mal.'

A woman was standing on the steps.

'You coming or going, miss? You look as if you're in a trance.'

'No.' Emilie recovered quickly. 'I was looking for a room. Are you the landlady?'

'Sure am. But I don't take the likes of you.'

'I beg your pardon?'

'No offence, miss. But I have enough trouble with the toughs and boozers without bringing in women. Don't know what you're thinking of even asking me.'

'I'm sorry. I do need accommodation. Perhaps you could recommend a suitable place.'

'In this town?' The woman laughed. 'Have you been living under a rock? I can tell you this straight, miss, ain't no lodgings or boarding house in this neck of the woods where a girl like you would be safe in bed. Too many men here starved of women. Better you get back to where you came from.'

But Emilie had already burned her bridges at the house. She couldn't face backing down to Mrs Manningtree, asking for her room back.

'There must be somewhere,' she pleaded. 'Can't you recommend a decent place?'

The woman squeezed her face into a grimace to assist her thoughts. 'You could try the Prince of Wales Hotel. It's for toffs and new gold money. You'd be safe enough there, love, but it'd cost you.'

Emilie recoiled at the thought of living in a hotel. 'Isn't there anything else?'

The woman shook her head. 'You take my advice, love. Keep outa lodging houses. You look like a nice girl. Go on down to Mrs Mooney at the Prince, see what she can do.'

There were several problems in calling on Mrs Mooney at 'the Prince', not the least being the fear of what it might cost her to stay at a hotel. Emilie wished she hadn't been so hasty. Then there was her village upbringing. People of her class did not frequent hostelries unless in the course of travel, where there was no choice, and especially not an establishment like this. The Prince of Wales was a large, two-storeyed building, but a saloon catering to rowdies opened right on the main street. One would have to pass that even to enter.

As desperation directed her across the road towards the front door of the hotel, Emilie could almost hear her sister protesting, demanding she turn back before her reputation was ruined, but she could not. She averted her eyes from the saloon and scuttled up the front steps into a carpeted hallway.

It was surprisingly cool, and when her eyes had adjusted to the dim light, Emilie hurried along the neat hall to a door marked 'Office' and knocked timidly. There was no answer, which gave her a good excuse to flee while there was still time, but as she turned, a woman coming down the staircase further along the hall called to her.

'What can I be doing for you, miss?'

She was a robust woman, tightly corseted into a plain black dress with a white lace collar. Her face was high-coloured, wind-burned like a washerwoman's, Emilie thought, but her brown hair was carefully dressed, swept back into shiny neat rolls.

'I was hoping to see Mrs Mooney.'

'That's me.' She was a head taller than Emilie, and the voice was direct, purposeful, as if she had no time to waste.

'Oh. Mrs Mooney, I'm Miss Tissington . . .'

'Good Lord above! The governess. Violet Manningtree's governess.'

'Yes. I was wondering if you had a room. I should like to take a room.'

'For how long?'

'Oh! As a permanent guest.'

'Then I'll not be able to help you. I don't take permanents, you see.'

Emilie was already backing away. Almost relieved. 'I'm sorry, madam. Please excuse me.'

'Just a minute. What's the rush now? I thought you were live-in up there.'

'Yes, I was, but a lady is coming to visit . . .'

Mrs Mooney laughed. 'Oh, sure, so she is. The Countess! And haven't Violet and Bert Manningtree been crowing about it to all that'll listen. Are they pushing you out then?'

'No. They do need the room, so I suggested I find alternative accommodation.'

'Then you'd not be permanent?'

'Well, yes, really. I thought that it might be a nice change for me to stay elsewhere once I made the move. Find a place for myself, you see.'

Emilie hated to have to be explaining all this for no reason. She wished the woman would let her go.

'You'd still be teaching her children then?'

'Of course. They're very nice children.'

'Glad to hear it. I answered the advertisement for you girls too, but that agent fellow said you were placed. Violet had that to crow about too,' she grinned. 'Beat me to the punch, you could say.'

Emilie quaked, remembering that she and Ruth had declined to work in a hotel, this hotel, or for a Catholic family, this family. She was glad Julius Penn hadn't passed on their reasons.

'I'm sorry,' she mumbled.

'Not at all. Worked out for the best. I sent mine off to boarding school, let the nuns take care of her for a while. Can't say my Marie was too happy about it, but it's for the best.'

A noisy cheer came from the bar rooms beyond the wall, and Mrs Mooney eased Emilie towards the door.

'I have to go now, miss. Busy day, Saturday. But you come back and see me tomorrow afternoon, when all's quiet, and we'll see what can be done for you.'

Emilie wanted to protest, to tell her not to bother, but she couldn't get a word in.

'Two o'clock? We'll have a talk and you can tell me all about yourself.'

She hurried away and left Emilie standing at the door. Why couldn't the woman just have said no and left it at that, instead of complicating her life with inane chats? She sighed. Nothing for it now but to go back to the house and admit to Kate and Nellie that she hadn't met with any success yet. And the Countess only a week away. But she certainly wouldn't mention calling at this hotel, where they didn't take permanents, and making an utter fool of herself.

In all the time she had been in Maryborough, Emilie hadn't taken much interest in the town, chiefly because of the wild-looking inhabitants, but on her walks with the children she'd become somewhat braver. It was as if their presence gave her a reason to be out and about, as their guardian, and therefore made her less likely to attract attention. There were so many men in this town, and relatively few women, that on the few

136

occasions she had stepped out alone, she'd felt like an intruder into a male domain.

On this Sunday morning, though, Emilie made a conscious decision to change her attitude. To stop being such a mouse. It was laughable, she knew, to be hiding behind the children's skirts, because they had the run of the town. Except for their governess, no one seemed to mind where they roamed when they went wandering off on their own to join other children, and obviously they were quite safe. They loved to go down to the wharves to see all the ships, taking no notice at all of the throngs of poorly clad Aborigines and South Sea Islanders, the silent Chinese coolies, not to mention the gangs of white men toiling there in the heat, bare-chested and barefoot. Despite Emilie's protests, they darted in and out of warehouses and stores, running through the port bond store to hide behind the huge kegs of rum and whisky until their so-called guardian gave up and found some inconspicuous spot to wait until they were ready to reassemble and move on.

Across the road from the Manningtree House in Lennox Road, botanical gardens were being carefully nurtured, and Emilie found that very interesting, often chatting with the curator, but only little Rosie would walk there with her. The other two found it boring, and indeed, Emilie had to admit, the overgrown grounds of their own home were far more fun for children to gallop about, playing hide and seek, than the neat paths and young trees of the gardens, which were being established on land that had previously been cleared for sawpits and a boiling-down works.

Emilie stood at the gate and thought she would much rather make a visit to the quiet gardens again than head into the centre of the town, but there was no turning back now. She felt she owed it to Mr Willoughby to remain in Maryborough, at least for the time being. If she left she'd lose touch with him altogether. Apart from the money, she worried about him, about what would become of him.

'So,' she said to herself as she set off towards Sussex Street, which would take her down to busy Wharf Street, 'if you are to live here, it's time you took stock of this town instead of trailing about with the children.'

The first thing she did, stepping into the new era, was to take off her gloves and stuff them into her handbag.

Before she met with Mrs Mooney this afternoon, Emilie needed to continue her search for accommodation, so she planned to walk the streets methodically, hoping she could find a room to rent somewhere.

More than an hour later she found herself at the other end of Lennox Road, only blocks from the Manningtree house, on the outskirts of the small town, and still no further advanced. She had seen two signs in windows advertising rooms to rent, but the houses were so desperately poor-looking that she hadn't even bothered to enquire.

Tired and hot now, she took off her bonnet and ruffled out her damp hair for coolness, no longer caring that ladies of her class did not go hatless in public. As she marched up the dirt road, it occurred to Emilie that she really should stop wearing these hot stiff bonnets and invest a shilling in one of the woven straw hats she'd seen in a shop window. She could keep her ribboned boater for best. Why not? A lot of women wore them here.

There was no choice now but to see Mrs Mooney and then, tonight, ask her employer if she might stay on, sharing with the children. The thought depressed her so much that she began to have second thoughts about remaining in Maryborough. She could travel out to Nanango and visit Ruth, or go directly to Brisbane to search for another job. But how to tell Mr Willoughby of her whereabouts? She wished she could see him again. Talk to him about her dilemma. He would understand.

How could anyone possibly think that a nice young man like Mr Willoughby could actually kill people? It was all too horrible to contemplate.

The hotel seemed quiet, but as Emilie entered the front hall, she met a tide of folk leaving the dining room and had to step aside to allow them to pass. Some of them, friends of the Manningtrees, recognised her and wished her a good afternoon in friendly fashion. Emilie responded politely, heart sinking, knowing that madam would soon hear that her governess had been seen in the Prince of Wales Hotel. Then she realised that, apart from curiosity, her employers, heavy drinkers, would hardly see anything askance in her presence here.

Suddenly, Emilie found herself giggling, the first time anything had amused her in a very long time . . . No one in this topsy-turvy world would care that she'd entered a hotel . . . though her sister would! Ruth would be shocked. Come to think of it, a lot of things were happening in her world that would cause her to be more than shocked. Furious, in fact.

'There you are!' Mrs Mooney was down the hall, calling to her. 'Punctual too, Miss Tissington. I like people to be punctual, but in this town they've never heard of the word. Have you had your lunch?'

'Yes, thank you.'

'Cup of tea?'

'No thank you.'

'And how's Violet going? Has she put down the red carpet yet?'

Emilie shook her head, not knowing whether the woman was joking or not.

'She bought one, you know. True as I'm standin' here. A genuine red carpet for to welcome the Countess. What do you think of that now?'

'I really don't know, Mrs Mooney.'

'Ah, get out with you! A young lady like you'd know full well it's altogether the wrong thing, but you're too polite to say so. Well then, come along with me. I've been worryin' about you. People say she's bunged the kids into your room to make way for the Countess and that's why you're looking about for a bed.'

Trotting along the hall behind Mrs Mooney, past the staircase and into a narrow corridor, Emilie tried to damp down the blunt statement.

138

'Not exactly . . .' she began, but Mrs Mooney stopped and turned back to her.

'No need to cover up for her. Everyone knows everyone's business here, and everyone knows Violet. She's a selfish bitch. You mustn't let her get away with it.'

Emilie stiffened. 'I am in Mrs Manningtree's employ. It is her home. I have a duty to comply with her wishes or to make other arrangements that meet with her approval.'

Mrs Mooney gave a hoot of laughter. 'What a little love you are. I think my Marie has missed out on a grand teacher.'

She plunged into a large and noisy kitchen where a half-dozen women were working, practically hauling Emilie after her.

'This here's Miss Tissington,' she called to them over the racket of pots and pans and loud talk. 'She's an English governess, the real thing, so you lot mind your manners if she decides to grace our dining room one day. I'm goin' out for a while and I want you all back here for high tea by four, because we'll be busy. Four, I said, not half past, and not tomorrer. Now get on with it, and you girls set those tables right, not forgettin' the cake stands.'

They all nodded, grinning, obviously not fazed by the imperious tone, and their two visitors swept past, out the back door to a wide veranda packed with crates, spare chairs, empty butterboxes and bins of sweating vegetables.

'I've got something to show you,' Mrs Mooney said as they descended the back steps to where an old blackfellow was waiting with a pony and trap.

'You want me to drive, missus?' he asked.

'No thanks, Toby. Only room for two of us, and I'm taking this missy with me.'

Before she knew it, Emilie was sitting up beside Mrs Mooney and the neat trap was spinning steadily from the hotel yard into a back lane, then out and around to Kent Street. They left the main streets behind as they turned down a narrow lane that seemed to follow the winding course of the river, past paddocks yellowing with maize, and all the while Mrs Mooney was telling her about her late husband, and how he loved to go fishing along here.

They turned a corner, passing a quite splendid two-storeyed house, far more attractive than any Emilie had seen in the town. It was even painted, she noted with a wry smile.

'Who lives there?' she asked, intrigued.

'Paul Dressler. He's on the town council. Came here on his uppers with a party of Germans brought in by Pop Hamburger to help populate the district. Funny story there. They'd been expecting a shipload of immigrants from the old countries and there'd been great excitement in the town, farmers, sugar planters, loggers, graziers, all turning out with the councillors and locals to welcome them. They even lined up a brass band. This was a big occasion. After all, they were expecting eighty from the British Isles and ten from Germany, with their families if they had any. So the ship comes round the bend and hauls into the wharf, and the band's playing and everyone's wavin' like it's St Patrick's Day in Dublin, and down trot ten German blokes, all smiles and grins – well, wouldn't they? – never speaking a word of English.

'But everyone's lookin' past them. Like, where's the rest? Turned out all the rest, fed up with a voyage that long . . . you and me both, we know all about that . . . well, anyway, they took one look at Brisbane and decided that was as far as they go. They all decamped the ship and bad luck, Maryborough missed out.

'And then you should have seen Hamburger's face! Talk about the cat that swallowed the canary! In between shaking hands with *his* immigrants, the good old Germans having stuck by their promise, he laughed his head off.

'Dressler went logging for a while, here and over on Fraser Island, across the bay . . . they raft the timber from there and up river to our saw mills. Your boss, Bert Manningtree, says he gets his best timber from there, blackbutt and kauri. But Dressler was really a shipwright by trade. He started with a small repair dock down by the wharves, opened a chandlery as well, then went into ship building himself. Never looked back. Still making a mint . . . but here we are.'

The property at the rear of the Dressler house met the river, so they came to a dead end down this sandy lane, confronted by thick bush.

'Where?' Emilie had to ask as they climbed down and Mrs Mooney secured the pony.

'Over here,' she said. 'See this gate? Dressler owns all this land except for a quarter-acre down the bottom, on the riverfront. It was my Paddy's favourite fishing spot and he was real put out when Dressler bought the whole forty acres round here, but Paul's not a bad bloke. He tossed Paddy for this patch and Paddy won.'

She opened the gate and they walked down a short, overgrown path to the rear of a small – unpainted – bungalow.

'Paddy used to call this his fishing lodge,' she laughed. 'Back to front, isn't it?'

'It seems so,' Emilie admitted.

'That's because he wanted his little veranda on the front, overlooking the river, see.' She unlocked the door and they walked into a tiny two-roomed house, but Emilie hardly noticed the interior, because there were tall windows across the front that led the eye over the mangroves to the river.

'Oh,' she said, surprised. 'It's a lovely view, isn't it?'

'The best you'll get round here. The house isn't that bad either. I never come here any more, too busy, but I have the maids keep it nice.'

Emilie looked about her. The floorboards were unpolished but softened by large, attractive rugs.

'Them rugs are Indian.' Mrs Mooney smiled sadly. 'Keep in mind that my Paddy, God rest his soul, furnished this place himself with bits and pieces he picked up . . .'

Emilie saw the pain in her eyes as she spoke of her late husband, and found herself envying the woman that experience, of an enduring love, especially since she seemed doomed to the life of an old maid, living in the back room of her employer's house with no chance of a social life.

But Mrs Mooney was explaining. 'He put in the necessities, table and chairs, a comfy sofa, and a good bed inside there. But he wouldn't have curtains. You ever heard such a thing? Said they would spoil the view.'

'They would rather,' Emilie said, and Mrs Mooney beamed.

'You think so?'

She opened two doors wide enough for them to step out on to the veranda, where several worn canvas chairs were splayed lazily in the sun. 'Now isn't this just lovely?'

'It is, Mrs Mooney. Very restful indeed.' A rugged path led downhill to the water's edge, where a muddy bank indicated that the mangroves had been cleared away to allow direct access to the river and a small jetty.

Paddy's fishing lodge was truly a lovely spot, with the ruddy afternoon glow on the river and the acclaim of rainbow lorikeets hustling in nearby trees, and Emilie began to wonder how far she was from town. From the Manningtrees' house in Lennox Road. She'd become turned about down these lanes.

'The kitchen's off to the side there,' Mrs Mooney said. 'By the water tank.'

Deep in thought, Emilie studied the steep incline to the river.

'I was thinking of renting this place until I sell it.' Mrs Mooney offered.

'And that's why you brought me here?'

'Just wanted you to see it. Think about it. No obligation at all.'

'Where are we, Mrs Mooney?'

'Not too far from town. Are you a walker?'

'Back home we walked a lot. I don't do much any more. Just into town and back with the children. We had a lovely Sunday walk, nine miles it was, over the fields and back through the forest . . .'

'Good God alive, nine miles here would take you into the bush and we'd never see you again. From the back door here, on the front what's supposed to be, you cut up through the Dressler place, past the house on the other side on to the lane, and across to the park, and thence to Lennox Road.'

'Is that all?'

'Well, I brought you from Kent Street down along the river so you'd get your bearings, but I think I must have mixed you up.'

Emilie laughed. 'You certainly did. I thought I was miles away.'

'Then I'll take you back that way so you can see.'

As they left the house, Mrs Mooney locked the door and looked wistfully about her, as if she was seeing this scene for the last time. Emilie felt sorry for her.

'Are you really too busy to come here, Mrs Mooney, or does it have too many sad memories?'

The Irishwoman nodded. 'It's that and all. We'd come here, Paddy and me, to get away from all the yabber and the carryin'-on in the pub. Your life's not your own in a pub, you know; no matter how grand you think it is, there's always somethin' day and night. He'd go fishin' and I'd come down later, and nights we could sit out here in the quiet and be us. Just Paddy and me and our thoughts and our memories, and we'd talk about the folks back home . . .' She sighed, and summoned herself back to the present. 'That's all gone now. I'm busy, doin' the work of two to keep the hotel going and up to standard, so it's time to let go. I was thinking about you, and how maybe you'd like to see the place.'

'And rent it?'

'Up to you, Miss Tissington. It was just a thought. I know you're accustomed to grander living . . .'

Emilie took the older woman's arm as they walked to the gate. 'I would love to have a place of my own. It is very difficult for me to live in another person's house. The more I think about it, Mrs Mooney, the more I realise I am not cut out to be a live-in governess, although my sister would disagree with me. She copes very well, but I feel imprisoned.' Suddenly Emilie heard herself pouring her heart out to a woman she hardly knew. They had reached the gate, and the pony and trap were in sight, but Mrs Mooney made no attempt to open it. She simply stood quietly and listened.

'This is no reflection on Mrs Manningtree,' Emilie explained. 'It's just that when my mother died and my stepmother moved in, I had the same feeling. It was as if I didn't belong anywhere any more. I don't suppose I have any reason to complain . . .'

'Not a matter of complaining,' Mrs Mooney said firmly. 'Nothin' to do with it. Your trouble is you've lost control. I can see it in your eyes. You're an intelligent girl with a downtrodden look about you if ever I saw it. Apologisin' for living. You been through some bad times, have you?'

Emilie nodded, thinking of their misery in London. The damp room, the cold and the hunger while they tried to preserve a brave front.

'Well, all I can say is, face the world a bit harder, girl. I know you've been brought up different from me, with the hard knocks comin' later – we suffered as kids, what with we had little schoolin' – but it all works out the same. You have to stand your ground. Growing up, the hard school calls it.'

She pushed open the gate and looked back. 'So the question is here. Now that you've seen the place. I've been wonderin' if you'd like to rent it, until I sell. No obligation. I wouldn't be hurt if you decline, or you're too nervous to be living alone. Not that there's anything to worry about. The Dresslers are just up the hill . . .'

Mrs Mooney didn't realise that the only thing holding Emilie back from this wonderful opportunity to have a place of her own was the ever-present worry of respectability. She was afraid that a single girl living alone might cause talk, and it took an effort on her part to mention this, because she was also afraid of offending Mrs Mooney.

'Respectable?' boomed the Irishwoman. 'I wouldn't have offered you

142

the house, my girl, if I'd thought to damage your reputation. In these towns it's a case of take what you can get. People understand that. Propriety has its place, but survival comes first. You don't know much about the bush, do you?'

'No,' Emilie said meekly.

'Do you good to see how women live out there, and not too far from here. But for now, you set your own standard . . .'

'So you think it would be all right?'

'I do. But you make your own decision. If it doesn't sit well with you . . .'

Emilie took a deep breath. 'I'd be very happy to live here, Mrs Mooney.'

'Well then, we've had a successful afternoon, have we not? We'll go back to the hotel and have a cup of tea.'

Emilie almost ran up the drive, eager to tell Kate her news, but she'd hardly stepped into the kitchen before Kate had a question for her: 'You been down at the Prince of Wales Hotel?'

'Yes. How did you know?'

'The missus heard it from one of her pals. Got her rattled. She was in here asking us what you were doing there, and I said I dunno. She thinks you was looking for a job there.'

'What job? Mrs Mooney's daughter is at boarding school.'

'She knows that but she reckons she beat Molly Mooney to getting you as her governess, and Molly might be trying to get you just the same, and bring Marie home . . .'

'What nonsense. I only went there looking for a room.'

'Cost you a pretty penny to stay there!'

'I know, I didn't understand the hotel arrangements.'

Kate put a hand on her hip and laughed. 'Anyway, you got the missus rattled. She don't want to lose you to Molly. So she come back in here a little while ago and left you that envelope on the bench.' The cook gave Emilie a hearty slap on the back. 'I reckon you got some pay at long last!'

The governess would have preferred to open the envelope in private, but Kate, still crowing her delight, waited expectantly.

Emilie found eleven pounds and fifteen shillings in the envelope, and presumed it was part of her annual salary, less the five shillings advance, since her employer had not had the grace to enclose an explanation.

'Heavens above,' she smiled. 'It never rains but it pours.'

'Whaddya mean?'

Emilie recovered quickly, cross with herself for almost referring to Mr Willoughby's money. Mal's money.

'I mean I found somewhere to stay. A house. I'll tell you about it shortly. I must change for tea.'

Chapter Seven

Jollied along by the company of Mrs Stanfield senior, whom she found a charming and cultivated person, Ruth was feeling so much better now. Her appetite had returned, she was enjoying her walks and was in excellent spirits. Time to return to work; the girls had been permitted a holiday all these weeks, and there was a lot of catching-up to do.

Duly, then, Ruth presented herself to Mrs Stanfield, though still unable to address her as Leonie, to inform her she was ready to begin lessons again.

'Oh, Miss Tissington, I'm so glad you're better. We were very worried about you, that fever is so hard to shake. But you've come through with flying colours.'

'I'm grateful to you, Mrs Stanfield, and can only apologise for being such a burden but the enforced rest did give me time to consider our curriculum. I'm full of new plans for the classroom and eager to begin lessons again.'

'Ah, yes. I wanted to talk to you about that.'

'Good. I think the girls could profit by instruction in Greek and Latin roots, to assist their spelling and understanding of the meaning of words. I could list them but textbooks would be far more beneficial. They're only small books and I should appreciate it if you could send for them. Then the girls would always have them. The printed word, you know . . . they'd carry more weight than my . . .'

'Excuse me, Ruth, just a moment. I did say I wanted to speak to you about the girls' education. I've been waiting until you were quite well to discuss this with you.'

'By all means. What do you have in mind?'

Mrs Stanfield appeared nervous. 'Come into the parlour, Ruth, we can't talk out here in the hall.'

The governess was pleased. They did need to talk about Jane and Jessie's education. It was long overdue. Mrs Stanfield had to be told that for their ages, the girls were not up to standard. They would have to settle down to really hard work from now on. No more excuses.

When they were seated, Mrs Stanfield took a deep breath. 'Ruth, I have to tell you how impressed we all are with you. Jack's mother says we were so fortunate to have a person of your qualifications come all the way out here . . .'

Ruth preened. 'Thank you.'

'But it is just not working.'

'I beg your pardon?' Ruth stiffened.

'To cut a long story short, Ruth, we have decided to send the girls to boarding school. You've tried hard, I've tried to help you pull them into line, God knows they need it, but they're not co-operating. In a boarding school . . .'

Ruth interrupted her. 'Am I to understand that you no longer require my services, Mrs Stanfield?'

'Ruth, you must see that they need the discipline. We were embarrassed when Jack's mother referred to them as brats . . .'

'That's not my fault.'

'Of course not. But don't you see . . .'

'When would you like me to leave?'

'Oh, Ruth, there's no hurry. We'll provide you with excellent references and a bonus as well as your salary . . .'

'I am not in need of charity.'

'We don't regard such things as charity, Ruth. Only recognition of your dedicated work. One day Jessie and Jane will come to regret the loss of a teacher like you.'

'I doubt it, Mrs Stanfield. Now, if you'll excuse me, I shall pack. I will be ready to leave in the morning.'

'You're welcome to stay here until you find another position.'

'I told you, I don't take charity. I shall be returning to Brisbane at the earliest opportunity. Now . . . if you would excuse me . . .'

With as much dignity as she could muster, since her head was reeling and she felt weak again, Ruth stormed away to her room. She had been dismissed! She would not allow, would not admit, even to herself, that the Stanfields might have made the right decision, that she was not the right teacher for their stupid daughters. She blamed them for not giving her the support she needed to control the wretches. To make them work. The humiliations of her poverty in London paled in comparison to this affront. How dare these colonial upstarts, country bumpkins, dismiss her? And send her pupils off to some half-baked boarding school . . . she hadn't bothered to enquire which one . . . run by women with barely a decent education among them.

Within two days the governess had left Lindsay Station with hardly a backward glance, despite entreaties to stay awhile. She was Brisbane bound, only because she couldn't think of anywhere else to go. How she envied Emilie, so well settled with the Manningtree family in that northern town, teaching three delightful children. But she must not worry Emilie. It was just a matter of stiffening one's resolve. She'd find another situation. At least she had local references as well now. That was something.

Mrs Medlow was surprised to see the elder Miss Tissington back on her doorstep, but there was no explanation. The young lady, as reserved as ever, took a single room at the back of the house, making it plain that she preferred to dine alone. She did not wish to share a table with other guests.

★ ★ ★

Superintendent Jasper Kemp and his wife had moved out of the Belleview. Not that Ruth would have noticed. Mrs Kemp was delighted with the new house on Wickham Terrace, their 'residence', she called it, and she was now very busy establishing their status on the social scene.

Jasper, though, was wondering if he had bitten off more than he could chew. Though the politicians talked grandly about law and order being a priority in the new state of Queensland, to impress the voters and muffle the press clamour, the gentlemen on the Treasury benches were tardy in approving much-needed funds to support a reliable police force. It hadn't taken long at his desk for Jasper to grasp the enormity of his task, and to realise that the Premier could pour all of the contents of his state coffers into a law-and-order programme here and it would hardly make a dent.

Until he'd come face to face with the problem, Jasper hadn't grasped the sheer size of this state. It was a thousand miles from the capital, Brisbane, to the little settlement of Somerset up on Cape York, most of the territory unexplored. No wonder bushrangers were running wild. They were a minor problem for Jasper, though.

'How the hell can I organise the force when towns are being overrun by gold prospectors and immigrants? It's difficult to pin down the true extent of the permanent population in these places.'

Daniel Bowles, the Attorney-General's secretary, sympathised with him.

'I quite understand, sir. My Minister is being plagued by demands from graziers out west and in the north to send troops to defend them against attacks by tribes of Aborigines, and this at a time when we're trying to phase out troopers and replace them with policemen.'

'Defend them?' Kemp muttered. 'From what I've read, there's a range war going on out there. No quarter given on either side. Why can't they have a pow-wow with the blacks? Sit down and call a truce?'

Daniel shifted uneasily in his seat. This wasn't why Mr Lilley had sent him. He had an important message to deliver. Daniel was a pragmatist. He figured the matters Mr Kemp was complaining about would sort themselves out in time. If people wanted to go to these outlandish places and get themselves robbed or killed, they only had themselves to blame. They shouldn't come crying to the government for help.

'Ask your Minister this,' Kemp said. 'If the government is phasing out troopers, the military, from civilian duties, then why can't those funds be transferred to the police budget?'

Daniel smirked. 'You don't understand, Superintendent. The government simply can't afford to support a military presence. There are no longer provisions in the budget for anything more than a token military corps and, of course, our navy.'

'Our what?' Kemp exploded.

'Our navy, sir. We have an immense coastline. It has to be defended. Our Premier has already commissioned two ships, and there'll be more to come. It's quite a feather in our caps, don't you think?'

146

'Poppycock! Who's going to attack us, for God's sake? Mars?'

'We, in the House, look at the matter in a global sense.'

'I see. In the meantime there are no funds available for even the most basic management of crime in our towns. The crime rate in Brisbane alone is alarming.'

'Only in the poorer suburbs, Mr Kemp. The papers make far too much of it. If I may, I would like to turn to a matter that does have Mr Lilley greatly concerned.'

'A matter? I should have thought he'd find a dozen off the top of his head without scratching it.'

'Yes, of course.' Daniel thought of this man as a jumped-up police sergeant, quite the wrong person for Mr Lilley to have appointed. There were any amount of gentlemen in Brisbane who could have handled the post without making waves. Kemp simply did not understand the political situation. To stay in office, the government had to appease the right people, and that meant moneyed people who were demanding better port facilities, better and safer roads, better hospitals and all the necessary accoutrements that came from turning towns into cities. And yes, the status of a state navy. Daniel was very much in favour of Queensland having its own navy in the British tradition. He even saw himself as the Secretary of the Navy one day.

He had shuffled Kemp's impetuous reports into oblivion, providing Mr Lilley with his own version of the contents, which irritated his Minister and made no impact on the budget. Few people realised, Daniel often mused, just how much power a civil servant could wield without even raising his voice.

Kemp's complaints and propositions were endless.

'If the government is dispersing trained troopers, putting them out of work, when unemployment is a huge problem here anyway, why can't they be transferred into the police force? They already understand discipline. They could be a great help to me.'

'Dear me. British military men are highly regarded. Most will be heading home or for India, they'd hardly stoop to . . .'

'I didn't ask for your opinion, Mr Bowles. I ask that your Minister give credence to the suggestion. There could be fellows, even officers, who might appreciate the opportunity to remain in this country.'

Another request that will find its way into the archives, Daniel smiled.

'As you wish, Superintendent. Now for the matter in hand. My Minister – and, I have to say, a great many of his supporters – is outraged by the murders and gold robbery that occurred in the vicinity of the port of Maryborough. The robbery, as you know, did not gain the outlaws too much, not in comparison with the amounts stolen from bigger goldfields than this Gympie place, but word is out now that the Charters Towers fields will have a massive gold output. There is already an indication that this rush will put Ballarat in the shade. Even South Africa. Syndicates comprised of some of the most powerful gentlemen in the country are already being registered. They have to know that the gold being transported from that place will be safe.'

147

'I see,' Kemp said, glowering.

'So, the Minister wants something done about that robbery.'

'Not about the murders, just the robbery?'

'Well, them too. Of course.'

'I am conversant with that raid. The Sergeant in charge of that investigation, Pollock is his name, is, as far as I can see, a capable man.' He frowned at Bowles. 'One of the few I have at my disposal until such time as I am able to train more men. When the funds are available.'

'Well, he might be, but my Minister is concerned that he is not making any progress on this heinous crime. He allowed one of the outlaws to escape and nothing has been heard of him since, or of his associates, or of the missing gold. The matter has become an embarrassment to the government, and of great concern to the aforementioned syndicates. We need investors, not only from this country, but from overseas. They will not invest if they are led to believe that we are overrun by bandits. That a situation has arisen wherein we cannot guarantee that the gold will reach civilisation safely.'

'Are you quite finished, Mr Bowles?'

'I was simply trying to explain the situation to you, sir.'

'As you say. But I do not need your intelligence. I am quite aware of the situation you refer to, and of the overstated implications. It has been my experience, in dealing with southern goldfields, that investors can't plunge their cash fast enough into viable gold mines in this country. They'd invest in a field in the bottom of the ocean if the gold was there, regardless of how it was to be transported to safety. Knowing full well that the gold had already been sold to banks that are on the field for that very purpose. Don't tell your grandma how to suck eggs, Mr Bowles. The loser here is the government. But I work for that government and it is my job to put a stop to these holdups. I'm endeavouring to do just that.'

Daniel was not perturbed; nothing that this policeman said could have any impact on a man who worked from the seat of power itself.

'I am sure you are, Superintendent. But these outlaws have to be apprehended. As an example. To show that the government is very serious in its programme to stamp out bushranging, and what better example could it have than in this incident? It has gained a great deal of press.'

'Thank you, Mr Bowles.' Kemp was dismissing him, ungraciously, Daniel thought, already turning back to his files. 'Please tell your Minister that I appreciate his interest.'

'I shall do so, Superintendent. Mr Lilley will be pleased, because Cabinet has decided that it would be efficacious to be able to inform the newspapers that you are taking charge of the investigation yourself.'

Kemp nodded. 'Fair enough. I'll be keeping a weather eye on it.'

'No. They want more action than that. It is requested that you go to Maryborough and take charge. That way the government can be seen to be regarding the matter as of the most serious moment.'

Daniel stood, facing Kemp across his rather mean little desk, not half as large or as imposing as Daniel's own, back at Parliament House.

'You are to go right away, sir,' he pronounced, and departed with a flourish.

Now that he was mixing in such illustrious circles – the Premier had actually referred to him by his Christian name yesterday – Daniel decided he needed a more salubrious address. Boarding with the Timmons family had suited him while he was just a clerk in the Public Service, but since his elevation to secretary to a Minister of State, it simply wouldn't do.

Unfortunately, and foolishly, as he now realised, he'd been involved in a rather passionate affair with the Timmonses' daughter, Joan and there was every indication that the family expected an engagement to be announced, which was another reason for him to make an exit from their clutches as soon as possible. Joan had been a convenience, that was all, a pretty girl, buxom and willing. And it was that very willingness, he told himself, as he prepared to disappear into the sunset, that branded the girl a slut. Not a fit person to be married to a gentleman of his calibre. Daniel was ambitious. He was fast learning about the political scene. One day he could even become a Member of the Parliament himself. And in that world there was no place for the likes of Joan Timmons.

He planned his departure very carefully, announcing that shortly he would be travelling interstate with his Minister on House business, knowing that Parliamentary affairs were a great mystery to these impressionable people. He paid his rent to the last day. On the eve of his departure, he stayed out late, hoping to dodge the girl, but she came knocking at his door, regardless of the hour.

Daniel, feigning sleep, let her knock, knowing she wouldn't make too much noise for fear of waking her parents, and in the morning it was easier to let her smooth his hair in the hall and brush his new brown suit and straighten his bow tie, while exchanging sweet nothings. He promised to write to her. To come 'home' as soon as possible, and accepted her parting gift of cheap cuff links with a peck on her cheek.

Then he was gone from the dreary house next door to the smelly butcher's shop, and heading across town. He had heard that Kemp and his wife had been staying at the Belleview Boarding House over near the botanic gardens, on the right side of town, and had decided that if it was good enough for the Superintendent of Police, it was good enough for him. One needed the right address to meet the right people and get on in life.

Mr Bowles arrived in time for dinner, and since the dining room was crowded, he was placed with a Miss Tissington, who, it was plain to see, did not appreciate the intrusion, but she was a well-mannered young lady and accepted his presence with a regal nod and a 'Good evening, Mr Bowles.'

He studied her over the soup and liked what he saw, guessing she was in her mid-twenties, and English. She had light-brown hair and a pleasant, slim face; she was slim all over, in fact. Her clothes, though plain, were well cut, reminding him that his brown suit, compared with her navy-blue outfit, was pathetic, ill-fitting, sloppy. He would have to remedy that if he was to move in the right circles. Miss Tissington's hands, he noted, were beautifully manicured; in fact, everything about her was immaculate, even to the fine pleats in her white silk blouse. And she wore no rings. Daniel decided he'd have to get to know this lady; she could be an asset.

The lady, though, was reserved. She had nothing to say, so Daniel took his lead from the politicians he'd seen in action. Smile. Talk. Flatter. And above all, be self-deprecating.

'I hope you'll forgive me,' he began. 'Nothing worse than having a stranger dumped on one when all one asks is to be able to enjoy a meal in peace.'

Her response was predictable. 'That's quite all right.'

But her voice was so English, so cultivated, it made his toes tingle, and almost intimidated him. He heard himself trying to round out his own vowels so as not to appear too much of a yokel in her company.

The waitress was slow bringing the main course, so Daniel grasped the moment.

'How very good of you to say so. I wish my Minister could be so tolerant.'

She gazed at him, unblinking, and Daniel noticed that too, realising that it was the secret to her regal attitude. The unblinking gaze, obviously natural to her, was quite a trick. It sort of pinned one to her attention. He was busting with curiosity about her.

'Your Minister?' she asked, head high, hands neatly placed in her lap.

He almost grinned. That had caught her attention.

'Oh, dear me, yes. My Minister, the Honourable Charles Lilley, is Attorney-General of the state of Queensland. I hope I didn't give you the wrong impression. For a minute there it sounded like a minister of religion. I'm so sorry if I embarrassed you. Religion can be such a controversial subject these days.'

'You didn't embarrass me, Mr Bowles. I'm at a loss to understand the connection.'

'Of course. Forgive me again. I'm just a small cog in the great wheel of government. I'm private secretary to Mr Lilley. My Minister, you see. We all refer to them like that.'

'Really? How interesting.'

Mr Bowles and Miss Tissington became friends. They were both hugely impressed with each other. Daniel learned that she was a governess with the highest credentials. He was amazed that she spoke French fluently, and, as he told her, wildly jealous that she'd been able to perfect her accent by spending several months, at the age of sixteen, in Paris, a city he'd longed to visit.

Although until now, the very idea was beyond his scope.

While she waited for a suitable appointment, and worried about the lack of opportunities, Mr Bowles took her on a tour of Parliament House, and even to an afternoon tea party on the lawns in front of the House. A very gracious occasion, for which Ruth felt it necessary to invest in a lovely afternoon gown of white muslin with a pleated bodice and trailing flounced skirt. Quite the frothiest dress she'd ever owned, but matched with a large straw hat that she'd overstitched with folds of muslin and some artificial yellow roses, she felt she looked the part. Even Mrs Medlow was impressed at the transformation of the governess into a fashion plate, as she and Mr Bowles walked out together.

While she'd never admit it in her weekly letters to her sister, Ruth was quite impressed to receive such a compliment from Mrs Medlow that day, but she still kept her at arm's length. Ruth was not interested in any of these people except for Mr Bowles. He was gentlemanly, pleasant, though obviously of the lower middle class, or worse, she was wont to worry at times, but he had the makings, as she often reminded herself. And he took no offence at corrections. Here was a man, only five years older than herself, who needed, wanted, to learn how to better himself. And who more suitable to help him than his friend, the English governess?

She corrected his accent, his grammar, his choice of clothes, his table manners . . . there was no end to it . . . and Daniel, as she now knew him, pressed her to keep at it. Miss Tissington had found an appreciative pupil. She even taught him enough French to recognise menus in restaurants where French dishes were all the rage. Not that she went with him to those places, where he was at the beck and call of his Minister, but it was interesting to hear of these eminent people and their associates. And astonishing, Ruth pondered without comment, that such highly placed gentlemen should mix so readily with common people, as was the case in this town. She was not sure that she approved.

There was no romance between Mr Bowles and herself, more a measure of mutual usefulness, and respect, of course, she allowed. After her dismissal – she would accept no other interpretation – the company of Mr Bowles had contributed somewhat towards easing the hurt, and in her own way Ruth was grateful. However, he did not seem to understand, or care, that it was essential for her to find a new position as soon as possible. Admittedly he was a busy man, but she had hoped that since he did move in moneyed circles he might be able to help with a word in the right place. When this didn't eventuate, Ruth resumed her daily visits to the office of Julius Penn, but nothing had changed there. He kept assuring her he would find her a place any day, irritating her with empty promises, until on one of those days she arrived to find the office closed.

Bewildered, Ruth hurried to the little café on the corner to enquire as to Mr Penn's whereabouts, only to be told that his landlord was also seeking him. The agent had disappeared owing six weeks' rent.

At dinner that night, Mr Bowles did eventually notice that Miss Tissington was quieter than usual.

'Is anything wrong?'

'My agent has disappeared without a word. Simply closed his office and left.'

151

'Oh well, you said he wasn't any good anyway.'

'That's not the point. I shall be forced to advertise again now.'

'Something will turn up,' he said, digging into his sausages and mash.

'And in the meantime I'm supposed to live on air,' she retorted angrily.

He sat back and looked at her. 'Why? Are you short of money?'

Ruth could not bring herself to admit that the payout she'd received from the Stanfields was fast dwindling, and as yet she hadn't repaid one penny of the loan from the Society in London.

'Are you so wealthy you can afford to live without your salary?' she snapped.

'No, Ruth, definitely not,' he replied, and they lapsed into a moody silence.

Eventually, though, he did have some advice.

'You are immigrants, you and your sister. Have you applied for your Land Grant?'

'I beg your pardon? What would that be, Mr Bowles?'

'Good Lord, you're wasting your opportunities. Immigrants who have paid their own passage to this country are entitled to a grant of twenty acres of land. I presume you were not recipients of free passage paid by the government?'

'No, we were not,' she replied, quaking a little, reasoning that assisted passage by other means would not disqualify them.

'Well then, you may select forty acres of land between you.'

'And we would own that land?'

'Exactly.'

'But we're not farmers. What would two ladies do with such an outrageous amount of land?' Forty acres was almost beyond Ruth's comprehension.

'You could always sell it.'

'Good gracious! Is that legal?'

'Of course it is. The state doesn't have much capital but it does have a massive oversupply of land. The grant is a carrot to entice immigrants, since we're seriously underpopulated. Some take up farming, others sell. It's as simple as that. I'll get the papers for you.'

'You'd do that for me?'

'It's no trouble.'

'Oh, Mr Bowles, I'd be most grateful.'

That night Ruth sat down to write to Emilie to tell her of this sudden good fortune. Some weeks back she'd been forced to tell her sister that she had returned to Brisbane, to the Belleview, because the wretched Stanfield children were being packed off to boarding school, but she was in good spirits and in possession of excellent local references, which would make more of an impression than the Society references. She'd been well paid for her time at Lindsay Station, so there was no occasion for concern.

She was now able to admit to Emilie that so far she had not been able to find a new position, since the ubiquitous Julius Penn had run off, but prospects were good. Also that she had met a gentleman, Mr Bowles, about five years her senior, who was secretary to the Attorney-General, no less, and who had kindly offered to make all the arrangements about the land. She had ascertained from Mr Bowles that if they chose well, there was every chance it could be sold for almost two pounds an acre, and she hoped that Emilie would be amenable to the sale, so that they could share the proceeds.

Their letters crossed. Two days after Ruth had posted hers, Emilie advised her sister of her new abode, that she was now living in a dear little cottage on a small property in Ferny Lane. She went into raptures about the house before enlightening Ruth as to the reason for leaving the Manningtree household.

Ruth disapproved. She was appalled that her young sister should be living alone in a wild town like that. What could she be thinking of? Even if she did have to share her room with the children temporarily, she had her reputation to think of, and she ought to return to her employers' home immediately.

This she wrote in a long, angry letter, and rushed around to the post office to mail it right away.

For her part, Emilie was delighted to hear about the land but cautious about selling. From the talk she'd heard, land values in this country increased at an alarming rate, since so many thousands of immigrants were arriving by the boatload. She herself had seen them disembarking at the Maryborough wharves, and so it stood to reason that even more would be landing in Brisbane.

However, if Ruth needed money to tide her over, she wrote that she'd be only too pleased to send some, since she'd been able to save quite a bit.

This last line had Emilie nervous. She had plenty of money but it really belonged to Mr Willoughby, although he had said, quite decisively, that it was hers. At a pinch, she was sure that he wouldn't mind if she used some to assist her sister.

But she couldn't possibly tell Ruth anything about that. This was a very awkward situation.

The Countess was a sprightly woman with an angular face and shoulder-length grey hair which she never bothered to pin up, or even tie back with a ribbon. It was simply allowed to blow free like a wiry cloud about her face. In some ways it seemed to Emilie that the wild hair gave a true indication of the woman herself, right from the start, because her clothes were plain, devoid of fripperies, and her step was firm.

Because of this, Emilie wondered how on earth she could put up with Mrs Manningtree, whose affectations were an embarrassment, but the guest seemed not to notice.

During the first week of her visit, the household was placed in mourning as the memorial service for Captain Morrow came and went, and his mother, naturally, was very quiet. But then she announced that she liked to ride and wished to see more of the countryside now that she had journeyed to this far port.

Since her hostess did not ride, several of Captain Morrow's friends volunteered to escort the lady, and it was then that everyone realised that the Countess loved adventure. After exploring the town, she expressed a wish to visit the goldfields, and an expedition was arranged. She was gone for days that time, with Mrs Manningtree left home fuming, though pretending to be happy with these arrangements. When she returned from Gympie, she retired early each night and steadfastly refused to allow her hostess to go to the trouble of arranging soirées and dinner parties for her.

'I wouldn't dream of inconveniencing you, my dear. It's so kind of you to allow me to stay in your lovely home.'

Then she was off on another jaunt with her trusty companions, who were delighted that she thoroughly enjoyed camping out in the bush on their travels.

Emilie didn't see much of her, and nor, for that matter, did Mrs Manningtree, but during these weeks Emilie too was enjoying her living-out situation. Walking to the house early in the mornings was good exercise and a great pleasure, only exceeded by the joy of returning to her own little house of an evening. She'd even had the children stay overnight with her one Saturday, and that, to them, was a great adventure. All in all, the Countess's visit was turning out to be a great success for everyone but the hostess. Her husband didn't even mind. He was busy at his mills and relieved that the Countess was such an easy-going guest.

By the time the Countess eventually departed, nothing was said about Emilie returning to her room, so she stayed on in Ferny Lane, hoping that Molly Mooney would never find a buyer.

In spite of Ruth's dire warnings, Emilie was not nervous in the house, and no one saw anything untoward in her living there alone. Compared with some of the rough dwellings in and around the town, and the harsh conditions in camps endured by newcomers, her place was quite appropriate. Mr Manningtree, who'd come to inspect her new home, had told her that wives of timbergetters lived very lonely lives deep in the forests, with their husbands away for weeks on end, so she passed this information on to Ruth. It didn't help.

'You are not the wife of a drover, or of a timbergetter,' she wrote. 'You are a young lady placing your reputation in jeopardy. You are to return to that house or to a boarding house forthwith!'

She sent the papers regarding the application for land for Emilie to sign, advising that with the help of Mr Bowles she had found suitable land in an area outside Brisbane, known as Eagle Farm, and insisted that, once acquired, they ought to sell. On that point Emilie disagreed, but postponed arguing about it for the time being so as not to upset her sister even more.

One evening, though, when she was carrying water from the tank to the tiny kitchen, she heard movement in the nearby bush and froze, remembering tales of wild Aborigines who still roamed the scrub. A tall man emerged, a rough, ugly fellow with matted hair and a thick beard . . .

Emilie tried to scream but no sound came out, which was just as well, she realised later, because this apparition was Mr Willoughby!

'Don't be frightened, Miss Emilie,' he said softly. 'I look a fright, I know . . .'

'Oh my heavens! Is it you? You look dreadful. Are you all right?'

'Sure I am,' he said, standing back timidly.

'You'd better come inside.'

He reached over and took the bucket from her, following her into the kitchen.

By the lamplight Emilie saw that he'd grown his hair and now had a reddish curling beard, but his blue eyes were clear and he did, in fact, look surprisingly well.

'I'd never have known you,' she told him.

He laughed. The same infectious laugh. 'That's the point. I don't need people to know me.'

Emilie stood there, hands fluttering, not knowing what to do with him.

'Are you hungry?' she asked, hoping he would be, to give her something to do. They were standing in such close proximity in the small space, and he was so large, she felt short of breath.

'If you can spare something.'

'Of course. I'll put the kettle on. I've eaten but I've got some cold lamb and bread and pickles, will that do? I've not got much else at the minute.' She giggled foolishly. 'I'm afraid I'm not much good at stocking a larder properly yet.'

'That'll be fine, Miss Emilie. I'll put the kettle on. Your stove needs a bit of a stir up.'

While he stoked the fire with some twigs she'd collected, Emilie took the meat and butter from the wire safe, then it suddenly hit her . . .

'How did you know I was here?'

'Followed you,' he grinned. 'I was waiting outside the house hoping you'd come out, wondering how I could get in touch with you if you didn't, then blow me down, if you don't come marching out the gate and set off down the road at such a pace I couldn't go bolting after you. Not since I'm still on the run,' he added apologetically. 'So I just climbed back on the horse and trundled along, quiet like.'

'You rode through town? You could have been caught!'

'It was getting dark. Kept the head down. Plenty of rough old bushies like me about . . .'

'That's outrageous! Never do that again.'

'Fair enough. Then I saw you come in here and waited a few more hours. Thought you might be visiting someone. When you didn't come out I scouted around and came up from the riverfront there. Not spying on you, don't think that.' The wood crackled and he closed the stove door. 'I just wanted to see how you were going. Have you moved out? Are you really living here now?'

Listening to him, to the cheerfulness in his voice when he heard that she had made the move, it sounded to Emilie as if he didn't have a care in the world. As if the most important thing in his life was her little triumph. She hacked at the bread, almost cross with him for being so nonchalant about his fearful situation.

She sat him at the table, gave him the sandwiches and some orange cake and black tea, and he smiled, contented.

'Now that's a beautiful cake. Just about the best orange cake I ever tasted. You're a good cook.'

'No I'm not. Kate, the cook at the house, made it for me.'

'Well, she's a good cook. But tell me, how did this house come about?'

Emilie explained its origins and how she came to be there as quickly as she could, because there were more important matters to discuss.

'But what about you, Mr Willoughby?'

'Mal,' he corrected.

'Very well, Mal,' she said impatiently. 'Where have you been?'

He drank the tea and sat back. 'Well . . . I went out towards the coast thinking I'd be able to hide out in the bush until the beard grew, then I met up with some Abo lads, and they had the idea of robbing me but I didn't make much of a catch. No grub, no supplies of any sort, not even a gun, so I was a waste of time. But they like a bit of fun and I still had my stockwhip, so I taught them how to crack a whip, and they decided I wasn't such a bad bloke after all. Especially when I told them I was on the run. That tickled them. Big joke for them but not for me. I soon found out there were more settlers in that area than I'd counted on, and my new mates were there on business, raiding the whites for anything they could get their hands on.'

'What do you mean?' Emilie asked. 'Weren't they local blacks?'

'No. They'd come over from Fraser Island, across the bay. You would have seen it from the ship when it entered the bay before you went up river.'

'Yes. I've heard a lot about it since. A ship was wrecked there.' Emilie shuddered. 'The survivors were murdered by the blacks and only the Captain's wife, Mrs Fraser, survived. She lived with them under horrible conditions until she managed to escape.'

'Yes. She was famous. But that was years ago.'

'But there are still wild blacks over there; people say they're cannibals.'

'I don't know about that. They haven't eaten the missionaries yet. Anyway, the lads weren't having much luck with holdups, so unbeknowns to me they disappear one night, attack a shepherd . . .'

'Did they kill him?'

'I didn't ask. They robbed his hut, slaughtered a couple of sheep and were piling the carcasses into their canoe when I came across them. They were off home, pleased as punch with themselves. Well, you know what a hue and cry that would cause out there, leaving me stuck in the middle of it, so there was only one thing to do. I hopped into the canoe and went with them.'

'You've been over on the island all this time?'

'Yes. And what a great place it is. I'll take you over there one of these days.'

'I can't see that happening in the near future,' she said primly.

'No. I suppose not. Can we sit outside? You've got a fine spot here looking over the river. She must be a nice woman, your Mrs Mooney.'

As they went out on to the veranda and settled in the canvas chairs as if he was just a normal visitor, Emilie, still a little cross that he was treating all of this so lightly, decided that he really was a sweet person but absolutely foolhardy. Quite reckless, in fact. And she was terrified that one of the Dresslers might decide to visit, as they often did, bringing down some farm produce – eggs or milk or vegetables – for her. But he was sitting back, talking happily about Fraser Island.

'I've seen some beautiful places in this country in my travels, Miss Emilie, but that island beats them all.'

'Weren't you afraid you'd be caught over there?'

'No. It's too big, it must be sixty miles long. There are only the missionaries and some loggers over there.'

'And the blacks.'

'Yes. Hundreds of them. But you should see it. There's a blue lake in the middle clear as a bell to the sandy bottom. And the most marvellous bays. There's one on the ocean side with orchids in the bush almost to the shoreline, and sand as white as white, and the sea there like a jewel. I made up a name for it. Orchid Bay.'

He looked dreamily out over the softly flowing river. 'Now this is a nice spot, but down there it's just mud on the banks. Orchid Bay is clean, pure and clean, you know what I mean?'

Emilie nodded. She supposed she could imagine it, never having seen many beaches to compare.

He turned to her, serious now. 'I've been on the road since I was a kid. First with my dad, then on my own. I never gave any thought to settling down, but when I do, if I ever get the chance, things being as they are, that'll be my home. And I won't forget you, Miss Emilie; if it's ever in my power, I'll take you to see Orchid Bay.'

Mal was silent for a while and then he apologised. 'I'm sorry. I've been talking too much. But it's a blessing to be able to have a real talk with someone. The blacks don't know much English.'

'Why didn't you stay over there, Mal? You'd be safe there.'

'Not for much longer. Word gets out. White man living with the blacks? Questions asked. Besides, the beard's long enough, and the hair, to cover me. I always hated beards, still do. Now I'm stuck with one.'

Emilie sighed. It was almost impossible to keep his mind on serious issues.

157

'Your clothes don't look as if you've been living in the bush,' she noted.

'I guess not. By the time the blacks dropped me back on the mainland, I was wearing rags, so I borrowed them from a settler's hut.' He looked down at his checked shirt and dungarees with a satisfied smile.

'You stole them?'

'Times are hard,' he grinned. 'They fit all right but the boots are a bit big. No socks either.'

They sat and talked and Emilie marvelled at his complacence, finally having to bring him back to the real world.

'They don't mention you any more in the papers, but they're advertising a reward for you. Fifty pounds.'

He shrugged. 'I guessed that would happen.'

'Aren't you worried?'

'What's the point? I just have to keep a jump ahead of them. It could be worse. Three men were shot dead that day. Three good men. Bugger the gold. I haven't forgotten them, and I won't. Someone has to pay for that and it's not going to be me.'

His voice was so harsh she realised that his nonchalance had been for her benefit, and a fierce spirit lurked behind his youthful attitude.

Mal stood. He stretched and reached out to her, bringing her gently to her feet.

'I have to go. But I've been thinking of you for so long, do you mind if I kiss you?'

Emilie didn't mind at all. She'd been wondering all this time what it would be like to kiss him, to have his arms about her, but then he was apologising for the beard and it was all too much for her. How long could he stay alive with all the world against him? Her response, a flood of tears, was embarrassing, but then he was kissing her, consoling her, and it should have been the other way around.

'I shouldn't have come here, upsetting you,' he murmured, but she was in his arms, kissing him passionately, marvelling that his lips were soft and gentle, and he held her to him, so close she felt he was her protection. Then he was saying how beautiful she was and how much he loved her, and they were there on the veranda of the little house, folded together, and Emilie Tissington was excited, his cares and hers forgotten.

'Do you have to go?' she whispered at last, as he released her.

Mal looked at her sadly. 'If I don't, we'll be making for that bedroom of yours, Emilie, and I'm not sure you want that.'

Emilie clung to him, afraid for him.

'Can't you stay a little while longer?'

He took her by the arm and led her back into the house, closing the doors, and took her in his arms again, kissing her eyes, her mouth, her cheeks, and Emilie knew then that he was leaving, and she fought against it.

'Am I too respectable for you?' she challenged him. 'Too much your

Miss Emilie? It's a wonder you even kissed me at all, even though you know I care about you.'

But he wouldn't relent. He simply picked up the warm waistcoat he'd discarded earlier, sheepskin she noted, home-made, with the wool on the inside. He saw her looking at it.

'I made it myself,' he grinned, as he slipped his arms into it. 'I have to go, Emilie.'

Then he looked about him. 'You like this house?'

'Yes. It's all I need.'

'And you're renting until she sells it.'

Emilie was surprised he'd remembered that. 'Yes.'

'Then where do you go? You said you had trouble finding a room.'

'I don't know.' She was almost sulking. Feeling rejected.

'Then get in first. Buy it. It's a good spot. You'd never lose on the block even if the house is a bit odd, backwards like.'

'With what?'

'What about the money I gave you? Is it all gone?' There was no malice in his voice, just curiosity, as if he had no idea what ladies did with their money. Which was probably true.

'It's still there. I couldn't hide it so I put it in the bank. It's your money.'

'Jesus! You didn't put it in my name?'

'No. I'm sorry. I had to put it in my name.'

'Oh, thank God. What do you take me for? I gave it to you. It's yours. Use it.'

Emilie remembered another concern. 'My sister needs help. Would you mind if I sent her some money?'

He swept her into his arms again. 'You're a real babe in the woods, aren't you? Do what you like, Emilie. It might be a long time before I see you. Just take care of yourself. That's all I want.'

He gave her a peck on the cheek and left through the side door by the kitchen. No goodbyes. He moved too quickly for her to protest or even wish him . . . what? Safe journey, she supposed, wherever he was going. She'd meant to ask him that. She'd meant to ask him so many things, but now he was gone, and she was staring out into the darkness, and she'd never felt so alone in her life.

Emilie walked outside and sat on the veranda until dawn began to streak the eastern sky, realising that another very ordinary day was ahead of her. Just another ordinary day in the life of a quiet little governess.

It was just another day for Allyn Carnegie, another long and worrying day, with the weather now at its best, cooler nights and exquisite blue days, or so people kept reminding him as he passed them by. The former Gold Commissioner, hero of the ambush, couldn't care less about the weather; he would have been indifferent if it had snowed. He was too intent on walking the streets, even calling in at numerous hotels and dives in the hope of sighting his partner.

For quite a while he'd been a familiar figure on the wharves, feigning interest in the ships decanting wide-eyed immigrants from Britain and Germany, watching stevedores loading endless supplies of wool, tallow and timber to fill the holds on their return journeys, but all the while he searched for Baldy Perry, for the hard, mean-faced brute who should have been working there, constantly fighting the temptation to enquire as to his whereabouts.

It would have been an easy thing for Baldy to jump aboard one of these ships and disappear, Carnegie knew, but he couldn't allow himself to believe that and face utter despair while it was still only hovering, like a hawk, waiting to strike. An anonymous letter from him naming Baldy as the murderer would put the fool on the run for the rest of his life. Somehow, the Commissioner knew that was the last thing the brute wanted. He'd talked incessantly about retiring to Tasmania with his gold. Round and round Carnegie went until his head ached and his nerves caused him to break out in hives.

So he took to riding again, to have the locals used to seeing him on horseback, sometimes even talking pleasantly to the ferrymen delivering passengers and supplies across the river, his eventual destination. Now he knew he had to go to check that tree, to find out, once and for all, if his partner had absconded with the gold.

In the meantime, congratulating himself on his cunning, Allyn had gone out of his way to make the acquaintance of sugar planters who worked their plantations over the river, using kanaka labourers, and was, of course, invited to visit and observe their interesting endeavours.

Finally, his mind was made up. He would head off that way, mentioning the plantations to the ferrymen, and detour for the gold stash. If it was there, he'd empty his leather saddle bags and fill them with treasure. Brazen, but practicable.

None of this subterfuge was necessary, Allyn understood that, but guilt and fear still held him in tight rein, almost asphyxiating his brain. Every night as he tossed and turned, trying to sleep, he found himself inventing more and more plausible reasons to cross the river, while a calmer edge of his brain endeavoured to explain that no one cared where he went or what he did.

The eve of his determined visit to that hiding place found him sitting by his window with a brandy, hoping that Baldy would arrive at long last. There would be no recriminations for him taking such a time, none at all; they would simply share the gold and the notes and sovereigns from the bank boxes, and that would be that. There was no one about. They could sit in the kitchen and sort it out as quickly as possible and it would be over. Dear God, he prayed. Let it be over.

When the gate squeaked, he turned away for a minute to replenish his drink. He forgot that his partner was supposed to sneak on to his premises, not come by the gate; it was hard to recall their detailed arrangements now, what with the worry, and his hives, and the liquor he'd had to consume to get through this, but they didn't matter now. His visitor had arrived. At last!

He raced to the door, but his visitor was a stranger. A large, barrel-chested man in a black uniform of some sort.

'Mr Carnegie?'

'Yes?'

'I'm Superintendent of Police for the state of Queensland, Jasper Kemp. I wonder if I could have a word with you.'

Allyn felt as if his bowels were about to give way, but he hung on and mustered dignity.

'I'm afraid I'm not prepared for company, sir. The daily maid has gone off.'

'I won't keep you long, Mr Carnegie. Just a few words to see how you're getting along after your dreadful experience. I would have come sooner, but I've been busy here the last few days.'

'Oh. I see. Yes. Then by all means, do come in. I retire early, sir, I was just having a nightcap. Would you care to join me?'

'Don't mind if I do,' Kemp smiled. 'Man in my position, difficult to have a quiet drink without giving a bad example to the locals.'

They adjourned to the small sitting room and Carnegie gathered enough strength to control the conversation by welcoming the Superintendent and plying him with questions about the case, which, he said, had been badly mishandled. He, along with the residents of Maryborough, felt the police were not doing enough to capture the outlaw, Willoughby, and his accomplices.

Kemp remarked on the excellent brandy, and Carnegie was able, with a conspiratorial grin, to direct him to the Customs House, where confiscated goods were often auctioned and excellent wines could be obtained at a decent price.

They talked about the town and the port and the fact that Maryborough would have to be proclaimed a city within a few years at the rate it was growing, and Kemp, whom Allyn found a most interesting conversationalist, and no threat to a gentleman at all, admitted his surprise.

'To tell you the truth, I had no idea this town was such a bustling metropolis. I think I expected a shanty town lining the river, but it has been well surveyed and the surrounds are a picture. That's the trouble trying to run things from Brisbane, so far south. When I saw what poor Sergeant Pollock was trying to cope with, I telegraphed for six more police constables to be sent up here immediately.'

Carnegie tried not to shudder. 'I'm so pleased to hear that. And how is Sergeant Pollock?'

'He's well. But as you would know, there have been two more raids by outlaws on the same stretch of road down from Gympie, and another by a gang of Aborigines who just stole food, and we are hard pressed to know how to put a stop to holdups, beyond searching out the criminals from the hills and bringing them in.'

'You could bring in troops.'

Kemp sighed. 'I'm afraid the government does not see this as a military matter.'

'I read that that outlaw McPherson held up a mailman on the Gympie road, so he's still in the district. It is beyond my comprehension that this murderer has not been detained. He's thumbing his nose at the law. Would you care for another brandy?'

'Don't mind if I do.'

Carnegie hid his sniff. Hardly the response of a gentleman. Kemp was a nice fellow, someone who had obviously come up through the ranks, but another plodder from the lower class. However, the brandy was mellowing Allyn now, and he felt quite paternalistic towards the fellow, a new chum in an outlandish society of misfits, endeavouring to make sense of it all.

'That's quite odd,' Kemp was saying. 'The description you gave fits McPherson like a glove. He's our man all right, or another one, with Willoughby, but why would he rob the mail after pulling off a raid that brought him more than eight thousand pounds in gold and coin? I mean, is the man a fool?'

'The criminal mind is not known for intelligence, one would have to say.'

'True. But his last holdup was *after* that horrific raid, where you were shot. How is your arm, by the way?'

'Wrecked. I'll never be able to straighten it again, the bastards. The ache is ever-present and I can't accustom myself to sleeping with an arm that just won't adjust to a comfortable position.'

'I'm sorry to hear that. But as I was saying . . . McPherson held up the mailman out on a lonely road. He went through all the letters, stealing any money enclosed, gave the man the residue of torn mail and sent him on his way. He didn't need the pathetic spoils of that holdup and he made no attempt to hide his identity. What do you make of that?'

'Exactly what it said in the papers. That he enjoys making a fool of the police. But keep in mind that he did shoot a man at the Carrington Hotel on the Houghton River . . .'

'Yes, but that was an altercation. Not the sniping operation that you experienced. It just doesn't sound like McPherson.'

'You forget that he has been captured and escaped so often that everyone knows what he looks like. The man's past caring.'

'And you still think it was him?'

Carnegie almost wavered. Maybe he could admit he could be wrong. But no. He had to keep the local police and this chump pointed in a definite direction. 'Yes. I saw the bastard. It was him.'

'Thank you. I find that a big help. McPherson is known to act the clown. Maybe he was just showing off. But at least we know he's still round here somewhere. I hope. But what about Willoughby? You knew him?'

'Yes. He seemed a nice lad. How was I to know he was in cahoots with an outlaw? Pollock and I went to a lot of trouble, with poor Taylor's help, to see that none of the guards knew each other, so we'd have no insider conspiracies, no chance to gang up on us.'

'I realise that. I understand it was Pollock's plan, not yours, to ride out and escort your shipment down the last leg of the Gympie track?'

'Indeed it was.'

Kemp savoured his brandy, nodding. 'It worked other times. Maybe once too often.'

'You can't blame Pollock,' Allyn said, hoping that might have this senior man beginning to wonder about his sergeant.

'No. But Willoughby . . . according to Pollock, people speak highly of him. But in Taylor's notes, he lied about himself. We've checked those stations. He never worked as a shearer. He was rather a ne'er-do-well, known as Sonny Willoughby, neither a criminal nor clear. He was just a drifter, a card sharp, quite well known at fairgrounds.'

'So there you are. He obviously fell into the wrong company.'

Kemp nodded again. 'Could have. But my officers have been talking to fair people and gypsies in New South Wales, that's where he comes from, and no one has a bad word for him. One report said he was more gypsy than the gypsies. Hardly likely to turn into a killer. You see my problem?'

In righteous mood, Allyn was angry. 'I see only that the police cannot apprehend these murderers. I see myself face down in the dirt, bleeding, my arm shot to pieces, swallowing my own vomit rather than allow I'm alive, not knowing from the shots who's dead and who's alive, turning my head only enough to see Willoughby and McPherson, not daring to move in the other direction to see how many others there are, expecting to die any minute . . .'

'Hush now. I'm sorry. I didn't mean to put you through all that again. It's just that the reading of a report never gives a man the full story. You understand why it was essential to talk to you, Mr Carnegie?'

'I don't understand! It's all forgotten now. The gold has gone. Three men are dead. And no one cares what happened to me. I'm too shattered to work. I've had to resign my commission . . .'

'Your wife cares, Mr Carnegie.'

Allyn came up with a jolt. 'I beg your pardon?'

'I thought you would have returned to Brisbane by this, so I called at your home. Mrs Carnegie told me you were still in Maryborough, and she's very concerned about you. She was very upset. She thinks you should come home.'

'So I will. As soon as possible,' Allyn mumbled.

'What's keeping you here? You really ought to go. There's little more you can do, if anything.'

Allyn wanted to say it was his business where he was and where he was not; it was personal and nothing to do with red-nosed police officers, no matter what their rank. Who did this fellow think he was? Instead, he nodded.

'I shall be returning shortly. I had hoped to see the end to this, but apparently the police are not up to the challenge. I don't consider that my wife, who comes from a very upper-class family, would find this town, or any of the accommodations, especially this temporary hovel, bearable. I should not dream of bringing her here.'

He was relieved that they parted on good terms, and even agreed to lunch with Superintendent Kemp the next day, which blew apart his careful plan to cross the river by ferry and ride to that tree, but another day didn't matter. Another chance for his partner to materialise. Allyn was already praying that Baldy would be careful to keep out of sight in case this fool with his airy-fairy theories of criminal personalities decided to revisit. He walked Kemp to the gate, agreeing that the weather, the damned weather, was indeed balmy.

'By the way,' Kemp asked, 'do you know a fellow called Clive Hillier?'

'No. Why?'

'Thought you might have known him. He was a miner for a while, out on the fields.'

'Never heard of him.'

Clive came down from the goldfields in a party of thirty men, relying on their own firepower for protection rather than the sparse efforts of the police. Not that he had much to protect, except for his person. Every time he made a decision to leave, a new chum just like Mal would come along and he'd be back at work, turning over abandoned digs with his partners, finding a little colour, but nothing worthwhile. None of them had Mal's luck.

And that was a moot point, he mused. Mal's luck had run out. Had come to a grinding halt, poor chap.

But Clive still had a few pounds, enough to keep him going for a while, so when his companions rode merrily down the main street of Maryborough, deciding which pub would be honoured with their patronage, he stayed with them, and soon a rip-roaring party was under way at the Saddler's Arms.

Sobering, two days later, he took a room in a dingy boarding house, lazed in a Chinese bath house, waited in a long queue at the barbershop, bought himself a white duck suit, striped shirts, a thin bow tie and a Panama hat, and further down the street haggled over the price of a pair of snappy riding boots. Then, feeling like his old self again, the young Englishman set out to explore the town. And ask about Fleur.

He found the country town, masquerading as a port, a very pleasant place, but then, he mused, after the dirt and dust of the goldfields, any town would be pleasant. It was such a relief to find the trappings of civilisation again, and shade from the sun, and decent meals in clean surrounds, that he began to regret his choice of accommodation, but wisdom prevailed. His funds wouldn't run to the smarter hotels that would normally be his first choice. But there was no sign of Fleur. Some men he met in the bars knew of her, but could not give him any information, other than that she had probably shipped out with 'the old bloke'.

Disappointed, Clive turned away and was about to go to the shipping office to enquire about ships sailing to Townsville, from where he could trek out to the latest goldfields at Charters Towers. According to the local papers, that area was being heralded as a massive field, so there was time yet. But then he remembered he'd promised to let Sergeant Pollock know of his whereabouts, so grudgingly he made for the police station.

Pollock wasn't available, but when Clive stated the reason for his visit, the constable at the desk retreated suddenly, and returned with the Superintendent of Police no less, who informed him he was visiting from Brisbane and would be interested in a chat.

'Better still,' Clive said. 'Nothing like starting at the top, sir.'

'At your service.' The genial man smiled. 'Come on in and take a seat. I won't keep you a minute.'

Clive sat on the hard chair across from Kemp, who took his time going over some files, occasionally asking Clive to bear with him. At last he looked up.

'I see from Sergeant Pollock's notes that you believe your former partner, Mr Willoughby, is innocent?'

'That's right. But Pollock had the cheek to imply that I might not be. That I was in cahoots with Mal on that raid. Did he put that in his report too?'

'Sergeant Pollock has to look at this serious matter from every angle, Mr Hillier.'

'Does he now? And has he looked at Carnegie?'

Kemp's genial smile did not waver. 'Mr Carnegie was a victim of this crime, as I recall. Why would you say that?'

Clive knew better than to implicate Mr Xiu, since the Chinaman had obviously heard from Mal in some manner. He didn't wish to send the police off harassing Xiu. Since that meeting he had made his own enquiries and discovered that the Chinese were great gamblers and were also known to be moneylenders, though fierce in recovering outstanding loans. He had begun to wonder if Carnegie was a gambler, and if he'd borrowed from Xiu. There was no way he could establish the latter, but he'd soon learned that Carnegie was indeed a heavy gambler.

Clive took a chance. 'What if Carnegie himself needed money?'

'What for?'

'What else do people need money for? To pay off debts, of course. Gambling debts.'

'You think Mr Carnegie owed gambling money?'

'I heard he was a big player. Did Pollock check that?'

'You'll be pleased to know that the Sergeant did look into that matter and was unable to come up with anyone on the goldfields or in this town to whom Mr Carnegie owes even a penny.'

Damn! Even if Pollock had approached Xiu, he wouldn't have prised any information out of him. Clive was baffled. Should he mention the Chinaman? But after all, he was only guessing at the significance of Xiu's remarks.

'So what?' he growled. 'I still say Carnegie had a hand in this, and others out at the fields say so too.'

'Really. I can find no mention of that in the reports. Who exactly made this charge?'

'I don't recall, it was just talk out on the fields. Anyway, with all due respect, Superintendent, I've done my duty. Checked in as Pollock instructed me to do, so I'll be on my way. I may be leaving for Townsville shortly.'

'You're going to Charters Towers?'

'If I'm permitted. I'll let you know which ship.'

'Yes. Please do that.'

'So I'm not off the hook yet. And you haven't got a thing on Willoughby except Carnegie's accusation.'

'First-hand evidence, Mr Hillier.'

Clive stood and pushed back the chair. 'Then I think I'll trot along and have a word with Carnegie myself. I hear he's still in town.'

That jolted Kemp. He closed his files firmly. 'I'd prefer you did not do that, sir.'

'Why not? I won't attack him, I just want a few words with him, since you people seem hell bent on hanging an innocent man. What if Carnegie made a mistake?' He found himself echoing Xiu. 'Sometimes mistakes are not what they seem.'

'What exactly does that mean?'

Clive wasn't sure himself, but now he tried to explain. 'Maybe the mistake was on purpose. To keep your eyes on the wrong target. Have you thought of that?'

Kemp rose to see him out. 'It might be a good idea for us to have another talk before you leave, Mr Hillier. But you are not to discuss any of this with Mr Carnegie.' His voice hardened. 'Keep away from him.'

When the Englishman had left, Kemp resumed his seat and made a few notes of his own. He considered Hillier's visit very interesting. He recalled his own visit to Carnegie's home in Brisbane, where he'd found the wife distressed that he hadn't come home. She'd wept, finding all this hard to bear.

'Especially with all our worries,' she'd sobbed.

Being a kindly man, he listened to her woes, encouraging her to talk them through, finding that the Carnegies were up to their ears in debt, that their house would have to be sold, and so on.

'And now that my husband has been forced to retire from his salaried position, we have no income at all. I know I should feel so sorry for the families of the poor men who were shot in that terrible affray, but those outlaws have ruined us too!'

Strange that Carnegie seemed unconcerned about his financial situation, lazing about up here when he could be home with his wife. Oh no, if anyone was to discuss this matter further with Mr Carnegie, it would not be Hillier. He might put the rabbit to fright and then nothing would be gained. Why *was* Carnegie still here?

Kemp scratched his head, answering his own question. Because he's not up to facing the music back home. Simply postponing the problem.

Then why all that talk about gold shares?

Then he laughed. The poor fellow could be just posturing. A pitiful attempt to preserve dignity, nothing unusual about that. If only Willoughby hadn't escaped. Threatened with a sentence of death, he would have given up his partners in this heinous crime.

Kemp turned back to his own report. From now on a police escort would be provided on a monthly basis to deliver gold and bank deposits from Gympie to Maryborough, and private escort firms would continue to be employed from Maryborough to Brisbane. He wished he could recommend promotion for Pollock, but Willoughby's escape could not be overlooked. It would be a long time before the Sergeant was able to live that down. Unless he captured him, and that was hardly likely. The rogue would be long gone from this district now.

Living away from the Manningtree household had given Emilie new energy. She enjoyed the brisk walk early in the mornings, beginning to recognise trees that lined her route and make an effort to learn to identify others. She decided she would draw some of them, resume sketching as a hobby.

More often than not, the children were waiting for her at the gate with renewed enthusiasm, which she took advantage of in the classroom, knowing the novelty would wear off. For the fun of it, she had them march across to the classroom and began the day with singing, then writing lessons, while they were at their neatest, then moving on to spelling and sums. It kept her busy, teaching three children at three different levels, but they all worked happily together.

Sometimes Bert Manningtree would look in with his usual jokes and winks, asking if they were behaving themselves, pleased to hear the chorus of 'yes' whether they were or not. Emilie didn't mind his visits, but his wife's rare appearances were a different matter. She brought her lady friends with her, and they stood inside the door watching the classes, giggling, telling the governess not to mind them, exchanging anecdotes about their own schooldays. Miss Tissington wished she could remind them that talking in the classroom was still not permitted. She knew that Mrs Manningtree was only showing off, using the fact that she had a governess as a status symbol, so she suffered in silence, feeling silly, as if she were on stage.

Not long after she'd moved out, down came the lady again with two friends, chatting in loud whispers on the sidelines while Emilie was sitting with Rosie, teaching her baby sums with coloured blocks. She heard them talking about her, and pretended not to notice.

'She doesn't live in any more?' a woman asked.

'No,' Mrs Manningtree said. 'I really couldn't spare the room. I can't put important guests like the Countess on the roof. I've been at Bert to build a guest wing for me. It's not as if we haven't the space.'

'Where's she living?'

Mrs Manningtree giggled. 'You won't believe this. She moved into

167

Paddy Mooney's hut on the river. Quite a come-down from my home. Next thing she'll be taking in washing.'

'And she doesn't mind being there?' the woman whispered.

'Apparently not. It'd be cheap rent.'

Emilie had the children stand and wish the ladies good morning as they left, and tried to concentrate on teaching Rosie to count. Offensive as it was, she was not upset by the conversation, because she found it interesting. Molly Mooney had been right. These people were not concerned that a single woman was living alone, something that would have given gossips a field day back home. They only seemed surprised that a governess of her calibre would take up residence in such a place.

'It's not a hut anyway,' she muttered. 'It's quite a solid little house.'

'What is?' Rosie asked.

'Never mind. If I take these five blocks, how many are left?'

'Five!'

'Right, you are a good girl. Jimmy, stop staring about you. Have you finished your sums?'

'Not yet, miss.'

'Then carry on, or Rosie will catch up with you.'

He grinned and put his head down, scratching at his slate.

Cheap rent is it? Emilie mused. We'll see about that. Mal had told her to buy the place. It was on a lovely block of land, with a view of the river, more than this house had. She *would* buy it.

Thoughts of Mal came flooding back, but she pushed them away, postponed them. These dear children were entitled to her full attention.

That night, as she was walking out through the gate, Mr Manningtree came up the street in his buggy.

'Do you want a lift home?'

'No thank you, sir. I wouldn't put you to the trouble.'

'No trouble at all. Hop up.' He wheeled the buggy about and took off at his usual pace, rattling over bumps and potholes as if they were to be attacked not avoided.

'Do you know where I'm living?' she asked.

'Sure I do. Many a good time I spent down there with Paddy. Fishin' and cookin' the catch and downing a few jugs.'

'It's quite nice inside,' she said, a little defensive.

'Molly would see to that. She'd never let Paddy's place go to rack and ruin.'

'She intends to sell it.'

'Does she now? That's a surprise.'

'She's too busy to use the house now, but I do believe it also has too many memories for her . . .'

'That'd be right. They were close, Paddy and Molly. Sweethearts all their lives.'

Eventually he reined in the horse. 'Here you are, miss. Home, James. You sure you're all right here?'

'Oh yes.' Emilie saw her chance to do a bit of politicking. If she bought

168

this house, his wife would soon find out, and one never could gauge her reaction, though Emilie could foresee spite following surprise. It might be a good idea to get in first. Mrs Manningtree might run the house, but Bert was the real boss. He held the purse-strings.

'Could I ask you something, Mr Manningtree?'

He sat back, nursing the reins while the horse snuffled and blew from the exertions. 'You can an' all. Everything all right up home?'

'Oh yes, of course. But since Mrs Mooney is selling this place, and I wasn't able to find suitable renting accommodation other than here . . .'

'I told Violet that. I warned her she could lose you if she pushed a nice girl like you into one of them bogholes that pass for lodgings in this town . . .'

'No. It's not that. I just thought, since the house and land are for sale, do you think I should buy it?'

He frowned. Balked. 'What? You want to buy it?'

'Well, the house is all I need, and it is in a lovely position.'

'Buy it?' he echoed. He smelled of sweat and sawdust on this humid night, but Emilie had learned to respect the results of honest toil, where once the Tissingtons would not have associated with so much as a farmhand. This man worked hard. He left for his mill at dawn and was never home until sunset.

'What would you use for money?' he asked. 'Do you want a loan?'

Emilie smiled sweetly. 'Oh, no, sir. I do have some money. My father, you see, he gave us, my sister and I, a little nest egg each . . .' The lie came easily to her. A lie that she couldn't use on Ruth. Another one. God knows how she'd ever explain any of this to Ruth.

Bert Manningtree was laughing. 'Well, I have to say this for you, girlie. You're a smart one. And why wouldn't you be, with your education? That's what I keep tellin' Violet. Our kids will need a decent education or it'll be easy come, easy go, with my cash.'

Emilie had heard that lecture before, so she nodded agreement. 'I would appreciate your advice, sir,' she said, though she already had his answer. 'You know this town. Do you think it would be appropriate?'

'What do you mean, appropriate?' He had trouble pronouncing the word.

'I mean the right thing to do.'

Oh Lord, she thought, I'm becoming so sly . . .

'Why not?' he barked. 'I reckon it's the smart thing to do. Bloody smart. You can't lose on it. This town is going to take off like a cannon shot. It'll be a city before you can spit. That's why I'm buyin' up property right smack in the centre of Kent Street, costing me a heap now, but you just wait. With my other investments I'll be worth a heap the day I retire.'

'Thank you, Mr Manningtree.' Emilie gathered up her skirt to climb down.

'Hang on.' Her adviser had the bit between his teeth now. This transaction interested him mightily. 'What's she asking?'

Emilie slid back into her seat. 'Oh! I don't know.'

'You don't know? And you're going to buy the place? God, you women! Now let's see. What have you got here? A half-acre if I remember Paddy's talk. But there's your little house. It's not as rough as it looks. And got a good big water tank, one of the best. Will see out a lifetime.'

She let him meander on with his assessment until he came to a conclusion. 'I'm betting she's asking ten to fifteen pounds. Offer her eight. You might have to go up a bit, but tell her you want the bush cleared round the house, and a proper path from the gate down to the door. In the wet you'd break your neck skidding down there. And an awning over the front door there, which isn't a front door the way bloody Paddy looked at it. But it has to look like a front door, facing this way. See what I mean?'

Emilie was horrified. 'I don't know about that. Mrs Mooney has been so nice to me, I couldn't possibly . . .'

'Don't worry about Molly. She's a tough bird. Not short of a quid either. You sure you've got the cash?'

'Yes, sir.'

'Then leave it to me. I'll work it out with her. I'll fix it up for you before someone else jumps in.'

'I hope she won't mind.'

'Don't worry about it. I'm pleased to do the deal for you.'

'That's very kind of you, Mr Manningtree.'

He tipped his hat back on his head and grinned. 'It's my pleasure, missy, because it tells me another story.'

'I beg your pardon?'

'It tells me that you're staying, doesn't it? And for the sake of my kids, that's the best news you can give me. I mightn't never think to say the right thing, missy, but you're doing a fine job with them and they love you. That's what counts in my book. Now you hop down and scamper down there before it gets dark. I'll see Molly tomorrer.'

The deed was done. Emilie was the proud owner of Lot 759 in the Parish of Maryborough at the end of Ferny Lane, and more nervous about it than excited, realising that she could never invite Ruth to visit. Not unless she told her the truth about the source of the purchase monies, and she could not do that.

'Oh dear,' she sighed. 'This is becoming very complicated.'

Mr Manningtree had secured the purchase for her at nine pounds plus the improvements he had requested, and Mrs Mooney had not taken offence. She had been pleased that 'Paddy's place' was now owned by a young lady who would appreciate it, so everyone was happy, except, of course, Mrs Manningtree, whose caustic remarks about 'people getting above themselves' were not unexpected. Emilie marvelled that she was able to cope so well these days with the woman's spitefulness and discourtesy, the attitude that had so distressed her earlier, even causing her to react angrily. Now, though, it all went over her head, and Emilie felt more confident in herself. Probably, she decided, from being pushed out to fend for herself, and from a belated admission that her own attitude had needed revision. She and Ruth had been too stuffy, far too reserved to fit in with people in this country, in this town anyway. It had been necessary to bend a little, be more sociable. She supposed Ruth had come to the same conclusion.

This very matter was brought home to her with an uncomfortable bump when a burly man had stopped her in the street outside the Prince of Wales Hotel.

'Why! If it isn't Miss Tissington! How nice to see you again.'

Emilie blinked, unable to place the man, thinking he was probably one of the Manningtrees' party guests . . .

'Kemp,' he said. 'Jasper Kemp. Don't you remember me? Mrs Kemp and I were staying at the Belleview Boarding House the same time you were, with your sister.'

She felt the heat of a blush on her cheeks. She did remember them, and she also remembered that she and Ruth had cut his wife, even though she had addressed them politely. What on earth were we thinking of? she worried. Those people must have thought us incredibly rude.

Embarrassed, she rushed her response to try to make up for the slight. 'Mr Kemp. Yes, I do. How nice to see you again. Are you keeping well? Lovely day, isn't it? And how is Mrs Kemp? Is she with you . . .'

He smiled. 'I'm very well, thank you. And no, Mrs Kemp is not with me. I'm just visiting, here on business. And you? Do you live here now?'

'Yes.' Emilie calmed down. 'Yes. I have a position as a governess with a local family.'

'Good to hear. And do you like the job?'

'Thank you, indeed I do. The children are very good.'

'And they're lucky to have an excellent teacher, I'm sure.' He looked about him, at all the men striding about and the rows of horses hitched to rails along the street and bullock wagons rumbling down towards the wharf. 'I would have thought this place to be a bit wild and woolly for you.'

Emilie smiled. 'So did I when I first arrived. All these strange people petrified me, but one accustoms . . .'

Just then Mrs Mooney came down the steps of her hotel.

'Ah, Emilie. I see you've met the Superintendent.'

'We're old friends, Mrs Mooney,' he said. 'My wife and I met this young lady in Brisbane. How is your sister, Miss Tissington?'

'She has just arrived back in Brisbane, as a matter of fact. Back at the Belleview. She's very well, thank you.'

As she spoke, Emilie registered the word 'Superintendent', and she remembered that this man was a policeman. Dear God, and a high-ranking one at that.

Mrs Mooney was all for a chat, but Emilie apologised to them both, explaining that she was in rather a rush. She bade Mrs Mooney goodbye and turned to Kemp.

'How nice to see you again. I hope you enjoy your visit. I really must go.'

She walked away, resisting the temptation to run, to flee from that man, from the law, guilt pushing her along like a blustering wind. Only when she was well away from him did she stop, leaning against a fence, her heart pounding. Sheer foolishness, she knew, to be so jumpy about the police, but she was simply unable to control her reactions.

Emilie wore a wide straw hat these days, brightened with navy and white ribbons to match her working outfit of white blouse and navy skirt. She jammed it down on her head and plunged on. The episode had brought Mal to mind, and she didn't want to think of him now. She was only just managing to banish reminders of her own behaviour that night. Her shame. She had all but invited him to share her bed! What must he think of her? This time a real blush burned her face. But he'd had more sense. Emilie had always believed that only men got carried away with passion . . .

'Well, you were wrong,' she muttered, stamping along, head down. 'But real ladies don't behave like that.'

Their lovemaking had been such bliss, though. She could still feel his strong arms about her and his lips on hers.

Tentatively, she allowed her thoughts to drift ahead into her bedroom, as if she were an onlooker. What if he had stayed? And in the throes of love shared her bed; would she have allowed him to make love to her then? To have sex with her? She tried to tell herself probably not, but then again . . . she had wanted him, no denying that. There had been an excitement about being with Mal in such romantic seclusion that had aroused her so much, it was embarrassing to think about it now.

But was it love? Or was she so heartily sorry for him, so anxious to comfort him, and be comforted by him, that she could not differentiate? He seemed to cause a clamour in her all the time, and yet he wasn't the sort of man she ought to be attracted to. Definitely not. At the best of times Ruth would not approve of him. But he was sweet, and obviously he cared very deeply for her . . .

Emilie had missed lunch to go into town to buy some new shoes, but in her dash to escape Mr Kemp, she'd turned on to the familiar route back to the house, forgetting all about her shopping.

Another time, she shrugged, walking up the drive, noticing that several of the trees had burst into snowy-white blossoms, even though it was now winter, so-called. The grounds were looking quite splendid on this warm, sunny day.

Mrs Manningtree was standing on the front porch. To her it definitely was winter. She wore a gaudy wool shawl over a brown serge dress. She beckoned to Emilie, who wondered what was wrong now.

But her employer was all smiles. For a change.

'You have a visitor, Miss Tissington. In the parlour.'

Since she'd been thinking of Mal all the way home, he was the only visitor Emilie could envisage. She was so shocked, her head reeled.

Surely he wouldn't be so crazy as to come into this house!

'This way!' Mrs Manningtree hissed, indicating that Emilie was to be permitted to enter through the front door. Mystified, and very, very, nervous, Emilie mounted the steps, crossed the porch and made for the parlour.

While he was waiting, Clive had to suffer the company of this awful woman, Mrs Manningtree, who had quizzed him at length, forcing him to become inventive, since he could hardly say that Miss Tissington's friend, an outlaw, had asked him to call on her.

'You're English, Mr Hillier? Do you know Miss Tissington from home?'

Home to a lot of these colonials was England, even if they'd never been there.

'Unfortunately, no. We have never met. I'm a friend of the family.'

'She never mentions her family, only her sister. Who is a governess also.'

'Ah, yes. So I believe. People speak well of both ladies.'

'What does their father do?'

'Retired,' he said blithely. 'A fine gentleman. Misses the hunt, though. Had a fall, you know.'

'Really? And what brings a young gentleman like you to our shores, Mr Hillier?'

At least he was on solid ground here. 'Came out to have a look about and decided to have a bash at the goldfields . . .'

When that subject was exhausted and he was considering leaving, he had to listen to her waxing lyrical about some countess who'd been visiting recently.

'Do you know the Countess?' she enquired.

'Afraid not,' he said, casting hopeful glances at the door.

'What a shame you missed her. A charming lady. My dearest friend. I am considering voyaging to London in the near future. Where exactly is your home?'

'Reading.'

'Really. And is that anywhere near Nottingham? That's where the Countess lives.'

'Nottingham is further to the north . . .'

And so the inane conversation laboured on until she spotted Miss Tissington coming up the drive.

'Here she is. I'll fetch her for you.'

Clive waited, wondering why he was bothering with these people, and what he was supposed to say to the governess. Mal's girlfriend. But when she walked in looking so sweet and shy, he changed his mind. Mal's Miss Tissington was lovely. She was a dark-haired girl, not very tall but with a neat figure; her skin was creamy and flawless, and she had marvellous eyes, wide, deep-blue eyes. No wonder Mal raved about her. How on earth had Mal, the bushie, managed to win a girl like this?

Her employer was hovering in the doorway behind her, so Clive spoke quickly.

'Miss Tissington. I'm Clive Hillier . . .'

She nodded cautiously. 'How do you do, Mr Hillier.'

'You don't know me, but I'm a friend of the family. They asked me to call on you.'

She seemed confused, and well she might be, he mused. For all I know she may not have any family apart from the sister. Her employer was still there, so he couldn't explain.

He stepped forward. 'It's such a beautiful day, would you care to take a walk outside?'

'If you wish,' she said primly, while Clive turned to Mrs Manningtree. 'Your gardens are quite lovely, madam.'

She stepped aside, thanking him for the compliment, having no choice but to allow them to pass by her and leave the house.

'I'm so sorry, Miss Tissington,' he said, as soon as they were out of earshot. 'I don't know your family. I had to think of something to say. I'm a friend of Mal's. Mal Willoughby.'

'I see.' She didn't appear impressed with that introduction either.

'I had a letter from him. He asked me to call on you.'

'For what purpose?'

'He seems to think you might be unhappy here.'

'That is not correct.'

'I'm glad to hear it.' He sighed. 'Look, I'm just the messenger. He thought you might be lonely, that you might appreciate some company.'

'So he sent you, Mr Hillier? But who might you be?'

'I was his partner at the diggings. We did quite well for a while but Mal got bored with it, decided to leave. That was a very unfortunate decision. He came in with the gold escort. I presume you know what happened after that?'

'Yes, I do.'

She was heavy going. 'Forgive me,' he murmured. 'Am I to understand that you no longer consider yourself a friend of his? If you were ever that in the first place.'

He expected her to defend herself from the obvious charge that she was a fairweather friend, not inclined to admit to friendship with a wanted man, but she merely glanced at him with a proud tip of her chin.

'And what about you, Mr Hillier? Are you still a friend, or simply a curious messenger?'

'Both,' he said firmly. 'I don't believe for one minute that Mal was involved in that crime, and I've made a statement to the police to that effect.'

'I don't believe he would be either,' she said quietly, and they continued their walk with that established.

'Have you heard from him?' he asked.

Emilie resisted confiding in the stranger. That meeting with Mal had been private. 'He doesn't write to me, Mr Hillier. And I'd prefer he didn't.

174

I'm surprised he took the risk of writing to you.'

'The letter came through friends.'

'I won't ask you where from.'

He shrugged. 'It didn't say. It was just a note. I destroyed it in case the police searched my tent. As his former partner I've had them breathing down my neck too. They haven't bothered you?'

'Why would they?' she asked coldly. 'You're the only person who knows that we are friends. I met him in Brisbane, and we stayed in touch.'

'But he doesn't write to you?'

'I've already said that.'

'I know. I meant it as a sad comment on his situation. Poor Mal. God knows what's to become of him.'

'Isn't there anything you can do to help him?'

'Apart from making a statement, I wouldn't know where to start.'

'I suppose not,' she said glumly.

Next thing a young lad came chasing up the drive after them.

'Miss Tissington!' he called. 'Mum said you have to get back to our lessons. It's after two.'

'Yes, I'm coming, Jimmy.' She turned. 'I'm sorry, Mr Hillier. I have to go.'

'You can't go yet,' he grinned. 'We have all the family things to talk about yet.'

'What family?'

He winked. 'They'd be hurt if you didn't let me deliver all the news of home. You know, how your father doesn't hunt any more and all the rest of it. Mrs Manningtree and I had quite a chat before you came. What time do you finish?'

'She leaves at seven.' Jimmy was pleased to help.

'Very well. I'll call for you at seven, Miss Tissington. The family will be so pleased I've found you. Good day to you, young fellow,' he added, patting Jimmy on the head. Then he strode off towards the gate.

'Is he your boyfriend?' Jimmy asked.

'Certainly not. I only just met the gentleman.'

'Mum says he's gentry.'

Emilie laughed. What next? A title for Mr Hillier to impress Violet Manningtree? To add to the litany of lies that she seemed to be embroiled in.

If not a boyfriend, then at least a suitor. That was the opinion of everyone in the household, despite Emilie's refusal to discuss the matter, because he always seemed to be on the doorstep, waiting for the governess. And Mrs Manningtree was delighted. As it turned out, Emilie smiled, Clive did not have a title, but his father was a colonel and that was good enough for Violet. She invented chores to delay Emilie so she could have her time in the parlour with Mr Hillier, insisting he partake of a glass of sherry or whisky with her. And Emilie, with an elegant gentleman friend, was no

175

longer denied access to the house through the front door, a change that had the kitchen staff in fits of laughter.

'You're really comin' up in the world, missy,' Kate teased.

While not exactly a suitor, Clive was entranced with Miss Tissington. He found he had to work to make her smile, to break down that reserve of hers, to make her talk about her present employment and that family back home, but they did have a lot in common. They both came from England, they were both well educated and they could share their culture shock experiences in coming to this strange country.

For a start, he'd simply walked her home a few times, to the little workman's cottage by the river. Then he'd persuaded her to dine with him at a hotel, but she'd only go to the Prince of Wales Hotel, where she knew the proprietor, Mrs Mooney. On a Sunday afternoon he took her to a band concert down at the end of Wharf Street, and she seemed to enjoy that. Hard to tell. She never enthused about anything.

How the hell then, he worried, had Mal Willoughby got close enough to her to make her a friend? Miss Tissington was a real mystery. A challenge.

In the meantime, tales of hazardous conditions on the northern goldfields had filtered back, and Clive, a fastidious man, was fast losing interest. When he was offered the job of manager of the busy bond store in Wharf Street, he took it gratefully – the decision made for him. Something to do while he pondered his next move. While he was enjoying the company of Emilie Tissington. She was quite a find in this sub-tropical outpost. Poor Emilie. She'd come from a gentle world where it was considered ill-mannered to draw attention to oneself, but it was her neatness, her ladylike demeanour that caused heads to turn in this town, and she was totally unaware of the interest she created.

But where did Mal fit into her scene? Not at all, as far as Clive could make out. She had acknowledged that he was a friend, she believed he was innocent, but that seemed to be the end of it. Emilie never mentioned his name, not voluntarily anyway. And when Clive spoke of him, wondering where and how Mal was, in an attempt to draw her out, she changed the subject very skilfully. It became obvious to him that Mal had exaggerated this relationship. A typically one-sided affair, with Mal starry-eyed about her – and why wouldn't he be? – while she saw him only as a friend, maybe just an acquaintance. And that, he concluded, made sense.

After all, he told himself, I'm more her sort.

Emilie thought so too. She was flattered by Clive's attentions and quite pleased to have a gentleman like him to step out with. At least Ruth would approve of him, as did the Manningtrees. They even invited him to dine, and allowed Emilie to join them, where the inevitable happened. She had to play the piano for the company. That irritated her, but Clive saw no reason for her to be upset.

'I enjoyed the evening,' he said. 'An excellent meal, and though his wife's a bore, old Bert's all right. When in Rome, my dear, you have to make the best of it. And you do play well.'

When he took on the management of the bond store, Clive moved into the Bush Inn, another well-known hostelry that catered for male boarders, and insisted she dine with him there. She was not keen on the idea but trusted his judgement. They had a very pleasant evening and afterwards he walked her home.

This wasn't the first time he'd walked her to her gate, but it was the first time he'd given her a peck on the cheek before he departed, and Emilie thought that was very nice, very sweet. She really was becoming quite fond of Clive; he was such a gentleman, so dependable. It was refreshing to have him around, and a relief that he understood her position without the necessity for any discussion. Living alone, she could not invite him into her house; they both knew that the proprieties had to be observed.

Once inside, though, lighting her lamps that night, Emilie shivered as if with a chill. There was always the possibility that Mal might be waiting for her, and that would require explanations she could do without right now. She hadn't forgotten him. She still worried about him, cared about him, but he seemed to be fading from her life. As Clive had said, there was nothing they could do to help him, they wouldn't know where to start. He was still at large, but where? It seemed unfair that she and his friend should be able to enjoy a normal life while poor Mal was out there battling to survive. Even disloyal.

Emilie went to bed depressed, dreaming not of Clive, who had given her such an enjoyable evening, but of Mal Willoughby and his farewell kiss.

She couldn't bring herself to tell Ruth that she owned the cottage. It was too soon. Ruth had only recently accepted that she intended to remain in her 'rented' accommodation, not without misgivings, though. Her letters still resounded with advice on propriety, no matter the loose-living attitudes of the local populace. Emilie had to smile – her new freedom had given her the opportunity to explore the town, no longer agitated by the presence of darkies in the streets, or by large men, booted and spurred, who tipped their wide hats as she passed by. As for loose living, she knew Ruth would have a fit of the vapours if she heard that this town had as many houses of ill-repute as hotels. And that her sister was aware of them.

At first she'd hurried past those houses to avoid the stares of loud, vulgar women lazing about the verandas, until one of Cook's whispered remarks about all the bordellos opening up in Maryborough caused her to realise with a shock what those women were. She still hurried past them, but always on the other side of the street where possible.

Anyway, Ruth seemed happier these days, less concerned with Emilie than with her own affairs. There was a possibility of a teaching position at the Brisbane Ladies' College for which Ruth considered she was eminently suitable. She had called on the headmistress and the interview had gone well. She was sure her application would be approved by the board.

Even more interesting was her constant talk of Mr Bowles. Her friend. Her dear friend. So kind and helpful. They seemed to be inseparable. And Mr Bowles even sent his regards to her sister. Emilie was thrilled for Ruth and wrote asking for more news of this exciting development, only to be reprimanded for unseemly personal remarks. Ruth explained that Mr Bowles liked to read her letters, and she'd had to hide the last one to avoid embarrassment.

'Try to be more circumspect in future, Emilie,' she admonished.

Circumspect? Emilie sighed as she set out that morning, still thinking of Mal, *her* friend, the outlaw. Obviously he'd never measure up to the perfect Mr Bowles.

Chapter Eight

It happened in the main street, right in front of the post office, on the eve of Kemp's departure for Brisbane, and renewed the anger and indignation about the murders at Blackwater Creek. The former Gold Commissioner took a heart attack and fell from his horse. Had not an agile young chap sprung forward to rescue him, Mr Carnegie would have been run down by a passing wagon loaded with timber.

The incident roused great sympathy for the man, whom people claimed had suffered enough, and it was soon discussed on street corners and in the pubs by the good citizens of Maryborough. Within hours crowds had gathered in the police paddock, beside the station, demanding action, demanding that the outlaws be brought to justice. What with all the other holdups by outlaws and roaming gangs of blacks, as well as the brawls and thievery common in the town, the protesters claimed they were no longer safe in their beds, blaming the police for inaction and ineptitude.

Pollock was pleased that Kemp was still in town. As his superior it was up to the Superintendent to address the mob with the best excuses he could muster, because the truth of it was, they'd not received so much as a wink or a nudge as to the whereabouts of the two wanted men, Willoughby and McPherson. But Kemp put up a good show, his rank inspiring confidence, while he promised more police officers and intimated, with a mysterious note in his voice, that investigations were proceeding . . .

But he still boarded his ship the next day, bound for Brisbane.

Before the ship sailed, the two men slipped down to Kemp's cabin to study the local newspaper, which harangued the police in no uncertain terms, depressing Pollock, who was to be left to face the music.

Kemp pushed his copy aside. He was beginning to think like a politician.

'Well, they would, wouldn't they?' he remarked.

'Would what?'

'Give us a blast. That's their job. Don't worry about it.'

All very well for him, Pollock thought, though he could hardly say so. Instead he came back to their mutual worry.

'What do we do about Carnegie?'

'Hope he lives. He's a witness.'

'Why is he still here?'

'Because his creditors are in Brisbane, I'd say. I tried to persuade him

179

to come back with me, but he wouldn't budge.'

'And he still holds to his story?'

'Word for word.'

'You believe him?'

'I'm inclined to, yes. It's no crime to be broke.'

'I suppose not.'

Frustrated, they drifted into a silence, listening to the soft slap of the waters and the muted voices of other passengers as they found their way aboard.

'You'd better go,' Kemp said, 'or you'll be sailing with me.'

'Yes. I know. There's just one other thing I've been trying to recall, and now it hardly seems worth mentioning.'

'What's that?'

'It's not in my report, because I forgot it at the time, with the shock of finding those bodies, but I do remember Willoughby shouting that Taylor hated Carnegie. Something like that . . .'

'So?'

'Well, Carnegie claimed that he was devastated at Taylor's death. He keeps saying that. He claims that they were best mates.'

'Yes, he told me that. But keep in mind that sudden death can swiftly remove rancour.' Kemp lifted his bulk from his bunk to see Pollock out.

'I know. But why would Willoughby lock on to something as trivial as that, at a time like that? I saw him turn in surprise when Carnegie first claimed Taylor as a mate. It was genuine surprise.'

Kemp shook his head. 'Even so, Carnegie's reaction was natural. Now that you've had plenty of time to think this through, where do you place Willoughby?'

'Hard to say. I met him. Rode with him. He's a likeable bloke, but so are a lot of those criminals out there. I wouldn't have picked him as a killer, had not Carnegie pointed him out.'

'We haven't proved he *was* a killer. Just one of the pair or the gang.'

'True. And there's that other thing. I never did find out where Willoughby got to between the time he arrived in town and contacted me, and when we left to ride out and escort the contingent back to town. I've asked around. No one saw him. He was running late by the time he came back to the station.'

'Are you saying he could have been in touch with one of the gang right here in town? Hardly likely. After a raid like that they'd head for the hills.'

Pollock nodded. 'Yes, you're right. That wouldn't happen. I just don't like gaps, if you know what I mean.'

'Surely do.'

The ship swung out into the river and Kemp stood up by the rails, clearing his head in the gentle breeze as it toiled towards the coast. The river had cleared a path through mangroves and deep forests that gave no hint of the activity beyond. From his vantage point the land seemed uninhabited. By late afternoon they had crossed the wide bay and followed the colourful cliffs and shores of famous Fraser Island before plunging out into the open ocean and heading south.

Kemp dined with the Captain, hearing once again the fascinating story of Mrs Fraser, the surviving castaway, and her adventures, and of the magnificent island and all its beauty. The Captain had actually explored the island; he'd been one of the party sent to search for other survivors after Mrs Fraser had escaped to civilisation with the help of an escaped convict who had lived there with the blacks for years. Kemp was sorry now that he hadn't taken the opportunity to visit the place and view the crystal-clear blue lake that everyone talked about, but he'd had more important matters on his mind. So he was content to share excellent brandy with the Captain and be a good listener.

In the morning, though, strolling the decks, he thought of Taylor, the clerk. The man with impeccable credentials. The man who had been taken in by Willoughby, enough to approve his appointment as a guard on Carnegie's recommendation. The man, he quickly recalled, who had kept meticulous notes and books. The man who had a wife in Brisbane too, A widow, he corrected himself.

The sea was choppy, exhilarating, with a fair wind blowing and not a cloud in the sky. The few passengers aboard were polite and the Captain an excellent companion. But Kemp was eager to get back to Brisbane. He prayed that Taylor had been on good terms with his wife, because, being so meticulous, he would have written to her. He would have given her some insight into his sojourn on the goldfields. He might even have mentioned Carnegie.

Jasper Kemp lay down to sleep that night with a mild comment: 'Well, he might have.' It was worth, perhaps, a little of his time.

How else could he help Pollock? As their friend Allyn Carnegie had said, the rogues would be well gone from the Maryborough district by this.

Though Allyn was conscious, his eyes were wearily closed. He was lying on a bed as hard as a slab in the morgue. And as cold. He could do with another blanket but would not ask. Suffering was his life. His destiny. What were a few more hours of pain to a doomed man? The slightest movement made his head throb, and his body was all of an ache. Agony, he was in agony, and no one cared. He knew he was in the wretched bush hospital, a foul place, stinking of metho and phenol, the 'before-and-after' smells, his mother used to call them, as she saw out her last days in a miserable country hospital like this. The one to revive, the other to disinfect, after the soul had flown.

Well, thought Allyn, I can't wait for my soul to fly. I shall welcome the release from my suffering, from those matter-of-fact voices around me, talking as if I'm already a corpse.

'Heart attack,' they were saying nonchalantly, as if this heart was a fort that had only sustained a few arrows, as if attacked hearts were trivial, routine and not deadly serious.

181

'Nearly killed him,' he heard, and gave a mental nod to avoid further spasms of headache, as they stamped round his room, jarring his bed, while his heart fluttered to its end. The poor heart, out of sight, out of mind.

All his life it had been sorely tested. So much effort, so many failures, it was a wonder it had lasted this long. Tears came into his eyes when he recalled his last, his final endeavour, and he tried not to think about it, but the travail was too recent. He saw himself boarding the ferry with his horse, rattling down the ramp on the other side of the river, relieved that there was no necessity to explain his destination to the ferryman, who hadn't even bothered to enquire. He was just another passenger. Irritating to realise that he could have made this journey earlier.

He took off down the road with a cheery wave that belied the pounding of his heart, heading for the plantations, but soon detoured down the dirt track that followed the river. A lonely track, not much use to anyone bar fishermen or as the back entrance to a plantation, because it was known to flood, and it ran smack into a jutting hill. A dead end. So Perry couldn't have missed the tree. It was there on the left, the massive Moreton Bay fig, its huge branches extending out over the muddy waters of the river. And there for anyone but a blind man to see were the signs that Carnegie himself had carved into the trunk. Just VVV. They meant nothing. They wouldn't have interested any observer except Perry. Innocuous letters carved by an idle hand. VVV. The haul from the robbery should be stuffed in the hollows formed by the mangled, above-ground roots of this tree.

Allyn looked about him and shivered. He sensed danger in this desolate spot but forced himself to dismiss the fear, which he knew had come from the reminder of what he was about. Fear of being caught in the act of retrieving the haul. Fear that Perry had robbed him. Taken the lot and absconded.

He climbed down from the horse and squelched through the mud towards the tree. Last time he was here, the banks had been drier, the muddy bank at this level caked and cracked, much more accessible, but today he'd just have to put up with the mud. He hoped that Perry had placed the bags in the hollows above the water level, worrying, as he began to search, that the banknotes could be ruined, though the gold and coin would survive.

The base of the tree was yards in diameter, hidden by writhing, extended roots, and the first time Allyn reached in, feeling about the hollow, his heart sank. Nothing. From then on, searching and searching in every nook, hope fading, desperation set in. He went round the tree again, clambering over the slippery roots, praying, cursing, even looking higher, among the tough, leafy branches, but nothing. No sign of bags of any sort.

Finally he stood back, hissing at the tree, calling Perry every foul name he could think of, then, making allowances for Perry's idiocy, his lack of brains, he surveyed other trees in case the fool had got it wrong. Only

182

Perry could make a mistake like this. But there were hundreds of trees. If he'd hidden the haul in one of them, surely he'd have had the sense to blaze it with the agreed VVV sign, which was as clear as a bell on the huge fig. Allyn kicked at the base of other trees in a haphazard manner, knowing he wouldn't find the treasure, knowing, without a shadow of a doubt, that any further searching was a waste of time. Baldy Perry had double-crossed him. By this it didn't come as a surprise. Just a horrible, miserable sense of defeat.

His horse, waiting patiently up there on the track, reins hitched casually to a tree, gave him the warning. It suddenly snorted, pawed the ground, spooked, and instinctively Allyn looked up the track, expecting company.

He couldn't be caught fishing round down here without good reason, and he certainly didn't want to draw attention to this particular neck of the woods, so he moved quickly up the grassy bank, slipping a little, grabbing at tufts.

But the horse wasn't just spooked. It looked crazed, nostrils flared, and in that split second Allyn saw terror in its eyes. He looked back to the river and saw the reason. A huge crocodile, at least twenty feet long, was already out of the water, plunging towards him.

'Oh, Jesus!' he screamed. 'Oh, Jesus!' Fear gave him wings. He flew up that bank, knowing how fast crocodiles could move, not daring to look back again until he was well on to the track and higher still, past the horse, which was rearing and screaming by this. It burst its leather straps and shied away to safety, to stand shuddering down the track.

As Allyn watched, the monster came to a halt, the heavy snout with its meshed teeth menacing the area, cold eyes waiting. Then the huge body on its fat claws turned about. Having missed its prey, it waddled away and slid silently into the water. Even then, even though he was safe, Allyn, mesmerised, was afraid to move. His heart was pounding so hard he thought it would choke him. The monster hadn't gone away; it was only half submerged in the shallows, knobbly head and eyes still visible. Allyn wondered wildly if this monster or one of its mates had got Perry. They could take a man with ease. They could, and had, taken horses. That animal up there knew the danger only too well.

Everyone knew these northern rivers were alive with crocs. Why hadn't he thought of that? Because the last time he was here he'd been too busy with his plans, and besides, the river had been lower.

'Oh, God,' he moaned, feeling battered and bilious at his narrow escape. That brute would have killed him. Would have dragged him into the river, rolled over to drown him, and killed him, and nobody would ever have known that Allyn Carnegie had met such a frightful end. He vomited into the spiky grass.

The horse was docile, comforted by his presence, willing to be ridden away from that place with half of a single bridle strap to direct him, and no one on the crowded ferry returning to Maryborough even noticed. They were too busy trying to cope with about twenty kanakas, fleeing a plantation in protest at ill-treatment, who had boarded the ferry, refusing to pay, demanding they be taken back to town.

Allyn was too shattered to care what they did. He squatted on the deck beside his horse, his only friend in the world, like an old bushie, like a tramp, with no future and a past not worth mention.

By the time he rode back into town he had no destination; he just sat his horse and let it wander the familiar streets. The horse had recovered, but its master had not. He rode, unseeing, uncaring past his house, so the horse took charge. It was headed for home, for Grauber's stables and a good feed, when suddenly its master fell off, and they'd only been plodding along.

The doctor was tapping him. That doctor, that bloody witchdoctor, fit only for veterinary work, was tapping him.

'Mr Carnegie. How are you?'

Allyn was irritated by this intervention. Couldn't a man die in peace?

'How are you?'

A response was essential to get rid of the fool.

'How do you think I am?' he muttered angrily, barely able to muster enough strength for even this effort. 'I've had a heart attack that almost killed me, and . . .' he sucked in breath to continue, 'my lungs have given out. Leave me be.'

'No, we can't do that. You have had a mild heart attack, but that won't kill you. Though the fall from the horse, almost under the wheels of that wagon, nearly did.'

'A fall from my horse?' Allyn could raise words now without effort.

'Yes. You really are in the wars lately. A bang on the head, a cracked rib and a few more bruises, but you'll be all right. Out of here in a few days.' He laughed. 'Only the good die young, sir.'

'What's that supposed to mean?'

'A joke. Now you rest and take some nourishment and I'll see you tomorrow.'

Never before, in all his life, with the trials and tribulations he'd suffered, with people letting him down, and brilliant plans going astray, had Allyn Carnegie ever wished that tomorrow would not come. But he did now. He wanted to die, but as usual he was failing even in that simple ambition.

While not quite out of the district, Mal was well on his way, climbing steadily into the hills past Gympie. At the same time Pollock was returning to Maryborough with a prisoner, a forger who had been creating havoc by issuing fake sovereigns in busy hotels and taverns for the best part of a year.

Mal pressed on for days, heading north-west into the back country where folks living in isolated farmhouses or loggers' huts were never averse to a yarn with amiable travellers. He had assumed the role of a prospector, not for gold this time, but for land, knowing that country folk liked nothing better than a chance to expound on the fortunes and misfortunes of trying to tame the bush. And he was, above all, an amiable traveller, with a ready smile, an honest face, a shy manner about him and a readiness to give a hand where needed, accepting only a meal in return for his services.

He dug wells, helped men in the onerous chore of removing huge tree roots from cleared land, sawed timber, gathered firewood for the women, and even better, being a non-drinker, declined their kind offers of a glass of rum or whisky. To these people, barely surviving in their rough huts, liquor was precious and his reticence was appreciated. Somehow, though, over a campfire or a billy of tea in the bush, he always managed to bring up the name of McPherson, watching carefully for a reaction. Most had heard of the Scot, since he was becoming part of folklore, but beyond that there was little interest, so Mal moved on.

The search was slow and disheartening. What with the frequent stops, Mal had been moving north for nearly three weeks but had only covered a few hundred miles as the crow flies. He marvelled that McPherson had covered five times the distance to get to that northern town of Bowen. But then the Scot would not have had a mission, as Mal did. He would simply have been keeping out of reach of the law. As Mal himself should be doing. But he had to find McPherson. It was all he could think to do, because if McPherson couldn't help him, he'd be on the run for the rest of his life. Or until they caught him, he brooded.

One night, though, when he was almost ready to turn back from this hopeless task, having decided there was one place where he could hide out in safety, at his uncle's property in the far west of New South Wales, it occurred to Mal that McPherson must after all have travelled as he was doing. The same way. He would have needed help too, not only for himself but for his horse. Mal's horse had already thrown two shoes. White men couldn't live indefinitely in this rough country without help, relying totally on bush food, and the Aborigines out this way were by no means obliging. So who had helped him? He must have mates out here somewhere. If he was in the area at all, Mal thought dismally.

That night, with a hot, dry wind blowing and the unmistakable smell of bushfires in the air, Mal decided against lighting a campfire, which could easily spark a bushfire, and contented himself with a tin of beans and an apple he'd been treasuring for days.

In the morning he climbed a rise to see if he could locate the fire, but smoke furling from distant hills told him it was a long way off. Then he saw another curl of smoke, coming from a shack almost hidden deep in a valley. He shrugged disconsolately and decided that that might as well be his next port of call.

This time he was not so welcome. A worn-looking woman, in her thirties he guessed, with a small girl hanging on to her skirts, greeted him at the door of her log hut with a shotgun as he rode up.

'What do you want?' she shouted.

He held up both hands. 'No trouble, missus. I'm not armed.'

'I asked you what you wanted.'

'I'm just passing through. Going north.'

'Well, keep going.'

He sighed. 'I hoped you could spare us some water. My horse is dyin' for a drink.'

She wavered and he smiled to himself. They'd let a man die of thirst, but not a horse.

'There's a creek down the hill.'

'And if it's on your property, I'd still be trespassing.'

'What?'

'Begging your pardon, missus, I don't want to be trespassing. I mean you no harm. Did you know there's fire in the hills?'

'There's always fire in these hills this time of the year.'

'I suppose there is. Would you mind not pointing that gun at me. It makes me nervous. I've come from Jake Raymond's place, I'm on my way to Rockhampton.'

'You're well off course . . .'

'Can I get down? I think we're frightening your little girl.'

The child did look scared, so the woman allowed him to dismount. 'But keep your distance. What's your name?'

'Mal.' Had she insisted, the surname would have been an invention.

'You one of them loggers?'

'No. Not me.'

It took some cajoling, but he finally managed to convince her that he was not the enemy, and he was allowed to lead his horse over to the trough, where it drank greedily.

'Why are you so fearful of loggers?' he asked quietly, and she turned on him, still holding the shotgun.

'Because they're drunken bastards. They came through here two days ago and treated my house like a tavern. Shoutin' and roisterin' . . .'

'They didn't harm you?' he asked, genuinely concerned.

'Didn't get a chance.' She put the gun down carefully, so he guessed it was loaded. 'Me and the child spent the night in the barn with the gun pointed at the door. Any of them had come in, they'd have got what they deserved. A nice mess they made of my house, and rode off without so much as a sorry. I've been cleanin' up ever since . . . the bastards.'

She was so suspicious of him, he didn't dare ask where her husband was, but she did relent, and gave him tea and reheated stew.

Her name was Mrs Foley and the child was Angela. They sat at a home-made table under a timber awning clothed in purple wisteria, and encouraged by the visitor, Mrs Foley was as keen for a chat as any of his previous hosts. She enthused about the serenity and beauty of the area, and told him proudly that they had bought more than eighty acres . . . 'for a song'.

'You can grow anything in this country, it's fine farmland. It's harder to keep down everything else that wants to grow alongside our crops. In time we'll have big orchards here, you mark my words.' Though they had shade, they were not sheltered from the wind that gusted across the

186

clearing, and her hat blew off, scudding towards a two-rail fence beyond which nestled a long, neat strawberry patch. Mal retrieved it for her and turned the conversation to her, and the lonely life out here, but she laughed.

'We're never lonely. Too much to do. Them loggers is the only trouble we've had here. My husband called a truce with the blacks when we first got here, so they don't give us no bother. They take him hunting sometimes, and they're good to our Angela here. She wandered off a few months ago, got lost, we were nearly out of our minds with worry, but the blacks brought her back. I could have kissed them all.'

The girl squirmed. 'I weren't lost. I were just lookin' about.'

'Sure you were,' her mother grinned.

While they talked about visitors and neighbours, she was careful to give him no hint of her husband's whereabouts, as if to convey the impression that he wasn't far off, although Mal guessed he was away temporarily, probably helping out a neighbour with heavy work, as was often the case in these outlying districts. Or delivering produce to a pickup point. Otherwise he'd have been here to confront the loggers.

But the conversation being on visitors, he dropped the name of McPherson, remarking that outlaws were said to favour this area, and she was immediately on the defensive.

'What's it to you?'

'Nothing. I just wouldn't want to run into one on a dark night.'

That response didn't work. 'Are you with the police or something?' she asked him. Suspicious again.

'Me? No fear. As a matter of fact, I met McPherson once. In Brisbane. Got along all right with him. But I'd be a bit wary of the others.'

'Why? They got no quarrel with you.'

Mal smiled. 'You mean I'm not worth robbing. I guess not. But I'd better be going now.'

She didn't disagree. 'You can get yourself some water from the tank before you go if you like. Me and Angela got work to do now.'

Dismissed, he filled his waterbag while she watched, thanked her for her kindness and strode over to his horse.

More out of mischief than hope of a breakthrough, Mal bade her goodbye as he mounted, then called back to her with a grin:

'If you ever see McPherson, tell him I said hello.'

Riding down the track away from the farmhouse, he blew the hot wind from his face in a faint effort to gain some fresher air, because the acrid smell of burning eucalypts was so strong, with smoke wafting over from those distant bushfires.

About a mile down the road he came to a narrow creek, crossed it and looked at the track that wound through the scrub, up the steep hillside. He'd forgotten to ask Mrs Foley where this road led. Not that it mattered; he'd find out sooner or later. Another farm, another lonely inn or the loggers' camp. He was tossing up whether to tackle the steep climb right away or cool off in the stream first when he heard the familiar crackle of fire in the bush. It was so loud, it had to be close. He glanced all about him, but could see very little at this level. The trees stretching above him to the blue skyline were green and still, giving no indication of fire, even in the undergrowth, but the menace was near, that was certain, probably just over the hill.

Mal was no sightseer. He didn't need to climb a hill to see another bushfire; there was nothing to be done about them out here, they just had to burn themselves out. He decided that retreat was the better part of valour, turned the horse about and was easing it through the rocky shallows of the stream when he heard a whoosh, almost like a large engine letting off steam . . .

'Jesus!' he shouted. 'Here's your bloody fire all right.' The wind was showering the treetops with smoke, and flying leaves danced about in a confused flurry seconds before the fire burst over the ridge. The skyline up there looked like a figure with its hair on fire. He waited just long enough to see that it was a huge inferno, a great line of flame across the hills, storming fiercely down the tinder-dry valley, the wind lashing it on.

He put the horse to the gallop and tore back along the track to the Foley house, realising that the fire was travelling equally as fast, racing down towards him.

She knew. She was out front of her house, tossing buckets of water at the timber walls, while Angela stood by, refilling the buckets as fast as she was able.

'No time for that!' he shouted. Heavy smoke was bearing down on them already. 'Come on, get on the horse.'

He made a grab for Angela, but her mother screamed at him. 'Leave her alone. Come and help me!'

Frightened, the child ran to her.

Mal jumped down from his horse and grabbed the woman by the arm. 'Leave it, the fire's coming. It's too big. You haven't got a hope here.'

She was screaming at him to leave her alone, that she wouldn't leave her house, when he saw that another branch of the fire, probably lit by flying sparks, was well under way in the bush to the rear of the house, flames leaping high as it devoured a field of maize.

The horse reared, panicking, and Mal had to hang on to it while he forced the woman to give up the hopeless task, dragging her away.

By this time the heat was intense. He was back on the horse, finally managing to pull her up behind him, thanking the Lord that she was a slight, skinny woman, and holding Angela in front of him, when the fire roared into sight. His horse didn't need any urging; it took off with a jolt that nearly unseated them all, but they hung on, pelting down the track only to find the fire had crossed the road further down and was confronting them, threatening to engulf them in a firestorm.

'Cover your heads,' he yelled, as he jerked the horse to a halt. 'We have to go through.'

'We can't,' screamed the woman, but he pulled off his shirt, and dumped it down over the horse's head, and before the animal had a chance to react, kicked it into action. The horse bolted wildly, trying to rid itself of the cloth that was blocking its sight, and they went on through in seconds, emerging to blackened fields and scarecrow trees as the fire, behind them now, surged on.

Mal had crouched over Angela to protect her, so she was untouched, but his hair was singed and Mrs Foley was frantically brushing hot ash from her hair and clothes, and from him, except, he realised as the horse halted, shedding the blindfold, that she was thumping him. Thumping his back.

'What did you do that for?' she sobbed, still thumping angrily. 'You could have killed us. You could have killed Angela.'

'It's all right,' he said quietly, calming her. 'You can hop down now.'

Then they were walking miserably along the desolate road, leading the horse, trying not to look at the burned carcasses of small animals that littered the scorched land and hung, ghastly black forms, from stripped, scarred eucalypts. At least the trees will burst into life again, Mal thought, but I'm betting her house and their crops are finished.

Angela finally broke the silence, her voice wavering still from fright. 'Where are we going?'

'I don't know,' he said. 'We'll just have to keep walking until we're past the burnt-out patch and then we'll see.'

The gloom of smoke was clearing as they tramped on through the wasteland, but nothing could lift the woman from her misery. Mal saw the tears running unchecked down her grimy face, and took her arm to assist her round the blackened debris strewn on the track, but she soon broke away and he let her be. She would have to deal with this calamity in her own way.

He gave Angela a drink of water from his waterbag and was settling her on the horse again when three horsemen came galloping down the road towards them. They were all heavily bearded bushmen, and by the look of their blackened faces and battered clothes they'd been fighting fires elsewhere.

One of the men, obviously Mrs Foley's husband, leapt from his horse and threw his arms around her.

'Thank God you're safe. And Angela too. Thank God.'

'Everything's gone,' she wept. 'The fire. It came too fast. I couldn't do anything. I'm sorry.'

'Now, now. It's all right. It can't be helped. As long as you're both safe, it doesn't matter.'

The other men dismounted to comfort her while Foley ran over to his daughter, forcing a grim smile.

'Look at you, riding the big horse while your daddy was worrying about you.'

'We rode right into the fire,' she said, 'and it was hot. I thought we'd get burned but we didn't. That man made us. Mum didn't want to.'

Foley nodded to Mal. 'Thanks, mate. I'm beholden to you. I couldn't get back here in time.'

'It was moving fast,' Mal said. 'Roared up out of those back hills. You wouldn't have seen it until it was too late. Nothing you could have done.'

The party rode moodily along the track, which verged east, until they topped a rise and Mal looked about him in surprise. The other side of this hill was untouched, and the sweet fragrance of bushland spread out below them was almost too strong after the dank and sour smell of smoke. The men looked back at the destruction behind them, shook their heads and rode on.

Several miles on, they emerged from the bush and rode into the fields of a banana plantation. Silently Mal bet that the owner of this place was thanking his lucky stars.

As it turned out, the owner was with them. They called him Ward. Mal didn't know whether it was his Christian name or surname, but it was of no importance. Ward led them through an avenue of tall, frayed banana palms until they came to his farmhouse, and his wife came running, arms outstretched in relief, to see to Mrs Foley and Angela.

Eventually, when they'd sorted themselves out and explanations and introductions were over, Ward announced that a drink was in order, so the men gathered for the ritual by the water tank, handing out mugs of rum.

'If you don't mind,' Mal said, 'I don't care for rum. Water will do.'

The host was shocked. 'You can't have water, Mal. Have a rum, it'll put meat on your bones.'

'Not much of a drinker,' Mal explained. 'Can't say I like the taste. Water will do. I've got a mighty thirst.'

None of them had washed, and they were all blackened with soot, but drinks by the tank had priority while they talked over the events of the day. Mal knew the women would be making tea inside, and he yearned for a cup, but in this company to ask would not be appropriate, even though they'd already voted him a hero. The other man, whom they called Bill, hadn't had much to say before this, but now he took a swig of rum, wiped a hand across his bushy mouth and peered at Mal.

'What did you say your name was?'

'Mal.'

'The hell! I been wondering whcrc I seen you before. Now I got it. You're the pansy that don't drink. And I've got your name too, you bloody pipsqueak!'

The quiet voice had turned into a familiar roar, and Mal knew he'd found his quarry, but had already upset him.

The Scot lunged at Mal and grabbed him by the shirt. 'The name's Ned Turner, isn't it? Bloody cheapskate. Swapped me a watch for a horse but never told me the bloody watch was engraved. Name all over it. Had to ditch the thing.'

Mal reacted angrily, pushing him away. 'It was my horse. You stole it in the first place.'

'You calling me a horse thief?'

'I'm calling you McPherson, and your name's not Bill either.'

The other men stood by with benign grins, Ward still holding the mug

190

of water he had poured for Mal, while Matt Foley propped himself, interested but unconcerned, against a long fence.

'Never ye mind my name. What are you doing skulking round out here, Turner?'

'Looking for you. I've been more than a month on the road looking for you.'

'Is that right?' He turned to his mates with a guffaw. 'Did ye hear that? And we'd better look out, because he's going to take me in, all on his own, and claim the reward. Do you reckon I ought to go?'

'Yeah,' Foley laughed, but there was menace in his voice now, Mal's previous status as the hero under serious threat. 'You run along with him. Maybe you could split the reward.'

'Or maybe I could split his head open right out here, where no one would miss him.'

'Unless he's in cahoots with the traps,' Matt warned. Traps was a bush name for police.

Mal moved away from them. 'Ease up. You've got it all wrong. My name's not Ned Turner.'

'The hell it's not,' McPherson growled.

'Well it's not. It's Mal Willoughby.'

'This week!'

Mal turned on the Scot. 'Why don't you shut up and listen. Don't you read the papers? Mal Willoughby!'

'What's the papers got to do with it?' McPherson snapped, and then he reacted as if he'd been bitten. 'Jesus bloody Christ. Willoughby! From the holdup on the Gympie road? Where you dropped me in it? I'll kill you, you bastard.' He was spluttering in rage. 'I never had nothing to do with that. Me and Matt, we were up in Bundaberg then, weren't we?'

Matt nodded, and it was then that Mal began to understand why Mrs Foley had given no reasons for her husband's absence. He'd probably been away on a job with the Scot. Judging by the calm acceptance of McPherson's identity, all of these men were involved in the outlaw business, with their farms as ideal hangouts. He remembered Mrs Foley's tears about the loss of their farm, and Matt's response.

'Never mind, love, we'll start again.'

'With what? We're ruined.'

'No we're not.' He'd winked at Ward. At the time Mal had only taken the wink as apology for a gentle lie, but now he knew better. And so did Mrs Foley, had she stopped to think about it. A couple more raids would put them on their feet again while the farms gave them cover as responsible citizens, battling the elements deep in the bush, hundreds of miles from coastal towns.

'I didn't think you were there,' he said quietly. 'Can I have a smoke?'

Ward reached for his pouch, rolled a smoke and handed it two-fingered to Mal. The kindness, the gratitude, had been extinguished from the eyes of these men now and he saw only their hard, uncompromising faces. Romantic tales of their exploits were only folklore, as men who'd been

191

robbed and bashed by them could testify. Mal knew he had to talk fast.

He nodded to McPherson. 'If you weren't there, who was?'

'How the hell do I know? You tell me. You're the one.'

Mal drew on the smoke. 'That's the trouble. I'm not. I wasn't there either.'

McPherson leered at him. 'Don't get smart with us, sonny. You were in on it all right, and now that you've come this far to pull me in, you won't be leaving until we hear who's using my name in vain, if you get the picture. We'd be right pleased to hear a name or two.'

'Good. I'll give them to you. But you have to hear me out. I'll tell you what happened. Right from the start. Can I have that water, please?'

Mal drank the water, handed the mug back and squatted on his haunches while he related the whole story, from the goldfields to his escape, smoothly sidestepping their irritating interjections.

'So that's it,' he said eventually. 'That's what happened.'

'Then what?' Ward asked.

'Well . . . I've been on the run and I . . .'

'Bugger you. What about the gold? Where is it?'

Mal stared. To them the question was obvious. To him it was the least expected. 'How do I know?'

'What's the point of all that rigmarole if you don't know who's got the gold?' McPherson barked.

'I dunno,' Mal said uneasily. 'I just figured I ought to come and have a talk to you. You're getting blamed for it same as me, and I didn't reckon you were in on it either.'

'Who cares what you reckon? You're just a small-time hustler.'

'I bloody care,' Mal retorted. 'It's my neck as well as yours. We have to clear our names.'

'Yeah! Right, lad. We'll ride down to Maryborough and tell them ourselves, then we'll go to the pub and buy you a raspberry cordial.'

Mal turned to Ward. 'Can't you make him see sense? This wasn't just a holdup, there were three murders. If they catch us we're gone. No jury in the world could save us.'

Foley intervened. 'You say you've been on the run all this time,' he commented suspiciously. 'How come you're so bloody smart? For all we know, you're a bloody informer, trackin' our mate here for the police. For all we know, you're not Willoughby. We never seen no pictures of you in the paper. Jimmy here said your name is Turner.'

Mal shook his head. He didn't like any of these men, but he was stuck with them. And with Bill, who was James McPherson, known to his mates as Jimmy.

'I pinched the damn watch from the toff. I wasn't about to give my real name to anyone. Give me a go. My name's Mallachi Willoughby and I come from west New South Wales. And I don't like being on the run for something I didn't do. You can take it or leave it.'

He helped himself to another drink of water while they refilled their mugs of rum and ignored him, talking among themselves.

'All right,' Foley said in the end. 'Give us another story. If you were on the run, who took you in? How did you dodge the traps?'

'No one took me in. I don't know anyone in that district. I couldn't go back to the goldfields and I reckoned the police would expect me to head for the hills, so I went in the other direction. East.'

'What's east?' McPherson snapped. 'You'd run into the sea.'

Mal grinned. 'Yeah. So I did. More sea than I've ever seen in my life. So I went across to Fraser Island.'

'Swam, I suppose?' Foley growled.

'No, in a canoe. I teamed up with some black lads and they took me. Had to let the beard grow.'

'Oh, Jesus, that's right,' McPherson said. 'Angel face he is, behind the fluff. We ought to shave it off.'

'Then I'm not moving from here until it grows again. You can give me a job out there in your plantation.'

'We got kanakas to do that,' Ward said. 'And that story of yours about this bloke Carnegie giving you a job. What was that all about? If you had no part in the holdup, what was the idea of him pointing the finger at you? According to the papers, he said he saw two men commit these crimes. One he says was Jimmy here, and you were the other one. Why you? He trusted you. He gave you the escort job. What was the point in fingering you?'

Mal sighed, relieved at least that they seemed to accept now that he was Willoughby. 'I've been trying to work it out myself. Why pick on me? The bastard.'

'Or me,' McPherson said, lighting his pipe and taking time to suck on it. He looked at Ward. 'Unless there wasn't anyone else to point at.'

'What does that mean?'

'What *I've* been thinking,' Mal said.

McPherson glared at him. 'You shut up, sonny, and let me do me own thinkin'. This bloke Carnegie says he saw two holdup men. Why two? Because it was too big a job for one bloke. He says there could have been more out on the road, but he didn't see them. Like they probably didn't exist. What sort of a gang, moving fast, would have their mates out on a road sitting their horses like ladies-in-waiting?'

'Doesn't sound too bright,' Matt conceded.

'Good. So only two blokes did the job. Now this bastard described me and sonny here. Why? Because I'm famous, and he could be placed on the spot by Carnegie himself.'

'By his lies,' Mal said.

'By his plan,' McPherson corrected. 'Sounds to me as if you walked right into it, you mug.'

'I didn't walk anywhere. I was on my way to Maryborough to bring back the police escort.'

McPherson stood back with a grin. 'And bloody sorry we are we didn't know you were there. We could have held up the coach, grabbed the gold, with your help, and we wouldn't have had to shoot anyone.'

193

Ward's wife came out to tell them to wash up for dinner. 'In a minute,' Ward told her, and turned back to McPherson. 'So what's the story here?'

'Carnegie's a liar. So that gives him the front seat. But who was his partner? Two men, he said. A dead giveaway. Him and someone else. But who? We have to get that bastard.'

Mal was excited. They were coming to the same conclusion as he had, but he dared not intrude. It was obvious they'd studied the newspapers far more than they'd previously allowed, which told him McPherson was disturbed by the charges. They talked openly about the problem in front of their wives, who went quietly about serving them soup and a thick stew at the long kitchen table, the saga of the fires seemingly forgotten. For the time being anyway.

'So who's got the gold?' Foley asked in the end. 'According to the papers, Mal's mate Carnegie is in Maryborough.'

'He's not my mate. I've been suspicious of him ever since he accused me, but why would a toff like him get mixed up in robbery and murder? And how do you know he's still in Maryborough?'

McPherson sighed, nodding thanks to the women, who had left the table and were serving the men tea. 'For gold, wet-behind-the-ears! No one's immune. Not the laird nor the lad. It said in the papers that there was a ruckus in Maryborough recently, with the good citizens complaining no one has swung yet. And your Mr Carnegie had a heart attack and fell off his horse. Can't you read?'

'I'm on my bloody own,' Mal retorted. 'I don't have hideouts and I don't have people to buy papers for me. And I'm sick of all this talk. What can we do? You lot reckon you're smarter than me, but they're after us, you and me, McPherson. If I can find you they will too. And sooner or later they'll get me. We're running out of time. I've come to you for help and all you can do is talk.'

The outlaws laced their black tea with rum. Mal had milk.

'We have to think about it,' Ward said. 'My missus has made a bunk for you in the stable, Mal. You go and put your head down. The women have taken care of your horse.'

Mal stood, dismissed, but Foley walked out to the stable with him. 'Don't go past here. The kanakas and their overseer live down that track. They don't need to see you. And thanks for taking care of my missus and the girl. Sorry we were a bit heavy on you, but . . .' He shrugged. 'You know. It ain't easy these days.'

The stable was warm. His bunk smelled sweetly of clean straw. Six contented horses were snuffling, comforting company. Mal slept well.

In the morning Mrs Foley came down to wake him, thank him and apologise for her ill-temper out on the road.

'I'd hoped with the farm that Matt would have been out of the other business, but now that it's gone,' she grieved, 'it'll start all over again. There seems no end to it.'

He muttered something appropriate for the thanks and all, but she hadn't finished. 'What do you think you're doing with them? They're old hands at the game, but you're only a young fellow. What in the name of God would your mother say?'

'My mother's long gone, Mrs Foley . . .'

'God rest her soul, to be looking down on this.'

'I didn't have anything to do with that holdup.'

'Maybe not. But I got ears, and did I not hear Jimmy say you stole a fine watch? You see now how things go? Started small and look at the trouble you're in now . . .'

It was no use arguing; she had the floor and her lecture had to run its course.

'Best thing you can do is move on. They're already talking about another raid, to help me and Matt out. Always another one, you see.' She sighed. 'Always another reason, and me knowing there's no end to it. Only the one I can't be bearin' to think about. So you be on your way while you can; this is no place for the likes of you. Now come up and have your porridge.'

She was right. As Mal took his spoon to a huge bowl of porridge sweetened with molasses and cream, the trio were already discussing the possibility of holding up a coach which carried wages for railroad workers somewhere to the north, and, to his horror, including him in their plan as if he'd now been accepted as a member of the gang.

'All very well,' he said, when he found a chance to speak. 'But the immediate problem is me and Mr McPherson.' He saw them grin that he addressed the outlaw formally but knew from past experience that these little gestures of humility won hearts, pleased people, delivered smiles. Gave him an edge.

And so it was. 'We're well aware of that, son,' Ward said kindly. 'You're in a bad spot, the both of you. Nothing we can do to help, bar keep you both hid up here, but Jimmy's got an idea.'

'You bet I have,' McPherson growled. 'And more than one bloody idea. The first is, we ought to go back into Maryborough and screw that bastard Carnegie's neck until he spews out the truth.'

Mal was stunned. 'You can count me out on that for a start. I'm not going anywhere near Maryborough.'

'Hang on. Let me finish. The second is, we're getting blamed for that holdup, so if we find that gold, it's ours.'

'Fat chance,' Mal said.

'The third is this. I'll write a letter to the *Maryborough Chronicle* . . .'

'He writes good letters,' Matt interjected.

'And tell them what?' Mal asked.

'Tell them the truth. That you and me are innocent. That Carnegie is a liar. A lot safer than going to town.'

'And then what?'

'We'd have to wait and see.'

They seemed to think it was a great idea. Mal couldn't see the point. 'What good is a letter?'

Matt Foley explained. 'Look at it this way. If you or me was to be writing the letter, it would be wastin' in a bin within minutes. But Jimmy here, he's famous. A letter from him would earn a front page.'

'Why?'

'Because that's how newspapers work. They've got to live, like the rest of us. A letter from Jimmy would be a sensation.'

'How do you know?' Mal thought all three ideas were hare-brained, but then he didn't have any suggestions of his own. He'd run to find McPherson for company, for solace even, believing foolishly that the Scot could somehow extricate him from this mess, but he knew now that there was no solution here. Or anywhere else. He'd just have to keep running. Maybe try to get out of the country.

Ward was explaining. 'Matt worked for a newspaper in Dublin in the old days.'

Mrs Foley, walking past the kitchen table, put in her threepenn'orth. 'Pity he isn't still there!' she said tartly.

Foley turned on her. 'What's this you say, woman? They'd have hung me there for speaking up for Ireland. Would you rather that? Would you rather be a widow starvin' back there? Or would you have been glad to be rid of me, so you could marry Dinny Murnane, who'd sell his soul for a penny?'

Angrily she slapped at him with a dishcloth and the discussion deteriorated into a domestic argument. With the kitchen in disarray, Mal moved outside, looking over at the banana plantation that climbed the adjacent hills in a profusion of green while he rehearsed his excuse for leaving. Mrs Foley was right. He was in enough trouble without throwing in his lot with these bitter men. The charges hanging over his head were bad enough without seeking more. But the decision depressed him. There was a lonely road ahead.

McPherson was far from pleased when Mal announced he was leaving, and immediately suspicious.

'Where do you think you're going? Have a mind to throw your lot in with the traps, eh? Trade your thick hide for Jimmy McPherson, would you?' He stood up, thumping a fist on the table. 'You're not going anyplace.'

But Mal wasn't to be intimidated by the Scot's rantings. He was no longer impressed by the famous outlaw. Besides, Mrs Foley was standing in the background, frowning at him, as if ready to give him a whack with the dishcloth too if he didn't make a move.

'Ease up,' he said crankily. 'I can't go near the police and you know it. I'm a stranger in these parts. It's better I keep moving. You don't want folk round here wondering who I am.'

'The hell with them. We've got a job for you. Being a stranger will come in handy.'

'I'm not coming in on that holdup, if that's what you've got in mind.'

'You'll do as you're bloody told.'

'Or else what? Do me a favour and use your head. I don't fit in here and that's the end of it. I'll take my chances on my own.'

'All right, smart boy. Where will you go?'

'That's my business. If I hear anything useful, I'll let you know.'

Ward interrupted. 'What about that gold? We never did figure who's got it. One thing's for sure, the police haven't, so there's a chance this bloke Carnegie's still holding it.'

'If he has it at all,' Mal said.

McPherson tramped round them to stand angrily by the fireplace. 'We agreed he's got it,' he said belligerently.

'We only think he might,' Mal corrected. 'And so what? I'm not after the gold. I just want to be cleared, and Carnegie's not about to help me.'

'There's only one way to find out,' Ward said with a grin. 'We'll have to ask him.'

Here they go again with their crazy ideas, Mal thought dismally. I never should have come here. If they go after the gold, I'll never be cleared.

He turned to McPherson. 'Leave it be. You touch that gold and sure as hell you'll hang. It'll tie you up to the robbery and the murders.'

Mal could see that McPherson was only too aware of the ramifications. He looked worried but he wouldn't allow Mal to have the last word.

'I'll make my own decisions. I don't need you, Wet-behind-the-ears, to tell me what to do.'

'Then I'm off. And I say good luck to us all.'

Mrs Foley went to the back door and called to Angela. 'Come and say goodbye to the gentleman who rescued us from the fire. He has to go.' Then she turned to her husband, her voice firm and decisive. 'You heard me. He has to go. The least you can do is see him out.'

Life, that unwelcome state, was sheer monotony now. Allyn had been informed that he was fully recovered from what was finally diagnosed as a fainting fit, not a heart attack, and that the pain he'd endured was the result of the fall from his horse. They were wrong, of course, Allyn was convinced of that. But what could one expect of these incompetents? It was a wonder anyone came out of that dingy hospital alive. He'd been close to death but they hadn't noticed, plodding about with their ointments and potions, seeing only his external abrasions.

Nevertheless, he had recovered, a disappointing anticlimax. Several of the town dignitaries, including the Mayor, had found their way to his bedside, to commiserate with him, to bemoan the fact that he was laid low again, and at the time, in his weakened state, Allyn had seen that as a fitting end. His demise, still the hero, would have warranted him a grand funeral. But now he was back in the cottage he'd come to hate, impoverished and alone, frozen in time, too afraid to make a move in any direction. He'd lost the gold and the other monies from the raid; that rogue Perry had double-crossed him. He would have to accept that now. But he couldn't go back to Brisbane, where, according to his whining wife, creditors were constantly on the doorstep. Once again she was

197

threatening to go home to her father, and he wished to hell she would.

Wearily he took himself out to the porch and settled in the morning sun to await the arrival of his daily maid, who seemed to come later every day. He was famished; she should have served his breakfast by this.

When at last he heard her bustling about inside the house, he banged on the wall with his stick.

'Coming, sir,' she yelled in response, and he sighed. The woman was a slattern of the first order but it would be too much trouble to find a replacement in this cowyard of a town.

He banged again, shouting, 'Where's my newspaper?'

She took her time, but eventually came waddling out to drop the paper in his lap.

'Do you want bacon today, sir?'

'I always have bacon. Crisp, not burned.'

The *Maryborough Chronicle* held little interest for him, but he read every line, even down to the price of poultry and pigs, to fill in time.

It was only when he took his first glance at the front page that he lost his appetite completely and almost suffered a real heart attack.

Walter Agnes White was a slight, stooped man with thinning hair. He wore wire-rimmed spectacles that lent glitter to mean green eyes . . . eyes that constantly darted, missing nothing. It was said in Maryborough that he had big flapping ears too, but that was not true. His ears were neat, well formed. The illusion was created by his ability to latch on to any rumour or hint of news in the town, and transfer it to his pen. For Walt was editor of the *Chronicle*. His style was flowery and long-winded, but the content was hard, and sharp to the point of being spiteful, and he spared no one. His front page was always dedicated to newsworthy issues, but a column on the back page headed 'Town Topics' was widely read because it was packed with malicious gossip and innuendo. Some were known to whisper, behind closed doors, that any lad forced to face the world bearing his mother's name would have to emerge with a chip on his shoulder, and that at least was true. The scourge of Agnes had made Walt's life miserable. He'd not had the wit nor the muscle to defend himself, so he'd retreated moodily into his studies, delighting his elderly parents.

The name trailed him through his apprenticeship with a Brisbane newspaper and on through his years as a reporter, where his colleagues tormented 'Agnes' unmercifully.

Release came on the death of his dear father. Few knew that old Jeremy White, a cabinet-maker, was a wealthy man, thanks to years of investing in the stock market, which had always fascinated him, so it was a surprise to all when 'Agnes' put on his hat and walked out the door without a word or a backward glance.

After a careful study of prospects, Walt used his inheritance to build a fine house in Maryborough, this up-and-coming port, and then bought the *Maryborough Chronicle*, lock, stock and barrel, positioning himself as editor. No one would ever call him Agnes again. No one would dare.

The editor spoke of himself as an opinion purveyor, but he was in fact an opinion wielder, lashing out at officialdom at every opportunity and boosting the careers of his few favourites, the latter never too sure when they would fall from grace.

He castigated the plantation owners for leading idle and dissolute lives, and for their treatment of their kanaka labourers, at the same time demanding that darkies of any race be barred from the town. He ranted against power-hungry squatters with their vast sheep and cattle properties and their fingers in 'the till of government', and he attacked long-suffering local councillors for their inadequacies in providing good roads and services, ignoring the obvious fact that funds were low.

But he reserved most of his venom for the police, for the lack of law and order in the town and surrounding district. The ambush and murders at Blackwater Creek gave him plenty of scope to keep that issue running, blaming Sergeant Pollock and his men for mishandling the case right from the beginning. It was Walt who, with suitable fanfare, posted the fifty-pound reward for the apprehension of the outlaw Mal Willoughby, since the police were already offering a reward for his accomplice, James McPherson, dead or alive. Then, when Superintendent Kemp left town without bothering to call on the editor, who considered himself the most important man in the district, he activated a petition, calling for Kemp's resignation.

Through all this, though, he stood by the other victim, Allyn Carnegie, claiming that the man's life and career had been ruined by the vile crime and suggesting that Carnegie ought to replace the Mayor, who, he wrote, was lazy and incompetent, bent only on lining his own pockets. It concerned Walt not at all that Carnegie had, on several occasions dismissed the suggestion. That wasn't the point. Walt was only interested in displacing a mayor who had called his paper scurrilous, and him a muckraker.

Nevertheless, Walt was happy with his paper and with its growing popularity, earning enough these days to consider selling up and taking the giant step towards purchase of a Brisbane newspaper.

Then one day, during a quiet time, when he was haranguing his staff for their failure to come up with some real news, a letter arrived in the mail. A letter heaven-sent, he decreed to his pop-eyed senior reporter, as he danced around in glee, waving it about like a hundred-pound note.

'Oh boy oh boy oh boyo!' he chortled. 'Wait till they read this. Just wait till they read this! Clear the front page. I don't care if we're late. This is gold. Sheer damn gold!'

'What is it, Walt?' the reporter asked.

'What is it? I'll tell you what it is. It's a letter from McPherson himself. And it's real. It's no fake. I'll stake my life on it.' He cleared his desk and smoothed the page. 'Take a look at that.'

His reporter squinted at the careful script. 'That's him all right. I've seen his letters before.'

'But not like this. And not to me!'

'Better watch out. You could be looking at libel if you publish the whole text. Carnegie won't be too pleased.'

'That's not my problem.'

'But he's a mate of yours.'

'No one's above the law,' Walt intoned piously, already envisaging the scramble for copies of this edition.

'But it might only be an attempt by McPherson to save his skin. It could be a pack of lies.'

'It's still news. It is my duty to report the news. The people can decide whether they believe it or not.' Walt laughed. He knew his gullible readers certainly would believe it; they believed anything in print. And he also knew the letter would throw the local police into utter confusion, providing him with an opportunity to drag this story on for weeks.

Carnegie read and reread the front page of the *Chronicle*, his heart pounding, eyes misting . . .

OUTLAW APPEALS TO THE CHRONICLE

Dear Sir,

I am writing to you to ask for a fair go. I am being blamed for the gold robbery and the shootings out at Blackwater Creek. I never laid claim to be a perfeck citizen in some ways but I never had nothing to do with that crime, you have my word on that. I never seen none of that gold and the same goes for Willoughby. He's innocent like me. Folk who know me know I'm not going to let the police pin the blame on me only because they can't solve the crime. I don't know who done it and neether does that Willoughby but we reckon Carnegie knows more than he's saying. I been asking about and I never yet hear of any gang of knowed outlaws who had any part in this. I say its an inside job and stick by that. Innocent men are being hounded while the police sit on their laurels.

I remain,

Your servant, innocent,

James McPherson.

While Allyn Carnegie was frantically packing, his breakfast forgotten, intent on quitting Maryborough on the first available transport, be it ship or coach, the town was in uproar. Walt was right. Most of his readers believed McPherson's letter, that he was innocent at least, because they wanted to. McPherson was a popular outlaw, his exploits had become folklore, and it was a tremendous relief to hear from the man, in his own words, that he was innocent of horrific murders that had upset the town.

People began converging on the *Chronicle* to read the letter for themselves. Ever obliging, Walt had posted it in a glass case by the steps to his offices, usually reserved for government proclamations, to avoid damage to this important missive. He had also telegraphed the complete text to the *Brisbane Courier*, and their response was immediate. By this time he knew that his coverage would make headline news all over the country, because he had decided to champion McPherson's cause and, by extension, that of Willoughby. He realised, as his pen flew, rewriting the story of the ambush and the people involved for interstate consumption, that if Willoughby was innocent it would save him the fifty-pound reward he'd posted in a reckless and far too magnanimous gesture.

Had McPherson known the nationwide interest now being created by his letter, which he'd had someone post in Brisbane, he'd have been delighted, but he was far from civilisation. Being so well known, he'd acted as lookout, or cockatoo as the expression went, while his mates robbed a tiny bank two hundred miles inland from the scene of the fires.

Sergeant Pollock came pounding into Walt's office, slamming the paper down on his desk.

'What do you think you're doing, publishing that letter? You should have brought it to me as soon as you received it.'

'Why? You're getting to read it same as everyone else.'

'Was there any accompanying note? Anything that might give us an indication as to his whereabouts?'

'No. Only the envelope, marked Brisbane. But I hardly think he'd be in Brisbane. I suppose you do.'

'I don't know where the bastard is, and if you do, you have an obligation to inform me.'

'Well I don't. And you ought to be pleased. He wrote to me, remember, not to the local police, so that he'd get a fair go. So that his letter wouldn't be hidden to cover up your failures. I think McPherson is right. I think you and Carnegie could have hatched up his name between you to get you off the hook.'

Pollock was livid. Too angry to use caution, as his superiors later admonished him. 'You bloody fool. We're not through with Carnegie ourselves. We haven't got anything to go on yet, but we're watching him. Now you've put him on the alert by using the guesswork, and that's all it is, of a bloody criminal.'

'Is that so?' Walt purred as he polished his spectacles. 'Tell me more. You've never mentioned this before.'

'Because there's nothing more to tell,' Pollock snapped. 'Just an uneasy feeling about the whole thing.'

'Like McPherson?'

'No. Not him. Because of Willoughby. He doesn't seem to fit the bill.'

'And yet you're hounding him to his death.'

'We're trying to find him.'

'Seems to me you have no idea what you're doing, Pollock. From what I hear, you're never going to see a promotion while you're in this town. Why don't you quit and take on a one-horse shanty town to fit your capabilities?'

As Pollock stormed out, Walt chewed his pen, savouring this extra bit

201

of information. Who'd have guessed the police had been suspicious of Carnegie all along? God bless McPherson for ferreting out that sideshow for him. Now he had to decide the best way to handle the news. Probably a polished editorial comment using Pollock's quotes, condemning the police for their secrecy in suppressing true accounts of the ambush from ordinary folk. One law for the rich, another for the poor. That sort of thing. But he had a day to work on that angle; right now, the letter was the big news.

By the time Pollock reached Carnegie's cottage, the gentleman had already left.

'He's going to Brisbane to see his wife,' the daily maid informed the Sergeant, 'but he'll be back next week some time.'

'The hell he will,' Pollock muttered, as he unhitched his horse from the gatepost.

He found Carnegie on the wharf, preparing to board the coastal steamer *Tralee*, bound for Sydney, and knew he had to tread carefully.

'Good day, to you, Mr Carnegie. Leaving us?'

Carnegie was in no mood for niceties. 'You know bloody well I'm leaving after that libel in the *Chronicle*. I'll sue Walt White for every penny.'

'Might I suggest that it does not look good? Your leaving now.'

'Who cares? I've had nothing but suffering in this town. I'm going home.'

'But this ship bypasses Brisbane. Wouldn't it be better to wait for a Brisbane berth?'

'I can get home more easily from Sydney.'

Yes, and you can depart more easily for any number of Pacific ports from Sydney too, Pollock thought. And from there disappear to New Zealand or the Americas.

He tried to reason with the man. 'This isn't the right thing to do, Mr Carnegie. You ought not to run just because an outlaw like McPherson published his gripe. You're entitled to your say as well.'

'Like hell. If I stay in my house I could get lynched, if people believe that tripe. I was a victim of that attack, no one seems to recall that. I am being driven out by that sewer rat White. He's a scandalmonger of the first order, you know that as well as I do. What choice do I have but to leave?'

'I thought you might like to move in with Mrs Pollock and me for the time being. These things blow over, and in the meantime you'll be well protected from any upsets.'

Carnegie picked up his suitcase and walked towards the gangway to join the groups boarding the ship.

'Sergeant Pollock, I am leaving now. You may not detain me unless you arrest me. And if you do, I am entitled to know on what grounds.'

The Sergeant could do no more. He watched Carnegie move into the queue, march up the ramp and disappear into the ship. As he turned to walk away, a reporter from the *Chronicle* accosted him.

'You're weak as piss, Pollock. My boss will love to hear how you came down to see Carnegie off. You blokes look after your own, don't you?'

Sometimes of an afternoon, Emilie would take the children on a nature walk through the sprawling gardens, observing the almost imperceptible changeover of the seasons. As she'd told Ruth in one of her letters, at first it had been quite amusing to have the children teaching her about the various plants, but now that she had become more observant herself, she was winning the game. She could spot the winter plants replacing summer blooms and new flowering gums, note the disappearance of many of the tiny honey-eaters and wrens, and list the appearance of such birds as spangled drongos and orioles which she found so exotic but the children took for granted.

Unfortunately, that letter was a mistake. Ruth had reproved her in no uncertain terms for her giddy attitude to her profession, pointing out that teaching was not a game, nor was it amusing to admit that children knew the subject better than she did.

As they strolled about, Jimmy pounced on the frangipani trees, calling shrilly that they'd lost all of their big leaves. Alice laughed.

'You said that last week. We know about that one.'

'Never mind,' Emilie said. 'It's still important to notice.' So they moved on.

She wished Ruth wouldn't be so strict with her. Sometimes she even sent Emilie's letters back with the spelling of a word corrected, and Emilie found that very irritating, although she never commented. Sadly, she felt that they were drifting apart; they seemed to have so little in common these days. Ruth was teaching French and English at the Brisbane Ladies' College and was very proud of being chosen from among a number of applicants. So much so that she now considered governessing beneath them and was constantly urging Emilie to quit her 'demeaning' position and return to Brisbane and the Belleview Boarding House so that she could take a decent teaching position.

Ruth was also still appalled that Emilie was living alone in that cottage, insisting that her sister return to the Manningtree house where, at least, her reputation would not be sullied.

To placate her, Emilie forwarded fifty pounds that she had 'saved' to be put towards the repayments Ruth was sending to the Emigration Society in London, relieved that her sister did not question the sum or even congratulate her on her frugality. Nevertheless, Emilie blamed herself for the rift, blamed the secrets she was forced to keep from Ruth, who would be shocked and angry if she'd known of her association with Mal Willoughby, and of the money he'd given her. She shuddered at the thought.

'Look! There's an orchid,' Alice said, and Emilie lifted Rosie up to view the brilliant white flower with its purple border which was attached to a tree trunk.

'What sort is it, miss?' Jimmy asked.

'I'm afraid I don't know. I'll have to find a book and look it up. They all have names but you have to be rather clever to know them all.'

'But you're clever, miss,' Rosie said stoutly.

Emilie smiled. 'Not that clever.' The flower reminded her of Mal, and of the place on the island that had entranced him with its orchid display. She wondered where he was and if perhaps he'd fled back to that island haven, since the police had not managed to apprehend him as yet. Poor man.

Still thinking of Ruth, she had some relief from her guilt in being able to inform her sister that she too had a beau. Ruth was all talk about her friend Daniel Bowles, secretary to the Attorney-General, and they seemed to be very close, while Emilie, by this, had become quite attached to Clive Hillier, who was charming and very attentive. She hoped Ruth would approve of Clive. That would be something.

In fact Emilie was fast becoming more than quite attached to Clive. She cared for him so deeply that on the few occasions that business took him away from the town, she missed him, looking forward anxiously to his return. Neither of them ever spoke of Mal now. Clive had no reason to, since Emilie had said that Mal was just an acquaintance, never daring to mention, even to Clive, that he had been to her house. For her part, the loving time, such a short time, she'd spent with Mal seemed a dream now, eclipsed by the reality of Clive and his constant flattering attentions. For everyone in town knew that they were walking out together, and they were often included in invitations as a twosome. It was very nice, she reflected, that both she and Ruth had at last managed enjoyable social lives. Something they'd never imagined could happen in their scary first days in the colony.

'There's Mr Hillier!' Alice cried as they left the garden to return along the drive.

'Where?' Emilie asked, surprised. It was only four o'clock. Clive never called to escort her home until after seven.

'Coming in the gate.'

She sent the children on ahead and walked back to greet him. 'What brings you here at this hour?'

'I had to rush up and show you this. I've been busy all day checking and costing shipments of the demon drink, so I only just came across it.' He gave her a peck on the cheek, his usual greeting now, and handed her the newspaper. 'Have you read this?'

Emilie shook her head as she scanned the paper, and then stood back stunned.

'This fellow is saying he is innocent and so is Mal.'

'I know, but it's hardly a recommendation, coming from a villain like McPherson. The local police might be having a rethink, though. I told them they should investigate Carnegie more fully, and now I believe he has left town. Sailed this very day.'

Emilie was studying the second page. 'It seems the editor believes the

204

letter. He even says here that the police have been wasting time chasing the wrong men. He's practically saying that Mal is innocent. That's marvellous.'

'I wouldn't take much notice of him. Walt White seems to make it his life's work to bait the police. And any other authority, for that matter. He could change with the wind.'

'But it must help Mal's case.'

'Emilie, he has no case as yet.'

She bridled. 'You sound as if you don't want to believe this man McPherson.'

'Of course I want to. All I'm saying is that the letter is interesting, but by no means gospel. It won't do Mal any good, but it will cause Carnegie to shake in his boots.'

'That's a start. Someone has to get to the truth before they apprehend Mal. It's all so unfair.'

Clive sighed. He was beginning to regret his hasty decision to bring her the paper. 'You have to remember that Mal brought some of this on himself. If he hadn't run off when he was in custody, the police would have had a chance to hear his point of view. As it was, he gave the impression of guilt by absconding.'

'How can you say that? He had no choice! They might have hanged him. You weren't here. Everyone agreed he should be hanged right away. I felt ill listening to people.'

'Goodness, Emilie, don't upset yourself. There's nothing we can do. I have to go back now, but I've got a surprise for you. I've bought a gig. A fine one with leather upholstery and a good sturdy roof . . .'

'How nice,' she said without too much enthusiasm, her mind still on Mal's troubles.

'Yes, it is. What say I collect you this evening and give you a run about town before I take you home?'

She nodded. 'Thank you, Clive. That will be very nice.'

'Better than nice,' he smiled. 'No more tramping home for my lady. You'll be travelling in style. Come on now, tell me you're pleased.'

'Of course I am. I'm looking forward to seeing it, but I must go now, Clive . . .'

It was indeed a very comfortable conveyance, and very smart, and it put Emilie in a much better mood as they spun about the town, which was already twinkling with lights, and then turned down towards her cottage. Despite their earlier mild disagreement, she looked very happy, enjoying the ride, and Clive was delighted. He'd always had a suspicion that she was rather too fond of Mal but had never voiced it. That afternoon, though, a streak of jealousy had caused him to do an about-turn, and instead of standing by their friend, as she was doing, he'd criticised Mal. That had been a mistake. Emilie had not appreciated his attitude.

Then again, he consoled himself as he pulled the gig up at her gate, Mal was no competition. For God's sake, he was only a bushie, not her style at all. And a wanted man to boot. Even though she might see him as a romantic figure, as did a lot of silly women when it came to outlaws, she was too level-headed, too prim, to become involved with that type. As for romance, he decided, now was the time. The gig was ideal for spooning; he would no longer have to be content with a quick kiss at the gate before tramping off home alone . . .

'Here you are,' he said gaily. 'Tell me it isn't the smoothest ride in town.'

'Oh it is, Clive. It really is.'

He put an arm about her. 'Then you'd better thank me nicely before you go.'

Soon they were in each other's arms, kissing passionately, and Clive congratulated himself on buying the gig, because this was the first real privacy they'd experienced. The first time he'd had a chance to woo her in comfort. Unfortunately, though, when he began to fondle her more intimately, Emilie decided it was time to go in, and he had to submit to her will. For the time being, he told himself, for the time being. The fires were lit now and he wanted her desperately. He was even thinking ahead to the possibility of marriage. It was unlikely he'd ever find another girl as sweet and lovely out here, and as well educated.

Clive was ambitious. He'd given up all thoughts of another miserable stint on the goldfields; there were too many opportunities unfolding in this fast-growing port for a man not content to settle for a mere wage. Folk still bought their clothes at the general store or by mail order through catalogues. Clive envisaged a gentlemen's outfitters, where people could purchase decent day and evening wear. While there weren't too many gentlefolk in the town yet, there was plenty of money and it had to be spent somewhere.

These thoughts were in his head while he renewed his courting of Emilie, careful now not to upset her by being too forward, but at last they had to part, so he helped her down from the gig.

'Goodnight, my sweetheart,' he said gallantly, opening the gate for her as she nervously set her hat straight.

'What's the point of that?' he laughed. 'No one will see you in there.'

Emilie smiled. 'I know, my dear. It's just habit.'

'So when am I to be invited to dine? I've never even seen the inside of your mansion.'

'Clive . . .' She rested a hand on his arm. 'You know my position. I can't afford talk.'

'Who would talk? Who's to know? They're probably talking anyway. I bring you home most nights. Emilie, you don't seem to realise how much I love you. You treat me like an acquaintance.'

This was the first time he'd told her he loved her. Whether it was true or not Clive wasn't sure, but it had an electrifying effect on her.

'What did you say?'

'I said I loved you. But surely you must know that.'

'No, I did not. I really do not know what I thought . . .'

'Am I wasting your time? I mean, I know I'm not a very important person, but I hoped you did care for me, Emilie . . .'

'Oh Clive, I do. I just didn't want to allow myself to . . . um . . .'

'To be hurt?'

She turned away, whispering, 'Yes, I suppose so. I mean, you're so confident and I'm only . . .'

'Emilie Tissington,' he laughed. 'My darling Emilie. Well then, if you won't ask me to dine, what about lunch on Sunday? Broad daylight. Surely you can invite me to lunch?'

'Of course I can.'

The decision made, he could feel her excitement, the pleasure in her, as he took her face in his hands and kissed her positively. 'Then I am honoured to accept.'

Chapter Nine

Heavy rain had called a halt to the ravaging fires, but it had also left the land sodden with ash, and a tangy stench still hung over the burned-out Foley homestead. Ward's plantation manager had put some of his kanakas to work clearing the site prior to rebuilding. The boss and his mates were away on business, the sort of business this man had no wish to enquire about. He had his own thoughts on the matter but kept them to himself, just as Ward left the running of the banana plantation to him. The job suited him, and for his lack of curiosity, no doubt, he was extremely well paid.

Nevertheless, he was pleased when the three weary men rode in, leading spare mounts, an indication that they'd travelled far and fast, because he was sick of Mrs Foley's interference. She came over every day to oversee the overseer, making certain the foundations were dry, requiring more fill on the slope because now that she had the chance she wanted her house extended, and, refusing to reuse the old brick chimney, demanded that the men build another . . . there was no end to her orders. He was glad to hand over to Matt Foley, leaving him six of his best labourers.

The construction work was of no interest to James McPherson, though. He hung about Ward's house, sleeping most of the time, waiting impatiently for news of the letter that he'd taken such trouble to write. It had only been on Ward's insistence that he'd included Willoughby's name, and that still irked him, but it was done now.

He was well out of sight when the mailman rode up carrying commiserations and mail for the Foleys together with the bulky plantation mailbag. McPherson thought the man would never leave, standing out there yarning with Ward as if they had all the time in the world to spare.

The *Maryborough Chronicle* had arrived, sent by a friend and addressed to Matt Foley, and inside was a short note.

McPherson was beside himself with delight. His letter, which he knew by heart after so many attempts at the writing, was on the front page with not a word omitted, not even that bit about Carnegie which Ward had thought the editor would not publish for fear of libel.

'I told you so!' McPherson gloated. 'I knew they'd print it all. I'm a man to be reckoned with, and by God, don't they know it? Folk won't let them hang me now. And look here on the next page, this here editor's a good fellow. He knows I'm innocent, and he's serving the blame for the mess on the traps!'

He poured himself a fine whisky, compliments of the manager of a small outback bank, and sat grinning into his beard, savouring the thrill of seeing his name in print, several times.

Ward scanned the note.

'Clancy says the folk in Maryborough are all your way, Jimmy. They're saying they knew all along you couldn't have done it. And he says Carnegie left town like a startled rabbit, escorted safely to a ship by the police, and folk don't like that neither.'

'What the hell did they do that for?' McPherson demanded angrily. 'I put Carnegie in their bloody laps; why would they let him get away? Unless they're in cahoots with him,' he added darkly.

Ward nodded. 'You shouldn't have been so fast firing off that letter. You should have let me and Matt slip into Maryborough and have a quiet word with that bloke Carnegie. We'd have wrung the truth out of the bastard. And found out where the gold's hid, if it hasn't already gone over to a fence.'

McPherson grabbed the note and glared at it. 'We gotta find out where he's gone.'

'Too late. He could be on his way to China by this. Wherever he is, he's out of our reach now.'

As soon as the *Tralee* had left the wharf, Pollock hurried back to his office and composed a long telegram to Superintendent Kemp in Brisbane, advising him of the contents of McPherson's letter but not bothering to pass on Walt's editorial comments, which he regarded as irrelevant. He also advised that Carnegie had sailed for Sydney claiming that he would travel from there back to Brisbane, despite Pollock's request that he remain in Maryborough. Under the law, Pollock emphasised, there was no actual reason for the gentleman to be detained.

When Kemp received the telegram, he too moved swiftly. The mild-mannered Superintendent had less regard for the letter of the law than the Sergeant. While he set no store by the pitiful pleadings of a known outlaw, who proclaimed his innocence without providing a scrap of evidence in his defence, Carnegie was another matter. There was every chance that the fellow could jump another ship in that busy port and disappear forever, if only to escape his creditors. Kemp had no intention of letting Carnegie out of his sights until this case was closed.

He telegraphed his counterpart in Sydney regarding this gentleman, a material witness to a crime, requesting that all efforts were to be made to make sure that Mr Allyn Carnegie did proceed on to Brisbane.

The Sydney police were even less kind.

Carnegie was shocked to be escorted from the *Tralee* in full view of other passengers by two burly policemen.

'Where are you taking me?' he demanded. 'Do you know who I am? I have friends in high places. I demand to see your superiors!'

Deaf to his pleas, his complaints and his threats, they collected his luggage and took him to the Cobb and Co. depot.

'What is this?' he shouted. 'I demand an explanation. How dare you arrest me without due cause? You'll be sorry, believe me. I wish to go to an hotel immediately, do you hear me? A decent hotel.'

The officer shrugged. 'I believe you are on your way to your home town of Brisbane, sir?'

'That is correct, but in my own good time. So take yourselves off, you flaming idiots.'

'We are here to assist you, Mr Carnegie. The interstate coach will be leaving shortly. Constable Shelley is putting your luggage aboard.'

Still furious with them, Allyn found an inner calm. At least he would be rid of them, and the journey to Brisbane was long, requiring many stops. They might place him on board, but he could just as easily leave the coach wherever he pleased. Brisbane was the last place he wanted to see, with creditors knocking at his door and that insidious Kemp hanging about, needling him with questions.

'You may be sure I'll report this outrageous treatment the minute I arrive in Brisbane,' he snapped. 'I do not require your assistance, as you call it. You may go now, but believe me, you haven't heard the last of this.'

When he was permitted to board the coach he took a window seat, facing the front, and sat down with as much dignity as he could muster, but then stared as the two policemen stepped up to join him.

'What's this?' he demanded.

The officer grinned. 'Didn't I tell you? We're travelling to Brisbane too.'

Though the big coach, drawn by four splendid horses which were replaced at every stop, was able to travel fast when they came to open plains, the journey took more than a week, and all the passengers, even Carnegie, were relieved to sight, at last, the quiet streets of Brisbane.

Stiff and sore from the long grind, Carnegie climbed down from the coach at the Brisbane depot, stretched his creaking legs and, ignoring his escorts, called for a porter to assist him with his luggage.

As he followed the porter out into the street where horsecabs were waiting, he was met by an unsmiling Kemp in full uniform.

'I thought we might have a chat before you go home, Mr Carnegie.'

'We certainly will not. I am humiliated and exhausted. I am going straight to my house.'

'Very well. We can talk there.'

The Carnegie house in south Brisbane was a two-storeyed sandstone construction and could have been called elegant were it not marred by a huge 'For Sale' banner plastered across the front porch. Allyn would have dragged it down had it not given him further opportunity to bewail his impoverished circumstances.

On the way to the house, Kemp had broken the news to him that he had been declared a bankrupt in his absence, and that to avoid the indignity of bill-servers Mrs Carnegie had taken refuge at her father's home, so by this stage Allyn hardly cared any more. Sale of the house might leave him with some cash, but in the meantime, genuine moans of misery over these events were a good cover for the very real fright of facing interrogation again after that damned newspaper had resurrected the story.

Impatiently he took Kemp into the parlour, made no effort to offer him refreshments of any sort and flung himself into an armchair, a picture of weariness and depression.

'Well now. You've seen how desperately upset I am, Kemp. What more can you do to me?'

'I just wanted to go over the details of that holdup one more time.'

'For the hundredth time, you mean. Hoping I'll get mixed up and make a mistake.'

As he snapped his answers to the same old questions, he took off his boots and his socks, but Kemp seemed not to notice the insult.

'You said you heard the outlaws ride away. Would that have been only two horses?'

'Yes.'

'I thought you said there could have been more out on the road.'

'There could have been. I don't know.'

'But you definitely saw and heard those men ride away?'

'Yes.'

'I'm asking you this because Sergeant Pollock has more men to assist him now, and they have scoured the area where you camped, even down the nearby slope to Blackwater Creek . . .'

'So?'

'So they noticed quite a few dead plants down the creek bank which had obviously been trampled some time back.'

'What has that to do with this matter? Anyone could have been fossicking down there, or fishing.'

'They could indeed. But Pollock took it into his head to detour around the other side of the river, right across from the site of the holdup, and just a way down river they found a small rowboat submerged in the mud.'

Allyn frowned, feigning boredom, while his stomach fluttered nervously. He wished now he had brought out the whisky; he could do with a shot. A double.

'Now the interesting thing about this rowboat is that the bottom of the hull was busted, smashed in, as if someone sank it deliberately. Makes you wonder who would do that.'

'Who cares about a bloody old derelict rowboat?'

'Ah, but it wasn't old. Apart from the injury it suffered it was near to new. Why would anyone sink a perfectly good rowboat, do you suppose?'

'For God's sake! How the hell do I know? Bloody kanakas, I suppose, they'd wreck anything they can't eat to get their own back on their bosses.'

'Yes. We thought it might be a case of vandalism, but the funny thing is, no one living along that side of the river is missing a rowboat.'

211

Allyn leaned back and closed his eyes. 'You sound devilish clever, Kemp, but I'm damned if I know or care what happened to some bloody rowboat.'

Kemp leaned forward, clasping his hands between his knees. 'Try this. What if the outlaws chose that spot for the holdup so they could take the booty down to the creek and escape with it by boat. Take it across the river, dump the boat, jump on a waiting horse or horses and make off with it. No one would be looking for them on that side of the river. They could ride quietly off into the sunset.'

Allyn nodded, interested. 'That could have happened. Unlikely, I think, but possible.'

'Right. But if you saw Willoughby and McPherson, and heard them ride off – in different directions, by the way, since Willoughby had to get to town. You did say they rode off in two directions?'

'Yes, I did. Of course. I would have.'

'Then there had to be a third man. The one in the boat.'

'By Jove. You could be right.'

'But you didn't hear another voice at all? No third man?'

'If I'd heard another man, I'd have said so.'

Kemp sighed. 'That's disappointing, because it would make more sense. You see, we know that Willougby's gun was not fired, which means McPherson shot all three, the guards *and* Mr Taylor. But he's not known to be a crack shot.'

'So one of the outlaws out on the road must have done the shooting.'

'And that makes a gang of at least four. Or maybe five. Maybe six, if you put another fellow on the other side of the river. Not that much to divvy up when it's all said and done. Hardly worth three murders for any self-respecting outlaw. A single man could do better with a payroll.'

Carnegie took out a handkerchief and blew his nose. 'All these theories of yours are giving me a headache. I don't know why you're foisting them on me. I was one of the victims, and since that day I've been unable to regain my health. I have enough worries, Kemp, without having to do your job for you. And do not forget, I intend to complain to the Premier about the way you have treated me.' He stood up. 'Now, if you'll excuse me, I believe I'm entitled to a rest after that nightmare coach journey.'

When at last he was free of Kemp, he poured himself a goblet of whisky and slumped back into his chair. After a few gulps he felt better, glad to be back in the comfort of his own home. He'd given up worrying about Perry and the gold, lost hope there, but as long as he stuck to his story, Kemp couldn't touch him, couldn't pin anything on him. He might be close with his theory about the boat, but what the hell? They couldn't place him anywhere near a boat. He hadn't gone riding off into the sunset as Kemp had said; he'd stayed right where he was supposed to be.

And McPherson and Willoughby could bleat all they liked. They were still the main suspects. All Kemp could have discovered was that they'd had partners in the crime. While the real partner, Baldy Perry, was obviously long gone.

As for the bankruptcy, that was a help not a hindrance. His creditors would have to be content with a few pence in the pound while he had several hundred quid put away for a rainy day under a floorboard in this very house.

'Do your damnedest, Kemp,' he sneered, saluting with his glass. 'You won't get any more out of me.'

Back in his office, writing up his report, Kemp was inclined to agree. Although he hated to be working on a hint from that damned McPherson, he was leaning towards the belief that Carnegie was definitely involved somehow.

He looked up at the photo of the Queen on the wall, and spoke to her.

'But he's a damned hard nut to crack, ma'am, if I may say so.'

Pollock was busy, though. He'd had the rowboat washed down and hauled aboard a yacht, which delivered it to a Maryborough wharf. From there it was lifted on to a wagon and carted about the town to various boatbuilders, large and small.

Eventually Karl Grossmann, a German immigrant with a fast-growing reputation as a skilful boatbuilder, even though his business was still in the backyard stage, recognised the dinghy. He was horrified that his handiwork should have been found at the bottom of the river.

'Good Gott!' he exclaimed. 'What happen to my boat?' He pounded the keel. 'Look! Solid! Best timbers, I use. Someone smash it, by golly.'

Pollock grinned. 'They sure did, mate. Sank it on purpose, wouldn't you say?'

'Bang bloody hole in it from the inside! Bloody fools.'

'Do you remember who you sold it to?'

'Sure I do. Big fellow. Fisherman, he say.'

'English?'

'No. Australian.'

'I meant, he wasn't a kanaka or an Abo or a Chinee?'

'No. What I said. One of your mob.'

'What did he look like?'

Karl shrugged. 'Same as I say. Big fellow. Fisherman. Piggy eyes. Straggly beard.'

'What colour hair?'

'Don't know. That fellow wore a knitted cap, same as all them fishermen wear. With the tassle on top, you know?'

'Did he pay cash?'

'Everyone pay me cash, no loans.'

'Did you put it in the river for him?'

'Yeah. I show him, float like a cork it did. Down the back lane there.'

'Anyone else see him take it?'

'Who's to see? He pay me, I put the boat in the river. It's his. I go away. I got work to do. I know he won't sink.'

'When did you sell it to him?'

'Ah. That we will have to see. Come inside, Sergeant. Maybe you like a glass of cider? Very good. Maybe you can tell me where we get more bottles so we can sell it.'

'Have a talk to Clive Hillier at the bond store in Wharf Street. He could probably set you right.'

'You don't say? You write that name down for me, eh?'

'Yes, of course.'

Pollock wrote the name in his notebook, tore the page out, gave it to Karl in exchange for a delicious glass of cider and wandered about the yard examining the rowboats and runabouts under construction, though he knew little about the business.

When Karl returned with a large ledger, pointing at an entry with his finger, Pollock shook his head.

'It's in German. You'll have to translate for me.'

'Ah, yes. I don't write so well in English. The date is March fourteen. He pay seven shillings.'

March the fourteenth? Three weeks before the holdup. Pollock was excited.

'His name? Did he give his name?'

'Yes. He spell it for me.'

Pollock looked at the spidery foreign writing, amazed. 'Does that spell McPherson? J. McPherson?'

'Ja. That is right. Mr McPherson. That was his name.'

The Sergeant was stunned. Was McPherson openly in the town at that time? And would he give his real name? The outlaw had more cheek than old Nick, but this would be pushing his luck.

'One more thing, Karl. Did this fellow have a red beard?'

'No, no, no. I remember him. Big tough fisherman. He had a beard like mine. Fair. Nordic, you people say, mean northern maybe. Fair. No grey neither. Plain fair. Needed a good trim, I tell him. Make it grow thicker.'

Pollock extended his hand. 'Thank you, Karl, you've been a great help, and thanks for the cider. Congratulate your wife, it's very good.'

'What about the rowboat? What you do with that now?'

'We'll keep it in the police paddock for a while, and when we've finished with it, you can have it back.'

'How much I pay?'

'Nothing. You can have it.'

Weeks later, Pollock, who had started off with such great expectations, was no further advanced. None of the fishermen he questioned knew anything about this dinghy, or the owner, and the description meant nothing to them. All he could report to the officer who had been appointed to take command of *his* police station was the certainty that this dinghy had been used in the robbery by someone who claimed to be McPherson, but his superior was not impressed. He considered the theory had more holes in it than the hapless rowboat and pointed out that the best real lead they had at present was that McPherson was an associate of

Willoughby's, otherwise why would he have included the younger man in his disclaimer?

'They're obviously mates,' he said. 'Holed up together somewhere. You take Constable Lacey and head for the hills. I don't care how long it takes, or if you have to go as far as Bowen, where McPherson has been seen at various times, but you find him. Take chits, offer rewards, bribes, but find them. Or one of them. We find one, we'll get the other.'

'But what about the boat? Someone must have seen this fisherman in that dinghy; we should at least figure out who he was, before we write that plan off.'

'It's already written off. Draw funds and supplies, and a packhorse if need be, but get out there and find them. By the way, I've been meaning to say, I'm sorry you had to move out of the police residence. It wasn't by my choice. I hope you're comfortable in that cottage.'

'It'll do,' Pollock muttered, rather than admit that his wife was thrilled to be living in a new cottage, away from the police station, where they had so often been awakened with complaints at all hours of the night. He was not looking forward to the almost hopeless task of trying to locate McPherson and Willoughby, since there was every possibility that they'd left the state, but that night he sat down with Mike Lacey and worked out a plan. They decided to visit as many country and coastal police stations as possible to enlist help in scouring those districts, checking on strangers, and reminding local folk that rewards were being offered for both of the outlaws. On the first day they headed into the hills, travelling north.

That was as well for Mal Willoughby, who was moving in the opposite direction. Keeping to the inland ranges, he had bypassed Maryborough and Gympie and was well on his way south, through the difficult terrain. His father had always said the kid had a compass in his head, and it served him well now, for he had a destination in mind. By the time he emerged on the plains, he was more than a hundred miles north-west of Brisbane and taking his time so as not to tire his horse. Occasionally he teamed up with other men on the lonely tracks, swagmen, bullock drivers, prospectors, sharing campfires with them, knowing these taciturn characters didn't mind a little company at times, but he kept well away from farmhouses and villages. Mal had no more need for information.

When he reached the great Condamine River, he grinned with satisfaction and began following it upstream. A signpost stood at converging dirt tracks in the middle of nowhere, reassuring him that the village of Chinchilla was some sixty miles further on. But he only needed half of that mileage. As the sun was drooping in the afternoon sky and flocks of parrots were speeding homewards, he turned down a narrow track that he remembered so well, and stopped to open the gate to his uncle's farm.

Mal gazed about him. The paddocks were dry, in need of rain. The last time he'd been here, years ago, the small dairy farm had been lush and green. But otherwise, nothing had changed. The farmhouse was as dilapidated as ever, greying timbers crying out for paint, glass missing

215

from a front window, and the usual junk was still strewn about; even the rusting plough that he recalled cutting his foot on when he was a kid still lay forlornly under a tree. Uncle Silver, so named for his silvery hair, was Mal's late mother's brother, and had never been one for neatness, or hard work, for that matter. The farm barely gave Silver and his wife a living.

Skinny dogs raced out yapping and protesting as Mal approached, and Silver ambled out of the house in what Mal's dad had always referred to as his uniform: a sleeveless flannel shirt, baggy dungarees held up by rope, and battered boots.

'What do you want?' he rasped.

'Thought you might have a spare cup of tea,' Mal grinned.

Silver peered at him through rheumy eyes. 'For Gawd's sake! Is it you, Sonny? I didn't know you behind that bushy beard. Well, for Gawd's sake! Where did you spring from?'

'Just riding past, Uncle. Thought I'd better stop by to see how you're going.'

'Good for you. Come on in, Sonny. The wife's not with me no more. Passed away last winter.'

Mal dismounted. 'I'm sorry to hear that. I always liked Auntie Dot.'

'So you did. So you did. But she got awful pneumonia and complications, the doctor said, couldn't breathe. It was a relief for the poor woman to go in the end, I can tell you.'

'Ah, that's bad luck. Can I settle the horse down first? We've had a hard ride today . . .'

'Yeah. Bring him round the back. Come a long way, have you?'

Mal nodded. 'You could say that.'

Two days later, Mal was earning his keep in his usual amiable way. Silver complained endlessly about his rheumatism, and handed the milking of the cows over to his nephew, as well as allowing him to do the cooking, which Mal was only too happy to do. He'd sampled Silver's stew on the first night and was in no hurry to try again.

To fill in the rest of his days he set to work weeding the overgrown vegetable garden that had once been his aunt's pride and joy, managing to unearth some potatoes and turnip patches that were struggling along unaided, and putting some order into the neat rows ready for replanting. At night he sat by the stove with his uncle, playing cards and amusing him with the old familiar tricks.

Finally, though, he felt the old man had a right to know the real reason for this sudden visit.

'I won't be staying long,' he began. 'I have to keep moving, but it's good to be able to rest up here awhile. The fact of the matter is . . .'

Silver smoked his pipe and listened intently as Mal told him that he was on the run, and how this had come about.

'That's about the size of it,' he said eventually. 'It's one big bloody mess and I'm in the middle of it.'

His uncle tapped his pipe on the fireplace bricks and sighed. 'I was wondering when you'd get around to mentioning it.'

'You know?'

'Course I bloody know. This isn't exactly the Dead Centre. I go into Chinchilla every so often for supplies and pick up a newspaper. You're famous, Sonny, even down here. They've even got a Wanted poster in the police station with your name large as life, and a fifty-quid reward.'

'The police haven't bothered you?'

'No fear. Why would they? I'm Silver Jeffries, not Willoughby. Nothin' to do with me.'

'That's good. I wouldn't want to cause you any trouble.'

'It's no trouble having you here, Sonny. But what will you do when you leave?'

'I don't know. Keep moving south, I guess. I was even thinking of heading right across to Western Australia. They'd never find me over there.'

'Forget that idea. You'd never cross that desert on your own. You'd need a camel train to make it. You'd die in your tracks.' He poked at the fire. 'You ever thought of giving yourself up?'

'No.'

'Why not? It'd be safer. With the charges hanging over your head, you could be shot on sight.'

'No.'

'Sonny, you ought to give this more thought. You can't keep running. You're well away from the roughnecks up north. If you turn yourself in down here you can get a lawyer, a fair trial. Make them see that you're innocent. I'll speak up for you, that you're a good lad. So will your sister. I had a letter from her, she's worried sick about you.'

'Have the police been to see her?'

'Yes. They're ferreting about looking for everyone who knows you, so you mustn't go there.'

'I won't. I thought that would happen.' Mal emptied his tobacco pouch and rolled a cigarette.

'Is that the last of your baccy?' Silver asked.

'Yeah. But I can survive without it.'

'No you won't. I'll go into town tomorrow, pick up some supplies, and I'll get you some. Anything else you want?'

'Only some matches and tea,' he said dismally. 'Don't have much call for anything else. I keep my swag light.'

'Sorry about that, Sonny. But listen, while I'm away, you give plenty of thought to what I'm saying. You been on the road all your life, I know that, but this is different. It'll go better for you if you give yourself up. You're not a real outlaw. Those blokes have got mates and gangs to help them and they still get caught . . .'

'You don't have to tell me about them. I've met them. And I don't want no part of them, They'd get me into worse trouble.'

Silver was fascinated. 'Who have you met?'

'You don't need to know, Uncle. They're a pack of lunatics.'

217

'Where have you been hanging out all this time anyway?'

'In the hills,' Mal said vaguely. He couldn't bring himself to mention, even to Silver, the delight of Fraser Island and his beach humpy at Orchid Bay. That time, and his time with Emilie, had become precious to him, his defence against depression. He daydreamed about it all the time, often putting himself to sleep by working out how he could take her there. First by boat to the Anglican Mission on the island, then borrowing some horses, for it was a long hike across to the ocean side, and then riding over with her and watching her face when he showed her the pristine beach and its pure white sand, then turning her about to look at the brilliant green of the rainforest with the orchids . . . all of those orchids displayed like jewels . . . Sometimes he fell asleep midway through the long, romantic idyll, but it didn't matter . . .

Silver was dozing in his battered old armchair, so Mal crept quietly away to bed down in the sleepout, noting that the nights were colder down here. He could probably cadge a few extra blankets from Silver before he left.

After his uncle had trundled off in his wagon early the next morning, Mal finished the milking and let the cows out into the paddock, then he lugged the heavy cans up to the far gate to be collected by the dairymen on their rounds, noting sadly that the farm was very poor thanks to Silver's lack of interest. He only had a dozen cows now, and no sign of calves, so the separator was rusting in the cowshed. The wooden churn was idle too, where once Auntie Dot had made, and sold, butter and cheese. He wished he could stay longer and help make something of this farm again, but it was not possible. Sooner or later someone would start to wonder who was shining up old Silver's place, and he couldn't allow the kind old man to be accused of harbouring a fugitive.

He laughed when Silver finally arrived home, stumbling down from the wagon in a merry mood, waving an empty rum bottle about, but at least he'd bought the necessities of tea, flour, sugar and a side of beef, as well as the tobacco makings, before imbibing. Mal humped him into the kitchen then returned to unload the wagon and release the horse. Silver had also collected some newspapers, but there was nothing in them about outlaws, so Mal read them gratefully while his uncle snored in his chair.

When he wakened Silver, they ate roast beef and baked vegetables and Mal suggested a game of cards, but Silver wasn't up to it, and that, he grinned, was understandable, so they both went to their beds, content, and all was quiet.

Sometime during the night Mal heard the dogs barking, but put it down to the moon, or maybe a skulking dingo, and went back to sleep.

When he awoke, frail dawn was filtering through the trees and two men were standing over him, the cold steel of rifle barrels pointed at him. Behind them, standing back, looking pale and troubled, was Silver.

'Out now, Willoughby!' one of the men said. 'Get up. Get dressed. Slow. Keep it slow.'

They backed away, rifles still trained on him while he dressed, and knowing this was the road to a chilly cell. Mal did go slow, pulling on his fleece-lined jacket over a flannel shirt and dungarees.

'You're under arrest,' his captor added, and Mal sighed resignedly. It was hardly a surprise.

As they herded him outside, Silver came round with Mal's horse. 'I'm sorry, Sonny,' he said. 'It's for the best,' and Mal turned towards him, startled.

'You gave me up?'

'It's better this way,' Silver muttered.

'For who, Silver?' said the police sergeant, who Mal later learned was called Moloney, and not a bad fellow. He spat at Silver's feet. 'You'll get your reward.'

Mal turned sadly to his uncle. 'I thought you believed me.'

'I do, Sonny. True I do.'

'Then why?'

'Come on, get mounted, son,' Moloney said. 'You're worth money to the bastard, that's why. He says he's your uncle. Too bad you don't know him like we do. Old Silver would sell his soul for sixpence. He's already booked up a feast at the grocery store on the strength of your fifty quid. Haven't you got anything to say to him before we go?'

'No.' Mal swung on to his horse and fell into line behind the constable, who was already heading for the road. Sergeant Moloney followed, deliberately leaving the gate open.

Moloney wasn't about to make the same mistake as Mal's first captor. Once out on the road he ordered the prisoner to dismount, searched him carefully for weapons, took his stockwhip and then allowed him to mount again.

'Your family call you Sonny?' he asked, but Mal could only nod.

He was then trussed to the horse and the constable took hold of the bridle to lead the prisoner into Chinchilla.

Riding beside him, Moloney noticed that Willoughby held his seat well on the horse, despite his bonds, even when the Sergeant eased the horses into a canter to cover the thirty miles as quickly as possible. This character, he mused, was a real bushie. His uncle had said Willoughby was about twenty-two, but he looked younger. Then again, Silver would have been lucky if he could add ten and ten. Except when it came to the reward. He'd be after every penny of that.

Moloney tried to talk to his prisoner when they slowed over the hills, but Willoughby was not very communicative, turning his head away as if the scenery was more interesting.

They entered the town along a back road and cut through paddocks to secure the prisoner in the single-cell lockup behind the police station, before, with a huge sense of relief, Moloney was able to make his way to the telegraph office and send the message to headquarters in Brisbane that he had the outlaw Willoughby in custody.

Within minutes word spread round the town and excited curiosity-seekers rushed to the police station to verify the news, and perhaps get a glimpse of the famous outlaw.

'This will put Chinchilla on the map!' they exclaimed with glee, hounding Moloney for more information, disappointed that there had been no shootout, that Willoughby had come quietly. The Sergeant left his constable to parry questions while he went out back and looked in at his prisoner.

'You all right?'

'Yes, sir.'

'Anything I can get you?'

'I'd like something to eat. And a shave.' He managed a weak grin. 'Doesn't look like I'll need this bloody beard any longer.'

'Righto.'

While Moloney's wife cooked breakfast for the men, including the prisoner, a reporter from the local newspaper managed to skip round the back and peer in at the prisoner, who surely did look a ferocious character, with a full beard and beady blue eyes. He was a big fellow too, a real live outlaw! He rushed away to find the town's only photographer, who specialised in family portraits, since the *Chinchilla Leader* did not, as yet, use pictures.

By the time he returned with his associate, who had fiddled about finding the right equipment for a portrait of this importance, the barber had been and gone. Instead of a fearsome rogue, all they had was a baby-faced kid who looked more like every mother's pride and joy, shiny-faced, with innocent blue eyes and soft blond hair.

After an argument with Moloney, in which the reporter demanded the right to take a photo of the prisoner, pointing out that the reputation of the town was at stake, that locals should be permitted first shot at a photograph because many more cameramen would follow, the Sergeant relented. He even allowed himself to be shown standing by his prisoner. After all, it wasn't every day that a country policeman beat his colleagues in two states to an arrest like this.

In the meantime, scribbling away in his little notebook, the reporter changed his story. He had heard Moloney refer to the prisoner as Sonny, which was more fitting and a damn sight more interesting than plain Mal. So the famous outlaw from then on became known as Sonny, the baby-faced kid who would not answer any questions except to say: 'I am innocent. I never hurt anyone in my life.'

That reporter, whose name was Jesse Fields, had the sneaking feeling that Moloney agreed with him, although he would not admit it. There was something about this kid that reminded Jesse of his young brother, who had been killed in a fall from a horse. He went back to his office, wrote the story of the arrest for his paper and wired the full text to the *Brisbane Courier* and the *Sydney Morning Herald*.

He then turned back to old copy, dredging up what little information he had on the holdup and the murders, noting that Willoughby's rifle had not been fired, although that was no excuse. He could have used another gun provided by his associate or associates. The story had gained so much public attention that various politicians had weighed in, demanding these fiends be apprehended, but he bypassed their opinions and went straight to the latest report, where that rascal James McPherson had written to some Maryborough paper claiming innocence, not only for himself but for Willoughby too. His editor hadn't bothered with the full text of the letter, and neither had Jesse. They'd simply reprinted comment from a Brisbane paper wherein it had been merely regarded as an interesting item, not to be taken seriously.

Moloney's instructions were not to delay. A telegram from the Superintendent of Police in Brisbane, one Jasper Kemp, ordered him to bring the prisoner in, forthwith. Extra police from the town of Miles were to accompany him over a journey of more than a hundred and fifty miles.

'Oh well, that's that,' the proprietor and editor of the *Leader* said as they watched the entourage ride out two days later. 'At least Chinchilla had its day in the sun.'

'No way. It's not over yet,' Jesse said. 'We can still have a hand in it.'

'Ah, give it away, Jesse. You kept me up all hours last night going on about this. What if the kid said he'd never hurt anyone in his life? He was still there. He was in on it.'

'So where's the gold? And the bank money? Willoughby was down on his luck. His saddle was thin as paper. If he'd had a quid he could have asked Silver to go buy him new gear.'

'Who'd trust Silver?'

'He did! Moloney said the kid could hardly believe Silver had sold him out. He reckoned if Willoughby hadn't been so shocked he would have got more out of him.'

'Well he didn't. We'll follow the story – everyone out here will want to know what happens – but we've done our part.'

'The hell we have. I'm going out to talk to Silver. Don't you see? He had the kid living out there, he must have talked. And for a few more quid, so will Silver. McPherson must know Willoughby, to speak up for him. I'm betting that the kid knows where the big fish is, and he could have told his uncle.'

Uncle Silver whined and protested to Jesse Fields.

'It's for the best, I kept telling Sonny that. I wanted him to turn himself in. I didn't want him shot down like a dog. He's a good kid. Look how he worked about my place, cleaning up things. God rid of that plough that's been lyin' about. Did the milkin' even.' And so he went on.

Jesse let him talk, carefully avoiding the embarrassing subject of the reward until he was able to mention Willoughby's claim of innocence.

'What happened?' he asked. 'Did he just turn up here on a family visit, you being his uncle?'

'Yeah, that's right. Just rode up out of the blue. I didn't recognise him with all the fuzz on his face.'

221

'And he never told you a thing about what he'd been up to?'

'Nothing much. Though I knew all along what he was about. I'm not blind, you know. And I can read. I knew it was me own flesh and blood mixed up in that big gold heist.'

'Looks like I've run into a dead end,' said Jesse. 'I was after the real story about that holdup, willing to pay a few quid too, but it seems as though Willoughby was as close-mouthed with you as he was with Moloney and everyone else in town.'

Silver leapt up from the kitchen table, where he'd been sharing a drink at Jesse's expense, blatantly ready to reconsider.

'What do you mean, he didn't tell me? I'm his uncle, ain't I? Took his time but he had to tell someone. Course he told me about the holdup.'

'What?' Jesse asked derisively. 'That he was just an innocent bystander?'

'A lot you know,' Silver growled. 'You got any more of that grog? Do you know, that bloody kid doesn't drink. His pa could put it away by the quart, but Sonny, he never touches the stuff. Turns up here without so much as a pint for his old uncle.'

Jesse pondered that as he went out to his saddlebag and brought in a half-pint of rum. Willoughby had eluded a concentrated police search for months; no one had even sighted him. Maybe, as a teetotaller, forgetting to bring Silver the accepted introduction of at least some liquor had been his first mistake. For Silver now beamed on his visitor.

'We'll have a quick tot of the rum,' Jesse said, making it obvious that the rest of it would leave with him. 'Then I'd better get going.'

'A lot you know,' Silver said again, savouring the liquor. 'Sonny told me the lot. From go to whoa. I reckon I'm the only person from here to the black stump who knows what really happened. And do you know why? Because Sonny told *me*. He reckoned since I was good enough to take him in, I was entitled, he said, entitled to know. What do you think of that?'

Silver jutted his jaw belligerently and Jesse nodded gamely, thinking he'd like to throttle the wretch.

'Ah, come on, Silver. I only came out here to get some background on Willoughby, his family and all that. Whatever he told you about the holdup has to be a pack of lies, since he's still pretending to be the good lad. Fair go, mate.'

Silver was insulted. 'Is that so? Well, you listen to me. Sonny sat in that very chair. He apologised for bringing his troubles to my doorstep, and he told me how it happened, as true as I'm sitting here. I only put him in because it was for the best, and that reward, you know. Well, it might as well have been me as anyone else . . .'

Jesse had his notebook out. 'What did he say, Silver? There's no money and no more rum until I get the story, and none of your embellishments.'

'Jesus! Why shouldn't I give you the truth, right from the horse's mouth? I got nothin' to hide. You can't be blaming me for anything. It was like this . . . He was out on the goldfields, didn't do bad either. He was always a lucky blighter, could always turn a quid, Sonny . . .'

As best as he could recall, Silver gave the astonished reporter the story of that ambush as told by Mal Willoughby himself. Jesse was so excited by the tale, and so intrigued, that he had to keep delaying the narrative to get the words down exactly. He knew he had not only a great story here, but one hell of a coup, so he rewarded Silver with an occasional tot of rum to keep him oiled. He knew the old man could never invent a story that sounded as simple and honest as this. Willoughby had not even been there. He had obeyed orders and gone into Maryborough to advise police, as instructed, that the gold shipment was *en route* and that they required escort over the most dangerous leg of the journey. A plan prearranged not by Willoughby but by the Gold Commissioner and the police sergeant in Maryborough, because the shipment dates were deliberately haphazard.

When that tale was completed, Jesse had more questions.

'What about McPherson? What did he say about him?'

Silver scratched his head and looked longingly at the rum bottle. 'Nothing. He said he had met some outlaws but didn't like them.'

'Didn't like them?' Jesse laughed. 'Was he supposed to like them?'

That offended Silver. 'You don't know Sonny. He must have met them but he didn't approve of them. He reckoned they were ratbags.'

'What outlaws?'

'How do I know? He never said.'

Jesse sat back. 'Silver, you've been very helpful, and I'll pay you. Here you are. There's two quid on the table now. But Sonny is small-time. I need information on McPherson. I'll double it for McPherson.'

He saw the pain in Silver's eyes as he stared at the money, but even Silver couldn't invent a tale of McPherson.

'Sonny never said nothing about McPherson. He's been out there on his own, Jesse, with no one to help him. All on his bloody own. No one. So I knew he couldn't keep it up. That's why I had to turn him in,' he whined. 'It was only a matter of time.'

'All right. One more thing. He must have had a hideout all this time. Where was he? If we knew that, we'd be closer to trapping McPherson.'

'Honest, mate, I don't know. I'd tell you if I did.'

'I'll bet you would. Now I want to start again. Tell me about Sonny, about his folks. Where did he grow up?'

Silver chuckled. 'I reckon Sonny grew up on the road. Traipsing around with his old man since he was in knee pants. Nothin' much to tell. His dad was a boozer but Sonny would never hear a bad word about him . . .'

Bit by bit, Jesse managed to elicit enough background to be able to sketch the character of young Willoughby.

'What about friends? Who were his friends?'

Silver shrugged. 'A bloke like Sonny, he had plenty of friends at fairs and things. Everyone liked him, but he was a loner.'

'Independent?'

'Yeah, that's the word. Never asked no one for nothin'. That's why he gave a hand round here, see . . .'

And that's where I came in, Jesse mused. Interview over. He packed up, left the money and the rest of the rum on the table and took his leave of Uncle Silver.

On the way back to Chinchilla he occupied himself composing a feature article that should find its way into leading newspapers as well as the local, and wrestling with a heading which could possibly be: 'The Life and Times of Sonny Willoughby'. Something like that. A real scoop. And there'd be more to follow.

Brisbane was shrouded in heavy rain on the night the shadowy figures in dark oilskin coats rode steadily through to the police barracks to hand over their prisoner. As they dismounted in the stables, Willoughby turned to Sergeant Moloney.

'Can I ask a favour of you?'

'Sure you can.'

'Will you take care of my horse?'

Moloney tried to be cheerful. 'You want me to mind him for you?'

'Depends how things go. If I don't come for him, you can have him. Striker's a good horse, and smart. I wouldn't want just anyone to take him.'

Moloney nodded, noticing the other mounted police turning away sadly, appreciating the thought.

'He'll be all right with me, Sonny.'

At the Belleview Boarding House there was great excitement in the air. The schoolteacher and the gentleman who was secretary to a Minister had announced their engagement to Mrs Medlow, and she was busy dispensing the news to all of her guests. She even suggested to Miss Tissington that, perhaps, an afternoon tea party could be arranged, at minimal cost, but the couple had turned down her offer, preferring privacy.

Ruth thought Daniel had put that rather well, that bit about protecting their privacy, but then Daniel moved in illustrious circles where diplomacy, as he himself often remarked, was a way of life. Parliamentarians, she now knew, thanks to Daniel's interesting observations, were particularly difficult people to deal with. Admitting that tact was not one of her own virtues, Ruth admired Daniel greatly for his response. She would have given Mrs Medlow a swift 'no' at such a vulgar suggestion; she had no wish to associate any more than was necessary with the strangers and busybodies who made up the complement of this establishment. In fact, Ruth was inclined to believe that it was the sustained nosiness and cheap remarks made by these same people that had led to Daniel's proposal.

For quite a while now, she and Daniel had spent a great deal of time together, looking into the matter of acquiring the two blocks of land to

224

fulfil the entitlements of the two immigrant ladies, and that had led to gossip, as people so often saw them stepping out together. In the end Daniel had said, in a rather amused manner, that the gossips probably thought they were having an affair.

Even now, Ruth blushed at such a dreadfully untrue suggestion.

'Oh, surely not!' she'd exclaimed, wondering wildly how they could put a stop to it.

But Daniel was unconcerned. 'The only way we can counter talk like that is to announce our engagement, if you would be so kind as to do me the honour, Ruth?'

She was flabbergasted. Flustered. Stuttering in surprise. 'Heavens. I don't know. Goodness, Daniel. Are you proposing marriage?'

'I'm sorry. I did intend to propose to you, dear lady, in a more dignified manner, and certainly not here in a public park. It just slipped out. But we do get along well, and as you know, my career is very important to me. I don't intend to be a secretary forever.' He smiled. 'Unless I become a Secretary of State. My little joke. And I will need a lady beside me, of the right sort, you understand. But of course you must have time to think about this, and I shall be patient.'

Ruth was immensely flattered. She knew exactly what he meant by 'the right sort' and considered herself ideally suitable. A man in his position would need a lady by his side, and a lady who could speak English without any of the rude accents that prevailed in this town, capital of a state though it be. It took her twenty-four hours to announce her decision to accept, and her fiancé was delighted. They exchanged their first glancing kiss on the darkened porch of the Belleview as they sheltered from the teeming rain.

Ruth was relieved that Daniel did not embarrass her by indulging in soppy love talk, because their relationship was built on a more solid foundation of mutual respect. Intimacy, which she dreaded, would come at the proper time.

To celebrate, Daniel took her to dine at the prestigious Royal Arms Hotel in Queen Street. She thought it frightfully expensive, but Daniel disallowed her qualms, insisting that it was important they be seen in the right places. He ordered wine, which Ruth agreed was excellent, but she demurred at the necessity for a second bottle, since she drank very little, and to her dismay Daniel became quite cross with her.

'You don't count pennies in a place like this,' he hissed.

She didn't like to say that it wasn't the pennies that bothered her, but the obvious fact that Daniel was getting tipsy. By the time he'd drunk the second bottle, insisting she have at least one glass, her fiancé was inebriated, talking far too loudly for her liking.

The next morning, though, he apologised to her, explaining that he'd been carried away with joy and excitement on such a momentous occasion, and of course Ruth forgave him. She found his crestfallen attitude rather sweet.

When he went to his office that day, Daniel had what he called, dismally, a 'momentous' hangover, and was relieved that his Minister was away on business. Gradually, though, as the day wore on, he felt better, and was immensely pleased with himself.

It had been a long and irritating business sorting out the endless paperwork involved in claiming that land for Ruth and her stubborn young sister. They'd visited the Eagle Farm area several times before finding and deciding on two adjacent twenty-acre blocks. It was rural land, rather flat and uninteresting, suitable for agriculture, the agent had told them enthusiastically, but Daniel, better advised, knew that the area, not far from the river, would soon become a suburb of the burgeoning town and port of Brisbane, and to be able to acquire forty acres at no cost was a windfall of some note.

The usual complications began as clerks in government departments placed as many obstructions in their path as possible. First there were objections to claims by women, single women at that, but Daniel was able to produce evidence that Land Grants were not confined to men. Then came a more serious objection. It was considered that the Eagle Farm district was becoming too expensive to be given in grants, and they were urged to look further afield, where settlement was being encouraged.

Ruth was disappointed, but she understood the logic of it. After all, a grant of such huge blocks of land was to her almost unbelievably generous, and the recipients should be grateful no matter where the blocks were.

Daniel saw it differently. He wanted Eagle Farm. After making some careful enquiries, he managed to find a clerk who would backdate the Tissington applications in return for two pounds handed under the counter. He knew that Ruth would never agree to paying a bribe, and he certainly had no intention of being personally out of pocket to the tune of two pounds, so he obtained the money from her by a simple explanation.

'Your application for the Land Grants at Eagle Farm has been approved but there is a surcharge for late lodgement of the claim, of one pound per block. I thought it better to pay that rather than have to search about for land in the backblocks, too far out for you to be able to continue teaching in Brisbane.'

Ruth readily agreed, though she hadn't given thought to actually living at Eagle Farm; the original idea had been to sell both blocks.

'How could I live there, Daniel? There's no house and I can't afford to build one.'

'Ah, but you could. I'll soon find you a buyer for Emilie's land. That will give you more than enough to build a nice home on your block.'

'Emilie may not agree. She wasn't happy about selling at all.'

'So you say. But Emilie has to think ahead. Imagine if you had your own home, your sister would have a home too. You know only too well how uncertain is the life of a governess. She'd be much better off finding a suitable position in a college as you have done, and thereby gaining independence from a domestic scene.'

'That's true. Our house would be jointly owned, since it would have been built with the monies gained from the sale of her land . . .'

'On your property.'

'Yes. It seems an excellent idea. I'm truly grateful to you, Daniel. I should never have been able to work all this out on my own.'

In the meantime Ruth had another worry. Her sister had sent fifty pounds, and Ruth had added twenty pounds of her own, to be forwarded to London as part of repayment to the Society that had sponsored them, but she was concerned that the money would not reach the Society, since the mails were known to be unreliable.

'It is such a large amount,' she said anxiously. 'I should despair if it disappeared *en route*. I feel miserable as it is that Emilie has managed to save more than I have; imagine how awful it would be if our payments didn't reach the Society. We could never replace it.'

'Leave it to me. I'll send it for you in a diplomatic bag. There could be no problem that way, unless the ship sinks . . .'

'Oh, Daniel! Don't even joke about such a thing.'

'Sorry. But all you have to do is address your letter in the usual way, seal it well and it will go with government papers. The Colonial Secretary's office will forward it to your Society.'

'How marvellous. It would be such a relief.'

Daniel did intend to send the money for Ruth, but he knew little about the operations of diplomatic bags, which he was sure did exist, and as he was pondering that problem, he gave thought to the Society. Ruth had only recently told him about their sponsor and he'd taken little notice, but now, with her letter and all that money in his desk drawer, he began to doubt the authenticity of the Society. What had they really done for the ladies? Paid their fares, that was all. Then let them down. They had not provided them with the promised positions or any measure of support whatsoever. They did not deserve her loyalty. Or her money.

The day after they announced their engagement, Daniel, as Ruth's fiancé, made a decision. He took the letter from the drawer, burned it and kept the money, some of which he used to pay for their celebratory dinner at the Royal Arms Hotel. Since he was soon to be head of this family, he was only doing what he thought best. They couldn't afford to be giving money away, especially since he had no savings and his salary only exceeded Ruth's by nine shillings a fortnight. She was a well-brought-up young woman; she wouldn't dream of enquiring into his financial situation, and thankfully there was no glowering pater about to put the question, so he was spared the need to mention the subject.

But then there was Emilie. Obviously a silly young romantic, she had gone into raptures on hearing of their engagement, congratulating them effusively and sending heartfelt greetings to Mr Bowles who was soon to become her dear brother-in-law. She also, shyly, broke the news that she and her English gentleman, Mr Hillier, might soon come to an arrangement, since a fondness had developed between them.

Ruth, the elder sister, worried about this, demanding to know more of Mr Hillier and his situation, and hoping that Emilie would bring him down to Brisbane to meet her before committing herself to any definite arrangement.

'She's rather flighty,' Ruth told Daniel. 'Heaven knows who the fellow is. She says he manages a bond store, something like Customs, I presume, but it hardly seems suitable employment for a gentleman.'

Daniel agreed. He didn't want some fellow horning in on the Tissington girls at this stage. 'You tell your sister to be very careful. All sorts of strange characters drift up to those northern towns. They're riddled with outlaws and confidence men. I, myself, personally, had to insist that Superintendent Kemp go up there to investigate the breakdown in law and order, and upon his arrival he immediately sent for more police to be stationed in Maryborough. I'm surprised you allow your sister to remain there.'

'What can I do?' Ruth worried. 'She insists she's quite all right.'

'Oh well, maybe she is, as long as she doesn't get involved with this chap before we have a chance to look him over. What does she say about the land?'

'She signed all the necessary papers and she now owns that block, thanks to your assistance, which she acknowledges, but she flatly refuses to sell.'

'Did you tell her that the sale of her block would be a windfall for both of you, and enable you to build on your land?'

Ruth sighed. 'She understands that but she doesn't believe we should sell either block. She says they'll be worth much more in years to come. I simply can't understand her thinking. Poor Emilie, she's only scratching along, saving every halfpenny. I think I taught her economy far too well.'

'Then you must inform her that under the law, anyone who accepts a grant must make improvement upon that property within a specified time. That means fencing or irrigation or even a house. Where will she find the money to do that? The alternative is to sell quickly and pass on the obligation to the buyer. They have inspectors to monitor grants, you know.'

'Yes, I remember you did tell me that, and I made sure Emilie was aware, but she insists there's no hurry. I'm afraid she won't sell, and that is her decision, but Daniel, there is nothing to stop me selling my block.'

'Oh, well done,' he said, marching over to stare out of the window of the Belleview's small sitting room. 'Then all your money goes in paying rent here. You have a chance to own your own home; you should insist on it.'

'But how?'

Daniel shrugged. 'It's not for me to tell you your business, but if I were

228

you, my dear, I'd try another suggestion. Your sister might be living cheaply in that one-horse town, but here in the state capital there is no such thing as cheap rent, and rent down here is money down the drain. Why don't you suggest that you sell your block and with the sale money build a house on her block? A house that would always be home to Emilie as well. I mean, goodness me, a house on twenty acres would hardly be noticed.'

Chapter Ten

Though it was only approaching noon, Bert Manningtree trudged out to the schoolhouse for a word with the governess.

'I think you'd better call it a day, miss. This rain's getting heavier by the minute. Best you get along home while you can.'

The children cheered and their father grinned. 'Stroke of luck for you, eh?' He turned to Emilie. 'Early for the monsoons, miss, but it feels like that to me. This rain could set in for days.'

Alice was dismayed. 'Will we still have our lunch at your place, miss?'

'It's only Friday,' she said. 'We'll have to see how the weather is on Sunday. I've invited the children to my house for lunch on Sunday, sir. Mrs Mooney agreed to collect them and bring them home. Surely it will have cleared by then?'

He shook his head. 'I wouldn't bank on it, but it's real nice of you to ask them. You kids will have to wait and see.'

'Never mind,' Emilie promised, seeing their disappointment. 'If not this Sunday, then the next.'

'Paul Dressler's up at the house,' Manningtree told her. 'Seeing he's in a neighbourly mood, he's offered to take you home in his gig, so you run along, miss. I'll stay here and hear out the scholars.'

Dressler was a charming man. He didn't mind at all when Emilie asked if he'd drive past the post office so that she could mail a letter. She was tired of arguing with Ruth about that land, and still feeling guilty for having lied about her so-called savings. And for not mentioning that she actually owned her cottage. Ruth needed the money from the sale of her block and she might as well go ahead, especially since she intended to use the sale monies to build a house that they could share on Emilie's block. She found the idea quite exciting when she'd had time to think about it. Anyway, her letter gave Ruth permission to build a suitable house, and now she was looking forward to seeing the plans.

As for the Sunday lunch, since she had invited Clive to lunch after he'd pressed her to allow him to visit, Emilie had extended invitations to Mrs Mooney and the children so as to observe the proprieties. Clive would see through her little manipulations, but there was nothing he could do about it. When he arrived they'd be there. However, according to Mr Manningtree, and now Mr Dressler, she doubted she'd be entertaining anyone, and in a way that was a relief. She liked to potter about the cottage on her own on Sundays, her only full day off.

Though she was wearing her long tweed overcoat, Emilie was soaked by the time she ran back to the gig. She hoisted herself aboard and Mr Dressler dropped a damp newspaper in her lap as they set off again, visibility poor through the driving rain.

'You'll have to dry it by the fire to get a read out of it, missy,' he said, urging the horse through streets already running with water.

Eventually they arrived at her gate. 'Now if you're troubled by this storm, missy, you come on up to us, you hear?'

'Thank you, Mr Dressler, but I'm sure I'll be all right.'

'Well, don't you be worrying. I'll watch the river. It can flood high, that's why Paddy built right up here, and it always bears watching.'

Emilie made up her mind to buy a sturdy umbrella and she trod carefully down the steps to the cottage, steps that had become a slippery cascade of water, ruining her shoes. She sighed, pushing open the door to be met by a gust of heat. Because of the light rain earlier in the morning, she'd closed all of the windows, and now the house smelled damp and musty.

'Damn,' she said, divesting herself of the soaking overcoat. 'I'll never get used to this climate! How can it be hot *and* teeming with rain?'

She decided to light the fire anyway, to dry her clothes, but the woodheap, also soaked, was no help, so she changed out of her wet things and ducked across to the kitchen, where at least the wood for the stove was dry. Though only mid-afternoon, the cottage was dark and dismal. She couldn't even see as far as the river, so she had no idea whether it was rising or not.

Feeling locked in, a rare experience in this cottage, with its views now well hidden, Emilie made tea and took some biscuits from their tin, munching on them miserably. They were dry and not very tasty, though she'd followed Kate's recipe closely.

'Obviously not as closely as I should have,' she remarked. Then, with nothing else to do, she decided to rescue the newspaper that she'd dropped somewhere in the house.

Learning to be resourceful since she'd become a bachelor lady forced to do her own cooking, Emilie had been amused to find 'colonial' cooking was more her style. When Kate was constantly preparing dishes for the family, Emilie found it easier, and faster, to grill and potboil on the top of the stove, using the oven for heating, so now, with a wry smile, she used the stove to dry out the newspaper. She emerged, pleased with herself, with six very dry, crackling pages, and folded them in order.

The front page shocked her.

SONNY WILLOUGHBY CAPTURED.

Sonny? Who was Sonny? Was it Mal?

The columns that followed soon made it plain that he had been apprehended in the south Queensland village of Chinchilla, and had been transferred to a Brisbane jail.

Through her tears, Emilie read every cruel line on the page, over and

231

over. They were gloating, horrible, the way they spoke of him. Not a word about the possibility of his innocence, just a rehash of the holdup, the murders, the gold robbery and his part in the heinous crime.

And over the page there was more. A dreadful explanation of his capture out on a lonely farm near the Condamine River, wherever that was. The outlaw – the outlaw? – had been apprehended in his sleep at that farm, as a result of a tipoff from his uncle, who was now entitled to the reward. Which would be paid, of course, by the owner of the *Maryborough Chronicle*, who had been demanding more attention to law and order on behalf of the residents for more than a year.

Emilie hated him. And Mal's uncle. How could they do this to an innocent man? On top of all that, the uncle had apprised people of Mal's nickname, a family name. Sonny. Was nothing sacred to that man? That awful man.

There was a description of the scene where Mal had been taken from that town, under guard, by extra police, through a barrage of abuse by local residents who had rallied to witness the event, and Emilie felt his agony, Mal's Calvary, as if it was her own. The humiliation must have been shattering.

Then she read that the prisoner had had nothing to say, nothing at all, and she wept again.

All the afternoon and evening Emilie waited. Regardless of the rain, she felt sure that Clive would come out to see her, to tell her about this, in case she hadn't read it. To commiserate. Mal was their friend and he was in jail for crimes he had not committed. Surely Clive would come. In this emergency, proprieties meant nothing.

That evening Emilie fell asleep on the long couch, still fully dressed, rather than receive Clive in her night attire.

On the Saturday, the rain continued to fall as if there was to be no end to it, and her only visitor was Mrs Dressler, who was cheerfully unconcerned about 'a bit of water' and who brought Emilie some of her delicious white pork sausages and a cheesecake.

Sunday, for Emilie, was more of the same. The *Chronicle* was not published at weekends so she had no further news of Mal. Rain came down in torrents, the roof began to leak, water rushed in under her front door, reminding her forcibly as she mopped and swabbed that this cottage had only been built as a fishing lodge. Venturing outside under a strip of canvas she'd found in the shed, Emilie saw that the river had indeed risen several feet into the garden but not far enough to be of any concern. Mrs Mooney sent her barman to make sure that Emilie was not expecting her for lunch, or the children, and she assured him she was not. Unable to concentrate on reading, or anything constructive, all she could do was pace the floor, grieving for Mal, willing Clive to come and comfort her, hating this town, this country, for its cruelty, for its appalling weather, for its injustice.

And then Clive came. Eight o'clock at night, as the rain was easing. Clive came, and Emilie threw herself into his arms.

'Oh my dear,' she wept. 'Where have you been? I've been out of my mind with worry.'

'Good Lord, Emilie!' he cried, taken aback. 'Did you really expect me for lunch? I wouldn't have put you to that trouble in this weather. But here, desist, dear girl, or you'll get soaked. Let me get rid of these wet things.'

He threw his hat and coat on to the couch. 'My papa used to talk about the rains in India, but I'm betting this weather would give him a run for his money! It's simply appalling, isn't it? Now give me a hug and tell me you're not angry with me.'

He returned her hug with a long, hard kiss and Emilie could smell liquor on him. It was difficult to extricate herself from him but she had to be firm.

'Not now, Clive, please. I have to talk to you.'

'What about?' One arm still held her to him and he nuzzled her neck. 'Have you missed me? I've been so blasted busy, hardly a minute to myself . . .'

'Will you listen to me, Clive. Please!' Emilie moved away from him. 'Didn't you see Friday's paper?'

Smiling, he rubbed his chin thoughtfully. 'Friday? What happened Friday?'

'They've captured Mal!'

'Oh, Lord, yes. Poor old Mal. But it was only a matter of time. He'd have known that himself.'

'But he's innocent.'

'And now he'll have a chance to prove it.' He wandered about the room. 'This place is much bigger than it appears from the outside. And it's very cosy on a rainy night.' He dropped into the big armchair and patted his lap. 'Come and sit here and tell me all about your weekend.'

Exasperated, Emilie kept away from him. 'Don't you care about Mal? I've been waiting all weekend to ask you what we can do.'

'We? Emilie, I'm sorry for him, believe me. But there's nothing anyone can do. It's up to the police.'

'They should arrest that Mr Carnegie.'

'Maybe they will, for all I know. Pollock said that Kemp interviewed him in Brisbane, making certain he doesn't leave there, but they can't charge him. They've got nothing to go on.'

'They must have something.'

'Can we talk about something else? This conversation is futile.'

'I don't regard it as futile,' she snapped. 'He's our friend. We can't sit back and let them hang him. An innocent man.'

'Oh, for God's sake. They won't take him out and hang him. He has to be formally charged, he'll go to jail for a while and then he'll get his day in court . . .'

'But he shouldn't even be in jail! It's dreadful.' She continued to worry the subject, demanding that Clive do something, though she had nothing constructive to suggest, until he lost patience with her.

233

He jumped up, grabbed his coat and hat and confronted her. 'I'll come back another time when you're talking sense. I won't have you blaming me for his misfortunes.'

'I'm not. It's just that I've been worrying all weekend. I hoped you would come to see me when you saw the paper . . .'

'And I told you, I've been busy. The world doesn't revolve round Mal Willoughby, though you seem to think it does. You hardly know the man, Emilie. You're behaving like a silly schoolgirl.'

She didn't want him to go. 'I'm sorry, Clive, it's just that it's all so unfair and . . . more than that. It's tragic!'

'Well, you keep your tragedy and I'll see you next week.'

He slammed out of the house, leaving Emilie in tears again. She realised she hadn't even offered him tea or coffee, or enquired if he'd had an evening meal, and was abjectly sorry about that. How could she have been so thoughtless? So discourteous? His first visit to her house and it had been a disaster. He'd probably never speak to her again.

Tired, depressed and desperately lonely, she curled up on her bed, clutching a pillow, hoping to end a miserable weekend in sleep.

Had she known it, another man was quicker off the mark as soon as he heard that Willoughby had been arrested.

'He'll talk, sure as hell,' McPherson told Ward. 'I've got to get out of here.'

'I think that's a good move. Next thing they'll have his photo in the papers and folks might recognise him. He said he'd been trailing about these hills for quite a while before he stumbled on you. But don't worry about us, we'll just say we've never seen him. Never heard of him.'

McPherson wasn't worried about Ward, or the Foleys. They could look after themselves. He had chosen a good horse and was already packing his swag.

'The bastards won't get me. I'm heading so far north I'll run them out of steam.'

Sergeant Pollock heard the news when he rode into the coastal town of Bundaberg, only fifty miles or so north of Maryborough.

Constable Lacey was relieved. 'Can we go home now, boss?'

'I don't know,' Pollock said sourly. He felt a fool, chasing Willoughby up here when the bugger was hundreds of miles in the other direction. Any hope of promotion for recapturing Willoughby was finished now. And obviously the two outlaws, McPherson and Willoughby, had not been travelling together. One had gone south. Had the other gone north? A possibility but he could have headed west. A thousand miles in any direction. Hopeless.

Though they'd started out searching the hill country, calling on farms and tiny remote settlements with a few local police, who resented their intrusion, they'd not even uncovered a whisper that McPherson was in those areas.

234

Pollock drowned his sorrows in a shanty pub half hidden by steaming palms glistening from recent rains. The roof was thatched, the earthen floor bare of boards, which by no means bothered the other half-dozen customers, none of whom wore boots. They were hard-looking men with leathered skin and cold, tired eyes, unimpressed at having a uniformed policeman in their midst, but Pollock didn't care. He ignored the glares and snide remarks, standing stolidly at the greasy counter, downing his third warm ale while he waited for Constable Lacey.

He had decided that they would return home. There was enough policing to be done in Maryborough and the surrounding districts without wasting time searching for McPherson, who was a will-o'-the-wisp at the best of times. And it would be better not to advise his senior officer, who was crazy enough to order him to keep going. Who had no grasp at all of the size of this damned state.

Having obtained no reaction from the bobby in the bar with their sidelong remarks, a red-haired fellow tried the direct approach.

'Hey, mister. You looking for Willoughby? Have you tried the dunny outside? He could be in there.'

Shouts of laughter greeted that witticism, but Pollock stared straight ahead, realising that the fancy bottles facing him from the shelf behind the bar were all just that, fancy decorations, probably filled with tea. He forced himself to appear genial.

'Willoughby's been captured. Anyone know McPherson?'

That brought a sudden silence, followed by more derisive laughter, but by the time Lacey wandered in, the men had lost interest in the newcomer.

'I've found us a couple of cots for the night,' the constable told Pollock. 'On a riverboat. But it's clear of bugs.'

'That'll be a change,' Pollock grunted, signalling to the barman for a drink for his colleague.

'And that's not all,' Lacey murmured. 'A little bloke I met down there told me that McPherson has got mates in Bowen.'

'So what?'

'Well, do you reckon we ought to go up there?'

'Jesus, Mike! It's five hundred miles if it's an inch from here. I wanted to get Willoughby. I've missed him. I'm not going after McPherson. We don't know for sure that he was even at Blackwater Creek.'

'You believe that letter?'

'I do and I don't. We're getting out of this mosquito nest and going home. When we get there, you wire the Bowen police to be on the lookout. It's your tip-off.'

Lacey was pleased. 'Thanks, boss. I didn't fancy a trek like that. Just thought I'd better mention it.' He drank his pint in a couple of swallows and leaned back on the bar.

'Hey. Any of you know where a bloke can get a feed here?'

The other men mellowed. Bundaberg was as yet only a parcel of a town. No police, no cafés, just a collection of shanties dug into the

235

rainforest by the Burnett River, not too far from the lonely coastline. A coastal outlet for more sugar plantations.

'Cookup outside on the campfires,' one man allowed grudgingly. 'Bring your own grog.'

Pollock awoke next morning on the gently rocking boat feeling very healthy considering the amount of liquor he'd consumed, but then, he'd eaten well. Fresh fish wrapped in palm leaves cooked under the coals while meat was seared above and pots of potatoes and corn bubbled from iron hooks . . . It had been quite a feast. After that night, he had fond memories of rough old Bundaberg. And so did Mike Lacey. He remembered to telegraph the police in Bowen, another sugar town.

After that wretched weekend, Emilie was glad to be out and about again, looking forward to the comfort and security of her own little schoolroom. And the distraction, she added ruefully as she walked briskly. The sun was out again, glittering harshly without a shadow of guilt for its absence over the last few days, and the lush greenery along her route steamed in response. Another monotonously hot day ahead. Sometimes Emilie yearned for a cold day, a really cold day, with roaring fires and woollen guernseys and socks and shawls . . . She sighed, depression lingering.

In the kitchen Kate and Nellie were all talk about the capture of the outlaw, while the children finished their breakfast, silenced by the appearance of Mrs Manningtree, who was in an exceptionally good mood, even chatting to Emilie about her weekend.

'What a shame you had to postpone your luncheon with the children.'

'Oh, yes, it was a pity to disappoint them, but if you're agreeable, madam, we'll try again next Sunday.'

'By all means. So what did you do with a whole weekend to yourself?'

'Very little. I couldn't do much in that rain. I usually enjoy a little gardening.'

'Heavens above. If you stay here you'll have to get used to rain. The wet season hasn't even begun yet. We never let rain spoil our social lives.'

As she rattled on about their busy weekend, the Friday-night dance at the Masonic Hall, and the Mayor's birthday party, Emilie began to wonder if she was being reproved for cancelling her own weekend arrangements. Sensing something was amiss, Nellie disappeared into the house and Kate drifted across to the pantry, out of the firing line but not out of earshot.

'We had a simply wonderful weekend really. Damp, I admit, but that made it all the more fun. Just about everyone turned out for the Mayor. I was surprised you were not there. It was a gesture of support for the Mayor, who of course, as you know, is a dear friend. Your Mr Hillier was there, cutting quite a dash, I might say.'

'That's nice,' Emilie said flatly, understanding now.

'I was curious about his partner, though. I mean, since he is, or is supposed to be, your boyfriend . . .'

'Mr Hillier is a friend.'

236

'Of course. But you can't blame me for being curious, so I had to ask. Maybe you know her, a tall girl with red hair, rather good-looking in a flashy sort of way.'

'No, I don't know her.'

'Oh. Are you sure? Her name is Fleur something.'

Emilie shook her head. 'No. But I'm really pleased you had such a lovely weekend. Would you excuse me now, madam? I really must attend to the children.'

Who was Fleur?

Although Emilie had not given her employer the satisfaction of appearing concerned, she was furious. Clive had lied to her. Busy all weekend? Obviously he had been, but not with work as he'd implied. Then he'd had the cheek to argue with her for caring about Mal, while he'd been squiring another girl about. And he'd left in a huff. Disappointment affected her concentration nearly all day. She hated the term 'boyfriend' but it was true that she did regard Clive as more than a friend, and this news was very hurtful. Emilie hoped Clive would have some simple explanation. Maybe this girl was a relation of some sort. In which case, why hadn't he mentioned her before?

Who *was* Fleur?

She'd been working as a barmaid in Brisbane when she met the suave Englishman. He was on his way to the Gympie goldfields but was so smitten with Fleur that he kept delaying his departure until she suggested accompanying him.

Clive was astonished. 'Good heavens, no! From what I hear, conditions on the diggings are quite rough. You couldn't possibly come with me!'

'Why not? Plenty of women are going up there. I can ride and I'm a good bush cook. I'll bet you're not.'

'Even so . . .'

'You can't work alone,' she said quickly. 'You need someone. You have to let me come! It would be such a lark. And imagine finding gold! Please, Clive – say yes!'

He didn't take too much persuading, Fleur recalled with a grin. It had been quite a lark for both of them at first.

Reality set in after a few weeks of living in the dusty, flea-ridden camp, surrounded by the noise and clamour of desperate diggers during the day and sheltering from drunken brawls and celebrations through the chaotic nights. They had both worked hard. Fleur kept her part of the bargain, finding supplies, cooking over a campfire and helping him on the dig, but she soon became heartily sick of it. Especially when they hardly found a speck of gold while others were doing well.

The lark became a daily drudge. Fleur shuddered, recalling that miserable time. They argued a lot, with Fleur blaming him for not finding gold, claiming he was hopeless, so he reacted by working harder, from dawn to dark, and collapsing on his bunk at night. He was so obsessed with the search, he was no company any more. Just plain boring.

Fleur made her own fun. She'd sneak out while he slept and join the mobs at the grog shops, and that caused even more rows, because he usually caught her.

But that was where she met old Stan Colman, a prospector with real experience of gold diggings.

By this time Fleur was looking for a meal ticket to get her out of the place. No point in leaving broke, with so much gold surfacing throughout the Gympie hills, so she planned her move carefully. It was too late to latch on to a digger once he'd struck it rich. He'd be off and away, maybe with his favourite whore on his arm – no, she'd have to place her bet on a likely winner.

She had had a feeling all along that this man was a rare digger who knew what he was doing, so she began to stop and chat with him whenever she passed his mine, which she managed to do as often as possible. Stan was flattered by the attentions of the 'pretty missy', as he called her, and Fleur was careful never to mention him to Clive. Not that her handsome partner would have seen any competition in a sixty-year-old digger with a white beard.

The minute word was out that Colman had struck it rich, Fleur found an excuse to go to the store, detouring to Stan's claim to congratulate him.

'You're a good girlie,' he said. 'That's real nice of you. I've hit gold all right, and as soon as I clear out this reef I'm gettin' out of here. There's enough colour here to fit me out for life.'

She sighed. 'I wish I could come with you. He beats me, you know.'

The lie had its effect . . .

Stan was shocked. 'Who? Hillier does? I'll give him a bloody hiding meself.'

'Thanks, but that won't help things. I'm stuck with him. Can't afford to get away.'

He winked. 'Don't be too sure. You hang on a little while until I give you the nod, and we'll both disappear. I'll give you a good time, you can bank on that. What do you say?'

'I wouldn't want to impose on you, Stan.'

'Impose nothin'. A girlie like you, I'd be real proud to take you along.'

Fleur glanced a kiss on the bearded face. 'You're a real gent, Stan. I'd be ever so grateful . . .'

They went to Maryborough and on to Brisbane, and while the money lasted they had a fine old time, staying at the best hotel as Mr and Mrs Colman, spending on anything that took their fancy, from smart clothes and cases of champagne to treating old and new friends in fine style.

When finally the cash ran out, Stan had no regrets. 'I've had the time of me life, Fleur. I'll head for fresher goldfields now. Do you want to come with me?'

'No fear,' she laughed. 'I've had enough of that dirt and dust.'

They parted friends. Stan hadn't left her stony broke. It never occurred to him to ask Fleur if she could return some of the pounds he'd stuffed in her purse with the regularity of a dedicated spendthrift; it just wasn't in his nature. And she still had some valuable pieces of jewellery, as well as trunks of fashionable outfits. But her old mate had conferred an even greater favour on the former barmaid: he'd introduced her to the high life, and now there was no going back to the drudgery. Not ever.

She soon found another gentleman friend, equally generous, and ten years younger than Stan, to keep her in comfort in the hotel suite. He was married, with a clutch of kids, and that suited Fleur; she didn't need him around all the time, she had to make plans

Finally she decided she ought to buy a hotel. Or, as her best friend Madeleine urged, she who had some experience of the business, a brothel. A high-class bordello. By this her rich benefactor was so enamoured of the saucy redhead that he readily agreed to back her, especially when she mentioned that a fast-growing town like Maryborough would be a good start. He was in shipping and, as Fleur guessed, to have his lady love ensconced in another town, which he was able to visit without inventing excuses to the wife, was daringly perfect.

The two ladies, Fleur and Madeleine, arrived at the port of Maryborough on a wet Friday afternoon, and struggling through the deluge to the Prince of Wales Hotel, Madeleine took an instant dislike to the town. She already had a bad cold and soon took to her bed convinced that she had caught pneumonia.

Fleur was of sterner stuff. She called for a maid to take their wet clothes and dry and press them, towelled her hair dry, settling it with pomade, and pinned it up in the elegant style she'd learned to manage in Brisbane. She chose an expensive dress of self-striped taffeta in green and black with a low-cut bodice, and added emerald earrings to the picture.

'If you're going downstairs, you ought to wear a hat,' Madeleine sniffed as she watched. 'It's done, and it isn't as if you're short of them.'

'Who cares? I'm not going out in the weather. I'll give them all a thrill. I make my own rules.'

She sailed downstairs, full of confidence, happily aware of stares from large hatted ladies as she wandered through the lobby, peering into the parlour and the busy dining room.

A waitress rushed forward, enquiring if the lady wished to be seated yet, since her company had obviously not yet arrived. It was not the done thing for ladies to dine alone, not even in Maryborough. Not in this dining room anyway.

'Shortly,' Fleur said imperiously. 'I suppose it's the rain. I'll take another turn about the rooms for a few minutes.'

'Oh, yes, madam. Everyone's late tonight. But you can wait inside here if you wish.'

Having made her point, that she could get away with dining alone, Fleur tripped back towards the foyer, admiring herself in a gilt mirror above a wilting palm. She could now claim that she'd been left in the lurch as a result of the weather and survey the other diners. From the women she'd seen so far, a dowdy lot, there'd be no competition tonight, and one never knew, there could be an eager gentleman within reach. Fleur was never one to spend her own money unless there was no alternative.

The alternative came up the hall from the direction of the billiard room and the lady with the red hair stepped forward, confronting him.

'Well, for heaven's sake, Clive! Fancy meeting you here.'

He stared. 'Good God! Fleur. I hardly knew you.'

Fleur preened. 'Quite a change from the dirty old diggings, wouldn't you say?'

'I would indeed,' he said with a wry smile. 'You're looking very well.'

'So are you, my dear.' She took his arm. 'It's so nice to see you again. You must buy me a drink and tell me how you are prospering.'

He looked about him. 'I really must go . . .'

But Fleur had no intention of allowing him to escape. She pouted. 'But you can't! You have to tell me all the news. Surely you can spare me some time. I'm staying here in the hotel and I'm bored stiff.'

He raised an eyebrow. 'On your own?'

'No. I'm with a lady friend. But she's indisposed.' She laughed. 'See – away with your wicked thoughts. Where can we have a drink?'

'I really don't know, Fleur. Hotels in this town don't run to ladies' lounges.'

'Never mind,' she told him. 'There's always the dining room. Now come along. It's damp in this hall.'

'Very well,' he said lamely, and Fleur was delighted.

'Marvellous. We'll have a good old talk.'

Clive didn't really mind being commandeered as a dinner partner. He was intrigued by Fleur's transformation from country girl to this figure of fashion. He thought she was overdressed and looking rather vulgar for his taste, but the outfit showed what she had in all the right places, the full bosom that he remembered so well almost spilling out before his eyes. She was as bold as ever and had regained the wild humour that had first attracted him, and that had been so quickly demolished in the squalid surrounds of the diggings.

Listening to her laughter and her unabashed hilarious tales of travels with old Stan Colman, he was surprised to find that he bore her no ill-will for deserting him. He'd been hurt at the time, and angry with her, but it was probably more a blow to his pride than his heart.

Nevertheless, when he realised that she was under the impression he was a prosperous businessman now, since he had mentioned vaguely that he was considering investing in the town, the same pride kept him from correcting that impression. Some recompense for her making a fool of him.

Old friends now, they dined well and were enjoying a third bottle of wine, ordered by Fleur, when they were interrupted by Walt White, who,

240

though he was addressing Clive, could hardly take his eyes off Fleur.

'Here you are, old chap! We need a favour, Clive. As you know, big party here tomorrow night. Support for the Mayor. Elections coming up.' He turned an ingratiating smile on Fleur.

'Have to tell you, dear lady – he's not much of a Mayor, but better than the alternative. So Clive, old chap, we'll present him with an illuminated address and we've chosen you to read it out to the company.'

Clive was unimpressed. 'Oh no, not me, Walt. Find someone else.'

'There isn't anyone else.' He turned back to Fleur. 'Wouldn't you say he has a wonderful voice – mellifluous.'

She agreed. 'Oh yes, so very English. You must do it, Clive.'

'Indeed he must. We won't take no for an answer and he must bring you along too. You'll be the belle of the ball.'

'A ball! Will there be dancing? Marvellous! We'd love to come. Thank you . . . um . . . ?'

'White,' Clive grated. His failure to introduce them had been deliberate.

'Then it's settled,' Walt said triumphantly. 'I'll seat you and this beautiful young lady at my table.' He clicked his heels and bowed to Fleur – 'Adieu, milady' – then hurried away.

'Idiot!' Clive said.

'Don't be like that, he's very nice. And it's obviously an honour for you to read that thingamajig for them. I'm looking forward to the ball. It will be fun.'

Clive groaned. 'Listen, Fleur, I have to get going.'

'So early?'

'Yes. I've got a busy day tomorrow.'

'Why don't you come up to my room for a nightcap?'

'No. I wouldn't dream of disturbing your lady friend.'

'She wouldn't care.'

'No. Come on, let's go.'

'Oh, all right. I'll need my beauty sleep for tomorrow night. You won't forget, will you?'

'I suppose not.'

She kissed him on the cheek as they left the table. 'Goody. You really are a dear.'

The next morning, from habit, Fleur was up early, though still confined to the hotel because of the rain. She lingered over breakfast, where she made the acquaintance of a charming Frenchman, who told her he was a planter, and a little while later she slipped into the bar, not for a drink, but in search of information.

Prior to opening time, a barmaid was polishing the glasses. She looked up in surprise to see a lady enter.

'I'm sorry, madam, we're not open. And . . .' whispering, 'we can't serve ladies here.'

'I know that,' Fleur laughed. 'I'm staying in the house, just wandering about for something to do. It's a very nice bar, isn't it? Quite large.'

In the course of conversation with the talkative barmaid about the hotel and the town, she mentioned Clive Hillier.

'Do you know him?' the woman asked.

'Oh yes,' Fleur said, making no pretence about her background. As far as she was concerned, people could think what they liked. She made her own rules, as she often said. 'I worked a mine with Clive out at Gympie.'

The woman was astonished. 'You did?' Then she stared. 'Good God! You're Fleur! I used to work in Salty's grog shop out there. I wouldna known you!'

'I got lucky,' Fleur grinned.

'Well, good for you. Do you want a quick nip?'

'Wouldn't mind a brandy. A pick-me-up after putting away too much wine last night.'

She swallowed the brandy quickly, so as not to cause problems for the barmaid, and slipped the glass back to her.

'Tell me about Clive. What's he up to these days?'

'He's the head man over at the bond store.'

'Works there?'

'Yeah, he's been there for quite a while. Got himself a steady girl. A schoolteacher. Nice little thing. Friend of Mrs Mooney's.'

'Well, she ought to be able to keep him in order.'

'Seems so. No accountin' for men.'

'You can say that again. Who's the Frenchman?'

'You mean Mr Devereaux? Isn't he the goods? Tips everyone like money's going out of season. Got a big sugar plantation over the other side of the river . . .'

A barman came in with a mop and bucket. 'You're late,' the girl snapped at him, and Fleur nodded to her, knowing it was time to go.

She pondered Clive. Doing well, are you? Looking at investments? I don't think.

The dining room had been enlarged by the opening up of folding doors, allowing the adjoining room to be set aside for dancing, and it was decorated with palms and colourful Chinese lanterns. A band consisting of a pianist, two fiddlers and a drummer was already romping into action when the first guests arrived. Clive kept his promise to escort Fleur to the ball, but he was moody and glum, by no means enthusiastic about either of his duties on this hot and humid night. Not that Fleur cared – he looked very attractive in his dark suit, starched collar and bow tie. An ideal escort for the lady who was the centre of attention as they entered the room. A quick glance told Fleur that none of the dowdy women in this company could compete with her – she was wearing her favourite dress and was delighted to have an opportunity to show it off. Madeleine, not a little miffed at being left out, had dressed her hair in a cascade of curls from the crown, with ringlets framing her face. Her ball frock, off the shoulder, was pink satin, with layered skirts trimmed with silver, and she wore

242

pearl drop earrings to complete the picture.

Mr White rushed forward. 'My dear, you look magnificent. You show us all up! Come along and join us. We can't let Clive out of our sight either.'

Clive thought the whole show was a bunfight, people smelling of damp clothes and mothballs crushing into the room and scrambling for free drinks. And Fleur looked ridiculous, despite Walt's gushing compliments.

In a whisper she told him that her dress had cost the earth, and out of politeness he ignored the remark.

The night dragged on. Mrs Mooney came by and snapped at him. Mrs Manningtree made a point of chatting to Fleur, and Clive, worrying about Emilie, took refuge in whisky.

A drum roll heralded the speeches, and eventually Clive read the wildly flattering illuminated address, but by that time no one was listening and he couldn't care less. He drank champagne, too much champagne, with the maudlin Mayor, and staggered back to the table to find Fleur singing ballads with old and new acquaintances since the musicians seemed to have fallen by the wayside.

Drunk and depressed, he whispered to Fleur that he was leaving.

'You can't go yet! It's early!' she laughed.

'I am going, Fleur. You don't need to be escorted home.'

'Oh, very well,' she sighed. 'But my friend Madeleine is feeling better. Why don't you take us sightseeing around the town tomorrow? She hasn't seen a stitch of it yet.'

'I can't. I'll be working.'

That brought hoots of laughter from Fleur and her friends.

'It's Sunday tomorrow, Clive!' she reminded him. 'Now do be kind. Poor Madeleine has had a horrible time here.'

'Of course he will,' Walt White added. 'You mustn't let the ladies down, Clive.'

'Very well,' Clive agreed. It seemed the only avenue of escape.

During the evening, Fleur had managed to catch the eye of the Frenchman, Mr Devereaux, who raised his glass to her, so once Clive had departed, she looked about for him, but unfortunately he too had left.

Walt White's attentions were becoming boring – he had taken to pawing her, and he had bad breath. He was full of himself, telling her he was an important man in the town, and when he whispered some suggestive remark in her ear, the old Fleur emerged.

'Push off, you bloody old creep!'

Mortified, Walt left the remains of the party, vowing vengeance. She wouldn't get a mention in his paper after all. Not one word. In his fuzzy head he was already rewriting his next social column, not forgetting that the Mayor, overwhelmed by 'sentiment', had had to be carried to his residence.

Sunday morning. Clive had slept like a log. An intoxicated log, he reminded himself, but he was feeling well, and glad he'd escaped early enough to survive the revelries without too much pain from the free cheap grog being passed about. He would have preferred further sleep, but shipping schedules were not observers of the Sabbath, so there was work to do.

He grabbed a towel, pulled on a pair of white duck trousers that he'd put under his mattress to be pressed, and headed down the hall, by-passing the dingy bathroom to make for the 'shower room', an outdoor contraption shielded by a low fence of corrugated iron. The water was warm but it had enough force from a high tank to act as a reviver of sorts. As he stood, soaking himself, he began to laugh, recalling the previous evening, that social event! It really had been a riot, with so many people fawning over Fleur that he was amazed at their naiveté!

'I must have enjoyed myself,' he mused. 'I drank enough to sink a ship.'

The rain had eased to a light mist and so the heat was gaining force as he made his way down the street with a square of oilskin slung over his shoulders. There was no one in sight this early except a gang of blackfellows shovelling manure into a cart – their daily chore in Maryborough – but by disturbing the droppings of horses and bullocks and the goats that roamed the town, they raised a sickly-sweet stench that sent Clive hurrying past them.

Already the wharves were busy loading cargo and passengers on to ships, but Clive was there to watch for the last-minute offloading of illicit liquor to avoid excise. Finding everything was in order, he accepted the invitation of the captain of the barque *Virginia* to join him for breakfast and the mandatory tot of rum.

With the day taking shape now, he unlocked the bond store and took refuge in his office to read interstate newspapers that he'd collected from the ships.

Then he remembered that he'd promised to take Fleur and her friend on a tour of the town, and that irritated him, though it wasn't much of a chore really. Besides, he was curious to know what these two women were up to. Fleur had said they were thinking of buying a hotel. Unlikely, with Fleur, but the other woman was an unknown quantity. It mightn't be a bad idea to talk them out of it.

This time he presented himself at the hotel with his gig. The ladies were already waiting for him. Fleur was showing no signs of wear from the night before, and she even looked presentable in a tailored brown suit with a smart hat to match.

She chatted happily as she introduced her friend to 'dear Clive'. One glimpse of Madeleine, an older woman, blonde and blowsy, told Clive that this pair were not looking for a hotel. Premises for yet another brothel, more like it.

While they drove about the town, Madeleine was full of complaints about the weather, the heat, the wretched hotel. And Clive agreed with her on every point.

'It's not much of a town,' he admitted, 'too many hotels as it is. Not much cash around since the gold rush, and at the risk of offending your sensibilities, ladies, far too many bordellos. Though the town council is busy lowering the boom on those establishments.'

By the time he returned them to the hotel, Madeleine had lost interest in Maryborough, but Fleur was still keen to stay.

Oh no you're not, Clive thought. Not if I have any say in it. Fleur was charmed, flattered even, when he offered to call back to see her that evening.

'Till then,' she said gaily, and disappeared up the steps of the hotel, pushing Madeleine ahead of her.

'He's no fool,' Madeleine said angrily. 'He knows what we're about, Fleur. And you said yourself, he hasn't got any money.'

'You just never know,' Fleur argued. 'He seems to be very popular. He could pull strings for us.'

'Rot. You heard what he said. There's no money in this town, just farmers and bushies. All tightwads. I don't know how I let you drag me up here. It's an awful bloody town.'

'It might not be. Now that you're feeling better, come and have lunch with me. The food's good, that's something.'

The staff had been working hard under Mrs Mooney's direction restoring the dining rooms to order, and all was in place when the two ladies presented themselves at the door, followed by Mr Devereaux, who insisted they join him on this miserable Sunday.

They learned he was a widower, that he owned sugar plantations in the area and others in Fiji. He was a jolly fellow, appreciating Fleur, who made him laugh, and was very disappointed to learn that the ladies had decided to return to Brisbane.

'Ah, but you can't go yet. You must visit my plantation. I can assure you my home is indeed comfortable. There is so much interesting to see, and I shall take great care of you.'

It was Fleur who took some persuading. Anything outside town limits was bush to her, and she'd had enough of that. Without wishing to hurt Mr Devereaux's feelings, she tried to convey to Madeleine, through pressure with her foot, that this was not a good idea, but by then Madeleine was enthusiastic.

'We should be delighted to accept your invitation, Mr Devereaux,' she said firmly.

It appeared that he'd come down to Maryborough to obtain more labourers, but apparently the ship carrying the South Sea Islanders had been delayed in Cairns, so he would be returning home that afternoon.

'But whenever you are ready, ladies, I shall send a vehicle for you.'

Further discussion followed as to when they should visit, until Madeleine announced that any time would be suitable for her. Finally, outvoted two to one, Fleur was persuaded that they might as well allow Mr Devereaux to accompany them this very afternoon.

As they packed, Fleur was cross. 'What did you do that for? I don't want to go out to some damned farmhouse.'

'Who cares? He's keen on you, Fleur. We haven't got anything else to do. Unless you really are interested in Hillier.'

'I am not!'

'Well then. Won't it be funny for him to come looking for you tonight only to find the bird has flown? Again.'

That brightened Fleur's day.

Mr Devereaux's vehicle, driven by a coloured man, was a comfortable carriage, well insulated from the inclement weather. The ferrymen took particular care of the party and, Fleur noticed as the coach and horses were delivered safely to the other shore, their new friend must have tipped them well, judging by their beaming faces.

They set off down muddy tracks through vast fields of blackened stubble as stark and depressing as a battlefield. Sullenly Fleur gazed out at rows of kanaka labourers picking their way across the dark landscape like grave-robbers.

She shuddered. She hated the place. It was only fit for blackfellows and the hundreds of garrulous crows that plodded sharp-eyed over the rough terrain.

Then Madeleine had to ask a stupid question.

'Has there been a bushfire, Mr Devereaux?'

Irritated, Fleur gave an audible sigh, but Devereaux was patient. He explained that they burned the canefields before cutting and went on to give the reasons, followed by the various stages of cane growing. Fleur thought she'd pass out from the steamy heat and the sheer boredom.

At the first gate, Fleur's heart sank. She knew it! Why hadn't Madeleine listened to her? The house confronting them was a typical bush farmhouse, neater than most, but still only a dreary timber cottage . . .

'That is my manager's house,' Devereaux told them as the driver closed the gate and started up again.

At least a mile further on they rounded a bend, and this time there was no mistake. Thrilled, Madeleine nudged Fleur. It was a large house, painted white, with tall black shutters, and it was every bit as elegant as its owner. A well-designed formal garden with clipped hedges, flower beds and fountains surrounded the house, adding quiet charm to the scene.

'It's beautiful!' Madeleine cried, and Fleur tried not to gape.

'I'm so glad you like it,' their host said as the carriage crunched up the gravel drive and coloured servants with umbrellas ran out to greet them.

Weeks later, all three were back in Maryborough to board a ship for Brisbane, where Madeleine would farewell Fleur and Mr Devereaux, who remained on board. They were *en route* to Suva, Fiji, to visit his other sugar plantations.

On that decisive Sunday evening, Clive headed for the Prince of Wales again. This time he would have a straight talk with Fleur. There was no need to be unpleasant, but he would point out to her quite firmly that he had his own life to live here, that whether she stayed or not they would go their separate ways. She should not expect him to be other than an acquaintance. All weekend he'd dreaded the thought of bumping into Emilie with Fleur clutching on to him. Not that there was any chance of that so far – Emilie did not frequent hotels, nor would she have been out on a drizzling Sunday morning. Only half remembering all the incidents of that boozy night in the overcrowded dining room, he'd completely forgotten Mrs Manningtree. In his eyes, the pathetic woman hardly existed.

More importantly, he would be stern with Fleur. If she and her peculiar friend had any ideas of opening up another brothel in this town – yes, he would come right out and say it – they'd better think again. A warning, or a threat – immaterial.

He might even advise her, as a businessman, since he had mentioned he was investing in the town – without specifying what business. It would be just like Fleur to pinch his idea. They obviously had funds. He would recommend that their line of business would be better served back in Brisbane or out at the newly famous goldrush town of Charters Towers.

He had to be rid of Fleur. She was too unpredictable, too clingy, to be hanging about Maryborough causing a nuisance.

Clive was taken aback when Mrs Mooney informed him that the ladies had departed. Had left town.

'Where did they go?' he asked, bewildered.

Misunderstanding his motives, Mrs Mooney was cool.

'I'm sure I don't know. Maybe they went off on a ship, Clive.'

'Not today.'

'Then perhaps they went by coach. One of the ladies suffered sea-sickness, as I recall.'

Mrs Mooney enjoyed watching what she thought was disappointment as Hillier made for the bar. How dare he two-time Emilie with that floozy! It wasn't a lie, she grinned. They went off by coach all right, but a private one. And that was Mr Devereaux's business.

But Clive was in the private bar reaching with a sigh of relief for a whisky. They'd gone! Thank God!

Several of the leading functionaries were also in the bar, reliving or recuperating from the previous night, and he joined them for a while before deciding he ought to go and see Emilie. It was still early, after all.

But the visit turned out to be a mistake. A waste of time. The whole weekend had been a waste of time from beginning to end. First Fleur and her demands and then Emilie with her fixation on Mal's troubles – or, maybe, on Mal. It was hard to know. Clive had had enough of the ladies for the time being.

He did not call for her on the Monday, even though Emilie, to give him time, fussed over the children and their dinner much later than usual. She was upset over so many things, she needed to talk to him, to try to sort out all her worries.

The cook wasn't fooled. 'Go on home, Emilie. Your Mr Hillier is probably busy tonight. You know the ships unload at all hours and he has to be there to see there's no trickery. And don't you be taking any notice of the stuff the missus has to say about him. She's plain jealous, she is. Wouldn't mind him for herself.'

Nellie, not known for her tact, looked surprised. 'But it is true.'

'What's true?' Emilie asked, cornering the girl so that she couldn't be intimidated by Kate's frowns.

'I told Kate earlier, when I came back from the messages. I met my sister in town, you know, the one who works as scullery maid for Mrs Mooney . . .'

'And what did she say?' Emilie asked quietly.

'Why don't you shut your mouth!' Kate snapped at Nellie, who reacted sullenly.

'Why shouldn't she know? I'd like to know if it was my boyfriend.'

Emilie was appalled at herself for listening to backstairs gossip, but not enough to overcome the awful need to hear more. She steeled herself.

'He was with her, that woman, all weekend. He even took her out in his gig yesterday, showing her off round the town. You ask anyone. And what's more, they say at the pub, she was living with him out on the goldfields before he came to town. Living in sin!'

'Damn pub talk!' Kate said angrily. 'You get the kids up. It's their bedtime.'

Nellie was defiant. 'It's true. That woman, Fleur is her name, she told Doris, the barmaid. Didn't care a jot.'

'Neither would Doris, I bet,' Kate snorted.

'No, she didn't,' Nellie said innocently. 'She thought it was a laugh. She said Fleur's a good sport.'

Emilie rushed to collect her coat and hat, leaving Kate and Nellie to argue the matter themselves. She felt like an eavesdropper who had earned due punishment for her transgressions. Before she left, Kate handed her the newspaper. 'You wanted me to keep this for you,' she said kindly. 'And here's some of my meatloaf for your tea. It's your favourite. Don't let that talk bother you.'

'I won't. And don't be cross with Nellie. It is important to know with whom one is dealing.'

She sounded so calm and self-assured again that Kate was pleased. 'That's the spirit. See you in the morning.'

A long editorial in the *Chronicle*, written by Walt White, took an interesting view on Mal's capture, maintaining the editor's previous assertions that, according to the letter-writer, McPherson, both men were innocent, and at the same time demanding justice for the families of the murdered men.

Emilie read the editorial thoroughly but found it confusing, more of a

248

tirade against the police than a real effort to arrive at a conclusion of any sort. She frowned. The essay didn't appear to have any point at all. It was simply a round-robin of opinions, as if he was trying to please everyone. Except the police.

She wished she had the courage to go to see that man, on Mal's behalf, and tell him what she knew, first hand. That Mal really was innocent. But she didn't dare. It occurred to her that this was something Clive could do.

Clive.

Emilie only felt a numbness. About him. About everything. She ate the meatloaf cold. Cut up a small, delicious pawpaw from one of the many pawpaw trees that grew so lopsidedly in the Manningtree garden, meaning to eat only a couple of slices, and ended up absently eating it all. She put the seeds aside for replanting, remembering that the gardener had pointed out the difference between the male and female trees so blatantly that she'd blushed, making a mental note not to bring it to the attention of the children.

But they were the most succulent, sweet fruits, and there for the taking. Along with bunches of bananas brought into the house by the hand, as they were called. A dozen or more on the one branch. A marvel for a girl from London.

If you had your life in order, she mused, this odd town wasn't such a bad place to live. Food was bounteous and cheap. There was no such thing as a real winter as she knew it, and summery clothes were also cheaper than heavier attire. She had learned to cope with her employers – he was kind, she could be ignored – and to see some sense in the confusion of nationalities that inhabited Maryborough, as well as the seemingly rough men who always treated her politely. Emilie also knew that it was time she invited Kate and Nellie to visit her home. An outlandish idea in her previous life, but imperative now in recognition of their kindness. They were her friends.

Ruth wouldn't understand, but then Ruth had her own life. It was sad that she had decided to settle in Brisbane. Somehow Emilie had hoped that they would come together one of these days, and obviously Ruth seemed to believe they would, since they would soon have the longed-for Tissington home, built on the second block in Brisbane.

Emilie sighed. She felt better. Firmer. She doubted it was all that pawpaw she'd consumed. But there was a stirring in her to be herself once more. To fight back against all this depression that had seemed so overwhelming lately. Her good sense told her that sitting about feeling sorry for herself had to stop. Weeping and wilting over Clive like a hothouse flower had to stop too. He loves me? He loves me not? That doesn't become you, Emilie. Where was it written that an attractive man like Clive did not have other lady friends, past or present? Hadn't she been secretive about Mal?

Right now, how she felt about Mal or Clive didn't seem to be of major importance. Clive had said that Mal would have his day in court. To prove his innocence, of course.

Emilie had little knowledge of courts, but she did know that a person had to engage a gentleman to solicit on his behalf. Who would Mal engage?

'Oh, dear God!' Emilie looked about the house that his money had bought for her, and out over the terraced garden to the dark swirl of the river. Those men cost money. The better they were, the more they cost.

Who would Mal engage? Did he have any money at all? What happened to people who could not afford to be represented by a solicitor, even with the meanest of credentials? Where was Clive? He would know.

Emilie took pen and paper and began to draw up a list of questions on the subject of a solicitor, and extended that to another list of submissions that could be made on Mal's behalf to prove his innocence, as she saw it. And a list of people who could attest to his good character. So far there were only three, including that dreadful uncle, but it was a start. At home with pen and paper, Emilie wrote all these thoughts and ideas for hours, determined to set them before Clive in the morning, despite his miserable behaviour, even if she was late for work, because it would be up to Clive to introduce her to a local solicitor. They would have him enquire if Mr Willoughby had engaged such a person, and if not . . . the response was obvious. Emilie Tissington would require his services.

She placed all the pages neatly in a folder, for future reference, turned down her bed and was brushing out her hair when, facing the mirror on the cumbersome dresser, the only other furniture in 'Paddy's' bedroom, another thought hit her.

'You are so dull!' she told the mirror. 'You've let your brain go to waste! Smarten up, girl. You don't need Clive. You need Ruth. And her fiancé. Hasn't she told you often enough, and so very proudly, that he is secretary to the Attorney-General? If they don't know a solicitor with the most excellent qualifications, who would? The answer has been there all the time and you have been too dull to see it.'

That night she dozed fretfully, too full of her plans to allow real sleep, but she still woke with a burst of energy, eager to set these plans in motion. Welcoming the day.

'What?' Mrs Manningtree exploded as Emilie put her case to them at the breakfast table.

'As I explained,' Emilie said calmly, standing by the table, 'it is usual for children to have a break from schoolwork. Holidays. They've hardly had a day off since I've been here.'

'What about last weekend? You didn't come in Saturday morning.'

'That is not a real break for them.'

'You mean you want a holiday? That's the real truth, isn't it?'

'As I explained, my sister has become engaged, and as she is my only relative in this country I should like to visit her and meet my future brother-in-law.'

Emilie knew it would make a good impression if she mentioned the name of Mr Bowles's employer, but she couldn't bring herself to do so, to bring herself down to the same level as the angry woman at the table.

'I am simply stating that it is usual for children to take summer and winter holidays.'

'All work and no play, you mean?' Mr Manningtree asked, chewing on a bacon rind.

'Yes, sir. And I thought this might be an opportune time.'

'Don't see why not. You got schooled, Violet. Didn't you have holidays?'

'Yes, but this is different.'

'How so?'

Emilie was dismissed while they discussed the matter, but later Mrs Manningtree came to the schoolroom to announce that she might take three weeks off, without pay.

'From the day I can find a ship sailing for Brisbane,' Emilie bargained.

'All right. I suppose so. Is Mr Hillier going with you?'

Emilie feigned bewilderment at that spiteful remark. 'Good heavens, no,' she smiled.

Chapter Eleven

When he found himself in a dark cell with a couple of old lags, Mal still wasn't talking. He was in too much of a daze. He'd never really faced the fact that he would be caught, let alone arrested, handcuffed, dumped in one cell after another and abused through towns by sneering crowds. He just hadn't believed it would happen. By this time they should have found the real outlaws.

But then his cellmates began to talk to him, dragging his story out of him to fill in the hours, and they came to like this Sonny Willoughby.

'If you're not going to stick up for yourself, mate, no one else will,' they warned. 'You better get off your backside and start yelling. Sulkin' won't do you no good.'

'Who'd listen?'

'Plenty of people. There's reporters out there breaking their necks to hear what you've got to say, and to get more pitchers of you . . .'

'What's the use? No one will believe me.'

'How do you know? You've gotta rattle the cage.'

The other man sucked on an empty pipe. 'He ain't about to do that. He's whipped. They got him beat.'

Mal hated to hear that. He lay on the bug-ridden bunk all night, smarting from the insult. Was he whipped?

'The hell I am,' he mumbled to himself, over and over. He doubted it would do any good, but he should try . . .

Smiling Sonny Willoughby became the darling of the newspapers. He talked to everyone who would listen, to reporters, to the police, and especially to the stern men from the Prosecutor's office, even though he knew they were building a case against him. Crowds came to the Brisbane jail daily, to catch a glimpse of him, some for, some against him, but all curious. Ladies sent him notes of encouragement, and one reporter, called Jesse from Chinchilla, seemed to be around almost every day, asking more and more questions.

Mal told them all he knew, so many times that he could almost recite the tale by rote, but he was insistent that he did not know McPherson, nor any of the Scot's mates.

On Jesse's advice, he asked to see Carnegie, to have the man accuse him to his face, but that request was not granted.

He saw his own picture in newspapers, read the reports, that seemed to have little bearing on what he had to say, and was shattered to discover letters to the paper demanding that he be hanged without further ado.

'I knew it wasn't any use,' he told Jesse. 'I'm not going to read those damn rags any more, and the warder said I don't have to talk to no one if I don't want to.' He'd had enough of being the circus freak.

'Then don't read them. And reporters are moving on to other stuff now.'

'I'm old news, am I?'

'Not to me, Sonny. Have you got any money?'

'What for? They're not charging me to stay here.'

'For a solicitor. Or better still, a barrister. You'll need one to represent you in court.'

'When will that be?'

'A while yet. They need to know more. The doubt is there that you didn't fire any shots . . .'

'How could I? I wasn't there.'

Jesse drew circles on the page and criss-crossed them with neat lines. He had talked with the Prosecutor, maintaining that there was every chance the kid was telling the truth. The prosecutor had replied:

'That's only your opinion. He's taken you in too, Jesse. He's a confidence trickster; he could sell the Brisbane River to a drowning man. And he's no kid. He's been knocking about, living on his wits for years.'

'But never been in any real trouble.'

'So he met up with bad company.'

'Like Carnegie?'

Jesse had meant that remark as an indictment of the man who had inveigled Sonny on to the scene, but to his surprise, the Prosecutor took it seriously.

'We're looking into that angle. Carnegie's not off the hook yet, but I don't want to see that in print.'

'Carnegie and Willoughby?' Jesse asked, amazed.

'Could be a plot gone wrong.'

'Well, where's the gold and the bank money?'

'Ask your mate Willoughby. We've got time to sit him out. A dose of St Helena Island prison might loosen his tongue. He won't get the kid-glove treatment up river.'

Now, still toying with his pencil, filling in the shapes, Jesse looked up at Mal.

'You're sure you haven't got any money?'

'Of course I'm sure. Ah, wait a minute! You think I'm suddenly going to produce some cash from the raid? Jesus! You're as stupid as all the rest.'

'No, I don't. But that haul has never been recovered, and because of the murders, there isn't a fence in the country who'd touch it with all that publicity.'

'Since when? Gold is gold. It hasn't got a brand on it. Grow up, Jesse.'

Jesse sighed. 'You were out on those goldfields. Can't you think who might have it?'

'No. I keep telling people that.'

'What about McPherson? Maybe he's got it.'

'So he goes to the trouble of writing to a newspaper? He'd be in China by this.'

'But if you don't know him, why does he claim you're innocent too?'

Mal's blue eyes didn't blink. 'Maybe he knows more than I do. He pointed the finger at Carnegie.'

Jesse gave up. But forewarned of Sonny's next destination, the dreaded St Helena Island prison, he decided to visit the island the very next day. A few shillings distributed among the warders for any information about Sonny Willoughby would be well spent. A stitch in time, he reminded himself.

One day at a time, Mal decided stoically as he clambered into the longboat and his leg-irons were replaced. He had heard enough from inmates of the Brisbane prison to know that the St Helena Island Penal Establishment was no holiday home, and the grim faces of the convicts shackled to the oars bore this out. He nodded to them but was soon shoved up to the bow, to sit alone, handcuffed, his back to the rest of the company.

'Try jumping overboard and you'll sink like a stone,' a warder warned, while another laughed.

'And ain't no one here goin' in after you.'

Mal ignored them. It was a fine spring day. He'd never been on this big river before so it would be interesting to explore for free, regardless of what awaited him at the other end.

Past the wharves there were some fine houses along the banks and even on the high cliffs of Kangaroo Point on the other side, then there were some cleared fields, and after that, as the river wound its way to sea, thick, rich bush. The clean, pungent fragrance was pleasure revisited after sour cells, and he felt invigorated, relaxed. Fish plopped, birds swooped and the expert oarsmen swept the boat along with the current. Hours later, they passed the mangrove-stained mouth of the river and headed out to sea.

Dreamily, Mal recalled his voyage to Fraser Island with its rainforest and tall pines, and his beautiful Orchid Bay, wondering if he'd ever see it again. When a speck of island appeared in the distance, he'd almost convinced himself that St Helena would be similar. As the boat veered into the wind, he set himself the task of working out how far it was from the mainland, figuring it was about four miles. Not that hard a swim for a fit man on a calm day. Except for the sharks. Hard to believe that shark story. He'd searched the waters all the way, and hadn't sighted one. Not being familiar with the dreaded monsters, he figured they must keep to the deep. Nevertheless, he would have been interested to see one.

This island, though, was not Fraser. It was small and flat, and as they neared shore, high brick walls loomed up ahead of them. A real prison it was, he realised, disappointed, true to its notoriety as being high-security, an isolated colony for the worst of the state's criminals. It was still difficult to comprehend that he was numbered among them.

The longboat pulled into shore and Mal looked longingly at the crystal-clear shallows, wishing he could plunge in and rid himself of the prison smell that assailed him permanently these days, but after some confusion caused by all the shackles, the prisoners were landed on the spiky grass verge.

After the boat was hauled up on to a slipway, the prisoners were herded up a road towards the prison, pushed and shoved along with the help of heavy truncheons. Mal, being the only one in leg-irons, kept stumbling, holding up their progress, and that seemed to enrage the warders, who cursed and kicked him to his feet.

'What's the bloody hurry?' he muttered to one of the other prisoners.

'They'll miss their dinner,' the man whispered. 'We've already missed ours.'

They passed through the gates into the gloom of the prison, and Mal shuddered. He stumbled again, as yet unable to control this shambling pace, and the others hurried on ahead, leaving him with a lone warder, who struck his back with his truncheon time and again as they crossed the stockade.

Inside the long cell block, prisoners stood at the barred windows, idly watching their progress, until one man yelled:

'Do you see who that is? It's the outlaw, Willoughby, what got all that gold in the raid up north.'

Baldy Perry sneered knowingly. They were all fools. He ambled over to take a look at the mug, Willoughby, then shook his head.

'That ain't Willoughby. His name's Ned Turner.'

'Ah, go on! That's Willoughby all right.'

'It ain't Willoughby, I tell you. I know that bloke, and his name's Turner. I met him with McPherson. They had a blue over a horse.'

The others jeered at him. 'Not that again, Baldy. You're always goin' on about knowin' McPherson. Looks like you can't tell one bloody face from another.'

'My bloody oath I can. That bloke's name is Turner, and you just wait. He'll be able to tell you I *am* a mate of McPherson's. Then you won't be so bloody smart.'

Maybe it was just an excuse, Emilie admitted, but because she hadn't seen him for days, not since their argument last Sunday, she felt it was only polite to inform Clive that she was planning a visit to Brisbane, so, nerves fluttering, she called at his place of business.

Clive was surprised to see her but obviously not displeased, and that gave her confidence.

'My dear! What a pleasure! Do come in.' He escorted her into the wide bond store past a short counter, beyond which clipboards bearing bills of lading hung in rows on the timber walls. The floor was also dark timber and her new shoes squeaked as they crossed the wide office, bordered by massive kegs sporting yellow seals.

'You're looking well, Emilie,' he was saying, ushering her into his office at the rear of the building. 'Come on in, this is my lair.'

His office was very plain, just a table and chair surrounded by benches overloaded, untidily, with official books, journals and more papers, but the view from the window caught her eye, and instinctively she walked towards it.

'What a magnificent view!'

'Yes, it's splendid. We're so high here, and so placed at the bend of the river, that we can look across it in both directions. The old Mary River looks her best from here, wouldn't you say?'

'I would indeed.' Eventually, she turned back to him. 'Clive, I just came to tell you I'm sorry we had that silly argument . . .'

'My dear, don't be. I had forgotten all about it. I haven't been able to call for you these last couple of days because I've been so busy. Ships that were held up by the storm have finally made it to port and kept me on the hop.'

She wished he hadn't mentioned being busy. Though she had promised herself that she would ignore the gossip, her irritation tumbled out.

'Yes, I heard how *busy* you have been.'

'What do you mean?'

'I hear you've been very busy socially too.'

'Oh, that,' he said impatiently. 'I suppose you've been talking to Mrs Mooney.'

'No,' Emilie said primly.

'You've been talking to someone, so you'd better let me explain.'

'I'm really not interested, Clive.'

'Then why did you mention the subject? The fact is that an old friend came to town.'

She turned to stare out of the window. 'I heard it was a young friend.'

'Do we need semantics? She was an old friend, in town for a few days with a lady friend who was ill. I hardly thought I would need your approval to spend time with her, but if you are offended, I apologise.'

Emilie was sorry she had started this conversation. Clive was always far cleverer with words than she was. He confused her.

'You don't have to apologise.'

'But I will anyway. I'm sorry if seeing an old friend upset you. I was going to tell you all about it on Sunday night, but we seemed to get off on the wrong foot altogether.' He closed the door and put his arms about her waist. 'Tell me you forgive me, dearest. I wouldn't hurt you for the world.'

He nuzzled into her neck, drawing her close, hugging her to him, and Emilie could not resist, all her arguments and resolves lost as he moved her gently about and kissed her with such longing that she felt weak in his arms.

They heard voices outside and Emilie pulled away quickly, afraid they might come in, but Clive laughed.

'It's only the delivery men.'

256

Emilie was already primping her hair into place under her hat, and blushing. 'No, I really must go. I only came to tell you that I am taking leave and going to Brisbane for a little while.'

'Why?'

She found herself blushing again. 'My sister has become engaged; she wants me to come down and meet my future brother-in-law.'

'That's very nice. Do offer my congratulations. I wish I could come with you, but I can only take leave when the powers that be give the word.'

'I wish you could come too,' she said softly, and she meant it. What heaven it would be to have him with her in Brisbane, even though she had a private matter to attend to. She would love to be able to introduce him to Ruth, and maybe, being together like that, away from here, a better relationship would evolve. Who knew what might eventuate with them in the romantic company of the engaged couple?

But it was settled, with Clive's blessing and his assistance. He made all the arrangements for her, finding her a single cabin on a coastal steamer, organising her luggage and even introducing her to the captain.

He was there at the wharf to see her off, kissing her fondly in front of everyone.

Emilie did not mention her other mission, for fear of upsetting him, nor was Mal remembered in all the excitement of her departure. But she did remember to go to the bank and draw out all of her money. Mal's money.

Clive didn't like to recall the way he'd treated Emilie. Bullied her. He'd lied to her about being busy over the weekend, and she knew it. He'd lied to her about his relationship with Fleur, and he was damn sure she knew that too. He wished she'd shouted at him, accused him of being untrustworthy, punished him and, by doing so, absolved him somewhat of his guilt. But Emilie was too timid, too logical, for histrionics, and he'd taken advantage. Clive was sorry about that now; he'd have to make it up to her.

He wondered if this sudden trip to Brisbane had anything to do with it. Was she deliberately distancing herself from him? He hoped not. Had she given him more time, he could have arranged to go with her – to meet the sister and her fiancé. After all, he worried, what was the rush?

He was sorry about Fleur, too. Sorry he'd made such a fool of himself over her. But it had been a surprise to see her again, and, he had to admit, a pleasure. She was a trollop, but very sexy, and his sex life of late was non-existent.

Still is, he shrugged. Fleur had treated him as badly as he'd treated Emilie. In all, a wretch of a weekend.

Mal met trouble in the chilly ablutions shed, not from the warders but from another prisoner, Baldy Perry, who felled him with a punch in his back.

Baldy was fighting mad at being proven wrong, his status in the community sorely dented.

'What's your name?'

Mal slithered about, trying to climb to his feet from the slimy green concrete.

'Willoughby, you bloody fool,' he shouted. 'Who the hell are you?'

'I'm a mate of McPherson's,' Baldy snorted, 'and I know you ain't Willoughby. You're Turner.'

While Mal conceded that no one in his right mind would want to be Willoughby these days, he had to defend himself from this madman, and Baldy was shocked by the result. He was in a weakened state from overwork, ill-treatment and malnutrition, but he had been in the company of men similarly weakened. This prisoner was not only younger, he was new to the island, and fit. He came up from the floor with fists like iron, battering Baldy into a corner until warders with their whips and truncheons took control.

Both men met again at the triangle the next morning for their punishment of sixty lashes each.

As Baldy was brought forward, Mal, shocked by the severity of the sentence, spoke to him.

'I'm sorry. I didn't know this would happen.'

Baldy ignored him. He shrieked when the first lash hit his bare back, a back that was already scarred, but was silent from then on, as the blood seeped down on to the stand.

In his turn, Mal was brought forward and fastened to the triangle, but he wasn't quiet. As the lash tore at him and the count went on, he screamed abuse at his tormentors, at the injustices that had befallen him, at his Uncle Silver, at the newspapers that made him out to be a murderer, at everyone he could think of who had betrayed him. His screams were a form of deliverance from the pain, from such agony that he had never believed could be inflicted on a human, while uniformed men with cold faces stared and talked and smoked with bored indifference. And they were a release, a deliberate release of the fear that had been building up inside him, ever since the day that Pollock had placed him under arrest.

As prisoners were ordered to untie him and lift him down, just as they had done for Baldy, so that his wounds could be doused in stinging salt, he listened to the warnings of a pompous superintendent about good behaviour, and then he spat at him.

Willoughby spent the next two weeks in a solitary cell, constructed inside another cell so as to allow some air but no light. Bread and water were pushed through a ground-level slot once a day, at about six o'clock in the morning, he reasoned. They might be able to shut out light, but they couldn't shut out sound.

There were no human voices to be heard, so he figured he must be well away from the living and working areas, having earlier seen hundreds of prisoners lining up for various duties. Most of them shackled with leg-irons.

At first he lay on his stomach on the cold stone to allow his back to heal, with nothing else to do but think and listen, preferring the latter. He realised that though this place must be hell on earth for prisoners, it was a haven for birds, and Mal knew them all. Kookaburras were pre-dawn. The tiny birds came next, with their loud twitterings. Seagulls were always about, shrieking, foraging. Magpies sang in the mornings, their clear notes penetrating, a joy. And so it went on. He heard the squawks of crows, the song of butcher birds and all the rest, the quiet of the afternoons and the regular traffic of the evenings as they prepared to rest, and so did he. Mal relied on the birds to regulate his day. When they were busy, he thrust himself up in the darkness and exercised. He practised copying their songs and whistles. He nibbled on the stale bread and took the water sparingly, and when he was released, he stumbled out, as cunning as a bird protecting her nest by feigning a broken wing, because he was not broken. He knew that if he were to survive this place he'd need his wits, and this was no time to be showing off. He seemed almost pitiful when they threw him from the blinding light into a normal cell.

The shillings were well spent, but the information was disappointing. A warder scrawled a letter to Jesse describing Willoughby's progress at the prison.

> Within a day, the prisoner was in trouble. He got into a fight with another prisoner by name of Baldy Perry and subsequently, both were flogged. The newcomer screamed like a pig but was then defiant, insulting the Superintendent, receiving solitary confinement. Upon his release he was found to be weak in the legs, falling down at assembly on several occasions, so was given light work in the dairy.

Jesse guessed that the writer was probably a retired police officer, given the form of this report.

> I myself made further enquiries as to the reason for that fight, which turned out to be nothing more than a stupid argument about who knew McPherson best. Prisoners are always claiming to know that outlaw. According to Perry, your man also travelled under the name of Ned Turner. I hope this information proves valuable.

Valuable? Jesse mused. Yes, I'll pay you, but what's this? Who knew McPherson best? Did Sonny know the outlaw after all? Had he lied? Damn him!. Jesse's disappointment almost caused him to pack up and go home. Had Willoughby made a fool of him? And what about that alias? Ned Turner. He shook his head, wondering why he'd allowed himself to be taken in by this rogue, who could easily be a confidence man, as the Prosecutor had said.

While he worried about his next move, news came that James McPherson had been up to his tricks again, robbing a mail coach and then a station owner. Witnesses were certain it was McPherson. Jesse rushed to police headquarters to find out where these crimes had taken place.

Prison gossip had muddled the cause of the fight, but whatever the conclusions, Mal knew he had to shut Perry up.

As soon as he could, he went in search of Baldy Perry, to slip him some cheese he'd stolen from the creamery. He remembered Perry now as the hulking lout who'd been with McPherson in that bar, but somehow he had to turn him round. He couldn't afford to have anyone placing him with McPherson.

Baldy wasn't one to exhibit a grudge when food was offered, though it lingered. He demolished the cheese in a second.

'I still say youse are Ned Turner,' he growled.

Mal grinned. 'Everyone needs another name sometime. But tell me, how did you get on to it?'

'I knew you was, all along,' Baldy crowed. 'Don't you remember the time in Brisbane you was arguing with my mate McPherson about a horse?'

'With *McPherson*?'

'Yeah. And he made you hand over his watch.'

'Jesus! That's right. You were there. But that other bloke, the one who took my watch and nearly got my horse. Don't tell me that was McPherson?'

'Surely was, mate.'

'God Almighty! I wouldn't have been so smart if I'd known it was McPherson. Don't tell me!'

Baldy was pleased: he'd got the name right and, better still, proved without a doubt that he was a mate of McPherson's while this fool didn't even know the great man when he met him. It would make a good story round here. Not that it mattered; he'd be out soon.

The kid was impressed. 'Did you do many jobs with him?'

'Plenty,' he boasted. 'Listen, I could tell you a thing or two. Me and Jim, we were great mates. We made a pile. I'll be a rich man when I get out of here.'

Mal almost laughed out loud, but he'd solved the problem and wanted to keep it that way, so he let the goat talk. He already knew that Baldy was said to be a terrible liar, so no one ever listened to him, but the new chum did; he was determined to stay friends with Baldy now.

'One of these days you'll have to introduce me,' he said, but Baldy laughed.

'Like when? You two are both headed for the rope.'

'Not me. I wasn't even there when it happened, and McPherson says he wasn't anywhere near Maryborough. So the papers say.'

He had pulled himself up sharply there. McPherson had told him that himself; he wasn't sure that any such thing had been written. But Baldy, enjoying the flattery, didn't notice.

'Forget the papers. Jim was there.' He gazed craftily about. 'I saw him meself.'

'Where?'

260

'In Maryborough, doncha listen?'

'I never saw him there.'

'Well, you wouldn't, 'cos you don't know him like I do,' Baldy chortled. 'Listen, you get any more of that cheese, give it to me and I'll look after you. There's some nasty blokes here that'd take a shine to a pretty boy like you, if you get what I mean.'

The hackles stood up on the back of Mal's neck as Baldy stamped across the yard. He was still trying to figure out what he'd heard when the bells clanged, their half-hour of recreation time over.

He filed through to the mess hall with the others, waiting patiently with his tin dish to be served the usual slop, took a hunk of mouldy bread and stood in the crowd shovelling the food into his mouth using his fingers and the bread. Then he lined up again to wash the slimy dish under a tap. The food didn't bother him, but that conversation did.

Baldy was a liar and stupid. What he had said might have made sense to him, but not to Mal. He welcomed the darkness as he lay on his bunk to think this through, hardly aware of the curses and mutterings around him.

Baldy couldn't have seen McPherson in Maryborough because he was not there. So that was just a lie.

But it was strange that he'd accepted Mal's claim that he hadn't been at Blackwater Creek without a blink, without even ridiculing him, though he had been arrested for the crime.

Then he'd said that Mal wouldn't have recognised McPherson in the town. And yet he was supposed to be McPherson's partner; Baldy had even said the both of them would swing.

It was almost as if Baldy knew that Mal hadn't been at the holdup. And if so, how did he know?

Baldy had been in Maryborough at the time.

Baldy had said he would be a rich man when he got out. If that wasn't another lie, the part about the earnings in company with McPherson was. Mal had seen for himself that McPherson wasn't cashed up.

He couldn't sleep, it was impossible to drop off with all the discrepancies in that conversation rattling about in his head. Baldy had accepted that McPherson was unknown to Mal when they met in Brisbane. Why then, if he knew they were supposed to have been partners in the holdup, did he believe Mal when he continued to protest his ignorance about McPherson's identity?

During the next few days, Mal made it his business to learn all he could about Baldy Perry's past. Since he was so thoroughly disliked, it wasn't hard. He'd done time before, for robbery under arms . . . and was in prison this time for bashing a man in Maryborough.

'Almost crippled him,' it was said.

'Do you think he could kill a man?' he asked an old fellow.

'That blockhead would do anything if he thought he could get away with it. Why? You scared of him, son?'

'No,' Mal said firmly.

261

'Oh yes. You're the one gave him a belting.'

One man, though, had a grudging respect for Baldy. 'I knew him in the old days, out west. He was always a bastard, but he was a good shot. Handy bloke to have on a hunt.'

Mal was aware that he could be digging for false gold, that desperation was leading him to search for a lead that did not exist, confusing Baldy's lies and boasts to suit his fancy. Misconstruing them.

But the suspicions had lodged in his mind and he could not wish them away. Because of this, he avoided Baldy, afraid of alerting him, until such time as he could think of something to ask him that would definitely tie Baldy in with the murders. But what to ask? He racked his brains, searching for a way to trip Baldy, but nothing came, and he began to wonder who really was the stupid one – him or Perry.

Time was running out; Baldy had only a month to go before release. Mal asked permission to send a telegram to someone, and the warders laughed.

'Get out with you, you mongrel. Who do you think you are? Lord Muck?'

His insistent demands led to several beatings, but he would not give up until the Superintendent, Captain Croft heard of it and sent for him, out of curiosity.

'What's this nonsense about? Prisoners do not have the privilege of telegrams.'

'But this is urgent, sir. I would be most grateful.'

'You don't say? Who has died?'

'No one, your honour. I only need to write one line.'

'I should think so. They cost money. And what is this all-important line? Can you write?'

'Yes, sir.'

'Then write it for me.' He pushed a page and pencil across his desk.

Mal wrote quickly: 'I have something to tell you. Urgent.'

'I see. And who does this go to? Your lady friend?'

'No, sir.' Mal wrote the name and address on the page, and Croft stared.

'If it's that important, why can't you tell me?'

'Begging your pardon, sir, I can't.'

'Are you being insolent? I have means of correcting that sort of behaviour.'

'No, sir. Definitely not, sir, I've learned my lesson.'

'In which case, you can take on hard labour now. You are dismissed. Inform your warder. I'll think about this.'

He stared at the telegram. The cheek of the fellow. But he'd been following this case with interest and he knew the police were having a difficult time putting it together. This sounded as if Willoughby was about to confess. It might not be worth his career to put obstacles in their way. And he had nothing to lose if what the prisoner had to say proved to be hogwash. Better to pass the buck. He would charge the recipient for the cost.

★ ★ ★

Constable Lacey showed him the telegram and was kind enough not to say 'I told you so'. Pollock slumped over the pile of paperwork on his desk. He had been relegated to the job of sorting out back files since they'd returned from their aborted search for the outlaws.

'Looks like the reward did its job again,' Lacey said. 'Someone gave McPherson up in Bowen.'

'So I see. I wonder how it came about.'

'I guess we'll hear in time, but now they've got both of them, something should break. Or someone. Willoughby is sticking with his story, but McPherson is sharper. Now that he's in custody he mightn't be so arrogant. Where do you suppose they'll take him?'

'They'd better be on their toes; he's escaped from custody once before. With luck they'll bring him here. We've got judges here now, and the new courthouse. The trial should be held here. And so should Willoughby's for that matter, but politics will have a hand in it, you bet.'

He found an excuse to escape the police station and his dreary role, calling in on his wife for a cup of tea.

'I feel a bloody fool,' he told her. 'I took the wrong road after Willoughby. I had the tipoff about McPherson headed for Bowen. I should have kept going.'

'But you warned the officers at Bowen he could be in the area.'

'No. Lacey did. He'll get a promotion for that while I sit and search through unpaid fines. I'm beginning to think I ought to give the game away. Do something else. Buy a farm, or get another job somewhere else.'

She brought him some buttered scones. 'No you shouldn't. You're a fine policeman, and you like your job.'

'I used to,' he said dully. 'But I think I'm in a dead end now, my love.'

He ate the scones. Drank his tea. Stared out of the window at their neighbour, a fisherman, who was mending nets slung over their clothes line. He thought of that boat, the good rowboat that had been dragged from the river and was now dumped in the police paddock, causing more irritation than interest. Nothing to be done about that. Another false lead . . .

Lacey was waiting for him back at the station.

'There's a telegram here . . .'

'I've seen it. They got McPherson.'

'No. This one's for you. It's from Willoughby. He wants to confess.'

Pollock grabbed the page. 'The hell he does! What's he up to now?'

'That's for you to find out. He says: "I have something to tell you. Urgent." '

When Pollock requested permission to respond to this telegram by leaving for Brisbane at the earliest opportunity, his senior officer flatly refused to allow him to go.

'Brisbane has any amount of efficient police officers. They can handle it. I shall advise them that Willoughby is ready to talk.'

'He could have done that himself, sir. But he has asked for me. I know him. I know the case. I believe it is important that I interview him.'

'Sergeant Pollock, you may know the case, but you've made no progress. Don't you understand that? And dare I remind you that you were the one who allowed that rogue to escape? Your request is denied.'

For Pollock, that was the last straw. He didn't care any more. As it was often said, this was Sydney or the bush. Win or lose on the turn of a card.

'In which case, sir, be advised that I will go over your head. I intend to wire Mr Kemp that I need to come to Brisbane on urgent business, giving him the reason.'

'You do that and you're fired!'

'It is not your place to dismiss me, sir. Mr Kemp might have something to say about it. He was here in Maryborough and he understood the case, if I may say so, far better than you do.'

'How dare you speak to me like that! You'll be a constable before the day is out.'

Pollock pushed a form across the desk. 'This is a temporary release from duty here; please sign it. I'll send in the application for expenses shortly. If you don't sign I'll wire Kemp. Either way I'm going and you can stick this station . . .'

His senior officer refused to sign. Pollock wired Kemp but did not wait for the response, which simply referred him back to the judgement of his senior.

But by then Pollock was already home and packing.

The joy of the renewed and, Emilie felt, stronger friendship with Clive didn't alter her determination to extend a helping hand to Mal. It is my duty, she told herself, with the fervour of a missionary, as she stood at the rails of the steamer waving goodbye to everyone.

She'd been surprised, and touched, that anyone would bother to come down to farewell her, especially when she was only leaving for a few weeks, but there they all were . . . Clive, Mrs Mooney and the Manning tree entourage. Mr Manningtree had packed everyone into his wagon and brought them to the wharf for the occasion: the children, madly excited, and even Kate and Nellie, though there was no sign of his wife. Emilie's neighbours, Mr and Mrs Dressler, came too, promising to keep an eye on her house for her, and Mrs Dressler gave her a lace handkerchief wrapped in tissue, with a pink ribbon. She found the unexpected kindnesses a little overwhelming, and reminded herself that she must bring some gifts back from Brisbane in return. It was almost as if they were family now; they'd shown her she wasn't alone any more.

When the steamer pulled out into the Mary River and rounded the bend, heading downstream, she went below for a cup of tea in the salon and then returned to the deck for a while to watch the ship's progress. She was more aware of her surroundings now, and she recalled her first voyage up this river, when she'd been so nervous, having only a vague idea of where she was going.

That afternoon, as the steamer left the mouth of the river and made out into the blue waters of Hervey Bay, Emilie's mood had changed, for ahead of her was Fraser Island, where Mal had taken shelter. As she stared at the coloured sands of the cliffs along the shoreline she could no longer think of her venture as duty, because she was reminded of his reckless grin and his bold blue eyes, and how much he cared for her. The worry for him began all over again.

Days later, the steamer rounded the point of yet another large island, which guarded the entrance to Moreton Bay at the mouth of the Brisbane River. This was more familiar. She felt like a seasoned traveller. The ship from London had brought the two unhappy girls across this bay, and she'd traversed it *en route* to Maryborough on that sad boat with the emigrant women. Now she knew exactly where she was going and was excited, looking forward to seeing Ruth at long last.

The bay had been choppy, causing a fair amount of sea-sickness, so there were few people on deck.

A gentleman whom she'd met on the ship joined Emilie.

'Not bothered by the swell, miss?'

She smiled. 'Not really. I find it wiser to stay up here in the fresh air.'

'It has been a very pleasant voyage, thank the Lord.'

'Yes, indeed.'

He pointed out an island they were passing. 'That's the prison.'

Emilie looked up, surprised. 'I thought it was a leprosarium.'

'That it was, years ago, but it's a top-security prison now. It's where they put all the bad lads. That outlaw Willoughby is in there, they say. The one who carried out that murderous raid back home . . .'

He continued to talk, as travellers do, expounding information: 'That little group of islands was known as the Green Isles back in the old days. The penal settlement was at Dunwich. They had an Aborigine prisoner there called Napoleon, because he looked like Boney, but he was a real terror, caused so much trouble, they exiled him to that island. That's how it got its name. St Helena . . . see. But he was smarter than Boney. He built a canoe and escaped. I don't know if they ever caught him again . . .'

But Emilie hardly heard him. She was staring at the forbidding brick walls, so incongruous on such a small island, in a state of shock. Mal was in there? Locked up with the most vicious of criminals. It was too terrible to contemplate. Too unfair. She had to turn away, tears in her eyes.

Ruth was waiting for her as the steamer docked, dear Ruth.

Emilie ran down the gangplank and threw herself into her sister's arms. 'Oh my dear. It's so wonderful to see you. It seems like years . . .'

Ruth stiffened, stepping away. 'Really, Emilie. Such emotion, in public! Control yourself. I am pleased to see you, of course, but we're not children.' She straightened Emilie's hat and did up the top button on her coat. 'Now, that's better. Your face is quite tanned. I warned you to keep out of the sun. Don't you wear a hat?'

265

Chastened, Emilie tried to explain. 'I do, but I walk a lot, and I suppose the wind . . .'

'Never mind. We'll find your luggage. I hope you didn't bring too much.'

'No, I only have this valise.'

'Good. You'll be sharing my room, I've had a bunk put in there, so we'll be rather crushed.'

'I've got some savings. I can pay for my own room.' Emilie would have preferred not to share, there was so much to think about.

Ruth was offended. 'Oh, I see. Now that you have a rental house, I suppose sharing a room with your sister is not good enough for you.'

'Good heavens, no. I'm very happy to share with you. I just didn't want to inconvenience you.'

'It's not a question of convenience, it's a question of money. I dislike wasting money. Since you have savings, though, you may pay half of my weekly rent.'

'Very well.' Emilie nodded meekly. Ruth seemed taller and thinner, and far more shrill than she remembered.

'Come along then. We have to walk quickly. I want you to meet Mr Bowles before lunch. It is fortunate that you arrived on a Saturday or you'd have had to make your own way to the Belleview.'

After all that time in a country town, Brisbane felt like a city to Emilie; people were so smartly dressed, and the shops were such a wonder, it was an effort not to stop and stare.

'I'm so looking forward to meeting Mr Bowles,' she told Ruth, as she stepped out firmly to keep up with her. 'It's very exciting.' She looked at Ruth's gloved hand.

'You didn't show me your ring.'

Ruth turned on her. 'Don't you dare mention a ring and embarrass Mr Bowles. It's such a juvenile attitude! I don't require trinkets.'

'No. I suppose not. No.'

He was standing on the veranda in a shiny black suit lightened by a starched wing collar and thin cravat. His hair was pomaded into a flat part over a long, sallow face and a large mole on the side of a beaky nose. He greeted Ruth cordially and nodded to Emilie as they were introduced.

'I'm very pleased to make your acquaintance, Miss Tissington.' He checked a fob watch and replaced it in his waistcoat pocket. 'We're already late for lunch, Ruth.'

'Yes, I'm sorry. Let's go in.'

He didn't offer to carry Emilie's valise, so she picked it up and followed them inside, where they were greeted by Mrs Medlow, who waylaid Emilie.

'How nice to see you again, my dear.'

'It is nice to be back.' Emilie smiled. 'You're looking well, Mrs Medlow.'

'Ah, yes, dear. Keeping busy. Do you enjoy living up north?'

266

'It's very pleasant. Very countrified after Brisbane, and different, I have to say, but one manages.'

'That's good to hear . . .'

Emilie saw her sister frowning at her from the door of the dining room. 'I'd better go. Could you put my valise in your office for me? I'll collect it later.'

'Don't bother. I'll have a maid take it to your room.'

'Thank you. That's very kind of you.'

Ruth was cross. 'Did you have to stand talking to *her*? Mr Bowles has gone on in.'

Emilie reddened, not for the rebuke, but because she recalled their attitude when they'd first arrived. She and Ruth had not deigned to associate with anyone here; in fact, they'd been quite rude to people. Since then she had learned that people of whatever class were just people, and kind words brought their own reward. Loneliness had forced her to be less critical, but even she hadn't realised how much she'd changed. Until now. Obviously Ruth hadn't faced a challenge like that, for she was still as reserved as ever. Emilie decided she'd better watch her step; after all, Ruth had her ways, and it would be a shame to upset her.

Over lunch Mr Bowles was content to allow Ruth to sing his praises, remarking on his important work in the Parliament, and he offered to take Emilie on a tour of 'the House', which she accepted, delighted. In his turn he spoke of Ruth's sterling efforts, teaching giddy girls at that college. Their mutual admiration pleased Emilie, but somehow she could not take to Mr Bowles. He was so serious, so self-important, with no humour in him. In fact, she thought dismally, he and Ruth were very much alike.

Emilie brought up the subject of their land, still thrilled by the windfall. 'We're so lucky. I'm dying to see it.'

'We'll go next weekend,' Ruth told her.

'Why not tomorrow?'

'Tomorrow isn't convenient for Mr Bowles.'

'But it's Sunday.'

He smirked. 'My Minister seems to need my presence no matter what day of the week. Sometimes I wonder how he'd cope without me.'

'So do I,' Ruth said. 'You'll just have to be patient, Emilie. Anyway, my block will be sold within a few days now.'

'Oh! So soon? How much are you asking for it?'

'We can leave that to Mr Bowles,' Ruth told her. 'He understands the marketing process.'

Emilie turned to him. 'I'm sure you do. But how much can Ruth expect? Roughly.'

'My dear Emilie, roughly does not come into it,' he said stiffly. 'I shall require the going price.'

'Which is?'

Ruth intervened. 'We are not aware of that as yet. But please don't imagine that Mr Bowles will stoop to bargaining. I shall be grateful for whatever we receive.'

After he had left, Emilie and Ruth sat in the bedroom, talking about old times, and Emilie felt much better. Her sister was far more relaxed, and there was so much to discuss.

'I wrote to Father,' Ruth told her, 'to let him know where we were and how we were placed, but he didn't respond.'

'He probably didn't see your letter. *She* could have burned it. Did you tell him you are engaged to marry?'

'Yes. I wrote that in a second letter. I felt he was entitled to know.'

'And still no reply?'

'There hasn't been time yet.'

Emilie shrugged. 'Don't bet on it.'

'Really, Emilie, what an expression! We shall just wait and see. I quite miss England,' she added wistfully. 'I can't wait to go back.'

Emilie was surprised. 'Mr Bowles might have something to say about that.'

'He already has. As soon as we can afford it, we intend to visit, and eventually we'll go home for good.'

'But it isn't his home.'

'He would like it to be. He has always longed to reside in the old country. But what about your Mr Hillier? He's English. How fortunate. You may even make it home before me.'

'I don't know about that. He's never mentioned going home.'

'Then you should encourage him. This country is so crude.'

Emilie laughed. 'Good Lord. If you think Brisbane is crude, you should come north. Maryborough is another world. It's pioneer country, but that makes it hugely interesting. I wish you could come back with me, even for a week or so.'

Ruth shuddered. 'I can't spare the time, and I'd be so much happier if you could return here. I worry about you.'

'No need to, you old darling. I manage.'

They talked for a long time and then decided to take a walk in the Botanic Gardens, since it was such a lovely day, neither hot nor cold. Just perfect, they agreed. Emilie made Ruth laugh, showing off her knowledge of exotic native plants, and Ruth unbent enough to amuse her sister with stories about her headmistress, who was quite eccentric, given to addressing the assemblies in French, where no one could understand her.

'Except you,' Emilie giggled. 'How is her French?'

'Frightful,' Ruth bubbled, 'but I don't turn a hair. I stand there nodding and smiling as if I'm impressed, because I heard a rumour she's thinking of making me deputy head.'

'Marvellous,' Emilie said. 'But you always could maintain dignity. I'd ruin it; I wouldn't be able to keep a straight face.'

They were so happy together, so involved in each other, with so much to talk about, they even walked arm in arm at times. When they eventually took a rest on a park bench, so that Ruth could tighten the laces on her shoes, Emilie knew it was the right time to mention Mal, to ask for her sister's advice. There was no question of Ruth's integrity. She was a stalwart when it came to what was right.

'Stay a minute,' she began. 'I want to tell you about a friend of mine who is suffering the most dreadful injustice.'

'What friend?'

'His name is Mal Willoughby.'

'You've never mentioned him before. What sort of injustice?'

'With the law.'

'Then he should engage a legal gentleman to solicit for him, and not some pettifogger.'

'I'm so glad you agree. I'll tell you what happened . . .'

Ruth was gracious enough not to interrupt, but as Emilie outlined the sorry tale she saw her sister's face turn white, and then cement into a stony frown. She couldn't stop, though; she had to explain this fully so that Ruth could understand.

'And where is he now?' Ruth asked, at length.

'In St Helena prison, an island at the mouth of the river. We saw it when . . .'

Ruth jumped to her feet. 'Stop. Stop this instant. I don't want to hear another word. I knew I shouldn't have allowed you to go off on your own. This is the most appalling story I have ever heard in all my life. Murders. Outlaws. Are you mad? Is this the sort of company you keep? You are not going back to that place. I will send for your effects first thing tomorrow.'

Emilie was hurt. 'Ruth. Please. Sit down and listen. I probably haven't explained this . . .'

'You've explained quite enough. And what about Mr Hillier? What does he say about this?'

'He believes Mal is innocent too. He was his partner on the goldfields.'

'Mr Hillier was a labourer on the goldfields?'

'All sorts of people dig for gold.'

'No one that I have ever been acquainted with. It's time we went back and you pulled yourself together. You have totally lost your wits. I don't want to hear another word about this. I can't imagine why you'd think I would want to hear such horror.'

Emilie refused to move. She looked up at her sister. Pleading. 'Mr Bowles has contacts in the legal world. You said yourself my friend should not hire a pettifogger. He could advise whom Mr Willoughby should employ.'

Ruth clapped her hands over her ears. 'Not another word. Do you hear me? Not another word. You may not mention this to Mr Bowles at any time, or under any circumstances. Your behaviour is disgusting.'

She gathered her shawl about her, as if the afternoon had suddenly become chill, and stalked away. Miserably, sadly, Emilie rose to follow her, wondering if she really had gone a bit mad getting involved with Mal . . . knowing, even as she'd recounted the tale, that a young lady of their class should not even discuss such matters, let alone admit association.

269

When she did catch up with Ruth, she was treated to a furious lecture – her behaviour was not only disappointing but embarrassing. Did she have no self-respect? Obviously not. And it was clear to see that it had been a dreadful mistake to allow her to go to that outlandish place on her own, since she had no idea how to comport herself without guidance. Ruth nagged and nagged all the way back to the Belleview and Emilie had no doubt it would not have ended there had Mr Bowles not been waiting for them on the front veranda.

As soon as the two ladies joined him, seating themselves elegantly in adjacent cane armchairs, Ruth announced that Emilie would not be returning to 'that place'.

He didn't seem too enthusiastic. 'I thought you were well placed in Maryborough?' he asked Emilie.

'It's really not suitable,' Ruth answered for her. 'I shall look about for a better position for her. In this town. I really think, from my own experience, that it is rather demeaning for either of us to have to cope with country bumpkins. They're just not the sort of people we are accustomed to associating with.'

'With whom,' Emilie corrected crankily, but Ruth ignored her.

Emilie sat, simmering with anger as they talked about this and that, until their conversation came round to the blocks of land at Eagle Farm.

'I shall draw up plans for our house next week,' Bowles said. 'I have already spoken to the tradesmen who built the extensions to the Minister's house, and they are willing to give me a fair price.'

'That's wonderful,' Ruth said. 'I'm sure Mr Lilley would have the best.'

Our house? Emilie was in no mood to allow them to take her for granted. His house? Who did Mr Bowles think he was, calling it his house? The house was to be built with the money from Ruth's land on Emilie's block. It belonged to them, not him. Only then did she realise what was happening. She'd been too involved in her own concerns to take much notice before. But of course, when he married Ruth, he would be entitled . . . Good Lord! As her husband, he would own Ruth's equity.

So where will that leave me? she asked herself. Ruth might think she'd made a mistake associating with Mal, but she wasn't completely stupid.

Emilie leaned forward, interrupting their chat. 'We will, of course, need a solicitor to draw up the necessary papers before the house is built on my land. To establish ownership.'

'You do not need a solicitor,' Ruth snapped, maybe thinking that Emilie was using this as a roundabout way to be introduced to a legal man.

Bowles was even firmer. 'There is no necessity to employ one. I am quite capable of handling the paperwork. After all, I am in the Attorney-General's office. There is no need for you ladies to be bothering your heads about it.'

So, Emilie thought, I am to have no say in this at all. And as it turns out, I wouldn't be sharing this house with my sister, but with them. And sharing the ownership with him.

She crossed her hands firmly in her lap. 'I am not sure that I want to build a house on my block just yet.'

His pale eyes blinked several times. 'I beg your pardon?'

Ruth flushed. 'Don't take any notice of her. She's not very well today.'

'I am well. And I should like the deeds of my block, Mr Bowles. I believe you have them in your office.'

'You're being ridiculous,' Ruth flared. 'After all Mr Bowles has done for us. You wouldn't even have known about acquiring land . . .'

'That's true, and I am very grateful for your advice, Mr Bowles, but I do not wish to build on that block. Not yet, anyway.'

'But I've sold my land!' Ruth cried.

'No you haven't. Not yet. But that's up to you. You may still do so if you wish and buy a smaller block somewhere else to build your house. I have no need for one at present.'

'Emilie! You can't go on living here. It's too expensive. We need a house.'

'You forget, Ruth, I'm only visiting. I have not agreed to leave Maryborough.'

'We'll see about that!' Ruth stood. 'Would you excuse us, Daniel? I think Emilie is confused.'

Ruth hustled her back to their bedroom.

'How dare you! How dare you speak to Mr Bowles like that! You will go right out and apologise to him. I do believe you have gone quite mad. And what's this about not wanting the house? We need our own home. Don't you realise how fortunate we are? When we first left home I thought we'd be living in rented rooms for the rest of our lives . . .'

'So this isn't such a bad country after all,' Emilie commented.

'That remark is uncalled for, and smug. It does not become you.'

'And your nagging is getting on my nerves.'

'I see. I am being punished for not permitting you to ask Mr Bowles to help this criminal friend of yours. But you may be sure that ploy will not work. Don't think for one minute you can force me into lowering my standards for your outrageous causes.'

'That has nothing to do with it. I shall attend to that myself. I don't wish to be unkind, but I feel it would be better for all concerned if you, as newlyweds, had your own home. Just leave me out of it.'

'You're jealous! That's what it is. You're jealous because I have found a decent man and you haven't . . .'

'Oh, stop, Ruth. There's the gong for tea. I'm going in.'

They were a tight-lipped group at tea, but Emilie had made up her mind. Relations would be grim with Ruth, and Mr Bowles, for a while, she supposed, but they'd get over it. Even, with luck, see her point of view. She felt lonely, stuck here with this disapproving pair. She missed Clive and her other friends in Maryborough. They were cheerful people at least.

271

Emilie looked about the quiet dining room, wondering who all these people were, and what they did. They seemed decent folk, as Ruth would say, but still her sister never addressed any of them except her Daniel. Then she remembered a face, the face of a large, kindly man who used to sit at the next table with his wife. Mr Kemp. Superintendent Kemp. He'd spoken to her in Maryborough outside Mrs Mooney's hotel, and she'd been petrified of him. Petrified that she might say something that would hinder Mal's chances of remaining free. But now that he was in custody, did it matter?

She still had no idea of how to go about choosing a solicitor who handled matters like this. Maybe Mr Kemp would help. Emilie shuddered at the thought, but at least she knew him. Better than gaining the attention of a legal gentleman who might not even agree to see her for weeks. She didn't have that much time. The more she thought about it, the more she worried that she might not have the nerve to call on Mr Kemp, but she'd have to try. First thing in the morning.

Pollock's first meeting with Kemp had not gone well at all. The ship had berthed early in the morning and the Sergeant had wasted no time hurrying up to police headquarters to await the Superintendent's arrival by the worn stone steps. He knew the old timber building well, having served his first years as a constable there. He'd been informed that the Superintendent was due at eight, and that was good enough for him. He lit a smoke and lounged about outside the building, watching weary constables leave for home after the long night shift that had been his own due, years ago.

When he saw the tall, familiar form striding up the street, he smartened up, straightening his hat and rubbing his boots against his trouser legs for extra shine.

'Good morning, sir.'

'By Jove, Pollock. You didn't waste any time. What's this all about? Hand in your papers and come on up to my office.'

Pollock blanched. 'Excuse me, sir, I don't have any papers, but I'm sure it will be all right.'

'What will be? You must have leave papers. Temporary transfer? Give them to my duty officer.'

'I didn't have time to get any, sir.'

Kemp frowned. 'Time? What do you mean? Am I to understand that you left your post without permission?'

'Yes, sir.' Pollock hadn't realised that Kemp could be so difficult. 'But it was necessary.'

'Then don't give me that nonsense about not having time.'

'I'm sorry, sir.'

'You are under detention, Sergeant. Report in immediately.'

Kemp was annoyed. He was interested in contact between Willoughby and this man, but he could not allow insubordination to go unchecked, no matter who it was. On his way to his office, he instructed his deputy to look into the matter.

He left Pollock to cool his heels until late afternoon and then sent for him.

'Your senior at Maryborough flatly refused to allow you leave to come to Brisbane . . .'

'But it is important, Mr Kemp. You know that. And I've already wasted a day.'

'Then you had better count the days you are wasting down here, because to settle the matter, you are now on unpaid leave.'

'The way I'm going, I might as well quit.'

'That's up to you,' Kemp said tonelessly. 'You had this telegram from the prisoner Willoughby. What have you in mind?'

'I need permission to visit him on the island.'

'You're asking my permission. That's reassuring. Well, you may visit the prisoner after I receive approval from Captain Croft, the prison superintendent.'

'There's no need for that. He wouldn't have allowed Willoughby to send that telegram if he hadn't known it was important, and expected me to respond.'

'You will still need written permission before you or anyone else can visit prisoners.'

'But that will take days. Can't you telegraph him, sir?'

'I'll think about it. Be here at eight in the morning.'

'What if Willoughby changes his mind? I'm certain he wants to confess.'

Kemp laughed. 'A few more days in that prison could make him even more eager.'

Three days elapsed before Pollock was able to board the prison longboat, handing over the official form signed by Kemp, and by that time he was convinced the police hierarchy was conspiring against him, blaming him for a murder case that could be neither solved nor forgotten.

Croft, elegant in a black uniform with silver buttons, obviously self-styled and tailor-made, made him welcome.

'Delighted to see you, old chap. I don't get many visitors. I've prepared a special luncheon for you, but first let me show you round. We're coming along here, you know. Practically self-supporting, one could say. Convicts here earn their keep, as it should be. A gentleman from the House of Lords, in London you know, visited St Helena two months ago – Lord Blessington, in fact, fine chap. He regarded this as a model prison. Although transportation of convicts from the mother country has ended, he feels it should be revived. We have hundreds of islands in Queensland, we could open another dozen prisons like this without upsetting anybody on the mainland, and earn the undying gratitude of the Britons, struggling for space in their jails . . .'

Jesus, this bloke can talk, Pollock sighed. His only interest was to find Willoughby, not spend the day socialising with Croft, but he couldn't afford to antagonise him, too . . .

273

He was marched out to the lime kilns and the canefield, and on to the sugar mill, and from there to view crops being tended by prisoners in their canvas garb, all the time hoping to catch a glimpse of Willoughby. The tour seemed endless, from the seawalls under construction, back through the high brick walls of the stockade to the workshops, where prisoners were engaged in bootmaking, sailmaking, candlemaking, and out the other side to the dairy and blacksmith. He passed stocks and triangles in the punishment court without a murmur, understanding the necessity for them, as Croft kept up his narrative like a practised tour guide, until he was finally forced to enquire after Willoughby.

'I haven't sighted him yet.'

'He's not far away. Don't worry about him. He's out digging pits for my new underground water tanks. Now what about a drink? I have some wine cooling.'

Lunch was excellent and interminable. The Superintendent had a very pleasant house and garden, which he was anxious to show off. At times Pollock felt sorry for the man, who so desperately needed company, and at others he was irritated by the time this was taking. The longboat on the beach was at his disposal, waiting to take him back to Brisbane, but Croft was pouring wine and outlining his latest plan to grow wine grapes on the island.

'They call this island a hellhole,' Croft confided after several glasses of wine, 'but one has to maintain discipline. Wouldn't you agree?'

Pollock did. As prisons went, this one didn't look too bad at all.

'They send me the worst criminals,' Croft added in his defence, and once again Pollock agreed.

'You must have a busy time keeping them in order. But if you don't mind, sir, I have to talk to Willoughby. This case is a real pain in the neck.'

'So I believe. The papers are most unkind to the police about it, that's why I decided I ought to try to help. I'll have your fellow brought up and we'll see what he has to say.'

Pollock hardly recognised Willoughby when he was escorted to the Superintendent's office. The burly, youthful body had given way to a skinny frame, and his thatch of blond hair had been shaved off, leaving an almost bald skull. His eyes – blue eyes, Pollock had reported in his description of the outlaw, as best as he could recall – now seemed brilliant, set in the shadows of a bruised face.

'Hello, Mr Pollock,' he said as he walked in, chains clanking, and Pollock remembered something else, the quiet, polite voice. How long was it since the same man had ridden up to his house in Maryborough to inform him that the gold escort was waiting for backup out at Blackwater Creek? It seemed like years.

'Hello, Willoughby. I believe you want to talk to me.'

'That's right, sir.'

The Sergeant turned to Croft. 'All right if he sits down there? I might need a written statement.'

'By all means.' Croft leaned back in his chair, interested. 'Now what was it you wanted to tell Sergeant Pollock?'

Willoughby stared. 'You know me, Mr Pollock. I said I wanted to talk to you. Not him.'

Pollock suppressed a burp. He'd eaten too much at lunch with Croft. He was not accustomed to five-course meals.

'It's all right,' he said. 'The Superintendent has a right to be here. As witness. You may speak freely.'

'The hell I can. What I have to say has got nothing to do with him.'

Croft slammed his desk with his fist. 'I knew it. This scum has brought you here to complain about the prison.'

Just as swiftly, Willoughby's voice changed from the demand to a purr, and Pollock listened, astonished.

'Ah, no, sir. You mustn't take it that way. I've got nothin' against your prison, except I don't belong here, you see. Now me and Mr Pollock here go a way back. I have to tell him something, and if he believes me, it's on his head. His, not yours. You see what I mean? I don't want you to be sorry for arranging this meeting.'

Croft saw, though he pretended not to. He blustered and argued, but with little conviction, and eventually left the room.

The Sergeant leaned against the windowsill. 'Someone told me you could talk the leg off an iron pot, Willoughby.'

'Did they now?' the soft voice asked. 'And who would have said that?'

'Clive Hillier.'

'And is he still a friend?'

'Yes.'

'That's good to know. I'm a bit short lately.'

'What happened to your face?'

'I said I wouldn't say nothin' about his prison.'

'Right. So what have we got to talk about?'

'Is that all?' There was shock as well as disappointment as Willoughby finished outlining his conversation with a prisoner called Baldy Perry. This wasn't a confession; it was nothing. It could cost Pollock his job. His bluff about quitting was reality now. He couldn't take this rot back to Kemp; his leave without pay would be extended to life.

'You've dragged me all the way down here for this?' Pollock snarled. 'For some bloody lunatic's raving. I never even heard of Baldy Perry!'

'He was arrested in Maryborough. You could have locked him up yourself.'

'I didn't. I must have been away. But so what? He claims to be a mate of McPherson's and no one here believes him. Not even the prisoners. Only a mug like you. Jesus, Willoughby, you've done me in well and good this time. I'll see you die here. You'll never get off this bloody sandbank if I have any say in it. Not until the day they come to string you up.'

Mal had known this wouldn't be easy; he'd had enough trouble convincing himself that Baldy had let something slip about that raid. He'd have to be very patient with Pollock. He had a right to yell.

He waited for the harangue to run its course. 'Can I ask you a question?'

The Sergeant shrugged, almost ready to give up and leave.

'If I am supposed to be McPherson's partner, why would Baldy take it for granted that I didn't know McPherson was in Maryborough when he did?'

'Because he's stupid.'

'Maybe.' Mal had avoided any mention of meeting McPherson in Brisbane or out in the hills; to do that would only dig a deeper hole for himself. He was still claiming to have taken no part in the raid, in the first instance, and, of necessity, that he did not know the outlaw. 'But I don't think so. He was so sure of himself, Mr Pollock. Let me try again. I don't believe for one minute that McPherson was in Maryborough before the raid. And you don't either. He wouldn't show himself in town.'

'Which shows Perry to be a liar.'

'Yes. You're right. But why would he deliberately place his *mate* there if he didn't have a reason. Like setting him up for blame. To take the heat off himself. I reckon Baldy Perry was in on that raid.'

'That's drawing a long bow.'

'Bears thinking about, though. And that bastard knows, sure as hell, I wasn't in on it. I saw it in his eyes. It was in his voice.'

Pollock sighed. He scratched the back of his neck. This tale was as weak as water, but Kemp had told him that though McPherson, in custody, had pleaded guilty to several holdups, he was still denying any complicity in the raid. He claimed he was in Bundaberg at the time and could prove it. Police were bringing him south now, through Bundaberg, to investigate the claim, and what was more, Pollock thought gloomily, they were inclined to believe him. That only left Willoughby and, possibly, Carnegie. Still a team.

'Where were you between the time you came to my house in Maryborough on the day of the raid and the time we left to go out and meet the escort?' he asked.

'I was just looking round the town. I'd never been there before.'

'Maybe *you* were alerting Baldy Perry.'

'No. I only met him in here.'

'So you say.' There was something else Pollock knew he had to ask, but he couldn't put it into words yet. Something. In the meantime he allowed himself to consider Perry as a suspect, with little else to go on. He *had* been in Maryborough at the time. But so had hundreds of other likely lads.

'All right,' he said. 'I'll have them bring Perry in and you can face him with these accusations. I'll be interested to hear what he has to say.'

Mal shook his head. 'Listen, I could have done that myself. Where do you think that would have got me?'

'A bashing.'

'No, that wouldn't help either. He won't talk, not to me and certainly not to you, Mr Pollock. He'd be on his guard.'

'So what's the point of all this? You claim he's a suspect but we shouldn't interrogate him. This is going nowhere. I'll decide what to do about Perry. Not you.' He reached for his hat. It was time to go. He couldn't keep the boatmen waiting much longer.

The boat. That was it. The boat. The German boat-builder had described the man who'd bought the new dinghy from him and then deliberately sunk it in the river. About the time of the raid. In the river, not far across from the mouth of Blackwater Creek where the raid had taken place.

Almost casually, he asked his next question. 'What does this bloke Perry look like?'

'A bruiser. Big bastard, you wouldn't want to turn your back on him. Pudgy face, with little squinty eyes. Bald as an egg, but he's got whiskers, and I'll tell you something else, a bloke here says he was a good shot. Out in the bush. You could get the boss here to point him out.'

'No need,' Pollock said drily, although he had every intention of doing just that.

'So what happens now?' Willoughby asked.

'What do you think can happen?'

'Perry gets out of here soon. You ought to follow him. See what he gets up to. He might lead you to the gold.'

'You're a dreamer, Willoughby. We've got better things to do than trail ex-cons.'

'Then you'll never find out what happened.'

'Oh yes we will. In the meantime, you enjoy your stay.'

Willoughby stared out of the barred window. 'Doesn't anyone believe me?'

The Sergeant was unsympathetic. There'd been no confession, only a vague accusation against another prisoner, not much to take to Kemp.

'If they did, you wouldn't be here,' he said, and called in the guards.

Kemp was not impressed by the Sergeant's report.

'I was expecting a confession and all you've got is a classic case of a prisoner shifting the blame.' He read through the pages again. 'Just like this fellow Perry is doing. Shifting the blame to McPherson while we now know that the rogue *was* in Bundaberg. He stole a horse from a farmer, who reported the theft to police but blamed his neighbour, starting a neighbourhood war. But now, of course, the Scot is only too pleased to own up to stealing the horse. He was riding the very same animal when he was apprehended. So that counts out McPherson, once and for all. And another thing . . .'

'Excuse me, sir. What you said back there is important. You said Perry was shifting the blame to McPherson. Now that is exactly the same sort of mistake, if you don't mind me saying so, that Willoughby picked up when he was talking to Perry.'

Kemp frowned. 'My mistake?'

'Yes, sir. Easily overlooked, sir, since I had to outline that conversation in my report. Takes a bit of figuring,' Pollock added apologetically. 'But you see, Perry had no need to shift the blame. He wasn't a suspect.'

'A boaster and a liar, though.'

'Agreed. But in my book, he is a suspect now. He fits the description of the man who bought that boat. It's in the report.'

He waited while Kemp took his time, this time, rereading the report, which hadn't shown much promise at first glance.

'All right,' he said at length. 'You're clutching at straws, but we'll bring him up to our jail and my officers will interrogate him.'

'Willoughby says we won't get anything out of him.'

'I don't give a damn what Willoughby says.'

'Could I take part in the interrogation?'

'Yes. I suppose that would be useful. But I have another item of interest to add to the file on Willoughby. A young lady from Maryborough, who is known to me, visited me yesterday.'

'Who would that be?'

'A Miss Tissington.'

'The governess? Works for Mrs Manningtree?'

'Correct.'

'What's she got to do with it?'

'Let me tell you. Apparently she is a friend of young Willoughby. A good friend. So much so that she has come to Brisbane to arrange legal representation for him.'

'Good God!'

'She's a very nice girl, and rather shy. She sought my advice on selecting a suitable gentleman, as she put it. But naturally I was interested in what she knew of Willoughby. That was a little more difficult. Miss Tissington hadn't bargained on being questioned and we had a few tears, but after a cup of tea it all came out. She met him casually in Brisbane. Then one day, as she was walking down the street in Maryborough, who should loom up but our lad. Delighted to see her. And do you know what day it was?'

'I've no idea.'

'The day of the raid, Sergeant. The morning! He walked her home and stood and chatted with the lady, at her gate. All very circumspect. Then he said he had to rush off . . .'

'That would be to join up with me?'

'Yes,' Kemp said. 'But before he left her, he arranged a rendezvous. To collect her at the same gate the following night and take her to see the sights of Maryborough.'

'Don't tell me! The silly bugger was only seeing his girlfriend. He's never explained where he got to. Said he was just riding about the town.'

'It seems he didn't want to involve her in the subsequent events.'

'So the lady waited at the gate the next night and he didn't turn up, because he was on the run by this . . .'

'Not at all. He was there. It seems to me that Willoughby is greatly taken with Miss Tissington. He was there, large as life, while you and your men were scouring the countryside. Looking in entirely the wrong direction.'

Pollock groaned, thankful that Kemp didn't add 'again'. He was beginning to hate Willoughby.

'This is another interesting part. He was saddened that due to circumstances he could not play the swain. But he told her what had happened. He was very upset, told her he was innocent of any wrongdoing, but now he was running away from the police, so he'd only come to say farewell. Then he disappeared. Miss Tissington believes him. She is adamant that he is innocent, and is very indignant that he is being treated so unfairly.'

Kemp sat back with a grin. 'So there you have it. The missing hour is accounted for. And Willoughby circled back into town just to say goodbye to his girl.'

'I don't know if she's his girl,' Pollock said. 'She goes out with Clive Hillier now. Who is also a friend of Willoughby's. What else does she know?'

'Nothing, except what is in the papers.'

'Still doesn't get us far,' Pollock shrugged.

Kemp agreed.

Emilie sat in the long corridor, eyes downcast, gloved hands neatly folded together, studying the toes of her shoes as they peeped out from her long navy skirt. She dared not look up. The corridor was busy with policemen striding back and forth, and so many had asked what they could do for her that she was embarrassed being there in public view. She couldn't move, though; she'd been told to wait there for Mr Kemp and she'd have to stay.

Everything seemed drab and brown. Brown lino, brown benches, walls painted beige with a brown trim. Even the policemen's boots were brown, despite their black uniforms. Anyway, the brown fitted her sombre mood, for she was worried that she'd said too much to Mr Kemp. She had only come for advice, and hadn't counted on bursting into tears. What a sight she must have been. But Mr Kemp was a kind man; he'd understood how difficult it had been for her to come here at all, to ask to see such an important man without even making an appointment.

And then it had all spilled out. How she'd met Mal, and then seen him again in Maryborough. And so on. She'd answered his questions truthfully and in doing so had gained a little confidence because he was so nice, just nodding politely at her responses with no criticism of her or of Mal. It was as if they were simply having a social conversation. It was much easier to explain to him than to Ruth. He wasn't shocked that a governess should have a friend like Mal. But that confidence helped her to assess where to draw the line. She did not mention that Mal had given her his money. He had said they would take it from him, and Emilie

279

wasn't taking any chances that she might be required to hand it over.

When she'd said that Mal had said goodbye to her and gone, because he was being pursued by the police, Mr Kemp had asked her why she hadn't told the police about that meeting.

That had given her a fright. She recalled going out of her way to avoid even walking past the police station.

'I was too afraid,' she answered truthfully. 'I didn't know what to expect. I've no experience in these matters.'

'No, my dear. Of course not. But he didn't stay on the premises, did he? I mean, on or near the Manningtree property?'

'Heavens, no. He disappeared. I had no idea where he was. Then one day I read he'd been captured. I hope I haven't done anything wrong.'

'I think we can overlook that. But it would have helped to know he was in the vicinity.'

Emilie gazed at him. 'The man is innocent. It did not occur to me to cause him even more trouble. I am at a loss to understand why he is in prison.'

'Ah, well, we shall have to see.' He wrote a name and address on a page and handed it to her. 'This is the man you should see on behalf of Mr Willoughby. He may be able to assist.'

So she waited, until Kemp's voice broke into her reverie. 'Miss Tissington. Back again? To what do I owe this honour?'

She jumped up. 'Oh, Mr Kemp. I am so sorry to bother you. But I did call at Mr Harvey's office, and unfortunately his clerk said he was ill. He's not expected back for quite some time. I wondered if you could recommend another gentleman?'

A reporter witnessed Kemp's interest in the very attractive young lady and watched as the Superintendent of Police ushered her into his office. Jesse Fields had been about to return to Chinchilla when he'd met the editor of the *Brisbane Courier* in a pub. The two men had struck up a friendship over their mutual interest in their favourite topics, politics and crime, and at the end of a long drinking session, Jesse had stumbled back to his hotel feeling on top of the world.

He had landed a job with the prestigious *Courier*! Farewell, Chinchilla.

Since he was *au fait* with the Willoughby story, it was left to him to follow it up.

'Keep on it,' the editor said. 'Old Walt White on the Maryborough paper says the police are making a real mess of this case. Getting nowhere, even though they've caught Willoughby. It wasn't a one-man job. Anything you hear, pass it on to Walt. Keep sweet with him so that we have both towns covered.'

McPherson was captured. McPherson had admitted to a string of crimes, but it had been proved that he'd been in Bundaberg at the time of the holdup. Jesse kept the story running. Sergeant Pollock was in Brisbane from Maryborough and the whisper was that he was following up on the same case. Doing what?

280

Jesse accosted Pollock, only to learn that the Sergeant claimed to be down here on leave.

'Rum sort of a holiday, hanging about police headquarters,' he snapped, but Pollock wasn't talking.

'Something's going on,' Jesse muttered to his editor. 'I know he's reporting to Kemp. About what? I might need a few extra shillings to cross palms down there.'

Knowing that the press was still hard on his heels over this case, Kemp ordered a clamp on Perry. Two of his trusted officers were sent to bring the man up river, bring him ashore out of town and deliver him, well chained, and hooded, not to headquarters but to a cell in the police barracks. He was still convinced that Perry's involvement was only a bone thrown to them by Willoughby, and he couldn't afford the press to find out they'd accused the wrong man again. They were taking enough abuse for blaming McPherson, not only from the papers, but from irate citizens, fans of the rogue Scot. Reporters were already hanging about, slavering for a chance to talk to that damn McPherson, who was playing up his role as the victim of police misjudgement. His progress south to Brisbane through coastal towns to certain imprisonment for his real crimes had become a triumphant procession, his police escort suffering heckling and the prisoner rejoicing in the cheers of encouragement from ordinary folk who turned out to wish him well.

Reports of this adulation infuriated Kemp. The man was a bloody criminal, even if he hadn't been in on this raid. What was the world coming to?

Even the Attorney-General wanted to meet McPherson. The request had come at a formal dinner.

'What on earth for?' Kemp had asked.

'I saw his picture in a newspaper,' Lilley said. 'I think he was the fellow who rescued me from a riot early last year.'

'McPherson? I hardly think so, sir.'

'Nevertheless, I should like to meet the fellow. Be kind enough to arrange it, Kemp.'

The world was truly going mad. McPherson was getting more publicity than an opera star. And Sergeant Pollock was still underfoot, nagging over Perry's stupid utterances.

'Sir, he has told several prisoners he's a rich man!'

'Well, ask him about these riches.'

'I have. He says he was only ribbing them. A joke. But the more I think about it, the more I believe that Willoughby is right. Perry is in this somewhere.'

'You can't convict a man on vague possibilities.'

'We can keep at him, sir,' Pollock insisted. 'He'll give something away eventually.'

'If you think so,' Kemp said wearily. He wasn't looking forward to the weekend. Another official dinner on Saturday night, a mounted police display on Sunday morning and an afternoon tea the same day, organised by the Ladies for the Advancement of Female Prisoners. Mrs Kemp loved these functions – they gave her a place in the hurly-burly of this town, a social status – but Kemp would have preferred to be home working in his new garden.

And here, on this Friday afternoon, was Miss Tissington, looking as pretty as a picture in her navy ensemble, a pert boater hat perched on her dark curls. The sweetness of her countenance and her innocent smile swept away, temporarily at least, the gloom of his day. No wonder, he mused, young Willoughby fell for her at first glance. Miss Emilie certainly was a sight for sore eyes. In fact, he thought it was rather gallant of Sonny Willoughby to have taken such a huge risk just to keep his appointment with her.

He looked up another name and gave it to her, adding: 'I'm sure my wife would be pleased to see you again. You must call on us at home before you go back.'

'Thank you, Mr Kemp. I'd like that.'

'Good. I'll ask Mrs Kemp to drop you a note. Now, if there's anything else troubling you, at any time, you come and see me, here or at home.'

She nodded, as if this needed thought, and Kemp imagined she had more to say, but the moment passed. A gentle smile replaced concern.

'It's very kind of you, Mr Kemp.' The voice was sorrowful, though, as if carrying a great deal of hurt, and his heart went out to her. If his daughter had lived, maybe she would have become a sweet girl like Miss Tissington.

Jesse was a sprightly fellow, and he managed to duck out of the way in time to avoid being spotted by Kemp, but he did hear the exchange between them before the Superintendent took the girl into his office. Her voice surprised him. English, and not long off the boat by the sound of it. What would she be doing here? Waiting so patiently for Kemp.

'My, she's a looker,' he exclaimed to a passing constable. 'A local girl, I hope.'

He grinned. 'No such luck, Jesse. She's from Maryborough.'

'A friend of the boss?'

'Could be. I don't know.'

Nothing more to learn there. Jesse had hoped to find out her name, but her home town was far more interesting. He didn't set much store by coincidences. He decided to leave by the side entrance, which necessitated passing the desk of a friendly officer.

'What about a drink at the Pig and Whistle at six?' he asked.

'Good idea.'

Jesse looked about to make sure no one was listening. 'Who's the girl from Maryborough?' He winked. 'I'd be interested to know about her.'

The police officer smirked. 'I'll bet you would.' He went back to rubber-stamping pages and Jesse drifted away.

'She's what?' he cried, astounded.

Senior Sergeant Ellis downed his pint and pushed the tankard back across the counter for a refill.

'Thought you'd like it. She's Willoughby's girlfriend. Come down to plead for him, they say. Her name is Miss Tissington. She's a governess. Not bad going for a bloke like Willoughby, eh?'

'You can say that again.'

'I could say a bit more too, but it'll cost you, Jesse. And no mentioning where it came from.'

'Righto. Five bob.'

'Kemp's none too pleased with Pollock. Seems the country copper made another blue. Not only did he let Willoughby escape, but while he and his men were out all night searching the bush, young Sonny, cheeky as you like, rides back into Maryborough to see his lady love!'

'Ah, go on!'

'It's true.' Ellis laughed. 'It's on record. One of my mates saw the statement. No doubt about that Sonny, he's a smart kid. The lads reckon if his uncle hadn't given him up, he'd still be at large.'

'What does Pollock say about this?'

'He's not saying nothing. And I'll tell you what, his files have suddenly gone under lock and key in Kemp's office.'

'I thought he was on leave.'

'He is. Enforced leave. He took off from Maryborough without permission from his boss. So he's working without pay, lucky not to be in a cell himself, but Kemp needs him. He let him go down to St Helena and have another go at Willoughby.'

'What did he find out?'

'Nothing, as far as we can make out.'

'Then why are his files locked up?'

'Good point. Something must be going on.'

Not long after that, Jesse was back at his desk with a new twist to the story, and his editor was intrigued.

'Willougby's lady love, eh? Good on you, Jesse. So Sonny led the police a merry chase, taking time out to visit the girl. Old Walt White will love this story on his home turf. You write it up, send the gist to Walt and I'll get a photograph. I want a picture of her. Where's she staying?'

'I don't know.'

'Never mind. We'll find her. You get on with the story.'

283

Chapter Twelve

'Why is she doing this?' Daniel wanted to know.

'She's just trying to spite me.'

'I don't understand. I thought you two were on good terms.'

'We are,' Ruth said. 'Or we were. I mean, she's come down from that place with all sorts of funny ideas.'

'What funny ideas? Let me talk to her.'

'No. She's so stubborn it won't do any good. I've been at her all week. She won't listen to sense. She insists she has to have the deeds to her block. Did you bring them home?'

'I did not. I need a proper explanation of her behaviour.'

'Perhaps if she could just look at them, Daniel, it would make her feel better. She is so foolish, seeing them might put her in a better frame of mind.'

'You may be right.' He nodded. 'But what I did bring home is the contract of sale for your land. All you have to do is sign it, and your immediate worries will be over. You will have forty pounds in the bank, quite enough to build and furnish the house.'

Ruth was disappointed. 'Forty pounds? I thought I'd get at least three pounds per acre.'

'So did I, but it seems part of the block is swampy, not suitable for man or beast. That's understandable. You can't expect the very best land for free, and Brisbane itself is very swampy in places, being on the river. The dreaded mosquitoes that harass us at dusk are living proof, as you well know.'

'Even so, I thought a little more . . .'

'Then there's the agent's commission, my dear. And the stamp duty, it all adds up. I think you've done well. But if you don't wish to sign, I can go looking for another agent . . .'

'Oh, no, Daniel. You've done your best, I feel sure . . .'

'Yes. And another agent might drop the price.' He hurried out of the parlour to borrow pen and ink from Mrs Medlow, who knew better than to enquire the reason of Mr Bowles.

There was no agent. Daniel considered he was entitled to the agent's fees, plus a little more, for his time and effort. He had done well in achieving three pounds an acre for that block, and the money he'd held back was in their best interests. When they married, she'd be sharing it anyway.

Ruth signed with a sigh of relief. She desperately needed extra money to keep up with the rent and buy some new clothes. Darns were beginning to show and her linens were almost threadbare. If she shopped with care she would only have to spend a few pounds of the precious forty, but it was so good to know she didn't have to scratch for every penny now. She could even send a few more pounds, maybe ten, back to the Society.

'Thank you, Daniel,' she said, handing him the contract. 'You've been such a good friend to me.'

He smiled. 'Just don't go on a spending spree now.'

'Oh, no. I wouldn't dream of it. But what about tomorrow? Saturday. We did promise to take Emilie out to show her the blocks.'

'Why bother, since she's in such a mood?'

'I thought if we were nice to her – she's so childish – and we let her see, even have some say in where the house could be placed, she might change her mind.'

'If you insist. We'd better take her, I suppose. We did promise. But really, Ruth, you shouldn't have to put up with her tantrums. You ought to put your foot down. It is quite obvious she lacks your good sense.'

They'd hardly spoken to each other all week. Ruth had no idea how Emilie had spent her days and had been too angry with her to enquire, but now she decided that she would have to try a different approach. She would be nice to her, she had to be; it was humiliating to be placed in this position.

'I've sold the block,' she said. 'Did quite well after commission and stamp duty.'

'That's good, as long as you're happy with the result.'

'We'd still like to take you to see the area. You do want to see your land, don't you?'

'Of course. I'm looking forward to it.'

'Oh, I'm so pleased. We'll have a day out. Mr Bowles said we take public transport out there at ten o'clock in the morning. It's a horse-drawn omnibus like they have in London, and quite pleasant. The ride takes us down through Fortitude Valley and out along the river before turning inland to the Eagle Farm area, which is becoming quite progressive.'

'I read in the paper that the Brisbane Turf Club is building a racecourse out there.'

'Oh well, I'm sure it won't be anywhere near our blocks. But it spells improvement in the facilities.'

'This doesn't mean I want to build on the land yet.'

'Emilie, we went to so much trouble finding that land, just come to see it and be happy. It is such a thrill . . .'

At least, she mused, there'd been no more talk of that outlaw fellow.

With Kemp's permission, Sergeant Pollock decided to call on Carnegie, who was now living with his brother up on the Paddington slopes. Wattle trees, heavy with yellow blossom, hung over the narrow road and bees swarmed about them, their insistent buzz in the still of the day a warning to stay clear. Pollock did just that, riding warily around them. He was terrified of bees.

. Cleared patches on the heavily forested hills made way for large timber houses, but there seemed to be no pattern in their placement as yet. He rode up several dead-end tracks before a woman, trudging sturdily uphill, was able to direct him to the home of John Carnegie, a retired grazier.

The brother was pleased to welcome him. A talkative man, on hearing the Sergeant was from Maryborough he was more than ready for a yarn about that heinous raid and gold robbery carried out in broad daylight, especially since his own brother had been a victim of the dastardly attack.

'Allyn had a bad time of it,' he continued. 'Damn shame. And then to have a heart attack. Well, is it any wonder? The poor chap. Wife left him, you know. Damn bad show.'

Obviously John Carnegie had only heard his brother's version of the story, including that so-called heart attack, but Pollock had no wish to enlighten him.

'Did you have any trouble finding the house?' Carnegie asked.

'No, sir,' the Sergeant said, rather than prolong the conversation. 'I was wondering if Mr Carnegie is in.'

'Yes, yes, of course. Do come in, I'll fetch him for you.'

He was ushered into the parlour, a comfortable room with family portraits gazing down on solid cedar furnishings.

'That's my late wife,' Mr Carnegie said, nodding to a photograph of a plump woman which held price of place over the mantelpiece. 'Lovely woman, passed away nigh on three years ago. Heart, it was, she always had a fluttery heart, but never complained, mind you, never a word of complaint would pass her lips. In the end it got the better of her. We were out on the station then. Sheep, we ran sheep, did well too, but when she passed on I lost heart in the place, decided to give it up. My son . . .'

Carnegie was at the door. 'John,' he said sternly, 'I think the visitor is for me.'

'Yes, I was just coming to fetch you. Shall I ask the girl to bring us morning tea?'

'No thank you. I don't expect Sergeant Pollock has the time to be sitting about.'

'Are you sure?'

Pollock answered for him. The brother was a nice old chap, no need to upset him. 'I'm fine, thanks, Mr Carnegie. I just wanted to see how your brother here is getting along.'

'Kind of you,' he murmured, looking to seat himself, but Allyn Carnegie led him to the door. 'You can leave us now, John. I'll have a private word with Mr Pollock.'

The door closed firmly, Carnegie turned on Pollock. 'What the hell are you doing here? Haven't I suffered enough without you intruding on my family?'

'I won't stay long. Do you mind if I sit down?'

'Please yourself.' Carnegie remained standing by the open fireplace. 'What do you want?'

'I'm sure you know that McPherson has been apprehended.'

'So?'

'So we have to discuss the raid again. It has been established, without doubt, that he was in Bundaberg on that day. Nowhere near Blackwater Creek. Yet you claimed he was there.'

'Obviously it was someone who looked like him.'

'That's our problem. There aren't too many men around who look like McPherson, with the red beard and all.'

'Yes, Sergeant. It is your problem. Not mine.'

'I thought you might reconsider that description. You could have made a mistake. Understandable under such horrific circumstances . . .'

'I don't make mistakes. I gave you the description. If it wasn't that fellow, then it was someone like him.'

'And you definitely heard the attackers ride away?'

'Of course I did.'

'I thought you might have heard only Willoughby ride off.'

'And the rest stayed? Don't talk rot. I heard horses leave.'

As usual, Pollock was only covering old ground after that, until Carnegie refused to submit to further questioning.

On his way back to town, Pollock wondered what he could have expected from that conversation. About as much as he got, he supposed. He'd considered asking Carnegie if he knew a man called Baldy Perry, but decided that question could wait until they finished interrogating Perry. Something might come of it. Or nothing.

Willoughby was hungry. He was always hungry in this place, his belly rattling like an empty tin. It made hard labour in the pits even harder, his arms almost too weak to swing the pick, and his legs straining with cramps. There was food on this island, any amount of food grown by the prisoners, but they saw little of it. He looked longingly at the bush that crowded the outskirts of the prison. A man could survive there, fish would be plentiful on the shores and there had to be bush fare of some sort, but it was such a small island that beaters on foot would soon flush out absconders. When he wasn't thinking of food, Mal thought about escaping, of making a raft and paddling to the mainland, but the guards kept such a close watch on the prisoners that it was hard to figure out how to go about this.

He hadn't heard any more from Pollock, so he could expect no help from that direction, but there was one glimmer of light on the horizon. Word had got round the prison that McPherson had been captured. According to the warders, he'd pleaded guilty to so many holdups he'd be in one door of court and out the other in minutes and on his way to St Helena.

'You're on your own, Willoughby,' a guard taunted. 'Jimmy McPherson's been cleared of them murders. You might as well make the best of your time here. You'll go out a courtroom door to the gallows.'

McPherson. Mal desperately needed to talk to him. He was a cranky bugger but he just might help. Now that he'd been cleared, he could be interested in the whereabouts of the gold. He would be, Mal was sure of that. So the trick would be to steer him towards Perry. With the gold in mind, it was possible that the Scot could wheedle information out of Perry, or, as a last resort, because time was running out, they could join forces and beat it out of him. Mal had nothing to lose, and crafty McPherson had plenty to gain. He smiled grimly when Perry announced proudly that his mate McPherson was listed to join them.

One day shortly afterwards, however, as they assembled for Sunday service, Mal, still plotting to make that move on Baldy, noticed that the man was missing.

'Where's Baldy?' he asked a guard.

'Gone. He's done his time. They took him up river yesterday.'

Mal was stunned. 'Ah, the bloody fools!'

The guard jerked back. 'You cheeking me?'

'No.'

'Then shut up and get going.' The truncheon slammed across Mal's shoulder to keep him in line.

As the lay preacher, who was also the dairymaster, droned on, Mal sat, head bowed, according to the prison rules. It was an offence for any of these hardened felons to raise their heads in the house of God, punishable with the lash. He listened to the voice but not the message, trying to concentrate on how the hell he could go about making a raft, trying not to think of Emilie in this rare hour of quiet. Mal reckoned she must have given up on him by this. And why wouldn't she? The odds were heavily stacked against him now.

Emilie hadn't forgotten him; she just didn't mention him to Ruth any more, but on Monday morning she had another call to make, to the second legal gentleman recommended by Mr Kemp.

Her sister was in a cheerful mood as they dressed for breakfast this Saturday morning, even offering to lend Emilie her best summer straw hat, now relined with green to offset the glare of the sun.

'We should have an enjoyable day,' she said. 'And when we return from Eagle Farm, we may be able to take you for that tour of Parliament House. I want you to learn more about this town and what it has to offer. You don't belong in that dreadful place . . .'

'There's the bell,' Emilie said, glad of the interruption. 'Have you seen my gloves?'

'In the top drawer.'

Someone was hammering on their door.

'Who on earth is that?' Ruth asked, affronted by the clamour, but as she opened the door, Daniel pushed past her, barging right into their room.

From the dresser, Emilie stared, amazed, but Ruth was shocked.

288

'Really, Daniel! This is our bedroom!'

He ignored her, confronting Emilie. 'Who are you? What sort of company do you keep?'

'You shouldn't be in here,' Ruth was saying. 'Daniel, please, keep your voice down. What will people think?'

'Think?' he screeched, his face white with rage. 'They're already doing their thinking. She's already disgraced.' He hurled the morning newspaper at her. 'Have you seen this?'

'Seen what?' Ruth picked up the paper and stared at the front page, which spoke of more gold strikes in the north and plans for tramways in Brisbane. 'I don't see . . .'

'Look at the third page,' he gritted.

Ruth was all thumbs as she tried to unfold the pages. He grabbed the paper from her, slammed it on the bed and jabbed at an item with a thin finger that almost tore the page.

'What is it?' Ruth asked, then began to read out a heading: ' "Sonny's lady love comes to town." Sonny who, Daniel? For heaven's sake . . .'

'Willoughby. The outlaw,' he snapped, glaring at Emilie, who backed towards the window, shocked. Praying. Hoping against hope that her name wouldn't be mentioned . . .

Ruth read it swiftly. She reread it, shaking her head. 'A Miss Tissington, who says Sonny Willoughby is innocent . . . who is believed to have received a visit from Sonny right under the noses of the police.' She turned on Emilie. 'What have you done? You stupid girl. You promised me you'd put all this dreadful business out of your mind.'

'I didn't promise.'

Daniel now rounded on Ruth. 'You knew about this? You knew the sort of people she associates with?'

'No. I mean, I told her I didn't want to hear about such things. Daniel, I tried to stop her.'

'Why didn't you tell me? I'd have sent her packing. The man is a criminal. A murderer. And your name is associated with him. Your name! My fiancée.'

'Not my name . . .'

'Oh, I see. Now I have to rush off to my friends and God knows who else and explain that it isn't my Miss Tissington, it's another Miss Tissington. Do you think people will differentiate? They won't, you know. What have you done to me? She's your sister. Her name is in the paper! Don't think we're going anywhere today. I won't be seen with her.'

When he had slammed out, Ruth continued the tirade, and Emilie could only cringe before the onslaught. She was as shocked as they were. How could Mr Kemp do this to her? He had seemed such a nice man, and she'd trusted him. Now her name was in the paper. Ladies of their background did not have their names in a paper, any paper. The wound was deep. Drained of words, Ruth ended up in tears and Emilie wept quietly in the other corner.

Neither of them made any move to go down to breakfast. They simply didn't know what to do next. Both were too humiliated to show their faces.

Hours later, Emilie couldn't stand the room any longer. She mopped her face with cold water, patting away the redness of weeping.

'We can't stay in here for the rest of our lives. Would you like to go for a walk? We could buy some tea and cake somewhere.'

Ruth reacted viciously. 'I won't go anywhere with you. I don't want to be seen with you. The sooner you leave here, the better.'

'I'm so sorry, Ruth. I had no idea this would happen. I only went to see Superintendent Kemp because you wouldn't let me ask Mr Bowles for the name of a solicitor.'

'I see. Now I'm to blame.'

'No. Mr Kemp used to stay here, with his wife. He's a policeman, very high up. Superintendent of Police . . .'

'You went to the police? First it's criminals, now it's police. And the newspapers. I have never been so ashamed. And poor Daniel. It's horrible for me, but Daniel, in his position . . . He's innocent of any knowledge of all this, and now he'll be lumped with you. He must be devastated.'

'Oh, damn Daniel. I never trusted him anyway.'

'You watch your language, and don't you dare criticise him. You're in no position to criticise anyone. Daniel is a good man, trying to do the best for us . . .'

'The hell he is,' Emilie slammed back. She had learned a lot of words from her friends Kate and Nellie, and a few of the same from the Manningtrees. 'If you ask me, he's a bloody swindler. He wants your money to put a house on my block. A house he can call his own. What is he putting up? Nothing, as far as I can see.'

Ruth sprang to her feet. 'Get out!' she shrilled. 'Get out and take your common talk with you. And don't come back until you're ready to apologise.'

'I've already said I'm sorry, Ruth. I wouldn't have hurt you for the world. I had no idea this would happen.'

'Get out.'

Mrs Medlow must have been loitering, waiting for her. As soon as Emilie came down the hall she pounced.

'Could I have a word with you, Miss Tissington?'

Emilie's heart sank. More trouble. She allowed herself to be ushered into the landlady's sitting room only because she couldn't think of a truthful excuse to be on her way.

But it wasn't so bad, after all. Mrs Medlow had a twinkle in her eye when she informed Emilie she'd read the paper.

'I'm sorry about that,' Emilie began. 'I had no idea I should be of any interest to anyone. I don't know why they had to put me in the paper.'

'But you are of interest, my dear. You know Sonny Willoughby. Is it true? Do you really know him?'

Emilie blinked. 'Why . . . yes.'

'How exciting! My friends and I are all agog. You're a celebrity. But tell me, dear, what's he really like? I have his photograph here somewhere. I cut it out of the paper. He's so handsome. Now sit down here, and do tell. I'm dying to hear all about him. The papers say he's very gallant.'

To her surprise, Emilie burst into tears.

Mrs Medlow was up to the occasion, though. This was the most delicious gossip that she ever encountered, right here under her very own roof, and she wanted to hear everything. Knowing that the Misses Tissingtons had missed breakfast, she had a maid bring in tea and scones while she commiserated with the girl, learned she could call her Emilie, dried her tears and held her hand while, triumphant, she heard first-hand about a nice young man called Mal Willoughby who was gentle and kind, and innocent. The real story about the famous outlaw. All incredibly thrilling.

News travels fast. Even up and down the streets of a wild and woolly town like Maryborough, where disorder grew commensurate with the swift expansion of the river port, where nationalities collided and rustics clashed with tough seamen and port workers. Nights brought gaiety and a temporary truce until the fights started, and that gave Walt White plenty of copy for local news and more swipes at incompetent police. The story about the governess, though, was different, a change from violence, a new aspect on the Willoughby tale and, best of all, proof positive that the local police couldn't find a rat in a cage. He loved it. He hummed as he wrote it and did a little jig as he saw it planted front page in his *Chronicle*, not buried a few pages over as the *Courier* had done. This brought the story home to his readers again. Home to Maryborough. He didn't have to change much of the text sent to him by Jesse Fields, only a few lines here and there. Where Jesse had reported that Sonny had visited Miss Tissington, Walt rearranged it to read that Miss Tissington had entertained the outlaw. It meant much the same thing, he reckoned, but sounded better.

'By Jove,' he murmured. 'The governess, eh? You never know about those quiet ones.'

Mrs Mooney read it and shook her head. 'For cryin' out loud. Emilie's his lady love? I don't believe a word of it. And entertaining Willoughby while he was on the run? Stuff and nonsense. You'd think Walt could find some real news to write about, what with the fire at Barney's stables last night that nearly took half the street.'

No one on her staff would disagree with Mrs Mooney, but when she was out of earshot the gossip flew. It was in the paper. It had to be true.

Clive read it. He too shook his head. 'Good God, Emilie. What have you done now? Who have you been talking to down there?'

He lit a cheroot and studied the page again. He wasn't concerned by the claim that she was Mal's lady love. That was only paper talk. And that bit about her entertaining him didn't ring true either. But the article did say she was in Brisbane to help him. Now that did sound like Emilie, the silly girl. How she was supposed to help him wasn't stated. Clive wondered why that sister of hers had allowed her to talk to the press. Still, he mused, if she's as naive as Emilie . . .

The desk clerk stuck his head round the door. 'You've seen the paper, Clive? Looks like you've got competition there. And none other than Sonny Willoughby.'

'He's a friend of hers and a friend of mine. And I want those invoices tallied and on my desk in five minutes!'

Clive drew on the cheroot and stared out of the window at a sailing ship heading into the wide reach of the river. He wished he had gone with Emilie to Brisbane. Had he not lost his head for a few days over Fleur, he might have been able to invite himself to join her, but she'd been touchy and distant. He wondered if she'd had some mad plan all along to help Mal, as well as to visit the sister. Maybe she was considering finding legal representation for him, but Mal wasn't stupid. He would have thought of that. If he had any money. A barrister would be needed in his case and they didn't come cheap. Clive had heard they could charge up to two pounds a day.

He missed Emilie. He hadn't realised how much he would miss her and her sweet little ways. It had taken time for him to find the real Emilie under that prim and proper exterior. The woman, warm and caring. And too damn loyal for her own good.

One of these days he'd have to ask her just how she felt about Mal Willoughby.

Mal had had this giant crush on her, from a distance. But they'd never seen much of each other. Or had they? Now he was confused. Had they really met in Maryborough somewhere? Had Mal turned up at the cottage?

Even if he had, Clive knew Emilie. Knowing Mal was on the run, she wouldn't have told a soul.

'Not even me,' he murmured unhappily.

All supposition, though. He preferred not to guess at the relationship between them; it would be up to Emilie to tell him, once and for all, because it only stirred up the jealous feelings he'd had about Mal. About them. And they depressed him. So did this damn paper. He wished Pollock was in town so that he could find out what was really going on, not Walt's garbled tale.

This week, though, he'd had satisfactory talks with his bank manager regarding a loan to open a quality apparel store and it looked as if he could be in business very soon. Some new shops were under construction and leases would be available. If he could obtain approval and get the papers signed, he could go to Brisbane himself to start buying stock and, of primary importance, find Emilie at her boarding house to see what she was up to. It would have to be this week, though, otherwise she'd be back.

Maybe it would be better to just wait. He might miss her.

'Dammit!' he said, stubbing out the cheroot. 'Why couldn't she have talked to me first? And damn Mal and his troubles.'

★ ★ ★

In the kitchen, Kate and Nellie were working feverishly, keeping their heads down, because the missus was on the warpath. This very day she was having a luncheon party for her lady friends, including the Lady Mayoress, as she called her, and everything had to be more than perfect.

'Emilie said that's not right,' Kate whispered. 'She says she's just a Mayoress because her old man isn't a Lord Mayor.'

'Emilie'd know,' Nellie grinned.

But just then, Mrs Manningtree came storming into the kitchen, waving a newspaper about, screaming at Kate.

'Did you know about this? I swear if you did you're out of here at the end of the week. Out!'

'Beg your pardon, missus?'

'This! This! That wretch of a girl. The governess. She's been consorting with criminals right under my nose. In my own house! And today of all days!'

'What happened today?' Kate asked nervously.

'That's what happened!' She threw down the paper. 'Look at that. On the front page.'

Kate wiped her hands on her apron and scanned the page. 'Oh my Gawd!'

'Did you know about this? I want the truth.'

'No, madam. I don't know nothin' about it.'

Nellie was peering over her shoulder. 'Me neither.'

Their mistress was ropable. 'That damned little hypocrite. I always said she was too bloody good to be true. Sneaking about behind my back to meet that outlaw. That murderer. We could all have been murdered in our beds. Well, she's finished, I can tell you that. No wonder she went off to live down there in that cottage. A perfect little love nest, while she's up here preaching at my kids. She probably had that fiend living there with her all the time. God knows what I'm going to tell the ladies. Have you got the ducks on yet?'

'Yes, madam. They'll be ready right on time.'

'And the orange sauce?'

'Yes, it's ready.'

'See that it is. I want the ducks properly carved so that Nellie can serve. At least my menu will be up to standard, but I warn you, I never want that person's name mentioned in my house ever again. I knew something was odd about her right from the word go. But would my husband listen? Oh no. Sweet little thing, he said. Now he'll find out what sort of a sweet little thing we've had under our very roof. The cheek of her! The bloody little wretch.'

The missus stormed out and Kate turned to Nellie:

'Gawd! What a bloody carry-on!'

On the Sunday morning Mr Bowles paid his rent and informed Mrs Medlow that he was leaving the Belleview.

293

Guessing the reason, she was in no mood to accommodate him. 'I require notice for permanents,' she said. 'One week or the equivalent in rent.'

'I'll give you two days.'

She couldn't argue much about that, taking the extra. 'May I have your forwarding address for mail?'

'I'll call for it. Have my bags brought down.'

She wondered if his fiancée knew he was leaving. Miss Ruth was a standoffish person – it was the English in her, Mrs Medlow had finally allowed – but she was a good woman, and an excellent guest, paying exactly to the minute and never causing any bother. And dear little Emilie was a sweetie, so innocent, standing up for Sonny Willoughby. She had no idea, still, what a ruckus she'd caused.

As far as Mrs Medlow was concerned, Mr Bowles, with his smelly socks and dirty sheets, was no loss, even if he did have some high-falutin' job. The right type of women were always better guests, cleaner; gents without their mothers could be quite disgusting.

Miss Ruth was upset, that was plain to see, with Emilie taking meals in to her, so Mrs Medlow kept an eye out. When she did meet Emilie by the stairs, she beckoned her over.

'Did you know Mr Bowles has left?'

Emilie shook her head. 'Oh, no!'

That was how Mrs Medlow knew for sure that the fiancée had not been informed.

'Better off without him,' she told a friend. 'I never did like him. A toady if ever I saw one.'

Emilie broke it to Ruth gently, but Ruth wasn't surprised. 'It's very sensible of him. He doesn't need to be associated with scandal. Not in his position. And your presence here, in my room, would have caused him acute embarrassment. How could he possibly explain to me with you sitting there? You ask too much of people, Emilie, that's your trouble.'

The solicitor, Robert Lanfield, was a formidable man, with a shock of white hair, puffy sideburns and keen green eyes which bored in on her so intently that Emilie felt constrained in her chair. His voice was clipped, almost curt, with the result that her own voice was reduced to a whisper as she outlined her story.

'Speak up, miss. Are you a relative of this Mr Willoughby?'

She clutched her purse. It contained all that money, hidden in a deep pocket, and she hadn't let it out of her sight since she left Maryborough.

'No, sir. Just a friend.'

'Well, your friend seems to have got himself into a heap of trouble. You want me to represent him?'

'Yes, sir. He is innocent.'

Lanfield let that pass. 'If I take the case, I shall have to instruct a barrister. You understand that?'

She nodded, not caring what he did as long as he took the case. As long as he rescued Mal.

'And you're acting under instructions from Mr Willoughby, I presume?'

'No, sir. He doesn't know I'm here. I thought you could go to see him.'

'He's in the St Helena prison. I'm a busy man, Miss Tissington. A visit to the island would take me all day.'

Emilie was bewildered. 'How else could you see him? You must talk to him, Mr Lanfield. If you do you'll realise that he is innocent and all of this is dreadfully unfair. He shouldn't be in prison at all.'

He sighed. 'Very well, very well. But I can't go dashing off there until I ascertain that the fellow is willing to accept my services . . .'

Suddenly Emilie felt better, as if she'd found someone at last to share the burden. 'Mr Lanfield, he will, I know he will. I'm so grateful to you. I can't tell you what a relief this is. I've been so worried . . .'

'Let us wait and see. I shall write to Mr Willoughby via the office of the Superintendent of the prison and require a response in the affirmative before anything more can be done. I shall let you know in due course.'

'Thank you, Mr Lanfield. I was wondering, though, how long that will take, because I have to return to Maryborough at the end of the week.'

He sat back. 'Let me see. My clerk could find out about transport arrangements to the island, which are at best uncertain. He may be able to send a courier to hand-deliver my letter and bring the reply back the same day. It depends. But he'll do his best. That's all I can say for now. He will advise you at earliest.'

Despite his abrupt manner, the solicitor stood and ushered her to the door with a polite 'Good day to you, Miss Tissington.'

Emilie thanked him again and passed into the outer office, where the clerk sat, head buried in papers. She hesitated before him, wondering if she should offer some payment, but he looked up, nodded to her and went back to his own affairs, so she tiptoed out, glad to escape the sombre surrounds.

With nothing else to do and the strain of the interview over, she wandered back to the boarding house, only to find a strange gentleman lurking on the porch.

Before she had time to think, he called out to her: 'Look this way, Miss Tissington.'

Horrified, she found herself staring at a camera. There was a snap and a puff and he popped his head up. 'Thank you, miss.'

'What are you doing?' she cried. 'What is this?'

He gathered up the camera and its stand. 'Don't worry, love, you look a picture.' Then he was gone, scuttling past her down the steps and out of the gate.

Realising what had happened, she rushed through to her room and shut the door. 'Oh, dear God. Surely they won't put my photograph in the paper? It's so stupid. And pointless.'

She sat miserably on the edge of the bed, worrying about Ruth's reaction. Petrified at the thought of the row a photograph would cause.

She hoped Ruth wouldn't have to face problems over this at her college. Her sister seemed to think she would. Emilie worried too about Ruth's remark that she asked too much of people. Surely not? She'd only sought legal help for Mal. That was not meant to become public knowledge.

Later in the day, though, Emilie faced a worse blow.

Mrs Manningtree had dispensed with her services, due to her 'unsavoury background'. The telegram was sharp and cold.

'Bad news?' Mrs Medlow asked as she handed it over.

'No.' Emilie managed a smile. 'Just a request from a friend.'

'Did you see a solicitor?'

'Yes. It's out of my hands now, which is a relief.'

'That's good, dear.'

Emilie fled. She walked round the block to try to shake off the shock of being fired, relieved that she had a return ticket to Maryborough. At least she wouldn't be paying rent in the cottage. But what then? She shrugged, fed up with all this worry. She'd just have to find another job up there.

Doing what? Emilie had no idea.

When Ruth came in, she didn't mention the telegram.

'Is everything all right at the college?'

'You mean because of your behaviour, Emilie? I was asked if I was the Miss Tissington mentioned in the newspaper and was able to reply: "Certainly not." Nothing else was said. I hope that will be the end of it. But I would like to know how much longer you'll be staying.'

'Until next Sunday.' That was her original plan anyway, she mused, so she might as well stick to it, as long as Mr Lanfield was prepared to defend Mal. She had asked him, as she explained the charges against Mal, if it would be possible for her to visit Mr Willoughby, but the solicitor had been very certain about that.

'Definitely not. Visitors are not permitted. And it is no place for young ladies anyway.'

'Hey, Willoughby, the boss wants you. Get up here.'

Mal climbed out of the lime pit, wiping his hands on his rough cotton shirt. 'What's up?'

'Maybe he's going to invite you to dinner. How do I bloody know?'

The guard trotted behind him as he passed the row of cell blocks and headed for the administration office. Mal hated being herded about like this. You were never alone here, unless you got the other extreme, solitary. He yearned for the solitude of the bush, for its fresh, clean smell. As they passed a water pump, he suddenly thought this visit might not be trouble; it could be Pollock again.

'Can I have a wash first?' he asked, suddenly shamed, knowing he must stink, but the guard shoved him on. The Superintendent could not be kept waiting.

Croft was sitting outside the building enjoying the warmth of the sun, newspapers strewn on a nearby table. No sign of a visitor.

He looked up. 'Ah, Willoughby. You have been offered legal representation by Mr Robert Lanfield. He asks if you accept his services.'

'How come?'

'Answer the question,' Croft drawled.

'Yes. I suppose so, sir. But who is he?'

'Mr Lanfield is a gentleman of high repute. Well known to me, in fact.
You are fortunate to have him take an interest in you, so I wouldn't be
supposing in your boots, I'd be accepting with some grace.'

'Yes, sir, I understand, but I'm wondering how this came about.'

Croft laughed and showed him a page of the *Brisbane Courier*. He
inclined his head towards a photograph. 'Do you know that girl?'

Mal stared. It was Emilie. 'What's this?'

But the caption was clear. *Sonny Willoughby's lady love.* He flushed,
embarrassed for her. In the photograph she looked startled.

'Well?'

'Yes, sir. She is a friend of mine.'

'A governess, it is said.'

'Yes, sir.'

'There you are then. Your governess has engaged Mr Lanfield on your
behalf. You may go.'

'Excuse me, sir, what happens now?'

'You await Mr Lanfield's pleasure. Other prisoners have court cases
pending, but few have the luxury of representation. You will be advised of
his arrival, when you will clean yourself up and have a haircut. Dismissed.'

Mal hesitated. 'Do you think I could have that picture?'

'I said, dismissed.'

The guard jerked him away, but Mal shook him off, storming away
under his own volition. Emilie! She was trying to help him. She hadn't
forgotten him after all. But this legal bloke would have to be paid; where
was the money coming from? And what could he do but talk a lot? Mal
had scant knowledge of solicitors and not a lot of faith in them.

That night, though, hope was renewed. If this Lanfield was a good
talker he might just be able to get him off. In which case Mal vowed to
work at any job he could get to repay the gent, to pay every penny of the
bill, whatever it was. On the other hand, if Lanfield failed, he'd be the
loser, like his client. You can't get money out of a dead man.

But Emilie. How brave of her to come forward, to try to help. Mal
knew how shy she was, and what an effort that must have taken, and he
was overwhelmed. No one else in the whole wide world had cared, not
even his sister, who hadn't lifted a finger beyond writing a cautious letter
when he was first arrested. Wishing him luck. Fat lot of good that was.

Mal refused to tell anyone why he had been summoned to the big boss;
he wanted no mention of Emilie in this place. It would besmirch her
name. So the waiting began again.

Baldy Perry was angry. He had thought he was to be released, but here he

297

was in a cold cell underneath the barracks, with no one to talk to.

They'd told him there'd been a mistake, so he could sit out the rest of his term here, but he didn't buy that. Admittedly it was better than hard labour on the island, and the grub was an improvement, but a man had to be suspicious, being brought in hooded, and slipped from the boat into a closed buggy. Something was up and he had a damned good idea what it was. But how had they got on to him? Carnegie? He bet it was Carnegie, to pay him out for not delivering the gold, but Carnegie couldn't say much without incriminating himself, so Baldy figured all he had to do was sit out his time until they had to release him. Then he'd get the gold. All to himself. He would be a rich man and all those clowns on the island would be laughing on the other side of their faces.

It began the next day, the questioning, by Pollock from Maryborough – thereby tipping off Baldy that he'd better watch his step – and a couple of Brisbane coppers.

To throw them off, he grizzled and complained about everything he could think of, and for good measure claimed he'd served his legal term and should be free.

'Where will you go when you are free?' they asked.

Baldy snarled. 'Where will I go? Down to the wharves to get a job so I've got a shilling in me bloody pocket to get some grog.'

They went on and on about Maryborough. Where had he been at the time of the raid? That question was inevitable, and he was ready for it.

'I dunno. I was working there. What sort of a day was it?'

'A Sunday.'

'A bloody Sunday. How would I know? I wouldn't have been at work. I was probably sleeping off the booze. Then I'd have gone back to the pub.'

He was glad it had been a Sunday. There could be some old rosters about to prove him absent on a working day.

'Do you like fishing?'

'Me? No. Bloody waste of good drinking time.'

'You ever owned a boat? A dinghy?'

'What would I do with a boat?'

'Take it out on the river.'

Frightening memories came back at a convenient time. 'On that bloody river? With all them crocs? Turn it up.'

'Do you know a Mr Carnegie?'

'The one what got shot in the raid? No. I read about him, but . . .'

'You ever been to the Gympie goldfields?'

'Yeah. Me and the rest of the world. Did no good. Came into Maryborough for a job that got paid.'

'Do you know Mal Willoughby?'

'Yes. Met him at the prison. He'll swing for that raid.'

'You didn't know him before?'

'Yes. Now I come to think of it. Met him with McPherson here in Brisbane.'

'He was with McPherson?'

'No, I was. Jimmy's a mate of mine. Willoughby got into a blue with McPherson over a horse. Said his name was Ned Turner then.'

'Why would he do that?'

'Born liar, I suppose. He's a cagey character, that Willoughby. Guilty as sin if you ask me.'

As the questioning became more intense, the impatient police beat Perry unmercifully, achieving little but his curses.

Two days later Pollock joined the two Brisbane police officers in a meeting with Kemp. Inspector Greaves was all for sending Perry back to the island to serve his last weeks.

'He's a bad lot, no doubt of that. This is his third sentence for violent assault, but he *has* to be clear of that holdup. We didn't get a thing out of him. Just because he was in the town at that time doesn't fit him with the raid. There were more than a dozen known criminals in the area around then. We just haven't got the right one.'

'Yes we have,' Pollock insisted. 'I'm convinced we have. He had his answers all right, but I'm more interested in what he didn't say.'

'Like what?'

'The man's a whinger. He whinged about everything, but not once did he whinge about being *interrogated*. Not a peep out of him, because he caught the drift as soon as he saw me. He knew what we were on about; he just kept answering, smirking, until he collected a few punches. When we did mention the raid, his answers were all too trim, too smart . . .'

Greaves interrupted. 'We can't charge a man on what he didn't say.'

'But it was there, don't you see? It was there. He had the day off on the Sunday. He could have bought that boat and ditched it after the raid. He could have had a horse waiting the other side of the river to bring him back to town. I still say it's in his attitude, in his failure to resent the implications . . .'

Kemp sighed, turning over the pages of the file. 'You're beginning to sound like Willoughby.'

The Sergeant leaned back in his chair and nodded. 'So I am, come to think of it. So I am. But Willoughby smelled a rat, and so do I. The more I think about Willoughby, the more I'm convinced that he's being railroaded here.'

'Now you're trying to tell us Willoughby's just a farm boy. That bloke is known to every showie and fair folk across half the country; he's a confidence man . . .'

'And they say he was a sharpshooter,' the other officer added.

'No he wasn't,' Pollock said wearily. 'I checked that with some of the agricultural show folk who ran sideshows. They laughed. They said Sonny couldn't shoot a target from two feet. It was a trick to get the punters in. They gave him a prize that he took round the back and returned; meanwhile the punters were encouraged to step up and have a go. But listen here . . . Baldy was a good shot. That *has* been established.'

299

Kemp intervened. 'I haven't got time for this. Keep Perry at the barracks and keep at him. Change the tune. Tell him you've got him and he's going to be charged. Can't do any harm.'

'What about Carnegie?' Pollock asked. 'What if I go and see him and tell him we've got Perry in custody?'

'And he'll say "So what?",' Kemp retorted. 'Leave him be.'

'One other thing,' Pollock said. 'Could you ask the prosecution to delay moving on Willoughby until we've got Perry sorted out. Right or wrong, he couldn't have done it on his own. Even Carnegie bears this out . . .'

Kemp nodded. 'Fair enough. They've got plenty to do right now and Willoughby isn't going anyplace. But don't try their patience, Sergeant.'

That didn't work either. Perry continued to smirk. 'You've got nothin' on me or you would have charged me. I can give you the names of a dozen out-and-out felons who were hanging round Maryborough back then but you have to pick on me. Well, I can tell you, you're barkin' up the wrong tree. I didn't have nothin' to do with it, so you can stick your questions up your bums. I'm entitled to a proper prison with yard time; you've got no right to keep me penned up in here. I want to see your boss.'

The following days were the worst Emilie had ever experienced. Her photograph was in the paper and Ruth was so shocked she was bilious all night, with her sister trying desperately to comfort her. Some people in the boarding house snubbed Emilie; others were anxious to make her acquaintance. With all this unwanted attention, and Ruth's attitude a constant rebuke, she was fast losing confidence and finding it difficult to think what to do next. She wrote to Mrs Manningtree, regretting that any of her actions had caused discomfort to the family, but firmly rejecting any wrongdoing on her part.

Then she wrote to Clive, a rather confused letter, too dismal to post, tore it up and instead sent a short note advising him that she had postponed her return for a while. It had suddenly come to her with a thud that she would be going back to a town where everyone would know she'd been dismissed, and her face reddened at the thought. Mention must have been made of her in the local newspaper too! Humiliation upon humiliation.

She shook her head; she just wasn't up to facing people yet. Not even Clive, who would understand. But would he? What if he, too, had read that she was Mal's lady love? Was this too much to ask of him? She wanted to write to Mal, to tell him she was doing her best, but she had no idea of the address, and dared not ask. She hated the thought of addressing an envelope to St Helena prison, sure that someone in authority would read it and maybe the contents might be made public. Anxiety had her thoroughly shaken, until Mr Lanfield's clerk brought a message to inform her that Mr Willoughby had accepted his services and the solicitor would visit the accused at the earliest opportunity.

That helped. Emilie went to the shipping office to cancel her return ticket, and as she made her way back passed another boarding house, in Charlotte Street. It seemed quite pleasant, so, without further ado, she marched in and took a room. The situation with Ruth had become intolerable. They couldn't even converse without an argument.

Mrs Medlow was sorry to see her go, but Ruth was not. In fact she was relieved.

'I don't know what you're thinking of, not returning to Maryborough, but you seem intent on your own business, whatever it is, and I prefer not to know about it. I hope your employers approve of this extended holiday.'

'Really? Last I heard you wanted me to leave there and find a situation in Brisbane.'

'Don't be smart with me, Emilie. You know perfectly well, or you should do, if you have an ounce of sense left in you, that no respectable employer in this town would even consider an application from you. And I can't afford to support you.'

Emilie knew she was right, and that there'd be no reference from Mrs Manningtree, but she was tired of all this blame.

'That reminds me, Ruth. Has Mr Bowles given you the title deed to my land? I would like it.'

Ruth bridled. 'I haven't seen him.'

'What about the money for your land? You signed the contract a week ago.'

'That's my business. Mr Bowles will give it to me in due time.'

'Of course. But when you do see him, please tell him I should like the deeds before I go back.'

She finished packing. 'I don't want to be on bad terms with you, Ruth. I'll only be a block away. I shall call to see you of an evening, after dinner. Everything will work out. You'll see.'

'I hope so,' Ruth allowed, but she did not accompany Emilie to the front door.

Chapter Thirteen

Robert Lanfield had visited the island to interview clients before this, and he was also on the board of the State Prison Authority. He thought it was a great pity that such a pretty little island should house an ugly prison, but these things happened, and violent criminals needed to be kept in secure surrounds.

His clerk had provided him with enough information to be able to acquaint himself with Willoughby's case, and the charges laid against him, before he met the prisoner, so he was well prepared to hear the fellow out with an open mind. Depending on Willoughby's attitude he could still decline to take the case, but it was important. Three murders and a missing gold consignment rated nationwide publicity, and he already knew a Queen's Counsel who was keen to be involved.

The police case against this fellow was weak, in the absence of accomplices, so he would be pleased to see the case brought forward as soon as possible, though he had heard the prosecution thought otherwise. He smiled. He didn't blame them, but it was a bonus for him. And the prisoner, of course.

Superintendent Croft provided him with morning tea and then offered to take him on a tour of the prison, but Lanfield pointed out, politely, that he was wearing his legal hat on this visit and so could not accept. He asked about the prisoner, interested to hear that he was a bold fellow, showing no remorse at all for his actions, but was not causing any trouble at present.

'We see to that,' Croft said, and Lanfield nodded as if in agreement. Already judged and sentenced, he mused. The fellow was on remand and shouldn't even be here, but since he'd already escaped custody and led the police a merry chase for months, he doubted he could have him brought back to the Brisbane jail. Worth a try, though. Make life easier for me, he decided.

He wasn't impressed with the prisoner, though he was a handsome young fellow, despite the shaved head, with clear tanned skin and honest blue eyes. None of that cut any ice with Robert Lanfield. In his thirty years of legal practice he'd met too many rogues whose looks were their stock-in-trade, whose smiles would melt butter. Nor was he taken in by Willoughby's courteous manner. That too could be a façade. He wanted to find out who really lurked behind the eager grin.

302

Nevertheless, for a jury, appearances mattered. Lanfield made a mental note to ask Croft to allow the fellow to grow his hair.

Usually, prisoners on remand asked that their handcuffs be removed, but Willoughby either did not know about that right, or did not care. As soon as Lanfield announced himself and allowed his client to sit, Willoughby wanted to know about Miss Tissington. How she was and how their association had come about.

Lanfield explained briefly but Willoughby wasn't satisfied. 'If you don't mind, sir, I need to know about the money. Surely you don't expect her to pay you?'

Lanfield sighed. 'The lady volunteered to meet costs, several days ago, according to my clerk.'

'But that's not right. She can't afford this.'

'Then it is up to you.'

'But I don't have any money. Can I owe you?'

'Mr Willoughby, you can owe the lady. Now may we get on? I need to know all about you, and in particular every detail of your involvement in that raid.'

'I wasn't involved. I was not there.'

The solicitor nodded. That was a good start. He had deliberately used the word involved to see the reaction. He had learned to listen to thought processes behind the spoken word.

'Like it or not, Mr Willoughby, you are involved in the matter and it is my duty to see that you become uninvolved. Now where were you born?'

'What does that matter?'

'Bear with me.'

It was said of Lanfield that he was a hard, insensitive man, but had it been put to him, he would have argued that he simply lacked sentimentality. He regarded sentiment as womanish, something that had no place in the law, unless to be used as a last resort when appealing to a jury. So he was impassive as he heard of this fellow's upbringing, which he regarded as no worse than many a child of impoverished parents, but Willoughby seemed impassive too. It could be interesting to shake him up a bit.

'You disliked your father?'

'No.'

'But he was a drunk! Rather unfair on you at that age.'

'In what way?'

Lanfield's eyes glazed. Obviously the fellow knew no better. He moved on. 'It has been said you were a thief.'

'I suppose so, if you put it like that. But I didn't see any harm in it, a few things here and there like a watch or a wallet or something when I was down on my luck.'

'And you expect me to condone that?'

'Why would you? Come to think of it, I got robbed plenty of times myself.'

'As a result of the company you keep.'

303

'Probably.'

'It is an established fact that petty crimes lead to worse crimes.'

'Yeah.'

'Well. It could be said to be true in your case.'

'No. I never had the heart for it.'

They moved on to the Gympie goldfields, and to his surprise Lanfield learned that the accused and his partner had each earned about four hundred pounds on the diggings.

'I was flush,' Willoughby said. 'It was more money than I'd ever had in my life. Why would I want to rob anyone? That's why I took the job. I got robbed myself on the track north. I figured those roads weren't safe for a lone man with a fortune in his pocket. I reckoned I was on to a good thing going into Maryborough with the gold escort. And being paid.'

'But the next day you were arrested. What did you do with the money?'

For the first time the cool blue eyes wavered. The sudden shift was not missed by his interrogator.

'I chucked it away. Why give it to the police? If they'd caught me they'd have pocketed it.'

He was lying, but Lanfield let it rest. 'Tell me about this man Carnegie.'

In fact, Lanfield knew Carnegie socially, and had little time for him, but his opinion was of no consequence here. He bent over his notes as Willoughby responded, at length.

'You say you think Mr Carnegie inveigled you into this situation and then identified you as one of the outlaws to cover his participation in the holdup?'

'It seems like it to me.'

'Rather unlikely also. Mr Carnegie was the Gold Commissioner, a man of good reputation. It seems to come down to your word against his.'

'And I'm a nobody?'

'Exactly. You'll have to do better than that, Mr Willoughby. What was your arrangement with Miss Tissington?'

'What arrangement?'

'You called on her after you escaped.'

'I didn't call on her, I waited at the gate. Why did she have to mention any of this? She should have stayed clear.'

'Because she is concerned about you.'

'But why did she talk to the papers?'

'Apparently she didn't. She was simply enquiring of a friend of hers, Kemp, Superintendent of Police, about the name of a reliable legal representative. Her enquiry led her to me. It appears that someone in the police station leaked that information to the press.'

'Is she upset about that?'

'I believe so. But I need to know about this arrangement with her.'

'What bloody arrangement?'

'Put it this way. You are accused of robbing the gold coach. You escape custody. You take a serious risk in calling on a lady friend right in the town of Maryborough with police at your heels. One might ask, did you give her the gold? For safe keeping.'

Willoughby erupted. The chair went flying as he leapt to his feet and slammed his manacled fists on the desk. 'Don't say that! Don't even bloody think it! She's worth ten of you and ten of me, you bastard. She wouldn't consider such a thing . . .'

Hearing the commotion, two guards shoved clumsily through the door, diving at Willoughby, but his solicitor was calm.

'It's all right. Leave him be. You may go.'

When the room was quiet again, with Willoughby standing by the tiny barred window, Lanfield spoke.

'That was only supposition, Mr Willoughby. The sort of supposition that the prosecution might come up with, so you have to be prepared.'

'No I don't. I won't have this. I only called on her to apologise, to tell her I was in trouble, that I couldn't meet her. Oh, Jesus Christ. What have I done to her? Forget all this, plead me guilty.'

'That would only make it worse. The gold is still missing. Now settle down.'

Willoughby's reaction was a breakthrough. He had been entirely too cheerful, answering questions in that boyish way that had served him well over the years, that had made him a likeable person. It wasn't a façade, it was the way he'd learned to survive those years dealing with a drunken parent, no home and, by and large, no visible means of support. But it was not good enough. Prosecution could just as easily tear down the face of innocence and reveal an insecure and possibly violent man.

Lanfield asked him that question. 'Are you violent?'

'No.'

'You've never had to defend yourself in perhaps a dangerous situation?'

'Sometimes.'

'How? With a gun?'

'No. I never carry a gun.'

'With your fist then?'

'No. With a stockwhip.'

'I see. And you're a good hand with a stockwhip?'

'Yes.' The voice was sullen. Noncommittal. Lanfield read enough into that. He'd seen the damage that could be inflicted by men expert in the management of those long, snaking whips. This fellow was by no means the gentle character that he saw himself as being. It was quite intriguing.

'Tell me about this man, Baldy Perry.'

'You won't get it any more than Sergeant Pollock did. It was more in what he didn't say, that's what counted.'

Lanfield felt his man needed encouragement now. 'You might be surprised to know that it interests me a great deal. You behave as if you've had a fairytale life; even your association with this young lady doesn't appear to have any basis beyond a couple of casual meetings . . .'

'That's true,' Willoughby flung back.

'You accept without question Carnegie's instruction to leave the camp and go to town . . .'

'The others did too.'

'You disappear on Pollock for an hour that Sunday morning without giving any reason, before you take the police out to meet the escort . . .'

'How was I to know there was a raid on?'

'But suddenly you began to listen to the prisoner Perry. It appears to me, Mr Willoughby, that, for the first time, you started to do some thinking. If only by accident of acquaintance. I shall have to leave now. I suggest you start to take life more seriously. We shall begin with my account. Since Miss Tissington has come forward to underwrite your expenses, I am hereby writing an IOU in which you become indebted to Miss Tissington. Please sign here.'

Willoughby signed. 'I've written a letter to her. Would you take it for me?'

'No. It's against the rules. But I shall pass on your good wishes if you care for me to do so.'

'Thank you, Mr Lanfield.'

Lanfield collected his papers. 'It might be more helpful if you could give some more thought to Mr Perry and Mr Carnegie.' He frowned. 'And to who might have that gold. You were on the goldfields. Can't you think of anyone who could have been in league with Mr Carnegie, since you have him in mind?'

'No.'

'Well, if you do, you may communicate with me by letter, via the good offices of Mr Croft. I bid you good fortune, Mr Willoughby. I shall do my best for you.'

On the return journey, Lanfield mulled over Carnegie. He was a known gambler. If indeed he had been involved, this type of crime was not without precedent, although the previous example had been poorly planned. The reign of the fist and the gun in the northern backblocks was so rife that few of the perpetrators of such crimes were ever apprehended, but Gold Commissioner Griffen had been caught.

Some years back, Griffen, a compulsive gambler, had turned to crime. Escorting more than seven thousand pounds in gold and notes from Rockhampton in the company of two troopers, they'd made camp along the way, where Griffen had shot both men dead while they slept. Griffen later admitted to the murders and the robbery, and was sentenced to death. His story that his men had become lost in the bush and that they must have been set upon hadn't saved him. He eventually led the authorities to the cache he'd hidden in the bush.

A precedent. Lanfield nodded. A crime that another man might consider he could perfect, with an accomplice and more attention to detail. He had no doubt that Kemp and his officers were also aware of the Griffen crime, but that didn't necessarily lead them to Carnegie. There were other gold commissioners and an oversupply of gold escorts in these heady days. North Queensland seemed to be a veritable treasure chest of gold, with no sign as yet of it abating.

Was Carnegie the instigator of this crime?

According to Willoughby, yes. But only by elimination of any other suspect. In truth, he had nothing to go on.

Would Carnegie attempt such a thing on his own?

In Lanfield's opinion, no. Not without engaging the assistance of a criminal element. And this Perry? How to prove association? Willoughby said that Perry had been freed, therefore it was imperative to locate him. Imperative.

Miss Tissington was a nice girl. But foolish to have become mixed up in this business. What were her parents thinking of? As she seated herself neatly before the solicitor, she wore an expression of eager anticipation which he knew would soon vanish. It was unfortunate but necessary. He answered her questions about Willoughby patiently, but put her at ease. Yes, he was well and in good spirits. And he sent his best wishes, but . . .

'How did you come to meet the gentleman, miss?'

Her answer appalled him. They'd not even been introduced! He'd picked her up in the street like some common little type. Lanfield adjusted his glasses and peered at her. 'Did your father know about this?'

She blushed, explaining her circumstances.

'I see. And did your sister approve of this acquaintance?'

'My sister didn't know.'

'Pray tell me, then, why you took a liking to a fellow who was hardly more than a vagrant?'

'Are these questions necessary, Mr Lanfield?'

'Indeed they are.'

She shook her head, discomforted. 'I don't know. He was nice to me. Cheerful. When I met him in the street, in Maryborough, he seemed so delighted to see me again, by chance, he took my breath away. And . . .'

He saw the dampness in her eyes and intervened. 'Now we don't want any tears, do we? We're here to do our duty by Mr Willoughby.'

She gulped. 'I was unhappy. The lady of the house was difficult. I had no friends. I was lonely and he was very kind to me.'

He nodded. 'Ah. Was he your lover?'

'No! That was only the third time I'd seen him, when he came to tell me he was in trouble! Certainly not!'

'When was the fourth?'

'At my house when . . .' She stopped suddenly.

'Go on.'

'During the time he was hiding from the police, Mal did call on me. He was concerned for me.'

'And not about himself?'

'Not really. He didn't stay long. He said he had somewhere to go.'

'And you didn't inform the police on this occasion either?'

307

'No. Mr Lanfield, please, I didn't tell them about that visit at all.'

He clucked. 'Just as well. Do not mention it again. Now, did Mr Willoughby give you anything at all?'

'What do you mean?'

'Did he give you any money? The truth, please.'

She bridled. 'I am being truthful, and I can't see what any of this has to do with his case.'

'A large amount of gold and notes is missing, Miss Tissington. To this point you are the only person, known to the police, whom he encountered after the holdup. He took risks to visit you. You have made it plain that he trusted you not to inform on him, in which case it could be said that he entrusted you with the proceeds of that holdup.'

She stiffened in shock. 'No! Who would say such a thing? No. He didn't steal the money and he didn't give it to me.'

Her tears were inevitable. 'That's a terrible thing to say,' she wept. 'I didn't even realise I was doing the wrong thing in not reporting that Mal had waited for me at the gate after he'd escaped.'

'Come now. You might have been shocked and upset at the time, on hearing of his troubles, as you call his situation, but it must have registered later. You are an educated young lady; you must have known that it was your duty to report to the police. Yet you did no such thing. Now, did he give you anything? Any money, Miss Tissington?'

She was shaking uncontrollably and he poured her a glass of water, which she managed to spill on her skirt. Still weeping, she fumbled in her handbag while he sat quietly, unperturbed, thinking she was searching for another handkerchief, since the one in use was already damp from tears, but instead she dragged out a bundle of notes and dumped them on the desk.

'Here! Take it. This is Mal's money. His own. He earned it on the goldfields. He gave it to me because he said that if he was caught the police would take it from him. He said he'd rather I had it.' She slumped back in the seat, sobbing. 'I was embarrassed. I didn't want to take it but he insisted it was to be mine. It's not stolen money, it's not! I brought it down to pay for his legal defence. To pay you, Mr Lanfield.'

He clasped his hands together, pleased. So Willoughby hadn't chucked it away after all. In fact, it was a sensible move. Maybe there was hope for the fool yet. Nevertheless, he should never have involved this girl. Lanfield was convinced now that he had on his hands a pair of silly goats. She should never have gone near the police, no matter how kind Kemp was, and as for Willoughby, maybe he had been wrongly identified. Or set up, as he said. Lanfield was also inclined to believe that escaping mightn't have been a bad idea given the circumstances. He could claim that Willoughby had good reason to fear his life was in danger in that town at the time. But he should have given himself up to the police somewhere else.

'Did you talk to anyone else about your friendship with Mr Willoughby?'

'Yes. With Mr Clive Hillier. Who is also Mr Willoughby's friend. They were partners on the goldfield.' She looked up defiantly. 'Clive believes Mal is innocent.'

'Does he know about that money? Or that Mr Willoughby visited you while he was on the run?'

'No.'

'That's a relief. He can give evidence as to Mr Willoughby's good character, I presume?'

She nodded, exhausted. 'Yes. May I go now?'

'Of course. You've been very helpful, Miss Tissington. Questions like this can be an ordeal but you've come through very well; there's nothing to worry about. Now, you take your money back. It is yours. Nothing to be ashamed of.' He walked round the desk, picked up the roll of notes and handed them to her.

'If you wish, you may pay my clerk ten pounds, for my services to date. I shall have to brief a barrister, though, and that will cost quite a bit more, so you ought to be prepared.'

He smiled. 'It seems Mr Willoughby has invested in his own defence. He is fortunate to have a friend like you.'

Allyn Carnegie might have felt strong enough to treat the oaf of a policeman from Maryborough with the disdain he merited, but the frock-coated gentleman in his parlour was a different type altogether. As soon as Carnegie had sighted Robert Lanfield stepping down from his gig, he knew it was trouble, and nothing to do with his debts. A solicitor of Lanfield's stature did not venture out of his rooms on errands. He hunched his shoulders and affected a shuffling step as he made his way over to an easy chair.

'The heart, you know, not the best since I was shot, Lanfield. Would you care for tea? Or a brandy, perhaps?'

'No thank you, Mr Carnegie. I'm sorry to hear you're not well. I wanted to talk to you about that business. I have to inform you, in the first instance, that I am acting for Mr Mallachi Willoughby . . .'

'I have nothing to say to you.'

'That is hardly the attitude I expected of you, sir. I imagined that you would be anxious to assist me, since you were the victim of that vicious attack. I realise that it is a horror you do not care to dwell on, but I would appreciate it if you could let me have your account of those events.'

Lanfield's fluffy sideburns did not disguise the hard-set jaw and cold green eyes. He terrified Allyn, who decided it would be better to have him on side than against. After all, he could practically repeat his story by rote now, so he had nothing to lose.

'I am so tired of all this,' he muttered. 'Over and over the same thing. You surely don't expect me to bear witness to the good character of the man you are defending. A murderer. I mean, that's laughable.'

'Not at all, my dear fellow. You misunderstand. I simply need your side of the story, since Willoughby claims he was not present.'

'He can lie until the cows come home. He was there, I can assure you. He came back with them.'

'Them?'

'Whoever his associates were.'

After a preamble, Lanfield managed to hear Carnegie's story, being careful not to interrupt, since it was obvious that the teller of the tale was practised.

'You were wrong about McPherson. Is it possible you were also wrong about Willoughby being there?'

'Definitely not. I knew him. I hired him, God help me.'

'It is said that it was your deputy, Taylor, the gentleman who was shot, who actually hired Mr Willoughby, on your recommendation.'

'That is so.'

Lanfield looked intently over his glasses. 'And yet Mr Taylor was known to be a sharp man. One who was known to be a fairly good judge of character.'

He had come across this little gem in close scrutiny of statements in the police files and newspaper clippings, made by a bevy of enthusiastic Maryborough locals, and found it interesting, since Willoughby was under the impression that Taylor and Carnegie had not been on the best of terms.

But Carnegie drooped, sadly. 'That mistake cost poor Taylor his life.'

'So it seems.' Lanfield suddenly brought the interview to a close. 'I appreciate your co-operation, Mr Carnegie. I had hoped that you might have had second thoughts about my client.'

'How could I? Wounded though I was, there was no mistaking him at all.'

'Of course not. It was kind of you to give me your time. I shall have to prepare the case as best I can for the QC.'

Carnegie blanched. 'What QC?'

'The gentleman you'll meet in court,' Lanfield said sadistically. 'Mr Willoughby will have a QC; I'm only a lowly fellow in the scheme of things. I'll leave you my card, Mr Carnegie. I ask no favours but I see you are a fair man. If there is any chance at all that you might be mistaken as regards Mr Willoughby, do come to me. It's not too late to set the record straight.'

'I have already done so,' Carnegie said nervously.

'So you have. And one good turn deserves another. Have you heard of the Griffen case?'

'Griffen. No. What's that?'

Lanfield almost applauded. That was exactly the reply he needed. There wasn't a Gold Commissioner in existence who did not know of the Griffen case. This man was a liar.

'Oh, just a bit of history,' he murmured. 'Not relevant, I suppose.'

He settled back in his gig and drove down the sharp slopes towards the river and the turnoff back into town.

'Tit for tat,' he said, as if addressing the prosecution. 'You sneak up on my young lady for information, so I sneak up on your gentleman. The court will no doubt give her a bad time, but that will be child's play compared to what my QC will do to your witness.'

Lanfield was even more certain now that Willoughby was innocent. He had no idea who had committed the crime. It was possible that Carnegie was involved, but he was not a detective; it was not his job to detect the real perpetrators of the attack. That was up to the police. His brief was to clear Willoughby.

He followed the river to the quay and sent his gig spinning up Queen Street towards his club, where Allenby QC would be waiting. Allenby liked to win, and this case was not only winnable, it was high stakes in the publicity department. There was a lot of foolish public sentiment riding on Willoughby, thanks to the handsome photographs in the paper and the juvenile name of Sonny that had been attached to him, but the pot had boiled over in his favour when it had been revealed that his own uncle, whom he had trusted, had given him up for the reward. The best thing the uncle could have done for the fellow, as it turned out.

Lanfield couldn't believe his luck that Miss Tissington had walked in through his door. Allenby would take the brief. He'd jump at it. But they ought to have a discussion about the girl. She should be sent back to Maryborough. Out of reach for the time being.

He worried about Miss Tissington. She might make a good character witness, if she didn't pass out on the stand with stage fright. But then Willoughby himself would be an asset. What better time for the fellow to put his winning ways to good use? Lanfield wished ladies were eligible for jury service.

'Oh, for the weekend,' Lanfield sighed. All this dashing about was bad for the liver. He had promised to take his family to their house at Sandgate by the seaside on Saturday morning, on condition that there were to be no hangers-on, his word for guests. He was in no mood for company, old or young. Sometimes he thought the life of a beach-comber could be quite pleasant if one didn't have a wife and three daughters to support. That thought brought him abruptly back to the present.

He had called on Kemp, found him an obliging fellow but a man who held his cards close to his chest. He appeared to have no opinion on either Willoughby or Carnegie, and made no mention of Miss Tissington, which suited Lanfield – he hoped they'd forget about her. But hardly likely. He was then passed on to Sergeant Pollock, who had an axe to grind. He was the fellow who had allowed Willoughby to escape and was still suffering the consequences.

Unlike Kemp, who had steered their conversation on to other matters, the Sergeant was like a dog with a bone. He was determined to solve the case, which Robert thought was admirable, as long as he wasn't able to prove Willoughby's involvement.

However, Pollock made no bones about his suspicion that Carnegie might have planned the raid. An inside job. Which didn't mean, he'd

311

insisted, that Willoughby was off the hook. Allenby would be pleased to hear Pollock's opinion; he wanted his day in court, looking forward to tearing down Carnegie's story, right or wrong.

The good news, though, was that the criminal Perry was still in custody, not lost in the mire of freedom.

'So you believe Willoughby on that?'

'It's possible, that's all.'

'Could I see Perry?'

'Not without Kemp's permission. Not a good idea. We've been interrogating him at length but so far we can't break him.'

'It seems to me, Sergeant, that since you have Perry stowed away somewhere, still under interrogation, it is more than possible for me to see him.'

Pollock relented. 'Look, Mr Lanfield. To be honest, I think Perry's connected. But the other officers down here don't share my opinion, so it's dicey, if you see what I mean. If you start pushing to see him, I might lose him. It's all I can do to keep the pressure on him now.'

'Good. After all, we do have the same aim, Sergeant. The perpetrators of this crime have to be brought to justice. So I should tell you that I sincerely believe Carnegie is a liar.'

'You've talked to him?'

'No law against it.'

'What did he say?'

'Everything you'd expect him to say.'

'What? How? I mean, did he put his foot in it anywhere? I've been racking my brains . . .'

'Let us just say that I heard a lie from him. On the other hand, I have not detected a lie from Willoughby.' Not unless one counted the tale about chucking away his goldfield earnings, he added to himself. 'The prosecution had better watch their step. Willoughby is innocent; he won't be easy prey. What have they got without Carnegie?'

Lanfield believed in the law, which was why he'd demanded of Kemp that Willoughby be removed from the penal settlement and brought to the state prison on the outskirts of town. Kemp had said he'd consider the request.

If he didn't agree, there was always Attorney-General Lilley to turn to, if only on the grounds of access to one's client. Travel to the island was a waste of a full day.

The solicitor frowned and called in his clerk.

Mr Lanfield's clerk called at Emilie's new address to deliver the message that she was free to return to Maryborough.

'What does that mean?' she asked anxiously. 'Mr Lanfield will proceed with the case, won't he?'

'But of course. My gentleman has everything in hand.'

'I thought I should stay in case he needed me.'

'Absolutely not necessary, miss.'

Emilie looked at him keenly. 'Why is it of any interest to Mr Lanfield whether I stay or go?'

The clerk coughed, embarrassed. 'I am simply delivering a message, Miss.'

'No, no you're not. I just know it. Does he want me to go? Am I a nuisance? I wouldn't intrude, believe me.'

Lanfield's clerk was a serious young man who liked to see himself as a budding Lanfield, with the stern jaw and the imposing glance, but he'd read the files, and thought the attachment between the accused and this young lady headily romantic. Far from being an outlaw, Sonny Willoughby was coming over as gallant, and Miss Tissington a true friend. He wished he had a lady friend like her; looking at the sweet girl now, he wished it *was* her.

'Oh, heavens, no, Miss Tissington. You wouldn't intrude.' He glanced over his shoulder, as if to make sure he couldn't be overheard. 'I think it is for the best. You have to trust Mr Lanfield; he's trying to protect you. The courts, you know. They are not nice places to be. You ought to keep your distance, if I may say so.'

In all of this dreadful business, it had never occurred to Emilie that *she* might have to appear in court. She felt faint. Hardly able to whisper the words.

'Does he think I might be called to court?'

The clerk nodded miserably, sharing her hurt. 'Not by Mr Lanfield, you understand. The other side.'

'Oh, dear God! What have I done? Oh, heavens.' She clutched his arm.

'Are you all right, Miss?'

Emilie's sigh was almost a sob. 'Yes thank you. You've been very kind. Would you excuse me. Please. And thank you. I shall send you my address in Maryborough. If you don't mind, I don't feel quite up to it now.'

She fled down the passageway and across the courtyard to her room, a much airier room than the one she'd shared with Ruth. It even had a private balcony where she could sit outside of an evening and contemplate the events of the day in peace, but now it was just another lonely hideout, no different from all the other miserable places she'd inhabited since they left home. And further back, since their dear mother had died.

Emilie took refuge in hate. She hated the woman who'd married her father. She hated him for his indifference. She hated Ruth for her priggish self-interest, but most of all she hated Mal Willoughby. He had brought all this humiliation upon her. He had caused her to lose her job, to become a figure of gossip in a town that didn't even meet the standards of normal behaviour. He had alienated her sister. He had done everything, all of this, because he was a madman. A person she should have shunned in the first instance, when she knew better . . . or should have.

God, how she hated him. Emilie wept. She didn't want to know about him, or his money, which she would insist on giving to Lanfield in the morning, or ever to see him again. She shook with fright at the very thought

313

of being dragged into a witness box in front of people, with the world staring at her, the worst thing that ever could happen to a person. She would never forgive Willoughby. Never. Not as long as she lived. In wild thoughts of escape, she even gave thought to boarding a ship, not for Maryborough, but for London. Emilie desperately wanted to go home. She hated this place.

Ruth found her sister unusually quiet, even contrite, when she came to say she would be returning to Maryborough on the next available ship. She wasn't surprised. It was about time Emilie faced up to her responsibilities.

'I hope you will take more care in the company you keep from now on.'

'Yes, I shall. Have you heard from Father?'

'No. Apparently he is not inclined to write, so that's that.'

'What about Mr Bowles?'

'What about him?'

'Have you heard from him?'

'You have to realise he's a busy man . . .'

'Too busy to see his fiancée? I'm sorry, Ruth, but I really do want the deeds to my property. I should like to take them with me.'

'Then you go and ask him,' Ruth flared. 'You can't expect me to chase after them.'

Suddenly she was in tears, and Emilie put her arms about her. 'What is it, my dear? What's wrong now?'

Ruth fished in her pocket for a letter, and flung it at Emilie. 'There! Are you satisfied now? I'm sorry you ever came down here. You have ruined everything.'

Her sister didn't have to guess the contents. It was brief. Bowles had broken off the engagement because of 'social differences', and extended his best wishes for Ruth's future.

Emilie was silent. What could she say? Obviously she had caused this break by bringing scandal into their lives, but she felt there was more to it. She didn't want to upset Ruth further by suggesting that the loss of a house that would have cost him nothing might have had something to do with Daniel's change of heart. She sighed. The blame was hers to bear, for the time being, to make it easier for Ruth.

'You'll get over him,' she said, eventually, but Ruth stiffened.

'Of course I'll get over him. He didn't even have the decency to address me personally. But the humiliation is another matter. Everyone knows I am engaged. How can I explain this? What will people think?' She slumped into a chair. 'I even wrote to Father to tell him I was to be married. His wife will know now that I have been jilted . . . that woman will know!'

'She doesn't have to know. Write and say you changed your mind.'

'Lie? You expect me to lie!'

'Yes. For goodness' sake, Ruth. Start thinking about yourself for a

314

change. You're not short of money now, everything will be all right. You'll see.'

'But he's got my money!' Ruth cried.

'That's all right, he'll return it.'

'And I shall have to face him! Oh my God! Oh Lord, what else can go wrong?'

'Nothing,' Emilie said firmly. 'Nothing. If you don't feel like facing people here, why don't you come to dinner at my boarding house tonight. I'll pay . . .'

'That's another thing that has been worrying me. How can you afford to be staying down here all this time, while you're still paying rent up there? I'm totally mystified. Your clothes too, some of them are quite new.'

'I know,' Emilie soothed. 'It's a long story, I'll explain to you later. But it's all above board, believe me. Right now we just have ourselves to worry about. Now put your hat back on and we'll go round to Charlotte Street. They have an excellent table.'

Fortunately Ruth was past arguing, too weary to care any more, and Emilie smiled, thinking of Mr Lanfield.

'I am not a depository,' he had told her that morning. 'You may not leave the money here for Mr Willoughby. He gave it to you in good faith. It is yours. You should budget for your costs of about a hundred pounds if the worst comes to the worst, and the bill will be forwarded to you. Otherwise, Miss Tissington, I have no interest in your finances. Or Mr Willoughby's. It has been my pleasure to meet you, but now run along. And when you get home, kindly do not discuss this case with the police.'

She liked Mr Lanfield. He was such a domineering man, he'd terrified her at first, but now she knew he meant well. And he exuded confidence. Some of which she hoped would rub off on her when she confronted Mr Bowles. There was no time to waste now.

The gatekeeper at the side entrance to Parliament House passed her on to a doorkeeper down at the rear of the imposing sandstone building. He inspected his staff lists and called to a steward to fetch Dan Bowles. Emilie was left to cool her heels outside, disappointed that she wouldn't have an opportunity to inspect at least some of the interior.

Eventually Bowles hurried out.

'What are you doing here?' he hissed, drawing her towards a tall hedge.

'I'm leaving shortly, Mr Bowles, and I should like the deeds to my land, if you please. And the monies that should have been paid to my sister for the sale of her land.'

'This is unpardonable, Miss Tissington. How dare you come here!'

Emilie stood her ground, trying to emulate Mr Lanfield. Or at least his clerk. 'It is unpardonable that I should have no choice but to come to you. Please do as I ask.'

'They're not here. Tell your sister I shall forward them.'

'No. You will get them. Today. I will be back at five this afternoon, and you will have them here . . .'

'Oh, go away,' he said, disgusted, turning back to the door, but Emilie called after him:

'If not, I shall take legal action.'

Bowles stopped in his tracks. The doorman, alerted by the tone of her voice, looked over, interested. Bowles rounded on her.

'I want no more of this nonsense. You are a dreadful person.'

'Very well, I need not wait any longer. You will be hearing from Mr Robert Lanfield, possibly as soon as this afternoon.'

His face was white and his voice conciliatory. 'This is most inconvenient . . .'

'I find it inconvenient also. You will be here at five?'

He shrugged. 'As you wish.'

'Good. And I also require a copy of the contract that my sister signed. Be on time, Mr Bowles.'

Having made that huge effort, Emilie almost ran for the gate to breathe a sigh of relief. It had worked.

Bowles was frantic. He had her land title, and Ruth's money, but the contract would show a discrepancy between the amount he'd quoted to her and what she was really owed. There was nothing for it but to duck out to the bank and withdraw the balance from his meagre savings. That blasted girl. She'd ruined everything. Who else would marry her frigid sister anyway? They really had tickets on themselves, that pair.

At four o'clock that afternoon he handed the doorman a sealed envelope and told him to give it to that woman, Miss Tissington, when she came. Terrified that Emilie would run to a lawyer if the cash enclosed did not meet the exact figure as stated on the contract, and its receipt, after stamp duties, he made sure the right amount was enclosed. They would probably see that there hadn't been an agent, but what did he care? He could claim that Ruth was so stupid she couldn't remember what he'd said. And good riddance to them.

The same longboat that had brought Mal from St Helena to the Brisbane jail returned with another batch of chained convicts, among them the famed 'wild Scot'. His reputation allowed him a better reception from the guards than the likes of Baldy Perry earned, but the Superintendent was not impressed. McPherson had been sentenced to five years on the island, so he was ordered straight out to hard labour.

'To become acclimatised,' Croft smiled grimly.

Four weeks of breaking rocks for a seawall under the burning sun was too much for McPherson. This was hell on earth. He soon rebelled. First he stole a tomahawk, binding it to his waist under his canvas jerkin. Then he hacked a hole in the rear of the timber latrine and was off, racing for the bush.

He tore through the trees into heavy virgin scrub, until he was far enough away to select the tree he needed. Not so thick round the girth that it would take him a week to cut down, but solid enough to float and keep a man moving towards the mainland. To hell with the sharks; he'd take his chances. He knew there was a whaling station on the other side of the bay and figured that if the sharks had any sense they'd be over there where they'd have plenty of grub.

But Croft's men were well practised in this exercise. As soon as the alarm was raised they fanned out through the bush and McPherson was recaptured dragging the stripped log to the beach. He was first taken to the triangle to be flogged and then thrown into the solitary cell. He never attempted to escape again.

There was a gale blowing as Emilie's ship ploughed out into Moreton Bay, and the passengers were warned to stay below.

Emilie was relieved. She couldn't bear to see that island again. To even think about Mal until she recovered from the trauma that had been her visit to Brisbane.

There was a jolly crowd on board and she was befriended by a missionary couple who were returning to Fraser Island. They were interested to hear she was a governess, and unemployed. Very interested, as it turned out. The little mission settlement had been established to bring the Aborigine population to God and they had achieved some success so far, but they desperately needed another teacher, to concentrate on English classes.

They were rapturous in their description of the beautiful island, with its rainforest, its glorious blue lakes and its brilliant seascapes.

Despite herself, she found herself remarking that a friend had visited Fraser Island, and that he too had spoken of its beauty.

'Do you know a place called Orchid Bay? I believe it is on the oceanfront.'

The woman shook her head, but her husband thought he did. 'There is a bay that could be named after the profusion of orchids that grow in the rainforest nearby. That's probably the place. You should give our invitation some thought, Miss Tissington. It really is an idyllic life, and there's no need to worry about the natives. They wouldn't harm any of us; they're cheerful people. More curious about us than God, I fear, but everything takes time.'

Emilie did think about it. Life over there sounded so peaceful, a welcome retreat from the barbs she had yet to face, and the uncertainty of how she would cope from now on. Shelter.

There were several ships in port, and the wharves seemed to be in total chaos, but Clive knew his way around now, and he was easily recognisable in his white duck suit and the smart pith helmet he now sported. He grinned. Headwear sorted out the players on this stage. Poor women wore scarves or shawls, the better heeled afforded hats. Labourers and seafarers wore sweaty bandeaux, planters affected flat straw hats, while the countrymen, bosses and stockmen, lorded it in wide-brimmed rawhide. Immigrants and prospectors made do with battered felts, and the few professional men, bankers, lawyers and their ilk, preferred top hats. Clive was noticing all of these fashions now, because his dream was about to take shape. His loan had been approved, and he'd reserved a lease on one of a row of shops being erected in Kent Street, owned by none other than the mysterious Mr Xiu.

The agent informed him that Mr Xiu had a myriad business interests, and rarely came to this town.

'There is no need for you to meet him, Mr Hillier. I can handle any of your enquiries,' he said pompously.

'Nevertheless you will pass on my felicitations. Mr Xiu is known to me personally.'

'He is?'

'Kindly tell Mr Xiu that I should be delighted to have him dine with me next time he is in town.'

'By all means, Mr Hillier. By all means.'

Clive had no idea if Xiu deigned to dine in public, or even if any of the hotels would serve a Chinaman, but he had made the offer and could probably arrange a private room. The fellow intrigued him, and since he was investing here, he would be a good contact for a budding businessman.

Clive moved swiftly through the crowds with his clipboard, a pencil stuck behind his ear, and a piece of chalk in hand to mark cases and kegs of liquor, and then he saw her. Emilie! Burrowing her way around groups of people and their luggage.

He raced after her, calling to her until she looked back and saw him, but there was no smile for him, no pleasure in the chance meeting, just a nod. But at least she waited for him.

She really is quite lovely, he thought as he approached, with that pretty little hat perched on her dark hair. He couldn't resist throwing his arms about her and kissing her.

'Oh my dear! I'm so pleased you are home. I was worried about you. Did you get my letter?'

'No.'

'It must have missed you. You've been away so long I wondered if you would like me to come down and join you. Are you all right?'

'Yes, Clive. I'm quite all right.'

'You don't sound it.'

'I suppose not,' she said bitterly. 'Do you mind if I go? I don't want to stand around here.'

'Yes, I do mind.' He led her over to the shelter of the customs shed. 'Wait here a minute and I'll take you home.'

'There's no need. I can walk from here.'

'Emilie, it's getting late. There'll be no fresh food in your house. Now do as I say. Wait here. I shan't be long.'

She refused to leave his gig, so he shopped for her, packing whatever the storekeeper thought she would need, and adding a bottle of German wine and a fat German sausage, which Clive had lately come to enjoy.

He opened up the cottage and put her bag in her bedroom while she stood about, seeming disoriented, so he poured two glasses of wine, handed one to her and instructed her to sit at the table.

'Now tell me all about it.'

'You know I've been dismissed?' she said dully.

'Yes, I heard. I spoke to Bert Manningtree, gave him a good telling-off, but he said it was all his wife's doing. He had no idea. He's all for taking you back . . .'

'It doesn't matter. I wouldn't go back.'

'Emilie, it's just as well. You can do with a good rest now. But for the life of me I can't understand how you became so involved. I mean, it's one thing to care . . .'

'I owed Mal,' she whispered.

'What do you mean? Owed him?'

'This house, for a start.'

'What?'

'You remember that Mal left the goldfields with quite a lot of money, about four hundred pounds or so?'

'Yes. He did. That's right.'

'Well . . . he gave it to me.'

'Gave? Why?'

'Clive, I'm tired. I'm tired of having to explain this, over and over. I'm just not up to it now. You're very kind but I really would appreciate being left alone tonight.'

He sighed. 'Very well. But you mustn't think of hiding yourself away here. You've done nothing wrong. Chin up now. I'll be back tomorrow.'

Over the next few days he managed to prise out of her the series of events that had brought her to a state of nervous exhaustion. He wished she had consulted him before dashing off on her errand of mercy, but he made no comment. Even though her naiveté had brought her to public notice, she was fortunate that Kemp had treated her kindly. Since she *had* seen Mal while he was on the run, they could have charged her with withholding information regarding a wanted felon. She still didn't seem to realise what a risk she'd taken in her willingness to tell all, in the hope of proving his innocence.

Was she besotted with Mal? Hard to say, as yet. She was still worried about him, but Clive thought he heard a tinge of irritation in her voice at the problems he had caused her.

Clive wanted to ask if Mal had ever visited her at the cottage, but he did not dare. Emilie wouldn't lie. If Mal had been here, he didn't want to know. He cared deeply for Emilie now, but he had to step carefully; she was badly shaken, she needed his friendship and support, not an impatient lover.

Then he heard about her family problems. The sister had been outraged by her involvement with an outlaw. As he listened, Clive stifled a laugh. Of course she would have been. His own sister would have ordered him from the house in the same circumstances. But Ruth's fiancé, ex-fiancé, was a different story.

'I don't like the sound of that chap.'

'You'd hate him. He's an awful person. Ruth is better off without him. I don't think she ever loved him, it just seemed like a convenient arrangement.'

'Mutual.'

At last Emilie managed a smile. 'But at least I have the deeds of my land and Ruth has her money. More than she expected. He had tried to diddle her out of some of it. An awful man.'

Clive wondered if that was all. These two ladies had entrusted Bowles with a payment to the Emigration Society, which he'd said would go to London in a diplomatic bag for safe delivery. He doubted that a staff member would have access to official mail for private purposes, and he wouldn't be surprised if that payment was still in the pocket of Mr Bowles. But no point in upsetting Emilie with that conclusion now. Time would tell. Months, in fact, and by that time she'd be better able to deal with it. If it didn't arrive at the Society, being a large sum of money, then perhaps Emilie's lawyer, Mr Lanfield, who sounded quite efficient and worldly, could be called upon again.

Gradually Emilie began to emerge from her self-imposed isolation, encouraged by her neighbours, Mrs Mooney and, of course, Clive, who took her for long walks down the country roads away from the town. She was terrified of being stared at in the streets, of having to walk in the footsteps of her own shameful reputation, and nothing they could say would induce her to become part of the community again. Clive's kindness overwhelmed her, and she saw her previous behaviour as mean-spirited and unbecoming. She'd had no right to judge him over that woman, Fleur. It would have served her right if he had taken the same attitude as Ruth and Mrs Manningtree, and God knows how many people in this town. He had been jealous of Mal, and she'd given him more reason to be upset . . . a great deal more than any gentleman could be expected to put up with, and yet he continued to stand by her. Dear Clive.

A kindly letter arrived from the missionaries on Fraser Island, begging her to accept the position of English teacher for the natives, a post which they assured her would be uplifting and a great service to the Lord. Although she hadn't mentioned it to anyone else, Emilie was considering the offer. It would be interesting, a real challenge, something immensely different to shake her out of this awful feeling of inferiority that stultified her days. And hadn't Mal said that the island was incredibly beautiful?

Mal again. She had overcome her irrational annoyance with him, but the anxiety remained. She could only pray for him. The papers seemed to have lost interest in the case, but she knew the story would erupt again any day, and she had to steel herself for that, somehow.

Then Mr Manningtree came to call, bringing the children with him. They ran down the path and threw their arms about her, and Emilie wept while their father stood by, beaming.

They had brought her gifts of their drawings, and a blackberry tart from Kate and a pineapple with a pink bow from Nellie.

When the excitement had died down and the children were off exploring her terraced garden, Mr Manningtree, in his forthright manner, wanted to know what she was doing now.

'Nothing much,' she said, embarrassed.

'So they say. I never see you in town. Never see you nowheres. You turnin' into a hermit or something?'

'Oh, no.' Emilie looked away nervously. 'I just don't go out much.'

'Why not? I can't do nothing about your sacking. She's put on another girl, belongs to one of the planters, and I don't reckon that lass knows much. Can't even play the piano. But getting back to that other business, seems to me from what I read, you thought you were doing the right thing by that bloke.'

'Yes, Mr Manningtree. And I still believe he is innocent.'

He nodded. 'Well, if he is, missy, he's having a bad trot, I'll say that. But what about you? Are you gonna stay shut up in here feeling sorry for yourself?'

'I beg your pardon?'

'It's true, isn't it? You're too scared to show your face. I thought you had more grit than that. You're making too much of this. You're not the first, nor the last, my missus gives the push. You're not letting that get you down?'

'It wasn't pleasant, Mr Manningtree, a shock really. But the papers were worse.' Emilie felt a sob rising. 'It's hard really.'

'So what? I never thought I'd see you losing sight of things that count, and you an edjicated woman.'

'I don't understand.'

'Then you'd better think about it. People round here have met real tragedies and got back on their feet again. Pioneering ain't no joke: it's kids who die, it's fightin' to survive against everything this bloody country can throw at you . . . I'm no good talker like you are, but you been here long enough to see nothin' comes easy in this neck of the woods.' He strode over to look at the children, diving in and out of the shrubs.

'We lost our first kid,' he said bitterly. 'No doctor. I thought my missus would go mad. He was only one year old. A little treasure he was . . .'

'I'm so sorry.'

'Yeah, well. You ought to look around you, that's what I'm trying to say. But there's something else. I've donated a block of land in March Street for the council to build a school. And they're gettin' on with it at long bloody last. It's only a one-room school, I've seen the plans, but the best we can do for now. You should get in fast and apply for the job.'

His speech over, he turned away again. 'By cripes, this is a damn good spot here, with the view and all. Old Paddy knew his onions. Good bloke, Paddy. I better be taking the kids home.'

Emilie walked over and linked her arm in his. 'You remember when you picked me up from the boat when I first arrived? I can tell you now I was terrified of you. I didn't realise what a nice man you are, Mr Manningtree. You must have thought me an awful prig.'

'You were a bit,' he acknowledged. 'Get up here, you kids! We have to go or we'll be late for dinner.'

Clive was astonished when she agreed to come into town, walking, on her own, to have lunch with him at Mrs Mooney's hotel. But it wasn't easy. At each corner she had to fight off the urge to turn back, concentrating instead on the morning . . . It was hot already, and that reminded her of Ruth, who had complained about the weather.

'It's either hot or hotter, Emilie. What wouldn't I give to see sleet and snow again.'

'You used to hate it, and our house was always so cold . . .'

When she entered the town, Emilie had no idea whether people were staring at her or not. She'd worn her straw bonnet, not just because the ribbons matched her summer dress, but because it acted as blinkers; she couldn't see to right or left. She pondered Mr Manningtree's rebuke, not really convinced that she was indulging in self-pity but stirred enough by his remarks to make this effort. She felt she was starting all over again, walking down the main street of Maryborough with the same acute shyness she'd experienced during her first days here.

Maybe I do have to start again, she mused, but then she saw Clive ahead of her, waiting outside the hotel, and she was so relieved she almost broke into a run. Dear Clive, he looked so handsome, so self-assured, and yet there was no mistaking his fondness for her. As soon as he sighted her, his face lit up with such an expression of delight that Emilie blushed; she thought he might actually kiss her in the street. He did not, of course, but when he took her arm, so firmly, Emilie experienced a quiet joy of her own. She loved being with Clive.

Mrs Mooney joined them for lunch and they talked easily about their own affairs. Mrs Mooney, on the advice of German friends, was arranging to have tables and chairs placed in the gardens beside the hotel so that she could serve customers out in the fresh air.

'And weren't they ever horrified when I said I'd have to put a roof of some sort, held up by poles, at the side,' she laughed. 'They said I'd be altogether missing the idea, but it's them who're missing my point. Hot it would still be, warm enough to sit out there, but not without a roof when the rains come. I never seen such torrents as our summer rains.'

Clive and Emilie agreed it was a grand idea, but Clive too had his plans. After lunch he wanted to take the ladies down to see the shop he had leased, and hear their ideas on fittings before he called in a carpenter. He had also received his first catalogues of gentlemen's outfits from a Sydney warehouse, and a sales representative would be calling shortly.

'I thought you would be going to Brisbane to buy your stock,' Emilie said.

'So did I, until I had a chat with Mr Xiu.'

'Who's Mr Xiu?'

'A Chinese gentleman, an absolute font of knowledge. He made some enquiries and was able to advise me that Sydney wholesalers are cheaper and more reliable.'

'That's very kind of him.'

Mrs Mooney nodded. 'Smart too, you know. He can't have his leaseholders going broke on him. But Clive will do well, you mark my words. We can do with a good shop like he's settin' up.'

While they talked, Emilie noticed other diners coming and going, but there were none of the sly glances she had expected, no untoward interest in her at all, and gradually she relaxed, feeling that the worst was over. For the time being, anyway.

'I hear they're building a school at long last,' Mrs Mooney said, 'and a little birdie told me that you might be our first schoolteacher, Emilie.'

'Oh, no. Really. I'm sure they'll need someone better qualified than I. How is your daughter enjoying boarding school? Have you heard from her lately?'

Emilie managed to change the subject, but as they strolled back to the cottage, Clive was curious.

'Did you know about the school?'

'Yes. Mr Manningtree told me. He wants me to apply for the position as teacher. But I wouldn't dream of it. I'd have to submit my application to the town council and I'm sure they would not even consider me, after all this unpleasantness.'

'I don't know about that. And you are qualified.'

Emilie stopped and turned to him. 'Clive, be honest, dear. I can't apply. You do know that the reputation I've brought upon myself would precede me. Some people might be kind enough to overlook it, but too many others would not. Were I on the council myself, looking at this objectively, I should not approve. I've no intention of placing myself in the position of being rejected. So may we forget about the school?'

'Of course. I'm pleased to forget about it. I don't expect my wife to have to go to work.'

Emilie stared. 'I beg your pardon?'

'Oh, Lord, that just slipped out! Now I'm making a mess of things. I wanted to wait until you were feeling stronger . . .'

'Your wife?'

He shrugged ruefully. 'That's what I said. And I meant it, but I did intend to propose in a more romantic setting, not standing here at the corner of the lane. I love you, Emilie, and beg you to do me the honour of becoming my wife.'

Emilie was so taken aback she felt foolish just standing there, not knowing what to say.

He took her arm and began walking with her down the lane. 'I shouldn't have popped it on you like that. You don't have to answer now, or even next week.' He smiled. 'We can leave the proposal tabled for the time being, if you like.'

'Yes, thank you,' she said quietly. 'It was rather a surprise. I . . . sort of . . . hadn't thought about marriage. I suppose I've been too concerned with my own worries.'

'Is it Mal?'

Emilie shivered. 'Mal? I don't know. I really don't know, Clive. I just can't help worrying about him. He is innocent. It's so cruel.'

She was relieved that he didn't pursue either subject.

'We'll talk about it another time, Em. But do keep in mind that I love you. I believe we could be very happy together, but you have to decide on that.'

He didn't stay. He kissed her on the cheek and left her at her door, and Emilie was disappointed. In herself. A proposal was hardly an everyday event. She could at least have shown some emotion, instead of floundering about in confusion. She hoped she hadn't hurt Clive's feelings. And what had she said about Mal? She couldn't recall now. It was difficult to explain her feelings for Mal, even to herself. The night he'd come to the cottage had been so romantic, so exciting. As if no one else in the world existed.

She walked to the windows and looked out over the river. The world and its peoples did exist, and there was a big difference between the paths that these two men would choose. But there was also a big difference between friendship and love. In her own way, Emilie admitted to herself at last, she did love both Mal and Clive. But she wondered if her feelings for Mal now were just based on loyalty. She really didn't know him very well at all. If she could only see him again, talk to him . . .

An uncomfortable thought lodged. What if Mal had lost interest in her? He might be thankful for her help but he'd had a dreadful time, and his affection for her could have faded. Emilie sighed. What would Ruth think of Clive's proposal? Not kindly. She hadn't approved of him either.

Emilie took off her bonnet, dropped it on the table and wandered aimlessly about the cottage. It wasn't much fun being a lady of leisure with nothing to do all day, and no one to talk to. She really would have to think of something to do to occupy herself. Suddenly she missed her home in Brackham, the family life they'd taken for granted before their father remarried, the village, knowing everyone . . . There was always something to do in Brackham, if only a visit to Mrs Collett's Lending Library. Here there was no library, no bookshop . . .

'Only the butcher, the baker and the candlestick-maker,' she said ruefully, and wondered what this place must have been like twenty years ago when the first settlers came.

'Hell on earth,' she shuddered. According to Mr Manningtree, most of those first settlers were still here. It would be an interesting exercise to record their experiences, dealing with hostile Aborigines, hacking a settlement out of bush as dense as any jungle, with no supply line to support them. Why on earth, she wondered, would people, mostly immigrants, take on such a hazardous experience? It could be interesting to find out from them, first-hand. Perhaps Mr Manningtree would introduce her. It would be something to do.

Chapter Fourteen

Quentin Allenby QC was terse. 'Don't you see, old chap? Our client is slipping back into the field. Carnegie might well be the only man in creation who hasn't heard that Gold Commissioner Griffen shot his own guards. Or it could have slipped his mind. But that doesn't make him a murderer. Keep in mind that he was a victim, therefore he is having no trouble in rounding up upper-crust witnesses to his good character to impress the judge and jury. If they are needed. Keep in mind that he is not on trial.'

Lanfield nodded. 'I understand that, but it was my expectation that you would be able to break his story. He's already very nervous . . .'

'Nervousness is not the prerogative of the guilty in a courtroom; many an innocent man can be shattered by the ordeal.'

'I know that,' Lanfield said testily. 'But surely you can trip him . . .'

'On what point? From what you tell me, he is still adamant that Willoughby took part in the raid. It will be almost impossible to shake him on that one question. The police are still smarting at public rebuke on this matter, so they need a conviction and Willoughby is their man. They'll paint him as a thief, a confidence trickster, a desperado who shows no sign of remorse after committing such a heinous crime.'

Although Allenby claimed he was only discussing this case in its worst light to place his own arguments in order, Lanfield had the impression that the barrister was regretting having taken the brief, and it depressed him. Until now he'd been certain that Willoughby would be cleared by proving that Carnegie was, at best, mistaken. That was all they needed. The police case had seemed weak, but now it was building into a strongly reasoned position.

As he made his way back to his rooms, he recalled Allenby's parting remarks.

'Since it is evident that suspicion of Carnegie does reside in all quarters, I will go over his statements with a fine-tooth comb. He is a bankrupt. The sale of his house settled only his most pressing debts, and as for his gambling debts, well, my dear fellow, they're hardly regarded as criminal in society. Which is all beside the point anyway, since he is not on trial. But as for the gentleman himself, I have to say that either he is innocent of any involvement, and therefore, as a known victim, has every right to resent cruel suspicions, or he is a lot smarter than he has been given credit for. You see my difficulty?'

Lanfield was surprised to find Sergeant Pollock waiting in the lobby. 'What can I do for you, sir?'

'I need to talk to you, Mr Lanfield. Urgently. I have to go home shortly but my work here is not completed.'

'Surely that's a matter for your superiors. But do come in.'

He placed his top hat and cane on the hallstand and took the Sergeant through to his office, impatiently glancing at a bank of files that his clerk had placed on the desk. He sat down and motioned to Pollock to do the same, facing him with a frown.

Pollock lowered his lanky frame into the chair and leaned forward. 'Mr Lanfield. There is a possibility that the Willoughby trial will begin next week.'

'So I believe. We'll be ready.'

'I'm pleased to hear that, but can you win?'

'We're confident.'

The Sergeant shook his head. 'I wish I was. Carnegie's the key, I know he is. But you won't get any more out of him than we have. Will you be calling Baldy Perry?'

'You know we can't do that. He has nothing to do with this case.'

'I believe he does.'

'So what would I do with him? Witness for the defence? Ridiculous. I wasn't permitted to interview him for fear I'd ruin what little chance you had of connecting him to the crime; now you're suggesting I call him.'

Pollock shrugged. 'No, I'm not. Not really. It's just that I'm getting bloody desperate. If you get Willoughby off, the case is still open . . .'

'I'm afraid that's your problem.'

'And if you don't, I reckon it would be a miscarriage of justice.'

'You think he's innocent?'

'He could be, but even so, he couldn't have carried out that raid on his own, so it still isn't over.' He took out a battered leather pouch and rolled a cigarette with practised ease, lighting it with a cupped hand as if he was still out in the bush, not seated in this closed office.

'Look, Mr Lanfield. There is something we haven't tried. I've been keeping an eye on Carnegie . . .'

'You've been following him?'

'Not all the time. I didn't want him to spot me. I've had a bloke from the Chester Agency on the job too.'

Lanfield was astonished. 'The police are paying a private detective?'

'No, I am,' Pollock said fiercely. 'I told you, I'm desperate, my job's on the line. The gold and the cash from the raid could still be out there.'

'And you thought he might lead you to it. To a private stash some-where? You must be desperate.'

'I didn't know what I was looking for. Something different. Some-where he might go. To a sleazy jeweller, maybe. I don't know. Or someone out of the ordinary he might associate with.'

'And what did you discover?'

Pollock shrugged. 'Nothing. Except that he goes to his club for lunch on Thursdays and to church on Sundays. The Anglican church in Paddington. The rest of the time he hangs about the house with his brother. They have all their provisions delivered. Absolutely nothing suspicious.'

The solicitor was disappointed but gave no indication of a fresh hope dashed.

'I can't see what all this has to do with me.'

'There's still a chance. I need a favour. It's unusual, but your co-operation would be essential.'

'In what capacity?'

'I believe you are also a member of his club. If you could go out of your way to meet him, casually, on Thursday and drop some information on him. Some important information . . .'

'Oh no, I hardly think so. I never go there on Thursdays anyway; the club is rather crowded with retirees on that day, and the service is poor.'

'Please, sir. Just this once. I want you to tell him that the police have a man in custody who is boasting that he's a rich man . . .'

'You mean this Perry fellow?'

'Yes, but for God's sake don't give him the name. Just say he's a criminal type with no known means of support, but suddenly he's rich and the police are suspicious of him. They think he might be the other wanted man . . .'

'Are you mad, Pollock? This isn't unusual, it's outrageous. You expect me to walk into my own club and play-act. No, definitely not.'

Pollock persisted. He argued forcefully, even angrily, but still Lanfield refused.

'Jesus!' Pollock said eventually. 'It's not much to ask. Just a few words to him. Some news. You could tell him kindly. No need to play-act, as you say. It's true. I just don't want the name mentioned. Not yet anyway. He may ask. You say you don't know. It's just something you heard.'

'Then what?' Lanfield said, relenting.

'His reaction could be important. He'll be interested, that's sure. Maybe scared. What if he believes we have *his* partner in crime? Who could talk. The possibilities are endless. And I'll be outside to see where he goes afterwards. You never know.'

'Highly improper!'

'But you'll do it?'

'Does Kemp know about this? Or anyone else?'

'No. Just you and me.'

'Well, keep it that way. If the opportunity arises I may say something,' he snapped. 'I don't know. I can't promise.'

Pollock was on his feet, obviously keen to depart before his man had a change of mind. 'Just do your best,' he said firmly. 'I'll be grateful, Mr Lanfield. Somehow we have to rattle the truth out of Carnegie; he's deep in it, I reckon.'

The Gentlemen's Club in Edward Street buzzed with the burr of muted voices, of voices theatrically muted because few members were accustomed to conversing quietly, as the rules required. In the smoking room an occasional hoot or guffaw raised heads or eyebrows, or the irritated shuffle of a newspaper, otherwise all was normal this noon as Robert Lanfield sat by the casement windows trying to appear occupied in the pages of a stockmarket bulletin. He hoped Carnegie would give this Thursday a miss and thereby release him from the probability that he was about to make an utter fool of himself. A steward brought him a sherry.

'Will you be staying for lunch, sir? Not your usual day. Should I reserve a table for you?'

'Thank you, no.' He took a pencil and wrote meaningless memos about gold shares in a slim notebook, and sighed, considering escape. But then Carnegie came in the door, right on time, just as Pollock had predicted, and what was more, he was heading straight for Lanfield. For one awful minute Robert thought the fellow intended to join him, but Carnegie nodded recognition to someone beyond and was walking past when Lanfield spoke. He stood, as if he was about to leave, barring Carnegie's way with a surprised greeting. Feeling a fool.

'I say, Carnegie. Good to see you out and about. Feeling better, are you?'

'A little.'

Lanfield hesitated before stepping aside, as indeed he was hesitating as to whether or not to go on with this farce, but curiosity got the better of him. By this he was interested in Carnegie's reaction.

'Just a minute. I heard a spot of news that might interest you.'

'What is that?' Carnegie responded unenthusiastically.

'Step aside here a second. I must tell you! It's quite exciting.' Robert had risen to his role now. 'The police believe they have picked up another one of those outlaws. Your attackers.'

'Who?' Carnegie said coolly.

'Didn't get the name. Apparently he's a criminal type, some sort of bruiser who raised their suspicions by boasting that he was a rich man. Typical of these wretches, not known for common sense. Can't account for his sudden wealth . . .'

Carnegie's pale skin was turning a shade of green.

'. . . No visible means of support, but in the money! They say he was in Maryborough at the time too.'

'You don't know his name?' Carnegie croaked.

'Can't for the life of me think of it. Never heard it before. But you'll see them hang yet. Thought you ought to know . . .'

'I daresay I'll hear in good time. Thank you.' Carnegie slipped away from him, heading for some gentlemen in the far corner, and that was that.

'Damned waste of time,' Lanfield muttered to himself as he put his notebook in his waistcoat pocket and went on his way.

Later that day Pollock was back to compare notes. 'Nothing unusual again. He stayed on until after three, then went straight home.'

'Silly idea in the first place,' Lanfield snapped. 'I can only tell you that he did look decidedly green at hearing the news, asked for the name, but otherwise no reaction at all. So you keep this quiet, Pollock, or I'll be a laughing stock.'

But Pollock wasn't disturbed, or even disappointed. 'You've let him know. That's the first stage.'

'What first stage?'

'We have to follow through now,' he grinned, 'or your good work will be wasted.'

Lanfield listened, astonished, as the Sergeant outlined the next step. 'Impossible! Out of the question!'

'No it's not. We have to do this. You have to do it for Willoughby's sake. I have to try, I *have* to try!'

'Kemp would never allow it.'

'Kemp's one for the rules, on the surface, but he's from Sydney. I reckon he'd be an old hand at bending the rules if he saw merit. He could have sacked me, but he didn't. He's a fair man. I know he doesn't trust Carnegie, and it rankles with him that even he couldn't take a rise out of the fellow.'

'What do you want me to do anyway? There's no part for me in this escapade.'

'Yes there is. You have to persuade Kemp. I'm only a lowly bush copper.'

'I wouldn't dream of taking such a plan to Kemp.'

'Willoughby will swing. I don't want that on my conscience.'

'You can't predict that. And anyway, what if this charade doesn't work?'

'Then you've got a tough fight on your hands, believe me. I heard this morning that Lilley wants a conviction, quickly. Our Attorney-General is taking a pounding in the press.'

Lanfield had invited Kemp for a drink at his club. Kemp had accepted, out of curiosity, but declined to meet in the club; he preferred pubs. He was standing in the bar of the River Inn, wearing civvies, when the lawyer came in, looking about for a hook to hang his top hat, but of course there was none. Lanfield looked like a fish out of water in the noisy bar, mostly frequented by working-class men, but, Kemp smiled, that was his problem. He had been wondering if Allenby had put the lawyer up to this meeting, to sound out the possibility, off the record, of a guilty plea before raising the matter with the Prosecutor's office. Advice. Was he after advice, or information? Kemp was not comfortable with the case against Willoughby, although his mate Lilley had said it was iron-clad. Not comfortable at all. And another thing. Lilley, ever the politician, had wanted to be photographed with the captured outlaw, McPherson, but Kemp had forgotten the request. By the time Lilley reminded him, the famous Scot had been sent down river to serve his time on the top-security island. The Minister was unimpressed.

Kemp shrugged that off and welcomed Lanfield. 'What's it to be?'

'Brandy and water, thank you, Kemp. Good of you to see me.'

'A pleasure,' Kemp said. 'I like this pub. A good drop of ale.'

They talked about Brisbane's mild and sunny winter, about a now discovered mutual interest in gardening, about the exotic plants flourishing in the Botanic Gardens, about this and that, and Kemp watched, interested as a couple of brandies relaxed this aloof fellow, who obviously had something to say but was taking his time getting to it.

It was Friday evening, and the western sky was awash with the spectacular pinks of sunset. Mrs Kemp would be waiting for him, but Kemp wanted this man to make the move. Or decide against it. Maybe this was, after all, just a social meeting.

But eventually it came. 'I wanted to discuss something with you, Superintendent. It is rather out of the ordinary, and I shouldn't be at all surprised if you rule against it, out of hand, but I should very much appreciate a hearing.'

'By all means.'

Kemp listened as Lanfield outlined his suspicions of the former Gold Commissioner, but in the end he shook his head.

'I'm sorry. This is old ground for me. I've been over and over it. I can't do any more.'

Lanfield nodded. 'Yes. My barrister, Allenby, believes that Carnegie has outsmarted the police at every turn.'

Kemp had just picked up his tankard of ale. He jerked his head at that remark. 'I wouldn't say that! We're not unaware that there could be something there.'

'Of course not.' Lanfield's voice was soothing. 'But you know Allenby. He's rather put out that the police won't say yea or nay on the matter of Carnegie. It puts us all in limbo, so to speak.'

'Not at all. Once Willoughby is convicted, we should hear the whole story. He won't go down solo, you mark my words.'

'But Willoughby won't be convicted. We shall see to that, and that leaves the police force looking at more public derision.'

Kemp frowned. 'What is your point? This is a very serious case, a shocking crime, but we're only on the sidelines now. We have to let justice take its course. The Crown versus Willoughby.'

'And Carnegie?'

'Damn Carnegie! His statement will be heard and that's that.'

'I'm disappointed that you give up so easily, Kemp. I heard great things of you from Lilley before you arrived.'

'What else can I do?'

'There is one thing.'

'What?'

This time it was Lanfield who outlined the plan, making a determined effort to be convincing, expecting little. He lacked Pollock's desperate plunge for the brass ring.

Kemp stared. 'What? You want me to what?'

Once again Lanfield explained the idea and the possibilities.

'That's all it is,' Kemp said. 'A bloody game. A fairground rort. Who thought of this? Willoughby? It sounds like him.'

'No. I saw him this morning. Great relief to me to have him back in our jail where I don't have to waste a day . . . but no. He has no part in it at all. We thought since none of us can get so much as a serve out of Carnegie, from his very definite statements, we should try another angle.'

Kemp took it for granted that Lanfield meant he and Allenby, and was intrigued by their audacity.

Lanfield continued. 'What have you got to lose? Nothing. A couple of hours of your time. No one really has to know if it doesn't work. I can't say honestly, Kemp, that I was enamoured of such a plan myself, it's really only an experiment. It could be interesting . . .'

The Superintendent saw the sky gush red as the sun slid into the hills. He turned to watch lanterns being lit and hang, glowing, from the timber beams. He saw the lights of a ferry begin to twinkle as it drifted by. He thought of Carnegie and the sleepless nights that miserable wretch had caused him. And he started to laugh. Heads turned, accommodating him, grinning, accepting his humour as their own.

'What the hell!' he said. 'It's bloody mad, Lanfield. But why not give it a go? But listen to me. If it falls flat, not a word. We keep this very quiet.'

Lanfield was at pains to agree. 'Believe me, I won't want to ever hear of it again.'

'What about Sunday, at the church?'

'I shall be away at the weekend. But I think that's a bit soon, anyway. We thought of next Thursday at his club.'

'You're cutting it fine.'

'Indeed. But it's only an experiment.'

'All right. Thursday.' Kemp was under the impression that Allenby had pushed a reluctant Lanfield into this plot, but was not concerned. Allenby was known to be a radical sort of fellow. Quite the actor in court. It would be interesting to see how the scene panned out.

'Probably nothing,' he told his wife later. 'I don't know how I let myself agree to it. But pray to God something happens. We have to make a decision about Carnegie.'

'That's true,' she said. 'If the poor man is innocent, you should let him get on with his life. He has suffered enough.'

The nightmares had begun again. Allyn had believed himself free of them once he'd settled into the tranquillity of his brother's home, his woes behind him. While his wife was alive, John had steadfastly refused to lend him any more money, but since then it was plain to see that his brother's mental capacities were deteriorating. When he returned from the north, Allyn had been quite shocked to find John wandering about his house, confused and disoriented, and he readily agreed with their pastor that it would be a fine brotherly gesture for him to move out here and take care of the old gent as soon as he'd sold his own house.

The pastor was not to know that here was the refuge Allyn desperately needed, although he was aware that Mr and Mrs Allyn Carnegie had separated. That subject was carefully avoided.

Then came another shock. Allyn discovered that his brother was not as well-off as he'd imagined, and for this, in darker moments, he blamed his nephew. He was convinced that John's son, in taking over the big pastoral property, had duped his father out of a fortune, but he made no complaint. He couldn't afford to antagonise his nephew for fear that this house and its half-acre grounds would be sold, and the old man whisked back out west. Leaving him homeless again. He and John now had enough to live on and Allyn was enjoying life as a gentleman retiree. After all his dreadful troubles, he felt he deserved the quiet life. He had lost his interest in society and in gambling, but made his weekly visit to the club to keep up appearances and chat to old friends.

When they captured Willoughby, he knew that he would have to bear witness in court and that worried him for a while, but he'd become stronger in these peaceful surrounds and so reassured himself that he would only have to repeat the same story, for the hundredth time, and walk away. A courtroom couldn't possibly be any worse than the harrowing interrogations he'd had to endure in Maryborough, when he really had been ill with worry, and suffering the fierce pain of his wound.

He'd become even more confident after he'd overcome the anxiety caused by Pollock's visit, because the country policeman hadn't achieved a thing. He had known, as Allyn had, that the interview had been a waste of time. He was too smart for that oaf.

Then there was Lanfield, fishing about on behalf of Willoughby, hoping he'd admit to a mistake. It was of no moment that he had made a mistake in identifying McPherson; that was easily explained. He did not know McPherson. But he was on solid ground accusing Willoughby. No mistake there. There were times when Allyn congratulated himself for implicating Willoughby. He truly believed that was a stroke of genius. And the arrest of Willoughby had proved it. He'd given the police their sorely needed scapegoat. If he hadn't done that, after all this time with no arrests in sight, Allyn had no doubt they would have harassed him even more. He was concerned, however, at Lanfield's snide reference to the Griffen case. Of course he knew about it, that was where he'd found the idea to stage his own robbery. Griffen had been a fool. Inventing some stupid story about his guards becoming lost in the bush, while he was innocently wandering about searching for them. Idiot. He deserved to hang.

Allyn knew he should have admitted knowing about the case. Everyone knew about it. But so what? And who cared? Lanfield too had been sent away with a flea in his ear. Another waste of time. Until he'd bumped into the lawyer in the club.

Lanfield had thought he was passing on some good news, but Allyn had nearly fainted. Only these long months of keeping his equilibrium in the face of cruel questioning had saved him from giving the game away. His heart had been pounding, his mouth dry as dirt, and yet he'd managed to stroll calmly away and join his friends as if nothing had happened. A truly remarkable effort of self-control. He'd dined quietly, sedately, determined not to allow that anything was amiss, though stabs of stomach pain held him in mortal fear that his bowels might give way. He sympathised with his friends' misgivings about the introduction of a new-fangled telephone system, the main topic of the day, struggled on to the pudding and left at his usual hour.

He collected his hat and cane, stepped out into the street and turned left, walking briskly along the front of the building, then turned again into the lane that would take him through to the mews where his horse was stabled. Halfway down the cobbled lane, he stumbled, and leaned against the wall for support, desperately fighting off an urge to vomit.

But he'd made it home, and by that time the biliousness had left him, to be replaced by wave upon wave of anxiety.

Who had the police arrested? Typical of that idiot to forget the name. What had he said? The fellow was not well known. In other words, not on the wanted lists. That could be Perry. A bruiser type, spouting off about being rich and unable to explain the source of his wealth. That sounded like the oaf. He had all the gold and the money from the raid, and he was stupid enough to boast about it, probably spending like a madman.

But maybe not. This fellow in custody could be anyone. A plain thief who was, naturally, not inclined to admit to successful robberies. There was really nothing to worry about, Allyn told himself, he was imagining things, making a mountain out of a molehill, getting the jitters over the arrest of a common thief.

That night he dreamed that the dead men were in his room, standing about, muttering, their voices rumbling like thunder, and other people joined them, strangers. Taylor took off his hat, handing it about to get up a collection, but Allyn had no money. He tried to explain this to them, but the menace in the room became so terrifying he shrieked for them to get away. Get away from him.

His screams woke John, who came shambling in to ask if he'd heard anything.

'No. Go back to bed.'

For days he scoured the newspapers for any mention of this arrest, of this suspect, unable to decide whether this was a good or a bad omen. Lanfield had said the fellow came from Maryborough, or was there at the time. He'd been over this conversation so often he'd lost the exact wording. But that could mean Perry. How he hated Perry. He could see him gloating over that haul, gloating over the way he'd outwitted Allyn Carnegie, sitting in bars and beer halls and brothels making a big fellow of himself, boasting ... with thousands of pounds, a fortune, at his disposal. Allyn prayed the good Lord would strike him dead. He was a murderer. Hell was too good for him.

But he was also a coward, a bully and a coward. What if the police did have him? What else had he done to draw attention to himself? Any number of things. What had he said? And what would he say if they did charge him with the murders? Oh God, what would he say to save his own skin?

By day Allyn went for long walks to wrestle with this fear, and by night he was beset again with awful dreams. He tried to ward them off with brandy, some help, but then he woke with fierce headaches and even more anxiety. And all the time he waited, fearful that a man in uniform might ride up to the house, but no one came.

Knowing that the appearance of normality was all-important, Allyn took his brother to church on the Sunday morning, as usual, and exchanged pleasantries with the pastor, even promising to attend the spring garden party in the church grounds on the following Saturday . . . 'if John is well enough.'

Whether it was the house of the Lord, or all the cheerful people about him, Allyn didn't know, but a great sadness fell upon him as he drove the buggy home. He wasn't exactly repentant – he felt nothing for the men who'd lost their lives – but he did regret that adventure from the very core of his being. He was sorry he'd ever taken on such a risky business. Even bankruptcy and the inevitable disgrace would have been preferable to the hell he'd put himself through, as a result of what he'd so stupidly seen as the perfect crime. The aftermath left a bitter taste. His partner had stolen the money, so it had all been for nothing. The pain, the useless arm, the endless anxiety, the fear of the law . . . all for nothing. Self-pity was breaking his heart.

Still nothing in the papers. On the Thursday morning he dressed with care, pegging his longish hair at the back in the style of a country gentleman, pinning John's gold watch and chain across his waistcoat, fussing over the arrangements of his white silk cravat and calling the maid to brush his dark frockcoat so that not a skerrick of dandruff or fluff marred its shining surface. And rather than ride in this attire, he took the buggy. This day was important; he had to appear unconcerned, of course, but he hoped to encounter Lanfield again and somehow arrange a casual conversation, during which he would enquire if the police had any more news of the suspect. And he could say, in all innocence, 'What did you say his name was again?'

Something like that.

He rehearsed the conversation over and over as he drove down the steep hills, past the police barracks, and spun out along the river towards Roma Street, trying not to shudder as he passed the police headquarters – would he ever be free of this anxiety? Turning up Turbot to Edward Street, he manoeuvred the buggy into the narrow mews. Stablehands rushed out to take over as one of their club gentlemen alighted, hardly giving them a second glance. Allyn straightened his hat, jerked his coat into order, took his cane and strode over to the lane. Today he might be able to find out exactly what was going on and make his preparations, he told himself. He had to know. His nerves were shot to pieces thanks to this frightful week, every sound made him jump and he had developed a bad tic in his left eye. He kept telling himself it couldn't be Perry, it had to be someone else, but even apart from all that, the very thought of Perry enraged him. Perry had beaten him; that oaf had succeeded where the police could not. That double-crossing bastard.

'What's all this then?' Perry had asked as Pollock and the bossman had walked into his cell and thrown the clothes down on his bunk.

'This is Superintendent Kemp,' the Sergeant said, 'and you'll do exactly as you're told if you know what's good for you.'

Perry stared. 'Them's street clothes. Am I out?'

Kemp nodded. 'You could be. Clean him up, Pollock, and bring him back here.'

The prisoner didn't take kindly to having his head shoved under a cold tap while a constable scrubbed him with stinging soap. 'Hey, mind out. You're gettin' soap in me eyes. What are youse doing to me?'

They weren't inclined to explain. He was given a rough towel to dry himself, and shunted along the cold corridor to his cell, where Kemp still waited.

'Now get dressed, in these clothes.'

Perry was mystified. Prisoners on release never got natty duds like this, but he was smart enough not to complain. They were real gent's clobber, these were, but probably these uniformed galoots wouldn't know the difference. The island had reduced Baldy's waistline and his beer belly had disappeared, so the trousers fitted well. The shirt was striped, and had a good feel about it, and Baldy looked at the other duds, betting they never paid for this stuff, betting it had belonged to a dead 'un. They were flash, real flash. They even gave him a waistcoat, red, with shiny gold threads, and a smart jacket that matched the trousers. It was tight across his broad shoulders, but it would do.

'Here, you might as well have this too.' Pollock tossed him a fancy spotted bow tie to add to the outfit, and polished boots.

Dressed in this finery, Baldy preened. He looked as smart as any of them showy blokes that spruiked at fairs. Smarter even.

'Can I go now?'

Sour-faced Kemp stood in the doorway. 'Your time's not up yet, but you might get lucky. We've got a job for you, but if you muck up you'll go back to the island. Consider yourself on parole.'

'What's parole?'

'Ticket of leave.'

'Yeah, I get youse. If I don't muck up, do I get to keep these duds?'

Kemp shrugged. 'Yes.' And Baldy could see he wasn't too pleased about it, but he had his rights. A man couldn't walk out in prison canvas, they had to give him some duds, so he might as well have this lot.

'What sort of a job is it?' he asked, suddenly suspicious of this parole business.

'Legitimate for a change, for you,' Kemp growled. 'Bring him up,

335

Sergeant. No handcuffs, but if he attempts to escape, shoot him.'

'What?' Baldy yelled. 'I'm going quiet, like, you got no need to shoot me. You just take me to that job.'

Bald and bewhiskered, scrubbed and smart in his expensive suit and loud accessories, Perry was taken up the cold stone steps and through an arched doorway set in the wall of the barracks, to emerge breathing free air at last.

A driver waited nearby with a buggy, and as they approached, he handed Pollock a gun belt and handgun. Baldy watched sulkily as he strapped them on, worrying that a bullet hole would ruin the best suit he'd ever owned.

With Baldy sitting warily in the buggy, Kemp called Pollock aside. 'Don't lose this one, Sergeant,' he gritted.

He watched them leave, shaking his head, still concerned about this coming charade, which seemed to be an exercise in futility, but he had agreed, and he might as well get on with it. No show without Punch, he mused as he went back into the barracks, bolting the gate behind him. Then he grinned. Baldy had looked the part all right, Pollock had seen to that. There was a rumble of laughter in him as he made his way out to the stables.

His mount was ready, as were the three armed troopers he'd already briefed. He took out his watch . . .

'Good. We've got plenty of time. Just remember, I want you all on foot. Get the horses out of the way. One each end. And you, Forrest, you give Pollock the whistle when it's time to go. Don't use a police whistle. Get your signals right and keep out of sight. We only get one chance at this.' He swung on to his horse and looked back at them. 'Watch out for Perry. Don't let him get away, for Christ's sake.'

For mine too, he added as the heavy gates were swung back to allow them to ride out. Losing Perry would take some explaining.

They stood by the buggy in busy Edward Street, near the entrance to the Gentlemen's Club, a building that held no interest for Baldy Perry.

'What are we doing here?' he asked.

'I'm not sure if this is the place,' Pollock said, stalling for time, but then his man from the Chester Agency rode by and nodded to him. Good, Carnegie was on his way. The Sergeant felt a surge of relief. He'd been afraid the ex-Commissioner would change his mind about coming in today, or change his schedule. He might even have had reason to walk through town, which would have made the meeting difficult, but not impossible. But no. So far, so good.

He lit a cheroot, and looked to Perry. 'Want one?'

'I reckon I would, Sergeant.' Perry was pleased with himself as he lit up with a sigh, luxuriating in this unexpected bonus.

Then Pollock heard a low whistle, and steeled himself. He had to get this right somehow. He took Perry with him and walked along the street past the club, moving towards that lane.

'Oh, Jesus,' he said suddenly. 'I knew I was in the wrong place. Look, you go through there to the mews, and no tricks, I'll be right behind you. I'll go back and tell Jack to bring the buggy round the back.'

'What?'

'Just get going!'

'Righto.'

Still enjoying his cheroot, Baldy sauntered into the lane. He didn't care what this job was, he was out, that was the main thing, and this was no time for tricks. He wouldn't be surprised if they had a job for him working in one of these rows of stables out the back here; he knew the area well. He'd stay just as long as he had to, so bugger them, and after that he'd take his time, meander back to Maryborough to collect something that had been waiting for him for a long time. He sniffed the aroma of the cheroot. And he'd buy himself a hundred of these here smokes, for a start.

From the dank dimness of the lane he saw a gent coming in from the other end, his top hat silhouetted against the light, a swell, a real swell. Habit caused him to take a quick look behind him – Pollock had not caught up yet – this used to be a favoured spot for footpads. Still could be, he thought meanly, but he was on his best behaviour today with a cop on his tail . . . He turned his saunter into a swagger, flicking the cheroot stub ahead of him, because he was a gent himself now, and was wearing the glad rags to prove it. He was as good as this bloke and he wasn't about to make way for him. Baldy moved into the centre of the lane, where flat bluestone formed a shallow gutter and strode on.

They were only a few yards apart when he recognised Carnegie. Carnegie! Jesus wept! And Pollock coming up behind him! He dared not look back; instead, he bent his head, looking away, trying to shield his face from the man ahead of him. They were not supposed to know each other. He had to keep walking . . .

Allyn had seen the large figure coming towards him and was a little nervous at first; gentlemen had been mugged in this lane, but rarely in broad daylight these days. And anyway, the fellow, he could see, was flashily dressed, hardly likely to be a footpad, just a spiv of some sort. He seemed familiar. There was something familiar about him. Carnegie kept his head high but was eyeing the man nevertheless. For some reason the fellow frightened him; he was very large. Carnegie grasped his cane to defend himself in case the spiv tried to strike him from behind as they passed.

Then he stared. He knew the man. He stared again and recognised Perry, who was now shielding his face hoping Allyn Carnegie, his former partner, didn't recognise him. He'd almost got away with it, dressed up fit to kill, and wouldn't he be – Allyn's mind was racing – and wouldn't he be, with money to burn? But no amount of money or new clothes could hide that cheap thug.

Allyn saw red. All that suffering, frustration and fear were released as he attacked Perry with his cane, with a violence that he had never known

337

he possessed, screaming at the bastard: 'You pig! You filth! Thought I wouldn't find you one day. I'll kill you, you bastard . . .'

Perry was pushing him away. 'No! No! Keep going, you bloody fool. I don't know youse! Get away from me.'

In his frenzy, it didn't occur to Carnegie that the big man was not reacting normally, that the thug could have flattened him with a blow. Finding that Perry was only trying to get away from him, Carnegie grabbed his shirt to prevent his escape, at the same time clawing at his chest, screaming obscenities at him. The cane bounced from his hand but he didn't care; he flung himself at Perry, kicking and clawing, grabbing him by the collar as if he hoped to strangle him, refusing to disengage, and all the time Perry was frantically trying to prise him off . . .

'Get away, you fool!'

Suddenly there were troopers trying to rescue the thug, and Carnegie was even more enraged. 'This man attacked me,' he shouted, his voice shrill, echoing and echoing, as a stillness settled and Perry stood, shaking his head dismally.

'You're mad, Carnegie,' he said. 'Stark ravin' bloody mad.'

Halfway down the lane the door to the service entrance of the club opened, and Carnegie squinted, seeing another familiar figure. It was Kemp. What was he doing here? He wasn't a member. Still, he had his uses now. 'This fellow attacked me,' he called. 'Arrest him.'

'Is that right?' Kemp asked Perry.

'Yeah. I attacked him. He aggravated me.'

Carnegie was puffing, flushed, still agitated, his suit in disarray, his cane and hat lost someplace. He searched about for them as the enormity of the situation dawned on him, as he realised why Perry was being so conciliatory.

The troopers waited. Kemp picked up Carnegie's cane and handed it to him. He seemed in no hurry. A policeman came pounding down the lane, a tall, gangly fellow. Pollock! Allyn looked at him, bewildered.

'I believe you two gentlemen know each other,' Kemp said, at length.

'Don't know him,' Perry said, and Carnegie, regaining his balance, nodded wildly, rushing to agree.

'Never seen him before this.'

A trooper intervened. 'He called him Carnegie.'

The other one gave his opinion. 'I was coming in from the mews, I saw Carnegie attack Perry.'

'That's not true,' Carnegie shouted. 'Not true.'

'It is so,' the trooper argued.

'Never mind,' Kemp said wearily. 'I heard it all. You men take Perry to the lockup. And you, Mr Carnegie, will have to come along with us. You've got some explaining to do.'

'About what? I'll do no such thing! How dare you!'

But Kemp did dare. Ignoring Carnegie's protests, he instructed Pollock to bring the ex-Commissioner to police headquarters forthwith. He noticed that, for once, the Sergeant was speechless. He'd gambled and won, by the look of things, and now he seemed to be having trouble taking it all in.

Kemp strode through to the mews to collect his mount, still mulling over Pollock's astonished reaction.

'Well I'll be damned! I don't think that rogue really thought it would work. It was just a last-ditch stand and he sucked me into it.' Kemp had suspected all along that the idea hadn't originated with Lanfield. But he had also known that Carnegie's nerves were not up to a sudden shock; the man was a walking ghost, as believable as a two-headed penny. Kemp would never have allowed Carnegie out of his sights.

But now, he frowned, let's see to Carnegie and Perry. And if we've got it right this time, the Sergeant deserves the credit.

Baldy lost his good suit. He was back in the rough canvas prison duds, back in the Brisbane jail but fighting off all comers. He denied, he lied, he doubled back and became thoroughly confused about whether or not he knew Carnegie, and how and why. The interrogations began all over again, thanks to that lunatic Carnegie. Baldy knew now that it had been a setup, and that if Carnegie had had the brains to keep walking he'd have been a free man within a week or so. But he had had nothing to do with that raid. Nothing. He must have seen Carnegie at the goldfields; that was how he knew his name. And he had mugged him in that alley. Why not? He'd looked like a good mark and no one was watching. Stupid? With cops about? All right. But he just didn't think. So what?

Baldy, the survivor of interrogations and beatings, was still a hard nut to crack. Pollock was ready to bring down the German boat-builder.

On the other hand, Carnegie was distraught. Humiliated. He demanded his lawyer be present at all interviews, and that request was granted, but he was forced to remain in custody for questioning, and by this Jesse Fields had stumbled on the biggest story of his career.

The *Courier* ran the headline: 'Former Gold Commissioner taken in for questioning'. And the town was in uproar. The ambush and murders at Blackwater Creek had become sensational news again.

Mal was in the same jail, but he was suddenly switched to another block when Baldy was brought in. As soon as he read the paper that was being slipped about the prison, he called for his lawyer.

'There's nothing we can do right now,' Lanfield told him. 'We just have to wait and see what emerges.'

'But I want to talk to Carnegie. I want to confront him. I'll make the bastard talk.'

'Not possible. The best you can do is sit tight. I've asked for an adjournment on your case and it appears it will be approved.'

'And I have to sit here. I'm innocent. I didn't do anything wrong. My life has been wrecked. It's not fair.'

He asked about Emilie. He wanted to see her. 'Are you sure she has gone home?'

'Yes, I told you that last week.'

339

'I wish she'd waited.'

'Mr Willoughby, that young lady has been a good friend to you. I don't think you have any idea how awful it was for her to find herself photographed, written up in the newspapers, the butt of gossip, from her association with you.'

'Yes, I do, and I'm sorry about that.'

'If you'll forgive me for saying so, you do not know. Young ladies of her class would find publicity of any sort, let alone the sordidness you've inflicted on her, excruciating. Your values are far removed from hers. She has repaid your kindness to her by underwriting all of your legal costs and I suggest you leave it at that.'

'What do you mean?'

'For God's sake, leave her alone. Can't I make this any plainer?'

'You like her?'

'I do. There's every possibility now that you might escape this charge, but whether or not you do, if you care for Miss Tissington at all, don't force yourself on her any more.'

'You think I'm a waster?'

Lanfield rubbed a finger behind his ear and looked closely at his client. 'You are what you choose to be. Miss Tissington is what she chooses to be. You are not her kind. You would be doing her a great favour if you understood that.'

Mal had plenty of time to think about that unwanted advice. He had dreamed of being freed, of finding Emilie again, and now he began to understand what a pipedream that had been. But he still loved her. How could he not love her? She was his world. What was left? He had written her a long letter, apologising for causing her this trouble, thanking her, and with the courage of the pen telling her how much he loved her and how everything would be all right once they were together again. But how could he send it now? He dreamed of her sweetness and innocence, and saw himself as he really was, practically a vagrant, not fit to follow in her footsteps.

When Pollock came to see him with more and more questions, all hopped up about netting Carnegie, Mal's responses were dull, disinterested. He didn't care any more.

The Sergeant was surprised. 'What's the matter? You could be cleared.'

'And who'd care? You tried to hang me, you bastard.'

'I was only doing my job. I was trying to protect you, remember, and you bolted on me. But your mate Hillier stuck by you. He gave me hell, sticking up for you.'

'So where's he now?'

'Maryborough. He's the manager of the bond store.'

That news didn't matter much to Mal at the time, but later he thought of an idea. If he shouldn't write to Emilie, he could at least write to Clive. Ask him how she was . . . ask him about her . . . they were in the same town. Dear Emilie.

With his four cellmates, Mal lined up dutifully as the barred gate was unlocked, and shuffled out to join the queue of hundreds of prisoners headed for the mess hall, burdened more by his own thoughts than by prison discipline.

Carnegie's lawyer was a short, dumpy man with pudgy hands that he kept slapping on Kemp's desk as he huffed and puffed about this insult to a fine, upstanding gentleman, dragged off the streets like a common offender. He threatened to sue for wrongful arrest. He warned Kemp that he was a newcomer to Brisbane and so would have to learn that he could not treat gentlemen like Mr Carnegie in this manner, not in this town. He spoke of friends in high places who would not tolerate this high-handed treatment of a good, kind man, and he went on so long that even Carnegie, sitting miserably by Kemp's desk, was becoming restless. He could see this was going nowhere.

Eventually Kemp, unimpressed, asked him to be seated.

'In the first place, sir, your client is not under arrest as he seems to think; he has simply been detained for questioning. You have had time to talk to your client, so you must know this is a very serious matter.'

'He doesn't know any such thing,' Carnegie exclaimed. 'I have no idea why I'm here.'

'You don't? That surprises me. But so that everybody knows what's happening here, you are being detained, Mr Carnegie, on suspicion of implication in the crimes of murder and robbery at Blackwater Creek outside Maryborough.'

The lawyer rocked back on his heels, stunned. 'Preposterous! This can't be right.' He spun around to face Carnegie. 'They can't do this to you, Allyn. They can't! It's preposterous!' He was stuttering, and Kemp guessed that Carnegie's man was already out of his depth.

'Of course it's preposterous,' Carnegie snapped. 'I wish to leave here immediately.'

'All in good time,' Kemp said. 'We have a man in custody, a known criminal, who we now have reason to believe took part in that crime and who, we also have reason to believe, is an associate of yours, Mr Carnegie.'

'That's a lie!'

'Nothing could be further from the truth,' his lawyer echoed, bewildered.

'We shall see. I have two officers waiting to interview your client, sir. One of my inspectors, and a sergeant from Maryborough who is known to Mr Carnegie.'

'I refuse to be interrogated and I certainly will not talk to Pollock. This is more harassment; I've put up with this for far too long.' Carnegie stood. 'I wish to leave.'

Kemp ignored him. He left the office and gave the Inspector and Pollock their instructions. 'No pussyfooting about any more. Hit him with everything you've got. Perry's story is full of holes now. Rerun the raid as you see it, right down to Perry escaping by boat with the gold. As

341

if Perry has enlightened you. Bring up the Griffen case; that will frighten the hell out of his lawyer.' His voice was harsh. 'People talk about the big gold haul, but three men died there. Don't forget that. Every instinct tells me that these two were in cahoots; it's up to you to find out.'

He turned to the Inspector. 'Carnegie is slippery; let Pollock take the lead but listen to every bloody word. Wear the bastard down. I don't care how long it takes.'

Allyn tried to contain the storm that was gathering about him. There was menace in this room, worse than any nightmare, and he pleaded with his lawyer to put a stop to these accusations and lies, but all the fool could do was offer comfort, telling him it wouldn't be long now. They were not accusations, they were just questions. Allyn screamed at him that this was not so.

'Can't you see what's happening here, you damned fool? I'm being railroaded. They've got two of the outlaws. Perry and Willoughby; *they* did it! Not me. I was shot!'

'So you agree now that Perry was one of the outlaws?' the Inspector asked quietly.

'I didn't say that. How do I know?'

The questions seemed to come in waves, like the nausea, and all the time they kept returning to Perry and what he'd told them, insisting that Carnegie did know Perry, that was established, so why had he lied about it? And that Perry had been at the goldfields with him.

'Not with me,' he whined. 'No. Never. I never saw him before in my life. This is atrocious. I am not well. I need a doctor.'

They brought in tea and biscuits and lit the lamps. The two faces across the desk from him seemed to enlarge grotesquely and then recede, and Allyn had to turn his head away. He wished he could faint, or fake a faint, but even that was beyond him.

Pollock sat back. 'How can you say Willoughby was there when Perry admits he was not?'

'Perry's got it wrong. He knows Willoughby was there.'

Allyn heard his lawyer suck in his breath and plant those fat hands, with an ugly ruby ring on show, on the desk. 'I think enough is enough for today.'

But Pollock was firm. 'If we don't complete this interview now, your client will have to be held overnight.' He looked at Allyn. 'In the cells.'

Allyn sat with his head in his hands as they argued over that, but then the Inspector intervened. 'One thing interests me. The gold. Perry's a rich man, he says so himself. He's laughing about it, he says he can afford the best barristers in the country. How are you placed, Mr Carnegie?'

'What's that got to do with me?'

'With Perry's evidence, a great deal, I'm afraid. It looks like being a long-drawn-out case; these matters usually are. Perry says Willoughby was not there. He had to have a partner. He has implicated you by association, Mr Carnegie, and you have returned the favour by acknowledging that you know him. Why *did* you attack him, Mr Carnegie?'

'I did not. You heard him say I did not.'

'We have witnesses . . .' the Inspector said drily.

The questions went on. Allyn felt himself crumbling. He wept, not in self-pity but in rage, that Perry was a rich man, that Perry had ruined everything from sheer greed. That Perry would drag him into court, not like this, a detainee, but as an accused. He could see it now, and he cringed. He sobbed. His lawyer, the fool, more interested than dismayed, made futile whimpers as those two men, with their grim faces, pounded at him over and over, dredging up dead men, dredging up Taylor his clerk, a good and honest man who had a wife and three children, and Allyn saw the nightmare again of those men muttering in his room and realised that the other people with them had been their children. He had read that between them the guards and Taylor had nine children, and he had seen them at the funeral. Those children, standing emptily with the widows . . .

'I didn't shoot them,' he screamed. 'You have to believe me. I didn't shoot them. Perry did. Then he shot me. He's got the gold. Every penny of it.' He grabbed his lawyer's arm. 'Tell them. I've got nothing. You know that. He's my cousin. He knows I'm broke. Tell them . . . I had nothing to do with it. How could I?'

The two policemen sat silently as the weeping man collapsed into his lawyer's arms, still appealing to his cousin to explain, to make them see that this was all wrong, that he was a victim, couldn't they understand that?

Days of confusion followed for Allyn's lawyer, his cousin George, another Carnegie. He had neither the skill nor the heart for a case like this, he was unaccustomed to being rowdied by reporters and he was horrified that his own family name was being dragged in the mire. George was furious with Allyn for getting him into this. Had he been given the slightest hint of why Allyn had been detained, he'd have made himself unavailable very smartly. Unfortunately, other legal gentlemen that he had approached on Allyn's behalf were quicker off the mark than he was, and were all otherwise engaged.

Finally he decided to call on John Carnegie, to discuss the serious nature of these charges and perhaps mention the delicate matter of his fees, since it was known in the family that John held the purse strings. His heart sank, though, when he saw two men on the front veranda. He'd hoped to talk to John in private. Worse still, the two men who welcomed him gravely were Pastor Trimble and young Tom, John's son, a churlish fellow at the best of times.

It didn't take long for Tom to cut through the small talk and insist they get down to business, as he put it.

'In the first place, my father is under the impression that Allyn is facing the bankruptcy court, so we'll leave it at that. I don't want this matter discussed in front of him.'

'Quite.' George Carnegie nodded.

'And on no condition should he be expected to pay any or part of my uncle's legal expenses.'

George shrugged unhappily, wondering who else in the family he could approach.

'I'm glad you came, though, George. What the hell is going on? Is there any truth in the accusations that are flying around? Can you give me the gist of it? Sounds bloody mad, the whole thing.'

George did his best, outlining the case and the difficulties and the unfortunate admissions made not only by the other fellow, Perry, but by Allyn himself, battling through young Tom's angry criticism of his part in all this. Cheap and easy advice in hindsight from this young upstart on how he should have done this or that to protect his uncle, until George protested that this case had been foisted on him.

'It's no use blaming me,' he snapped. 'I had no inkling that suspicions existed regarding Allyn. I was shocked. It's all too frightful. I don't normally handle criminal cases.'

'But you will get him off? The whole thing is obviously a fabrication. He's a Carnegie! The family would be tarred for generations with a scandal like this.'

'Then the family will have to help me. Unless you want him sent up for murder, you'll have to pass the hat around. I need a barrister, if not a local gentleman then someone from Sydney. You can't expect me to carry the load, I can't do it.'

'You have to. To hell with barristers. You know Uncle Allyn, you know he is not capable of conniving in such a hideous affair.'

George was quiet. He resented young Tom's attitude. He knew that Allyn had brought this on himself, that his own responses to police questions had been seriously incriminating, and he dreaded a long-drawn-out trial. If the Carnegie name was mud now, it would be a lot worse before this was over.

The Pastor intervened, gently. 'Could I have a word?'

'By all means,' George said. At least Trimble had allowed him to explain without interruptions.

'Would you say that Allyn is guilty, George?'

'Of course he's not,' young Tom snapped.

George looked out over the veranda rails at tall, still gumtrees standing sentinel down by the gate, and he heard the whip-whistle of a kurrawong, and the answering call from somewhere in the distance. 'It's not for me to say.'

'We all seek the Lord's truth, George. There is no other way. I have to ask if you are defending a guilty man or an innocent one. You should be clear on this.'

'What difference does it make? I'm stuck with defending him. Can't you see that?'

'Then I urge we kneel and pray for truth.'

Neither George nor Tom was in a mood for prayer, but Pastor Trimble soon had them on their knees for the Lord's Prayer, followed by an impassioned plea to God to reveal the truth, his voice lifting to a cry, just before he turned the Lord's attention to George.

'Let your servant speak! In the name of Jesus, speak, George! Only the truth will be our comfort. You dare not lie to the Lord. Thou shalt not kill, sayeth the Lord, and who dares to defy Him? Thou shalt not steal, sayeth the Lord, to you, George. Has his servant Allyn broken these commandments?'

'God help us, he has,' George intoned. 'What are we to do?'

'Amen,' Pastor Trimble said triumphantly, climbing to his feet and dusting off his trousers.

The other two stood, and Tom reached for a tobacco pack on a bench. 'That's bloody lovely. What do we do now?'

The Pastor knew. 'There is only one course. Allyn has to confess to the Lord and to his accusers. He has to beg forgiveness while there is still time. I know George would not have come to that conclusion lightly, and in listening to your account, George, neither did I.'

'He still has to defend him,' Tom insisted, but Pastor Trimble could not approve.

'The Lord is judge. George may not use trickery. Too many of our courts are the refuge of sinners. Criminals lie, perjure themselves in their fight for freedom, and they pay lawyers to encourage, nay, assist, in twisting God's truth for their own ends. Many men of your profession sacrifice their godliness on the altar of deception, George. You must not turn yourself into a sinner, even to save your dear cousin.' He bowed his head. 'God's will be done.'

'You think he should plead guilty?' George whispered, looking nervously at Tom.

'If he is guilty, he must. There is no alternative.'

Tom was listening carefully. 'It would get this mess over quickly, wouldn't it?'

'But they'll hang him,' George protested.

Tom shrugged. 'From what you tell us, they've got him, George. They'll hang the bastard anyway. Excuse the language, Pastor.'

Trimble nodded forgiveness. 'We should go, George, go together. We will see Allyn and pray with him. We will give him trust in the Lord, for that is what the poor man needs now. He must tell the truth, all of it, without recourse to legal machinations, for the love of God, for our dear Lord will never desert a repentant sinner. We are all in the hands of the Lord.'

Rumours flew around police headquarters that Carnegie had confessed to employing Baldy Perry in an ambush even more cold-blooded than the plot hatched by that other Gold Commissioner, Griffen. They talked of the doggedness of Pollock, the sergeant from the bush, who'd even taken on the brass in his determination to track this crime to its conclusion, betting that he'd be up for a promotion now. They laughed, delighted by the whisper that Superintendent Kemp had pulled a radical stunt in forcing a confrontation between Perry and Carnegie, at a time when they were not aware they were being observed. The troopers who had witnessed the setup, and the set-to between the two miscreants, swore it was true.

'The game was up then,' they said. 'By God, this Super might have seemed slow and a real plodder, but he's smart. This is a real feather in his cap.'

Where was the gold then? No one seemed to know.

What about Willoughby? His lawyer had been wearing out a track to Kemp's office to have all charges against Sonny dismissed, and it seemed certain that Kemp would approve once he had the statements of the other pair signed and sealed.

The mounted police took note. They felt sorry for Willoughby and decided to help. They sent a telegraphed message to Sergeant Moloney out at Chinchilla, the man who'd brought Sonny in.

Upstairs, Kemp was trying to wade through a backlog of work that had built up over the last few busy days. A sudden gust of wind sent loose papers flurrying, so he launched himself from his swivel chair to close the window, taking the time to look down into the gloom as the gas lamps flared, seemingly lit by an invisible hand. He caught sight of a tall, lanky figure crossing the road and sighed. He hoped Pollock had something definite to report this time. Since Carnegie had got religion and revealed the whole miserable plot, Perry had owned up to his part in it, but there was still the gold, and hundreds of pounds in English banknotes and Australian sovereigns. Where were the proceeds of that robbery? What had they done with the loot?

He was still standing there when Pollock came in. 'Well?'

'So far, no good. Perry says he did exactly as he was told. They slung the gold and cash into satchels. Carnegie helped him drop the satchels down into the boat. He rowed across the river with the haul, just as I guessed he had, to where his horse was waiting.'

'After he shot Carnegie?'

'Yes. Old Baldy's savage about Carnegie. He wishes now that he'd shot him dead and got away on his own. He's bleating and whining now. No remorse about the other shootings, none at all. Apparently Carnegie screamed blue murder at him . . . Baldy was only supposed to give him a flesh wound, not bust his arm.'

Kemp smiled grimly. 'Sounds like he wavered.'

'Yes. Another reason why Carnegie is so livid with him. Anyway, Carnegie couldn't be seen with any of the spoils, so Baldy was instructed to take the haul to town. Which he did. He rode down the other side of the river, crossed on the ferry without any bother.'

'That'd be right. Just another horseman crossing with other traffic. Then what?'

'Then he took it, as he was told to do, and buried it under Carnegie's house.'

'God Almighty! Have you got a search going?'

346

'Yes. I telegraphed the station. I reckon they'll be digging under lamplight already. Anyway, Baldy says he was told to lie low for a few weeks, until the fuss died down. Then he had to go back to Carnegie's house, in the dead of night again, so that they could divvy up the take. But he didn't make it. He went back to work on the wharves, got himself into that drunken fight and ended up in jail.'

'That means Carnegie's got it.'

'It would seem so. Carnegie told him under no circumstances to make contact with him, except by that prearranged late-night meeting, so Baldy couldn't let his partner know where he was. He thought the haul was safe; he just had to sit out his sentence and then call on his pal for his share.'

'And Carnegie couldn't afford not to share with him.'

Pollock laughed. 'Not with a bloke like Perry. Not unless he wanted to get dead too. No wonder Baldy was sitting about in jail crowing that he was a rich man.' He leaned against the window ledge as Kemp moved back to the seat at his desk. 'But we still have a problem. Carnegie reckons he never saw the satchels. That Baldy didn't carry out his side of the bargain. He says he waited and waited but Baldy never came. He reckons he was double-crossed.'

'We'll just have to see. I hope it's still there. Carnegie could have moved it.'

The Sergeant nodded. 'I hope it's there too. Baldy's story has got a ring of truth in it. He's got nothing to lose now. He knows he's for the rope. But that bloody Carnegie, he seems to think that if he pleads guilty and because he didn't shoot anyone himself, he'll get off with maybe a light sentence.'

'Where did he get that idea?'

'Putting his trust in God. He says he never saw any of the haul so he can't be charged with robbery.'

Kemp scowled. 'A damn good reason to keep it hidden. To know nothing about it.'

'In his eyes. And with us nosing about all the time, to let the haul stay hidden until what he calls our harassment finally petered out. He could afford to wait.'

'And Willoughby? Carnegie's definitely lying here. He's trying to hang on to some truth in his story. Sometimes he remembers Willoughby, then when we rerun the tale he forgets all about him. But surprisingly Baldy came good. He said, "That dumb Willoughby don't know nothin' about it." '.

'He says Willoughby was a bunny, served up by Carnegie to keep the police busy.'

'Willoughby's been saying that all along.'

'Of course he would. But hang on, our Baldy told me he didn't even get a look at the kid. He just heard someone ride off about dawn. And it was just as well! Hard enough to plug two blokes fast without trying for a third . . .'

'Two!'

'Yes. I thought you'd like that. He only shot the guards. Carnegie shot Taylor in the back.'

'The lying bastard!'

Pollock grimaced. 'God isn't going to like that, Mr Carnegie.'

The following afternoon Maryborough police informed Kemp that they had dug up every inch of land under and around Carnegie's house, right to the boundaries, and had also searched his house thoroughly, but had found nothing. Kemp was so exasperated, he sent his deputy to confront Carnegie.

'Don't waste any time with him now. Tell him we know he shot Taylor, and that he is in possession of the stolen gold and the bank cash. Make it clear to him that he'd better say his prayers because he will get the death penalty. So he might as well make a clean breast of it and reveal the whereabouts of the proceeds of that robbery. They have to be returned to their rightful owners.'

The deputy returned to admit failure. 'He still claims he didn't shoot anyone and he doesn't know where the money is. Or the gold.'

'Oh well, leave it for now. When it gets closer to the day, he'll squeal. Once he realises he really is headed for the gallows. It probably hasn't sunk in yet.'

But there were to be no more interrogations for Allyn Carnegie. No more fears and humiliations. No more prison cells. At dawn, when the iron doors began clanging open, he was found dead in his cell, hanging from a window bar with a rope made from mattress ticking. Allyn Carnegie had decided to take his chances with the Lord instead of the courts.

They were all in the same prison. When Baldy heard, he laughed fit to kill. He even sought out Willoughby in the yard.

'Do you know, that bastard tried to blame me for shooting Taylor? And I never did.'

'So what?' Mal said angrily. 'You shot the other two. And you tried to fit me up with it too.'

'Not me, mate, Carnegie. I never said you were there. I done you a favour. I reckon you ought to thank me. I told 'em you were the bunny. That bloody Carnegie just gave the coppers a hare to chase. You're clear, mate.'

'Well why am I still here? You're lying, Perry. Why would you do that for me?'

'Because I want you to do me a favour. You owe me now. Jimmy McPherson's down on the island. He got five years.' He took Mal aside and whispered, 'After I'm gone, you get a message to him. You tell him I died a rich man. I done better than any of them.'

'What are you raving about?'

'Never mind,' Perry growled. 'Just give him the message. And before you go, get me some baccy.'

The day was interminable as Mal laboured under doubts that he had been cleared, and the night brought impatience and anger. He kicked at his cell door, shouting at the guards to let him out. They ignored him, leaving it to his cellmates to threaten him with a bashing if he didn't shut up.

Lanfield was in court the next day but he hadn't forgotten Willoughby. He sent his clerk with his apologies . . .

'Mr Lanfield didn't want you to have to stay in prison a minute longer than was necessary,' he explained. 'The police have dropped the charges against you, you're a free man.'

'It's over?' Mal asked breathlessly, as a smiling guard unlocked the gate. 'Are you sure?'

'Yes, sir.'

'Ah, God bless you! And you will thank your boss for me?' He almost danced along the stone corridors with the clerk, through gate after gate and on into the courtyard. Then he remembered. 'Listen, could you get me some tobacco? I promised a prisoner . . .'

'Certainly. Mr Lanfield instructed me to look after you. I'm afraid you'll have to wait here a little while until I complete the paperwork, but I'll bring the tobacco back with me.'

The courtyard was small and bare, like a high-walled stone box, with barred gates at two sides, but above him was a patch of blue, and Mal sighed. It was a fine day. A truly fine day.

Just before he reached the opposite gate, which a guard was unlocking for him, the clerk turned back.

'Mr Willoughby. Forgive me. I am so excited at having the honour of arranging your release, I almost forgot. I have a letter for you.'

Mal took it gingerly. He saw the neat, precise handwriting and guessed it had to be from Emilie. Who else? Despite the joy of hearing from her, he opened the envelope as carefully as he could with large, clumsy hands, trying not to tear it any more than necessary . . . but it was from Clive. In answer to his own letter. Quickly he scanned the bottom of the page to see if there was a greeting from Emilie, but no such luck. Still, it was nice of Clive to write, he decided, resigned.

Clive was glad to hear he was well. Clive was sure that with the good offices of Mr Lanfield he would soon be freed, so he hoped to see Mal when all this was over. Clive was leaving his present job at the bond store shortly and opening a shop in Maryborough . . . Mal skipped over the explanations of that venture because he'd seen Emilie's name ahead.

Emilie sends her best wishes. We are proud that we both believed in your innocence from the very beginning of your travail.

Mal guessed what travail meant, but this talk of them *both* sent up warning signals.

You ask about Emilie. She is much better now, but she was naturally

349

very upset at being set upon by newspapers, quite a shock for her, I must say, though she insists you are not to blame. She's a brave girl and I do believe she would still have gone to Brisbane on your behalf, regardless of the personal cost.

Mal nodded. She was a brave and lovely girl, but he didn't need Clive to tell him that. Thank you.

She had a bad time of it for a while. Her sister has ostracised her. She was the butt of gossip in this town too, and was dismissed from her post as governess. All quite unfair, but even here scandal thrives.

'Oh, Christ, I'm so sorry,' Mal groaned. 'Poor Emilie.' He read on. What else could they do to her?

But now we're all settling down again with the welcome news that Carnegie has been apprehended with his henchman, which should facilitate your release. I have to tell you that I have asked Emilie for her hand in marriage. I am aware that her cottage does, in fact, belong to you and wish to reimburse you for the purchase price . . .

Mal crushed the letter in his hand. Clive was going to marry Emilie? No! NO! 'Emilie's my girl!' he cried, appalled. How had this come about? Then he remembered he'd told Clive to make himself known to her. Bloody hell! He'd done that all right. What a bloody fool.
    'We'll see about that,' he vowed as the clerk returned. 'Have you got the tobacco?'
    'Yes. I hope it's the right brand.'
    Mal shrugged. Who the hell cared what brand? He banged on the gate. 'I forgot something.'
    The guard looked enquiringly at the clerk, who nodded. 'All right. Get a move on, Sonny. You don't need to hang about here any more.'
    He ran through the deserted block, glancing up at the tiers of cells above him, with their long, railed walkways, and surprised the guard at the yard.
    'Can't bear to leave us, eh?' he laughed.
    'I promised a bloke I'd get him some tobacco,' Mal said.
    'All right, give it to me. I'll hand it on.'
    Mal's eyes twinkled. 'Ah, come on, mate. Let me do the right thing. I don't want to welsh on a promise. They've got me thinking like a bloody convict now.'
    'Go on, then. Five minutes. In and out, or you'll get caught up in the count.'
    He sped through the mobs of men mooching aimlessly about the great yard, quickly spotting Perry's bulk leaning against the wall of the building. Perry was on his own, and Mal remembered with a shiver that other convicts were apt to avoid men destined for the gallows. Bad luck,

they'd told him, but he guessed it was more than that; few had the gift of the gab. They wouldn't know what to say to them.

'Here's your baccy,' he puffed, surprised that he was out of breath from such a small exertion, blaming it on the months of inactivity he'd spent in this place.

'Good on youse,' Baldy said, taking the package. 'You won't forget my message?'

'No, I won't forget. But you know McPherson. He'll want proof. If you get what I mean.'

'Yeah,' Baldy sneered. 'But he can take a running jump like all the rest of them. It's mine. And the crocs'. No one will ever find it. Just make sure you let him know I died a rich man. I beat him. I always knew I could.'

'All right.'

'And you listen here, kid. Don't think you can go flappin' your mouth off to the coppers, because it won't do no good. The whole bloody circus went down with Carnegie.'

'Oh well. I wish you luck, Baldy.'

'Don't call me Baldy,' he sniffed. 'The name's Angus.'

Mal sprinted back to the waiting clerk, who informed him that the next stop was the front desk, where he had to be signed out. That over, the clerk ushered him towards the rear of the building, but Mal balked.

'I never did nothing wrong. These bastards have taken half a year out of my life and I've not got a bloody thing to show for it. I'm entitled to walk out the front door.'

'Bear with me,' the clerk said. 'This is just to save time.'

There were no more guards. They walked calmly through the cramped administration offices and out, at last, into the sunlight. He was free! Mal wished he felt good about it, but he didn't. He frowned as a policeman walked towards him. What did they want now?

'Don't you remember me?' he asked, and Mal squinted.

'Ah, yes. Moloney from Chinchilla. I was coming out to see you . . .'

'No need,' Moloney grinned. 'Take a look here.'

Other mounted police gathered about, clapping as they led out his horse, Striker, all dolled up too, mane plaited, coat ashine, rigged with a new saddle and bridle.

'Oh, Jesus!' Mal gulped as Striker made straight for him, nudging and pushing at his friend.

'I told you I'd take care of him,' Moloney said. 'The lads let me know you were due for release, so I brought him in for you.'

Shaking his head, Mal fondled the horse. 'God Almighty, Striker! I didn't think I'd ever see him again. Thanks, mates. For coppers, you're a decent lot.'

The little ceremony over, the men drifted away, but Moloney stayed. 'Are you all right, Sonny?'

'Sure I am,' he said tersely. 'Except for the stripes on my back to remember the island by.'

'I'm sorry about that. I was only doing my job bringing you in. No hard feelings?'

'No.'

'Well, if you're ever in Chinchilla, you look me up.'

'I don't think I could trust myself to go there,' Mal grinned. 'You might find my uncle hanging by his heels in the chookhouse.'

Then there was only Mal and Lanfield's clerk.

'That was very touching,' the clerk told Mal. 'And what a fine horse.' He took out a carefully folded five-pound note. 'Mr Lanfield wants you to have this. You can't walk out of prison with nothing.'

Mal looked down at it. 'Whose money is that? Lanfield's or Miss Tissington's?'

'Oh! Dear me. I suppose it will go on the account.'

'The account being paid by Miss Tissington?'

'I expect so.'

'Then I don't want it.'

'But you have to have something, Mr Willoughby.'

'I don't want it.'

To break the impasse, the clerk dug in his pocket. 'Look here. I've got a few shillings. Nine shillings . . . please take it.'

'Can you get it back from your boss?'

'Oh yes, sir. Reimbursement. Daily expenses, plus the tobacco.'

'Good. Just see that Miss Tissington doesn't have to pay. It has cost her enough already.'

They shook hands, and the young clerk watched as the famous Sonny Willoughby rode out the gate, a free man. Then he corrected his thoughts. The formerly famous Sonny Willoughby. The public was quick to forget. And no one would care what that innocent man had suffered. How he'd been hunted and incarcerated not only in this jail but in the dreaded St Helena. No one would be interested.

At first he was all fired up to ride straight to Maryborough, only a couple of hundred miles north, but it was such a joy to be free, to be able to go wherever he pleased, Mal's old ways soon took precedent. He couldn't resist a fairground, and after only a day up the coast road he was again wandering the tents and stalls, being greeted warmly by old friends. He knew he shouldn't delay, that he had a mission. Clive had only said he had asked for Emilie's hand in marriage. Not that she had accepted. It was important that Mal talk to her himself. But he dreaded the meeting, dreaded to hear that he had lost her to Clive, and most of all, wondered how he could have had the cheek to think a lady like Emilie would consider him as a suitable husband.

Mal's confidence had deserted him. The degradation of the prisons had done its work, it would take time for him to recover from the crushing humiliations he had suffered, and then Lanfield had delivered the almost mortal blow, pointing out cruelly that Emilie was too good for him. Clive, in his arrogance, had allowed the same thing, giving no thought to the alternative: that Emilie might be interested in Mal, not him. Taking it for granted that Mal wasn't even in the picture. It was what he hadn't said that annoyed and depressed Mal. Just the cold news of his proposal, as if a bloke like Mal didn't count. And in Emilie's eyes, maybe he didn't. Thinking of her troubles mortified him even more. He wished Clive hadn't told him that she'd lost her job and had been upset by the publicity. Mal knew he'd have to bear the blame for that, and one day he would apologise. Try to make it up to her.

When all the stallholders and sideshow people and the ever-present gypsy fortune-tellers moved on, Mal went with them. After all, they were moving north to another town. He seemed to be the same happy-go-lucky bloke, but a lot of his cockiness had been knocked out of him. He needed these people, their reassurance, their easy acceptance of him, and he really needed some fun again. Their laughter was a tonic, and he took great comfort in sitting about their campfires late at night, listening to their yarns, and their mad disregard of convention.

They detoured inland to a few country towns and then wound their way back to the coast towns, and Mal stayed with them. He gave a hand with the animals, the camp equipment, sometimes accepting payment of a few shillings, other times just being helpful. He operated gleefully as a 'gatc', winning prizes which were returned, to encourage the crowds to try their luck, and he played cards with well-heeled gents, using marked cards, not caring that he could probably have won without cheating, because it was obvious that the young blokes who swaggered up to the tables could have done with a few lessons in the game.

Mal had no pity on them. He watched them in their tweedy coats and cord pants and pricey boots, with their lady friends on their arms, having a jolly old time, and envy crept in. They hadn't been hunted across the country, slung into jail, flogged and chained, and then set free without so much as an apology. As if they were some sort of animal, let loose, casually, from a muster.

Girls offered him respite from those cheerless times. They flocked about him. Some recognised him as the famous Sonny Willoughby, which his friends laughingly called 'an added attraction'. One spruiker even wanted to use Sonny's fame as a drawcard for his flea circus, but Mal wouldn't come at that. Mal's hair had grown to its thick blond thatch again and the handsome young roustabout with his baby-blue eyes became a target for single and married women alike. The gypsies said he'd become more 'manful' now, because of his ordeals, and warned him to beware of bad women, while he smiled at the flirts and sometimes took them to his tent for a few hours. They were solace, their bodies soft and giving, and Mal was sorry for them, for himself. Once upon a time he would have slapped their bottoms and left the tents with them, arms about, laughing, understanding the fun of it, but now he was moody, confused, not much company any more. His gleeful spontaneity left behind somewhere.

Allora, the gypsy matriarch who, though she must have been in her sixties, had long jet-black hair garlanded with gaudy beads, worried about him. She said he was living under contrary stars that could not talk to each other. Too many of them. They only babbled at him. Wanting their own way. She said she saw a fine lady, and beauty, the spice of his life, beauty, wherever he found it. His private joy. All the colours of the rainbow. It was the gypsy in him.

As usual, Mal couldn't make any sense of it; he paid her his penny and gave her a peck on the cheek.

'You're leaving us,' she said.

Mal nodded. 'Yes. I have to be on my way.'

'From a cruel island to a kind island?'

'I think so. I have a lot to think about.'

'You will do what you will,' she said, giving him back the penny. 'I can't help you, dear boy. Think of us sometimes.'

Chapter Fifteen

For days the *Chronicle* had been running tantalising paragraphs about developments in the Blackwater case. Walt White had been unable to learn much himself, but he figured that since this waiting was making him wild with curiosity, then it was having the same effect on his readers.

When he did hear from Jesse, at last, that two men had been taken in for questioning, he couldn't contain his impatience. Angrily he sent a telegram to the Brisbane reporter: *Not good enough. Who?*

When the reply came, he stared, unbelieving ... *Angus Perry and Allyn Carnegie.*

He couldn't care less about Perry, whoever he was, but Carnegie! Now that was news! Front page. He went into his usual scramble, shouting orders, diving into files for all he could find on Carnegie's background then grabbing for a pen to write this himself, for hadn't he always said that Carnegie was implicated? Or had he? He couldn't remember. But it didn't matter; his pen flew.

After almost a week of agonising waiting, he was able to write, to crow that Carnegie had been charged! Along with a thug called Angus Perry, who was of no consequence to Walt as yet. He'd get to him later. But what of Sonny Willoughby? No mention of him so far. This was a Maryborough story. Walt hated hearing it in bits and pieces. He haunted the police station, demanding more information, but all he could glean was the theory that Carnegie had masterminded the raid, employing Perry to spring the attack. To Walt's pen it wasn't theory, it was fact, and he led with a cry of outrage against a man who had viciously betrayed the trust placed in him. The following day his front page demanded to know the whereabouts of OUR gold. Had the police forgotten the robbery?

He was so busy with all of this excitement and the daily reports he was receiving from Jesse that he had almost forgotten Willoughby, until he came across a casual line. 'Charges against Willoughby dismissed. Freed this morning.'

Walt nodded thoughtfully. No one was interested in Willoughby any more, but he could make something of it. He went in search of Miss Tissington.

When she opened her door, he wished her a good day and began to introduce himself, but she interrupted him. Coldly.

'I know who you are, Mr White. What can I do for you?'

'I wondered if I could have a chat with you? About events unfolding now, the Blackwater business.'

'You may not, sir. I have nothing to say.'

She was a very pretty girl, the dark hair and fair skin accentuating deep-blue eyes, but her severe attitude spoiled the picture. Walt sighed. It would take more than a miss like this to keep him out.

'My dear, I have some interesting news for you. Don't tell me I shouldn't have bothered.'

'Whatever it is, you may tell me now,' she said, resolutely guarding her door.

'By all means, but it is rather hot out here. Could I at least have a glass of water?'

Walt hid a smile as she relented and allowed him into the house while she fetched him a drink of water.

He took it with feigned gratitude while he looked about him. 'My word, you have made this room very pleasant. A change from Paddy's days. Nothing like a woman's touch, I always say. It occurs to me now that I ought to have a woman's touch in my paper too. The *Chronicle* could do with a lady's point of view.'

'Is this what you wished to discuss, Mr White?'

'A thought, my dear, an interesting thought. I can't let it pass. An educated young lady like you might be just the person to write for me, about women's affairs, household matters, correct furnishings and fashions, that sort of thing . . . We'll, ah, talk about that another time. But I want you to keep it in mind. May I sit?'

She could hardly refuse, but she remained standing as he perched on the couch, his hat beside him.

'Well now, Miss Tissington, I thought you'd like to know that Mr Willoughby has been released. All charges against him have been dropped. It will be in the *Chronicle* tomorrow.'

Obviously this girl had had her fill of reporters. Her expression didn't change. 'I'm pleased to hear that.'

'So you should be. You have shown you were a good judge of character, since you have always believed in his innocence. You must be greatly relieved.'

'I have nothing more to say on the matter, Mr White.'

'But don't you think he has been cruelly treated by the police? An innocent man, hounded all over the country. Imprisoned on St Helena?'

'Would you excuse me now, Mr White? I have things to do.'

He shrugged and got to his feet. 'By all means. I didn't wish to intrude. I just thought you would like to know.'

She walked to the door, opening it, dismissing him. 'Thank you.'

'Will he be coming back here now? I should like to interview him. His point of view should be very interesting.'

'I have no idea.'

Oh well, he thought, I can still make something out of this. Not a total loss. Miss Tissington pleased to hear the good news, and so on and so forth . . .

From her doorstep he turned back. 'I was serious about that column. Would you be interested in doing a little writing for me, Miss Tissington? You would be paid, of course.'

She seemed relieved that the worst was over, and allowed herself a small nod. 'I'll think about it, Mr White.'

'Good. You pop into my office and we'll have a talk. Don't leave it too long.'

A smile from her at last. 'Thank you.'

When he arrived back in his office, he decided to go quietly on her after all. He didn't want to offend her now. She might be far more useful as a contributor to the *Chronicle* than as a scrap of fleeting news in a big story that would not be short of angles.

'Yes,' he said to himself. 'Who better than a classy young English-woman to write for our ladies? Who better?'

Emilie flopped into a chair at the table, feeling totally washed out. Exhausted. It was over. She'd always imagined that on the day Mal was finally exonerated, if it ever came, she'd have been thrilled, dancing with joy, rushing out to tell the world, but instead there was only relief, wearied relief. She was happy for Mal, pleased, as she'd said in her guarded answers to Mr White, but the slow release from Brisbane of news regarding Carnegie and that other fellow had become a journey of its own. It had been a harrowing experience to scour the papers each day for facts, not suppositions, as police enquiries dragged on until decisions were made and the two men charged. Even then no hint had been given as to Mal's fate, until, suddenly and so unexpectedly, Mr White was at her door.

She had known immediately that his intention had been to involve her again. He hadn't come to tell her the news out of kindness, and now she resented his intrusion. She had been pleased then, delighted for Mal, but Mr White had forced her to remain passive, afraid to show any emotion for fear her reactions would be reported in an unseemly manner. He'd blocked spontaneity as surely as if he'd confronted her with a stone wall.

But Mal. Free. Where had he gone? And how did he feel, for God's sake? She wouldn't be surprised if he'd left the prison hurt and angry. He had every right to be. But then, basically, he was a cheerful person, he had a disposition that would assist him to bounce back. Emilie knew he would need a very positive attitude now to overcome his grievances, but if anyone could do that, it was Mal. She could still see his wide, unabashed grin, so full of life and confidence, and wished she could write to him to wish him well. Maybe he would come to Maryborough now that he was free. It would be such a relief to see him again.

Farmers down the road had opened a small co-operative dairy, so Emilie decided to take a walk down there to stock up on butter and cheese and, as she'd heard, their excellent bacon. An outing would do her good, clear her head, allow her to breathe in the happiness she should be feeling. Mal was free. She and Clive were very comfortable in each other's company now. Emilie felt she'd known him forever, there was always so much to talk about, with their common background as immigrants to this country. And, she reminded herself, what about Mr White's offer to write for his paper? She would love to accept. So why not?

When she returned from the dairy, Clive was waiting for her, excited about the news that had spread through the town, thanks to gossip from the telegraph office.

'I know,' she said. 'Mal has been freed. Mr White came down to tell me.'

'Blast him. I wanted to bring you the good news. Poor old Mal, what a bloody time he's had of it. I wonder what he'll do now?'

'I hope he'll come here, Clive. He'll need friends after all he's been through.'

Clive's face clouded. 'You don't really know him, Emilie. He'd have plenty of friends all over the place. He was my partner on the goldfields, remember? He's a likeable chap, people took to him. Or is it that you particularly want to see him?'

'I'd like to know he's all right. I wouldn't want him to think I've forgotten him.'

'He won't think that. I did as you asked, I sent your best wishes in that letter via his lawyer. Your lawyer. He would have received it. But are you expecting him to come back here to thank you for your help?'

Emilie turned away. 'I don't need his thanks. You know it was his money all along.'

'I'm very much aware of that,' he grated. 'But you want him back, don't you? You're hoping his gratitude will draw him back. I'm becoming very tired of this situation. Of always having Mal standing between us . . .'

'He's not standing between us. He's a friend and we should care about him.'

'Oh no. He's more than that. He was mad about you, we both know that. He probably still is, and you like it. Mal never was your style, but you won't admit it. You were flattered by his attentions, romanced by him! Are you in love with him or not? It's time we had this out.'

Emilie really hated admitting the truth. She wished Clive had just let the matter drop. She'd known for a long time now that her affection for Mal had been a phase, more excitement than anything else, spurred on by that sense of loyalty she'd already identified. She sighed. 'No, I'm not. And I wish you'd stop pestering me like this. You know I love you.'

He was thrilled. He took her in his arms and swung her about. 'Then that's all there is to say! Will you marry me, Miss Tissington?'

'Yes.'

'Great! Good! Wonderful!' He kissed her. 'Let's set the date. When shall it be?'

But Emilie was cautious. 'We will set a date, Clive, and soon. I'd like that. But listen to me. I don't want to upset you again talking about Mal, but it would be nice, if we knew how to contact him, to let him know.' She was worried that Mal might turn up here again, out of the blue, only to find that she had married his friend.

'He knows,' Clive said, unconcerned. 'I told him in that letter that I had asked you to marry me.'

Emilie was appalled. 'You told him that while he was in prison? Clive, how could you be so cruel?'

'I wanted him to know how I felt. He was entitled to know. Would you rather he believed you were sitting here waiting for him? He would have read between the lines that we must have become more than acquaintances. It's better this way.'

Emilie shook her head. 'Oh, dear. I don't know what to think. I just feel so sorry for him. Does it sound conceited of me to hope that he has forgotten he was keen on me?'

'No. Realistic.' Clive smiled. 'Though I would find you hard to forget. This is our happy day, Emilie. Let's keep it that way.'

The Lord moved in mysterious ways. When the letter arrived, Ruth fell to her knees by her bed to thank Him, to assure Him that she had always placed her trust in His dear hands. She took the time to say a prayer for the departed, and even apologised to Him for her insensitivity, nay, seeming callousness, but she explained that it had to be tempered by the other news, by the resultant effect this sad event would have on the lives of the two Miss Tissingtons, so far away. And so desperately homesick.

After Emilie left, things had not gone well for Ruth at the college. A new headmistress had been installed, a woman who had actually attended a school of education in London, and emerged with distinction in teacher training. She was appalled that several teachers in the college, including Ruth, had no training at all, pointing out that such training had been available in Sydney since 1850.

From that day, Ruth had been put on notice. The New South Wales government had now established a teacher training course in Sydney, and, as a result, a teachers' register.

'I can't keep you on, Miss Tissington. I must have trained teachers. However, you're young enough; you should go down to Sydney and enrol in the course. It is only one year for primary classes, and I feel very sure that you will pass with flying colours.'

'But I teach older girls French, literature and music. You know I am well qualified in those subjects.'

'I understand that. And those girls have been fortunate to have your guidance. But Brisbane will be a city one of these days, and we have to keep up with the times. Our fees are not cheap, as you well know. In return I have to offer the best teachers available. Qualified teachers. Not tutors. Every teacher in my college will be a graduate of a teaching academy. You may be pleased to know that I have not made this offer to the other ladies I am replacing, Miss Tissington, but if you return to me with a diploma in teacher training, I shall find a position for you without delay.'

'But I can't afford to reside a year in Sydney without an income. And I imagine there would be fees . . .'

'I expect so. Miss Tissington, if such a course does not interest you, then you should return to governessing. Families out west would be grateful for your services and I should be only too pleased to recommend you. But there's no rush. I shall be seeking graduates as they become available . . .'

Ruth was offended. She couldn't see how trainees, deficient in the subjects that she commanded, would be better teachers. Teacher training establishments! They were not colleges of education, only places where men and women were advised how to behave in a classroom. A week of that would be enough.

She had been given a brochure by the headmistress which explained the curriculum. It made little sense to her, but she was horrified to read that she would be spending her days in classrooms with men as well as other girls. None older than thirty. With the sale of her block, she could probably afford to get through the year, but the very idea of Sydney, that strange city, and possibly having to share a desk with a male, like some peasant child, sent her into a panic. And the very thought of having to 'go west' again and live with some lunatic family in the bush made her nauseous. She would have to warn Emilie that these new rules were bearing down on them, but she supposed that such innovations would take time to reach her sister in her pathetic outpost.

What to do? Panic-stricken, she did nothing. She did not apply for the course in Sydney, nor did she request references from the headmistress to enable her to look to her future. Ruth had come to the end of her resources. To the end of the line. She had already sent the balance of her debt to the Society, including the final payment that Emilie had given her. She didn't want to know how Emilie had managed to find that money without selling her land, because, despite their differences, she knew Emilie was a good girl. She was foolish, quite silly, caught up in her ridiculous adventures, as bad as those women who took off into the Levant chasing romance.

But that was all it was, she knew, Emilie rushing to the defence of some hard-done-by rake. Oh, yes, Ruth had read the papers. She'd gone to the public library and read back issues on the famous Sonny Willoughby, and she'd kept abreast of the news after that. She'd seen his photographs. He was handsome in a rakish way. The sort of fellow their father would have ordered from the door. But Emilie, in that uncivilised environment, had lost all sense of propriety, and the sooner she was rescued from there, the better.

Ruth was convinced that the Lord had guided the hand of a kindly neighbour, who had written to advise them that their stepmother, Mrs Tissington, had passed away. Succumbed to smallpox, as had five other poor souls in the village. As she reread the letter, Ruth still couldn't summon any sympathy for the woman, but she was concerned for her father. Apparently he too had been gravely ill, but had pulled through only to be left in a weakened state, with no one to care for him. He had been heard to say how much he missed his daughters . . .

Ruth missed him too. She blamed that woman for driving a wedge between them, for causing all the grief.

Then came the question . . .

The poor man is an invalid, and the doctor believes he will remain so. The late Mrs Tissington hired Meg Glover as their daily and she is still there, but not the best person . . .

'Meg Glover!' Ruth snapped. What had her stepmother been thinking of, employing that slummocky old drudge? She was fat and lazy, and far from honest. Everyone knew that. Nastily, it occurred to Ruth that no one else would work for the new Mrs Tissington, her being such a witch herself.

. . .to be in charge of a household, as you would understand, but we may not intrude. Meg sees to that. Mr Tissington is a kind gentle-man, well respected, and it worries us to see him in need of better care. I am sorry to be the bearer of sad news but one wonders if you could make better arrangements for your father? I know it would cheer him no end to see either you or Emilie.

Ruth was jubilant. Here was a reason, not an excuse, to return home. To leave this dreadful place and return to where they belonged. To their own home. And a reason to remove Emilie from company that would be the ruin of her. They would return to Brackham as celebrities, she rather thought. They'd travelled to the other side of the world, had interesting experiences and been able to pay their own way back to London, first-class. Thanks to the sale of those blocks of land. Mr Bowles had had his uses, she smiled. And all the right people travelled first-class. The return voyage would be simply wonderful. Ruth was already planning to make enquiries about the right ship to choose.

For the first time in her life, Ruth was truly excited, looking forward to a pleasant voyage and a triumphant homecoming. They would invite friends to hear of their travels, and she might even write some pieces for the local newspaper, leaving out the unfortunate side of their experiences. And certainly putting behind them Emilie's notoriety. No one need ever know about that.

She did spare a thought for their father that evening, before she sat down to write to Emilie to tell her that they would be returning to England on the first available, suitable ship, because they were urgently needed at home.

As a dutiful daughter, Ruth was worried about her father, but she had to allow that he had brought this situation on himself. He'd been so enamoured of that awful woman that he'd taken her side against his own kin. He'd become a different person. Sometimes Ruth had listened, furtively, to them in their bedroom, next door to hers, and had flushed in shame at what she'd guessed was going on, judging by the squeaks and bumps. Even then she'd been certain that sex had turned his head, at an age when such behaviour should surely have been an indignity, but she could not say this to her young sister. The woman had seduced him thoroughly, the old fool, taken over his life, his fine home, and evicted his daughters. With his weak compliance.

'Well, old man,' she said, 'now you need us. It is truly said that you reap what you sow. She's gone and you have no one.'

When she did write to Emilie, she pointed out that their father was fortunate that his daughters had forgiving natures. She hoped he was well enough to thank the Lord that they were coming.

Winds of change were blowing through the town, with an extension of the wharves to accommodate more ships, and the arrival of more and more immigrants, all eager for work. Ship-builders were firmly established by the Mary River and it seemed that all activity stemmed from its steady flow. Wharf Street was gaining new shops and hotels, and fanning out from there, other streets were becoming busier, vacant town blocks fast disappearing. As Emilie walked up the street towards Clive's new shop, taking note of all the changes, she felt that her life too was becoming more settled at last. It was a good feeling, reassuring, to be part of the growth of the town, to know so many people and be recognised as a local, taking for granted now casual greetings in the street.

She was wearing an engagement ring, a small sapphire set in gold, locally crafted. 'Charming,' people said.

Although neither she nor Clive had thought to put a notice of their engagement in the *Chronicle*, the editor had chosen to write it up as news, with Clive described as an energetic young businessman and Miss Tissington as 'our very own', since Emilie had agreed to write a weekly article for him, two of which had already been published. One contained cooking hints, gleaned in their entirety from her enthusiastic neighbour, Mrs Dressler, and the other carried advice for immigrant ladies endeavouring to settle into this new environment. As a result of the announcement of their engagement, Emilie had been bewildered to find ladies, most only acquaintances, stopping her in the street to wish her well and ask to see the ring, but she was adjusting easily these days and had learned not to take offence.

She marvelled that they both seemed so busy these days, as if the engagement had hastened the pace of their lives. Clive had found setting up shop, as he called it, not as simple a proposition as he had imagined. The stock he'd ordered from the catalogues had fallen far short of expectations. He complained that they were dumping shoddy clothes on him, thinking the buyer in this outpost wouldn't know any better, and finally decided he would have to make a quick trip to Brisbane to do his own buying. As well as that, with the carpenter at work hammering in fittings, the shop seemed too small, and worse, Clive was upset that a bootmaker was moving in next door. He hated the idea of odours from leather and glue permeating his serene atmosphere.

Emilie laughed. She knew he'd sort out his problems, and judging by the interest already shown by men in the town, he would do well. Nevertheless, she had persuaded him to forget the rather grand names he'd proposed for his shop. She didn't think Maryborough was quite ready for a Gentlemen's Outfitters, or an Elite Gentlemen's Clothier. A simple 'Menswear' wouldn't frighten off shy customers, and it was still an improvement on the market-style shops that spilled their wares into the street beside saddles and boots.

She was busy too, with her writing, and plans for the cottage, since they had decided to build extensions on it before they were married. Certainly it did need a decent kitchen, not just the tiny annexe, and a few other improvements to house a couple. Emilie wished she didn't feel guilty about that. It still seemed to her that the true owner was Mal. But where was he? It had been weeks since his release and no word from him at all. She wanted to talk to him. To tell him herself about their forthcoming marriage. To find out how he was now. How he was coping.

Clive wasn't at the shop, but Emilie chatted with the carpenter, who promised that he would start work on the cottage as soon as he'd finished this job. From there she looked in at the draper's shop, trying to work out what linen a married woman would need. Most girls her age, back home, would have a glory box, filled with hand-sewn fineries preparatory to marriage, but, she smiled, Emilie Tissington, globe-trotter, hadn't had time. Nor could she be bothered today. She bought a few white towels and wandered out.

There was the wedding dress to think about too. Emilie was still waiting impatiently to hear from the dressmaker, who had ordered bolts of white silk and lace from Brisbane, but obviously they hadn't arrived yet. She sighed. Her wedding dress! She'd always expected to marry in the historic Brackham church. Who would have thought to see her stepping down the aisle of a tiny timber church set in the middle of a bare paddock?

Next stop the post office. She'd written to Ruth announcing the engagement, and suggesting that they could set a date for the wedding during the school summer holidays, so that Ruth could attend and, if she would be so kind, serve as her bridesmaid. Emilie remembered that Ruth hadn't been pleased to hear mention of Clive in the first instance, but everything was different now. When she met him, Emilie knew she'd like him.

Once again her thoughts drifted back to Mal, and suddenly she had an idea where he might be. Fraser Island. He'd loved that place, especially his 'Orchid Bay'. Maybe he had gone back there. It would be easy enough to find out. She would write to her missionary friends . . .

Ruth's letter, her response, was waiting for her, but Emilie could hardly

363

tear it open in the busy post office; she had to place it in her handbag for the present, although she was dying to open it. What a surprise it must have been to her sister to read of the engagement and forthcoming wedding! And that she was invited to visit Maryborough. At last. Emilie was so excited, she couldn't wait until she reached the cottage. Instead, she seated herself on a bench outside the Mary River chandlers and slipped open the envelope.

There were two letters inside, both neatly folded into place.

She opened the first, a single page . . .

Dear Emilie,

I had just written the enclosed letter to you when I received yours of the fifth, so herewith an addition. As you correctly state, news of your engagement did come as a surprise, but given your erratic ways of late, I wonder why. Surely you do not expect me to approve? I do not know this fellow, nor do I wish to. One cannot help but think you must have had a touch of the sun to get yourself into another entanglement so soon after your last disastrous escapade. Fortunately I am able to provide you with a feasible excuse to extricate yourself from this situation, as you will see in the other letter. You must give notice to your employers immediately, and return to Brisbane as soon as possible, so that we may return to England together.

Emilie was stunned! What was Ruth talking about? Returning to England? Angrily she unfolded the other pages, learning that their stepmother had died, that their father was in desperate need of their care, and of Ruth's plans for their return voyage and their future back at home among the right type of people.

Confused and hurt, Emilie made her way back to the cottage. She hadn't told Ruth that she'd been dismissed from her post as governess, but that didn't matter now. She resented Ruth's attitude, her offensive remarks about Clive, who certainly wouldn't be permitted to read that letter, and her disregard of Emilie's wedding plans. As if her sister was too stupid to choose wisely.

'Just because you made a mistake,' Emilie muttered darkly as she stamped down the road, 'doesn't mean I have. Clive is a fine man. There's no comparison between him and that awful Daniel Bowles.'

But Father . . . She agreed with Ruth's response there; he was a sick man now, and they should not dwell on past grievances. He did need care, obviously, but why *their* care? Ruth could go home to look after him, since she was keen to return to England anyway, but he didn't need both of them.

Emilie's first reply to her sister was an angry outpouring of her own pent-up emotions. She pointed out that she had been right all along about Mr Willoughby, and that the outcome had not been disastrous but a vindication of her stance. She accused her sister of being callous and disloyal, and plunged on in defence of Clive ... but later she tore that letter up and began again, in a calmer mood, having rid herself of the spleen. Ruth was her only sister. It wouldn't help to be hurling insults at her. What was the point in creating a wider breach?

She was proud of her dignified response. Of course Ruth must go home to Father, now that he needed her, and take with her Emilie's expressions of affection. However, her fiancé was a good and decent man and she did intend to marry him. Therefore she asked Ruth to come to Maryborough before she sailed for England, to be part of the joyful occasion of her sister's wedding. The date to be set to fit in with Ruth's plans of departure.

Emilie hoped her wedding dress could be made in time, since it seemed that Ruth was resigning her teaching position right away.

A fortnight had elapsed before she heard from Ruth again, and this time her sister was more conciliatory, but she presented Emilie with another concern.

> You seem determined to marry Mr Hillier. That you are very much in love. In which case I am sure Mr Hillier will not stand in your way when you tell him that it is imperative you return to England as soon as possible. Father is an old man and very ill. He has expressed a wish to see his daughters. Possibly in your case, for the last time, since you seem to be set on making your home in this country. I hardly see that you can deny him this wish, nor that Mr Hillier would deny you leave of absence at this time ...

'Leave of absence!' Emilie sniffed. Such a visit would take the best part of a year, giving Ruth hope of a cancelled wedding, not just a postponement. But could she refuse to go?

Emilie discussed the problem with Clive, but he would not make the decision for her.

'It's up to you, Em. I'll be disappointed to have to postpone our wedding, but if you feel you ought to go home at this time, then you must go.' He shrugged. 'I'll still be here when you get back.'

Emilie agonised over her decision for days, and it was only when Clive announced that he would be leaving for Brisbane at the end of the week, and would escort her down to meet up with her sister, that she made up her mind.

'I was thinking it would be nice to have a wedding on Christmas Eve,' she said shyly.

He was surprised. 'But didn't Ruth want to leave before then?'

'Yes. But she'll be travelling alone.'

'You're not going?'

'No. I've written a long letter to my father, he will understand. He'll have to. I told him to take care of himself, since Ruth is on her way home, and that at a later date, when we're more settled here, you and I will sail for England together. I'll be bringing my husband home to meet him.'

365

Clive breathed a sigh of relief. He put an arm about her. 'Thank God. I didn't really want you to go, but . . . never mind now. Christmas Eve, did you say? Darling girl, I'd be honoured to marry you on Christmas Eve. Do you want to come to Brisbane with me, to farewell Ruth?'

Emilie shuddered. 'I don't think so. I'm safer here. She'll be furious, I don't want another row.'

'Then I shall call on her, introduce myself and make your apologies. At least we'll have met.'

Emilie laughed. 'Don't be surprised if you get the cold shoulder.'

He looked at her firmly. 'That won't happen. I shan't allow it. By the sound of things, your sister has to learn to be a little more amiable.'

There were so many strangers on the roads these days that no one took much notice of the lone bushman as he rode through Gympie, surprised that the main goldfield track had evolved into a village street that already had an air of permanence about it. Mal kept going, though, following the road. He'd only been over it once before, physically, but in his mind's eye he knew every inch of it. He'd had plenty of time to think about it.

He made camp at Blackwater Creek, well in the bush to avoid company and the inevitable conversations about what happened there. There was no emotion left in him about the raid. None at all. Dispassionately, with all the time in the world to spare, he poked about the bush, looking up at trees that overlooked the clearing, one of which would have harboured Baldy, the sniper. Then, with a shrug, he slid down the bank of the creek and gazed at the spot where, according to the police, Baldy had hidden his boat. At the escape route. There had been no riders, no outlaws, only stupid old Baldy. And there were no ghosts here, only the softly shifting breeze in the tall trees. Mal rolled out his swag and settled down for the night. He slept well.

In the morning he rode on towards Maryborough, but avoiding the town, he crossed the river by ferry to the plantation side. When he returned, he made a decision. He would not call on Emilie and Clive. He was on his way to Fraser Island, the most beautiful place in the whole world as he knew it. He needed to go there again, to rid himself of the stink of prison, of civilisation. To immerse himself in the wondrous rainforest, so full of mystery, and to hear again the pounding of the surf on the sweeping beaches, where footprints were a rarity, where he could shout and shout and shout and no one would hush him. Mal knew, with animal certainty that he had to grasp at this retreat to restore his soul, to cleanse himself of thought, to be physical again. Run. Fish. Swim. Challenge those huge waves. Sleep. Just plain happily tired. And wait.

The message from Pastor Betts, head of the mission station on Fraser Island, came while Clive was away. In response to her enquiry, he wanted her to know that Mr Willoughby was on the island.

Emilie didn't hesitate. She had to see Mal. It was time they had a talk.

She hurried along to the wharves to ask how one might obtain transport over to the island. The supply ferry wasn't due to leave for a week, but she was directed to a ketch that belonged to a timber company operating over there, and the master agreed to take her the following morning.

'We leave at first light, miss. Can you be here at that hour?'

'Yes, of course. But excuse me, sir, what time would that be?'

He laughed. 'About five, miss. But it'll be a fine day for a trip across the bay.'

And it was. A glorious day. Emilie was the only female on board, but the crew treated her kindly, and once the ketch left the Mary River and headed out over the blue waters of the bay, she sat contentedly in the small cabin, interested in the uninhabited islands they were passing, until at last the ketch manoeuvred into position by a long jetty.

Pastor Betts was there, surprised to see her. 'Good heavens! Miss Tissington! But how nice to see you! Can you wait a few minutes? I have to have a word with these gentlemen. Then I'll take you up to the mission.'

Emilie looked to the shoreline. The tide was out, and though there appeared to be white sand beneath the tufted grass, the beach was muddy, pockmarked with crab holes. Not at all the sweeping white expanses that Mal had described. Bordering the beach was a wall of dense forest, and Emilie was suddenly nervous. She should have given more thought to this expedition. Waited for Clive. This was a frightening place, home to wild Aborigines. All the terrible stories she'd heard about murder and mayhem on this big island surfaced again, and Emilie wished she could run back to the ketch, but by this, Pastor Betts was ready to escort her ashore.

As they trudged up a sandy track through the cavernous forest, the Pastor expounded on the beauty of their surrounds, but Emilie was far from comforted. She agreed that the giant trees were magnificent, but they only allowed sunlight to trickle down from aloft and this path was dark, so heavily bordered by muscular rainforest plants it seemed as if the gloom itself was green. A trick of reflected light, she supposed edgily.

When they finally rounded a bend and came upon the mission, that too was a shock, as if the walk through the wilderness had taken her back in time. She wondered what she had expected . . . a trim white church and schoolhouse, and a neat residence for the Pastor and his wife, probably, something like that, anyway, but certainly not a settlement of log huts, still only thatched, squatting dimly amid the trees.

'Here we are,' Betts said proudly, 'home sweet home.'

As they approached, some Aborigine children came running towards them, giggling excitedly at the sight of the visitor, and then older blacks came out to stare and smile as they passed by. Emilie noticed, curiously, that they were all dressed in the oddest ill-fitting clothes, as if they'd been handed their apparel willy-nilly from a poorbox, and then she realised that this was most likely correct. The missionaries' endeavour to clothe naked bodies. But no one seemed concerned. She returned their smiles

367

graciously and allowed two little piccaninnies to take her hands, leading her towards Mrs Betts, who was standing outside a hut, hurriedly removing her apron.

They were disappointed to hear that Miss Tissington had decided not to join the mission, but still delighted to have her visit, so she was soon taken on a tour of their primitive facilities.

Walking about with them, Emilie was impressed by their dedication and their pride in the mission, and wished she'd thought to bring them some gift, some offering, because it was obvious they needed so much of everything. The mission was very poor but her hosts didn't lack in enthusiasm, and they seemed incredibly happy.

Over morning tea in their little hut, she told them she'd come to find Mr Willoughby and, feeling they were entitled to an explanation, related his background.

Mrs Betts was astonished. 'We've heard of him, of course. The papers called him Sonny Willoughby. We read about him in Brisbane. Is that who he is? Oh, the poor man! What an ordeal for him. And you say he was hiding out here on the island while the police were searching for him? How very clever!'

'No wonder he came back here, after a term in prison,' her husband said. 'I've been to St Helena Island on a pastoral visit, and it's a terrible place, even for hardened criminals, but it would be soul-destroying for an innocent man. How is he bearing up now?'

'I don't know, but I feel, as a friend, I ought to make an effort to find out.'

Mrs Betts nodded. 'Good of you, Miss Tissington. I wish we'd known who he was; we might have been able to offer counselling if he'd needed it. But he did seem quite cheerful.'

'Would you know where he is now?'

She shook her head. 'This is a very large island. About sixty miles long, for a good part unexplored. He could be anywhere.'

'He did say his favourite place was Orchid Bay, but I think he made that up. It's over on the ocean side of the island.'

Betts tapped his fingers on the table. 'We spoke of this before. It was only a guess on my part, but there's Indian Head, and a few inlets where creeks dribble on to the ocean side. As for orchids, they do grow abundantly in some places here. Unfortunately, neither Mrs Betts nor I are proficient enough in botany to make a study of them, though we are sure there are varieties here as yet unknown to the experts. However, back to Mr Willoughby. Let me make some enquiries. Our blacks come and go, they might be able to throw some light on his whereabouts.'

While they waited, Emilie suggested to Mrs Betts that she might be able to instigate a collection in Maryborough to assist the mission. Either in funds or foods.

'We should be very grateful, Miss Tissington. We manage to grow most of our food but we should appreciate school primers, writing utensils and most importantly medical supplies. The loggers are very kind. They often give us food parcels when their fresh supplies come over from the mainland.'

While Mrs Betts chatted about their work on the island, blithely recounting stories of raids by 'difficult' blacks who resented their presence, Emilie was astonished, wondering whether these people were brave or foolish.

'You said the loggers have settlements here. Why don't you have your mission closer to them?'

'Oh, no. That would defeat the purpose. We can't have our girls mingling with loggers. Goodness me, no.'

Betts returned, delighted. 'I've found him. Two of our boys know where he lives. He's not at a logging camp, but at a place, I gather, almost directly east of here. It's quite a hike, so if you don't mind riding a donkey. I'll take you over there.'

Emilie swallowed. 'A donkey?'

'Yes, but don't worry, they're quiet. Rather sweet, you'll find.'

Oh well, Emilie thought as they set out on their safari across the island, Mr Betts and herself riding, while two of their 'boys', grey-haired blacks, strode ahead to lead the way, it's an experience, I suppose. But now she worried about Mal. If they found him, would he consider this an intrusion? After all, he hadn't made any attempt to contact her.

Her little donkey padded steadily on, over small hills the guides called jump-ups, and delicate creeks, deeper and deeper into the forest, noisy with the chatter and whip calls of birds. At every twist in the narrow track, Emilie expected wild blacks to appear, but they saw no one. It was as if they'd left the world behind. Was that why Mal had come back? If so, what was she doing here? This was a terrible mistake.

Emergence from the dim reaches of the bush on to the oceanfront was so sudden that Emilie was momentarily blinded by the glare. Even her little steed tossed its head, trying to accustom its eyes to the light.

From the high sand dune Emilie stared in awe at the sweeping arc of wide beach and the great ocean beyond. The beach was so empty, so uncompromising, as if they had no place there, that her sense of intrusion heightened, and she could only follow dully as the Pastor gave his instructions.

'We'll leave the donkeys here, Miss Tissington, and walk down. The boys say Mr Willoughby is camped a little further to the north of this track. As I thought, by a creek. For water, you see.'

She slid down from the donkey and patted its head, unwilling to part from it, dreading the outcome of the long trek whichever way it went. To have missed Mal would be a let-down, but seeing him again could be worse. He had every right to be irritated, or even amused, to have her chasing after him like this. Her face flamed.

Emilie had missed what Betts was saying to her and he took her blush to be ladylike concern.

'It's all right,' he said. 'We'll go on ahead.'

'I beg your pardon, Mr Betts?'

He smiled. 'So that you can remove your shoes and stockings. Otherwise you'll never cope in this deep sand, going down the dune. Barefoot is appropriate in these circumstances.'

'Oh. Yes. I see.'

It was not only appropriate, she found, but fun, to be able to proceed down the dune in this childish fashion, her feet sinking and sliding in the warm sand until she came to the beach. Even then, as she tramped after the men, she enjoyed the squeak of the shiny clean sand against her bare feet; it relaxed her. At every step she felt better. She wanted to run across the beach and paddle in the sea, to feel the coolness of that wonderfully inviting water, but, she reminded herself, you're grown up now, behave yourself.

They found his camp, a bush hut made of titree and palms, and the Pastor frowned. 'I'm glad we came. It's one thing for Mr Willoughby to come here for respite, for a holiday, so to speak, but we can't have him going native. That won't do at all.'

But Emilie was entranced. She looked into the hut, finding it bare but for a few rush mats and his belongings slung casually in a dim corner. It reminded her of the tree house her father had built for his daughters when they were little, though they hadn't had a view like this. An uninterrupted view of the ocean, of the rise and fall of powerful green surf out there, thundering in like a constant roar of trains. As she stood and listened, she revised that thought. Never before had Emilie encountered a massive beach like this, a surf beach, and she wondered what it must be like at night, under the stars, to hear that sound, never-ending. Like listening to infinity. She had to make a conscious effort to draw away and explore the rear of the hut as the men walked out on to the beach.

There was yet another of the clear sandy creeks and, sure enough, orchids of all colours shone shyly in the greenery. Some had tendrils of yellow blooms reaching out from their tree-hugging bases; purple orchids, others blue, or white, sat majestically in place; and across the creek she saw pinks, the palest pinks. Until now, Emilie had only viewed orchids in books; she wished she had her paints with her to capture some of them. This was truly his Orchid Bay, with just the right climate for these blooms to flourish, and Emilie felt humbled that Mal, easy-going Mal, cared so much about natural surrounds. She doubted that Clive would even notice.

But then the Pastor was calling to her. 'Some people are coming!'

Emilie ran down the beach to the water's edge to join them.

'Down there.' Betts pointed. 'The boys saw them. I can only just make them out. Who is coming?' he asked.

'Blackfellas,' one of their guides said. He shaded his eyes and squinted. 'Blackfellas comen. Fishin' men alonga white man.'

The Pastor was nervous. 'Perhaps you ought to go up to the hut, Miss Tissington.'

But Emilie was intrigued. She could see them now, far away in the

370

mist of spray from the surf, ghost-like figures, elongated, out of perspective. It was hard to tell whether they were stationary or moving, in any direction.

The guide rolled his eyes. 'Better you an' missy stay, boss. We go see if them good blokes.'

Emilie watched them run down the beach and turned to the Pastor. 'Are we in danger?' she asked him squarely.

His 'No, no, no!' wasn't too reassuring, but strangely, Emilie was not afraid. She reasoned that if the blacks down there were hostile, there wasn't much they could do about it. They could hardly run and hide, leaving their footprints across the flawless sand. But she did hope that if there was a white man with this group of blacks it was Mal, not a stranger gone 'native'. It seemed like hours before the figures down there could be defined as tribal blacks, and even before the Pastor spoke, Emilie knew that Mal was with them; she recognised his walk, that easy lope, and his shock of blond hair.

'Please go up to the hut, Miss Tissington,' Betts said. 'Those blacks are not clothed.'

With that, he ran towards his guides, who were beckoning him on, to intercept the newcomers and spare the lady the sight of naked men.

Emilie did turn away, reluctantly, torn with the urgency to make sure it was Mal and not her imagination, willing it to be him. The tide was out, and she walked heavily from the hard, wet sand on to the soft, dry expanse, swishing her long skirt aside, fighting off rebellion. What if it was Mal? It was the widest beach she'd ever seen. And the loneliest. But people were approaching. Incongruously she thought of Ruth, who in these circumstances would have been racing for cover, shielding her eyes from the oncoming disgrace, but then Ruth would never have lowered herself to be here in the first place. Ruth would never have chased after a man as Emilie was doing. Nor would she have been romping about barefoot, despite clogging sand. How had they grown so far apart so quickly? Was it this country? Or had they always been different people, their attitudes not clearly defined until they were forced to go their separate ways? Emilie thought of her mother, a woman with an enquiring mind, who had to know about everything, who had been a painter of distinction. She would have loved to see this place. But not her father. He was firmly anchored in Brackham, where he'd lived all his life. As was Ruth. She belonged back there.

Emilie wrenched herself away from Ruth well before she reached Mal's hut, and turned back. She didn't care if a battalion of naked blackfellows were advancing on her; she had to know if Mal was there among them.

And then she saw him. Streaking across the beach towards her, all of the others left far behind. He was bare-chested, wearing only rough dungarees, wet to the knees from the sea, and he looked so well, so tanned and happy and so . . . male. She quaked. But there was no time left to think; he took her in his arms in a bear hug, swinging her about with

371

such exuberance, sand from his hair and his stubbly unshaven face grazing her cheeks.

'Emilie! It is you! God Almighty! I hoped you would come.'

'Put me down. How did you know I'd come over here?'

He released her, standing back, grinning. 'Betts told me you'd been asking after me. And here you are.'

Emilie regained her dignity. 'You could have come to see me, Mal. It was cruel to let me go on worrying about you. And it wasn't easy for me to find you. I had to get up before dawn to find transport to the island and ride for hours to this place. I had no idea it would be so difficult or I would never have come. If it hadn't been for Pastor Betts, I'd never have stepped ashore here, so don't be thinking this has been a pleasure. It has not. And I still have to get myself back.'

'You could always stay,' he teased.

'Don't be facetious. I was worried about you, and now I know I needn't have bothered.'

'Oh. I could have sworn you were pleased to see me when I came up the beach. Was I wrong?'

He was still teasing, but she had to admit he was right.

'Well then.' He took her arm. 'What about a truce? I'm sorry to be such a nuisance. Again. Come on up to the hut, it's cooler there. Betts might have found himself some new converts, but I don't like his chances. I can give you a drink of water at least, and some fish, if you want to stay for lunch.'

'I don't know,' she said, uneasily. 'I think Mr Betts has our lunch.'

'Good. We'll have a picnic.'

Emilie turned on him. 'Mal! I didn't come here for picnics. I was, I am, worried about you. How you are, really, after what happened to you? After all that . . .'

'I don't want to talk about it,' he said suddenly, harshly, but as he turned, Emilie saw his back, criss-crossed with scars, and she knew, immediately, what had caused them.

'Oh my God! They flogged you! Oh, Mal, I'm so sorry.'

'Don't be,' he flared. 'The last thing I need is for you to be feeling sorry for me. So they flogged me. Who gives a damn? Everyone got flogged on St Helena, it was the entry fee.' He ushered her into his hut. 'No chairs, but the mats keep the sand out. Do you mind sitting in here?'

'No, not at all.'

He kissed her on the cheek before she sat down. 'You haven't given me time to tell you that you look prettier than ever, Emilie. And I am grateful to you. I owe you for sending Lanfield to rescue me. As long as I live, I'll owe you.'

His sudden change of mood nonplussed Emilie, but she was now very much aware that his personality had altered; something was a little askew.

When he returned with a mug of water for her, and sat cross-legged beside her, they talked in desultory patches dominated by silences . . . like old friends at ease with each other. It was very restful in his hut. They

372

talked about the island, the orchids, the mission. Emilie said she was no longer working for the Manningtrees but was writing articles for the *Chronicle*, and Mal was impressed. He said he'd probably get a job as a logger on the island and, more confident now, he raised the subject of Lanfield.

'How did you get on to him? He's a tough old bird, but smart.'

Emilie began to explain, but then found herself telling him how she'd walked into all those tangles with the police and lawyers, and the publicity, and how her sister had been affronted, and it all sounded so confused that they were suddenly laughing, because it was a release for her to look back on that time.

'Worse was to come,' she said. 'I met Ruth's fiancé, a perfect horror of a fellow, secretary to Mr Lilley, a Member of Parliament . . .'

'Lilley? I met him once. Didn't know who he was at the time. He was on the stumps spruiking to a mob . . . that was the day I met you. There was a riot. I told you to turn back . . .'

'Good heavens, so you did! And did you meet his secretary, Daniel Bowles, that day?'

Mal grinned. 'No. I didn't hang about.'

'Oh, well. Mr Bowles was so cross that I was in the papers that he broke off the engagement.'

'What did it have to do with him?'

'Nothing at all. A ploy, I think. He was busy cheating my sister out of her money. But we got it back . . . only because I threatened to call in Mr Lanfield.'

'All this because of me?'

'Not really. At least we got rid of Ruth's fiancé before it was too late.'

He reached over and took her hand. 'And what about your fiancé, Emilie. Is this an engagement ring?'

She nodded. Embarrassed.

'Clive wrote to me. You're going to marry him?'

'Yes.'

Slowly Mal climbed to his feet and stood in the doorway looking out to sea. And then he shrugged. 'Oh, well. I suppose you could do worse. Like me.'

Emilie scrambled up to stand with him. 'Don't say that, please. You know how much I care about you, Mal.'

'Then why?' he demanded harshly.

Emilie was upset. 'I don't know why. The way I love Clive, it's different from the way I care for you, that's all.'

'I didn't mean it to be, or I wouldn't have sent him to look you up. You were my girl. I wanted to be with you.'

She took his arm and smiled up at him. 'Are you sure about that? Did you really want to settle down in Maryborough with a schoolteacher? Wouldn't you have found it a bit boring?'

'I would have, if that was what you'd wanted!'

That said it all, and they both knew it then. Emilie laughed. 'Mal!

You're such a dreamer. You'd hate being tied down, and I'd feel guilty.'

They walked over to the water's edge and, to her delight, paddled in the shallows, daring the surge of waves to catch them. Then they were hand in hand, just strolling along.

'I have this thing,' she said eventually. 'I always feel guilty about something. I never seem to be right about myself.'

'Why? Like what?'

'About you, for a start.'

'I'll survive,' he said drily.

'Then there's my sister. And my father. He's ill. They want me to go home. If I don't go and he dies, I'll never forgive myself.'

'Oh, Jesus, Emilie. What if he dies on your way back to England? Then you'll look stupid. Stop trying to manage everything. You can't control how the cards fall, you just have to play your hand as it is, right there.'

'I suppose you're right,' she said, knowing he was. 'But there's something else. The cottage. It's yours, Mal. And you still have money in the bank. You need it now.'

He stopped. 'You paid Lanfield. And if there's any money left I don't give a damn about it. It was always yours. But you listen to me. That cottage is yours. Not Clive's. And you see it stays that way. For a rainy day, my love.' He peered down the beach. 'Looks like Betts is coming back. We'd better forget the picnic. I can't talk to you with him around.'

She nodded. 'I have to get back anyway. I don't want the ketch leaving without me.'

He put an arm about her as they retraced their steps. 'I'm glad you came, Emilie.'

'And I'm glad we'll stay friends.'

'I don't know about that. We'll see. But you did say you cared for me. That was the best part of the day.'

She nodded, uncertainly. 'Yes, but you know what I meant.'

'I guess I do. But brotherly love isn't my deal.'

He put his arms about her and drew her close. 'Kiss me goodbye, Emilie. I won't be around for the wedding.'

Pastor Betts was approaching them, but he turned away suddenly as he saw the young couple caught up in the sweetest embrace. He whistled to his black boys to get the donkeys. It was time to leave.

Coda

The big Chinese junk in full square sail was heading north along the Queensland coast, in waters sheltered by the Great Barrier Reef, *en route* to China. The crew was working hard. They all knew that having left Maryborough there would be no more ports of call until they were well clear of Australian waters, and even then, stops for provisions would be lonely islands, not listed as ports by customs officials. The only cargo the junk was carrying was a sorrowful contingent of coffins containing the remains of Chinamen of varying status that had to be returned for burial in their homeland; men who had died in their market gardens or on the goldfields, wherever. They had to be brought home to their ancestors. There were even the bodies of ladies of note among them. A sad but necessary voyage.

The crew also knew, but dared not remark, that an unknown number of those remains hid gold for the families, gold undeclared and undetected, escaping custom duty much enjoyed by officialdom. On board also were five passengers, four of whom were Chinese gentlemen and the other a white man of obvious importance who had been brought aboard in the dead of night at the mouth of the Mary River, before the junk crossed Hervey Bay and rounded Fraser Island to head into the open sea. The five passengers had comfortable private quarters towards the bow of the junk, and stewards to attend to their meals and their needs, which was all the crew had to know. Although it was said that one gentleman was Lord Xiu and another his secretary, so highly placed that he rated his own cabin. It was commented, however, that the secretary, a huge man with a bald pate and pigtail, was also a bodyguard, adroit in the martial arts, so he too was treated with deference.

Taking all of this for granted, as if it was an everyday occurrence to voyage into the unknown on a magnificent Chinese junk, was Mallachi Willoughby. It amused him that the shabby junk was so well appointed below. Mal liked the Chinese cheek. It had always appealed to him.

Now, as he stood on the high deck, the scenery astounded him. It seemed that at every step in his life he had seen places that he'd thought to be the most beautiful in the world, but each time yet another place had captivated him. He was astonished by the jewelled seas of this Whitsunday Passage, the name told to him by Mr Xiu, who seemed to know all about these waters. The sea was sapphire blue, a shock of colour, and the islands were emerald green. He could stand here for hours on end, just soaking up the colour as the brave old junk laboured on.

The breeze brought a lightly spiced smell of island forests and humid blooms, of salt and baking shores . . . a fragrance, like lavender, like the little pouches his mother had kept under her pillow and in her dresser drawer. A female smell, dreamy. He would have liked his mother to meet Emilie, they'd have got along. That would have been nice.

Mal sighed . . . a daydream to carry with him wherever this lavender breeze led.

It hadn't been hard to find Mr Xiu. Letters to the newly established post office, which he had noticed in Gympie, and to Maryborough, and even to Cooktown, base port for the new goldfields. A start anyway. But one of them had reached the gentleman who had responded to the address given: Care of the Methodist Mission, Fraser Island.

Mal thought of his horse. He'd sent Striker up as a gift to Mrs Foley, warning the stablehand he'd paid to deliver the animal that the Foleys and their mates were a hard lot, up there in the hills. If Striker wasn't delivered in prime condition they'd come after him and shoot him down like a dog. McPherson wouldn't see the light of day for a few years yet; maybe the woman would have a more sane life without him around. She'd be surprised to get the horse, but pleased, and Mal hoped she'd remember him at times. He'd liked Mrs Foley.

He'd thought of sending the horse to Clive, for a wedding present, but thought better of it. He wasn't that forgiving.

And as for Emilie . . . Well, as he'd said, you can't control how the cards fall. If she'd chosen him over Clive, faint chance, he'd have to admit, things would have been different. Emilie would have seen to that. Emilie and her guilt. She couldn't have handled it. She'd have taken him post haste down to Pollock . . . Mal laughed. God, she was lovely. But so out of place on that island, little white feet tripping about the sand, the neat white blouse and navy tie that matched her skirt all so much in order. He'd wished at the time that he'd been able to fall into the warm waves with her, clothes and all, and have her not give a damn, just roll about with him in the sea for the sheer fun of it.

She'd never know that he'd almost pushed her in, not from malice, but to try to break through the wall of respectability that stood between them. God, he loved her! He wished she was with him on this marvellous adventure. But wishing never made things happen; you had to figure things out for yourself.

Emilie. He'd listened to her talking about her sister. How they seemed to be worlds apart, and that had made her so sad. She hadn't realised that she'd been spelling out the same sort of gulf that existed between two other people, Emilie and Mal. But Emilie and Clive were birds of a feather. Had he always known that? Maybe he had.

Mal walked across the deck to look back to the mainland as it fell away from sight. Old Baldy was gone now. Gone to his maker. Proud that he'd won. Proud that he'd pulled off a robbery that left any of McPherson's exploits in the shade. And he and Carnegie had taken the secret to their graves, so the story went. The cash and the gold were never recovered. Gone. Lost.

But old Baldy had been bursting to tell someone. To prove he'd won the race. He couldn't give up the secret, because then he would have lost. Dying with that haul still his, still allowing himself to boast that he was a rich man, was to hold the winning hand right to the end. But he'd had to tell someone, even a hint, and Mal had been listening. There had been a little moment when the earth had stood still. When Baldy had played the clown. 'It's mine. And the crocs'.

That night, when Mal had revisited the scene of the Blackwater Creek murders, he'd stood and looked across the Mary River, knowing it was infested with crocodiles.

The next day, avoiding Maryborough, he crossed the river by ferry and rode back along the shores of the river until he was opposite the mouth of the creek. With all the time in the world to figure this out, he'd camped high on the bank for two days. Just poking about. He saw the crocs dozing, yellow eyes alert. Baldy's crocs. They missed nothing. They moved fast, jaws snapping. Monsters. They'd have been watching Baldy. Doing what? Burying the haul, of course. Somewhere around here. Baldy never took the haul into town. He'd double-crossed Carnegie. Birds of a feather again. The haul was treasure beyond his wildest dreams. But he'd got drunk, got himself jailed. So what? The treasure was still his. Waiting for him. He was a rich man. Mal was certain of that.

He surveyed the area carefully, allowing for drift in a light dinghy. You didn't just dig a hole, you couldn't disturb the grass or trees or shrubs for someone to notice, you needed to take more care. Tree roots. Trees around here, especially the old figs, were so ancient they had root structures as thick as a man's arm. Mal had nothing to lose. No guilt shadowing him now. He kept his eyes on the crocs while he hacked and dug into the roots of those trees, one after another. Snakes, disturbed, lunged at him, mosquitoes swarmed, spiders ran up his arms as he plunged them deep into hollows, searching, feeling about for something that didn't belong . . .

'Jesus,' he murmured, shaking his head. 'I almost gave up. But those bloody crocs were always down there, smart alec bastards, as if they knew something I didn't know.'

One dived at him. Racing up the bank. It was then that Mal realised that Baldy wouldn't have invited them; he would have gone higher. Well out of reach of the crocs.

'You were wrong, Baldy, you murdering bastard,' Mal said with a sigh. 'You died poor. You lost. I won.'

All the time Emilie had been sitting with him in the hut, his swag had been tossed carelessly in a corner. The bedroll was thick, padded with kapok, but since that day by the Mary River, Mal had never allowed anyone to carry it for him. He was strong, and whenever he lifted that swag imbedded with treasure, he gave the impression that it was light. As it should be. No trouble at all for a man to lump it over his shoulder.

377

A dead weight, he remembered, smiling, but who took notice of a swag? Xiu had taken his commission, of course, and made all the arrangements, guaranteeing his safety on the voyage.

Chung Lee approached him, bowing. 'His Excellency Lord Xiu requests your company to dine, sir.'

'Yes. Tell him thank you. I'll be down in a minute.'

Mal looked over to the mainland again. 'You'd better take care of her, Clive. Or I'll be back.' Then he swung down the steps from the deck in one jump, his old exuberance in full flight. 'What's next, Mr Xiu?'